Whispers of the Ice

THE BEACON CAMPAIGNS • BOOK FOUR

Whispers of the Ice

JENN GOTT

WHISPERS OF THE ICE

This is a work of fiction. Names, characters, businesses, places, events and incidents are either the products of the author's imagination or used in a fictitious manner. Any resemblance to actual persons, living or dead, or actual events is purely coincidental.

Copyright © 2018 by Jennifer Gott

ISBN 979-8-4258-7469-6 (hardcover)
ISBN 978-0-9908914-6-8 (paperback)
ISBN 978-0-9908914-5-1 (ebook)

Whispers
of
the Ice

Chapter One

"*Praxis* Fellows? Don't think I've ever heard of a *Praxis* Fellows."

"She's not on the list."

Uh-oh. An uneasy feeling settled over Kaedrich Mannly as, in front of her, the cold line of Praxis's shoulders drew even sharper. This wasn't going to be good.

"List?" Praxis said, lips curled up in distaste. She spat the word into the faces of the guards at the gate. "What list? Since when do we use *lists*?"

The guards exchanged a meaningful glance. There were two of them, one on either side of the golden bars that marked the entrance into the Fellows household. They were both young, though the one safely tucked inside was clearly younger, and both were built like granite blocks. The gray leather uniforms they wore reinforced this idea, and the thick fur of the vests layered over them added even more bulk to their shape. White animal hairs stood from the shoulders of their vests like spikes of armor, rising just about to their ears. Though both Praxis and Kaedrich were tall, these men were taller—and broad enough that, to Kaedrich's eye, either *one* of them could probably wrap both Praxis and Kaedrich in their arms at once, and crush them with ease. Their snow-white Yandosian hair was cropped near to the scalp, and the older one, on Praxis and Kaedrich's side of the gate, had a scar going across the bottom of his jaw, a whisper of white against the porcelain of his skin. Somehow, the delicate color of their features only added to their sense of muscle, as if they had been crafted of eggshells and *still* managed to dish out more beatings than they took.

Thinking this, Kaedrich was grateful she'd kept herself at a respectful distance away from the gate. She stayed by the . . . carriage, she guessed you could call it, though it was more sleigh-like than the word implied to her. A wide runner slid across the rough ice of the carved out "streets" of Yandosia's underground cities, and four massive white hounds, more wolf than dog, were tethered to the front. *Bruskers,* Praxis had called them, and Kaedrich's eyes widened now as one of them yawned, its long teeth flashing in the light. The driver had dismounted, and was ruffling up the dogs' deep fur and inspecting the sharpness of their claws. Behind them, traffic ambled past, both on foot and by sleigh, and so far, at least, their argument at the gates was drawing only the most cursory nosy glances.

"I'm sorry, miss," the younger guard said now, and Kaedrich reined her attention back, "there's just no record of you." He held a fat ledger in his hands, as he'd apparently been double-checking the infamous list spread out across the pages inside.

He seemed genuinely apologetic, his rough face suffused with an un-expected kindness, but Praxis either didn't see it, or didn't care. She took a single, threatening step toward the bars.

"No *record*? I don't need a *record*, you pointy little bureaucrat—this is my *home*, and if you don't let me in *right now*—"

Kaedrich darted forward, grabbing Praxis by the elbow. "Praxis!" Sparks had already begun to appear, hopping from one of Praxis's gloved fingers to the next, and Kaedrich knew a palmful of summoned flames could not be far behind. What would happen, Kaedrich wondered, her throat closing up with fear, if Praxis lost her temper in a place like this? It was bad enough back in Durland, where the buildings were flammable and a sufficiently angry Praxis could turn a whole block into an inferno. But here? Kaedrich's nervous eyes glanced at the ice, ice, ice. Miles and miles of ice, above, below, surrounding. How sturdy was it really, all these tunnels stacked upon caverns upon tunnels? Enough to support the rest of it, if one of the walls melted through?

She could only pray they'd never find out.

Praxis was ignoring Kaedrich, jaw set as she fumed and glared daggers at the two guards standing in their way. Kaedrich felt the tug of muscles that meant Praxis's fingers still twitched in irritation.

"Praxis," Kaedrich repeated, dipping her voice low and slightly scold-ing in Praxis's ear.

Her muscles stilled. Praxis took a deep breath, the sparks going out. "What about Geller?" Praxis asked, her voice carefully level. "Is he still in charge of security?"

"Who?" the younger guard asked, while the older one barked out a laugh.

"He's not been here for *years*."

"Fine, then who *is* your boss these days?" Praxis snapped.

"Prommel Fellows," the younger guard said with no shortage of pride. His chest puffed up. "My father."

The older guard turned, just enough to cut him a fast glare. "That's not relevant."

Apparently it was a *little* relevant, though, at least as far as Praxis was concerned—she took a quick step back, her eyes wide as she drank in the sight of the younger guard. Her face, already pale, had gone paler still, as if she'd seen a ghost. "Your *father*?"

"That's right," the younger guard said. He beamed at Praxis now, their situation momentarily forgotten as he held his hand to his broad chest. "Micadel Fellows, at your service."

The older guard rolled his eyes at Micadel. "Your *step*father, Mica. It's not the same."

"You're just jealous," Micadel said with a shrug, "because you're only *sort of* related."

"I'm more related than you!"

Micadel grinned. "Not anymore."

"Okay, okay," Praxis said. "Listen. Micadel, was it? Yeah: you may be Prommel's son—"

"Stepson," the older guard muttered.

"—but I'm *his sister*. So why don't you run and get Daddy, and then I guarantee he'll open this gate regardless of that infernal list of yours."

For a second everything stopped, as the two guards absorbed this.

It was kind of funny, Kaedrich decided, how they had managed to get all of this way with no issues at all, but now, literally on the Fellows' doorstep, now they were having trouble. Their trip down had been uneventful—a steam liner to the southern tip of Tjalava, transport on a cargo ship to the barren borders of Yandosia's shore, a caravan of heavily laden sleds across the endless stretch of frozen surface. From the instant they'd transferred to the cargo ship, it seemed as if the mere name "Fellows" had gotten them everything they wanted, no questions asked.

Then again, if you were surrounded by nobody *but* "Fellows," the power of it must diminish somewhat. Kaedrich squirmed, suddenly uncomfortable. If they were used to this much pomp and opulence, what were these people going to think of *her*? Her plaid green suit, the one piece of clothing that she still had after fleeing the capital city of Monfort with literally just the clothes on her back, felt shabby now, even though it had once been a fine bit of tailoring that had cost a full month's wages. Okay, fine, so Praxis had already bought her a leather jacket, warmer and longer than her plaid suit coat, and a thick fur coat that currently draped over her shoulders and trailed down to the back of her knees, to replace the full-bodied bundle she'd worn as the caravan crossed the surface. A pair of borrowed gloves, "gifted" to her by the cargo ship's captain after a weighted look from Praxis. These pieces were all finely crafted, as far as Kaedrich could tell, but it didn't hide *everything*. She was still mix-matched, half Durlish and half Yandosian fashion.

She tried to tell herself it didn't matter, that these people wouldn't be judging her for *herself*, anyway—not really. Praxis and Kaedrich had talked about it at length on their long journey down here, and decided it was probably best if Kaedrich kept up the pretense that she was actually a man. For one thing, Kaedrich (technically Kaedriella) was used to it, and didn't really know who she would be anymore if she presented herself as female. For another, it made . . . them . . . easier to explain to Praxis's family.

"Most Yandosians aren't exactly, um . . . open-minded," Praxis had said, twining her fingers in with Kaedrich's. They were wedged together on the narrow bed of their cabin, the covers kicked into a heap on the floor. Kaedrich was listening, because she knew what Praxis was saying was important, but she was also trailing the silhouette of Praxis's side with her eyes, the hills and valleys of Praxis's waist, her hip, her legs. It had been two weeks since they'd left Durland's shores, two weeks since all of this had happened, and Kaedrich still couldn't quite believe at times that Praxis was finally hers.

Kaedrich shook her head, shooing the memory away. Micadel had taken a step toward the gate while she'd been distracted, and now he was staring down at Praxis, searching her face as if looking for something familiar.

"Wait, you're . . . *that* one?" he asked.

Praxis shrugged. "Sure—you don't know my name, but you know I'm 'that' one. Not exactly a great legacy, but I'll take it."

"But . . . but you're dead!"

"What?"

The older guard gave Micadel a glance, visibly nervous. "Maybe we should get Prommel after all."

"That's what I've been—!" Praxis started, but the snap of a voice from somewhere behind the guards cut her off.

It carried easily across the distance, robust and commanding. Kaedrich craned her neck, trying to be discreet as she peered through the gold bars protecting the Fellows' property. From what she could tell, the space beyond was a cavernous "courtyard" of sorts, sculpted trees and shrubs lending it an outdoorsy feel even below ground. She did not see the speaker, however, not until he was *there*, on the opposite side of the bars, an imposing slash of black clothes and glinting eyes, as sudden as a thunderclap. Kaedrich froze, terrified without knowing quite why. The man rested his hand on Micadel's shoulder, asking a fast question in Yandosian.

Praxis, however, breathed an exaggerated sigh of relief upon the sight of him. "Prewish, thank goodness. Can you please tell these whelps to let me in?"

Prewish took his time in turning his gaze upon Praxis. He just stared at her for a moment, studying her features as if he didn't quite know what to make of her. He'd moved his hands to his hips, the broad sweep of his midnight fur coat drawn back. Beneath that, his black, fur-lined jacket came all the way down to land somewhere near his knees, which were covered by tall leather boots. A pattern of overlapping Xs were embroidered into his jacket, which was then tied together with a low-slung leather belt. Fellows gems dotted his appearance in tasteful moderation— a ring, a pin, a jewel on his belt buckle.

It was easier for Kaedrich to study his clothes than his face. His face, which already looked familiar, was marked by harder versions of Praxis's features; something in the eyes, the flat line of the brow, the vague scowl of suspicion that tied it all together. A pointed goatee and thin mustache gave him the look of a stage-show villain. Kaedrich found herself averting her gaze, as if, instinctively, she knew that he would never deem her worthy enough to look upon him.

Praxis, however, was having no such difficulty. Spine straight, she put her hand impatiently at her own hip. "Well?"

Prewish said not a word. With nothing more than a glance, the guards sprang into action. Micadel drew out a key from the depths of his fur vest, and the older guard moved aside, touching his three central fingers to his lips as he motioned with his other hand for Praxis to pass.

Praxis's right thumb twitched, and then she linked her left hand with Kaedrich's, guiding them through the gate. Faint clicks echoed off of the ice as they moved, a light undercurrent to their footsteps.

"That's better," Praxis said, as soon as they were on the other side.

The corner of Prewish's mouth twitched upward, just a fraction, drawing his mustache along with it. "Sister dear, did you forget how to speak?" His voice was surprisingly soft, now that he was not calling from a distance, and for a second Kaedrich wondered how it had managed to carry at all.

Praxis brushed the comment aside. "Durlish is more comfortable for me these days."

A lie. Praxis had been speaking it for Kaedrich's benefit, ever since they'd arrived. Many Yandosians were bilingual, Praxis explained, since Durlish was such a global language of trade, and Yandosia dealt almost entirely in exports.

It wasn't clear how much Prewish believed this, but he let the subject drop. He reached out to touch Praxis's hair instead, raising one of the short locks away from her scalp. "You cut your hair."

"You lost yours."

A bark of laughter escaped Prewish. He released Praxis's hair, running his gloved hand across the shining dome of his own head. Not even the scrape of stubble remained. "Times change."

"Indeed."

"You know Mother isn't going to like it," Prewish said. He raised an eyebrow, a pointed expression at Praxis.

Praxis shrugged. "At least I'm not dead."

"Ah, yes," Prewish said. "Speculation, naturally, but you understand. I'd say only about half of us ever believed it."

"Did you?"

Prewish was silent for a moment. He stroked his beard, once, before shrugging.

Kaedrich glanced uneasily between Prewish and Praxis. True, Kaedrich's only experience with siblings was with her twin brother when they were growing up (the real Kaedrich), but this didn't exactly seem . . . normal. Kaedrich's heart squeezed, remembering her brother. Oh, what she would have given to have him standing in front of her, telling her that *he* wasn't really dead . . .

Abruptly, Prewish turned back to Micadel. "See that you add her to the roster at once." He glanced at Kaedrich. "Get her servant's name, as well, and send it to the lower entrance. We wouldn't want him making the mistake of coming to this one again."

Kaedrich's cheeks flared hot as Micadel nodded and moved to make the notations. She started to slide her hand from Praxis's grip, but Praxis's fingers only tightened around her.

"No, wait," Praxis said, and something in her voice stilled Micadel.

He turned back, curious, as Praxis straightened her spine. "Kaedrich isn't my servant. He's my guest. You will add him to this entrance."

Micadel's gray eyes popped. They flicked down, to where Praxis's hand was still linked protectively with Kaedrich's.

A cold dread swept over Kaedrich, remembering the sea of ghostly pale faces she'd passed through in order to get this far. It wasn't just that darker people were rare—there had been *none* of them as they'd arrived at the shore, as they'd arranged passage into the vast network of tunnels. Kaedrich had tried to tell herself that she wasn't attracting funny looks, that it was just her imagination, but the truth is she knew better. She'd known from the instant they'd arrived. Part of her wanted to pull herself back, put some respectful distance between herself and Praxis, but Praxis had only gripped harder, keeping Kaedrich by her side. An unspoken *Stand your ground* passed between them, in the clutch of Praxis's hand.

Prewish chuckled. It rumbled low, reverberating against the ice. "Oh, Praxis . . . Mother isn't going to like *that*, either."

"I don't care," Praxis said, so fiercely that Kaedrich's heart swelled.

"You might," Prewish said. "After a while."

"Never."

Prewish made a noncommittal "hmm," neither agreeing nor arguing with his sister's assertion. He took one last look at Kaedrich, barely sweeping his eyes over her before he nodded at Micadel. "Not that this hasn't been lovely," he said, taking a step to the side, "but if you'll excuse me, I was on my way to the lapus lumeni division. Some of us have a company to run, after all."

"The lumeni?" Praxis asked sharply. "What do they need you for?"

Prewish smirked. "They're gems and I'm a geologist, Praxis, it's not that big of a stretch. Or have you forgotten while you've been off . . ."—his gaze flicked to Kaedrich, just for a second—"exploring?"

"I haven't *forgotten* anything," Praxis said. "But they're magical gems, and you're not exactly a wizard."

"Yet here I am." Prewish spread his arms as he stepped away. His fur coat flared when he turned his back to them, the dark hairs waving farewell in the breeze of his movements. "Welcome home, Praxis," he called over his shoulder. "Try not to cause too much trouble this time, all right?"

HOME.

Everyone kept using that word, but Praxis scoffed at it as they set off through the Fellows' courtyard. What did it really *mean*, anyway? It was nothing—a collection of sounds and letters, a jumbled attempt to express the place where you lived and shat and kept your belongings. Praxis blamed poets. Sentimental fools attempting to make simple concepts sound grander than they really were. Let's not get bogged down in false expressions of longing and nostalgia: this was a household, a dwelling, a shelter. Praxis used to live here, and then she did not.

She should have known it was a mistake to come back here, but what other choice did they have? In the aftermath of Pon Lanali's rise to power in Durland, Praxis had panicked. She was fleeing, scrambling to make arrangements, tending to a vulnerable and unconscious Kaedrich as she recovered from her . . . ordeal. Praxis had barely had time to stop at Brindlewood and make arrangements for the care of Brex—his species did not care to be underground, and while she had no idea how a creature from the jungle would have handled the cold, she was willing to bet it wouldn't be good. At the time, it had felt like enemies were advancing from all sides, like the chokehold was tightening in on her. Praxis had needed safety and protection. Simply hopping the border wouldn't be enough, not with Lanali in charge of Durland's military forces.

It hadn't taken long for Praxis's mind to turn toward Yandosia. Its frozen depths were about as far from the danger up north as you could get, but perhaps more importantly, the Fellows had power and resources, influence and security. The bottom line is they needed safety and protection, and to Praxis, there was only one place she trusted to provide that.

So here they were.

Still, this did not do much to ease the knot that had been growing in her stomach ever since she'd stood aboard the deck of the cargo ship and caught her first glimpse of the slab of white that signaled her return. The shore sat atop the blue-gray of the sea, snow and ice blending in perfectly with the thick clouds above and the ocean depths below. Only two faint lines marked the division. The captain was beside her at the time, directing his crew as they churned through the ice floes that led up to the mainland. He was a Yandosian himself, and his chest swelled with pride as they approached. *"Happy to be going home, Miss Fellows?"* he'd asked in their native tongue. There was that word again.

Praxis hadn't answered, just turned away in search of Kaedrich.

Whose hand was linked with hers now, in the courtyard, although between both of their gloves, Praxis could barely feel it. For Kaedrich, they provided extra warmth, but for Praxis it was more to conceal the other, mechanical "glove" on her right hand. She tried to shift her fingers with as much subtlety as she could, though there was nothing she could do about the faint click of the gears running down her leg. Another complication, one she'd been stewing on for ages now as they'd made the long journey down: how in the name of sanity was she supposed to hide her disability from her family? The glove was . . . feeble, she knew, but it was the best she could put together.

It wouldn't be enough.

What if none of it was enough?

Praxis jerked around. The thought had entered her head without summons, slipping into her mind as a whisper. Praxis peered around the sculpted garden of ice, not even really sure what she was looking for, as a shiver ran up her spine. But there was nothing to see, of course. Just the sigh of conjured wind, slipping like chimes through the crystalline leaves. It must have been Praxis's imagination. The combined efforts of fatigue and stress, finally coming to collect.

"I can't believe the level of effort this must have taken," Kaedrich said, drawing Praxis's attention back to the moment; and the concern, like the memory of the whisper itself, slipped effortlessly from her mind.

She and Kaedrich stopped, partway up the courtyard path. Kaedrich leaned in, examining a twisted vine that snaked up the side of a tree. All crafted of ice, all glittering beneath the soft blue glow of the lapus lumeni crystals embedded throughout the courtyard. Kaedrich's finger hovered just over the petals of one of the flowers blooming on the vine, so thin it was almost vapor.

"I mean, how do you even carve something this delicate?" Kaedrich said. "Wouldn't it break?"

"It would, and that's why you don't. I had to shape each piece as it was forming."

"You?" Kaedrich turned, her lips parted in wonder. "You did this? What, with your magic?"

Praxis nodded. "I was thirteen. I'd seen a picture of a Durlish garden, and thought it looked like a sufficiently complicated project. I was wrong—it took me a year longer than I'd planned."

Kaedrich's eyes widened. "Wait, you did *everything*?"

Praxis's cheeks flushed, but she forced a nod. "I was showing off," she said, trying to sound dismissive. She didn't like the way Kaedrich's face lit up at this information, the way she turned in place, taking in the garden slowly. The way her lips held themselves apart, wonder taking her breath away. Standing there, surrounded by the frozen replicas of trees and flowers and shrubs, a magical wind teasing the air so that the leaves chimed like bells, imported white doves flitting beneath the high ceiling, Kaedrich looked beautiful, a fairy princess in a magical kingdom.

"Come on," Praxis said gruffly. She grabbed Kaedrich's hand, dragging her away in an attempt to break the spell. The twisting paths of the courtyard beckoned them at every turn, and Praxis fastidiously avoided them. The scar on Praxis's wrist burned, embedded flames twisting themselves around in a fast track beneath her skin. She could not look at anything—not a branch, not a flower—without remembering the hours she'd spent crouched on her knees, teasing water out of a bucket and hurrying to shape it before it froze. Moc, her tutor in magic, would watch over her shoulder and scold her whenever a leaf came out lumpy or misshapen. He'd be dead less than two years later.

Instinctively, Praxis pictured her other wrist. The skin, and the tattoo it bore, was hidden beneath layers of leather brace and thick glove, but right now just knowing it was there was a help. She'd spent a long time staring at it, on the trip down here, grounding herself against what was to come. The tattoo, crisp black, depicted a simple drawing of a bird's wing, surrounded by stylized licks of flame. It was a much more refined mirror image of the same symbol she'd burned into her other wrist, and together they represented the two most defining moments of her life in Yandosia. Neither of which she was ready to think about, but there wasn't a lot she could do about that now. Not here, with every glance bringing her back to one point or another.

It was almost a relief to reach the door.

A pair of servants stood to either side. Nondescript in their crisp white uniforms, they had either been informed of Praxis's return already, or else they recognized that anyone who got through the gates was perfectly welcome to step inside. They touched three fingers to their lips as Praxis approached, and swept the double doors open with a flourish. And so here it was: the final threshold. Though Praxis had been moving steadily closer and closer to this moment for about three months now, a part of her must not have believed she would ever actually *make* it.

She plunged through before she could question herself. There was no more turning back—perhaps there never had been.

With this last step taken, Praxis's eyes opened up to her family's home. She and Kaedrich stood in the doorway, boggling at the sweeping view that unfolded before them. Everyone had always commented on the Main Hall, but Praxis had never seen it before, not really.

She saw it now.

The room was *massive*, the rounded ceiling so far overhead that artificial clouds had no difficulty drifting past. Arched hallways branched off both on the ground floor and for three levels up, balconies ringing the hall. Whale-bone trim ran as pale highlights down all the lines, acting as railing, support beams, accents. At the far end, a towering staircase twisted both up beyond the clouds and down into the floor, leading way to the rest of the household. Her family had redecorated in the long years since Praxis had left. Fat crystal chandeliers hung down at regular intervals all along the length of the room, glittering with both lapus lumeni and traditional gemstones. The ice of the walls, ceiling, and mighty pillars had been polished so much that they were almost mirrorlike in their reflection of the light, which bounced off and then back through the many crystals at just the right angles to splash the walls with luminous murals. The rest of the walls, and the ceiling itself (if Praxis's squinting was to be believed), had been filled in with their own murals: great sprawling landscapes and portraits crafted of *thousands* of tiny flecks of gemstone.

"Perlandra's breath," Kaedrich whispered beside her, and Praxis could only nod in agreement.

Clearly, business had been good to them over the many long years.

They were so busy staring at it that they did not hear the voice immediately, careening down from one of the many branching hallways. Kaedrich's ears actually perked first; she tipped her head, glancing at Praxis with a curious expression, a question of "Is that . . . ?" forming on her lips.

Then it reached Praxis. Breathless and repeating, a voice Praxis would recognize anywhere. Her throat seized up, listening. *"Out of my way, out of my way, out of my—!"*

Her father burst into the Main Hall, leather boots skidding as he rounded the corner.

Prawl Fellows drew to a halt, eyes popping at the sight of them. *"By the stars, it's true."*

A sharp jab hit Praxis's chest as her scar flared hot on her wrist. It was only the stoic nature drilled into Praxis by her mother's intense social training that kept Praxis rooted in place. Her father. Gods, he'd been one of the only members of her family that Praxis had actually *missed*, on occasion. His cheerful grins, his thick and jolly beard, his easily flushed cheeks. His warm embraces, his laugh. Praxis tapped her middlemost three fingers to her lips, a formal greeting that was much too impersonal for what the situation warranted. "Hello, Daddy."

"Oh, no," Prawl said, shaking his head as he switched seamlessly to Durlish. "No, my opal, this is much more than 'hello'!" He ran forward, and before Praxis knew it, he'd thrown his arms around her so tightly that she almost couldn't breathe. The fur of his coat tickled Praxis's nose, the smells of leather and ale and his spiced cologne wrapping their own familiar hugs around her. In a burst of enthusiasm that defied his age, he lifted his daughter up and whirled her around once before dropping her back in place, laughing the whole time.

When they finally parted, he held her at arm's length as he took in the sight of her. Prawl's face scrunched. "Is . . . this what women are wearing up north these days?"

Praxis fought against a blush, running her hands absently over the front of her vest. The clothes had been tailored to her female shape, but were still undeniably masculine, and not even her long, slate-blue overcoat could hide that she was wearing trousers instead of a skirt.

"Not . . . exactly, no," Praxis said.

Prawl grinned, his thick beard crinkling up around his smile. "Well, it looks good on you. It's nice to see people setting their own trends."

Praxis raised an eyebrow, taking in the details of Prawl's own suit. Rusty-red pants and a dusky-gray jacket hid beneath a sweeping coat of fox fur, while a heavy chain of gold hung down from shoulder to shoulder, supporting a bold spread of diamonds. No doubt the cut was of the latest style, a little longer and a bit more puffed at the sleeves than Praxis was used to. Praxis reached out, smoothing down the fur at his shoulders that had gotten ruffled in the force of their reunion. "I don't think Mother would agree with you."

"Don't you worry about your mother," Prawl said, waving his bejeweled hand in dismissal. "She fusses too much."

This was, perhaps, the understatement of Praxis's lifetime. She choked back a snort as Prawl smiled and then, finally, turned his attention beside her. "And you are . . . ?"

Kaedrich squared her shoulders, but it was Praxis that spoke.

"Daddy, this is Kaedrich Mannly," Praxis said hurriedly. She stepped into line beside Kaedrich. Their fingers interlaced and Praxis found herself staring up at Kaedrich's face, ensnared, just for a second, by her profile. Praxis shook her head, refocusing. She motioned forward. "Kaedrich: my father, Prawl Fellows."

One of Prawl's bushy eyebrows twitched upward, and for a horrible second Praxis feared they might have a repeat of the gate incident all over again. But as quickly as the panic began to stir, so did it settle. Prawl broke into a wide grin, extending his hand. "Indeed! 'Kaedrich,' you say? Am I pronouncing that right?"

"Just about right," Kaedrich said as she accepted the handshake, slapping their palms together in the efficient way of businessmen.

Prawl's other hand wrapped warmly over Kaedrich's as he pumped them up and down. "Such a pleasure to meet you! I have to say, you must be quite the extraordinary young man to have turned my Praxis's head."

Kaedrich blushed, a tint of coral layering beneath the lush brown of her cheeks. "The pleasure is all mine, sir—it's an honor, truly. Praxis speaks very highly of you."

"Ha! When she talks of us at all, I bet," Prawl said, laughing at himself, though Praxis flinched.

"Oh, no," Kaedrich started, "I wouldn't say—"

Prawl waved his hand. "I appreciate that you're honorable enough to rush to my daughter's defense, but can we make a promise to always be honest with each other, Kaedrich? I find that business works best if it's built on a foundation of honesty, don't you?"

To anyone else, it might have looked as if Kaedrich's "of course" was seamless, though Praxis noted the tiniest slice of hesitation.

"Then in the spirit of honesty," Prawl said, "I think it's safe to assume we were often the last thing on Praxis's mind these past however-many years—and that's exactly as it should have been, my dear, stop looking as if you're going to pass out! You had your own life you were building; we understood that."

"If that's the case," Praxis said, "why does everyone think I'm dead?"

"Dead?" Prawl frowned. "Oh! Yes, I believe I did hear that rumor, once or twice. Never paid it much attention myself. Your bank account kept needing to be refreshed, and the dead don't tend to do much shopping."

"And you didn't think to tell anyone that?"

Prawl shrugged. "There seemed little point, to be honest."

Praxis took a step back, torn equally between incredulous and amused. Here he'd known all along, and he just sat back and let the rumors persist? If it wasn't exactly the kind of thing Praxis might have done in his place, she would have been incensed.

Prawl tossed her a wink. "So!" he said, clapping his hands together. With a discreet nod into the distance, Prawl signaled at a servant, tucked away against the walls, who unfolded himself from his post and stepped forward.

The servant tapped his lips. "Sir?"

"Prepare my daughter's old room, and a second suite on Emerald Level for her guest." Prawl turned, regarding the two of them. "Do you have any luggage with you? Anything we should bring in?"

"No . . . ," Praxis said. She glanced once at Kaedrich, gathering her strength before she plunged on. "And—just the one suite on Emerald will be fine for us, please. Mine can stay as they are."

To his credit, Prawl merely nodded at this information. He waved his fingers, indicating that the servant should update his assignment and go, but the servant, it seemed, was not exactly eager to comply.

"Sir . . . ?" he asked, glancing to Prawl as if hoping to be saved from something. A wrinkle marred his nose. "Are you sure, I—"

"You heard my daughter," Prawl snapped. His hand lashed upward— he would not ever strike the servant, not really, though Praxis felt Kaedrich tense beside her, as if anticipating that he would. Instead, his hand caught the light of the lapus lumeni, each one of his fingers decked in a ring bearing a gem whose color twisted and shifted as they watched. Fellows gems, reserved for only the innermost circle of family. Never offered for sale.

The servant averted his eyes. "Sir," he said, his teeth gritted. But he pressed his fingers to his lips again, backing up until a sufficiently respectful distance had been laid between them, before turning his back and retreating down a hallway.

When the servant was gone, Prawl heaved a weary sigh. He looked at Kaedrich, reaching up to put a hand on her shoulder. "Welcome to Yandosia," he said, his voice apologetic. "I hope you're ready for it."

PREWISH FELLOWS CROUCHED at a table, in a small office just off the main labs for the lapus lumeni division. His hands were spread on the tabletop, and he drummed his fingers against the whale-bone slats so hard that he could feel the vibrations underneath his chin.

The object in the middle of the table didn't move at all. Not underneath the steady rhythm of Prewish's drumming, nor when he grabbed the table and jostled it, nor when he lifted the edge and tipped it just slightly. He straightened back up, folding his arms over his chest, burying his hands in the warmth of his thick black coat. He looked up.

"Who else knows about this?"

The other two men in the room glanced at each other. Stamm, the head of Excavation and Prewish's highest ranked subordinate; and Trendall, the wizard in charge of the lapus lumeni division.

"Couple of the grubs," Stamm said. "We've already put them in quarantine, told Praine they had the Aulish flu. They were the ones who dug it up, and brought it to me. I took it from there."

"Anyone else?"

Stamm pointed: you, me, the wizard. "No one else."

"Good. Let's keep it that way for now."

Prewish knew Stamm wouldn't have a problem with that and, indeed, Stamm nodded as if this was the most obvious order in the world. Of course he wouldn't blab, it was his job not to blab, but Stamm wasn't the one Prewish was worried about. No, it was Trendall that drew his attention. The wizard had been hired less than a year before, and it still wasn't entirely clear who had won the auction of his loyalties. Prewish nodded at him. "What's your assessment?"

Trendall glanced up, almost as if he was surprised to have been addressed at all. He was leaning against the wall in the corner—not far away from the rest of them in a physical sense, yet somehow the gesture seemed to isolate him. Something about Trendall had always unsettled Prewish, though Prewish couldn't say why. Certainly Trendall had been thoroughly vetted, both by Praine—who, as the head of staff, was in charge of that sort of thing—and by Prommel, making sure he was reputable enough not to steal from the company. Really, there was no reason for Prewish's dislike, yet there it was.

Was it just his dislike of wizards in general? The Fellows family had been thoroughly burned by them, in the past, though no one else seemed to hold a grudge against their own little "star," the once-shamed daughter who had seemed to not only be forgiven, but grow into a private legend in her absence. Prewish frowned, remembering Praxis's sudden reappearance at the gate. Was that all it was? His suspicion and annoyance at her, projected now at Trendall?

Trendall gave Prewish a moment, as if sensing the tempest of his thoughts. But that was impossible, surely . . . Prewish cut him a glare, and the wizard pushed himself off from the wall. There was never a single hair out of place on Trendall, on either himself or the fur coats he wore into work, coats that were much too expensive for a man of his station in life. "If you're asking me if this is a new phenomenon, I'd have to say yes. To my knowledge, no one has recovered a gem like this before."

"You're saying it is a gem, then."

Trendall chewed on his lip for a moment before answering. "Nothing crafted could have possibly made its way to where this was found," he said finally, and this was true. The tunnel they were excavating was one that Prewish himself had found not two months before, a branch-off in the deepest depths of a system they'd only acquired in the last year. The gem, then, was buried in a layer of rock, twenty feet or more in, which had been slowly chipped and chiseled for days, flecks of sediment flaking off and dusting the ground beneath the grubs' knees. The odds of them finding it were slim enough—the odds of someone placing it there were nonexistent.

And yet here was another undeniable fact: no one that knew of its existence—not the grubs who had been responsible for chipping it out and hauling it back to the main level, not Stamm, not Trendall with his books and years of higher learning, not Prewish with decades of experience and family mining connections going back generation after generation— had ever heard of anything like this object.

It wasn't natural. Its perfectly spherical shape, the outer layer so much like glass. The light that twisted inside of it, writhing and clawing its way around the bubble that held it as if searching madly for a means of escape, any means of escape. When you tried to roll it, it stayed put. When you held it, it seemed to weigh nothing at all. When you hit it with a hammer (because of course they had hit it with a hammer), it did not break, not a single crack darting out across the impossibly delicate surface. When you stood for a while in silence and stared at it, you could have sworn it was somehow staring back at you, even if you knew this was foolish and impossible, even if you didn't dare admit to this feeling out loud.

None of it was natural, and yet it had to be.

Prewish forced himself to look away. "Keep examining it," he said to neither man in particular. "Let me know if you find anything else." He waited just long enough for both of them to acknowledge this order before he left the room.

It wouldn't be easy to keep this discovery under wraps, Prewish thought. Rumors had a way of leaching through the ice, spreading like a great network of cracks, but Prewish could not afford to let that happen here. Not now, with everything riding in the balance. He made his way out of the lapus lumeni division slowly, painfully aware of the vibrations emanating each time his boots touched down. How much did a person give away, just by moving about, just by setting things down and picking them up? If someone was skilled enough, he sometimes wondered, and listened hard enough, would they be able to tell everything that was going on, just by pressing their ears against the great slabs of ice that connected every piece of their empire?

Was it even possible to keep a secret in a place like this?

Chapter Two

THE FAST CLACK of excited footfalls brought the rumor to Prett Fellows's attention.

He was in his law library, positioned about halfway up the stacks via a sliding ladder. At the moment, his nose was buried in a book so fat that it took both hands to balance, his arm looped through the ladder's rails for support. A stray lock of white-blond hair hung beside his eyes, just enough to distract him. He wore his a little longer than the rest of his brothers, those who still *had* it, anyway, long enough to curl along the line of his ear. That was fine—he was still fairly young, young enough for his winning smile and roguish looks to do the family favors. Prett glanced at the stray bit of hair, annoyed. He was always pushing it back, but he dared not now, with his balance so careful on the ladder.

Prett didn't bother to look up as the footsteps raced into the room. He listened to them, tracking their movements with half an ear. Women's shoes, chiming against the ice in much the same manner as his mother's, but younger and lighter and somehow softer than Prestina, even in haste. They entered the room, skittered to a stop. Tapped slowly, as if their owner was turning in place to look for Prett. Then they started up again, quickly, in his direction.

"Prett!" a breathless young voice said. "Prett, you'll never believe this!"

"If that's true, then you should save yourself the trouble of telling me."

Prett flipped a page, still attempting to be engrossed in his research. Only when the voice gave a quiet "ugh" of frustration did he bother looking up—or rather, down. Annelle, his research assistant and one of his many nieces, was staring up at him with exasperation written plainly over her face. Prett allowed himself a smile. "What's your news?"

"Your sister has come back!"

The words burst out of her, as if they were simply too amazing to be bottled up for another second longer. And yet, they did not land with the intended impact on Prett. He looked quizzically at the book still in front of him, wondering why Annelle would have referred to her own mother in such a roundabout way of phrasing. Not to mention the question of why such news was noteworthy to begin with—to Prett's knowledge, Prenna came and went from the household with the same regularity as the rest of the Fellows family, so the idea of her *return* being a surprise was odd, to say the least.

"Um . . . okay," Prett said. He shut the book, sliding it back into place on its shelf, and only then did Annelle's words finally settle in Prett's mind. His *sister*—he did, technically, have more than just the one.

Prett's eyes widened as he whipped his attention back to his niece. Annelle was beaming at him, looking as if she had just excavated this news from the depths of the mines herself. But despite the surge that had coursed through him at the idea, Prett held himself reserved for a moment, steadying himself against the ladder. For seventeen years, Prett had waited and wished for something like this, and he was not going to be mistaken on this point. "Annelle . . . where did you hear this?"

Annelle laughed. "Grandfather is going around telling everyone. He says he's *seen* her! He says—hey, wait a second! Where are you going?"

Prett didn't bother to answer. He had leaped from the ladder and begun to charge out of the law library, all sense of decorum and safety be damned. The soles of his leather boots slid here and there as he navigated down the wide hallways of his family's expansive home, but Prett barely felt it as he crashed into the occasional pillar or servant. Praxis, Praxis, Praxis. Could it really be true?

It was easy enough to find her. Even without stopping to ask the servants, Prett could tell he was getting closer by the spark of delight in their eyes, or the clamped lips as he appeared, their gossip cut off by his presence. He strained his ears, listening. The whisper of movement, the dramatic murmur that rose up again in his wake. Annelle chased after him, calling for him to wait, but Prett ignored her. There was only one voice he was interested in hearing, though would he even recognize it after all this time?

As it turned out, yes. It was accented with an odd mix Prett couldn't quite place, and the tone had lowered a notch or two, but it was undeniably familiar. The sharp pitch of it echoed out from one of the ballrooms, just ahead, and Prett drew himself to a sudden halt outside the doorway. "No, this one's the smallest," he heard her saying, the Durlish words harsh and discordant. Prett was straightening the cut of his jacket, smoothing out the rich, royal-blue fabric as Annelle caught up with him. Unlike most of his family, he didn't bother with a heavy fur coat, not unless formality forced his hand. The many layers of his suit were enough.

"Wait here," he told Annelle, whose face fell open in unrestrained despair.

"But—!" she started, but Prett held up a single finger. Annelle clamped her mouth shut, crossing her arms over her chest. She slumped dramatically against the wall, the high, fanned collar of her dress mashing against the twists of her hair.

Prett turned away. Okay; he could do this.

"I don't know," Praxis was saying as he entered. "Probably when they—"

She cut herself off, staring opened-mouthed at the doors. At Prett.

In a family of eight children, Prett had only ever had one younger sibling. He was too close in age to remember when Praxis was born, of course, and so while they were growing up, Praxis had always insisted that Prett being older didn't matter since they were both the youngest at the end of a long line. Prett knew better. It didn't matter that he only had a year's lead time on her—Praxis was his responsibility, always had been.

His baby sister. He hadn't gotten a chance to say goodbye when she left.

Time had changed her, as it would, but perhaps not as much as Prett expected. The trappings of her hair and clothes aside, her face looked exactly the same as he remembered. It was so much like his own, as if they were mirror twins. Gods, but he'd missed her. He hadn't even realized how much, until now.

Prett felt the shy pull of his lips as he nodded at her. "Praxis," he said, while her mouth soundlessly formed the name, "Prett?"

Then, two voices at once: "What are you doing here?" Though they were asked in two separate languages.

Prett laughed, ignoring the question—both his own, and the one posed to him. He ran forward and wrapped Praxis in a one-armed hug, thumping her hard on the back. "I never thought I'd see you again," Prett said as he stepped away.

It was meant more out of sentiment than reproach, though his voice caught and turned it harsher than he'd intended. Praxis looked away, stepping back so that she once more aligned with the man she'd been speaking to when Prett interrupted.

Prett hadn't bothered to regard the man before, though now he tried to pay attention as Praxis made introductions. Praxis called him "Kaedrich," and he was by far the darkest man Prett had ever laid eyes on, much more so than even the tutor Praxis had as a child. It was hard not to stare. Kaedrich wore a trim suit, plaid green trousers sticking out from underneath a longer brown jacket and a suspiciously new fur coat. Prett glanced at the way Praxis leaned toward this stranger, her gloved fingers linked easily with his. He made note of it, but he did not comment. Prett accepted Kaedrich's handshake when offered, and he tried to issue a warm smile in return. Kaedrich was holding himself perfectly still until called upon, but hidden underneath his calm façade was a look of utter terror, as if the very walls around them might break apart and start attacking at any moment. Most people probably wouldn't notice it, but Prett had seen that exact behavior so many times, standing across from people as they argued their case to the magistrate; he had seen it so many times in the mirror as he practiced his own arguments and tried to mask it.

"It's a pleasure to meet you," Prett said, trying and failing to put Kaedrich at ease. The Durlish language felt awkward on his tongue, all staccato consonants and lazy vowels.

There were a million questions Prett wanted to ask, and yet as he looked back to Praxis, there was only one that actually made its way out. Only one that mattered.

"Have you called upon Mother yet?"

Frost chilled the air between them.

Prett leveled Praxis with a steady look. "You can't avoid her forever."

"I can try."

"Prax. You know that putting it off will only make things worse."

Praxis said nothing, just turned and looked at her shoes.

"Come on," Prett said, his voice laced with tenderness. He held out his arm, the way that someone from Durland might if he wished to escort a lady of quality. "I'll go with you. We'll face it together."

WHEN KAEDRICH FIRST learned they were heading to Yandosia, she thought she had some idea of what to expect.

After all, she had experienced a memory of it from Praxis, back when they'd plunged into the land of the dead to stop Pon Lanali and remove her as Lady of Souls. A delusion of these very halls had been spun as a bubble around Praxis and Kaedrich, and Kaedrich had seen for herself the opulence of the Fellows' dwelling. She was prepared for the endless tunnels that would lead here, she was prepared for the size and ostentation of the household, she was prepared for their excessive use of whale bone in place of the much more expensive imported wood, she was even a little prepared for the cold. Neither the grandeur nor the lighting nor the faces particularly surprised her.

What she was finding difficult to reconcile was, ironically, the most familiar thing of all: Praxis herself.

She carried herself differently here. Praxis had always been somewhat arrogant and haughty, and Kaedrich assumed this was a direct result of her upbringing—and maybe it was, but if so, you would expect an increase in her superiority the closer toward home she got. Instead, what Kaedrich had been observing could only be described as a kind of shutting down. Despite the brief outbursts of joy at seeing her father and Prett, or the indignation necessary when she needed someone to listen to her commands, Praxis spent most of her time since dropping beneath the ice acting as if she was trying her hardest to become part of the frozen walls around them. She spoke little, her face a controlled blank. Only a handful of times could Kaedrich catch her attention, and in those instances she had tried to smile at Praxis, send some kind of reassurance to guard against a thing she didn't even have a name for. The most Kaedrich got in response was a squeeze of the hand.

Praxis wouldn't take her hand now. She walked ahead of Kaedrich, arm linked with her brother, leaning against him as if steeling her strength. Once, Praxis seemed to almost stumble, her braced leg buckling for a second before she caught herself. Kaedrich lurched forward, her pulse leaping, but Prett had already steadied Praxis, already glanced to make sure she was okay. Cold air swept in Kaedrich's face as she hung back, following them through the labyrinth of the Fellows household. The three of them spoke not a word; not her and Praxis, not Praxis and Prett.

By the time they reached another massive set of double doors, Kaedrich's heart had worked its way to her throat. Two men, tall and willowy, stood on either side in exquisite uniforms of silver and blue. They tapped their lips, as expected, and then they nodded—no, Kaedrich realized, they *bowed their heads*, bending slightly at the waists—as they reached between them and swept the doors open with a flourish. Kaedrich reached up, as they passed through the doorway, and grounded herself against a pin that she wore on her lapel. The wavy rays of a sunbeam, a reminder of Perlandra's love, were soft and well worn under her fingers. She tossed a fast prayer out; she had a feeling they'd need it.

On the other side of the doors, another uniformed man, hair tied back in a tidy ponytail. Same build, same uniform, though his jacket bore a silver signet above the breast. He regarded them with no apparent surprise, just tapped his lips without a word, and motioned for them to follow as he turned toward the room.

If the rest of the dwelling was fit for a king, then the room they found themselves in next could only have been the heart of court. Kaedrich was actually surprised, upon first entering, that there weren't a pair of thrones at the far end. The décor was done in much the same styling as the Main Hall, mosaics and chandeliers and gems encased deep in the ice, pale support beams cutting panels into the walls. More clouds overhead, more birds chirping near the ceiling. A soft white carpet, shimmering as if woven with diamonds, led the way all down a long and narrow chamber, to where a raised dais supported a massive white desk.

It was difficult for Kaedrich to unlock her knees enough to walk forward, but she dared not be left behind in such an environment. She hurried to keep up as the uniformed man led them to a place several feet back from the dais.

They were announced, or so Kaedrich assumed. Even if she could speak Yandosian, she doubted she'd be able to pay enough attention to understand what he'd said, because all of her attention was fixed on the chair that sat in front of the desk.

Or, more accurately, the figure occupying it.

Prestina had her back to them, opposite to what Kaedrich was used to. Her desk clearly was not intended to have visitors sitting across from her: everything from the high-backed chair, to the positioning of the desk, to the enormous collar rising up behind Prestina's head, was designed to let you know that you were unimportant. All you could see were jewels and feathers and furs, though they did shift in response to the man's announcement.

He was already slipping back toward the door, and Kaedrich was suddenly burning with envy that his task in this matter had ended.

Prestina, still ignoring them, said something, her voice turning up at the end like a question. Gods, it sounded so much like Praxis's—the dip of the accent, the way it bloomed outward through the room, demanding attention.

Kaedrich watched as Praxis stiffened. "Yes, Mother, it's true. Though I would appreciate it if you'd speak in Durlish."

A slight trill of laughter, followed by another brief question.

"Because I *asked* you to," Praxis snapped.

Prestina sighed, as if already exhausted by this exchange. "Very well, dear, you don't need to get so snippy about it." And only now did she turn, rising from her chair with a great sigh of dresses and robes.

Kaedrich's breath caught in her chest. Almost two years ago, a magical creature had been conjured up, designed to pose as Praxis from more than twenty years in the future—and it had been such a perfect replica, so easy to see how Praxis would settle into her age. For the briefest second Kaedrich's head spun at the sight of Prestina, nearly convinced that the same creature had risen from the dead and found her way here.

She *was* Praxis—older, though the ethereal glow lent to Yandosians by the lapus lumeni hid many of the years from her face—and yet, in this setting, with these clothes, with her hair swept into elaborate knots and dotted with diamonds, she was also a queen. Something even resembling a crown was nestled atop her head, spikes of ice rising up almost as high as the collar that framed her living portrait. White feathers trailed down her pale blue dress, glittering with hidden gems. They shifted with her, rippling with life, as she descended the dais.

Praxis was the sole focus of her attention, and for the moment that was fine with Kaedrich. Even Prett had stepped to the side, so that nothing would interfere with this reunion. Prestina stepped forward, placing her hands on Praxis's shoulders and gracing a kiss upon the top of her daughter's dipped head.

Then Prestina took a single step back, folding her jeweled hands neatly in front of her. "My poor darling, were you set about by bandits?"

Praxis's face twitched with a barely repressed flinch. "No, Mother. This is just how I look now."

"Ah, well. No matter—that's easily fixed."

"Very funny."

"Was I joking?" Prestina asked.

Praxis cleared her throat, ignoring that. She motioned behind her. "Mother, may I present Kaedrich Mann—"

"How long are you planning to stay?"

"I . . . don't know," Praxis said. Her hand fell, and though she was clearly upset by the change in topic, Kaedrich was just as glad to have the attention diverted off of her.

Not that Prestina had given her even the slightest bit of attention in the first place.

"Kaedrich and I haven't really discussed it," Praxis continued. "We've had a long trip."

Prestina smiled. Poised and perfect. "Of course. Well, there's plenty of time to settle that later. For now, you're just in time! I'm throwing a party this evening, and it will be lovely to present you again."

"A party?" Praxis asked. "Mother, I don't think that either of us is up to a party right now. We just *got* here. I haven't even had a chance to clean up. I don't—"

"Oh, nonsense, a little relaxation will do you good. I promise you it's a modestly sized party—in the Onyx Room."

"The—?" Praxis shook her head. "You call *that* a modest party?"

Prestina rolled her eyes. "Praxis, my darling, you've been gone for years. You really can't oblige me just this once? It's *one* evening. It's important to me. I hardly think it's going to kill you."

"It might," Praxis muttered.

"Don't be so dramatic. You have three hours to freshen up and rest."

Kaedrich glanced over. There was clearly no way Praxis was going to let herself be bullied into something like this, especially when the day had already been so long and fraught. From the instant Prestina had suggested it, Kaedrich knew the answer was going to be "no," that the answer had to be "no," and yet as Kaedrich watched, Praxis was offering up no immediate refusal. Instead, she was grinding her teeth together, so subtly that she might not even be aware of it. Neither she nor her mother said anything for a while, a long while, time suddenly dragging on so that Kaedrich was aware of each nervous breath forced from her chest.

Finally, Praxis's jaw settled. "I'm afraid I couldn't possibly," she said, "as I don't have a single thing that would be appropriate to wear to such an . . . *important* function."

"Ah." Prestina nodded, and for a second it looked like Praxis had found the one vulnerability in her argument.

But then Prestina looked Praxis up and down. Once, with military-grade precision. She nodded. "You can wear something of mine. It looks like we're about the same size these days."

Even being new to this family, Kaedrich could tell something significant had just happened. Praxis took a step back, her eyes nearly popping from her head, and Prett drew in a sharp breath. Prestina, meanwhile, was looking as calm as ever, as if it was nothing at all.

Praxis cleared her throat. She was obviously trying to think fast, and she grabbed at the first thing she found. "What about Kaedrich?"

Prestina frowned, just the slightest crinkle in her brow. "Who?"

"*Kaedrich*, Mother," Praxis snapped. "In case you'd forgotten, I didn't arrive alone?" She turned, reaching back, and despite the jolt of fear in Kaedrich's heart, she found herself stepping forward. Taking Praxis's hand.

Prestina did not look over, did not even blink. Instead, a patient smile bloomed over her face. "Darling, you hardly need to bring your own servant along with you. There will be plenty to attend to you at the party."

"If you had given me the chance to do a proper introduction, you would know that he is *not* my servant," Praxis said. She stole a look at Kaedrich, their eyes meeting for the first time since entering the room. Praxis drank in the courage found there for as long as she dared, and when she did finally turn back to her mother, she spoke with the steel precision of a fine blade. "This is Kaedrich Mannly. My *sare l' dell*."

The switch was instantaneous, and terrible to behold. Like day crashing into frozen night, like rain transmuting to the cut of sleet. Prestina iced over, nostrils flaring, as she reared back and slapped Praxis—*hard*—across the flat of her cheek. The sound broke through the room, cracking like the shatter of glass.

Praxis staggered back under the force of it, her hand slipping from Kaedrich's like a drowning sailor losing grip on the last plank of wood. Prestina was shouting, words spilling out faster than Kaedrich could track, but Praxis's rebuttal was already roaring from her throat, charging into battle as she turned back.

There followed, then, a brief and violent exchange in rapid-fire Yandosian. Kaedrich flinched away, not daring to tread too close, and was relieved when Prett guided her another step to the side. She glanced at him, offering a nervous smile, only to find him studying her like she was something he'd never seen before.

Perlandra's breath, what had Praxis *said* about her? The phrase wasn't one Kaedrich had ever heard before, and she felt herself warming from fear and dread as, abruptly, Praxis and Prestina cut themselves off. Kaedrich looked over to find mother and daughter glowering at each other, the rage of their faces perfectly matched.

A stalemate.

But then, as if changing a dance, Prestina blinked and shook herself off. Her face wiped clean, a new arrangement of comportment and benign civility settled into place. She brushed by Praxis, extending a formal handshake in Kaedrich's direction.

It was all Kaedrich could do *not* to flinch away from it. Somehow, she managed to accept the gesture, though Prestina's fingers clamped so tightly around hers that it hurt. The one consolation was that this close, at least, it was easier to see the differences between Praxis and her mother. Not just physically, though Prestina bore more signs of her age than Kaedrich had thought from a distance; there was something cutting in her gaze, as if she was carving Kaedrich up into neat little pieces, taking note of every detail of her appearance all at once. The smile she gave Kaedrich appeared genuine, but it was every bit as polished and frozen as the ice walls around them. "Pleasure to make your acquaintance," Prestina said, though Kaedrich didn't believe that for one second.

"And yours."

There was the slightest uptick at the corner of Prestina's mouth as she pulled her hand back. She turned without further comment, her heels clacking against the polished dais as she stepped back up and settled herself in her chair.

And so, without another word on the matter, it seemed they were all dismissed.

Praxis did not move at first. She was watching the back of Prestina's high collar with an empty expression that sent a chill down Kaedrich's spine. More disturbing than the actions themselves, it was Praxis's response that Kaedrich worried about. For someone to have gotten a strike in at all . . . Ordinarily, Kaedrich would have feared for the life of anyone who dared to lay a hand on Praxis, but Praxis had just stood there, just taken it. She hadn't even healed it yet, the impression of each of Prestina's fingers stark pink against Praxis's cheek. Kaedrich *wanted* to reach out to her, and yet she did not—instead it was Prett, a moment later, who rested his hand on Praxis's shoulder, and then everything clicked back into place. Praxis scowled, twitching her fingers so that she spun on the heel of her braced leg, and the three of them moved back down the long room in silence.

Chapter Three

PRAXIS MANAGED TO hold herself steady all the way until they were safely into the outer hall. She kept her breathing in check, the spitting spark of magic burning angrily behind her eyes. One deep breath, two deep breaths. She focused on the stretch and curl of her fingers, the tension as the gears lifted her foot up and forward on command, one step after another. She waited until they were safely beyond her mother's suite, the heavy doors thunking shut behind them. Then, and only then, did she allow her muscles to sag. She collapsed against the nearest wall, the chill of the ice seeping some of the bitter heat from her stinging cheek.

How many times had she done this, standing right here in this very spot? With her eyes closed she may as well have been a teenager again, waiting for the ringing in her head to subside. Perhaps she was in trouble for talking back, or perhaps she had acted poorly at a dinner party, or perhaps it was because she had not flirted with the man they'd seated her next to. Praxis's thoughts were whirling madly around her, time collapsing and looping back over and over again, and for a second it was almost impossible to remember which were the memories and which was the present moment.

But then a familiar touch brought her back to herself, running through her hair and cradling the back of her head. Praxis gratefully leaned into the cup of Kaedrich's hand, allowing Kaedrich to draw her face away from the wall so that the raw of Praxis's cheek was exposed. Praxis still leaned her shoulder against the ice, too weary to move.

Kaedrich's brows drew together in tender concern. "Are you all right?"

All right. That was perhaps a bit more than Praxis could hope for at the moment, but she nodded anyway. All right enough. It would have to do, for now.

Prett cleared his throat. He'd been standing at a respectful distance, giving them a moment to collect themselves. Praxis turned her head. She was suddenly very aware of the way she and Kaedrich were standing, of the continued presence of Kaedrich's hand on the back of her neck.

Of the fact that Prett had heard *everything* she'd said in their mother's office.

Not that Praxis had made any attempt to hide her relationship with Kaedrich, nor did she plan to start. But neither had she ever expected to openly *declare* herself like that. Granted, neither of them knew of Kaedrich's true identity as a woman—still. Praxis flinched, remembering the words. *My sare l' dell.* It was not a phrase to be thrown around lightly.

Praxis straightened up, the tiniest of gaps appearing between her and Kaedrich. "I'm going to my rooms, if it's the same to you," she told Prett.

"Absolutely," Prett said, as smooth as his trim blue suit. "I'm sure you must both be very tired. Will I see you at dinner, then?"

It was spoken as a question—it really wasn't. Both of them knew what the answer would be. Barely back in the same tunnels, and already Prestina had coiled around Praxis like a miser snake. What would happen to Praxis if she stayed here, even just for a little while? Already, she hadn't felt like herself in days.

She forced a stiff nod. It was all the leave Prett needed. He made a polite goodbye and slipped off down a branching hallway, gone with barely a whisper.

"Come on," Praxis said, gruffly shoving herself away from the wall. Her coat lingered against the ice for a moment, the fabric already freezing against the surface. "It's this way."

She tugged her glove off and tucked it into her pocket. One hand cupped her tender cheek as they started walking, her fingers first warming and then cooling with a gentle healing spell. Her mother had never allowed Praxis to heal away the handprints immediately, always insisting that the lessons would never stick if they were wiped clean too soon. Leaving the mark had been an old habit, one Praxis hadn't even questioned, and realizing this now dragged her already foul mood down another notch.

The guest rooms were spread across three different levels, ranked according to which luxuries the Fellows wished to afford their visitors. Praxis moved without thought, the layout of her family's dwelling seared into her heart. She would never get lost here, no matter how many identical twisting paths and wide, level staircases there were. Emerald Level was reserved for only the highest and most welcomed dignitaries, and while Praxis never would have chosen it for herself, she was touched by the fact that Prawl had immediately given it to Kaedrich.

They didn't speak until Praxis found their rooms, though Kaedrich's questions swirled around her as an unspoken cloud. Praxis was grateful for her discretion as they passed the silent eyes of servants. A pair stood sentry by one of the guest suites, and they touched their lips and bowed as they opened the doors at Praxis's approach. Praxis took Kaedrich's hand when she hesitated at the entrance.

Growing up, Praxis had never had reason to set foot in this particular suite, but the inside was no surprise. A little smaller than her childhood rooms, the suite consisted first of a combination sitting/dining room, one wall full of nothing but books; to the left was a private sculpture garden, nowhere near as impressive as the courtyard but still; while the right held the bedroom, bathroom, and dressing rooms beyond. The lapus lumeni in the ceiling was scattered to vaguely represent stars, and they trailed down the walls in a slowly fading approximation of the horizon at dawn.

Praxis let herself through to the bedroom, collapsing onto the thick mattress. She did not care that her coat was probably leaving a layer of grit on the otherwise impeccable fur blankets, she just drew them up around herself and cocooned into a lump. A headache was blooming at her temples, and her disabled leg had been developing a dull ache the closer they'd gotten to the frozen air. It would just be her luck, Praxis thought with a snort, that the first twinge of feeling she'd gotten from it in three years would be discomfort.

It was several long minutes before Kaedrich's footsteps padded into the bedroom, and another before a weight settled on the bed next to Praxis. She perched along the edge and pulled the blanket away from Praxis's face. Her cool fingers ran along Praxis's head as if tending to a sick child.

"I'm sorry you had to witness that," Praxis muttered, talking into the thick fur.

Kaedrich leaned over, kissing Praxis's cheek. "I'm sorry you had to go through it."

Praxis squeezed her eyes shut, and drew her arms more tightly around herself. She should be used to Kaedrich's gentle kindness by this point—

even before they admitted their feelings to each other, Kaedrich had never been anything but tender and sweet—and yet, there were times when Praxis still reflexively braced herself against it.

So Kaedrich sat back up, giving Praxis her space. Which was almost as bad, the quiet understanding somehow even more loving than an outright embrace would have been. Though she still rested her hand on Praxis's side, a subtle presence to let Praxis know she was there for her.

They were quiet for a few moments after that. But finally, Kaedrich couldn't take the silence anymore. "What did you *say* to her, anyway?"

Praxis opened her eyes. The bedroom wall was inset with streaks of emeralds, a sort of abstract jungle clawing up from the floor. She remembered saying it—*my sare l' dell*—but another part of her still couldn't believe that she'd mustered the courage.

She rolled over, until she could look up at Kaedrich. "It's . . . difficult to translate," Praxis said. "Just trust me when I say it accurately describes the state of . . . us."

Please, Praxis thought, watching as her explanation settled itself into Kaedrich's mind. *Please don't ask me to be more specific.* Praxis knew that she would probably have to explain the meaning of it, one day, but she also knew beyond the shadow of a doubt that she could not manage it today.

Kaedrich studied her for a minute as she read all those conflicting feelings off of Praxis's soul. It still shocked Praxis, at times, the way Kaedrich seemed to just *know*, regardless of how hard Praxis tried to bury things.

"Okay, so . . . speaking of 'us,'" Kaedrich said finally. She cleared her throat. "Since you brought it up, I've been wondering . . . what exactly *is* our . . . 'state'? I mean," she added hurriedly, "I'm not unhappy, but—well, it's just gone so quickly, and—I don't know, are we courting? Should I discuss my intentions with your father?"

Praxis couldn't help it—she bit down on a giggle, just as it was beginning to slip out. Her chest loosened for the first time in days, looking up at Kaedrich's nervous expression. Praxis raised her eyebrows suggestively. "You have 'intentions' for me?"

Kaedrich blushed. "No, I just—I don't want to offend—"

"Shh," Praxis said. She wormed her arm free, reaching up to cup Kaedrich's cheek. "Relax, Ella. You don't need to speak to my father."

At the mention of her pet name, the façade of "Kaedrich" seemed to melt away, and Kaedriella's shoulders relaxed. It had been strange for both of them, getting used to addressing her as her proper name, but Praxis had insisted on using it in private whenever possible. *"The world has to think I'm in love with a man,"* Praxis had said, on the second day of their sea voyage, *"but you need to know that I'm not."*

Both of them smiled a little, seeming to remember the conversation as one.

Praxis drew her hand away. "Besides," she said, never wanting to dwell on sentimentality for long, "around here, parents don't really have as much to do with approving matches as the auditors. And even then, it's only when a couple starts talking about marriage. So we're fine."

She had meant it to be reassuring, and yet the silence that followed dragged on for just a second too long. Kaedrich frowned, and for a split-second Praxis's heart rate spiked—surely Kaedrich wasn't thinking about . . . ? So when she asked, "Who are the auditors?" instead, Praxis all but laughed in dizzy relief.

"Oh," Praxis said, waving her hand in dismissal. "They analyze a couple's financial portfolio, and create a series of projections as to how each person's bottom line would be affected by a merger."

Kaedrich jerked back, her eyes wide as if in horror.

"What?" Praxis asked.

"You make it sound so . . . cold."

Praxis raised her eyebrows, glancing obviously at the ice that surrounded them. "We're a cold people, Ella. It comes with the territory."

"That doesn't have to mean—"

"I know. But honestly, is it any worse than how things are done in Durland? Parents take this sort of thing into account just as much as we do when they consider whether or not to give their blessing. We're just upfront about it. And we have ledgers to back up our arguments."

Kaedrich frowned. "Ledgers don't have a column for love."

Praxis shrugged. It was true, but how was she supposed to explain to Kaedrich the way that such considerations didn't even factor in here? Marriage and love and lovers—it wasn't all so tightly wound together as the romantics of Durland expected. Seven hells, Praxis doubted her parents had ever loved each other, though neither had ever taken open lovers on the side.

Before she could even begin to broach the subject, however, she was saved by a sharp knock upon the outer door of their suite. Kaedrich started to get up, but Praxis stilled her with a touch to her shoulder. She unwrapped herself from her bundle of furs, stretching her fingers as she swung her feet off the bed.

Praxis was concerned, as she crossed the open sitting room, that some other member of her family had tracked her down for a reunion. Even the handful she'd endured so far had been exhausting, and though she was perfectly happy to greet the rest of them in turn, it was going to have to wait until she'd regained some of her strength.

So when she opened the door she was in luck, and not. Servants, not siblings, stood in the empty hallway—but in their hands were a pair of gifts, bestowed by Prestina. One servant carried an exquisite ballgown, the quality of which had the power to impress even Praxis; and yet she barely paid it attention, because the suit that came with it was clearly intended for Kaedrich. It could have been anyone's—her father's, or any of her brothers', or even Prenna's husband's—and the fact that it was borrowed did not in and of itself offer offense. Nor was it soiled, stained, or patched in any way, not even faded around the edges.

No, the problem was that even Praxis, having been gone for seventeen years, could tell this suit didn't match the current styles. And if *she* could tell, then everyone at the party would be able to as well. And although Praxis hated herself for even noticing, hated still more that she *cared*, she knew this had been done on purpose as a slight against Kaedrich.

Praxis straightened up, her lips drawn with a reserved disdain she knew the servants would recognize—she'd gotten it from her mother. Sure enough, a flicker of dread could be seen darting from person to person, no doubt wondering what they'd done wrong. "Return these to my mother," Praxis said, "and tell her only this: She takes us both . . . or not at all."

She did not wait for their acknowledgment. Praxis slammed the door in their faces.

PRENNA FELLOWS, THE fourth child in line and the only girl in the family aside from Praxis, had a head for numbers.

It was a natural gift. From the time that she was a small child first learning her sums, a sense of peace and understanding had settled over her. Truly, there was order to the world after all. She attacked her lessons with all the ferocity she had to repress in the rest of her life, and as she grew, numbers became her silent companion.

Of course Prenna knew what was expected of her, as a woman and a Fellows both, and she accepted her duties gracefully. While her baby sister, seven years her junior, was already putting up fusses whenever they tried to trap her in a dress, Prenna would take extra care in her appearance. When Praxis would throw a tantrum, Prenna would try to shush and soothe her. When Praxis was stubborn, Prenna would try to negotiate. And as the two girls grew, so too did their differences. Prenna kept herself quiet, polite, deferential. She played girls' games with other girls living in Bolt, and she learned how to sing, how to dance, how to flirt. Her sums were her only small rebellion, but even that was so silent it was easy to keep hidden. Besides, it wasn't a terrible fault—merely useless, as far as most people were concerned, for a woman of Prenna's standing to bother with. What did she need to understand numbers for? She wasn't even going to cook.

And then, one day when Prenna was fifteen, Prestina brought her into her office, sat the girl at the enormous desk, and taught her how to balance a ledger.

It shouldn't have been a surprise, but it was. After all, it was common family knowledge that Prestina kept track of not just the household accounts, but maintained her own records of the Fellows' company ledgers as well. It was not the sort of thing one talked about, though—certainly never in public—so for Prestina to encourage her oldest daughter to follow in her footsteps, well. It carried weight, the significance pressing down hard on young Prenna's shoulders as her mother began her lessons.

Thus Prenna learned, slowly, how to handle the finances of the family empire, and by the time she was seventeen, was well on her way to becoming an official bookkeeper for the business. Such a thing should have turned quickly to scandal, and in any other family it might have; perhaps the Fellows were so enormous that they were allowed the occasional eccentricity. Besides, it wasn't as if Prenna was becoming an outcast. She still socialized with the other youths, still attended all of her parents' balls, still flirted where she was told to flirt, still danced where she was told to dance. And when a young man from a respectable family came courting, she happily accepted his proposal. They married a few months later, and Prenna was a mother within a year.

Through it all, though, she kept up her numbers. Her one private condition with her new husband, before they were married, was that he would not attempt to interfere with her working in her family's company. She would be a loving wife—dutiful, bear his children, stand by him in his own ambitions—but she would never abandon what she now viewed as her duty to her family.

She was lucky, really, in her choice of husband. She realized this only years later, just how much. Quite apart from protesting at her terms, Lorric had accepted and even embraced Prenna's interest in the company, and when Prenna was made the head accountant, he was no less proud than if he'd achieved it himself.

So Prenna's children—a son, two daughters, and then another son, years later—were raised more in an office than a nursery, but that was fine with them. Prenna kept their bassinets and cribs and fenced-off play areas right beside her desk, stopping often to swoop in and attend to them whenever they fussed. She rejected every nanny offered to her, even when her children were sick, even when the workload grew enormous. She balanced books with a baby in one arm, and her pen scrawling along from the other. Even once her children were too old to be tended to constantly, they often barged in and played near her feet, old habits keeping them close.

Only one was still a child anymore, though, and even he was bordering on too old for games. Still, Prenna looked up expectantly when her office door opened, sure that one or another had come asking for her attention, for her counsel, for her mediating abilities to settle a dispute between them. Old habits died hard, and it was so rare for anyone else to bother her in the middle of the day, that it took her a second to process the sight in front of her.

"Mother!" Prenna was on her feet at once, her pen dropped on the desk in her haste. Prestina Fellows took up most of the open doorway, between her wide collar and wider skirts, and Prenna rushed around the desk to approach. "Is something wrong?"

There must be something wrong, for Prenna could think of no other reason why her mother would ever call upon her directly like this. Instantly, Prenna thought of her children: Rommand, dead; Julaine, dead; Annelle, dead; Hanshaw, dead. So when Prestina held up her hand, shaking her head at the idea of tragedy, Prenna nearly fell to her knees in relief.

Prenna nodded, trying to calm her racing heart. "Then . . . what brings you here?"

"Forgive me," Prestina said, "but I have need to borrow one of Lorric's suits. May I trouble you to assist me in selecting one?"

"Of . . . of course. Please, this way."

She did not ask what her mother wanted it for; you did not ask Prestina anything, not directly, not if you knew what was good for you. Prenna merely turned, leading the way through her office. It was far less grand than her mother's suite, and far smaller—set up directly adjacent to her own and her children's bedrooms, a relatively small little hub off the main trunk of the Fellows' master household. Prestina followed without a word as Prenna led them through, breezing straight past the bedroom and into the large selection of closets beyond.

Lorric's suits were laid out in seemingly endless rows of fur and cloth woven thick with patterns. Prenna stepped aside, allowing her mother access. Though Prestina swept through with unwavering confidence, somehow Prenna doubted her mother had *ever* set foot inside of a closet; certainly not in recent memory, Prenna was sure of that. That was what servants were for—not to mention the fact that Prestina probably hadn't worn the same dress twice in her entire life.

Prenna could not deny the curiosity bubbling open on her face for anyone to see. "Is there something in particular you'd like?" she asked, hoping the question was helpful enough to not be considered prying.

Prestina ran her hand along the sleeve of one particularly fine coat, deep ocher with rows of diamond piping. "Your sister is going to be attending the party tonight."

Prenna laughed. She didn't mean to, but the absurdity of her mother's comment had yanked it out of her before she could contain it. "I see. Are we also to be entertaining the Star Fairy while we're at it?" she asked, adding to her mother's joke.

Only, when Prestina turned, there was nothing joking about her face. Prenna's hand flew to her mouth. "Mercy's sake, are you serious?" Prestina nodded.

"Oh my—! I thought . . . but . . . Mother, she's not dead?"

Prestina frowned. "Don't tell me you ever believed those rumors."

"I . . . I didn't know what to think," Prenna said, too stunned to even be bothered by her mother's chastising. "I have to go see her!"

Prenna had already gathered up a fistful of her skirts when her mother's hand landed firmly on her shoulder. "You will not," Prestina said. "Your sister has had a long journey, let her rest. You can see her at the party tonight. In the meantime, you can help me pick out a suit for her"—Prestina hesitated, her mouth twisting up—"companion."

"Wait, you mean that Praxis . . . I'm sorry, but—Praxis . . . brought a *man* with her?"

"Of a sort," Prestina said, snorting under her breath.

"I see." Prenna fell silent, watching as her mother continued to survey Lorric's suit collection. Was it possible, Prenna wondered, that Prestina didn't *know*? The idea of one of them being able to keep a secret from their mother was almost unfathomable, and yet . . .

Then again, Prenna had only suspicions herself, so maybe it wasn't that odd for it to have gone by without their mother's notice. Praxis had been careful, when she'd lived here, to keep her inclinations to herself. Only the occasional overlong look here, a bit of reluctance there, had ever tipped Prenna's curiosity. And maybe . . . Prenna doubted it, but maybe she'd been wrong, to think that Praxis preferred the company of women—though the presence of this mysterious "companion" certainly lent credence to that. Either way, she decided, striding forward to help her mother select an appropriate outfit, it would certainly prove to be an interesting evening.

KAEDRICH HADN'T MEANT to fall asleep, but she did so anyway. Weariness dragged at her like an undertow, lulling her as she laid down in the very spot that Praxis had vacated when she went to answer the door, as Kaedrich buried her face in the thick pillows to block out the light, as she slid into dreams.

When she woke up more than two hours later, a part of her was convinced she was still dreaming. Kaedrich jerked awake, a gentle hand resting on her shoulder. For a moment, she could not place where she was, and the blinding light and piercing cold seemed to flatten her to the bed, unable to move, unable to think. She squinted up, trying to clear her vision. An image of Praxis came to her, glowing as if caught by the light of Perlandra herself, and in it Praxis was changed: she wore a gown of cream satin and rose-tinted velvet, curls of white fur ringing the neckline and the wide cuffs of her sleeves; a high collar fanned out behind her head, dotted with diamonds as clear as stars, and rubies polished until they were drops of blood.

"Ella," the vision said, shaking her gently. "It's time to get up. You have to get ready."

This is when the world came back to Kaedrich, all of their journey kicking her in the stomach at once, and this is when Kaedrich realized that it was no vision after all. Praxis was really standing over her, done up like a queen.

She's home, Kaedrich thought, her chest instantly squeezing tight around her heart. She pushed herself until she was sitting upright—and, seeing this, Praxis abruptly turned and stalked to a vanity in the corner, a wide array of jewelry and makeup spread out across the surface like an alchemist's laboratory table.

Kaedrich couldn't stop gawking. Praxis's skirts rustled with each step, sighing as she settled herself in front of the vanity. Three angled mirrors stood tall before her, and though the high collar of Praxis's dress blocked most of the reflection from view, there was one tiny corner unobstructed. Praxis was frowning, staring at the spread before her. Her hand shook as she reached across for a tiny jar.

"You don't have to do this," Kaedrich said, understanding rushing through her. Hatred sprung hot on its heels—hatred at Prestina, for insisting that Praxis come to the party, for sending a dress for her to wear. Kaedrich knew it ran deeper than that, that somehow Prestina held a kind of sway over Praxis, and she hated her for that, too. She remembered the way Praxis had just stood there, allowed someone to strike her. Kaedrich was on her feet before she realized her intention to stand, and she raced to Praxis's side and took her wrist, to still her from opening the jar. "Praxis," she started, but Praxis only shook her head.

Praxis wrapped Kaedrich's hand in hers, prying it away. "It's all right," she said, though she was clearly lying. She drew Kaedrich's hand to her lips, pressing a kiss against her fingers. "Please don't fight me on this. I've made up my mind to go, and I know it's asking a lot for you to come with me, but—"

"I would never let you go alone."

The relief that poured out of her was heartbreaking. Praxis shut her eyes against it, kissing Kaedrich's fingers once more. "Thank you." She turned a moment later, suddenly composed. "There's a suit for you, over there. I think it belongs to my brother-in-law, but it looks like it will fit."

Kaedrich nodded. Her grip was released, and Kaedrich traced her fingers along the curve of Praxis's cheek before stepping away.

Getting dressed took Kaedrich longer than she'd expected. Perlandra's breath, a proper Yandosian suit had so many *layers*. Long undergarments, two sets of socks, fur-lined pants in light brown. An undershirt, then a white shirt woven of something that looked like silk, but was stiflingly hot once she slid it on. The collar covered her whole neck, choking her. The cuffs were snug as irons on her wrists. On top of *that*: a lightly quilted jacket, sunflower yellow in Kaedrich's case, a belt that tied around the waist. Praxis came over, adjusting the belt so that it rode, loose and useless, over Kaedrich's hipbones, the tails trailing off-center down the top of her leg. Was that not enough? Surely it must be, but no, for next came the coat, heavy fur dragging down Kaedrich's shoulders and trailing loosely around her like a cape. Praxis selected a variety of gems from her vanity, pressing two rings into Kaedrich's hand, a chain that would cross her chest and hold the opening of her coat in place, and an overdone pin that seemed to weigh half a pound. Kaedrich sighed, adjusting it all.

She'd have much preferred the pin she normally wore on her lapel, the symbol of Perlandra to keep her safe, but one look and she knew that Praxis wouldn't have it. Praxis had returned to her vanity and Kaedrich slid her rings on. She made a fist so that the array of stones caught the light.

As she stared down at them, green and amber and even one in jet black, she did feel a flicker of doubt at the whole enterprise; not just the party, but Yandosia in general. But then she looked across at Praxis, just now standing up from the vanity. Though she was done to perfection—short hair combed back to create the illusion of being both longer and drawn into a bun, a plume of crimson feathers rising a good foot-and-a-half above her head, her neck encrusted with the finest layer of gemstones— there was the smallest hint of the real Praxis skirting about the edges of her eyes; and she was scared.

There was no other place in the world Kaedrich would ever be, not now, not when Praxis needed her. Kaedrich approached with her arm offered, and after Praxis slipped her gloved hand around Kaedrich's elbow, they paused for a minute to look at themselves in the mirrors. They were almost unrecognizable, the king and queen of a land Kaedrich had never heard of. The mirror framed them as if it was a portrait.

Praxis was the first to look away. She guided Kaedrich out of their suite, past the servants at the door. The two of them walked stiffly, neither one comfortable in these clothes that felt more like disguises. Through an endless series of corridors and wide, sweeping staircases. At several points the walls opened up, revealing a pit of balconies and railings, a dizzying number of levels hollowed out through the ice like a great mine shaft. Kaedrich lingered at one, leaning over—she couldn't see the bottom.

At the base of a different set of stairs, Praxis stopped. Music had begun to filter out from somewhere up ahead, interspersed with trilling laughter and the clink of glasses. Her grip tightened on Kaedrich's elbow, and Kaedrich put her hand over Praxis's. "You don't have to go," Kaedrich repeated.

Praxis shook her head, wincing as if she was in pain. "No, it's not that. Kaedrich, I . . . I'm sorry, but I had to tell my mother that you were a lord."

The words were so unexpected that at first they didn't even make sense. It took Kaedrich a moment to sort out exactly what Praxis had said, understanding settling over her like an executioner's hood. She swallowed. "You . . . what?"

"I know, I know." Praxis turned, her face spilling over with embarrassment and remorse and panic. "I'm sorry, but it was the only way I could get her to let you stay. So just . . . just don't say anything to contradict it."

"What, like *anything real about my life*?"

Praxis flinched. "I'm sorry," she said again, as if being sorry would magically fix the situation. "If . . . if it makes you feel any better, I picked a minor title—so you don't have to pretend to be a duke, or anything like that. You . . . you have an estate, but nothing more."

"Oh, well," Kaedrich said, rolling her eyes, "so long as I don't have to pass myself off as a *duke* . . ."

Though, actually, even as she lashed out at the idea, it did offer some small degree of reassurance. She sighed, the obvious discomfort that radiated off of Praxis softening her own annoyance. Kaedrich drew Praxis in, wrapping her into a hug. She hesitated for a second, trying to find a free area upon which to kiss Praxis's head; finding none, she ducked and landed one on her cheek instead.

"Please don't hate me," Praxis mumbled into the fur of Kaedrich's collar.

Kaedrich shook her head. "Never. I mean," she added, her voice softening, "unless you make me pose as a *duke*."

Bravely, Praxis tried to smile. Kaedrich stepped back, arranging Praxis by her side as if she were a porcelain doll. Together, they held themselves tall, backs ramrod straight. Praxis squeezed Kaedrich's elbow, and Kaedrich patted her hand in return. Kaedrich gave a firm nod. "All right. Let's get this over with."

Chapter Four

PRAXIS WORE THE clothes, the smile. Though she'd been terrified approaching it, the role came back to her as easily as taking a breath. In the glamour of the Onyx Room, the walls splashed with plates of polished black and dotted with white bone carvings and beams, Praxis all but glowed with a vibrancy she barely recognized. In some ways, ironically, it would have been easier to live with if it was harder to do; with each greeting she exchanged, each false cheer exclaimed at seeing a face that she'd hoped to never encounter again, Praxis felt a tiny part of herself die inside, like slowly encasing her true heart in a thick layer of ice.

Kaedrich hung tightly by Praxis's elbow, an untouched drink in her hand and a permanent stony smile etched into her face. She said little, nodding at introductions and awkwardly trying to mimic the Yandosian hand-to-lips gesture, ignorant of when it was and wasn't appropriate. It was obvious to anyone that she didn't belong, that she wasn't comfortable—Praxis noticed it, then hated herself for noticing it, then hated herself for hating herself, because of *course* Kaedrich didn't really want to be here, and who could blame her?

At first, it was a seemingly endless parade of faces. Some Praxis knew, some she didn't. Prestina introduced them around to old and new alike, her wayward daughter Praxis, returned to us at last!, and yes, this is Lord Mannly, from Durland. Never a hint in her speech that Praxis and Kaedrich had anything to do with each other, and so eventually Praxis started to keep a permanent hold on Kaedrich's arm, just to make things clear.

She was reunited, in turn, with the rest of her siblings—all but Previn, though that much was to be expected. Prommel was there with his new wife and the two sons from a previous relationship that she'd brought into the family with her; including Micadel, who would happily regale anyone who would listen to the story of Praxis's sudden appearance at the gates. Pranders, attending alone, had gotten doughy around the middle, his face stilted as he tried to smile at Praxis. His suits were ill-fitted, as always. Prenna, on the other hand, looked immaculate, her yellow gown glowing like the warm sun. She threw her arms around Praxis so tightly that she almost choked her, and when she composed herself, she brought out a teenage girl and a middle-sized child, introducing them as her *youngest* daughter and son, Annelle and Hanshaw. Praxis could only boggle— Prenna's oldest, the only two Praxis had ever met, were apparently living in other parts of Yandosia these days. A few minutes later Prewish appeared, parts of his own long family in tow. Praxis accepted a reserved hug from his wife, Herrine. One of their sons, who'd only been seven when Praxis left, even brought with him his own wife and child, and Praxis tried to keep the shock off her face. Because, really, why wouldn't he? They were all so old now. Even Praine and Merylda, who hadn't yet been married a full year when Praxis left, introduced the twins that she'd been pregnant with the last time Praxis had seen them. The children—could you call them children anymore?—were tall and polished, preparing for their own coming-of-age ball.

Praxis reeled, trying to take it all in: the nieces and nephews, step-nieces and -nephews, all grown, some escorting small children. She didn't even try to remember them all. She felt ancient, suddenly, staring at the sea of relatives flitting about with the party guests. Her nieces and nephews looked more like the way Praxis remembered her siblings, their own older faces turned to near-strangers. How was it possible for her siblings to have families this large, children old enough to hold their own at dinner parties?

On the other hand . . . Praxis remembered, in a flash, being back in Aul, just after she'd struck out into the world. Her stomach twisted up on her, because she did not want to remember this, but if she hadn't stepped in and taken matters into her own hands, she would have a nearly grown daughter of her own to shock everyone else with.

It was strange to think about it in those terms, yet here was the simple truth: Praxis had fallen recklessly in love, Rinn had used an Aul spell (behind Praxis's back) that allowed the two of them to conceive, and Praxis had ended it, the relationship and the pregnancy both. And while she did not, for one instant, *regret* what she had done, it *was* a choice, and the alternate outcome was hard to ignore as she stood and tried to take in all of these teenage faces.

She had to excuse herself.

Praxis broke from the growing cluster that had been surrounding her over the course of the last hour, retreating with Kaedrich to a corner with a marginally smaller crowd. It was enough, barely, for her to steady herself. Kaedrich just stood there, a comforting presence, her hand on Praxis's shoulder as Praxis swallowed lungfuls of refreshingly cold air.

"Are you all right?"

Praxis forced a nod, and a few moments later she plunged herself back into the sea. Though this time she fixedly avoided her mother, thereby curtailing any further introductions Prestina might hope to make. She settled herself in a small group, where Prommel and his wife, a woman whose name Praxis couldn't remember, were chatting amiably with Prett.

Prett grinned as she approached. "So you've finally escaped the clutches," he said, stooping to wrap her in another of his one-armed hugs. Praxis accepted the gesture with far more gratitude than she normally might have. "How are you holding up?" Prett whispered, thumping Praxis once on the back.

Praxis nodded, the only response she could muster at the moment. Prett stepped back, and Praxis smoothed out the front of his royal-blue jacket for him.

They folded her into the conversation with the ease of a familiar embrace. Prommel reintroduced his wife as Sharmity, as if he knew that Praxis wouldn't have retained it. Praxis stayed quiet as they picked their conversation back up exactly as they'd left it. She listened with half an ear while they traded names she didn't know, stories she didn't understand, and she studied the changes in her siblings.

They were both familiar, and not. Faces shifted slightly by age, hair worn in unfamiliar sweeps—and yet, beneath . . . Prett's smile was infectious, his sly grin catching Praxis at odd moments; her own smirk responded automatically, like it knew exactly how this game was played. Prommel, even looking austere in granite- and steel-gray, his hair cropped military short, had a softness when he looked at his wife, an expression that Praxis recognized instantly. Sharmity was exactly what Praxis would have expected for him: elegant, stately, holding herself with a poise worthy of a Fellows. She wore shimmering black and pearly white, matching the décor of the Onyx Room around her, every piece of her appearance designed to make it look like she *belonged*.

She fit in, Praxis realized with a strange squirm, even more so than Praxis herself did these days—even with Prestina's dress to help her out. Of course, it would have helped Praxis's appearance if she wore a piece of the Fellows' signature gemstones, their shifting colors reserved for only the closest relations. All her siblings wore them on proud display, rings for most of the men, a bracelet for Prenna. Praxis had a matching bracelet, which her older sister had picked out for her just before Praxis's coming-of-age ball. It was one of the few things she'd managed to keep with her all these years, and it was still buried somewhere in the many pockets of her slate-blue coat in her room, but . . . somehow, it hadn't felt right to put it on.

But before Praxis could dwell on it for long, a polite little cough broke through the circle, and a polite little man edged his way into their ranks.

He was dressed in a graying green, like the distant sea. The features of his actual person were wholly nondescript in every way: average height, average build, a forgettable face. He cut into the semicircle their group had formed, exchanging bows and nods, hesitating only slightly upon sight of Kaedrich. Praxis was quite sure she had never seen this man before—or, if she had, that he was too unimportant to remember—and so she openly frowned as his attention fell at last to her. "Miss Fellows?"

"Which one?" Praxis asked, though apparently her sarcasm answered his question as well as anything.

The man bowed his head, tapping his hand to his lips in a respectful greeting. "Miss Fellows, my name is Huxley, and I bring you greetings and a message from my master, Lexthur Delford. He deeply regrets not being able to accept your parents' most gracious invitation this evening; unfortunately, he's being detained on important business. He wishes to extend to you a counterinvitation, to attend luncheon tomorrow, at his office in Bolt. Will you accept?"

Praxis could only stare. Huxley, in his gray-green suit, folded his hands behind his back and merely waited, his face pleasant and placid with unconcern.

Lexthur Delford. Of all the people she could have received word from upon her return, why did it have to be Lexthur Delford?

"No," Praxis said simply. She turned away from Huxley, ignoring him as he took this refusal in stride; she saw out of the corner of her eye as he bowed, tapping his lips again, before backing away from their group. The party swallowed him, even the distinct color of his suit soon fading away behind the layers of dresses and furs.

For a while—too long, really, to be innocent—nobody said anything.

Then Sharmity leaned in, lowering her voice as she said, "I cannot *believe* what just happened."

Praxis rolled her eyes. "I can't believe that Lexthur bothers to have an office. Whoever heard of a farmer with an office?"

A slight pause followed this pronouncement, the kind that might have gone unnoticed in almost any other social setting, and yet in the midst of a group of Fellows it spoke volumes. "What?" Praxis asked.

"You really don't know?" Sharmity said.

"Know *what*?"

Sharmity's hand flew to her mouth in open astonishment. Everyone else, save for Kaedrich, was suddenly staring at their drinks.

Prett cleared his throat. "Lexthur . . . he didn't go into the family business, Prax. He became a politician."

"Oh, that's even worse," Praxis said.

Prett smirked. "I'm not sure I would call being Archon 'worse,' dear sister."

Praxis's eyebrows shot up. "Archon? Lexthur Delford? The *same* Lexthur Delford?"

"Makes you think, doesn't it?" Prommel cut in. He glanced pointedly at Kaedrich for a moment before regarding his drink as if in thoughtful contemplation. "What you might have had. What you could have had, if you'd been sensible enough to accept it." When he looked up again, his wife was staring at him, and he gave her a single, solemn nod, as grave as his suit.

Heat threatened to bloom in Praxis's cheeks. Though she and Kaedrich had talked about a lot of things, in the idle first leg of their journey south, there were still parts of Praxis's past that she hadn't touched upon yet. Lexthur Delford was one of them. She kept her head down now, not wanting to look at Kaedrich.

"Now, be fair," Prett said. "None of us knew what kind of heights Mr. Delford would rise to. Can you honestly say at the time that you would have embraced the idea of our sister marrying into a family of farmers?"

"It doesn't matter what he's become," Praxis said, finally finding her voice. "I said 'no' then, and I would *still* say 'no' now. I'm very happy."

Only now did she allow herself to look at Kaedrich. It was funny, given the circumstances, but Praxis realized now that this might have been the first time she'd said that exact truth out loud: *I'm very happy.* So much of Praxis's life had been spent in isolation, in one way or another—alone even when she was in groups—so much of it bumbling from one kind of heartbreak to the next, so much dealing with disasters and their consequences. She wasn't used to thinking about her life in terms of its measurable happiness, for while it hadn't been *bad*, it had rarely been *happy*. But now, in Kaedrich's face, she saw it. *I'm very happy.* A swell of giddiness bubbled up inside of Praxis, so strong that she had to bite down to keep from laughing in sheer joy.

Kaedrich glanced at her drink, still mostly full. "Excuse me," she told the group, "I, um . . . I think this has gone flat. I'll be back in a moment."

"Kaedrich—" Praxis started, but Prett stilled her with a hand on her shoulder.

"Let me," he said softly. And before Praxis could argue, he, too, was gone, slipping into the crowd as if neither of them had been there at all.

KAEDRICH FLED TO the hallway just outside of the Onyx Room, and nobody stopped her. She didn't even really know what she was running from, because it's not like she didn't know that Praxis had lived a full and complicated life before they'd met. She was older, after all, by somewhere near ten years. There was a lot of life to be lived, in the time Before Kaedrich.

Still. You would think it would have come up, that she had almost *gotten married* before.

And to a man, no less.

Kaedrich took a deep breath, steadying herself in the comparative quiet of the hallway. Instinctively, she reached for her pin, only to find her fingers closing on nothing but the fur of her borrowed coat. Kaedrich shut her eyes, sighing. She tried to piece this new information together, to make it fit with her understanding of Praxis, but despite her efforts, it stubbornly refused to find a place to belong. None of it made sense, not a single thing that she'd seen or heard since coming to Yandosia—it was as if Praxis had been a wholly different person when she'd lived here, and suddenly everyone expected to see *that* face again. And Praxis, out of duty or habit or something in between, was showing it to them in bits and pieces, while all Kaedrich wanted was to see the woman *she* knew. It was all Kaedrich could do, standing in the midst of this endless stream of family members, to keep hold of the small thread of *her* Praxis, and the effort had exhausted her.

"It must be strange for you," someone said, and Kaedrich jumped, sloshing a bit of her drink. She still had the glass, despite her excuses.

One of Praxis's many brothers pulled out a handkerchief, passing it over. The youngest, and so far most pleasant one, the one who had accompanied them on the horrid visit with Praxis's mother. Longer hair, tucked softly behind his ears, and a vivid blue suit. Kaedrich thought for a second. Prett? Yeah, it must be Prett. The name sounded right, but it was hard to keep track. Whoever had thought it was a good idea to give them all such similar names, anyway?

Kaedrich nodded her thanks, taking the handkerchief and dabbing at the sleeve of her borrowed coat. The handkerchief was the same blue as Prett's suit, and made of the finest silk, so thin that it felt like nothing at all between Kaedrich's fingers. It seemed disgraceful to mop up spills with something so perfectly spun, but what else could she do?

"If it makes you feel better, I don't think she ever loved him," Prett said, rubbing his chin in contemplation. "And you *certainly* don't have any competition now, not after . . ." He trailed off, his fingers twirling as the words dissolved between them. "For what any of that is worth."

Kaedrich handed the handkerchief back. "Thanks." She didn't clarify which she was thanking him for, the handkerchief or the words, and he didn't ask.

"Can I ask you something?" Prett said as he folded up the handkerchief and tucked it out of sight.

"Sure."

"How did—" he started, but then a couple exited the black-and-white splendor of the Onyx Room, chatting gaily. Prett stepped back to allow them to pass, but instead they turned upon him, beaming.

"Prett!" they said, and then launched into a string of excited conversation, all Yandosian. Prett nodded, appearing to answer their question, offering something in return. And then he motioned behind them, to where Kaedrich was pressed back near the wall.

"Mr. Shail, Miss Demorra, allow me to present one of our honored guests for the evening. This is Kaedrich Mannly. Kaedrich, Mr. Shail is one of the ministers from Bolt's Minor Conclave, and Miss Demorra is part of a family that handles shipping and large-scale transportation for us."

The couple turned. The prearranged delight on their faces flickered into uncertainty as they spotted Kaedrich. But in an instant they'd covered it well, so smooth that anyone else might not have noticed. "So nice to meet you," Miss Demorra said, and the gentleman gave a little nod.

Kaedrich bit down on her tongue, exchanging polite smiles. Though she had every intention of playing this smoothly, for Praxis's sake if nothing else, the fact that Prett had failed to mention any connection between herself and Praxis, like Prestina before him, gnawed at her gut. She knew that's why Praxis had taken her arm during the first round of introductions, but Praxis wasn't here now, and there was no subtle hint Kaedrich could give. So she extended her hand, Durn-style, and after glancing at it curiously, they shook it in turns, and Kaedrich had every intention of letting the matter rest.

But then:

"Tell us, Mr. Mannly, how exactly do you know the Fellows?"

And, oh. Kaedrich should resist, she knew she should resist, but . . . how could she? She glanced once at Prett. She didn't need to know him well to understand the look he was giving her—it was so much like Praxis, she would have known it anywhere. *Don't say it.*

"Oh," Kaedrich said, shrugging as if it was nothing. Could she remember the term? She supposed that she would find out. "I'm Praxis's *sare—*"

"He's a guest of my sister Praxis," Prett cut in, instantly sweeping to his side. "A Lord, in fact, all the way from Durland! Can you imagine?"

"How delightful!" Miss Demorra said, while Mr. Shail stood by looking impressed. "A Lord? I didn't know they had that, for your kind."

"Yes," Prett said, talking fast, "apparently there are new things to be learned all the time. Oh, but if you'll forgive me, I'm afraid we really must be going. So many people to see. You understand."

With a smile that could cut ice, he grabbed Kaedrich by the elbow. "Ow," Kaedrich muttered, but she allowed herself to be led away; across the hall, where a second room held a smaller subset of partygoers, at tidy gaming tables and conversationally convenient sofas. In the corner, a guest was playing a stringed instrument much like a harp, but with a high, almost giggly sound to it. Was it simply the bone construction of the frame, rather than wood, that lent it such an odd tenor, or was it something else? Kaedrich tried not to boggle as Prett hauled her to a corner and released his grip.

"Listen," Prett said. He kept his voice low, his face lightly flushed. "Kaedrich. It's none of my business how you and my sister feel about each other—and I appreciate the awkward situation this must be for you—but just between the two of us, I'm going to tell you as a friend . . . that is *not* a term to be thrown around lightly. Do you understand?"

She didn't, but she was reluctant to admit so directly. *It accurately describes the state of us,* that's what Praxis had said, though now Kaedrich could see that she had clearly left a lot out of her explanation. So what *had* Praxis told her mother, and Prett? Kaedrich's skin crawled at the ignorance, but somehow she doubted that Praxis was going to be more forthcoming about it the next time she asked.

Prett, on the other hand . . .

He was still watching her, trying to read her expression as she worked all of this out in her head. So far, Kaedrich had to admit, he had been nothing but a friend to her and Praxis, and she could see easily enough why Praxis seemed to regard him fondly. Was there any harm, then, in testing the waters of his confidence?

"I'm . . . not entirely sure I *do*." She spoke carefully, trying not to give too much away—but Prett immediately straightened up, eyes popping wide.

"She hasn't *told* you?"

"Oh, no, of course she's *told* me, I'm not saying—" Kaedrich cut herself off, heaving a weary sigh at Prett's skeptical expression. "All right, fine. Not exactly, no."

"I see," Prett said slowly. Idly, he started fiddling with the ring on his hand, the only piece of jewelry he wore. Kaedrich recognized the row of gemstones instantly, the shifting-color pieces reserved only for Fellows.

Kaedrich paused, waiting to see if Prett would go on. When he didn't, she said, "Are *you* going to tell me?"

Prett shook his head—once, but decidedly firm. "No. I'm sorry, but it's not my place."

"Thanks a lot," Kaedrich mumbled.

"Look, I'm sure she has a perfectly good—"

"There you are!"

Kaedrich jerked around, startled and then calmed by the sight of Prawl Fellows's grinning face. As much as she disliked Praxis's mother, she found herself endeared immediately toward her father. There was an ease to the man, with his bushy beard like a storybook grandfather, and his fox fur coat that put Kaedrich in mind of fairy tales and kindly woodsmen. Only the gems, glittering on his rings and the chain holding his coat closed, betrayed his true status. Prawl veered through the room, determined as an arrow, and clapped a hand on Kaedrich's shoulder. "My boy, I've been looking all over for you! You certainly know how to hide yourself away."

"I'm sorry, sir, I didn't mean to seem as if I was avoiding you."

Prawl laughed, the sound booming out like a percussion accompaniment to the music. "Nonsense, nonsense! But listen, I've been wondering . . . my daughter hasn't taught you how to play Fiddler's Dash by any chance, has she?"

"Actually—"

Prett groaned. "Father, no. Please don't."

"Hush now," Prawl said. "Let the man speak. Well?"

Kaedrich glanced at Prett, waiting to see if he was going to offer up any further protests. But like Prestina before him, Prawl seemed to have a strangely subduing effect on their otherwise strong-minded children, and Prett only shook his head sadly.

"Actually," Kaedrich started again, "she has."

Well, in a way. Technically, Kaedrich was forced to admit, it was the magical creature *posing* as an older Praxis—but the "vacant" could have easily pulled the knowledge from Praxis herself. Either way, Kaedrich smiled at Prawl, happy to be able to surprise him. "I'm quite fond of it."

"Wonderful!" Another clap on her shoulder. Prawl's face was already flushed with joy. "Wonderful! I don't suppose you'll do me the honor of playing a round or two, then?"

"Don't do it," Prett said. "Seriously, Kaedrich, just . . . don't do it."

Prawl frowned. "Hush."

Kaedrich's only answer was to motion for Prawl to lead the way. He laughed again, with one more clap on the back for good measure, which he then morphed into wrapping his arm freely around her shoulders. "Excellent, excellent!" he was saying, already drawing Kaedrich through the gaming tables. Kaedrich eyed them, briefly confused, as they passed. Prawl clapped Kaedrich's shoulder again. "I *knew* that I liked you!"

All Prett could do was watch them go. He sucked in a cold breath through his teeth, already bracing himself. Sure enough, no sooner had the two of them disappeared from sight than the clack of shoes approached him from behind, a hand tapping him sharply on the back.

"Where's Kaedrich?"

Prett turned, his smile wedged firmly in place. She must have come in one of the other doors, probably had been searching for a while now. Prett's cheeks hurt, and Praxis narrowed her eyes, recognizing the look immediately.

"This is *not* my fault," Prett said, a surefire way to lose the argument before it began, but what the hell. With that look in Praxis's eyes, there was never any victory to be had anyway.

Praxis sighed. *"Where?"*

"He . . . went with Father. To play some—"

"Oh gods! And you *let* him?"

"I had no choice! You know how he gets when he's spotted a new mark!"

Praxis mashed her fingers against her temples as if fighting a sudden, raging headache. Prett watched from a safe distance, keeping a careful eye on her fingertips; they were encased in long silk gloves, but that didn't necessarily protect anything. Sure, he *assumed* that in the intervening years she'd gotten better at controlling her magic when it was inflamed by her temper, but he wasn't going to bet on it.

Abruptly, Praxis dropped her hands. He could see her steeling herself, the careful set of her jaw that she'd learned from their mother. Everything about her reminded Prett of their mother, and not just because of the borrowed gown. There was a cold ferocity that had grown in Praxis during the long years she'd spent away, which Prett would recognize anywhere.

"When he finally escapes," Praxis said, "will you please tell Kaedrich that I've gone to bed? I don't think I can take any more of this."

Prett nodded. "Of course."

Praxis didn't leave immediately, though. She glanced around the gaming room, as weary as a soldier finally stepping off the battlefield. Prett tried to imagine what this must be like for her, to have escaped for such a long time only to return *now*. They used to talk about it all the time, when they were kids—what they would do once they were free in the world, where they would go. While everyone else above them was content to live entombed in the ice, that had never been the plan for either of them, not really. For Praxis, her magic was the obvious out: she'd made no secret that she wanted nothing to do with the family's lapus lumeni division, and that was really about the only option for a wizard around here.

But then, well, things hadn't exactly gone according to plan for her. She'd gone on a ritual, one supposed to mark her transition from mere pupil into full-on learned wizard, only to return in tatters near to a year later, sobbing that her tutor was dead and that she was swearing off magic forever. Prett had been shocked, they'd all been shocked. He'd hung around outside of her bedroom suite for days, weeks, while Prestina tended to her daughter, nursing and coaxing her back toward health. But even once Praxis ventured out again, it was plain to see she was changed. It wasn't just that she didn't talk about leaving, or that her magic was buried so deeply that sometimes, in the year that followed, it was hard to remember she'd ever had it at all. Everything was different: she dressed the way Mother wanted, forced smiles where before she'd given scowls, moved and walked and talked wherever their parents pointed her.

Prett had never learned what made her snap, not *really*, though clearly Lexthur had something to do with it. But Lexthur wouldn't speak of that night, not even to Prett. All anyone knew for certain was that Praxis had stormed out of her coming-of-age ball, and had never come back. Prett didn't even know she'd gone until the next morning, when she wasn't at the breakfast table and Prestina calmly informed them, as if reading the latest financial reports, that Praxis had left, and no, she did not expect her to return any time soon. Then she'd picked up her knife and fork, and that was the last word either of their parents ever said on the matter.

Now she was back, as suddenly as she'd left, and with no greater explanation for her return than her departure. She turned, already several steps away when Prett called out to her. "Hey, Praxis!"

A single, cold glance over her shoulder; nothing more.

"What's with . . . ?" Prett asked, and he raised his right hand and wiggled the first three fingers, the way that Praxis curled and uncurled them with each step she took.

Praxis didn't answer, not at first. When she did speak, she only said, "Why are you still here?"

Prett fell silent, his face a carefully blank slate.

"Yeah," Praxis said, curling her fingers to set off once more. "I don't want to talk about it, either."

FIDDLER'S DASH WAS a game of calculated risk.

There really wasn't anything more to it than that. Take the cards you were dealt, assess the possible combinations you could make, and the strength of each of those hands; discard and draw through a careful series of moves that minimized your liability, attempting to build the best choice from your original options. Bet wisely, don't overestimate the odds in your hand, and you'll usually end up with a few more wins than losses.

Naturally, there were a lot of people that tried to tell you differently. Kaedrich had heard it all, by this point. Strategies and superstitions both, a whole litany of each that could be heard repeated from gambling hall to gambling hall, and parlor to parlor, all across the continents, over the oceans, and around the world. But really: calculated risk.

Prawl led Kaedrich down a long hallway and into one of a row of seemingly identical doors. The room beyond was far smaller than any Kaedrich had seen since entering the Fellows' dwelling, and tastefully appointed to be a cozy study. It looked so much like something from Durland that for a moment Kaedrich actually halted in the doorway, too surprised to move. There was a tidy desk, a row of built-in bookcases, a *potted plant*, and even a fireplace with a fake "fire" crafted out of lapus lumeni crystals. Though some of the furniture was still made of the ghostly whale bones that Kaedrich was trying to get used to, several pieces in the room gleamed the rich brown of dark wood, polished to a high sheen.

Including a small table with two chairs pulled up to it, which is where Prawl directed her. He took one seat, furling his rusty, fox fur coat behind him as he sat down, and Kaedrich perched on the other. Though she liked Prawl, she was still far from *comfortable* in his presence, even as he continued to smile genially. There was also the question of why they hadn't simply joined one of the games in progress at the party, which hung in the air like a cold dread and raised the hairs on Kaedrich's neck. Still, maybe Kaedrich was making something out of nothing. Prawl was as cheerful as ever, his thick beard curling up into a welcoming smile, as he drew out a deck of fresh cards from a drawer beneath the table. He tapped them idly against the surface as he began to shuffle them up, fingers dancing from years of practice.

"I'm so glad I have this chance to talk to you, my boy—man-to-man, that's how they say things up in Durland, isn't it?"

Kaedrich nodded. "Yes, sir."

Prawl raised a single jeweled finger, pausing his shuffling. "No formalities at the card table. That's the only rule."

"Oh," Kaedrich said. "Erm, yes . . . Prawl?"

Prawl grinned. "Much better." He went back to his shuffling, the cards sighing underneath his careful guidance. He shuffled the same way Praxis did, with a flick of the wrist that Kaedrich had never seen in anybody else's habits. "Of course," Prawl said, after a moment, "that's not exactly true in this case."

Kaedrich glanced up, from the cards to Prawl's face. He was watching what he was doing, paying no particular mind to Kaedrich—at least, not openly.

"Um . . . what's not true?"

"Man-to-*man*," Prawl said, and Kaedrich nearly fell from her chair in shock. She clutched the seat just to keep herself in place, both from falling and from bolting for the door, but Prawl continued as if nothing was out of the ordinary at all. He finished shuffling, cut the deck himself, began to flick cards back and forth between them. He shrugged. "I don't blame you for keeping it a secret—I'm sorry to say it, but you're probably right to. But we made a promise to be honest with each other, Kaedrich." He smirked. "Although that's probably not even your real name, is it?"

When Prawl looked up, it was all Kaedrich could do to keep herself steady. She was too warm, suddenly, even in these cold rooms and cold halls, the thick fur of her borrowed coat smothering her.

"Is it?" Prawl repeated. The cards were all dealt by this point, but they lay untouched on the table between them.

Kaedrich forced herself to shake her head. Just once, just enough.

Prawl smiled. "There, see? That wasn't so hard."

"How did you know?" Kaedrich whispered. She was so fragile, like a frightened bird, that she worried that even the question would break her.

Prawl set the rest of the deck down, scooping his own cards up in their place. He spread them, and took his time in assessing his hand. He did not even mention that Kaedrich hadn't yet picked up her own, just sat there and sorted his, grouping them in obvious pairs.

"I'm a dutiful father," he said finally, as if that explained anything. He shrugged again. "I may not have been there for the last seventeen years of my daughter's life, but I was there for the first seventeen. You learn a few things. In this case, I can tell you one immutable fact about my youngest girl." Prawl glanced up, looking directly at Kaedrich. "Praxis does not like men. Never has, never will. It wasn't hard to work it out from there."

Kaedrich tried to swallow, but her mouth was suddenly dry.

Prawl returned his attention to his cards, staring at them now, waiting. He glanced up only once. "Are we going to play?"

"Are you . . . are you going to tell anyone?" Kaedrich asked.

"No," Prawl said simply, and Kaedrich sagged in open relief. Prawl chuckled to himself. "Kaedrich, I have far more to concern myself with than the exact fancies of each of my eight children. So long as they're not doing themselves any great harm, what they choose to get up to in their own time is really not of any interest to me. Besides," he added with a smirk, "I have more than enough grandchildren already—but please, don't tell Prestina I said that. I'd never hear the end of it."

"Does *she* know?"

"Ha! Believe me, if she did, you wouldn't have to ask."

Prawl fell silent, and only now did Kaedrich feel marginally comfortable enough to pick up her cards. She spread them carefully, as if afraid they might lash out at her, and their numbers and suits swam and danced before her eyes, meaningless.

Prawl laid down the first move. "Since you bring it up, though, I will give you one piece of advice—which I *strongly* urge you to take. Stay out of Prestina's way."

Kaedrich snorted. "I intend to."

"No," Prawl said. He rested his cards, temporarily, against his arm on the table. "I mean it. This isn't an idle warning. You can't realize it yet, but there are things going on here that you do not want to get involved with— and even without knowing the truth, Prestina is *going* to hate you."

A chill ran down Kaedrich's spine. Okay, so it's not as if Kaedrich thought she was in Prestina's good graces, but *hate*? That seemed a little strong. She thought for a moment maybe Prawl hadn't meant it quite like that—he'd said it so casually, after all, and this wasn't his native language—but when she looked over, the way he was staring at her, his eyes pinning her in place like daggers made of ice . . . no, he had *meant* it.

Kaedrich cleared her throat. "Have I done something to offend her?"

She wasn't stupid—she knew it must have been about her looks, that Prestina hated her simply for having been born in the skin she was in. Still, if she was going to be casually insulted like that, she wanted Prawl to come right out and *say* it. If there was one thing Kaedrich hated, it was the way polite people danced around this issue, never openly addressing it, never wanting to imply that the words or actions of their peers were in some way *uncouth*.

Would Prawl admit it? It was hard to say. He studied Kaedrich, in no apparent rush, as he turned and picked at a stray bit of red fur that had migrated from his coat to the dark gray leather of his jacket beneath.

Finally, he shrugged. "In your case? Looking like you do?" Prawl drew another card from the stack, examining it for a moment before sliding it into its proper place in his hand. "Stealing my daughter's heart was enough."

Chapter Five

PRAXIS RETURNED TO the guest suite, and began to peel off the many layers of her borrowed gown the instant the door was shut. She wanted to plunge herself into a bath, scrub away the layers of perfume and makeup, scrub away all memories of the evening, but that would require summoning a maid to fill the tub, and the last thing Praxis wanted to do was see another Yandosian face. So she did the best she could without that luxury. She ripped off her gloves, yanked at the buttons that bound her into the dress, wriggled and kicked and cursed until the gown lay in a heap of silk and velvet and fur. The red accents of her dress spooled through the pile like ribbons of blood, staining the corpse of her evening. Praxis let everything fall, helter-skelter, on the floor: dress and hairpiece, jewelry, shoes. A silk handkerchief managed to scrub most of the color off of her face, and now, finally, she looked like herself. Her hair was even sticking up in the back, ruffled by the feathered hairpiece. She sat down to take off her brace, her attention lingering on her tattoo as she pulled the control glove off of her wrist.

She was in bed by the time Kaedrich got back, ages later. Trying to sleep, and failing. Lapus lumeni could not be turned off like a lamp, and though Praxis had a difficult adjustment when she'd first left Yandosia—to watch the sun set, to sleep in the dark—she was finding it almost impossible to sleep now in the light. The pink backsplash of her eyelids was a constant distraction, but burying her head underneath the fur covers was stifling her breath. She had just rolled onto her back, the crook of her arm thrown across her face in desperation, when the door clicked open. Even with unfamiliar shoes, Praxis recognized Kaedrich's gait as she loped through the outer chamber and into the bedroom.

Praxis just laid there for a while, listening to the sounds of Kaedrich's preparations for bed. The soft *tsk* as she spotted the mess Praxis had left behind, the slump of her heavy coat being laid down somewhere. There was a pause as Kaedrich unlaced her shoes, the cords nearly silent, and then the softer padding of feet across the floor. The click of cufflinks being set down, the almost imperceptible whisper of buttons being undone. The sigh of a jacket sliding free, and then shirts.

"So how much did you lose?" Praxis asked. She peeped out from underneath her arm, squinting in the bright light.

Kaedrich stood half-dressed, one end of her bindings trailing down her side. Her hand was pressed to her chest as if she'd been startled and was trying to calm her heart. "Gods, Praxis. I thought you were asleep."

"That would be nice." She propped herself up on her elbows, so that she was no longer speaking at the ceiling. "Well?"

"What makes you think I *lost*?"

Praxis snorted out a laugh. "Because you were playing against my *father*. Everyone loses."

Kaedrich scowled. She turned back to the process of unwrapping her chest bindings, in silence.

"Don't take it so hard, Ella. I think Moc was the only person to ever beat him at it, and he probably used magic to cheat."

"And that doesn't strike you as wrong, somehow?" Kaedrich shook her head. "I have *never* seen that many hands go that well for anyone."

Praxis shrugged. "He says he knows how to read people."

"No," Kaedrich said. She folded up her bindings and rested them on top of a dresser, then immediately dove into a thick nightshirt. Even a few moments in the cold had prickled her skin, and she furiously rubbed her arms for a moment. "No, that's what everyone *says* the game is about, but it's really not."

"And yet, *he* won."

"'Reading people' can't change the cards in your hand," Kaedrich snapped. She huffed in disgust, kicking the legs of her trousers off and letting them pile on the floor in an uncharacteristic display of slovenliness.

Praxis rolled her eyes. She laid back as Kaedrich burrowed into the covers beside her, being careful not to let in any more air than strictly necessary. Praxis stared at the ceiling for a moment, the spiraling twists of the veins of lapus lumeni.

"Though I grant you, he *is* good at reading people," Kaedrich added. She hesitated, clearly picking out her next words. "He knows, by the way. About . . . me. Us."

Praxis jerked, as if she'd been struck by electrical current. She rolled onto her side so quickly that a good portion of the covers came with her, cold sneaking up the back of her thighs. She ignored this, however, studying Kaedrich's face for signs of distress or concern.

She found none, not really. A gentle uneasiness around the edges, but nothing overly worrying.

Still.

"How?" Praxis asked.

"He's known of your tastes forever, apparently," Kaedrich said. "He says it wasn't hard to work out the rest."

Praxis went still and cold, trying to absorb this. She had never dared to breathe a word of her "tastes" to anyone while she lived here—only Moc, who had pressed her on the matter when he'd caught her staring at someone too openly, and then only the once. The discovery had left her jumpy for a long time after that, but eventually Praxis had let out a breath, convinced no one else knew. Moc was a wizard, after all, and it only made sense that he'd be able to suss out hidden truth. But now Praxis's skin crawled, wondering how many of them knew after all, how many more might secretly suspect. She'd brought Kaedrich here to protect her, but what if she'd saved her from one danger only to drop her in the middle of another?

"What—?" Praxis started, then paused. She swallowed, trying to figure out exactly what it was that she wanted to know. "Did he say what he was going to do with this information?"

"I don't think he's going to *do* anything. Why?" Kaedrich asked, seeing the look on Praxis's face. "You don't believe him?"

Praxis gave a nervous laugh. "I don't know. Gods, I honestly . . . I don't know."

Kaedrich's face softened. "Praxis, it's going to be all right. He didn't seem to care one way or another. Come on." She held her arm out, creating an open pocket for Praxis to tuck herself against Kaedrich's shoulder. Kaedrich wrapped Praxis in a gentle embrace, running her hand up and down the length of Praxis's side. "It's all right," Kaedrich murmured into her hair. "I'm here; it's going to be all right."

Despite herself, the tension in Praxis's muscles began to melt. She clung to Kaedrich's side, her arm wrapped tight around Kaedrich's chest. It was freezing in here, colder even than Praxis remembered it being, but snug beneath their covers, they'd begun to create a tiny promise of warmth. She tried to close her eyes, but the light just kept blasting against her eyelids, a constant reminder of what she'd gotten herself into.

"It's just . . . what if being here makes me forget who I am?" Praxis said. She hadn't planned on asking it, and the question slipped out so quietly it was a wonder her breath had formed the sounds at all.

But Kaedrich heard it. Always, Kaedrich heard it.

Kaedrich tipped Praxis's chin up, ducking her own head until she could brush their lips together. In and of itself, of course, this solved nothing, but Praxis let herself drink in the comfort of Kaedrich's mouth for a minute or two, her cares growing fuzzy and melting around the edges.

"That's what I'm here for," Kaedrich said, when they finally came up for air, though by that point Praxis's mind had already moved on.

She smiled at Kaedrich, her Kaedrich. The full lips and the wide stamp of her nose, the tall curve of her brow. Praxis's fingers traced these details, drinking them in through her touch. "Is that so?" Praxis asked, a purr curling the edge of her words. "In that case, I think I need a bit more reminding, don't you?"

Kaedrich's lips were already at Praxis's neck by the time the question was out. "Oh, absolutely."

KAEDRICH WOKE UP LOST.

Cold air bit at her cheeks and the one foot that she had sticking out from underneath her covers, and someone had covered her face with what might have been a blindfold. Panic seized at Kaedrich as she jerked up—had she been taken prisoner, where was Praxis, how bad would things get—until she realized that the presence of her flailing arms and legs meant she wasn't tied up, at least. She ripped the thing off of her face, and found herself staring down at a sleep mask made of deep blue velvet and silk. Light washed in from all directions, catching each minor wrinkle and ripple of the fabric in her hands.

It all came back to her then. Yandosia and meeting the Fellows, yes, but also the trek across the vast expanse of ice and snow, and a long, increasingly tense sea journey as they tracked farther and farther south, and even before that: a large, sunlit room with tall windows, an endless battle, the crack of a gun, pain searing through her gut. The smell of flowers and gunpowder, the scent that should have marked the time as the moment of her death.

Years ago, Kaedrich had struck a magical deal to gain temporary access to the land of the dead, and the terms were such that the moment of her death became a fixed point in time, unavoidable, unchanging. When they'd charged into the Council's Crescent in Monfort to stop the vote that would grant Lanali the powers of temporary head of state, Kaedrich had been convinced that the moment of her death was upon her. She'd been ready, as ready as she could be, and when she was shot . . .

But she must have been mistaken, because she'd woken up two days later on the ship Praxis had booked for them. Whole and safe, completely healed.

Kaedrich turned, reaching out for Praxis, but the rest of the bed was empty and her hand settled on nothing but air and rumpled covers. She craned her neck, looking toward the bathroom, the dressing room. "Praxis?"

No answer.

Kaedrich sighed. It wasn't really a surprise that Praxis had gone off somewhere without telling her, though she'd rarely pulled this kind of thing since they'd gotten together three months ago. Kaedrich reached over to put the sleep mask back in the bedside table where she'd found it the night before, and shifted out from underneath the rest of the covers. She picked her nightshirt off of the floor and dove back into it while she sought out a pair of reasonably suitable clothes for the day.

Once she was dressed, Kaedrich yawned, stretching, as she headed into the labyrinth of the Fellows household. With no windows, it was impossible for her to tell what time it was; there *were* clocks in the guest suite, or at least Kaedrich assumed those were clocks, but they were of a style that she had no idea how to read. She did still have her pocket watch, but it was set to Durland's time, and Kaedrich had no idea how far off they were now. Back home it was four, although who could even say whether that was afternoon or early morning?

She wandered without much success for a while, seeing no one. Gods, she was going to have to ask if there was some kind of map to this place. She had no idea how Praxis navigated it so expertly, moving through the junctions and up and down the wide flights of stairs as if she knew exactly where she was. She knew, intellectually, that the odds of wandering forever without success were unlikely, though the hunger clawing in her stomach did generate a flutter of panic; surely she would find someone soon, right?

It was a great relief, then, when she rounded a corner and spotted a maid at work. Dressed in crisp white, on her knees as she buffed at the trim of what would have been baseboards in a Durlish building. Kaedrich cleared her throat as she approached, to announce her presence. "Excuse me, miss? I was wondering if you could help me with something . . . I'm trying to find Praxis, have you seen her?"

The maid said nothing. She put away the buffing tool and took a rag out of her pocket; then she leaned in to the bottom row of a mural of gemstones, polishing each gem one by one. If she had heard Kaedrich at all, she gave no hint of it.

"Excuse me?" Kaedrich tried again. She paused, but the maid only squinted, leaning in closer to her work, her iced-off face pinched in concentration. Kaedrich cleared her throat again. "Excuse me, I need your help, I . . . Oh . . . I'm sorry, do you even speak Durlish?"

Though a language barrier still did not explain why the maid appeared not to have even *heard* her. Unless, perhaps, she was deaf? Kaedrich stood back, studying the maid as she worked. She supposed it was *possible* . . .

She was just reaching out to try tapping the maid on the shoulder when a voice broke out from behind her.

"Is there a problem here?"

Kaedrich jumped, startled by the sound of Praxis's voice. Except, no, she reminded herself just before she turned around. Not Praxis.

Prestina.

She marched down the hall toward Kaedrich and the maid, her heels ringing out against the polished ice. She was dressed as if ready to entertain royalty, or perhaps as if she was, herself, royalty. Not a single hair was out of place, and she was adorned with a fresh variety of glittering jewels, mostly either diamond or the signature Fellows stone, the colors shifting in a mesmerizing display. Her gown was every bit as impressive as the one she'd worn to her party, delicate fabrics the color of ice and snow, the width of her skirts brushing against both the left and right sides of the hallway. "Mr. Mannly," she said as she approached. "I asked you a question: is there a problem here?"

"No, ma'am," Kaedrich said. She forced her back to stay straight, her chin held firmly level. "I was just trying to find Praxis. Do you have any idea where she is?"

"No . . . she didn't say anything over breakfast, I'm afraid. Then again, I don't expect she would tell *me* her plans. You there!" Here she addressed the maid, in open Durlish; but this time the maid sprang instantly to her feet, bowing her head respectfully.

"Ma'am?"

"Have you see my youngest daughter recently?"

Still bowing, the maid tapped her lips. "I believe she called for a sleigh an hour or so ago. Word was that she was heading into the city, ma'am."

Prestina smiled, as if she'd just conjured Praxis up out of thin air. "There we have it," she said to Kaedrich.

Kaedrich frowned. Praxis hadn't said anything the night before about going out this morning—which might not have bothered her, except for the idea that Praxis had also gone and attended a breakfast without inviting Kaedrich along with her. Still, Kaedrich inclined her head in as much gratitude as she could muster. "Thank you, Mrs. Fellows. I . . . I'm sorry that I wasn't able to attend breakfast with her. I was not informed of it."

Prestina *tsk*ed, dismissing Kaedrich's apology with the flutter of her hand. "Think nothing of it. It was a family meal, it was not your place to join us. Besides, I've already made it clear to everyone that we're to be respectful of the fact that you will no doubt be ignorant of many of our ways of doing things. We must all be patient with you. We understand." She smiled beatifically.

"How . . . kind . . . of you," Kaedrich said. "Um, but since I did miss it, I don't suppose there's a way we could arrange something for me? I haven't eaten yet, and . . ."

"Oh!" Prestina said. "Oh, of course, my dear. I believe the servants are almost ready to eat their own meal, and I'm sure you'd be welcome to join them."

While the idea of eating among the servants did, in some way, hold a certain appeal, having come from a serving background herself and by no means comfortable being waited upon, Kaedrich knew there was no way she could possibly accept. Not if she intended to maintain even the slightest bit of grudging respect in the eyes of the Fellows. Besides, no doubt this was intended as a slight upon her person.

Breathe, Kaedrich reminded herself. "I was thinking more like a tray. I can eat in my rooms."

Prestina blinked. "If that's what you wish. I'm sure someone can help you put it together, and you'd be very welcome to bring it back to the guest suite."

Kaedrich bit the inside of her cheek, just to keep from sniping. "No . . . thank you, that won't be necessary. Never mind."

"Very well," Prestina said with an indifferent shrug.

"Right. If you'll excuse me, then," Kaedrich said. She turned and hurried back down the hall, hoping that she was at least going vaguely in the correct direction.

She was almost out of sight when Prestina's voice caught up with her. "Oh, Kaedrich! One moment, please." The chiming of Prestina's heels approached, easily falling into step. Kaedrich had slowed, but did not stop. Prestina walked beside her in silence for several long strides, until they rounded the corner and fell out of view of the maid.

Her grip pinched Kaedrich's elbow with surprising force. Kaedrich stopped. She could have easily wrenched her arm free, but for the sake of keeping the peace, she allowed the hold to remain.

"Since we're alone, there is one thing I wanted to discuss with you," Prestina started. She kept her voice low, so that it did not bounce freely down the empty halls. "As a lord of Durland, you are, of course, a welcomed guest in our home, and I hope you know that we will do all we can to accommodate your eccentricities."

"Eccentric—?"

"In regard to my daughter, however . . . Let's just say that as a member of this family, Praxis has certain obligations to live up to. Standards, if you will." She glanced at Kaedrich, taking in the whole of her appearance as the faintest crinkle appeared over the bridge of her nose. "You may not realize it, but appearances matter a great deal in business, and I would consider it a personal favor—and one I can reward handsomely for—if the two of you were to decide to part company. The sooner the better."

Kaedrich did not react immediately—not outwardly, at any rate. She held Prestina's look, an indignant fire in her chest lending bravery to her carefully modulated expression. Who did this woman think she was? Fine, so she may *look* like a queen, but that didn't *make* her one; and even if she was . . . did she honestly expect that she could bribe Kaedrich into giving up Praxis? Kaedrich wasn't sure, at first, whether to just be angry that someone would try it, or insulted that they thought it might work.

She pulled her arm free. Slowly, giving Prestina plenty of opportunity to try to increase her grip if she wanted to stop her. Kaedrich would not be aggressive; she would not rise to Prestina's bait. She would not give this woman more of a reason to look down at her. "Thank you for your *generous* offer," Kaedrich said, "but I'm afraid I'm going to have to decline. At any rate, even if I was willing to stoop to your level, Praxis makes up her own mind."

Prestina smirked, the same smirk as Praxis. "Not while she's living in my home, she doesn't. Think about it," Prestina added, backing up as she began to move off. "I won't be so generous in the future."

Chapter Six

I WAS ONLY a half-mile stretch from the Fellows' main gate to the heart of Bolt. Although the city technically sprawled for miles and miles, a complicated series of tunnels that led to all sorts of districts full of shops and homes, museums and music halls, laboratories and manufacturing hubs and offices—many of which were held, in one way or another, by the strong arm of the Fellows empire—the actual core of the city was nestled firmly in the middle, a heart in the center of a great and frozen life system. It was the point where everything connected.

Praxis leaned against the window of the sleigh, watching everything go by. When she was a child, the height of looking down the inside of the great spiral of Bolt was terrifying; now Praxis regarded it with a calm detachment as the brusker dogs dragged her ever higher. She supposed it was an impressive feat of design and engineering: a seemingly endless shaft surrounded by a wide and lazy slope that coiled up the walls, arching tunnels branching off at regular intervals. Certainly Kaedrich had been impressed by it as they'd passed through on their way to the Fellows household. But to Praxis, the spectacle was as familiar as her own face. She remembered the way Prett used to lean far over the whale-bone railing, making himself dizzy, until their father would race over, red-faced, and yank him back by his coat. The way Prewish used to pretend to crash into the rest of the siblings, as if he was going to tip them over the edge. The time one of their cooks had taken a day off, no one thought anything of it, only to learn later that he'd walked all the way to the highest rotation, slipped over the rails, and leaped to his death. Bolt was considered a place of culture and art, but to Praxis the city itself meant only a nameless fear that pulled at her heart until she wanted to lean over the railing too, just to see how it would feel.

She rapped on the front of the sleigh now. "That's far enough."

They were two rotations from the top when Praxis called the sleigh to a halt. While she'd been willing enough to utilize her family's transportation for the longest part of the journey, the last thing she wanted was to make a grand entrance at her destination, a Fellows sleigh cresting the final slope, all eyes turning at once. Just the thought made Praxis shudder. No, it was much better to pull over here, and Praxis hopped out and rounded the front of the sleigh, where the driver was watching her nervously. Praxis ignored his discomfort as she drew out two rubies and held them toward him.

The driver's eyes popped. "Ma'am! Thank you, ma'am!"

Praxis nodded. She understood his shock; her family did not tip drivers and service workers, considered their base salaries more than fair (even—especially—when they weren't). Praxis tugged at her gloves. "I pay my own way," she said, more for her own sake than for his. The driver was just watching her, steady and quiet, proper in his uniform and leather jacket. "I'll meet you by the secondary junction of level six in about four hours," Praxis said. "If you promise to be punctual, you're free to do whatever you like in the meantime."

The driver said nothing, merely tapped his lips in respect as Praxis moved to ruffle the fur of the team of bruskers that had done the actual work of bringing her here. They were purebred, as was only proper, descendants from a line that had once served the ancient reign of princes. Their coats were diamond white, and soft as a thousand strands of silk. They nuzzled the cup of Praxis's hand, and she smiled at the warmth of their breath in her face as one hopped up to lick her cheek.

Then all that was left to do was to finish the journey.

Praxis took her time. Her dismount had drawn the expected attention of passersby, but Praxis did her best to ignore their curious, even startled, looks. She drew her long coat tighter around herself, pinching it shut at the neck, as she curled her fingers and started out. For once, she actually wished the sun reached this place, so she'd have an excuse to hide behind the spectacles she usually wore, their lenses tinted so dark as to be nearly black. She wondered, briefly, what people would think if she donned them here anyway—they were still somewhere in the pockets of her coat, after all—but her ragtag appearance was already keeping her in too many people's sights. Best to ease to the side, hope that she would somehow manage to "blend in" to the myriad of bodies, the shifting mass of seal leather, furs, and tarbon-fiber coats. Praxis did her best to dart behind another sleigh, and in this manner, she managed to lose most of the attention she had garnered.

Too soon, and not soon enough, she reached the top. Around the final bend, and the spiral opened up to an enormous cavern beyond. A wide open space, the largest open space that Praxis had ever seen before going to the surface with Moc, the top of the spiral was the seat of government in Bolt. Sometimes, it was inadvertently even referred to as the seat of power, but everyone who was anyone knew the true power actually lived below, in the sprawling tunnels of the Fellows' mines. The cavern was swarming with workers, rushing around and shouting at each other, their voices crashing up to the ceiling and tumbling down to be swallowed up by the spiral.

Praxis paused for a moment, taking it in. In the middle of it all, rising tall out of a sea of bureaucracy, there sat an enormous column, which Praxis used to think looked like a tree trunk, before she'd seen an actual tree. It was here that she set her sights, for it was here that housed the Archon's office. Praxis had never been inside before, but she knew it resided at the top of the column. As she approached, Praxis wondered if he was up there even now, if he was looking down, if he could see her coming. She did not dare look up—she would not give him the satisfaction.

Through the doors to the column's interior, and from there it was easy enough to get someone to escort her to the top. Once she told them her name, they leaped to it with military efficiency. An intern was sent running on ahead to announce her arrival while a distinguished bureaucrat in a thick fur suit offered Praxis his arm.

She ignored it. Jerking her head in the direction of the lifts, she asked, "This the way, then?"

They took a silver lift to the top. The bureaucrat, at least, knew enough to keep his mouth shut and not engage Praxis in small-talk. In fact, while he respected her status, he clearly did not find it that impressive; but then, Praxis mused, he was probably used to dealing with important people, including Prawl himself. Hells, for all Praxis knew, this man might have dealt with him on a regular basis.

Finally they rattled to a stop, and with a nod to the lift attendant, the birdcage-like doors opened. Praxis strode out without the bother of her escort, taking in the room with barely a glance.

Huxley was already waiting for her. Dressed in purple this time, he was the model of neatness and punctuality. He smiled at Praxis, bowed his head just enough. "Miss Fellows, we are so honored you changed your mind. Please, if you'll follow me."

Praxis nodded, and Huxley went over to a set of double doors and opened them with a flourish. Beyond them was a curving staircase, and Praxis followed the tails of his coat as they ascended.

The Archon's office. Praxis raised her eyebrow, impressed despite herself.

They rose up in the middle of the room, straight through a gap in the floor. The "office," if you could even call it that, was really more of an open patio at the top of the central tower. Massive ice support posts ringed the outside, with nothing but the view beyond. An elegant desk *was* present, and a cluster of chairs and chaise lounges clearly designed for meetings, but most of the space more closely resembled a private art gallery than anything else. Five large paintings were suspended by thick wires from the ceiling, scattered in a loose circle around the perimeter of the office; landscapes, all showing the Yandosian surface under a cloud-covered night's sky. Praxis almost dismissed them, until the picture on one of them *moved*, like a snowdrift buffeted by a sudden gust of wind. She went over to inspect it despite herself, leaning in close.

"I'm glad you like it."

Lexthur Delford had been standing so still that he was almost another piece of furniture.

Praxis straightened up. "I didn't say I *liked* it. It merely drew my attention."

"I'm sure you would like them, though, if you took the time to study them," Lexthur said. He motioned at the paintings. "They've been enchanted to show the current weather conditions of this exact spot on the surface. An artist's rendition, of course, and not an accurate view. But essentially, they're my office windows."

"Ah." Praxis nodded. "That explains it. It's a nice trick, though hardly the most sophisticated wizardry I've ever seen."

Lexthur smiled. Mild, and polite. "I'm sure."

For a moment they just stood there, regarding the changes in each other. Despite the massive rise of his status, Praxis couldn't help but thinking that he looked more like his teenage self than she'd expected him to. He bore no real signs of age, though he had grown a beard, tightly trimmed against his face. Perhaps it was meant to help him look older than he would otherwise, but it did not hide the dimple as his smile increased, nor did it distract from the boyish twinkle of his eyes. He still had all of his hair, combed straight back, and his narrow strips of eyebrows still seemed to cut his face in half. The only real change was his clothing: whereas before he wore whatever was popular at the time, it seemed now he'd taken on a distinct style of his own. He wore a plain suit, white like an Aul's, but cut in the Durlish style so that it was narrow in the chest and hips, made of a light material that did not seem anywhere near warm enough.

"Please," he said, extending his hand in the direction of the furniture. "By all means, have a seat. Shall I order lunch? Do you still like zesty piconda?"

In fact she did, though she hadn't tasted it in years. Saliva sprang up at the mere mention of it, the rich, nutty flavor flooding her mind, but Praxis shook her head firmly. "I didn't come to socialize. I have business to discuss."

"There's no reason not to do both. Huxley, bring up my usual, and an order of piconda for Praxis—in case she changes her mind."

Huxley bowed at the waist. "Yes, sir," he said, and disappeared down the stairs.

Lexthur started moving toward the furniture, not bothering to wait for Praxis. "I have to admit, I was . . . shocked, frankly, when I heard you were back," he said as he sat on a long couch.

It was the one seating option that wasn't really clustered with the others, positioned to look out and marvel at the view beyond, and so Praxis was forced to come and join him on it. She sat, on the farthest cushion from Lexthur.

He might want to play the game of long friends catching up, but Praxis was quite serious when she'd said that wasn't her purpose for coming to see him. For even if it was in her nature to make social calls, the last time she'd seen Lexthur . . . Well, the fact that he seemed pleased to see her spoke well of his character, she would grant him that. Rejecting a marriage proposal wasn't exactly considered polite.

"I really didn't have much choice," Praxis said, and when he looked slightly confused she added, "To return? Have you not been made aware of the situation in Durland recently?"

Lexthur leaned back, crossing one leg so that his ankle rested casually on his knee. "I've heard there's been some significant changes, yes. Prince Hemmerick has been ousted, correct?"

Praxis nodded. "They've put Pon Lanali in charge, to oversee the formation of a new Governance Council and to determine a legitimate heir to the crown."

"Fascinating."

"Horrific is more like it," Praxis said. "Pon Lanali is a con artist, and has all but declared open warfare on magic use."

"Ah." Lexthur nodded. "So, not exactly friendly for someone of your skills."

Praxis took a deep breath. "Yes, but more than that, she's . . . Lexthur, she caused the ghost crisis three years ago. On purpose."

This, at last, caught his attention—as she knew it would. The ghost crisis, arguably the single most defining point of history, had not been limited to Durland's borders. Millions of ghosts had sprung forth from the land of the dead, sucking down the souls of the living. It didn't matter that Praxis and Kaedrich had fixed it, that upon seizing control of the Beacon of Souls for herself, Praxis had ordered a reversal of the process and everyone that had been taken was given their life back; this wasn't the sort of thing that anyone truly recovered from. Though people and nations alike had shaken themselves off, tried to put on a good face and march forward like old times, thousands of cracks and ripple effects were still being felt all over the world. Lanali's sway on the public consciousness was really only *one* of the many problems still working itself out over this.

Lexthur was clearly struggling as Praxis recounted a brief version of this story, but he held himself together. It didn't take long to explain the reasons why Praxis hated Lanali, and then she got to the heart of the matter: she wanted Yandosia to provide an army, to rip the power straight out of the Pon's greedy hands.

Though he raised an eyebrow in surprise, Lexthur listened carefully as Praxis laid out each argument. He said little, asking for clarification only on some small point or another, and then he would merely nod and motion for her to continue. He was a good listener, Praxis remembered suddenly, always letting her speak her full mind before he would offer his opinion. Even after she was done, he did not offer up an immediate reaction; Lexthur always sat on what he'd just heard, processing it, never hasty to pass judgment. In the amiable silence that followed Praxis's plans, she felt more confident than she had since arriving in Yandosia. Surely he would agree to help her—how fortunate, really, that he'd changed his career plans in these long years, carving out a position of influence for himself. Praxis was not so self-deluded as to imagine that he'd done it just so he could be a friend to her should she ever return, but the luck that it provided had buoyed her flagging spirits. It was easy, in moments like these, to remember why she had liked him in the first place, why she'd almost convinced herself that she could live this life.

Finally, Lexthur cleared his throat. "It's not that I am unsympathetic to the people of Durland," he began. He picked at the couch as he picked through his words. "But I'm not sure you'd get the support you're hoping for, if I put this to a vote in the Major Conclave."

"Well, I know I would be in for an argument, certainly."

"A bit more than that, I would think," Lexthur said. "Despite the trouble this . . . Lanali?—has caused, it's not exactly in Yandosia's interest to get involved in the politics of another nation."

Praxis nodded; this wasn't an unexpected point. "See, that's where you're wrong. Look, I'm not going to even *try* to argue about The Right Thing to Do, morally. I know how we operate here."

Lexthur smiled, gave a half-nod of acknowledgment.

"The bottom line is that if Lanali is allowed to go unchecked, she is not likely to stop at Durland. *This* transition was fairly peaceful, but when she turns her sights on, oh, Rolmstan? Or one of the leftovers from the retreat of the Marcovallan Empire? They're not going to go quietly into her rule."

"Your point?" Lexthur asked, a surprisingly sharp edge to his voice.

"How many trade agreements are we willing to risk? If the region dissolves into war and chaos—"

Lexthur raised a finger. "'If.' That's a big assumption."

"Not as much as you'd like to believe," Praxis said. "I know who we're dealing with. If we sit back and do nothing, the financial impact will be far worse than the cost of sending some troops *now*."

"Nonetheless, it would be a significant expense."

"Technically, yes, I suppose. In the short term. In the long term—"

"The short term is, however, of more immediate concern. Look, Praxis," he added when she began to sputter in protest, "I'm not saying 'no.' It's *possible* you could convince the Conclave of the urgency, with luck, and I'm open to the idea of helping you out on this."

"Then you believe me?"

Lexthur shook his head. "Praxis, I have always believed you. You're not a liar, nor are you delusional. You say there's a threat, you say it's in our own best interest to intervene—your word is enough for *me*." He reached over, resting his hand across hers. "It's not me you need to convince, though. Mounting something on the scale you're discussing is going to take quite a committed patron, for one."

Praxis slipped her hand free, waving it dismissively in the air. "My parents can handle that."

"Maybe," Lexthur said.

Praxis bristled, narrowing her eyes. "Are you saying the Fellows family can't *afford* it?"

"On the contrary, I would never dream of making such an insult," Lexthur said. "Only . . . your parents, they've *agreed* to this? They've actually *said* they're willing to back this enterprise?"

"Not *yet*, no, but—"

"Ah."

"They will! I'm going to speak to them this afternoon. My mother might be a bit of an issue, but I'm sure I could get my father on board."

"No. I really don't think you can."

Praxis frowned. "I think I'm a better judge of that than you are, Lexthur."

Lexthur shrugged. "Perhaps not. Under ordinary circumstances, I would be inclined to agree with you, but . . ." He paused, taking a moment to look down at his fingers. His signet ring was set, Praxis noticed, with stones he'd purchased from the Fellows. "Praxis, how much of your family's recent business have you looked into?"

"What are you implying?"

"Only that the glory days of the Fellows empire are . . ." Lexthur cleared his throat. "There's been some difficulty, these past few years. Two of their largest mines have dried up, and the output of a third is beginning to dwindle. They're pushing deeper underneath the crust, but it's getting more and more expensive that far down—and significantly more dangerous. There have been tunnel collapses, and numerous financial losses as a result."

"None of which is much cause for alarm. These things happen—they'll buy new mines, absorb a competitor. It always works out."

"Yeah, they've . . . they tried that, Praxis. A new mine was discovered last year, in prime real estate. Your parents invested quite a significant sum into securing the rights to it."

"There you go, then."

Lexthur winced. "I'm afraid not. The mine was a dud." He looked up, making sure to maintain steady eye contact. "They lost a small fortune on it."

To say this was a surprise would be somewhat of an understatement. Praxis kept up a cool face, even while she absorbed the full impact of this news. It wasn't so much the loss itself—loss happened, sometimes, in business, and it was true the Fellows had recovered from worse. No, what made this hard was more the idea that Prawl and Prestina had made a *mistake*, and an amateur one at that. Prewish should have easily been able to tell them of the viability of a new mine, so, what—did they ignore his advice, or just go ahead under the assumption that they didn't need him to inspect the new purchase? Neither option settled well with her, and despite her history of detachment over concern for the family business, Praxis felt a sense of unease creep up her back.

"Even if this is the case," Praxis said, speaking calmly and evenly, "the family cash reserves *alone* are enough to fund the patronage."

"But for how long? And how, exactly, is the company supposed to replenish it once it's run out? Your parents have a business to protect— a *dynasty*. They're not going to jeopardize the financial security of their own company for strangers half a world away."

"Oh, please. The reserves are not *so* small that we've reached this point yet."

"No, you're right. Unfortunately, your parents are *not* going to see that. You *know* they won't. I'm sorry, Praxis, but from their perspective, it just doesn't make sense to fund a war."

Praxis scowled, but she did not immediately argue this point. Though she was loath to admit it, Lexthur was right—the family might still be able to do it, but if they were feeling threatened, there was no way they actually would.

Which left what, exactly? There was no one else Praxis could appeal to, no other source of money to tap. Did that make this entire trip worthless, then? In which case, there very likely would be no one to step in and stop Lanali from trampling across the entire continent. A shadow of despair fell over her, and only Praxis's strict social training as a child kept her from revealing the depths of her emotions.

A friendly hand rested on Praxis's shoulder, but she shook Lexthur off.

"Believe it or not, all hope is not yet lost," Lexthur said. "Your parents' difficulties may yet prove to be the key to getting exactly what you want, although it depends on how far you're willing to go for it."

Praxis looked up sharply. "How?"

"You could petition the oversight committee to open up inheritance bidding on the company."

A single bark of laughter cut through the office, bouncing off the domed ceiling and sweeping out over the top of the bureaucrats below. "Oh, please. They would never agree to that."

"They would, actually. My ministers have been itching to do exactly that for more than a year now—it's just that no one is willing to openly move against Prawl and Prestina. But if a direct *family member* was to make a petition, they would be legally obligated to open up the floor."

"I—" Praxis started, but the rest of her sentence dissolved before it ever made it up her throat. She stared at Lexthur for a moment, trying to read the seriousness of his expression. The idea of the Minor Conclave's oversight committee wanting to wrest control of the company out of her parents' hands was, perhaps, more shocking than even the idea of financial difficulties in the first place. Most of the ministers had been appointed under the good graces of Prawl and Prestina's funding.

Praxis shook her head. "Even if that was so—and I'm not saying I believe it—I can't see where that would help us. What makes you think any of my brothers would be more willing to become a patron than my parents?"

As she said it, she realized just how true it was. Instantly, she thought of her brothers, the ones most likely to win the inheritance bidding. Prewish and Prommel, Praine . . . Prett didn't stand a chance, but even he, her closest ally, would likely never see the sense in funding something like this.

"You're right," Lexthur said. "The only way to guarantee control of the Fellows financial empire is for you to take charge of it yourself."

Praxis jerked back, eyes wide—but then she burst out laughing. Oh gods, she should have realized this whole thing had been a joke. She had to admit, Lexthur had been convincing. The level of craftsmanship of this prank was worthy of Prett himself, and as soon as Praxis could rein in her laughter, she would have to congratulate Lexthur on the skill of his ruse.

Only Lexthur wasn't laughing along. "Praxis, I'm serious."

"No, you can't be," Praxis managed to gasp out, still laughing. Lexthur was still staring at her, deathly even, and suddenly Praxis's mirth shriveled up. "Lexthur, you *can't* mean that. For sanity's sake, I haven't even *been* here in seventeen years! That's hardly a winning endorsement for a bid."

"On the contrary, the very *fact* that you've been gone gives you leverage. You've clearly had no involvement in your parents' recent choices. Nor can anyone insinuate that you've been manipulating the situation to your own advantage in the hopes of a takeover."

"But . . . I'm not even allowed."

"Technically, you are. All wizards are men under the law—surely you must be fully aware of that fact?"

Praxis fell silent. Of course she'd been fully aware of that—she'd been using it to her advantage for all these years, maintaining Yandosian citizenship so that the other countries they had diplomatic agreements with would have to allow her full access to her rights and privileges. But never once had Praxis actually given thought to what this legal truth would have meant for her if she'd *stayed*: the opportunities it would have opened up for her, the kinds of things she would have been allowed to pursue. And even though the idea of actually making a petition, much less putting in a bid, much less actually seizing control of the company for herself, even though none of it held any appeal to her, she did find herself idly curious anyway.

"Just . . . purely for the sake of argument," Praxis started, "let's say you're right. Do you really think I could win it?"

Once again, Lexthur did not answer right away. He shifted in his spot on the couch, uncrossing and then recrossing his legs. "Honestly?" he said at last. "No."

Praxis scowled. "Then why the seven hells did you bother winding me up like that?"

"Because," Lexthur said, "while I don't think you could win an inheritance bid *at present*, I do not think your obstacles are insurmountable. You have a strong case, but where the ministers will vote against you is that you lack influence in Yandosia. No one owes you any favors. You do not control anyone's secrets. There's nothing you can use as leverage against your financial opponents."

"I see. And I suppose you just happen to have some information for me that I would be able to use in this case?"

"Not exactly. But now we come down to the heart of the matter, and this is where you need to decide just how far you're willing to commit to this venture. Because I honestly do not think there is any chance you'll get the money you want without it being yours to invest as you see fit, and I *know* that you would ultimately lose as you stand right now."

"Okay. So what's your grand proposal?"

Lexthur's mouth quirked up in an amused smile. "It's funny you should choose *that* word."

"I don't understa—" Praxis started, but then it hit her. Her eyes widened. "No. Oh, no—no. Lexthur—"

"I'm not proposing a romantic entanglement, if that's what you're worried about. I haven't exactly been sitting around pining after you for seventeen years, hoping you'd come back to me. What I *suggest* is a political marriage."

"What you *suggest* is out of the question."

"Have you *really* been gone for so long that you've forgotten how to think like a Yandosian? With my influence, you would be a clear choice for successor. With your patronage, I could vote an endorsement in the Conclave to authorize military action.

"I know you've taken a lover," Lexthur added, and Praxis held up her hand as she stood and turned away from him, "and I would never interfere with that! There would be no reason for us to ever share a bed." Lexthur paused, just for a moment. "Tell me you don't see the logic in this. Go ahead, say it."

Praxis stood with her back to him. From this perspective, she could just about see the top of the spiral of Bolt, could just about hear the teeming chatter of the city over the shouts of government. It felt so strange, thinking of the curving spiral and the great sprawling tunnels as a "city." Everything in Yandosia felt strange. A sense of claustrophobia had been clinging to the edge of Praxis's awareness ever since they'd returned, following her like the cloud of a bad odor. Maybe Lexthur was right, maybe Praxis had forgotten how to think like a Yandosian. Knowing this type of loveless marriage of convenience was routinely practiced was one thing—the idea of it applying to herself was quite another. And, oh, the way he had described Kaedrich! *I know you've taken a lover,* so cold, so dismissive, as if sex was the only consideration of Kaedrich's involvement. Praxis hugged her arms to herself, her fingers digging into her coat.

She kept her face steady as she turned back to the office. To Lexthur, still sitting on the couch. "I don't see the logic."

"Liar."

"No. *No,*" Praxis repeated, raising a finger to still him as he began to stand. "Do not think that because we used to be friends, that means you have any insight into my mind these days."

"We were a little bit more than that, my sweet," Lexthur said. He pushed himself resolutely off the couch, his narrow limbs unfolding as he straightened up. "Just think about it. In the meantime, I'm going to write to the other members of the Major Conclave, and inform them of your request."

Praxis raised an eyebrow. "What, you mean . . . you're going to help me? Even though I've turned you down?"

Lexthur frowned. "I'm not a monster, Praxis," he said, a touch of hurt lining his voice. "Of course I'm going to help you. I don't think it's going to do any *good* . . . but if this is what you really want, then I'll do everything in my power to make it happen." He motioned at his desk, where sometime while they'd been talking, Huxley had brought up and deposited their lunches. On cue, the enticing smell of piconda, spicy and warm, drifted over Praxis. "And please, help yourself. I certainly can't eat all of this on my own."

THE FIRST TIME Praxis had met Lexthur Delford was at a dinner party her parents were throwing in celebration of the marriage of some local politician. Ordinarily, a family such as the Delfords might have never gotten the chance to visit the Fellows, but it turns out Lexthur's mother was a cousin of some relative of the bride, and there they were.

It wasn't that the Delfords were a bad family. Indeed, the production of crops along Yandosia's underground thermal vents was obviously a high-priority enterprise, and the families that oversaw it were respected for their time and effort. It's just that, in the complicated dance of rank and status, there really was no contest: mining brought in more profit. *Much* more profit, and so the Delfords arrived with nervous smiles and polite deference to the virtual monarchs that were the Fellows.

They met formally for the first time in the receiving line. His mother introduced him; and Praxis, stationed next to her own mother, accepted his lip-tap with a polite nod of acknowledgment. Prestina was already studying him as he smiled at Praxis and said to her, "This is so kind of your parents to invite us. Thank you."

"It will be our pleasure, I'm sure," Praxis said. She was getting good at this, by now, having been home from the disaster of her Qol Nar ritual for six months, and thrown herself at the mercy of her mother's social training.

Lexthur smiled again, and started to move on to Prestina, when Prestina abruptly cut in. She held up her hand, halting him before her daughter. "Lexthur, was it?"

Lexthur tapped his lips. "Yes, ma'am."

"Lexthur, I'm sure my daughter is getting bored with just standing here; young people should never stay in one place for so long. Why don't you take pity on her and invite her over to dance?"

"Oh!" Lexthur's eyes popped, his cheeks flushing infinitesimally along the upper line of his jaw.

It was obviously a setup, and everyone knew it. But Praxis extended her hand, allowing herself to be drawn from the receiving line without the actual formality of Lexthur asking her if she'd like to. Poor Lexthur's flush was growing, spreading out to tint his ears, creeping up his forehead.

They went through to the next room, where most of the floor had been buffed to skating quality. "We might as well make our parents happy," Praxis said, untying the skating blades from where they hung off her wrist via a thick velvet cord. "Though I will admit I'm really not much of a dancer." She gave Lexthur her best disarming smile.

Lexthur's own smile was somewhat shaky, and fast to boot. But he was trying, as he bent to assist Praxis in clipping her skating blades to the base of her shoes. "I'm surprised to hear that. Don't all you ladies learn the finer points of dancing?"

Praxis shrugged. "I guess I wasn't a very good student."

And this was technically true, though only half of the problem. Dancing lessons had drifted down the priority list when Moc had come into her life, and with him, the news of Praxis's magical abilities. A wizard was not often called upon to perform the tedious errands of a life in high society, which had suited Praxis quite well—up until recently.

She didn't bother telling Lexthur any of this. She assumed that he knew it, that he'd heard the gossip about her as it swirled through the tunnels of Bolt and possibly beyond. This wasn't vanity, not really—the Fellows family was too important for a scandal like her to stay quiet.

The rest of the evening was pleasant enough, as these things go. Praxis and Lexthur were stationed next to each other, and they made polite conversation, even lapsing once or twice into genuine giggles over some observation or another. Lexthur knew how to play the game, but his family had only recently gotten enough capital to be invited to take part in it, and so he had a somewhat unique perspective on the various social rituals and customs. Once he had relaxed a little, Praxis discovered that he was smart, and even funny, and he seemed to know exactly when Praxis was repressing the urge to roll her eyes.

Still, when he left at the end of the evening, Praxis never expected to see him again, and he disappeared from her thoughts by midmorning the following day.

So it came as quite a surprise when he turned up a few days later.

He arrived at their door on business, or at least that was the cover story. His parents had sent him. He had some papers or other, some meaningless excuse that was concocted to get him inside. Prawl and Prestina received him in the visitors' office, a room in the business trunk and separate from the rest of the household—but once their quick matter was easily dealt with, Prestina found every excuse to show him around the main dwelling, where she just *happened* to run into Praxis. And then, once she did, she "suddenly" remembered that she was needed elsewhere, and perhaps Praxis could take over for her?

Praxis rolled her eyes, but she accepted her charge without protest. Prestina strode out, heels chiming softer and softer as she left the two of them alone, and then Praxis began to stroll down the hallways, looping through the standard tour. She apologized for her mother, and Lexthur apologized for *his* parents, readily admitting that his errand wasn't actually the point of his visit.

"Oh, I'm well aware of *that*, Mr. Delford," Praxis said as they passed the bust of one of her long-dead relatives, and she motioned at it like it was worth paying attention to.

Lexthur nodded vaguely, glancing at the bust for only a second. "Yes, I'm sure you are. But . . . well, I just wanted to say, although I did agree to come here to please my parents, that was really only part of it. I genuinely did enjoy talking to you the other night. And . . . if you'd be amenable to it . . . I'd very much like to continue to enjoy our conversations in the near future."

Praxis stopped walking.

It shouldn't have been a surprise, and yet it was. No one had made such a direct overture to her yet, given her reputation, and she found that she didn't quite know what to make of it. True, this was now part of the plan: since giving up her magic, Praxis had resigned herself to living a "normal" life among the social elite, and that meant she'd eventually need to allow herself to be courted, and married. The true and inner longings of her heart and body did not matter—there was no alternative, for someone like her. However, up until now it had always been an abstract concept, something to accept as part of her future without having to look at too closely yet.

It was looking at her now, the idea tied to a physical face, a living body. Praxis found herself studying him more closely: the tidy knot of his belt, the boyish face, the delicate hands. She tried to imagine those hands running along her, and a heavy pit settled in her stomach.

"I . . . I realize that I might not be the *first* choice for someone of your position," Lexthur continued, hurrying on, and it was only then that Praxis realized he had taken her hesitation as a partial refusal. "But—"

"Oh, no, I'm sure nobody in *my* family would have cause to object," Praxis said, trying to spare him the effort. "My parents view me as something of damaged goods these days, I'm afraid. At this point, I think they'd be happy to see me in any marriage—not that I think that's what you're suggesting!" she added, her cheeks warming. "It's just, you know how parents see these sorts of things. Any advancement is half of a proposal in their eyes, isn't it?"

Lexthur blinked. For a second Praxis feared that she'd scared him off, and even though the prospect of him intimidated her, the idea of losing him before it had even begun was somehow worse. But all that he said was, "How could anyone view you as *damaged*?"

Praxis blushed fully now, and she actually looked away for a moment. "You flatter me, Mr. Delford, but surely you've heard my story by now."

"I haven't heard anything," Lexthur said, and when Praxis raised an eyebrow pointedly he added, "My family has only recently expanded into this area, remember? Local gossip hasn't exactly been a priority."

"Oh."

Surely he deserved to know, then.

Praxis held out her hand. "Then come with me," she said, "and I'll show you."

Though he looked a little nervous, Lexthur accepted the gesture, and without another word toward the rest of the tour, Praxis led him up to the main level.

This was the easiest way that Praxis could think of to explain it, for she was not about to break her vow of abstaining from magic to demonstrate her point. She led him in silence up three flights of stairs, down two additional hallways, finally exiting through the main doors of the household. No doubt Lexthur had passed through the ice garden on his way in, but he hadn't understood what it meant, what it was. The doors shut behind them, and Praxis drew Lexthur on, through the twisting side paths until they were buried deep in the middle of an alcove of frozen hedgerows and overhanging trees. Individual leaves of ice swayed gently in a crafted breeze, clinking together like chimes.

She let go of his hand, and gestured at the work that surrounded them. "This is mine."

Lexthur glanced around, taking it in. "It's remarkable craftsmanship," he said. He strolled over, examining the fine strands of ice that twisted together to create the impression of moss growing up a tree trunk. "Truly remarkable. Whom did you commission for it?"

Praxis shook her head. "No, you misunderstand. I did not commission it. I *made* it."

Lexthur whirled back, mouth and eyes agog. "You're a *wizard*?"

"Former wizard," Praxis said hurriedly. "I gave it up. It's a long story, and I'd rather not get into details if you don't mind. Suffice it to say, my life's path has taken a somewhat unexpected turn since then. I'm afraid that I'm not very well schooled in the 'womanly' arts—dancing, you already know."

The silence that followed this declaration was, in some ways, even colder than the ice around them. Praxis dipped her head, her eyes instantly catching on the tiny curl of scar that poked out from the end of her sleeve. The pain trapped underneath her skin flared as if summoned as Praxis pulled the fabric a little farther over her wrist.

She didn't know *what* she expected from him, not really. His shock was evident enough, and it was clearly taking him a moment to process what she had just admitted to. She wondered how badly this changed her esteem in his eyes. Here he thought he was attempting to win the interest of a *Fellows*—a high prize by any standard—and this was still true, and yet . . .

Prestina was right, Praxis was never going to get herself "settled" in her current state. Not that this should have upset her, because it wasn't as if Praxis was interested in marriage for romantic reasons—but if she ruled that out, what did that leave her? Living under the grace of her parents and whichever brother won control of the company when the time came? Sitting around sipping tea and entertaining guests that looked upon her with unabashed pity—or worse, entering into the family business in some fashion? No, she had to move on toward marriage at some point, and Lexthur was the first man not to dismiss her out of hand, given her tainted history.

She almost jumped out of her skin when he took her hand. She'd been so lost in her own self-pity that she hadn't realized he'd moved at all. When she dared look up, she found that, far from appearing distressed or dissuaded, he was watching her with a gentle smile.

"I won't ask you for the story," Lexthur said, "though if you ever want to tell me, I am more than happy to listen. But I will say this: Your garden is one of the most beautiful pieces of art I have ever had the privilege of setting my eyes upon."

Praxis blushed. "Oh. I, um . . . thank you."

"As for the rest of it, I cannot say I'm sorry to hear that you don't partake in all of the same dull fancies as the other ladies our age engage in. Already, you and I have had far more lively conversations than I've ever shared with a woman, and I would still like nothing more than to continue to enjoy your company. Besides," he added, the hint of a grin curling his lips, "you might not have noticed, but I'm not really much of a dancer myself."

"You . . ." Praxis's throat threatened to close up on her, and she paused for a moment to swallow down the lump that had formed. "You mean you really don't mind?"

"I really don't mind," Lexthur said, and something that had once been held back now burst inside of Praxis. She shut her eyes, trying to steady her rapid breathing. He didn't mind. He didn't mind!

In that brief moment she might have even loved him, despite the inherent shortcomings of his being a man.

And so, it seemed, Praxis Fellows was now being courted.

Chapter Seven

KAEDRICH FOUND HERSELF a library, mercifully devoid of both servants and Fellows. Naturally, it was enormous. Gentle curving bookshelves went up what would have been at least three stories in a Durlish building, though here every room was so tall that relative scale tended to get distorted. But there were several clusters of large, soft chairs scattered around the room, thick fur blankets draped over the back of each one, and the spines of the books were immaculate and inviting. Kaedrich shut the door behind her and made her way to the base of a gold ladder, leaning up against the endless rows of books.

There was only one problem, and it should have been obvious as soon as she'd entered the room: the books were all written in Yandosian. Oh well—it would still serve as a respite, even if not quite as comforting as the one she'd hoped to find. Kaedrich ran her fingers along the spines, selecting one at random. She flipped it open, taking in the comforting spread of text, the occasional illustration breaking up the words. It didn't really matter that she didn't know how to read it. The act of sitting in a chair, of flipping pages, had become a kind of meditation for her over the years.

Unfortunately, without the words to distract her, there was nothing to keep her thoughts reined in. Kaedrich stared blankly at the pages, fuming. It started as anger at Prestina, at her bribe, at the fact that she was motivated to try to separate the two of them to begin with, but it quickly bubbled over. Everything about this place was *wrong*, from the unnatural light of the lapus lumeni, to the false smiles and words of the Fellows, to the fact that, while it was certainly cold (gods, it was cold), it didn't seem nearly *as* cold as it should be when walking around in the middle of a glacier. And then, spinning even further back, the wrongness continued. Praxis's moods the closer to her home they got, withering from the elation that had oozed from her on the first boat, to the quiet that had settled into her on the second, to the downright testiness she'd started exhibiting on the caravan trek across the ice. Further still: the fact that somewhere behind them, Lanali was ruling over the people of Durland, advancing whatever sick scheme she'd been planning; that they had *fled* from an injustice, rather than staying to fight.

This last one caught in Kaedrich's chest, like a stitch from running too hard. She hadn't even stopped to think about it before, but it must have been bothering her in the back of her mind for some time now. It's not that she begrudged Praxis her choices: Kaedrich had been unconscious, after all, recovering from a wound that had nearly killed her, and Durland *wasn't* a particularly safe place for them to be, given the circumstances. She knew, also, that Praxis had some hopes of trying to convince people here to act on Durland's behalf. They had talked about this a lot, in the first leg of their trip down, and Kaedrich had gone along with it willingly. And yet . . .

She couldn't shake the feeling that she was responsible, somehow. She just kept thinking about their failed plans to stop Lanali—how they'd gone to the Council's Crescent, how they'd put up a valiant fight, how they'd been so determined to keep this very thing from happening.

This is when her thoughts really ran away with her, because thinking about the Crescent meant thinking about everything that had happened inside of it. Kaedrich frequently had dreams about it, dreams that left her sweating and shaking, dreams that Praxis would wake her up from and hold her close, whispering that it was fine, it was fine, it was nothing. In the darkness, Kaedrich would gulp in lungfuls of cool air and nod and try to focus on the present moment instead—on Praxis, on the smell of her skin and the warmth of her body—but they were so hard to let go of, impossible to let go of, because Kaedrich's dreams *weren't* nothing.

It wasn't just that she had nearly died. It wasn't even that she was convinced at the time that she would die, that she *must* die, that the fixed moment of her death that she'd bargained in order to help stop Lanali years ago had finally caught up with her. No, her own death wasn't the problem. She'd been wrong then, but it still loomed somewhere in her future, and she'd made her peace with it a long time ago. When it happened for real, she would accept it with grace.

But Kaedrich had killed people.

The fact that it was in defense of herself and her comrades—in defense of *Praxis*—made little difference. The fact that it was a combat situation made little difference. The fact that those people worked for Lanali made little difference. None of it changed the fact that there were people who were alive several months ago, people with lives, people with families, people with hobbies and jobs and friends, people that went out to dinner, or liked art, or could sing, people with belly laughs—*people*—and now there weren't. Because of her.

This is where she always ended up, whether in the middle of the night or in the middle of the library. She was a person who had taken a life, and nothing good that she ever did in the future would change that fact.

Kaedrich slammed the book shut. She dropped it on a table next to her and leaned her head between her knees, trying and failing and trying and failing to get their faces out of her head. Not even her pin gave her comfort in times like these. Despite the teachings of the Attendants, Kaedrich knew on some deep, primal level that Perlandra would judge her—and she'd be right to.

Unfortunately, these thoughts kept her wound so tense that when someone touched her shoulder, she reacted out of instinct: the training from her time at Falconridge Academy roared to life, and Kaedrich was on her feet before she even realized it. A shriek split the library, and she found herself staring down at a young Yandosian girl, pinned somewhat awkwardly over the armrest of the chair Kaedrich had just been in.

"Oh gods, I'm so sorry!" Kaedrich said, already dropping her hold and backing up several large paces. She tried to hold her hands up in a non-threatening way, though it was hard to tell how much that was helping.

The girl was, quite understandably, staring at Kaedrich with open terror, even as she scrambled back to her feet. She stepped behind the armchair, keeping something solid between the two of them.

"I'm really, really sorry," Kaedrich said again. "I didn't mean to do that, I just . . . You startled me. I'm sorry."

The girl frowned, but she nodded in what Kaedrich supposed was a sort of acceptance of her apology. She was still a little shaky, breathing in rapid bursts, but at least she wasn't running from the room screaming. She looked vaguely familiar to Kaedrich, but then they all did. This was clearly one of the nieces, her lilac dress far too ostentatious and her collar fanning far too high behind her head to be a servant.

The girl cleared her throat. "I was *asking* if you were . . . acceptable? Is that the word?" Her accent was thick, the vowels clipped and the *L* of "acceptable" drawn out lazily on her tongue.

"'Acceptable'? You mean, if I was all right?"

The girl nodded. "Yes. Allll right. You looked upset."

Kaedrich's face softened, guilt over her reaction making her even more touched by the girl's concern than she would otherwise be. "I'm fine. Thank you. That was very kind of you to ask."

Another frown. "It was less kind of you to strike me for it. But you're welcome."

Kaedrich winced. "I'm Kaedrich," she said, trying to change the subject. She held out her hand, but the girl merely looked at it. "Oh, right," Kaedrich said, and she brought her fingers to her lips.

"I know," the girl said. She inclined her head in acknowledgment of Kaedrich's gesture. "We all know. I'm Annelle," she added, holding her hand to her chest.

"That's a pretty name."

Annelle raised an eyebrow, and it was so much a Praxis-gesture that Kaedrich almost burst out laughing. The family resemblance between them was strong; in mannerisms and tone, mostly, though there was something familiar in the line of her brow as it settled back in place. Kaedrich wondered what Annelle was doing here. She did not seem to be in a hurry to resume whatever had brought her into the room. Indeed, she was apparently quite content to merely stand there and study Kaedrich, as if Kaedrich was some sort of new painting that had been commissioned, one she wasn't entirely sure if she liked or not.

"Am I not supposed to be in here?" Kaedrich asked, after a long and uncomfortable pause.

"Grandfather says that you can be anywhere you want," Annelle said. "He says you're a close friend of my aunt, and a lord besides, but . . ." Annelle pursed her lips. "You don't look like a lord."

Kaedrich felt herself flush. She ran her hands across her suit, tugging uncomfortably at the jacket. "I, um . . . I'm afraid that I had to leave in a hurry. I didn't have much time to pack more clothes."

"Clothes? Oh. Yes, you should talk to one of the tailors. They're on Sapphire Level. But, no . . . I mean . . . the lords that come from Durland, they don't . . . *look* like you." And she pointed, right to Kaedrich's face.

This was hard to deny. Kaedrich bit her lip, mulling over what to tell Annelle. It's true that in recent decades a *few* people with darker skin had managed to do something that deserved enough favor from the Crown to be granted a minor title—but it wasn't common, not by any stretch of the imagination. The lie that Praxis had told felt very fragile suddenly, and for the first time Kaedrich worried about how long it would take Prestina to make inquiries about the name "Mannly." If the Fellows regularly entertained Durlish lords . . .

Thankfully, Annelle did not seem to be asking a question so much as merely pointing out a fact, for a moment later she asked, "Are you in love with my aunt?"

Which might not have been any more comfortable, but at least it was easier to answer. "Yes."

Annelle grinned, and suddenly her whole demeanor changed. "I knew it!" She leaned over the chair, lowering her voice as if trading special secrets. "There's a rumor that she's *declared* you, though Grandmother says that idea is . . . um . . . '*plegmoska*'—I'm sorry, I don't know how to say it in your tongue. But I know. A woman knows."

Kaedrich forced a smile; she didn't know what it meant to "declare" someone, but she assumed it had something to do with what Praxis had called her, when they'd spoken with Prestina.

Annelle had straightened up by now, so smugly pleased with herself. She picked at the seam along the back of the armchair. "Don't worry, I won't tell anyone. I know what it's like for your heart to belong to someone that people won't approve of."

"Really," Kaedrich said. She did not intend to encourage the girl, but Annelle smiled anyway.

"Oh, yes. It's *horrible*—and yet, so wonderful, isn't it? Only don't ask me who. I'll never say."

"I won't."

Annelle's nose wrinkled. "Well. I should get back to work. Prett asked me to retrieve a book on the Native Revolts for a case he's working on. He's very good, you know. With the law. Everyone says."

"I'm sure he is."

Annelle nodded. She turned toward the shelves, but then stopped again. "Are you coming to dinner today? You and my aunt?"

Kaedrich tried to keep her shoulders from slumping, though she didn't have much luck at it. "Gods, don't tell me there's another party."

"No," Annelle laughed. "You weren't at breakfast, though. It's a *family* dinner," she added, raising her eyebrows meaningfully. "If you love her, you should come. Trust me."

"I . . . Thank you," Kaedrich said. "I'll think about it."

Annelle nodded, apparently satisfied. She turned and lost herself in a nearby set of bookshelves, and by the time she came out again, Kaedrich had already left.

PRAXIS DREW A sharp intake of breath through her teeth, trying hard not to cry out in pain.

"I'm sorry," the doctor said to her. "Did that hurt?"

"Yes, dammit. Did you think that jabbing a needle that deeply under my kneecap somehow *wouldn't hurt*?"

The doctor smiled, shaking his head. "You're the one that tells me you've felt no sensation there for three years." He drew the needle out, now loaded with fluid, and pressed a small, soft cloth onto the puncture mark.

"I'm not paying you to get cheeky with me," Praxis said.

"And that's not my intention, Miss P, I assure you."

Praxis scowled, massaging her knee as the doctor moved off to set the vial down on a small table.

She knew she was taking a risk in coming here, but what choice did she have? If you could afford it, Yandosia had some of the finest medical knowledge in the world. This particular doctor had come highly recommended when Praxis had made some discreet inquiries at the bars and socialite clubs that littered the spiral of Bolt, and he was willing (for an additional fee) to keep no record of her visits, and ask no unnecessary questions. This included not asking for her name, hence the "Miss P" moniker that Praxis had suggested to his secretary. She didn't kid herself into thinking the doctor wouldn't be able to figure out her identity—and sooner rather than later—but damned if she would give it up straight to his face.

The doctor pulled over a fine leather armchair, settling in as he began to prod deeply at Praxis's knee with his thumbs. "The fact that you're in pain now is actually encouraging," he said finally. "It suggests the joint is not *entirely* dead inside—just enough to prevent you from using it. I assume, by now, that you've sought out a wizard to try healing spells on it?"

Praxis nodded. "Yeah, that . . . doesn't help."

"And this was a *reliable* wizard?"

Praxis almost laughed at this, choking it down at the last second. "Yes," she said instead. "Quite reliable."

The doctor nodded. He was a slight man, with thinning hair and a narrow head that peaked as if the roofline of a temple was running down his face. Mostly an illusion brought on by his oversized nose, no doubt, but the bridge of his spectacles *was* bent slightly to accommodate his odd shape.

For a moment he just prodded at her knee in silence, his brow drawn together thoughtfully. Praxis tried not to wince whenever a flare of pain would shoot up her leg. She tried to look at it the same way the doctor had, as a sign that perhaps not everything was completely dead inside.

It didn't really help, though, when it felt like her knee was going to burst into flames.

Probably—almost certainly—Praxis should have told Kaedrich about this, but that was a thought Praxis shoved violently aside. She was sure that Kaedrich had already noticed, once or twice, when Praxis had difficulty keeping herself upright. It just . . . it wasn't the right time, Praxis told herself. Kaedrich was already overwhelmed, already dealing with so much. Why add to her burden, worrying about things that she could do nothing about? Once Praxis had some answers, then she would tell her.

The doctor sat back. He straightened his glasses, then squinted at Praxis like he still couldn't quite see her right. "I'm not going to lie to you: I've never heard of anyone surviving from this type of bite *at all*, so I can't say how likely it is we'll recover the use of your limb. But I'll see what I can learn from the fluid I drew. Give me a day or so, and I'll let you know what I have after that."

"Fine," Praxis said.

She made her way out of the office feeling slightly less miserable about the whole situation. She had to admit, her sojourn into the heart of Bolt that day was going better than she'd anticipated. Sure, her meeting with Lexthur didn't end quite as well as she'd have liked, but she'd gotten more than she'd expected. After that, it had been a long, uncomfortable walk into the residential districts, to track down a retired jeweler that used to work for the Fellows and discuss a commission—and that, at least, had gone off without a hitch.

Though . . . a part of Praxis still didn't know quite *why* she'd done it, like the suggestion had been whispered in her ear. Still, it could not be denied that the commission was an idea she should have had, that it could even be called necessary. Praxis had gotten back to the spiral right around the time for the doctor's appointment she'd booked that morning, and then, *even for that*, there was the possibility of answers somewhere in the future.

Maybe, she mused, just maybe, there might be something to be gained from this ill-conceived homecoming after all. Then she shook her head—

gods, what was that, *optimism*? Kaedrich must be rubbing off on her. That thought brought a faint smile to her lips, and for a while she lost herself in thoughts of Kaedrich as she made her way out of the branch-off tunnel and back to the main spiral.

She'd just reached the junction when a man rounded the corner in front of her with too much speed, the two of them crashing into each other. Praxis shouted, trying to leap back, only to find herself being steadied by a pair of familiar hands. She spotted a Fellows gem first, dotting the man's fingers, and her embarrassment turned to relief, back to embarrassment as she took in the sight of Praine's vibrantly colored coat, the furs dyed an electric mix of teal and purple and yellow.

"Why, Praxis!" Praine said as they both straightened out. "This is a pleasure, running into you here."

He held on to her shoulder as he spoke, a remnant from how he'd assisted in righting her. It took all of Praxis's self-control not to jerk out from underneath his grip. Instead, she eased herself out with as much grace as she could muster.

Praine was the third oldest of the Fellows siblings, and the first to be born after the gap Prestina had taken after . . . well, everything to do with Previn. Sometimes Praxis thought that her parents shouldn't have gone back to having children after that, if Praine was the result.

It was difficult for Praxis to even put a finger on exactly what bothered her about Praine. He presented a good face, but that was actually part of it: the sweep of his hair was always *too* neat, his smile always *too* straight and perfect. His smooth face looked as if it was sculpted like a statue of an ancient god, and while this had earned him the reputation as being the brother most likely to be swooned over by the fine ladies of Bolt, all it did was make Praxis's skin crawl. His eyes had a way of following you around the room, though you could never catch him outright *staring*. When he laughed, which he did frequently, it had the effect of making Praxis feel like someone was running their hands all over her body, whether she wanted them to or not.

And there were rumors. Nothing ever proven, no one ever willing to speak up. But when Praxis was eight, and Praine seventeen, a maid resigned from their service without warning, only to be spotted in Bolt about two years later with a little girl who had the Fellows eyebrows.

Frankly, Praxis had always questioned the family's decision, then, to put Praine in charge of staffing for the company, but her parents had incomprehensible blind spots at times, and Praine was one of them. *If I won, that would be the first change I would make,* Praxis thought, and then immediately scolded herself for it—she wasn't putting in a petition to open up inheritance bidding, no matter how much Lexthur might want her to. She just *wasn't*. If the Minor Conclave wanted to step in and yank control away from Prawl and Prestina, that was their choice, but she would not help it along, nor involve herself in the ensuing disaster.

"What are you doing here?" Praxis asked finally, when she realized that they'd just been standing there staring at each other for a little too long.

Praine smiled, and Praxis tried to avoid shuddering. "Why, I have business in the city, of course. Lots to do these days. Such responsibility. Anyway, I didn't really get a chance to see you at the party last night. Are you enjoying being back?"

"No," Praxis said. She did not elaborate further. She knew better than to engage herself in Praine's conversations.

He kept smiling. "That's a shame. We're all very glad to have you back, you know." He reached out and squeezed her shoulder, a glimmer of shifting color catching the light from the rings on his fingers.

"Thank you," Praxis made herself say. She clicked her thumb to reengage the brace system, intending to sidestep out of his grasp—and only then, too late, she realized she had forgotten to slip her gloves back on after her visit to the doctor's office. She tried to shift her hand back, out of sight, but Praine's eyes flicked down for just a second, his perfect smile never once leaving his face. Gods, she hated his face. Of all of her siblings, he had aged the least.

"I suppose I'll see you at home, then," Praine said, already stepping around Praxis. The colorful furs of his coat ruffled in the breeze of movement, swaying like peacock feathers. Praine snapped his fingers. "Oh, and do say hello to your friend for me, won't you? Kendrick, is it?"

Praxis took a breath, ready to correct him, and then thought better of it. "Yeah," she said instead. "Kendrick."

"Marvelous. I do like him." Then Praine gave a merry gesture that was a cross between a wave and a salute, and disappeared down the same tunnel that Praxis had just left.

As soon as he was gone, Praxis took her gloves out and tucked them hurriedly back on. She had intended to stay out and do a few other errands while she was in Bolt, but that would wait—all that mattered now was that she get back to Kaedrich, make sure that she was all right. *I do like him,* she heard again, over and over as she rushed out to where she'd arranged to meet her driver.

Chapter Eight

KAEDRICH WAS FINE, albeit somewhat confused by the flutters of panic, when Praxis caught up with her several hours later. *"Where have you* been?" Praxis hissed in her ear, after throwing her arms tightly around Kaedrich's neck.

"Um, right here?" Kaedrich said. "You're the one that went out." She bit back on adding, *Without telling me*, if only because it was obvious that something had rattled Praxis.

Praxis drew herself back, compressing as if embarrassed by her outburst of affection. "It's just . . . I couldn't find you. I've been looking all over."

"Why didn't your magic just tell you where I was?"

A flush passed quickly over Praxis's face. She waved it off. "It's not perfect, all right?" was all she had to say on the matter.

Kaedrich studied her for a moment, not entirely convinced. But it didn't feel like it was worth arguing over, not now anyway, and so Kaedrich let it pass. "Your father was giving me a tour," she said instead.

This was something of an understatement. Kaedrich had run into Prawl shortly after leaving the library, and it had started innocently enough: Kaedrich asked him for directions to the kitchens. Which apparently wasn't the right thing to say, because *Prawl* had no intention of shoving Praxis's guest off into the servants' wings, oh no, that just wouldn't do—*Prawl* had escorted Kaedrich personally to a small dining room somewhere off of Diamond Level, snaring a servant by the elbow as they passed and issuing orders for what felt to Kaedrich like enough food to host a dinner party. Kaedrich had opened her mouth to protest, but then decided that a lord of Durland, even a minor one, likely wouldn't object, and promptly shut it again.

So that was the start of it, but it didn't stop there. Prawl, though not hungry himself, had sipped on a glass of genuine Marcovallan ale while Kaedrich ate, regaling her with any number of meandering stories involving names she'd never heard of but nonetheless knew had to be wildly impressive. When the meal was done, Kaedrich figured that would be the end of it, but Prawl had drained the last of his drink and sprang eagerly to his feet, already going on about a tour as if it was the logical conclusion to events.

And then, gods, what a tour.

He took Kaedrich everywhere. Up and down what felt like a thousand staircases, through twisting corridors that glittered with wealth, from one end of the sprawling estate to the other. He pointed out works of art that were over a thousand years old, and busts of so many ancestors that it made Kaedrich wonder if Praxis wasn't related to the entire country in one way or another. She saw all three ballrooms, twelve different dining rooms of various shapes and configurations, a million sitting rooms. Libraries, gymnasiums, art galleries. Briefly, they stepped into a family crypt, the faces of Praxis's ancestors not just recreated, but preserved in various slow stages of decay behind the ice. Kaedrich tried not to let her skin crawl too much, and was privately thankful when Prawl moved on soon after. They found the tailor (*one* of the tailors, apparently), and spent a few minutes discussing Kaedrich's various needs, as Prawl saw fit. The tailor, an elderly man with narrow eyes and hunched shoulders, set his jaw when Prawl ordered him to measure Kaedrich for some suits, and held the tape about an inch away from Kaedrich as he worked. Which was probably just as well—Kaedrich always hated getting measured, so sure that someone would accidentally notice her secret while they were getting the sizing for her shirts and jackets—but the slight did not go unnoticed by Prawl. The smile hidden in his beard flattened, watching.

They moved on after that, more sitting rooms, more libraries and studies, more gems carved into various shapes, or embedded into murals that splashed the walls with so much color. Then, just when Kaedrich was beginning to feel hopeful that this was winding down, Prawl opened the door to what he called "the business trunk," and Kaedrich's legs groaned at the sight of more staircases.

"Wait," Praxis said, interrupting the summary that Kaedrich had been giving, "you mean that he showed you the actual operations of the business?"

Kaedrich shrugged. "I mean, he said that we didn't have time to see an actual mine, thank Perlandra, but . . . yeah, pretty much, I guess? Mostly there were a lot of offices, but we swung by Processing, and he introduced me to the gem inspectors, and—"

"You're kidding."

"No, why would I?" Kaedrich asked.

"He *never* takes people down there," Praxis said. "Not . . . gods, not *ever*. The whole of Operations is strictly limited to the workers themselves, and . . ."

". . . And?"

"And us," Praxis said. "Fellows, I mean."

"Oh."

Kaedrich couldn't look at her, suddenly, and so she looked at her hands instead. It's true that Kaedrich had gotten a number of overlong and somewhat disgruntled looks from the workers as they passed by, but she'd just assumed that it was the standard Yandosian distaste of anyone darker than ice. It hadn't seemed much worse, after all, than the nasty glares she'd gotten from the household staff.

She supposed that she should be flattered, but instead a knot of dread tied up inside her. The last thing Kaedrich needed was word of her tour to reach Prestina's ears, but how could that outcome possibly be avoided? A horrible thought occurred to her then: was this what Prawl had wanted? He'd been so ridiculously friendly toward Kaedrich ever since the beginning, but what if it was just a cover, a way to get Kaedrich to lower her guard? He was *married* to Prestina, after all—surely that signaled an allegiance of some sort, didn't it?

And what of Annelle's invitation? *You should come to dinner.* What if all of them, the whole tangled mess of Fellows, were conspiring to make Kaedrich look like the world's biggest fool? Maybe there was a *reason* why Praxis had grown up so cynical, so convinced that every kind gesture was a trap waiting to spring.

She couldn't voice any of this to Praxis, though. She *tried*, but the words died in her throat and she'd had to cough and come up with something else just to cover for it. Instead, Kaedrich allowed Praxis to lead her back to Emerald Level, to their immaculate guest suite, the one place Kaedrich felt marginally safe. They both skipped the family dinner, ordering trays instead, and Kaedrich tried to let the conversation stay light, stay safe. Praxis picked at her food, something obviously bothering her, too, and neither of them talked about either of their fears all evening.

The one thing she did eventually manage to bring up was almost irrelevant at this point, and yet it had been nagging at Kaedrich ever since the library. "Praxis," she asked a few hours later, when both of them were readying for bed, "what does '*plegmoska*' mean?"

Praxis jerked back, nearly dropping the jar of hand cream she'd been holding—in this type of cold, such things were a necessity. "What? Where did you hear *that*?"

Kaedrich shrugged. "Just . . . somewhere. Why, what is it?"

"It's . . . *vile*," Praxis said. "It's . . . well, literally it's the word for a pus that you have to sometimes drain out of an inflammation that can develop on a brusker dog's . . . anus. I'm sorry," she added, when Kaedrich cringed, "but there's really no polite way to explain that."

"No, it's fine," Kaedrich said, though it wasn't. She tried to laugh it off. "I asked, didn't I?"

"Seriously, *where* did you hear that? Was it one of the maids? Because my mother has strict policies against the use of that kind of language, and you shouldn't be subjected to it like that."

You mean the same woman who said it, apparently? Kaedrich thought, but she kept her mouth shut. She smiled, shrugging again. "I don't even remember. Forget I said anything."

Though Kaedrich herself had no intention of forgetting. Not once. Not ever. Instead, she let herself underneath the covers, her thoughts reviewing the day like a general surveying a battle map.

So it begins.

THE THING ABOUT living in a household as large and fully staffed as the Fellows' dwelling, is that when something happens, you can usually *feel* the impact of it before the real news finally reaches you. Ripples spread through the ice, carried on the whispers of servants and the nervous glances of those who had already been informed. The very air seems to grow somehow colder with dread.

So Praxis knew that something was wrong the instant she and Kaedrich stepped out of their chambers the next morning. Maybe it was the fast looks a passing maid gave them, watching: you could see the question in her face, *Did Praxis know yet?* Maybe it was the ache in her knee, somehow sharper than it had been the night before. Maybe it was the way her breath caught in front of her as a cold mist. Praxis grabbed Kaedrich's hand with her free one, squeezing tightly as they made their way down the corridor.

Kaedrich glanced down at the gesture. "What's wrong?"

"I don't know yet." Praxis paused, listening to a rapid-fire set of footsteps as they approached from down the hall. "But I think we're about to find out."

The first wave of the news, then, came from Prenna. Breathless, she stopped in front of Praxis and Kaedrich, clutching her sides as she told them in short bursts that Prawl and Prestina were summoning Praxis to the master study.

"What for?" Praxis asked, before Prenna had even had a chance to finish speaking.

Prenna shook her head. "I don't know," she puffed. "But it's not just you. Prewish, Praine, Prommel, Pranders, and Prett are all being sent for."

Praxis ticked names off of a mental list, her brow contracting as nearly all of her siblings were checked. "But not you?" Prenna was one of only two to be excluded from this elite roster.

"No," Prenna said. "I'm not sure if I should be grateful or scared."

"Grateful," Praxis said.

The first inklings of what was probably going on were starting to process through her mind, though she hoped desperately that she was wrong. Because the list of people being summoned were only the siblings with full legal status—Prenna, excluded for her sex, and Previn . . . well, even if he technically had a legal standing, there was no way he could ever act on it.

"I'd better go," Praxis said after a moment. Once her parents issued a decree, only fools ignored it. Praxis gave Kaedrich a fast kiss ("Good luck," Kaedrich said), and then she left the both of them behind, taking the death march to the master study.

She met up with Pranders halfway there. They didn't speak to each other, a quiet nod of acknowledgment more than enough. Though only three years apart, the two of them had never been close. Praxis wouldn't even have recognized him, if they'd met anywhere outside of Yandosia. His doughy face, scraped with a light beard, was unremarkable, interchangeable—even his suit, unobtrusive tan and medium brown, would have let him blend into the background of just about any other environment; only here was it out of place. Praxis held her back straight as she walked, trying hard to keep the sound of her leg brace to a minimum, and fighting the look of pain off of her face.

The master study. Even with their relatively sedate pace, they reached it all too quickly.

Once, when they were all much younger, Praine had given the room the nickname of "the bloody bath," because the Fellows siblings were only ever called there when they were in the worst of trouble. The master study was the very heart of the Fellows financial empire—the office out of which Prawl issued his decrees, met with his advisers, and kept the vault that housed the most sensitive of their sensitive documents. The naming of the study had earned Praine a fresh trip there, though it had stuck in the private vernacular among the siblings.

They stepped into the bloody bath together, Pranders and Praxis, the last ones to arrive.

It hadn't changed a single bit, in the years since Praxis had last seen it. The bloody bath was deceptive in its architecture and decorating choices—tastefully appointed, with a high vaulted ceiling and cheerful murals on the walls, the whole aesthetic designed to put you at ease in a way that you really should never be, sitting in this room.

The massive slab of Prawl's whale-bone desk sat at one end, the entrance of the vault on brazen display behind his seat of power. A semicircle of pale couches and comfortable chairs faced the desk, plenty of seating for whoever he had invited in to speak with him. Between the seats, a slab of ice rose from the floor as a low table, a tray of untouched drinks laid out. The rest of Praxis's siblings were already seated, arranged by unspoken loyalties: Prewish and Prommel, in their respective black and gray, beside each other as a joint force opposite the colorful splash of Praine; Praine, who sat back with ease, one elbow on the back of the sofa; Prett kept a calculated distance roughly equal between the two groups, a bright spot of blue like a lone flower tossed into the waters of the open sea. Pranders immediately went to sit beside Praine, and Prett waved Praxis over, patting the seat next to him with a masterful cheer that hid his apprehension. Praxis drew her battered coat tighter around herself as she perched on the cushion beside Prett.

Their parents stood in front of the desk. Not looking at the children yet, their heads bowed together as if in silent consultation. Prestina glanced up, her glare as cold as the icy blue of her dress, as the last of her children took their seats. But it was Prawl that turned to face them full-on.

Now Praxis knew they were really in trouble, and now she knew that her earlier suspicions had to be right. Far beyond the bloody bath itself,

Prawl only ever took the lead in a conversation if it was a matter of the most dire circumstances—and there was really only one thing Praxis could think of that would get him this mad.

Prawl held himself tall. There was no smile behind his beard, no twinkle in his eye. The only glimmer of his appearance came from the gems on his fingers, like the glint of a knife.

"One of you has anonymously petitioned the oversight committee to open up inheritance bidding for the company," Prawl said, his voice deathly level, and Praxis winced. Sometimes, she hated being right. "I want to know who, and I want to know *right now.*"

The silence following this proclamation was so complete that, if any of the siblings had the courage to breathe, it would have been as deafening as the screaming breaths of the deepest mine. They glanced at each other. Their faces were perfect mimics of equal parts shock and modulated control, though clearly at least one of them was lying. You could see the question flitting through the room: Is it you? Is it you? Is it you?

Prawl let them stew in their silent interplay of loyalties and suspicions for a moment, but not long. "Did none of you hear me?!" he barked, and everyone jumped. "I said I want a name!"

Another pointed silence. Whoever it was, they were in no hurry to confess, and none of the rest of them were eager to take the brunt of pointing this out.

Well. If it had to go this way, then Praxis might as well get it over with. She rolled her eyes. "Obviously whoever did it wouldn't have submitted the petition *anonymously* if he was willing to admit it."

She knew her mother's slap was coming, and she let it happen. Prestina shot forward, her hand cracking against Praxis's cheek before she could even blink. Praxis's head jerked to the side, the force nearly toppling her into Prett. She gritted her teeth and clutched at the searing skin as Prestina resumed her post at the head of the room.

"Does anyone else want to be funny?" Prestina asked, once she'd safely returned to Prawl's side.

Praxis shut her eyes, riding out wave after wave of pain screaming through her face. But at least now the conversation could move on.

Sure enough, it wasn't long before Prewish was clearing his throat. This was the dance, perfected over years of practice: someone, usually Praxis, would take the fall, and then Prewish, the oldest, would try to rein them all in and restore order.

"With respect," Prewish said, "I don't think that the question of *who* has done it is really the most pressing issue at this point. It has been done. What we need to do now is focus on where we're going—as a family, as well as a company—from here."

Praine smirked. "That is what the person responsible would say, now, isn't it?"

"Possibly, but it wasn't me."

"And we're supposed to just take your word on that?" Praine asked.

Prewish smiled. "I know it's hard for you to accept, but some of us *are* true to our word."

"Besides," Prommel cut in from beside him, "what does Prewish have to gain from acting *now*?"

"The same as any of us," Praine said with a casual shrug. "Control of the company."

"True, but doesn't the timing strike you as odd?" Prommel asked. He glanced farther down the circle, where Praxis was still cradling her cheek, slouching low in the couch, and trying hard to ignore the minutia of family bickering.

She snorted underneath the sudden scrutiny. "Yeah, in case you haven't noticed? Never had the slightest interest in this company."

"So you *say*," said Prommel.

"Times do change people," added Praine.

"Oh, please," Praxis muttered.

"Praxis would never be so subtle," Prett broke in from beside her. He shrugged apologetically at her when she raised an eyebrow. "It's true."

"Fair point," Praxis said.

"It wouldn't be Praxis."

Everyone turned, stunned by the voice that had issued this proclamation. Prawl, leaning now against his desk, was watching the interplay of his children. His arms were folded over his chest, and he was scrutinizing them as they bickered, no doubt looking for holes in their logic or their emotional masks. "It wouldn't be Praxis," he repeated. "She's telling the truth."

Praxis forced a tiny smile at her father, though Prommel was already rolling his eyes.

"That is what *you* would think," Prommel said.

Prawl turned, narrowing his gaze. "I beg your pardon?"

Prommel shrugged. "Come on. Don't we all know by now that you've always had a soft spot for her?"

"Your father loves his children equally," Prestina cut in, her voice slicing through the arguments like a finely sharpened sword. "I will not stand here and let you say otherwise—not after everything that he has done for *all* of you."

Once again, the room fell into silence. Once again, Prewish cleared his throat. Briefly, he stroked the point of his beard in thoughtful contemplation. "As much as it pains me to admit this, it might be a good thing that someone has finally done it. I know no one wants to say it," he added quickly, to hold the floor while he could, "but the company has been bleeding for years now. Father, Mother: I love you, and I'm sorry . . . but we need a change."

Prawl narrowed his eyes. Throughout the room, you could *see* each of the rest of the siblings silently thanking the universe that that look had not fallen upon them.

"And I suppose you think *you're* the right person to make this change," Prawl said. So quietly, and yet no one doubted his words—or his meaning.

Prewish, however, held himself straight underneath the glare.

"I do," he said. "And I hope most of you will support me when I enter my bid, but that really isn't the point. If not me, then perhaps Prommel—I will follow whoever is chosen, but that doesn't change the fact that we *need* this, if the company is to survive. And I promise you, anyone objectively looking at the numbers would tell you the same thing. You've made mistakes," he continued, his voice turning as low as a mine. "And they've cost us."

Prawl glowered at them. His jaw was clenched so tightly that several muscles and veins stood out on the side of his flushed face. Praxis tried not to think about how, if she had said anything remotely like that, Prestina would be making straight for her other cheek. *Soft spot, my ass,* Praxis thought. Since when had either of her parents shown her any favoritism?

The trouble is that Prawl could not directly argue with Prewish's point. Apparently. And while a more unruly father might simply lash out against any insolence, no matter how well justified, Prawl was simply too grounded to fly off the handle when presented with a cold, rational argument. Oh, he would never concede the base fight—that it was not time to hand over the company, that he'd been betrayed by his children— but the fact that he'd made mistakes . . . that was sadly all too true.

Praxis took the time to regard each of her brothers in turn now. It was easy for her to imagine any of them going behind Prawl and Prestina's back like this. Well—probably not Prett, who'd never had any more interest in the family business than Praxis; he was currently staring at his fingernails, without an apparent care in the world. And she doubted that Pranders, who had never stood up for himself in his life and tended to follow Praine around like a lapdog, would have ever had the guts to follow through even if he'd wanted to; already, his eyes were trailing toward the door. But the rest of them: Prewish, his hardened glare as dark as his coat; Prommel, stately and steady as iron, watching the room with the practice of a soldier; and Praine . . . She glanced at him, and he smiled, and Praxis remembered, suddenly, that Praine had been in Bolt just yesterday afternoon.

She sighed, slumping lower in the couch. Regardless of who had done it, it was done, and now there would be an automatic freeze on any major financial transactions until the matter was settled. Which meant that, even if she could convince her parents to fund a military intervention in Durland, it wouldn't do her any good. She was going to have to wait and see how this all shook out, and *hope* that whoever won would be amenable to using their new wealth for a greater purpose. She snorted, already disgusted with her prospects.

Tell me you don't see the logic. Praxis shook her head, chasing Lexthur's words away. No matter what was happening back in Durland right now, or how much it may have degraded since they'd fled, there was no way Praxis was going to break down and agree to that.

They were just going to have to find some other means of helping Durland, then.

Chapter Nine

So what *was* happening in Durland?

In the quiet shadows of a purple-gray mountain, at a sleepy country estate known as Brindlewood Hall, a man was just arriving home. His name was Quaith Vandervoon, and he'd been gone for five days.

He stood before the figure of the house for a moment, breathing in the fresh, open air, and took the time to finally brush the flecks of soot and choate-salt ash from the sleeves of his jacket. The greatest irony of his life was that, despite being the sole heir to a railroad baron's company, Quaith actually hated trains. He hated the filth. He hated the swaying, the way it turned his legs to jelly. He hated the squeal of the brakes, and the deafening blare of the whistle, and the shouts of the conductors reminding everyone to *Board!* and that this was the *Last stop for Monfort!/Styford!/New Hammond!* and the hiss of an engine as it cooled down at the end of the day. Most of all, though, he hated the weight of it: the responsibility of an entire company, the feeling that he should have all of the answers—even though the Board of Directors didn't seem to care what his answers were, even though they'd essentially been in charge ever since Quaith had inherited at only fifteen. Running a business had always been his father's dream, not Quaith's.

Well, then, good news! Quaith thought to himself, a bitter pang twisting up his chest. He scowled, and started up the gravel drive.

Quaith let himself in through the front door (they'd had to dismiss the butler last month), and was instantly greeted by the sound of four distinct shrieks. They pealed into the room from somewhere up ahead, the library probably, and rang through the foyer like temple chimes.

The first one—loudest and most distinct—came from his wife. Valinda gave another loud shriek of alarm, and then a second later she added, "Filthy, rotten, little vermin!" On the other hand Garen, the toddler, was shrieking with delight, laughter underscoring the rapid pounding of his tiny feet as he ran around the library, while Jillus, the baby, merely wailed in sympathetic discontent at all the commotion. Which left only one, a wild, animal cry that ripped through most of Brindlewood Hall with ease. Its short little bursts made it sound disturbingly like a laugh.

Quaith sighed as he quickened his pace. He reached the library just as a mad flutter of wings soared toward the doorway; Quaith reached up and snatched it right out of the air, drawing the creature close to his chest. He ducked, narrowly avoiding the wild swing of a broom as it *whoosh*ed over his head. "Valinda!"

"Get out of my way!" Valinda shouted. Her wild eyes had already settled on the bundle that Quaith cradled against himself, and she raised her broom in preparation for another swing. "That *thing* has gone too far this time!"

"*Valinda!*" Quaith wrenched the broom from his wife's grip, setting it easily aside. Brex, the tiny creature held fast before him, poked his iridescent-blue head out from the protective shell of Quaith's hand, his little nose sniffing wildly in the center of the ring of green fur that crowned his snout.

Valinda swung her fists by her sides like a child, a strangled cry of frustration filling the room. "It—!"

"Yes, I'm sure," Quaith said. He stuck his head out into the main hall and tossed Brex into the air, where the creature chittered happily and raced up the opening of the stairwell. "But my sweet," Quaith continued, turning back to his wife, "you really shouldn't be chasing after him like that in your condition."

"Exactly! Exactly! That's why you have to get rid of it!" Valinda cradled her ample stomach, her face pained. Though she wasn't even quite halfway through, she looked much further—twins, they'd been told, as if Quaith needed the additional expense.

He eased Valinda over toward a couch, murmuring softly to her. Garen, meanwhile, raced over and threw his arms around Quaith's leg, reducing Quaith to a shuffle. In the corner of the room, Jillus was still wailing from where she sat on the floor.

Quaith kissed his wife's head, brushing a loose sprig of hair away from her face. "You know why I can't do that," he said. He scooped up his son and crossed the room to his daughter, depositing one for the other as he carried the baby over toward Valinda's waiting arms.

"You don't owe that woman anything," Valinda said. "Does he?" she added to Jillus, now seated in what little space was left of her lap. "No, he does not. If it wasn't for *her*, you might even have a proper nanny right now."

Quaith massaged his forehead. The problem is that Valinda was not *entirely* inaccurate in her assessment, though Quaith would never assign the blame like that. *He* had been the one to take on Praxis Fellows to try to continue the work of his father's business partner, attempting to unlock the secrets of a more refined choate-salt to then power the more efficient engine designs that had been moldering in the attic for years. *He* had been the one to approve each additional expenditure in the last year, when she'd finally been making progress. *He* had been the one to reduce the household's expenses to pay for it, and when that wasn't enough, *he* had been the one to sell several dozen shares of his own personal stock of Orange Rail Lines, dipping him under fifty percent of the holdings. Praxis was right on the edge of figuring it out, Quaith knew that. It wasn't her fault that, in the wake of Lanali's rise to power, her life had been in enough danger that she'd needed to flee the country, the work still incomplete and therefore entirely without the profit Quaith had been anticipating.

Which had left him with a sizable debt, a skeleton staff for the household, and a bitter wife. And, of course, Brex, the small animal that she'd left in his care because he wouldn't be able to manage in whatever environment they'd been heading for.

And still, he would do it all again. It had been a risk, yes, and one that had blown up in his face in the end. But the successful development of the choate-salt and the old designs might have been the only thing that would have saved his company from the brink of disaster. If anything, his trip to Monfort these past five days had only solidified that conviction.

He sank into the couch beside his wife. Jillus had quieted, curling around Valinda's stomach and resting her head on it like a pillow. Valinda sat patting the baby's back, over and over and over again. Quaith leaned forward, his elbows on his knees, and stared at the spread of his hands for a moment or two. There really was no keeping this from Valinda, not for long, but Quaith would have given anything not to have this conversation.

"Oh, just say it," Valinda snapped. "You know I hate it when you brood."

"They're selling the company."

He didn't dare look at his wife as he'd said it, but he felt her stiffening beside him. "They . . . they can do that?"

Quaith nodded. *They can now,* he almost said, but thought better of it. Valinda didn't know about the shares, and there really was no point in bothering her with the information at this point.

Tentatively, Valinda rested her hand on Quaith's back. "Oh, Quaith. Is there really nothing to be done?"

"We've been bleeding money for years now. At this point, the Board feels it's better to just cut our losses and move on." Quaith sat up, giving his wife a brave smile. "We'll get a percentage of the sale. Enough to pay off the worst of our debts."

Valinda's brow crinkled. "How do you already know how much we'll be getting?"

Quaith's smile collapsed. "They've, um . . . they've already settled on a buyer."

"*What?* So soon?"

"They were approached," Quaith said. His mouth twisted up in distaste. "Apparently that's how this whole thing started."

"But that's . . . that's terrible! Quaith, you can't let this happen. This is *your* company. They can't just steal it away from you like that. It's not right! You need to petition the Transitional Council."

"Somehow, I don't think the government that just bought our company is going to be very receptive to my complaints," Quaith said.

He watched this information hit Valinda. The surprised arch of her eyebrows, her mouth gaping open and then shutting into a straight line, her lips pinching tight. Her eyes went soft as she considered this. Before the changeover, Valinda would have been as quick to criticize the government's decisions as anyone—all of Lanali's followers were. Everyone knew the old Crown was corrupt, that the Governance Council was squeezing the life out of ordinary citizens everywhere. But these days, Lanali held such a tight grip on the Transitional Council that criticizing anything it did was tantamount to criticizing the Right and Venerable Pon herself. *Some* people were still willing to do that. Quaith doubted Valinda was one of them.

"Well," Valinda said slowly, "I suppose if it's the Council itself making the call . . . I mean, they must have a very good reason for wanting to take over the business. And you did say we'd be getting a fair portion for our shares, didn't you?"

Quaith didn't know that he'd necessarily call the value of the sale "fair," no, but there was no point in arguing this with his wife. He patted her knee, neither confirming nor denying what she'd no doubt continue to believe either way. Valinda had been a supporter of the Pon from the very first days, when she'd just been a tragic figure voicing her calls of doom in the newspaper columns. Nothing Quaith said now was going to sway her, and he had long since given up trying.

Except that he knew the truth. Praxis and Kaedrich had made no attempt to hide what had transpired with the great ghost crisis, and exactly what Lanali's role in all of it had been. Valinda refused to hear it, and would attempt to snap down on Praxis's tongue the moment the topic shifted anywhere near that direction. But Quaith had listened, and despite Valinda's repeated attempts to convince him that it was nothing more than a story, that Praxis had personal reasons for lying, that she was unreliable anyway, and who are you going to believe, some *wizard* with a penchant for going behind your back whenever it was convenient, or your *wife?*— Quaith had still refused to be budged. He knew the truth.

It was for this reason, he realized now, that he'd thrown so much money at Praxis's research. Some part of him had been afraid of what Lanali was capable of, and some part of him had assumed that somehow a design buried in Abramm's notes would prove critical in preventing her rise to power. What he really thought Praxis would find in those dusty old notes, Quaith had no idea. He hadn't even known that's why he was doing it, until this moment. This moment, when he'd failed. This moment, when it was all too late anyway.

If only he had another chance, an opportunity to set things right . . . But that wasn't going to happen. His company was gone, Praxis Fellows was gone, and Valinda, for all the love Quaith bore for her, would never help him in this. Quaith slumped back on his sofa, inside of his grand house, a house that he had never deserved and would probably have to sell, surrounded by his family . . . but utterly and completely alone.

AND IN MONFORT, Durland's teeming capital city, a woman was alive who was not supposed to be alive.

Well. Technically, she probably wasn't in Monfort anymore—at least, Tol certainly hoped she wasn't. He had made it perfectly clear to her that she was never to set foot within a fifty-mile radius of the city, and in fact the farther she kept herself, the better. But there was nothing that *enforced* this perimeter, except for Tol's threats, and now Tol was seeing shades of the girl everywhere. His heart skipped at the appearance of every wisp of blond; every girlish giggle sent him whirling, trying to spot the source. Surely it couldn't be, surely she wouldn't be so stupid . . . ? And it never was. It had been a week, and it never was.

This did not comfort him, however. Instead, the longer it had been, the jumpier he was getting. He'd had too much time to think about it, too much time to consider and then reconsider and then reconsider *again*. Too much time to fret about the consequences. Too much time to concern himself with what-if scenarios.

He still could not adequately explain to himself why he had done it.

It was a normal enough assignment. Arrange for her death, make it look like a tragic accident. Tol hadn't been surprised when Pon Lanali told him to do it. Indeed, he was amazed that the girl had managed to last as long as she had. She had been the daughter of one of the family seats of the King's Court of State, sole heiress to the position; but because of her gender, she could not take the seat for herself. Her uncle had filled it until the time when she would marry a nobleman, and Pon Lanali just so happened to have an available nobleman under her control. The girl became Lady Hendril just in time for Lanali's takeover of the Crown, and now that they had gone through the various objections, now that the Court of State had ruled Lanali to be the legitimate ruler over the transitional government, now the girl was somewhat superfluous. Having completed a ruling, Lord Hendril's seat was secure. It probably would have been better to let the girl produce a child, just in case they needed longevity on their side, but alas, the new Lady Hendril grated on the Pon's nerves terribly.

So it was.

Tol had arranged for the girl to take a pleasure sail out in the middle of Abbney Bay. He handled the boat himself, dressed for the role of a lowly paddleboy. Summer had hit Monfort in full force, and everyone knew the storms were sudden and dangerous. The one that cloaked the bay that afternoon was worse than normal, so swift that there was no time to return to shore. Tol had made sure of that: reaching out with his magic, teasing an approaching front along, riling it up so it was raw and furious by the time it broached the crest of the protective city ridge. The wind tore up the surface of the bay. All around them, boats were trying to flee, but Tol's stayed where it was. They were smack in the middle of a calm patch, all of the world churning around them, rain and wind and thunder obscuring the view, but here in their tiny oasis they were still and dry.

"I'm sorry, but you're going to die now," Tol had said to her. His paddles were resting across his knees, water dripping onto the floor of the boat. He thought he was being polite. He tried to give his victims advanced warning, when he could. He wanted them to be able to make peace with their gods, if they believed in such things.

He expected the girl to panic, and plead for her life. Most of them did. It didn't save them one way or another, but most of them did. And Lady Hendril, so young, so girlish, so very, very naïve—if anyone was going to fall to their knees and blubber and beg, surely it would be her.

She didn't, though. Oh, she was afraid, certainly she was afraid. She had paled underneath her lady's tan, her heart fluttering so fast that Tol could see it thundering in her breast. Her eyes were wide and wet. When she spoke, her voice was small as a sparrow. But she did not beg.

"What did I do wrong?" she asked.

"Nothing," Tol said.

"There must be something."

"No."

"Then *why*?"

Tol shrugged. "Does it matter?"

"It does to me."

"It won't for long."

Lady Hendril frowned. "It's because she hates me, isn't it?"

Looking back, this might have been the first bit that led toward saving her life. Because this was something completely new, outside of all that Tol had been expecting. He'd blinked, startled. "What did you say?"

"Pon Lanali. She hates me, and now she's ordered my death."

"How—?" Tol started, and then caught himself. "Why would you think that?"

Lady Hendril was silent for a moment. She turned, staring into the chaos of the storm: the rain, so thick as to become a shimmery gray curtain around them, and the wind that refused to cross the circle. Their boat was shuddering now and then, the water colliding deep underneath the surface. The storm itself would not touch them, but there were still pieces that could get in, ripple effects that were beyond Tol's control. There were always pieces beyond your control, no matter how carefully you played the game, no matter how solid your strategy.

When Lady Hendril finally did turn back, she did not answer Tol's question. "She's not going to give up her power, is she? This government . . . it's supposed to be a transition, but she's never going to hand it over. That was her plan all along, wasn't it? That's why everything is taking so long to get started."

Tol honestly had no idea how to respond to this. Yes, that was exactly it; and it's not as if he had never considered the idea that someone might figure out what Lanali had been up to, but for *Lady Hendril* to have put it together . . . it was sort of like discovering that the household dog could do algebra.

He just stared at her. It was all he *could* do.

"I don't care, you know," Lady Hendril continued. "If that's what she's concerned about. I'm not going to expose her. Perlandra knows the previous Crown wasn't up to the job—maybe the Pon is a better choice. Either way, I'm not going to try to stop her. So if that's why she thinks I have to die—"

"It's not."

"Then why can't she let me live? I could help. I have friends."

Tol shook his head. "That's not how this works."

"Do *you* think I deserve to die?"

"*That's* not how this works, either."

And then, to Tol's infinite shock, Lady Hendril actually smiled at him. It was a perfectly crafted smile, innocent and disarming. She smiled with her whole face, dimples and bright eyes and arched eyebrows. The exact right tilt of her head. It was the way Lanali used to smile, back when she was just Frel, back before she had ever dreamed of this plan, back when they both still lived on the shores of Aul, and nobody knew who she was. Tol's head spun just looking at it.

"So you *don't* think I deserve it," Lady Hendril said.

It was honestly not a question Tol had ever considered. Lanali had ordered the girl's death, and Tol had been in love with her for so long that he did not question her choices anymore. That wasn't how this worked. He'd tried that, once, having opinions and expressing them, and Lanali had ignored them so often that finally, somewhere in the last few months, he'd just stopped thinking about it. Everything had worked out in Lanali's favor, after all, exactly as she'd planned it—surely she must have done something right.

But this wasn't part of any larger plan. This didn't help advance a play, or position the game board any differently. This was just . . . petty.

"No," Tol said finally. "I suppose I don't think you deserve it."

"Then let me go," Lady Hendril said, and as soon as the words were out of her mouth, Tol knew he was going to. Oh, he protested a little. He made various arguments in favor of her death, because he was supposed to, but they both knew on some level that his heart just wasn't in it.

The one thing he *had* stressed, with no hint of reservation, was that she was never to return to Monfort under any circumstances, nor reveal her true identity to anyone. "Lady Hendril must die," Tol said. "Here. Today. And if you don't agree, then *you* are going to die along with her."

The rest was just logistics. Tol smuggled her into the old quarter of the city, where she traded her fine dress for scrubby rags. He found a body at the Monfort Morgue, a blond girl with her face bashed in, and stole it in the middle of the night. By the time they fished it out of the bay several days later, it was bloated beyond recognition, gnawed at by fish, and clothed in the last outfit Lady Hendril had been seen in.

No one had ever known the difference. Pon Lanali had never known the difference.

Was she just so distracted, running her schemes, running her government, that she hadn't noticed, or had she *actually* paid attention and let this obvious farce slip by her? The idea occurred to Tol that maybe she trusted him so much that she didn't bother checking for herself, but it was so absurd that it nearly made him laugh out loud.

"Tol," Lanali snapped. "Are you even listening to me?"

Tol reeled himself back into the present moment: Lanali's private audience chamber, nestled just behind the throne room. Despite being handed temporary governorship of the Crown, Lanali had stayed out of the palace for a full month after her election. She'd worked from inside the Council's Crescent, trying to avoid accusations of using her influence to usurp Prince Hemmerick and the rest of the old royal family. Never mind that this is exactly what she'd done—being *accused* of it still wouldn't do. Rule ten: the truth is only dangerous if you cannot lie your way out of it.

She harbored no such concerns anymore. Tol had staged an assassination attempt on Lanali's life, and it was determined by the whole of the Transitional Council that the Pon must be protected in these fragile times. The palace was the most secure building in the whole of Monfort, and so, with deep humility and great reluctance, Lanali allowed them to move her headquarters inside of its walls.

It hadn't taken her long to make herself at home, though. In public, Lanali still spoke openly of her wish to relocate back into the seat of "the people"; but her actions in private, in front of Tol, even to a degree in front of Lord Hendril, those told a different story.

Tol looked at her now. They were both seated at a wide slab of a table, Lanali at the head and Tol a respectful distance halfway down one of the sides, but they could not have been more different from each other. Lanali sat in a specially designed chair, built up to compensate for her proportionally much shorter height than the Durns that the rest of the palace had been built for; Tol held himself rigid in a standard seat, the table uncomfortably high before his chest. Lanali had a spread of food laid out before her, everything from tarts and miniature cakes, to fruits of all kinds, to a platter of assorted roasted meats; Tol had a cup of plain tea. Lanali had slowly been replacing all of the austere aspects of her wardrobe—the demure, all-black dresses, the lace gloves—though she was keeping her signature black veil for now, the better to hide and lie behind. Her necklines were lowering, her bustle increasing; splashes of color were now woven into her dresses, often in the form of some rare gem or delicate silk ribbons. Tol still wore the signature formalwear of his homeland: a plain white suit, short-sleeved, with little adornments.

Sometimes it was hard to recognize her. If Tol squinted, he thought he could catch glimpses of the girl Lanali used to be, before she was the Pon, when she was still just Frel, still just a young woman from the island shores of Aul.

But that was probably just wishful thinking on his part. He made himself look at her openly, his eyes wide. This was what she had always been building toward, always been dreaming of, even back in those simple days at the beginning. When they were young and scared, when they'd just started out. When they'd needed each other.

Look at her, now. Look at what he had helped her to become.

Tol's face remained slack, his eyes tracking her with modulated interest. But in his lap, his hands had clenched into fists.

Chapter Ten

$\mathscr{P}$RENNA DID NOT wander off immediately. In the wake of Praxis's departure, she regarded Kaedrich for several long moments. She seemed to be studying Kaedrich, scrutinizing her as if she was some curiosity in a museum or a traveling carnival. Kaedrich shifted uncomfortably. She was trying to figure out some polite excuse that she could use to remove herself without causing offense, when Prenna abruptly reached out and touched Kaedrich's hair.

Kaedrich jerked back. "What the—?"

"I'm sorry, I didn't mean to startle you," Prenna said, but she was already reaching forward again.

Kaedrich leaned away; she had to duck and sidestep to get out of range of Prenna's pawing grip. "What do you think you're doing?"

Prenna frowned. "I'm just *curious*. You don't need to be rude about it." Again she moved forward, and again Kaedrich jerked to the side. Prenna huffed. She dropped her hand, resting it against her hip. She regarded Kaedrich as if she was some sort of disobedient child. "Will you please stand still?"

"Only if you're going to stop trying to touch my hair."

Prenna rolled her eyes. Normally, she and Praxis only had a passing family resemblance, but here it was impossible to deny the two of them being sisters. Despite the differences—Prenna's soft, billowing dress in sunshine yellow, the careful sweep of her hair, the demure jewelry arranged on her throat and ears—there was something deeply familiar about her. She was Praxis, if Praxis had behaved.

Kaedrich felt a pang somewhere deep in her chest. She realized now that being here was making her miss her own family. Her brother, her twin, who she would never see again, and her parents—gods, her parents. Her parents still probably thought she was dead, that they'd lost both of their children the night Kaedrich had died.

"Goodness, Kaedrich, are . . . are you okay?" Prenna asked. No doubt she'd seen the expressions that had passed unhindered across Kaedrich's face. Prenna reached out, as if to put her hand on Kaedrich's shoulder, then seemed to think better of it and withdrew. "I . . . I'm sorry, I didn't mean to upset you."

Kaedrich shook her head. "It's not . . . Never mind. Excuse me, I . . . I think I need some . . ." Kaedrich paused. Normally, she might have said "some air," but that wasn't exactly an option here. "Space," she said finally, which wasn't quite right, but would have to do. She darted around Prenna, mumbling apologies, and set off down the corridors.

She didn't know where she was going—she just knew she needed to move, to get away from people who looked like Praxis but weren't Praxis, to have ten minutes to herself without accidentally stepping on the outskirts of family drama. The very *air* here was thick with emotional history, only the tiniest fraction of which Kaedrich had any understanding of. She wished she knew more about what had happened here, when Praxis had lived in these halls. What, exactly, had driven her away. She wished she'd thought to ask, on their voyage down, during the long days with nothing to do. Praxis had been relaxed then, open and unusually talkative, and now Kaedrich regretted not asking more questions while she'd had the chance.

When she came to a stairwell, she arbitrarily chose to go up. She knew that somehow the household was divided up by hierarchy and some sort of order, with levels named after various types of gemstones, but damned if she understood the rankings or meanings. She stopped on a level where the trimmings were done up in diamond—which seemed interesting enough, but what really drew her attention was the *quiet*. Everywhere else, servants darted back and forth, bustling and efficient, but here the hall was empty. Kaedrich stepped in, and quickly realized it wasn't just that: The ceiling here was lower, and the decorations, while still opulent, felt somehow softer, more personal. Paintings depicted gentle rivers flowing through mountains, or even the occasional portrait of one of the immediate family. Kaedrich recognized Prenna's face, surrounded by her husband and children, including a much smaller version of Annelle. There was another one of Prawl and Prestina, obviously at the beginning of their marriage. Prestina looked so much like Praxis that it was jarring at first, and Kaedrich stopped and stared at it for a long, long time. She was actually *smiling* in the portrait, her whole face softer and kinder than Kaedrich had ever seen it.

She took her time, studying each of the paintings in turn. It was like stepping back through a family history. Eventually, she even found pictures of Praxis—with her siblings, by herself, with a short Aul man that Kaedrich recognized with a sickening twist as the person she'd watched Praxis kill, in a memory she was never supposed to have seen. Moc, Praxis had told her recently. It was weird, putting a name to the face after all these years.

Kaedrich rounded a corner. The paintings thinned out here, replaced by the usual sort of decorative bric-a-brac that filled the rest of the household. A series of doors lined both walls, and Kaedrich didn't pay them much mind as she passed them, until she was almost to the end of the hall. A tiny little plaque snagged her eye. Gold-plated and trimmed with diamonds, it shone with the look of something that had recently been polished after having sat stagnant for years. Kaedrich leaned in, not that she expected to be able to read it, and blinked in surprise as a familiar set of letters stared back at her. *Praxis.*

Indecision pinned Kaedrich in place. On the one hand, she knew she shouldn't be snooping—especially since she'd apparently stumbled into the Fellows' private chambers—but on the other, oh! How could she *not*? She remembered what Prawl had said, when they'd first arrived, about setting Praxis back up in her old room, and a surge of curiosity bubbled through Kaedrich. Her fingers hovered over the doorknob, hesitant but *dying* to take a peek inside.

She glanced down the hall—first to the left, then to the right—and pushed the door open.

Her eyes widened.

The room was . . . oddly disappointing. Lavish and beautifully appointed, Kaedrich wondered at first if maybe the family had emptied it out in Praxis's absence. It wasn't such a stretch to imagine, after all, given how long she'd been gone. Yet as she stepped inside, taking in the details, it became clear that they hadn't touched a single thing, had barely even taken the time to dust and clean. There *were* a few more books than Kaedrich would expect to find, and the few paintings and sculptures that hung about the space *were* a bit more interesting than what could be found in the main hallways and sitting rooms. But Kaedrich had come in here expecting to find something of the Praxis she knew, and there just . . . there *wasn't*. These rooms could have belonged to any one of the Fellows. Lots of useless space, lots of opulence. She *did* find an interesting little gadget sitting on a dresser in Praxis's old bedroom, something like a spyglass that showed various star formations when Kaedrich held it up to her eye, and there *was* one more portrait of Praxis in here. But beyond that, the rooms were cold and sterile, full of a dead sort of feeling that made Kaedrich feel like the walls were going to close in around her.

She hurried out, and as she clicked the door shut behind her, she wondered if she should have gone inside in the first place. Maybe it had been better not to know.

At this point, it's possible that she might have turned around and gone back the way she'd come. She was certainly considering it, after the disappointment of Praxis's old room, when the faint wail of a violin drifted around the corner.

Which is how she found herself, several minutes later, toeing open a partially cracked door a little deeper in the family chambers. And how she ended up meeting Previn.

PRAXIS WAS HEALING her stinging cheek outside of the bloody bath when Prett found her.

"Prax!" he said, jerking to a halt. He frowned, peering into the tiny little closet that she'd tucked herself inside of. "What are you doing in here?"

"Nothing," Praxis said quickly. She dropped her hand. "I was . . . looking for this." She picked up a random ice buffer off of the shelf, knowing how thin and stupid her excuse was, but somehow unable to stop herself from holding it out to Prett as if for inspection.

Prett rolled his eyes. "What is *wrong* with you lately?" he asked. He took the ice buffer from her and, in doing so, revealed the upturned palm underneath it.

Praxis winced. In her haste, she'd handed him the ice buffer with the hand that bore the mechanical "glove" to control her leg brace. And while most of the mechanism ran down the back of her hand, three of her fingers were still capped and ringed with narrow support straps, and pieces of the wiring could be seen along the edges of her fingers. Her thumb, too, was almost completely entrapped by the mechanism that allowed her to engage and disengage the tension of the system at will, and her wrist was covered in a thick patch of leather, only the curling ends of her tattoo visible around the edges.

So it was enough. Prett's eyes widened, and he'd grabbed Praxis's hand before she could withdraw it. Praxis cursed herself in silence—she'd only taken off her gloves to air out her palms while she worked, a brief moment of respite.

She tugged her hand, trying to free it, but Prett's grip was stronger than she remembered. "What in the world—?"

"It's nothing," Praxis said. She kept her attention fixed on the black ink peeking out, grounding herself against the tattoo that she could barely see. It was important for her to remember, to keep her strength.

Praxis tugged her arm once more, but unless she was really going to get violent with the force of her efforts, she wasn't getting her hand back. She heaved a resigned sigh, allowing Prett to turn her hand over, examine the complicated interplay of tension wires and gears.

Praxis's voice was soft as she said, "Don't tell Mother."

"Is this why you're always curling your fingers now?"

She forced a nod.

"What does it *do*?"

"Electric shocks," Praxis said, remembering the guess one of Kaedrich's friends back in Monfort had made. Though clearly, Prett wasn't buying that—he leveled her with a heavy look, and Praxis sighed. "It . . . controls my leg."

This time, when she withdrew her hand, Prett let her. She clicked her thumb, reengaging the tension, and curled her fingers one at a time to demonstrate: lifting her leg, shifting it back and forth, swinging it side to side.

Prett's eyebrows arched. "It's hard to believe that actually *works*."

"It takes practice," Praxis admitted. "And I don't always remember to time it right."

"But you're okay?" he asked. He looked at her, straight into her eyes. Her own eyes, or the nearest thing to them. A stray lock of his hair had fallen in front of those eyes, and Prett didn't even bother trying to brush it aside. His concern was genuine, and so raw that it made Praxis's chest ache.

She couldn't lie to him.

"More or less," she said. "The cold . . . the cold is bothering me some."

"You should see a doctor, then. We could—"

"I have."

"And?"

Praxis shrugged.

"Who did you go to? No offense, but you're probably not well-versed in who's reliable here anymore. I don't think my physician would necessarily have experience with this, but maybe Mother can arrange for you to see—"

"*No,*" Praxis said. She pressed her hand to his chest—her other hand, her free hand—pinning him in place to emphasize how strongly she meant it. "I'm not telling *anyone* about this, Prett, and neither are you. Do you understand? Not *anyone.*"

Prett frowned in confusion. "You don't need to be strong around us, you know. We're your family. We can *help.*"

"Exactly," Praxis said. "I know what this family's 'help' looks like."

"Huh? What do you mean by—oh." Prett's whole face softened with recognition. "Prax, you can't possibly think this is the same as—"

"It's close enough."

They fell into an awkward silence after that. Praxis took the ice buffer that Prett was still holding and returned it to its shelf. Then she tugged on her gloves, still damp from the sweat of her palms. She was finding it difficult to look at him at the moment; she didn't want to see the change in the way he watched her, with pity and curiosity and pain. Like she was something to feel guilty over, like she was something broken. She'd seen that face so much—too much.

"How is he, anyway?" she asked after a moment. She still wasn't looking at Prett, but it was clear enough to both of them which "he" Praxis was referring to.

"The same as ever, I suppose," Prett said. He adjusted the collar of his shirt, like it suddenly didn't fit quite as well as it had a moment ago. "Mother has been finding any excuse lately to have guests over for dinner, so it's not like we see him much unless we go to visit. And . . . I guess I haven't really been the best about that. I know Prenna goes to see him, at least two or three times a week."

"At least someone does."

Prett crossed his arms. "Be fair—have you even *thought* about visiting, since you got back?"

Praxis's scowly silence was more than answer enough. "I suppose I should," she said finally.

"He would love it."

Praxis rolled her eyes. "You don't know that. None of us knows what makes him happy."

"You're just saying that so you don't have to feel guilty about being gone so long."

"Maybe," Praxis said, and Prett cracked a smile. Instinctively, Praxis

reached her magic out, locating each of her family members in turn. Most
of them were still working their way outward from the bloody bath,
each going their own directions through the maze of the household. The
bubble around her expanded, reaching Diamond Level and the private
living quarters. Her senses reached his chambers.

Praxis's blood froze. Oh, of all the ironies of the fates. For another
presence, even more familiar than Previn's, was shining brightly in the
map of Praxis's mind, together with her older brother. "Shit," Praxis
muttered, her eyes widening as Prestina's path, still blaring in another
part of her awareness, reached the staircase. She looked in panic at Prett.
"Shit!"

"What—?"

"Come with me," Praxis said, grabbing Prett by the hand as she shoved
by him. "I need a favor, now!"

NOT THAT KAEDRICH knew it was Previn, at first. Nor would she have
even known who that was, if someone had been there to introduce them.

The door swung open. The music that had drawn her down the
corridor hissed and popped as it danced along, and instantly Kaedrich's
eyes settled on something she'd never seen before, not in person anyway:
a phonograph, playing merrily from atop a high shelf. Its brass horn
gleamed underneath the light of the lapus lumeni, the needle juttering
along on the track of the recording.

Looking at it objectively, she really should have realized that, if music
was playing, it meant someone was likely in the room listening to it.
Kaedrich was so enamored with the novelty of the phonograph, however,
that she stepped inside without stopping to consider this possibility.

There were several pieces of furniture in the room, so the only thing
she saw at first was his head, sitting tall over the back of a chair. He turned
immediately at the sound of her gentle footsteps, his eyes popping wide
at the sight of her.

"Oh!" Kaedrich said, realizing her error. "I . . . I'm so sorry, I didn't
mean to—to just barge in like this. Please forgive me, it's just, I heard
the music, and . . ." Her voice trailed off. Whatever her reasons, it didn't
justify her rudeness. "I'm sorry," she said again. "I'll . . . I'll go."

He blinked at her. His head cocked to the side, looking to Kaedrich
somewhat like a puppy studying something new. But while her sudden
appearance had no doubt caught him off guard, he did not appear *bothered*
by it, and this stilled her by the door.

She pointed at the phonograph. "I've never seen one of those before. I mean, I've seen pictures. Do you . . . That is, do you mind if I have a look at it?"

Another blink. But he still didn't say anything, and now Kaedrich suddenly realized what the reason for his silence might be.

"Oh. Um . . ." Kaedrich cleared her throat. *"Do you speak Durlish?"* she said in broken Yandosian, wincing at what she knew was her terrible pronunciation. At Kaedrich's insistence, Praxis had written down a handful of basic phrases for her yesterday, though this was the first time she'd tried to actually *use* it.

The man blinked at her again. A tiny frown appeared between his whisper-white eyebrows.

"I'm going to take that as a 'no,'" Kaedrich said. So she hovered just inside of the doorway; she knew she should probably leave, since she'd just barged in here without so much as a knock, but . . . something about the way the man was looking at her made her feel like he didn't want her to. His eyes were dancing across all of the points of her face and body, taking in every tiny detail—from the symbol of Perlandra pin sitting on her lapel, to the cut of her coat, to the way she'd slicked down her hair. Delight and surprise sparkled in his eyes.

He was certainly a Fellows. He had the right look about him, in the sharp line of his jaw visible even beneath a thick beard, and the soft lines of his long fingers, which he was currently running through the hair of his face as if applying cream. Though it was hard to judge his age, the lighting casting everyone in a state of perpetual youth, he was clearly younger than Prawl and Prestina, yet older than the flock of Praxis's nieces and nephews. So that left what, a . . . brother? A cousin? But he hadn't been at the party the other night, and Kaedrich had been led to believe that she'd been introduced to all the family that was still in Bolt.

Curiosity overwhelmed her. "Do you mind if I come in?" Kaedrich asked. She pointed at herself, and then farther into the room as she took a tentative step forward. He grinned at her, and so she let herself walk a little closer. She rounded the couch between them, and the rest of the man came into view. And now she understood why the family had kept him out of sight: the chair he was sitting in had large wheels on either side, and handles on the back to push him along. A thick fur blanket sat over his lap; narrow, bowed legs clad in thick pajamas poked out of the bottom. Of course such an image-conscious family as the Fellows would shut him away, pretending like he didn't exist. Kaedrich's mouth twisted up in disgust and anger, until she realized that it might look as if she was affronted by the sight of *him*, and so she quickly wiped it smooth.

She looked him straight in the face. "I'm Kaedrich," she said, holding her hand to her chest to indicate herself. "It's nice to meet you." She held her hand out, Durn-style.

The man looked at it. Kaedrich knew full well that he might have no idea what the gesture meant, so she pointed lightly to his own hand, a questioning look on her face.

"May I?" she asked, despite the language barrier. When he made no indications of protest, she gently took his arm and placed his hand in hers, watching carefully for signs that he was unhappy with this arrangement. Her fingers curled around his palm, and he made a low chuckle in his throat as he gripped her hand in return. Kaedrich shook their interlocked grip once, twice, and then released her hold. "That's how we greet each other where I come from," she told him as she straightened up.

The man's eyes flicked to another shelf. Lower than the phonograph, this one held a variety of odds and ends: some books, a few toys that looked designed for children, a handkerchief, and a globe. His hand shot forward, making grabbing motions, while the other hand rested against his neck, his fingers digging against the skin.

Kaedrich nodded. "Oh, right." She went over and picked up the globe, setting it down on his lap. He spun it once, then glanced at her, and Kaedrich smiled. She looked down at the world in miniature. "Right . . . here," she said, her finger resting on Durland.

It really was a beautiful globe. More colorful than the ones she was used to seeing back home, this one had been painted lush blues and greens and browns, sweeping lines dividing the world up into manageable chunks. Soft topography had been added to the mountains and valleys. Kaedrich's finger settled in the curl of Abbney Bay, the deep crater along the coastline that defined her country. A pang of fear and sadness stabbed at her heart, imagining what kinds of horrors were being played out there right now, under Lanali's rule.

Gods, what was she doing here?

"Kaedrich!"

Kaedrich jerked up. Praxis was rushing into the room, a frazzled look about her face. Her eyes were half-focused, some type of magic obviously distracting her.

The man made a squawk of either alarm or delight at the sight of her. He nearly dropped the globe, and only Kaedrich's quick reflexes kept it from crashing to the floor.

"Yes, yes," Praxis said to him. She switched over to Yandosian as she approached, her voice softening into tones of comfort and sympathy. She babbled at him for a moment, but she kept looking back over her shoulder, at Kaedrich, back over her shoulder. She was barely paying him any mind, even as she spoke.

"We have to go," Praxis said, to Kaedrich now. "Prett's distracting my mother, but she won't allow herself to be diverted for long, and she must *not* catch you in here, Kaedrich, do you understand? Come on."

Praxis was already dragging Kaedrich off. Kaedrich only just had time to return the globe to its place on the shelf before being yanked around the couch. "Praxis, slow down! I wasn't—and who is—? Gods, you're upsetting him."

"What?" Praxis paused. She turned back, irritation clearly splayed over her face. The man was gesturing wildly, and opening and shutting his mouth as if trying to speak, though only faint wheezes and creaks were making it out.

Praxis shook her head. "He's fine—he does that. Come *on*, she's getting closer!"

Kaedrich's arm would probably have been wrenched out of its socket if she didn't allow herself to be dragged forward. She looked back over her shoulder as she was yanked out of the door. "I'm sorry!" she called back to him, and then the door closed quickly in her face.

Chapter Eleven

"THIS WAY," Praxis said. Her fingers flexed madly, straining the top speed of her leg brace. Prett was still trailing along with Prestina, stalling her as best as he could, but they were moving forward once more. The distance between them was narrowing, and Praxis hoped to whatever gods might exist that the sound of her and Kaedrich's retreat wouldn't echo down the hallway. "Come on, come on, come on," she was muttering.

There was only one way in and out of Diamond Level—at least, as far as anyone else knew. Prett had tried to tell Praxis this, but she waved off his concern with a flick of her wrist. She didn't have time to explain, which was just as well, because Praxis had never told anyone about the secret passages that ran like a circulatory system through her family's tunnels.

She veered left, yanking Kaedrich down a side hall. At the end of the hall was an alcove with a large ice sculpture of a woman without a face. Family historians liked to report that she was based on a real Fellows that lived once, her name long since lost to the ages, though Praxis had her doubts about that. What kind of woman would allow herself to be recreated in ice without any defining features whatsoever? Her hair was hidden underneath a sculpted hood, hanging low over her blank face. She had on a flowing dress that the original sculptor had swept out into the hallway, hiding most of the shape of her body, and creating a trip hazard in the name of art.

Praxis drew up short in front of the statue. She yanked her glove off with her teeth, then reached up and cupped the woman's cheek, caressing it like a lover. Traces of magic teased out of her fingers, slipping deep into the ice. *"Solitude,"* Praxis said in Yandosian, snarling around the glove still hanging from her mouth.

The faceless woman nodded. Praxis withdrew her hand. She stood back, watching as the ice woman swept her skirts aside and took a wide step to her right, as elegant as a dance.

A hole was bored straight into the ice beneath her, a tightly wound spiral staircase beckoning. Praxis motioned for Kaedrich to go first, and then followed tight on her heels. Prestina, mercifully, had paused farther up the hallways, right in front of Praxis's old rooms. Praxis tapped the edge of the ice woman's skirts as she disappeared underneath the floor, and a moment later the statue had moved back into place.

At the bottom of the staircase was another hallway, narrower and less appointed than the one above them. The light of the lapus lumeni was dimmer here, the fragments diminished from years of neglect. But there was still enough light to see Kaedrich standing just inside of the hallway, her hands planted on her hips, a glower of reprimand on her face. "Do you care to explain that?"

"The statue? Magic activates the ice crystals, which in turn—"

"Not *that*! I meant—"

"I know what you meant." Praxis reached up, teasing a bit more energy into a vein of the blue crystal. Light spread out from her touch, down the long stretch of hallway like blood blooming through water. "His name is Previn."

"And . . . ?"

"And you cannot tell *anyone* that you met him," Praxis said. She turned back. "Seriously, not ever. Promise me, Ella."

"Is that why you didn't tell *me*?" Kaedrich asked. "Because you were sworn to silence?"

Praxis rolled her eyes. "No. It's just . . . we don't talk about him. Honestly, I don't usually think about him."

"You realize how horrible that sounds, don't you?"

"Oh, cut me some slack," Praxis said. "I've been gone a long time. I haven't thought about *any* of them much over the years."

It was the wrong thing to say. Praxis knew it the moment the words were out of her mouth. She turned her back on Kaedrich, just to avoid the mingled looks of pity, anguish, and disappointment staring back at her. She started walking. The farther they got from Diamond Level, the better off they would be.

Kaedrich's soft footsteps hurried along behind her. "Okay, but you're going to talk about him now," she said. "Who is he? Another brother?"

Praxis nodded. "Second oldest, just after Prewish. They think that my mother got pregnant again too quickly, that this is why he's . . ." She shrugged. "Anyway. I know that you want me to tell you about him, but there's really not much to tell. You saw him. That's all there is."

"There's always more to a person than *that*. What does he do? Is he married?"

Praxis laughed. It came out as a reflex, the idea so absurd that at first she couldn't even process it as a serious question. "No, he's not—He doesn't . . ." Praxis stopped walking. She turned around. "Don't you understand? He doesn't *do* anything. He can't."

"I understand that he can't do the *same* things as the rest of you, but you're acting like his life has no value at all."

"No, that's not . . . Well, yes, but—I mean, we don't . . ." Praxis fell short. An uncomfortable mix of emotions seethed in her chest like heartburn. "We make him very comfortable," she said, numbly parroting back the line that her parents had told her over and over, on the rare occasions that Praxis started asking questions. She scowled as she started off down the hall again.

Praxis knew even then that she would be stewing over Kaedrich's words for a long time, but for now she shoved them deftly into a back corner of her mind. Instead, she focused on where she was going, trying to navigate the secret passages from memory. Her wizard's sense was muddled by the pain in her knee, and suddenly every turn and junction looked the same. Praxis paused at the next corner. Her mind reached out, struggling through the fog of pain. Her sense found the exit, and Praxis released her grip on it, trying not to sigh with relief. She pushed forward, just a little ways ahead, and soon they were reentering the main hallways, stepping out from behind a large painting.

And that's when Praxis all but jumped out of her skin, because that's when they ran nearly headfirst into Prawl.

"THERE YOU ARE!" Prawl said. He'd veered at the last second, his hands springing up as if to catch himself. The danger passed, he now rested one onto his chest instead. "Depths, girl, don't go startling an old man like that."

Kaedrich flushed, but Praxis scowled. "You're not *old*."

Prawl laughed. "Oh, my sweet girl, if only that were true." He turned his attention, glancing at the edge of the painting that had just finished sealing up behind Praxis and Kaedrich. "I must say, I always wondered where you disappeared to as a child. I suppose I'll need to tell Praine that he was right."

"Praine?" Praxis frowned.

"Yes." A light shake of Prawl's head, a gentle chuckle under his breath. "His bet was on secret passages. Used to spend hours looking for them, but could never quite manage to find anything. They're sealed by magic, then? I don't see a mechanism."

Praxis shifted, uncomfortable. "That's right."

"Fascinating," Prawl said. He shrugged, apparently satisfied, as he turned to Kaedrich. Prawl clamped a hand on her shoulder—an iron grip that pinched down hard, far beyond the jovial greetings that Kaedrich was used to. "Anyway, I'm glad I ran into the two of you. I need Kaedrich for a moment. We have some important business to discuss."

Kaedrich blinked in alarm. "We . . . we do?"

"Daddy," Praxis said, "what's this all ab—?"

"That's none of your concern," Prawl said. He tossed his daughter a smile so well-rehearsed that it was almost genuine. "Don't worry, little opal, I promise to give him back to you in one piece."

If this was supposed to be reassuring, it had the opposite effect. Kaedrich exchanged a worried look with Praxis as Prawl turned away and began walking back the way he'd come—and then there was nothing to do but follow, because even Kaedrich knew that behind the jolly exterior lay an authority that you did not cross.

He led them back to the same quiet study where they'd played Fiddler's Dash that first night. The deck of cards, in fact, was sitting in the middle of the table, exactly where Kaedrich had left it after shuffling the last hand back into place.

It was too much to hope that this would be just another friendly card game. Prawl crossed the room, pulling down a bottle from a high shelf, and two thick-bottomed glasses. He deposited the glasses on the table with a heavy *thunk*, pouring out identical drinks.

"Sit," he said.

Kaedrich sat.

Prawl picked up a glass, sliding the other across the table toward Kaedrich with the bottom of his own. He did not wait for Kaedrich to take a drink, however, before he downed his and refilled it from the bottle still in his hand.

Kaedrich picked up her drink, giving it a tentative sniff. Whatever it was, it was clear and strong, curling Kaedrich's nose hairs. She took a sip and winced as Prawl downed the second, then a third.

He set the bottle down after that, it and the glass clinking together. "Did she tell you?" he asked.

Kaedrich looked up. Prawl was standing beside the table, his mouth a hard, bitter line, his hands clenching and unclenching by his sides. All the mirth and good humor had disappeared from his face, and without it he looked the picture of the stern king that Kaedrich supposed he was. Even his suit, red like royalty, was a richer, more bloody color than he normally wore.

It only made sense to assume that Prawl's anger had something to do with the mysterious summons Praxis had gotten earlier, though in the aftermath of everything that had happened with Previn, Kaedrich had forgotten to even ask about it.

She shook her head. "I'm—I'm afraid she didn't tell me. We were . . . Something came up. We didn't have a chance to talk yet."

Prawl gave a messy snort of disgust. "I would be insulted that something else proved more important to her than the fate of the company, but at least that does confirm my suspicions that she wasn't behind it. *One* of my children has convinced the oversight committee to open up inheritance bidding," he said, answering the question on Kaedrich's face. "I've been betrayed. My own children!"

He slammed his hands on the table between them. The glasses rattled, the cards shimmied. The gems of his rings gleamed angrily against the polished wood. Kaedrich jumped, and leaned farther back in her chair. "I'm . . . I'm sorry," she squeaked. It seemed the only thing she *could* say.

"Don't they realize how hard I've worked for this family?!" Prawl was all but shouting now. He picked up the bottle and threw it across the room, where it exploded against the ice. Fleetingly, Kaedrich wondered just how expensive this drink was, now freezing to the walls. She edged back, in case the glasses or even the table itself were next, but it seemed Prawl was trying to rein in his temper now. He had his eyes shut, and was taking long, deep breaths.

When he opened his eyes again, they were already settled on Kaedrich, as if he'd found her from behind the lids. "You need to audit the business. Find out what else my children are doing behind my back."

"*Me?* But . . . I don't know anything about the business! Or—or bookkeeping, or—"

"Oh, I don't need you to audit the *books*," Prawl said, waving his hand in dismissal. "I have a team that comes in quarterly to do that. No, you misunderstand. I want you to audit their *business practices*. Follow them around. Ask questions. Talk to their staff. Report back about anything that strikes you as odd, or inefficient."

Kaedrich's eyes widened. "You're *serious*?"

"I'm *always* serious. I need someone I can trust, and I need an outsider—someone that hasn't been corrupted by family loyalties, or bought off by one of my children already. That means *you*, 'Lord' Mannly. I'm appointing you as my personal assistant, as of right now. Congratulations."

"But—! I . . . I . . . I don't . . ."

Prawl smirked. "Well said."

"But I'm not even going to *be* in Yandosia that long!"

"Then you'd better finish quickly," Prawl said, and for the first time, Kaedrich was properly scared of him. Not of his temper, which had already startled her. Nor of his fists, which she could likely dodge or return with proper skill these days, anyway. Not even of his influence, the power and money that he had riding behind him, that made his every word law. Of *him*. There was something deep and dangerous in his eyes, a deadly look that reminded Kaedrich of Praxis when her control was slipping. Okay, so Prawl wasn't a wizard—that didn't help to reassure Kaedrich as much as it should.

Kaedrich nodded. Because it was all she could do, because agreeing with him was the only option that felt like it would let Kaedrich escape this room unharmed.

"Good man," Prawl said. He reached into his breast pocket, his hand snaking underneath layers of thick furs and fine leather. He pulled out something small, and flicked it into the air before Kaedrich had a chance to identify it. The thing spun over and over like a flipped coin as it arced across the space between them, flashing in the light. Kaedrich scrambled to catch it. When she opened her hands, she found herself holding a thick silver ring. A heavy gemstone sat nestled in the bed. Shifting colors stared up at her. Kaedrich had seen these gems plenty of times, of course—Praxis had a whole bracelet of them, and each of her brothers bore a ring just like this, which they wore on prominent display. But she had never seen them on anyone *else*. She tried to remember, now, did the spouses and the younger generations even have them? Did Annelle? Kaedrich couldn't recall.

Prawl jerked his chin. "Put it on."

Kaedrich's hands shook as she tried the ring on first one finger and then another. It fit comfortably on the middle digit of her right hand, as if it had been custom-made. She flexed her fingers, trying to get used to the weight of it. The pale of the silver was a sharp contrast to her dark skin, obvious even from a distance. Kaedrich's stomach jumped. *Everyone* was going to notice, she was sure of that.

"This will grant you free access to the whole of our operations," Prawl said. "I've already informed Prommel, so the guards will be prepared. There's an office being set up for you, in case you need to bring anyone in to ask them additional questions."

"Wait, wait, hang on," Kaedrich said. A wave of nausea had swelled up as Prawl had been speaking. "Isn't . . . I'm sorry, but isn't all of this a bit *much*?"

"No." Prawl shook his head. Only now did he relent to sit, pulling out his chair and crossing his legs at the knees, as if he and Kaedrich were having tea or discussing horse races. "I told you that business is built on honesty, Kaedrich. This family cannot survive if my children are going to plot and scheme behind my back. Their betrayal goes beyond this *one* incident. I need to know who I can trust." He pointed across the table, now, straight at Kaedrich's heart. "*You're* going to find out who's broken that trust. *You're* going to suss out the truth of their loyalties. And you'll never be able to do that if you don't have the full power and authority of my name behind your actions. For the purpose of this audit, you *are* acting as me, Kaedrich—behave like it."

"Sir, I . . . I don't know if I *can*."

Prawl shrugged. "Find a way," he said. He reached across the table, taking Kaedrich's nearly untouched drink and downing it in one. "Find a way," he repeated as he set the glass down silently between them, "or find yourself another place to hide from Pon Lanali."

Kaedrich stared. Prawl was regarding her with a slack expression, a perfect double of Praxis's cool indifference. Kaedrich's skin was crawling, and not just from the look he was giving her; they hadn't uttered a word about escaping Pon Lanali, not that Kaedrich was aware of anyway. She was forced to wonder: how much more did he know about their business, but wasn't saying? It seemed as if every time Kaedrich thought she had found a stable footing, Prawl managed to upend it.

He didn't wait for Kaedrich to answer. Prawl stood up, already heading for the door. "Start with Prewish," he said, holding it open for Kaedrich as if he was one of the guards. "Even if he wasn't behind the bidding . . . I know he's hiding *something*."

*   *   *

PREWISH HAD JUST finished closing the door to the lab when Prommel's voice caught up with him. "Prewish!"

Prewish straightened up. His well-practiced face was already wiped clean of the irritation he'd been experiencing, had been since before he stepped out of the lab. If their father had taught the boys anything, it was how to present themselves as they *wished* to be seen, regardless of how they were really feeling.

So Prewish was able to greet his younger brother with a convincing— if somewhat bland—smile. "Prommel. What can I do for you?"

Prommel drew up short. He jerked his head toward the lab, the presence of it behind Prewish looming larger than the physical door itself. "Is everything all right?"

It was the mark of a true Fellows that Prommel's first thoughts were toward the company's well-being, and not that of his brother. The lab was the heart of the lapus lumeni division, and the lapus lumeni division . . . well, that *was* the company, when you got right down to it. Selling attractive gems, and the spare minerals that they pulled up with them, shipping them out to all corners of the world—that was lucrative, no doubt. But without the light of the lapus lumeni, the whole of Yandosia would plunge into darkness. And without the Fellows, there was nowhere *near* enough of the crystal to go around.

The fact that there was *any* other source, though, was still a thorn in Prewish's side. One last rival company, one stubborn holdout that had refused to sell and couldn't be forced because they lived in a distant city-state, where the Fellows' influence was greatly reduced. His first priority, upon taking up the mantle of control (fates willing) was to marry off one of the next generation to their own. Two of his nieces were about to come of age, after all. It was time for them to prove their worth.

But at present, there were more immediate concerns. Prewish needed to *get* control first, and doing so would be a lot easier with Prommel's support.

Prewish started walking, drawing Prommel along with him. "You know that it's not all right, not these days," Prewish said. "But there's nothing new to concern ourselves over. What can I do for you?"

Prommel mulled in silence for a second, as if trying to figure out if he was going to allow himself to be diverted from the original topic. Prewish gave him the time and space he needed. Of all of his brothers, Prewish probably liked Prommel the best. He was sharp, without being devious. Loyal, without being blinded. Prewish had plans to take him out of security and offer him a position just beneath the top.

Prommel shook his head, clearly moving on. "I wanted to be the one to inform you," he said. "Because I didn't think you'd believe it, coming from anyone else. Father has . . . appointed an assistant."

Prewish stopped walking, Prommel following suit. The two brothers turned to each other.

"Not Praine," Prewish said, hoping more than anything else.

Prommel shook his head. "No, but I think you're going to wish it was."

"Tell me."

Prommel took a breath, but the sound of a distant door silenced him before he began. Both brothers instinctively turned toward the source. The lapus lumeni division was sealed off to only those with the highest security ranking, and so the hallways were free of all the usual bustle that went on in the layers below. In the long stretches of empty corridor, voices carried. It was always better to know who was within earshot.

The figure that rounded the corner was the last one Prewish expected.

Prewish groaned. "Can't we do something about him?" he asked Prommel. He stuck with their native Yandosian, knowing that Praxis's . . . companion . . . had come here without the slightest understanding of the language.

"Actually, that's what I was—"

"All right, that's far enough," Prewish said to Kaedrich, in the man's own crude Durlish tongue. He'd had to put up with Father giving Kaedrich a thorough and entirely inappropriate tour of the facility yesterday, but *this* was a step too far for Prewish's tastes. Besides, Prawl was nowhere to be found, at the moment.

"I, um . . . Actually, I'm sorry, but I need to speak with you," Kaedrich said.

"Then you should have informed a servant, and I would have them escort you somewhere appropriate when I had time," Prewish said. *"You cannot simply walk up here whenever you feel like it."*

Prommel cleared his throat. "He can."

"What?"

Prommel shrugged. "I told you, you weren't going to like it."

Prewish's attention flew back to Kaedrich. The young man was standing a respectful distance away, his dark hands folded neatly in front of him. A ring—one of *their* rings—glinted on his middle finger.

Fury coursed through Prewish. Only he and his brothers had ever been given rings like that before; not even Lorric had been granted the honor, not even Prewish's *sons*. Prewish made a move to rush at Kaedrich—what he was going to do, even he didn't know—but Prommel's strong grip found Prewish's upper arm. At fourteen, Prommel had overtaken all of his older brothers in both height and physical strength, and there was no way these days that Prewish, nearly ten years Prommel's senior and now pushing fifty, was going to overtake him. Prewish glowered at his younger brother, but Prommel would not be budged.

"It's official," Prommel said. "You know what happens if you touch him now."

Prewish's mouth set like a slash through rock. He forced a nod at his brother, and Prommel released his grip.

"Is there someplace we could talk privately?" Kaedrich asked. *"Assuming that you're done throwing your fit."*

"Look at it this way," Prommel said, talking in a low voice as both of the brothers regarded Kaedrich with distaste. "We'll only need to put up with it until the vote."

Prewish smirked. "Oh, you can count on that."

Chapter Twelve

"Here," Praxis said. She tossed a small box over as she entered the room, and Kaedrich scrambled to catch it.

The box was made of polished whale bone, hinged at the back. When Kaedrich flipped it open, a pair of diamond cufflinks, pure as perfect ice, winked up at her from a velvet base.

She sat up straight. She'd been sprawling on their bed for over an hour, trying to recuperate her strength after a long and extremely tense conversation with Prewish. When she got back to their rooms, Praxis was practically climbing the walls with anxiety over everything that had happened, but somehow, when Kaedrich explained what Prawl had done, Praxis hadn't really reacted much at all. "Oh," Praxis had said, and nodded like it was perfectly ordinary. She'd left a short while later, claiming that she had a headache and was going to get something to treat it with.

Now this. Kaedrich held the cufflinks: cold and sterile, sharp and perfect. They were nothing like the ones she always wore, the soft and soothing emeralds Praxis had bought for her years ago.

"What's this for?"

Praxis ignored the question, at first. She went over to the closet, her fingers curling as she guided her leg forward, and disappeared through the door for a moment or two. When she returned, she was carrying a heavy dress thick with furs, gemstones embroidered all over the bodice.

"They're for you. For dinner," Praxis said as she hung the dress from a peg near the closet door. She shrugged out of her coat and ripped off her gloves, tossing them both angrily onto the bed beside Kaedrich.

Kaedrich scrambled up. "Hang on, we're . . . we're *going*?"

Praxis rolled her eyes. "Of course we're *going*. We have no choice but *to* go." She began to unbutton her blouse. She was gnawing on her lip as she regarded the complicated layers of dress now standing before her.

"But . . . I thought you didn't want—"

"I didn't want a lot of things," Praxis said, "but it's too late to do anything about it *now*."

All at once, the bottom dropped out of Kaedrich's stomach. She sat back onto the edge of the bed, sinking heavily into the thick mattress. Prawl's ring, though it fit well, seemed tight on her finger. Choking. "Oh gods. This is my fault, isn't it?"

Surprisingly, Praxis's face softened. She still wasn't looking at Kaedrich, but her voice was gentle, bordering on tender, as she said, "Not really. If anything, it's probably mine. I knew what would happen if I came back. I tried to tell myself that we could stay out of things, that they wouldn't be able to rope me back in, but—"

"So let's leave," Kaedrich said.

It wasn't the first time she'd considered it. Coming here had been a good idea, Kaedrich supposed, but they weren't accomplishing anything. And though Kaedrich hadn't had any news from Durland, she knew the situation couldn't have improved in the three months since their departure.

Praxis shook her head. "No. It's not safe."

"To the darkness with *safe*," Kaedrich said, and *now* Praxis looked up: in shock and annoyance, her eyes first widening and then narrowing. Kaedrich didn't care. "I'd rather be risking my life and know I'm doing good, than be tucked away like some prized artifact gathering dust. We should go back."

"And do *what*, exactly?"

"I don't know. But running away isn't the answer."

"Neither is being stupid," Praxis snapped.

"Oh, so that's what you think I am?"

"No, but when you start talking like *that*—"

"I'm trying to do what's *right*!"

"So am I!" Praxis paused, shut her eyes and took a breath.

Kaedrich glanced at the floor between them.

"I'm . . . sorry," Praxis said. "Ella. I don't want to do this. I'm stressed, you're stressed, and I don't . . . I don't want us to take it out on each other. Please."

Kaedrich nodded. She was still holding the cufflinks. "I suppose that even if we *did* leave, it wouldn't get us out of tonight. We can't exactly just walk out the front door at a moment's notice."

"No. That's true."

Kaedrich looked up. Praxis had gotten as far as removing her blouse, somehow not acting at all cold despite the chill in the air. She had turned toward the mirror, already working on the row of buttons running down the length of each leg of her trousers, designed for easier access to her leg harness.

"So . . . um, how much time *do* we have before dinner, anyway?" Kaedrich asked.

Praxis's eyebrow was raised as she met Kaedrich's gaze in the mirror. Kaedrich was smiling, and Praxis's mouth fought against a match. "Not enough," Praxis said.

"Are you *sure*?"

"*Yes,*" Praxis said as she turned and threw her blouse at Kaedrich.

Kaedrich caught it, laughing, and vaulted off of the bed. Praxis yelped as Kaedrich wrapped her arms around Praxis's waist, lifting her and spinning her away before she could protest. When Kaedrich set her down, she slid around Praxis like a dance, and cupped her cheek in the palm of her hand. Her other arm was curled around Praxis's waist. Praxis's eyes were bright as Kaedrich leaned forward. "I think they can wait," Kaedrich whispered.

THEY WERE LATE for dinner.

Not very, but enough to be the last ones in to the Malachite Room, where the Fellows gathered for drinks before heading into the main dining hall. Praxis's body, already flushed, turned a deeper pink as she avoided her mother's gaze and made a straight line for the nearest glass. Prett was standing by the servant with the bottle, and he grinned openly at Praxis as she waited impatiently for her drink to be poured.

"I guess I don't need to ask how *your* day is going," he said as Praxis drained her entire glass in one.

She shot a glare at her brother. "Shut up."

Prett laughed.

Praxis held out her glass, and the server poured her another. When it was only half-filled, she nodded at him, and pulled her drink back. She forced herself to turn, to face the rest of the room.

A swirl of faces greeted her, and suddenly Praxis realized that she didn't recognize as many of them as she felt she should have. Her parents, obviously, her siblings, obviously, Kaedrich . . . Praxis's mouth quirked up as their eyes met across the crowd. The *look* in her eyes was enough to get Praxis to bite down on her lip and turn away, before her flush got any worse. But there were so many people here, the family dinners having exploded in number during Praxis's long absence from Yandosia. Some of the spouses, at least, Praxis *sort of* knew from before—even if she'd never bothered to get very well acquainted with them. As for the rest . . . there was a new breed of Fellows here, that was for damned sure. Bristling with youth and vitality, making everyone else look slightly withered with age. A tight knot of tiny children ran underfoot, playing simple games around the skirts and legs of the grownups; three or four of them, it was hard to keep them straight as they popped in and out of view. They would be shuffled off soon for their own meal, but for now they stopped in front of various members of the family, who would bend down and delight at some random inanity spouting from their small mouths.

One of them approached Kaedrich, naked curiosity splayed across his upturned face. He was the picture of childhood innocence, cherubic, as he gnawed on a finger and said something Praxis couldn't hear.

Kaedrich crouched down to his level. No doubt there was a language barrier between them—this boy was far too small to have gotten lessons yet in anything other than his native tongue—but Kaedrich's interaction with him transcended language. She smiled easily, talking in a soft voice, letting him examine her upturned palms, the shape of her nose, the soft curls clinging tightly to her scalp. The child was called away after just a moment, but Kaedrich stayed crouched as she watched him toddle off. The look on her face curdled Praxis's good mood.

She took another pull from her drink.

It was just as well that dinner was announced. Kaedrich found Praxis in the crowd, uncertain as to the protocol, and Praxis guided her in silence through to the dining room. "Are you okay?" Kaedrich asked at one point, but Praxis didn't get the chance to answer.

Prawl came up behind them. Praxis felt Kaedrich stiffen, no doubt concerned that he was looking for some kind of update about the ridiculous inquisition he'd set Kaedrich out on, but Prawl's focus was entirely on his daughter instead.

"Praxis," Prawl said, pulling her aside, "I hope you don't think this too presumptuous of me to ask, but I was hoping I could convince you to do a small bit of magic for us this evening."

Praxis hesitated. A flood of memories assaulted her: being trotted out for every visiting dignitary, every prospective buyer, every rival her parents had wanted to intimidate. Though magic was highly valued in Yandosia for things like the lapus lumeni division, so few wizards were born under the ice that when a member of a high family *did* exhibit talents, they didn't know what to do with them. Often, they became a sort of party trick. And while Praxis liked showing off as much as anyone, she only liked doing it on *her* terms.

As if reading all of this off her face, Prawl laughed. "It's nothing like that, I assure you. I understand there's a spell that enables everyone in a large group to be equally heard across a table—isn't that correct? You *do* know the one, don't you?"

"Of course I do," Praxis said. "Though I'm kind of surprised *you've* heard of it."

Prawl shrugged, his beard curling up into a soft smile. "We had a visitor here, ages back, that used it for us one evening. Delightful man, really delightful. From the Ashmorre highlands, I believe. It was so useful, it made me wish *I* could cast it, for the next time I met with the ministers. Maybe they'd listen to me, then."

"I'm sure you have no trouble making yourself heard," Praxis said.

"Ha! Too true, my dear, too true. So, you'll do it?"

Praxis winced, but Prawl was grinning at her so broadly that what was she supposed to say? She very nearly agreed, but just as she went to take a breath, she stopped herself. She held up a finger. "One condition. If I do this . . . *everyone* has to speak Durlish. The whole evening. I hear so much as a word of Yandosian, I take it down and cast everyone in a black haze hex as penance."

Prawl laughed. "Done."

"Oh," Praxis added, "and *you* have to tell Mother the terms."

"Ouch," Prawl said. He held at his chest, as if Praxis had physically wounded him. "You're a shrewd negotiator these days, little opal. Are you sure I can't convince you to work for us?"

"Not a chance."

"Very well, then." Prawl held out his hand, Durn-style, and Praxis accepted the deal. He motioned at the table, where everyone else had settled themselves and were trying not to look and listen in with *too* much open curiosity. "The show is yours, my dear."

To Annelle Fellows, the evening took on an air of a grand game: converse in a tricky language, no secrets at the table. Grandfather stood and explained the rules, a sparkle in his eyes, a youthful bounce in his voice that was quite at odds with his ancient face and stodgy red coat. As he spoke, Annelle could not remember the last time she was this excited. Oh, what would the evening hold? What kind of magical wonders would she be witness to?

She stole a glance at the rest of her family, trying to gauge their reactions. It was a large gathering—near to twenty faces, probably, Annelle guessed—though nowhere near the size it could have been. Nearly all of her aunts and uncles were present, and a number of her cousins, though some had already moved out, striking off for adventures unknown. But Prewish's son Tannem was still around, along with his wife, and of course Micadel had joined their ranks recently and worked alongside Prommel, so he wasn't likely to be going anywhere soon. Micadel's younger brother, too, just old enough to join them. Praine's twins, Maylin and Praine the Younger, sat to either side of their father, and somehow Annelle doubted either of *them* would be leaving after their coming-of-age balls. Annelle let her gaze shift between each of her family in turn, wondering, was anyone else as excited about this evening as she was? But, as Fellows, they were far too polite for something like *feeling* to show through. A series of carefully interested faces watched Aunt Praxis as she sighed and got to her feet.

A hush fell over the room, and Annelle returned her attention to the focal point of the evening. Her *aunt*—even just having Praxis here was something of a magic trick. Annelle had never been convinced that Praxis was dead, but that was more because Annelle had never given Praxis all that much thought to begin with. Her understanding of her aunt had been gathered through old stories, passed around like a battered mitten, so that by the time they'd reached Annelle, it was impossible to know what shape it had been originally. Praxis was a mythic legend. Look at her: there she stood, resplendent in a gown of silver and emerald green, like something out of a fairy tale. Annelle wanted her to reach into the depths of some other realm, revealing for a moment its glimmering secrets. She wanted something like the stories of old, when wizards carved the first tunnels of Yandosia, leading the original settlers to a world of safety and splendor. Annelle had read those stories obsessively as a child, her head filled to the brim with wondrous images of color and light and *magic* that seemed to ooze up through the pages.

That was not what she witnessed this evening.

A wave of the hand, a quick mutter of something under Aunt Praxis's breath. Nothing shimmered, or rippled, or quivered. The air did not change in temperature, nor did a *feeling* settle over the room. The only way to tell it had worked at all, in fact, was when Uncle Pranders sneezed a moment later, and the whole table jumped as the clap of it echoed out from each of the chairs at once.

"And there you have it," Praxis said, with a dismissive wave in Pranders's direction. A few chuckles sprinkled the table as Praxis sat back down, duty done.

Still, Annelle tried not to be too disappointed. Even if Praxis's magic was somewhat . . . lacking from its reports, her personality more than made up for any shortcomings. Even here, even now: the seating arrangements had placed her and Kaedrich on opposite sides of the large table, but Praxis had marched straight over to Annelle's father and booted him out of his place so she could sit beside her lover. Despite the embarrassment her father was no doubt feeling at the moment, Annelle had to admit that it had made her grin. She *adored* the boldness of her aunt's love for the dark, quiet lord from Durland. It was the way Annelle wished *she* could behave—and she swore she would . . . one day.

If she ever gathered up the courage to confess her love, that is.

Annelle shook her head, pushing such thoughts aside for the moment. Her family was reaching for their coin purses, preparing the customary offering to Prawl and Prestina for hosting the meal, and Annelle slipped hers discreetly onto her lap. She ran her thumb over the embossed head of some old Archon as she waited for the signal to begin. There was a time, not long ago, when just being old enough to be allowed at this table was a thrill beyond measure, and Annelle had loved taking part in the ritual. But now it just seemed stodgy, an annoying inconvenience to be endured before the meal began.

"Aw, shit," Praxis muttered, and Annelle looked up. Across from her, Praxis was patting down her dress, a light tinge of pink creeping into her cheeks.

Uncle Praine's chuckle drifted down from farther up-table. "Forget something, Praxis?"

Praxis shot him a nasty look, but it was Prett that got to his feet. "Allow me," he said as, ever gallant, he extended two coins in his outstretched fingers. Praxis stood up only long enough to snatch them away, passing one to Kaedrich.

"What's . . . ?" Kaedrich started, but Praxis shook her head once, a firm no.

Annelle flushed in embarrassment for her aunt as Uncle Prewish rose next. He held his coin aloft, letting the light catch its face. "Prosperity and growth," he said—the closest Durlish phrase, Annelle supposed, to the traditional grace. He kissed the coin, his pointed beard bristling on the metal, and set it in the middle of the table.

"Prosperity and growth," Annelle said, her voice joining with a chorus of others as they each repeated the ritual.

"I don't know why we actually still bother with that," Prommel said, once it was done. "It's not as if you've ever actually dismissed someone for not remembering."

"Perhaps we'll start," Grandmother said. She cast a pointed glance in Kaedrich's direction.

Grandfather shook his head. "Now, now. The point isn't so much the tribute itself, as the *tradition* of it. It's important that we don't forget our history."

"Maybe we should, though," Prommel said. "It's not as if most families still do it."

"*Most* families," Grandfather said, his tone suddenly sharp, "are not Fellows. It's important that we set a standard, even if nobody else chooses to live up to it." He nodded at the row of servants, still waiting by the door, and they stepped forward on cue.

"Father makes a fair point," Praine said as Grandfather and Grandmother were presented with the first trays of food that would be making their way around the table that evening. "Families like ours have to set an example for the rest of the community. Besides, it's far better than the excessive displays of mysticism that pass for mealtime entertainment these days."

"Oh, but Daddy, I love those!" Maylin cooed.

Praine tossed her a patient smile as the first of the servers reached him. "Yes, but not at the table, all right? Besides . . . maybe your aunt Praxis will show you some proper magic later."

"Not if I have a say in it," Praxis muttered, but Maylin was already gasping with delight over her. She clapped her hands together, squealing at the thought.

"Oh, Aunt Praxis, would you really? Really really?" Another gasp. "I know! We could have a séance!"

Praxis raised her gloved hand, one finger already held up. "Okay, first of all? No. And second, those are all a hoax. There is literally *no way* to communicate with the dead."

Maylin's eyes popped wide. "No, but that's where you're wrong! I was at—at a dinner with my friends, last month, and they had a demonstration from *the* Mistress Majesty. She was able to contact my friend Trinny's grandmother!"

Praxis shook her head. "No, she didn't."

"Um, *yes*, she did! I was *there*!"

"Then you were duped by a fraudster," Praxis said, "but that's hardly a novel occurrence."

Maylin's mouth dropped open. "You—! I wasn't—! How *dare*—!"

"Anyway," Grandfather cut in, "it's all a moot point, because there will be no séances in my household—real or otherwise. Is that clear?"

"But, *Grandfather*, that's not *fair*!"

"Fair or not," Grandfather said, "that's how it will be."

Maylin's face scrunched up. She was not, Annelle knew, used to being told "no"—Uncle Praine bought his children's love through spoils of affection and excess, and even now he was giving her a subtle nod, as if telling her not to worry about a thing.

Annelle stole a quick look at each of her own parents. It wasn't *jealousy*, of course, because there was not a single bone in Annelle's body that wanted to be the daughter of *Uncle Praine*—for sanity's sake, Annelle could barely stand being his niece. But . . . just once in a while . . . she did kind of wish that her own parents took the sort of stand for her that Praine was constantly showing for Maylin and Praine the Younger. Which isn't to say Annelle's parents weren't *supportive*, it's just . . .

Annelle's mouth twisted up. She didn't really know what it was—just that she didn't quite like it.

Uncle Prommel cleared his throat. He futzed with the cuff of his fur coat, stroking the gray hairs with his fingers. "Except that's kind of the point, isn't it? This isn't going to *be* your household. Not for much longer, anyway."

Annelle looked over, as subtly as she could. To the side, Grandfather's face had gone still, but he pretended to ignore the comment as he inspected and then approved of the next incoming trays. So much food, a constant parade that circled the table until everyone had eaten to the bursting point.

Prewish snorted. "It's not going to be yours, either, Prommel."

Prommel shrugged. "We'll see."

"Yes, we will," Prewish said. "And what we will see, is that the Minor Conclave is more interested in the strength of a bidder's proposal, and the quality of his history, than with how many among them are friends with your *wife*."

"*Excuse* me?"

"Oh, come on," Prewish said. "We all know that's why you really married her."

Annelle choked down on a gasp as the whole table stilled for a moment.

Far down to her right, her new aunt, Sharmity, had begun to flush, but Prommel remained as steady and calm as ever. He leveled his brother with a look as sturdy as steel as he rested his hand on his wife's shoulder.

"I'm going to ignore that jab, for the sake of family unity," Prommel said, his voice slow and even. "And I sincerely hope your comment was generated out of spite and jealousy, rather than any actual, genuine feeling on the matter. Because I would hate to imagine my own dear brother would think me so little, that I would marry such an honorable woman under selfish pretense."

Prewish rolled his eyes. He took hold of his wine glass, downing half of it—but, thankfully, saying nothing.

The pause that came next was colder even than the room itself.

Annelle's mother dabbed at her face with a napkin. "So, Kaedrich!" she said, her voice as bright as her dress. "Tell us about where you're from. What are its primary industries?"

Attention shifted, and Annelle could swear that the dark brown color of Kaedrich's cheeks turned, just a little. "It's . . . well, it's not that interesting, to be honest. I, um . . . I . . ."

"They're a farming community, mostly," Praxis said. "Mostly sheep, some pigs. Wheat, where the soil is good. Kaedrich's family has been there for six generations now. It *was* six, wasn't it, Kaedrich?"

"Six," Kaedrich muttered. "Right. Yes."

"Oh!" Maylin said, and Annelle groaned under her breath. "Do you know what *I* heard? *I* heard that Durns keep a rag soaked in rat piss under their pillow on their wedding night for good luck—is it true?"

Kaedrich raised an eyebrow. "Uh . . . no. No, it's not."

Annelle sighed. "Why would you even *ask* something like that?"

"What? I thought it was interesting!"

"'Interesting' or not, I don't think it's the most appropriate—"

"Tell me, then, Praxis," Annelle's mother cut in, and Annelle snapped her mouth shut with a scowl, "what do *you* think of Durland? It must have been quite strange, adapting to life outside of the ice."

Praxis shrugged. "Probably. Although, by the time I got to Durland, I was already used to it. I don't recall their culture as anything particularly noteworthy."

Annelle glanced up. "You mean you've lived other places?"

"Of course. I wouldn't have stayed in just *Durland* all this time."

"Hey!" Kaedrich said, but Annelle barely noticed; her breath was gone, her curiosity burning through her. She had to set her fork down, for fear she would drop it when she wasn't paying attention.

"Where . . . where all have you been?" she asked. She hoped the question wasn't impertinent. Certainly, Annelle would never think of posing one so direct to her Grandmother, and perhaps not even to her mother, but Aunt Praxis . . . there was something about Aunt Praxis. Something wild and dangerous, the way Annelle always pictured fire behaving. And seventeen years . . . the whole of Annelle's long life . . . how much was possible for Praxis to have seen, done, *lived*, in that endless stretch of time? The idea was intoxicating, hitting Annelle harder than the wine in front of her.

Praxis looked up. She looked at Annelle, right *at* Annelle, more directly than she'd ever done, and Annelle could swear in that moment that Praxis's face softened with a kind of recognition. For a moment she didn't say anything, but then once she did, her answer was both simple and infinite, all at once. It was, perhaps, the answer Annelle had been hoping for, what she didn't even realize she'd wanted. Praxis's voice went soft, almost sentimental, as she looked at her niece. She spoke only one word:

"Everywhere."

Chapter Thirteen

Everywhere.

The way Praxis said it sent chills down even Kaedrich's spine. Certainly Annelle was enraptured; the young woman sat there gulping down the possibilities, peppering Praxis with question after question—where did you go next, what was *that* like, when was *this*? Even the rest of the table fell quiet, listening to the bits and pieces of Praxis's story. It occurred to Kaedrich only later that this was the first time any of them had ever heard about Praxis's life in the outside world.

Everywhere. What had seemed like an exaggeration at first became more and more truthful as the minutes ticked on. Praxis was hesitant, at first, picking at her napkin as she answered Annelle's questions with the minimum amount of details; but eventually something began to soften. Kaedrich watched, as snared as the rest of them, as details began to pour out of Praxis. Countries and cities and temples, such a litany that it made Kaedrich's head spin. Praxis spoke with such reverence that you could almost see the places she was describing, hanging in the air above the table. Breezes seemed to drift by, fragrant with moss or fruit or muck. For the first time since they'd arrived, it was like Kaedrich had gotten a little piece of *her* Praxis back—the one that had talked, her voice dipping and laughing, as they lay sprawled in the little cabin on the boat. Kaedrich closed her eyes, not even caring about the words anymore; the *sound* of Praxis, her accent tripping up on itself in her enthusiasm, was what Kaedrich was craving.

And then, out of nowhere, a flush of silence.

Kaedrich opened her eyes. It had struck suddenly, the whole table seeming to collectively catch their breaths. Forks were held midway to mouths, one or two glasses of wine were tipped toward lips that had stopped drinking from them. Whatever had happened, it was so thorough of a shock to the assembled party that even the servants had paused in their motions—all but one.

It was this one that convinced Kaedrich that at least no one had cast some kind of malevolent spell over the dining room; that at least time had not, in fact, frozen them all into statues. The servant circled the room, and the only other motion was that of several heads turning in place to track his movements.

He did not appear in any way remarkable, at least not to Kaedrich. Dressed in the same basic livery as the rest of the staff, he could have been any of them. Whisper-pale and moving in ghostly silence, he took his time as he carried a glass tray. Kaedrich might have suspected that it was nothing more than another piece of the elaborate meal, but when he drew closer she could see that he was carrying something papery and bound in leather, like a book or a portfolio.

And then Kaedrich got a fantastically clear view of it, because he stopped right beside her. Or rather, right beside Praxis—he wedged himself in between their chairs, leaning over and resting the tray at Praxis's elbow.

It *was* a portfolio: bound in a gray leather, wrapped in a white ribbon, and sealed with a metal disk of some kind, like an overlarge coin. The disk had Yandosian writing around the outside, and an official-looking seal embossed across the bulk of it, the head of a penguin, something small clutched in its sturdy beak. It signaled nothing to Kaedrich, though it appeared quite stately, and she was the only one in the room in ignorance of its meaning. Even Praxis had drawn still at the sight of it, and she looked at it now, somehow even more pale than normal.

All the warmth that had begun to seep into her demeanor turned to ice. She looked away from the offering in front of her, back to the food on her plate. "Send it back," she told the servant as she stabbed at a piece of fish.

Nothing happened for a moment, except for Praxis chewing and swallowing, and then turning to glare up at the servant still standing beside her. She told him something in Yandosian, presumably repeating her instructions, her voice stern and cold.

The servant hesitated. He glanced at Prestina, who gave an almost imperceptible nod of her head. Only then did he dare to move off, bowing as he backed away from the table. Praxis had busied herself with her plate, and she took a long drink of wine—too long—as he left the room.

There was a lengthy pause after that, followed by Prawl clearing his throat. "Well."

"That was surprising," said Prewish.

"You have to admire his persistence," added Praine.

"Gods!" Annelle said. She looked fit to burst as she leaned forward over the table. "Aunt Praxis, how could you just *ignore* that?"

Praxis snorted. "Quite easily, I assure you."

"But that was—"

"I *know* what it was," Praxis snapped. She looked up sharply, her face a perfect impression of Prestina, and Annelle shrank back in her chair. Praxis kept her gaze steady on Annelle as she reached over and took Kaedrich's hand.

Kaedrich jumped. Praxis's gloved fingers squeezed tightly around hers, pinning her in place.

A frigid moment passed. Praxis regarded the rest of the table with her icy stare, *daring* anyone to question her. Several glances flicked in Kaedrich's direction, but most of the assembled Fellows studiously avoided looking at her. What any of this had to do with *her*, Kaedrich couldn't even begin to guess, but that did not make her heart stop racing, her palms stop sweating.

Kaedrich wished she'd gotten a longer look at the portfolio, or at least the seal that had bound it together. Maybe, she mused, she could find it in a book somewhere? Or she supposed she *might* be able to ask Prett, though it hadn't exactly gone her way the last time she'd tried to get him to explain something to her. After a long beat, the meal awkwardly resumed—forks and knives slowly going into motion again, mouths chewing through both the tension and meal in front of them—but Praxis's hand remained fixedly around Kaedrich's. And though no one mentioned it again, one thing was perfectly clear: Kaedrich's time here, always awkward, had just gotten a whole lot harder.

AFTER DINNER KAEDRICH was invited to another ill-advised round of Fiddler's Dash, and so that left Praxis to walk back to their rooms alone.

Which was frankly just as well. She took the long way around, looping through most of her parents' dwelling for no other reason than the fact that she needed time to process what had just happened, to decompress—

and, ideally, to burn off some of the simmering fury lurking just underneath her cool veneer. Because oh, there was a lot of it. Unimaginable pools of the stuff, thick and burbling. She stalked through the hallways, honestly surprised she was not melting the walls from the strength of her anger.

Of all the nerve. The *presumption* of the man! Honestly, if Lexthur Delford had been in front of Praxis at that very moment, she did not know if she'd be able to control the rage she felt for him. It was bad enough that he had gone ahead and filed for a marriage audit, bad enough that he'd had the results forwarded to her (favorable, of course, as indicated by the seal glinting cheerfully on the front of the portfolio), but for him to have timed it so that it would arrive at dinner . . . ! It wasn't as if he didn't *know* the Fellows' schedule. Everyone who was anyone knew the Fellows' schedule. No, that had been a step too far. What, did he think that somehow causing a public spectacle would make Praxis capitulate? Did he think that the gossip would somehow sway her? That she would bow to public opinion on such a personal matter? That there was anyone, literally *anyone*, who could change her mind on this matter?

"Oh, Praxis!"

Prestina's voice sprang around Praxis like a trap snapping shut over a mouse. Praxis shut her eyes, drawing a deep breath for support. *Not even her,* she thought to herself, and she grounded herself against the tattoo on her wrist. Not even her.

"Yes, Mother?"

Praxis had forced herself to stop walking, and now she turned around, every inch of control holding her face in the perfect mold of disinterest.

Prestina was striding up the hall toward her, heels ringing against the polished floor. All smiles, which was never good. "Praxis, *darling*, do you have a minute?"

"Not really."

"Excellent!" Prestina said, threading her arm as iron twine through Praxis's elbow. Her free elbow, Praxis noted, even though it was a farther step for Prestina to reach it than it would have been to grab Praxis's control arm. "Come with me, then, dear. Spare a few minutes for your old mother."

Praxis found herself moving forward automatically, as if Prestina was her puppet master and Praxis was nothing more than a marionette. She certainly felt like one, now especially—normally, her disability was merely something hovering in the background of her awareness, the curl of her fingers second nature to her. This time, however, she was painfully aware of the stretch and pull of her series of tension wires and gears, of the subtle click playing out underneath the chiming of her mother's shoes. It was foolish to think Prestina hadn't noticed, and yet the subject of Praxis's leg hadn't been broached even once.

Not that Praxis should even be worrying about such a thing right now. She had much more important things to worry about, which was probably the reason Prestina had drawn Praxis's attention to it in the first place. Misdirection, drawing worry from one place and moving it somewhere else, this was Prestina's specialty. Whatever she had planned, Praxis wasn't going to like it.

Prestina led way to her office, the same room where Kaedrich had first been presented to Prestina, the same room Praxis had openly declared her feelings in. Praxis hadn't been back in the room since then, and she looked at the door as if it was going to swallow her whole. In some ways, she almost would have preferred if it *did*.

The door shut behind them, and Prestina released her grip on Praxis. She strode cheerfully up to her desk, settling with calm grace at her chair. Praxis edged forward. She eased up onto the dais, inching around the desk until she was facing her mother again. A tiny chair had been set aside opposite Prestina, already waiting for Praxis.

She was expected to sit. She sat, as surely as if Prestina had pulled the strings herself.

Prestina smiled at her. She'd been waiting with her hands folded on her desk, and she held that pose for a moment, just long enough to let the dread rise like bile in the back of Praxis's throat. Then Prestina reached into one of her desk drawers, and pulled out a gray leather portfolio. The *same* gray leather portfolio, except now the metal seal had been removed. The long trail of white ribbon was undone, draped unceremoniously off of the edges.

Which meant that Prestina had read it. Somehow, in the limited time since they'd all left the dining room, Prestina had read it and then immediately sought out Praxis.

Praxis clenched her fists in her lap. Sparks of magic and rage crackled behind her eyes, threatening to burst out, and she struggled hard to keep them simmering just underneath the surface. "I told the servant to send that back," Praxis said.

"Yes," Prestina said as she spread back the cover. "And I clearly ignored your wishes." She studied the papers for a moment, though she was obviously acquainted with what they had to say. She looked up, sitting back casually in her chair. "I want to know if you plan to accept."

"No."

Prestina nodded. "I see. Care to tell me why not?"

"Why did you steal my portfolio, when I expressly wished it returned?"

"I'm your mother."

Praxis snorted. "That's not an answer."

"Actually, it is. It means I have to help you to see what's best for you, especially when others in your life might not be doing the same."

Others. Praxis narrowed her eyes. "You mean Kaedrich."

"Of course I mean *Kaedrich*," Prestina snapped. "He clearly has a conflict of interest in this matter."

"Oh, yes, not wanting the woman who loves him to marry someone she has no feelings for is a *horrible* conflict of interest, all right! Thank the gods you've stepped in to set me straight."

"Don't be snide, dear—it makes you look weak."

"No, what would be weak is accepting a shitty marriage proposal for my own convenience."

Prestina's mouth pinched. "You may not like it, but this is a solid match. You'd be a fool to dismiss it so blindly."

Praxis sighed dramatically. "How many ways do you want me to say this, Mother? I love *Kaedrich*."

"And what is *that* going to gain you, exactly?" Prestina asked. "Honestly, Praxis, stop being so *sentimental* for five minutes and think about this rationally."

"I *am*! It's not rational to chain yourself to a marriage that is going to make you miserable. I don't care if you don't like it, I am not going to make the mistakes you did! All you've ever loved is this company, and look at where it's left you. Look at you! You hate your life!"

Somewhere in the screaming, Praxis had gotten to her feet. With Prestina still seated, Praxis towered over her, and suddenly all of the power and strength that she'd always seen in her mother seemed to shrink down as well. She didn't even know if she had meant her words until they'd already been spoken, but now they seemed so obvious. Despite the wealth dripping from every pore, despite the economic power that she wielded with nothing more than her finger, Praxis could suddenly see nothing more than a miserable old woman, withered and bitter at her wasted youth. The shift was so jarring that it knocked the wind out of her, and Praxis had to sit back down again.

"I'm sorry," Praxis said.

"Are you done?"

Praxis nodded.

"Good," Prestina said. "Now, you listen to me for a moment. You're wrong: I don't just love this company. I also love this *family*. And right now, I have an opportunity to help them both, but I will never be able to do that if you don't have Lexthur's support when you place your inheritance bid."

Praxis's jaw dropped. "My . . . ? Wait a second, you want . . . *me*? To take over the company?"

"Well, perhaps not if you're going to make a habit of letting your mouth hang open like that, but yes. It's long past time we had a woman in charge of something important—a *strong* woman, good enough to prove that it can be done." Prestina clucked her tongue. "Oh, don't look so shocked at the idea. Why do you think I allowed you to be raised as an open wizard in the first place?"

Praxis's mouth continued to hang open. She honestly would not have been more surprised if Prestina had declared that they were selling the company and giving all their money to charity.

"Hang on . . . ," Praxis said. She was still trying to piece together what she'd just been told, still trying to make sense of things after her perception of her entire life had just been turned on its head. *Why do you think I allowed you?* Praxis could barely wrap her thoughts around it. "You mean to tell me this was your plan from *the very beginning*?"

"Of course it was. Honestly, Praxis, you never figured that out for yourself? That's disappointing, I have to admit."

"But . . . but when I came back . . ." She trailed off, though she didn't need to finish in order for both of them to understand. When she came back from her Qol Nar, half-dead and limping in through the doorway. Prestina had swaddled her in society, in parties and balls, in social lessons, not the slightest mention of her future beyond that of receiving guests and looking pretty.

Prestina shrugged. "You had renounced your magic, and that could have easily thrown your legal status into question. And frankly, you were broken. I'm pleased to see that you've since mended yourself. Now, I realize you're a little behind on recent matters, but with my guidance that can be overcome easily enough."

All words failed Praxis in that moment. Every argument she might have thought to make died before it ever made its way up her throat. The only thing she could do was stare at her mother. Her mother—Praxis didn't even feel like she knew her anymore. Her mother, who had never seemed to take much interest in Praxis's magical studies, who had regarded them with something bordering on cold disdain. Her mother, who had always found Praxis wanting, who had never offered the slightest scrap of approval. Her mother, who had spoken of nothing except finding an acceptable husband for her once Praxis came back battered and small. Praxis found herself turning these memories over in her mind, looking at them from fresh angles. Her mother, who had been trying to mold Praxis into the kind of woman that could prove herself against the harsh world of male scrutiny. Praxis's cheek suddenly burned with the impression of a thousand harsh slaps, each one designed not to put Praxis in her place, but to build up her resistance.

She found herself gripping the edges of her chair, as if it was the only thing keeping her upright. Maybe it was.

Praxis cleared her throat. "Mother . . . I'm sorry, I really am, but . . . I don't *want* it."

"I never asked you if you *wanted* it," Prestina said. "Do you think that I've *wanted* everything I've done in my life? Do you think that any of us women ever truly get what we *want*? You have a responsibility. To your family. To your sex. To your *country*. I don't care what you *want*."

"Then why should I care what you want?" Praxis asked.

Prestina sneered. "You would really be so selfish?"

"Yes."

"Fine," Prestina said. She rested her hands flat on the desk, smoothing out the wrinkle-free papers. "Fine. You want to play things that way? Let's play things that way. You do this for me—you marry Lexthur, you win the inheritance . . . and . . . and . . ."

Praxis raised an eyebrow. "And?"

"You can have him," Prestina said, her lip curling back in distaste.

Praxis blinked. "I can . . . ?" She trailed off, confused, until she saw the heavy glare her mother was leveling her with. Oh . . . *Oh*. Praxis's eyes widened. She could have "him."

Kaedrich.

With Prestina's extremely grudging approval.

"I don't—" Praxis started, but Prestina held up a finger.

"Provided you can assure me you have means at your disposal to en-sure that you will *never* become pregnant from him." Prestina paused, and swallowed, looking almost like she'd vomited into her mouth. "But beyond that . . . you can do with him what you will. You would hear no further objections from me, ever again."

Praxis sighed. She pinched the bridge of her nose, shaking her head at Prestina.

"I . . . *appreciate* what you think you're trying to offer me," she said, looking up, "but Mother . . . I'm going to be with Kaedrich regardless of whether or not you give me your approval. And when I don't accept Lexthur's offer, and I leave Yandosia . . . then frankly, your approval isn't going to matter either way."

"Isn't it?" Prestina smiled. She nodded. "That's probably true, yes . . . Assuming that you both make it back to Durland safe and sound."

A snap of cold, colder than usual, burst through Prestina's office as Praxis's eyes narrowed. "You wouldn't *dare*."

Prestina laughed. "No, I don't suppose I would. I'm just saying, darling, anything can happen. Your precious Durland isn't exactly a safe place these days. What if you *do* bank everything on Kaedrich? Let's say you turn this down, that you sail back thinking you're free and clear. What happens ten years from now, twenty, when he amounts to nothing? What are you going to do when you find yourself penniless, a world away from a place where your very *name* would grant you access to whatever you'd like?"

"He won't amount to nothing."

"Oh, please." Prestina rolled her eyes, the exact way Praxis did when an idea was too stupid to listen to. "Stop trying to change the subject and just humor me for two minutes, will you? Answer the question. What happens then?"

She didn't want to answer the question, because answering it—even thinking about it—meant entertaining the idea that Kaedrich would accomplish nothing of value with her life. She knew that, Prestina knew that, and this was exactly why Prestina had posed the question in the first place.

"I'll survive."

"Yes, congratulations, I'm sure you would. Of course you would. Anyone can *survive*. Surviving is easy, Praxis. Surviving is *small*. Is that really what you want to be? When you could have the company? When your achievements could be limitless? When you could do *whatever you wanted*?"

"I want to be with Kaedrich."

"And I'm telling you, *you can have that*. But why does achieving that need to prevent you from succeeding in the rest of your life?"

"I don't—"

"No, just shut up and listen to me for a minute," Prestina said. "I'm your mother, you owe me that much. Praxis, darling: I'm not heartless, despite how I'm sure you paint me in your head. I understand that you think you're in love, and I don't know . . ." She tipped her head to the side, her face gone oddly soft and thoughtful as she studied her daughter. "Maybe you are. I wouldn't profess to be an expert. All I'm asking you is, why does being with him need to mean sacrificing everything else? Doesn't love mean *mutual* support for each other's goals? Surely, if Kaedrich feels the same way about you as you do about him, then he'd want you to be able to achieve as much in your life as possible?"

"That would have been a good speech, Mother, but you're forgetting one thing: running the company isn't *my* dream. It's yours."

"Praxis, I'm going to tell you something, privately, that is perhaps the single most true thing I have ever said in my life. Running this company . . . it doesn't necessarily *have* to involve much of actually 'running' the company."

"But you just said—"

"I said I wanted a strong woman in charge. Part of being in charge is delegating tasks to those better suited than you are for handling day-to-day operations. Oh, you'd need to keep an eye on things, make sure that one of your brothers doesn't try to take it away from you in everything but name. You'd need to stay informed, make executive decisions. I'm not saying you could sit around doing nothing. I *am* saying that once you have control, what you choose to do with your wealth and power is entirely your decision.

"Think about it," Prestina went on. "The kind of things you could do with that. For yourself, for Yandosia—or Durland. For Kaedrich. Imagine what *his* life would be like, at your elbow."

It was supposed to be tantalizing, and on some small level, perhaps it was. Her mother had certainly planted an image in Praxis's mind, as surely as if she'd cast a spell to do just that. Praxis could see it—of course she could see it, she'd been *born* to see it. Herself in five years, ten, twenty: strong and commanding, draped in the glamours of the ice, using her power to advance the causes of magical inquiry, of women's equality, putting anyone that dared to question her in their place with a mere look. And Kaedrich, living in ultimate luxury, wanting for nothing. Free to read as much as she wished, pursue what she wished. Hovering in Praxis's benevolent shadow, tucked out of sight so as not to damage Praxis's image of authority. Sitting idle in the Fellows family's dwelling, trapped under the ice at the bottom of the world.

A sour taste filled Praxis's mouth. "I'd still have to marry someone else," she said. Which wasn't really the whole problem, no, but the only one Prestina might have a slim hope of understanding.

Prestina frowned. "A *Yandosian* marriage, yes. On paper. Technically. Seven hells, Praxis, you know no one is going to hold you to that in the bedroom."

"That's not really the point."

Prestina let out a huff of exasperation. She threw her pen down on the desk and leaned back in her chair, slumping so that the high collar of her dress actually mashed up against the backing. "So you would really do it, then? Throw away everything, chain yourself to a life of mediocrity and boredom, all to marry Kaedrich instead?"

Praxis flushed. She ducked her head, examining the stitching on her gloves. "I didn't say I was going to do *that* . . ."

It was a mistake to say this, one Praxis recognized immediately. She froze, horrified with herself for being so loose with her tongue. She could *feel* her mother's stillness, carefully measured as Prestina regarded Praxis.

Praxis looked up. She held her face slack, casual. "Not right away, at any rate. There's no rush, and that's assuming Kaedrich would want to marry me, anyway."

Prestina nodded. "I see," she said, and that was exactly the problem. She did see, with those scrutinizing eyes so very much the mirror of Praxis's. She saw into the tiny, vulnerable corner that Praxis had been so careful to hide in these last few months, a part of her that she did not even show to Kaedrich. Prestina cleared her throat. When she spoke next, her words were slow and concerned. "And . . . have you told Kaedrich this?"

"No," Praxis admitted. It was barely a whisper, more of a breath than a word. Her attention skittered back to her gloves, so that she wouldn't have to look at her mother. She shut her eyes and an image of Kaedrich's face—hurt, disappointed, laced with flashing waves of anger—filled her mind. It was as sure and as real as if Kaedrich was actually standing in front of her. It was *going* to happen, sometime, somewhere, somehow; Praxis held no illusions about that. And then . . .

"Listen, darling, all I'm asking is that you keep your options open. Can you do that for me? Don't say 'yes' to the proposal, just . . . don't say anything. Not yet. You can *always* turn him down later. For now . . ." Prestina sighed. "Well, who knows what will happen? None of us can see the future, now can we? Not even you."

DAY TURNED TO night, and night turned to day, and it was all the same underneath the ice. Only the patterns changed, traffic increasing and decreasing to an arbitrary rhythm that varied from family to family. The Fellows household quieted, everyone retreating home to sleep and rest and recuperate for another day.

Trendall did not. Trendall broke into a cold sweat as he held the mysterious object they'd found. He did not dare to give it a name, not even in his head. "The object" was plenty sufficient for his tastes. If he dared to tread any closer, if he should ever consider calling it what he was now convinced that it was . . .

He swallowed. The consequences weren't worth thinking about, he told himself, because that wasn't going to happen.

Time had slipped from Trendall, so he was not entirely sure how long the object had been in his possession by this point, but he still wasn't comfortable with it. From the moment it had appeared, long before he did his research, long before the understanding of what he held in his hands had begun to settle, long before he decided that it did not *need* a name, nope, not at all, he had felt unsettled by its presence. Neither Prewish Fellows nor his underling, Stamm, had appeared the slightest bit bothered, and so Trendall had kept himself collected. Besides, at the time, it was just a vague sense of unease; a tickle in the back of his mind, a whisper he couldn't quite hear. It was easy enough to ignore.

He had done his job. Prewish wanted to know what the object was, and Trendall had studied it. He'd subjected it to a battery of tests, both scientific and magical. He'd recorded its reaction: absolutely none. To anything. He'd frozen it, burned it, crushed it, boiled it. He'd assaulted it with magic—with spells to break things apart, and spells to bring things back together, with spells that only worked on living things, with spells intended for the dead. He'd sung to it. He'd whispered to it. He'd held it close, sleeping with it underneath his pillow. Once, he even masturbated while staring deep into its center—or at least he'd tried to, but the swirling, crawling mass of light that seemed to claw at the glass like a cage felt as if it was *staring* at him, and things didn't exactly, well, "work" after that. That was just as well, because by that point he'd been awake for . . . he didn't know how long—certainly more than a day, maybe more than two, and had barely eaten and bathed not at all, and he wasn't exactly thinking properly anymore.

Now the household slumbered, but he couldn't even think of closing his eyes. A second wind had seized him, and he'd been working for hours by this point, sequestered away someplace that nobody would find him. But now, finally, he was done. He dropped the knife, letting it clatter to his feet. With one hand, bloodied from where he'd accidentally cut himself, Trendall reached out to steady himself against the ice. The other clutched the object against his chest, the pads of his fingers caressing the glassy surface in a hypnotic pattern, over and over, and his mind whirled with a thousand horrifying possibilities. The truth had come to him in a dream, stolen when he'd fallen asleep standing up, his head frozen to the wall. He would probably never sleep again.

A Beacon. Trendall winced. The name had entered his head like a bullet, unwelcome and painful in his temples. *No,* he told himself, and tried to shove the name aside. But the name resisted. It bloomed, spreading through his mind. *A Beacon, a Beacon, a Beacon.* It sang its name, rich and clear as the ringing of a bell. A flare of pain split Trendall's mind, and he doubled over on himself, clutching his head. The Beacon lay cradled in his upturned palm, Trendall's body curled around it. He gripped his head so hard that his fingernails began to draw blood, though he hardly noticed. "Stop it," he muttered to himself, rocking where he stood, muttering and whimpering, while the Beacon just kept shouting at him—*a Beacon, a Beacon, a Beacon!*

Danger, it whispered, and Trendall whipped his head up. He reached out again, stabilizing himself.

His mind went silent. His headache receded to a deadened heartbeat.

A soft sound made him turn. A Fellows, appearing from around the corner. Somehow, impossibly, here in this secret place that should have been Trendall's alone. Panic scuttled up Trendall's spine as the Fellows stepped closer, and on its heels, a pressure ballooned up in Trendall's mind, scattering his thoughts. He could not identity the figure, and he should have been able to, and he knew that, but that knowledge did not help him.

"It's *true*," the Fellows said. This was not a question. His hands were clasped in front of his face, as if he could not believe the luck the fates had granted him. Gems glinted on his fingers, red and green and blue, fat and glistening like tropical fruit. The sparkles matched his eyes as they took in the sight of the Beacon in Trendall's grip.

The Fellows spread his hands, as if to indicate not just Trendall, standing there, but the corridor, the household—the whole of Yandosia, even. "It's true," he repeated. A broad grin was splitting his face—dammit, Trendall knew he should have been able to identify that face, he *knew* the knowledge of this was buried somewhere deep in his mind. Suppressed and muddled, certainly, but *there*, somewhere, if only he could access it.

There was no point in trying to deny the Fellows's statement. Briefly, Trendall felt the impulse to hide the Beacon behind his back, as if tucking it out of sight would accomplish anything. But that would have only dragged this encounter out. Instead, he clutched it tighter against his chest. "What are you planning to do with it?" he asked.

"That's not really your concern, now, is it?"

A typical Fellows answer. He reached out, his curled palm hungry and demanding. Greed poured off of him as thick as smoke, clogging up the air between them. "Give it to me."

The Beacon twitched. Trendall nearly gasped at the shock of it, the first reaction the Beacon had given to anything. He felt the strain as it tugged against his fingers, and he wrapped both of his hands around it as if trying to smother the thing. "No," Trendall said.

This was either a brave or a stupid thing to say. For all he knew, the Fellows could have had a gun on him. Trendall would be able to defend himself against such a common weapon, of course—unless his senses were as muddied as his thoughts. He tried to click a spark of magic to life inside of him, and his blood chilled when it did not happen.

The Fellows was grinning at him. His hand was still outstretched, still waiting, and the Beacon strained against Trendall's grasp. "Give it to me," the Fellows repeated, "or I will take it from you by force."

Trendall straightened his spine. "You cannot," he said. He hoped his voice wasn't shaking. Whoever this Fellows was, he had to know Trendall was a wizard—surely, just the threat of this would be enough to get him to back down?

The Fellows tipped his head. "Can't I?" And then he snapped his fingers, and a sputter of flames appeared in the cup of his upturned palm.

Trendall gasped. In his panic, he scrambled back against the wall, hunched to protect his treasure. He stood, snarling like a cornered animal.

What he was seeing wasn't possible, though he should have realized the presence of magic sooner, as soon as the Fellows had appeared. No one should be able to enter this place. And yet, and yet. He'd done his research on the family before agreeing to work with them, and only one of their ranks was ever born with the ability to perform magic. Trendall shook his head, as if denial would be enough to change the reality that was standing in front of him. "That's . . . that's not possible." The only member of the Fellows to do magic . . . she'd been gone for—

—No. She'd *returned*, that's right, he'd heard that rumor. But she was a *woman*, and the person standing in front of him was a *man* . . . right? Surely, he could not be so muddled in his thoughts as to be unable to distinguish the two. Trendall stared at the Fellows: the trousers, the long coat. *Man*, he thought to himself. Surely, it was a man.

Trendall clutched his head, pain and confusion raging now in equal measure.

"One last chance," the Fellows said.

"I can't," Trendall said. His voice cracked, open panic bleeding through. "Please, don't you see? This thing . . . I . . . It . . . If someone got their hands on it—"

A crack of laughter escaped the Fellows. "I know. That's what I had in mind."

There was little time to react. A burst of flame careened through the air toward Trendall. He leaped to the side, but his feet caught against each other, and a yelp escaped his lips as he went crashing to the floor. He landed hard on the knife, the point cutting against his hip. He ignored the pain. Trendall held the Beacon tight to his chest, quickly curling into the fetal position around it. "It's all right," he whispered to it, "it's all right, I've got you."

Danger, the Beacon whispered again, somewhere deep in his mind. *Sleep.*

Trendall closed his eyes. His mind was already slipping into dreams as the pain struck him, hot and fast, and by the time he would have opened his mouth to scream, he was already dead.

His lifeless hands slumped to the floor. The Beacon tumbled out of them, rolling across the ice until it bumped neatly into a pair of shoes standing nearby. "Why, hello there," a voice said to it, as it was scooped up as gingerly as a kitten.

Chapter Fourteen

"YOU HAVE TO admire how well the cold has preserved the body," Praxis said the next morning.

Several glares shot in her direction, but Praxis only shrugged. "What? You know he's thinking it, too." She pointed to the doctor, hunched over the frozen corpse of a Yandosian wizard that someone had called Trendall.

The doctor turned, shot his own glare up over his shoulder.

Kaedrich cleared her throat. "Tact," she whispered to Praxis, but Praxis waved her hand in dismissal.

"Tact doesn't bring back the dead."

"You'd know about that sort of thing, would you?" Kaedrich asked.

Praxis scowled. "No. Of course not." She folded her arms across her chest, her body shifting just enough to open the tiniest fraction of space between them. The gesture was so small that nobody else would have noticed, but Kaedrich's eyebrow ticked up almost imperceptibly, and Praxis *knew* she was making a careful note of it.

"So what's the verdict, Doc?" Praxis asked, hoping to distract from the moment. "Are the rest of us going to live?" Though even as she asked it, a certainty pressed itself into her mind. Of course it was fine. Of course there was nothing to notice, nothing to see. Praxis sighed, leaning back against a wall, already itching to go.

"Praxis, please," Prestina chided, though her heart didn't seem to be in it this morning. She held herself back from the corpse, one hand pressed against her stomach as if fighting a gag reflex, the other holding a delicate handkerchief near her mouth. Her skin was unusually pale and clammy, even for a Fellows—but then, Praxis mused with a sour twist of her lips, not everyone was as familiar with corpses as she was.

The doctor rose to his feet. "It doesn't appear to be contagious, if that's what you're concerned about, no. Poor man's heart seems to have gone out. It's unusual, certainly, in someone so young—but not unheard of. I wouldn't worry."

"I never worry," Praxis said. She met the doctor's steady gaze, her face and tone both deadpan. There was something she didn't like about the man, about this whole situation, but probably that was simply the terrible mood Praxis had woken up in. After all, she was certain there was nothing odd about the wizard's death . . . wasn't she? *Of course,* said a voice as her knee flared, pain radiating up and down the bones, until it felt like her shin was on fire.

Prewish cleared his throat. Almost the whole family had piled down here, out of concern and morbid curiosity, both. They wouldn't all be able to stay long—the lab wasn't designed to withstand this much body heat packed together—but for now, a thrill of the macabre got the better of them.

"And you're sure it wasn't something more?" Prewish asked. He ran his hand nervously across his bald head. "There's no reason to suspect . . . foul play?"

Prommel snorted. "'Foul play.' Listen to yourself, Prewish. You've been reading too many Durlish detective novels."

"I just want to make sure we're not overlooking anything."

"And I'm telling you," Prommel said, his voice as steely as his coat, "this area is one of the most secure in the whole facility. So unless you're going to start pointing fingers at *one of us*—"

"Enough," Prawl cut in. He'd been keeping quiet so far, standing nearby to Prestina. "Prommel, no one is questioning your security measures. Besides, you heard the doctor: this was the work of the tragic hand of fate, not man. There will be no more discussion of it."

Prewish frowned. "But—"

"No," Prawl said, raising his hand for silence. "I realize you'd love to make it seem as if this company is so uncoordinated that it clearly deserves your *excellent* leadership, my son, but that's simply not going to happen. The matter is closed. Do I make myself clear?"

Prewish's jaw tightened, teeth grinding together. He forced a hard nod.

"Good. Now, if everyone could clear out, please. I'm sure you all have better things to do than gawp over a poor man's demise."

Only a handful of stifled complaints drifted out from the crowd lingering in the lab. The family shuffled on, casting the occasional last look back.

Prawl cleared his throat.

"Not you, Praxis. There's something we need to discuss first." He glanced at Kaedrich. "Alone."

Kaedrich raised an eyebrow. She looked to Praxis, a silent question written on her face. *Will you be okay on your own?* Praxis gave a weary nod.

By the time everyone left, Prawl had knelt down beside the body, the same place the doctor had been a few minutes ago. He seemed to be studying the corpse's slack face, the peace that had settled in with the embrace of death.

"Such a pity," Prawl said softly. Then he pushed himself back to his feet, brushing his hands together. He returned his attention to his daughter. "There's no time to worry about being polite, so I'm going to be blunt with you, Praxis: I need you to take his place as the head of the lapus lumeni division."

Praxis's eyebrows shot up. She laughed before she could help it.

Prawl scowled. "I'm serious."

"I know," Praxis said. All of her mirth dried up, leaving nothing but a sour taste in her mouth. She shook her head. "I know, and I didn't mean to appear . . . dismissive. But, Daddy, you have to know I would never consider agreeing to that."

"I understand," Prawl said, nodding. "And believe me, my daughter, I am not trying to rope you into something you don't want to do. You have a life outside of this company and . . . I respect that, I really do. I'm not asking you to stick around permanently. I would never ask that. I just need you to keep things going for the next few weeks—a month, tops—while I sort some things out with the ministers of the oversight committee."

Praxis shook her head again, more forcefully this time. Though she didn't know, even then, if she was trying to convince her father or herself. "I can't. I'm sorry."

"Praxis, please," Prawl said. He took her hands, holding them up against his chest. Praxis watched her fingers curl through the thick fox fur of his coat, the better not to look at him as he pleaded. "Please, you have to help me. I can't *afford* to take the time to find a suitable replacement—not now. Not when *everything* is hanging in the balance."

"No. I'm sorry, I—"

"Please," Prawl repeated. "Please. I . . . I have a plan. If I can demonstrate the value of my leadership, then I might be able to convince the ministers to call off the inheritance bidding—but if I'm going to pull that off, I *need* someone I can trust in control of the lapus lumeni. I *need* you. Just for a little while."

Praxis shut her eyes.

This is what she was afraid of coming back to Yandosia for. The ice had a way of trapping you, wrapping its frozen embrace around a person until they were so fully entombed that there was no escaping it. Praxis had felt it trying to snare her from the minute her foot had set down on the outskirts of the tundra. Only her desperation to keep Kaedrich safe had driven her this far; but Kaedrich didn't need Praxis to be ensnared in family politics to protect her. Simply *being* in the Fellows' dwelling was enough.

"I can't," Praxis whispered. She opened her eyes, watching her father's reaction carefully. "I won't."

Prawl dropped his daughter's hands and turned away. He itched at his beard, fluffing it up, as he paced the lab like a caged animal. When he turned back, his face had the desperate edge of a dying man. "I'm not asking you as a businessman. I understand that you don't share our values. But can I appeal to you as a father, Praxis? We've always been close. Please do this for me."

Praxis shook her head. "No."

"Dammit, girl! What can I *do*?" He glowered across at his daughter, but Praxis had plenty of experience with making *both* of her parents angry. "I don't suppose I can threaten you."

"You're welcome to try," Praxis said. There was not a trace of anger or bitterness in her voice—she understood.

"I have a *right* to defend my company," Prawl said. "I have a *right* to fight for the future of my family!"

"I know you do. I wish you luck."

"But not enough to help me."

Praxis shrugged. "No. I'm sorry, Daddy. I really am."

If she was having this conversation with her mother, Praxis knew a slap would be coming next. As it was, Prawl could only stare up at her, his face shifting from rage to despair to desperation, looping back and forth and back again. For the first time, Praxis actually *appreciated* the way her magic was slightly unstable in her anger: the spit of flames that curled around her fingers, the crackle of the air, the way that minor storm clouds could rise like mist behind her. How disappointing it would be, to *feel* all this anger and not have it expressed in a way to make your opponents tremble. Standing beside her father, Praxis felt like a distant glacier: cold and untouchable.

She watched him draw a slow breath, closing his eyes for a moment to steady himself. When he looked back at her, his expression had stilled, and he met her gaze straight-on. "I will give you *anything you want*, if you agree to do this," he said. "Name your price."

This, she had to admit, she was not expecting. In a heartbeat, Praxis knew he was telling the truth. Her father did not make promises he didn't plan to keep, in business or in his personal life both. Nor did he tend to make open offers; this, more than anything else, spoke of his desperation in this matter. Here he was, literally holding out his open hand, all the power of *Prawl Fellows* at Praxis's disposal. Whatever she wanted.

All she had to do was take it.

Praxis's head was spinning so hard that she almost had to sit down. Both Lexthur and her mother had been insisting that the only way she would ever achieve her goals would be to seize control of the company for herself, but here Prawl had just presented another way. No marriage involved, no lifetime commitment involved. If she agreed to help him, if she asked for an army . . . Well. She would get her army, that was for damned sure.

She could rain hell down on Lanali's head.

She could keep Kaedrich safe.

A month, he'd said. At most.

Was that really so much to ask?

THE MARRIAGE PORTFOLIO made a satisfying *thwack* as it landed on Lexthur Delford's desk. It scattered several of his other papers, smeared the ink of whatever he was writing, toppled his ink pot. He had to jerk his hand out of the way as the portfolio crashed down in front of him. A pity; Praxis was hoping to splash some of his ink on that pristine suit of his.

Instead, he easily righted the pot, and then looked up. A pleasant smile spread across his face, neutral and controlled. "It's not what you think."

"Really?" Praxis said. "Because it looks to me like you went behind my back, purposefully trying to manipulate me into a marriage I've already turned down. *Twice*, I might add."

Lexthur set down his pen. "I admit, I can see how you might take it that way. I assure you, that was not my intention. I was simply exploring the potential of—"

"There *is no potential*! How many times do you want me to say that? Lexthur, *I am not marrying you*. Ever. Under any circumstances."

"I *understand* that," Lexthur said, and when Praxis started to laugh incredulously, he added, "Really, I do. But where is the harm in finding out the viability of it? For the sake of argument, if nothing else. If you really want to get aid for Durland—"

"I'll get it another way."

Lexthur shrugged. "I hope that you can. The last thing I want to do is make you unhappy, Praxis. But circumstances are happening faster than I think you're ready to accept. Several of your brothers have already placed their bids, and believe me, none of them are going to be open to helping your cause."

Praxis rolled her eyes. She waved her hand in dismissal as she turned away. Her fingers curled, guiding her forward. She went over to examine the magical paintings, enchanted to show surface conditions. The night stretched out into the distance, clear and cold. Stars littered the sky, thick as a snowstorm.

She was, perhaps, enjoying her newfound freedom from Lexthur's arguments just a little *too* much. Not that she would have ever agreed to them before, but . . . dammit, there *had* been a logic to what he said, and knowing that she had just kicked the legs out from underneath it had buoyed Praxis's mood immensely on her ride into Bolt. She was practically *polite* to the clerks and aides who parted at the sight of her, and she'd even been less than her usual amount of rude to Huxley as she breezed past his desk and let herself up the stairs to Lexthur's office.

There was no question she'd be admitted. She did not even ask.

Praxis ran her finger along the painting now, her perception shifted to study the magic tying it together. "Your concern for the success of my goals is *touching*," Praxis said, her back toward Lexthur. "But I don't *need* your help to get what I want. I've made my own arrangements with my father."

"That's . . . surprisingly agreeable of him," Lexthur said. "But, Praxis . . . you have to know there's nothing he can do while the bidding process is going on. Any major changes to expenditure and operations are frozen, until the conclusion of the inheritance."

Praxis nodded. "At which point, the ministers will vote to leave control exactly where it is."

"You're certain about that?"

Praxis turned, the Fellows signature scowl already in place. "I will bet on my father a thousand times before I put my faith into a marriage with *you*."

Lexthur smiled. "Fair enough," he said. He smoothed out some papers on his desk. "I sincerely hope you get what you want out of this. Prawl too, for that matter. I have nothing but respect for your father."

Praxis snorted. "Do you?"

"I do," Lexthur said. He opened a drawer in his desk, and picked up the leather portfolio. "That said . . . I'll be honest with you: I have severe reservations about his ability to pull this off. So, for your sake, I will keep this around for a while. Just in case you decide you need it."

"You needn't bother. I won't want it."

Lexthur shrugged. "Then it will waste a bit of space in my desk for a while, and no harm will be done."

"You're a right bastard, you know that?"

Lexthur smiled. Unconcerned, and perfectly collected. "I've been called worse. Just know I will always be here for you, Praxis. That's a promise."

AFTER PRAXIS AND Lexthur had reached their understanding, so many years ago at the beginning of everything, he came to the Fellows' dwelling just about every day. Just to talk. To stroll the long corridors with her, to explore Praxis's garden of ice. He folded himself so expertly into the day-to-day operations that the servants laid out places for him at the table before he even showed up. It was understood that Praxis's social calendar was always full now, and every other invitation she received, she could decline without worrying that her mother would slap her for her insolence.

For a while—two months or more—things were perfect.

But her birthday was approaching, heralding her coming of age, and things couldn't possibly stay the same forever. No matter how much Praxis might have wished them to.

"What's this?" Praxis asked, accepting the parcel from Lexthur. He had just arrived, and placed the parcel into her hands before he'd even said hello. Praxis turned it over, though the underside of a present wasn't much more obvious than the top. Thin paper painted with curling green leaves wrapped up a small box, while a silver ribbon tied it all together.

"It's for you—for your birthday. I know it's early, but . . . I have another present saved for the actual day. I didn't want to wait with this one."

Praxis smiled, motioning for Lexthur to sit. "You really didn't have to get me *anything*, much less two presents."

Lexthur nodded, though he made no attempt to take back his generosity. They both sat, on couches opposite each other in one of the Fellows' many, many sitting rooms. It was one of Praxis's favorites, gemstone fish embedded into the walls to give you a feeling of being under the sea. She liked to look at the bright splashes of color, half-visible through the icy blue, and imagine she could swim away with them.

There was no question that Praxis was expected to open the present now, and so she untied the ribbon.

The box—whatever it was—was too small to be a book, so right away Praxis felt a twinge of disappointment. Small boxes, in her experience, usually contained jewelry or other trifles, all the sorts of things that littered her bedroom and brought her no joy. Still, it was a sweet gesture, and clearly intended to make her happy, so Praxis kept a pleasant smile on her face as she slid her thumb underneath the flap of the paper.

Inside, a plain whale-bone box. This, she had to admit, piqued her curiosity; so few things in her life were plain, and in her experience jewels tended to come in packages encrusted with yet more jewels, or at least housed in boxes made of expensive imported wood. Praxis glanced up briefly, hoping to gauge Lexthur's expression, but he was just waiting, watching, and so she tipped back the lid.

Inside, a small brass cylinder like a spyglass, with tiny pinpricks running all along it. Somewhere from the depths, a scrap of lapus lumeni must have been fitted, because light poured through all the pinpricks. Praxis picked it up. When she turned little bits on the end of the cylinder, the metal underneath would shift in such a way that the points of light changed from one configuration to the next.

"It's a star chart," Lexthur said. "It shows you the night's sky over Yandosia. I set it to show you what it will look like on your birthday."

"Thank you. It's lovely," Praxis said, and it was. Lovely and different, though it wasn't his fault that the night's sky now brought to mind the stench of burning flesh and the memory of Moc's body, tiny ashes floating upward to mingle with the stars. Still, the gesture was nice.

She held it for a while, twisting the pieces this way and that, setting it to different dates and then peering through to see if anything looked familiar. She was so fixated on it that she did not notice that Lexthur had risen from his chair, nor as he leaned towards her, not until his lips pressed against hers.

The kiss was . . . wet. It felt rude, somehow, for Praxis to notice this, but caught off guard as she was, that became the only thing she could pay attention to. Was this how they were supposed to be, Praxis wondered, or had Lexthur been nervously overlicking his lips as he worked up his courage? In which case, good gods, then he'd been *anticipating* this moment, and what was Praxis supposed to do now? She was frozen in place, her neck twisted in a way that had felt perfectly comfortable until she was forced to hold it. Her eyes had been open when he'd struck and they stayed open now, the subtle pockmarks and faded blemishes of Lexthur's cheeks in painfully close proximity. He smelled different up close like this, his breath not unpleasant but far too *personal* for Praxis's tastes.

One of Lexthur's eyes cracked open, settling on hers. Lexthur flushed, and retreated in haste. "Forgive me, I—I didn't mean to be so forward, I just, I thought—"

There had to have been something in Praxis's expression. Her cheek stung in phantom anticipation of her mother's slap, an automatic response when Praxis let her emotions show through. Instantly, she'd wiped her look clean, replacing whatever he'd seen with a practiced society smile. "No, please, the fault is mine. I'm afraid you've caught me quite off guard, that's all."

It was clear he didn't entirely believe her, though he wanted to. And why not? It *was* the course Praxis had been steering him on, after all, and one she had entered into willingly. She could not be upset with him now that he had finally taken the bait. Just because she had chosen to forget about it doesn't mean she didn't know, all along, that this is where her efforts would lead her.

Besides, Lexthur was . . . nice. If she had to accept the company of a man, then she could do a lot worse than him.

Though her hands shook in her lap, Praxis forced a demure smile. She tipped her head, looking up through her eyelashes in a mimicry of her sister. "Mr. Delford—Lexthur," she said. She all but purred the words. She'd watched it played out enough, through Prenna and the rest of them. She knew the rules. "Please forgive my surprise. I promise that if you wanted to try again, I'd be more prepared this time."

Just like that, whatever reservations Lexthur had melted away. A sloppy grin split his face for just a moment before he managed to wrangle control of it. He cleared his throat. "Well . . . if you insist."

She did not insist, but neither was she going to point this out. Praxis raised her head, closing her eyes as she let Lexthur kiss her again. And again. At one point he cupped her cheeks, and that was nice enough she guessed, but her world did not stand on its head. No trumpets blared, no celestials sang, and the only flip of her stomach was one of nerves, realizing: seven hells, did this mean she'd have to *keep doing this*? He kissed her again and she began to wonder just how often she was supposed to allow this now—could she get away with narrowing it to once per day? That seemed fair, surely, for it's not as if she could remember ever seeing her parents kiss *at all*.

After what felt like it must surely be an appropriate length of time, Praxis rested her hand on Lexthur's chest, applying just enough pressure to indicate that he should step back. She did not want to risk him feeling reproached again, and so she was grateful when he took the hint, sitting back with a dazed sort of smile playing over his face.

He was evidently not content, however, to leave the romantic gestures aside. The gift and the kiss were surely more than enough for one day by Praxis's standards, but unfortunately for her, the apparently positive reception of these actions only seemed to embolden Lexthur. He took one of her hands in his, the same one she'd pushed him away with. Lexthur drew Praxis's hand up and kissed her fingers, then pressed her hand flat against his chest. She could feel the wild fluttering of his heart, pounding into the tips of each of her fingers. It matched the nervous jitter of her own, although for entirely different reasons.

"I'm afraid that I need to get back," Lexthur said. He reached over and brushed Praxis's cheek. "My parents have business they need me to take care of. But I just wanted you to know, Praxis . . . my sweet Praxis . . ."

She could see it coming now. Praxis took a sharp breath, which she tried to cover with a nervous little smile that she hoped looked expectant rather than terrified. The words entered Praxis's mind a split second before she heard them:

"I love you."

She'd tried to brace herself as best as she could, but Lexthur's declaration still struck her like the slamming of an iron gate. She *heard* the heavy *clang*, rattling through her mind, the snap of a lock being set.

She did not need to fake the heat that suddenly bloomed through her cheeks. It was easy to play it off as embarrassment, as modesty run amok; she'd seen enough girls giggle and dip their heads at sweet words from a boy, she knew it would not look wholly unexpected. She kept her eyes down to hide her expression, though now, unfortunately, she had a clear view out of the corner of her vision of Lexthur's trousers, and the budding tent that he was at least *trying* to hide with the cut of his fur coat.

Seven hells.

Praxis's throat closed up in an involuntary gag reflex, and she had to force herself to swallow just to clear it enough to speak. "Lexthur, I . . . I hardly know what to say. I fear you've put your affections into someone who is . . . greatly unworthy of your generous spirit."

"Nonsense," Lexthur said. He ran his hand along her head, coddling her as if she was a child, as if she was already his. Praxis's hands tightened into fists around the star chart in her lap. "I'm afraid I really do have to go, though, and unfortunately we'll be out of town for most of next week—but I promise I'll be back in time for your big day. I know you'll do wonderfully."

He said this with a smile, and he cupped her cheek. Praxis fixed a look of polite happiness on her face. *Come on,* she thought to herself as he leaned in and gave her a quick kiss. *Come on, see through this. Tell me that you know I'm lying.*

You have to know that I'm lying.

"I love you," Lexthur said again, grinning at the novelty of it. And he kissed her hand and backed out of the room, grinning the whole time. Oblivious, delirious, overjoyed.

He didn't know. He didn't know any of it.

Chapter Fifteen

Sometimes, people didn't realize just how difficult it was to be in a position like Lorric Fellows: to be one of them, but not *really* one of them. Which was silly, Lorric thought, because a generation earlier Prawl had married into the Fellows family the same as Lorric had, and nobody dared to question *Prawl's* authority.

Lorric sat across from his wife, watching her reaction. They were gathered for lunch in their small, private dining room just off of Prenna's office. It was important to Lorric that they have *one* meal together as a family every day—*just* their family, just him and Prenna and their own children, without all the politics and drama of Lorric's in-laws—and lunch, being one of two midpoints in the Yandosian day when half the population was asleep at any given moment, was the only meal not already spoken for by the Great and Mighty Fellows.

Of course, their lunches had gotten smaller in recent years. Their oldest children, Rommand and Julaine, had grown and moved out of Bolt to pursue their own interests. Lorric was proud of them for this, for not falling into the trap as Prenna and all of her brothers had done, though it still made Prenna weepy at times.

She wasn't weepy now. She finished chewing her bite of toothfish, the motions of her jaw slow and deliberate. When she was done, she rested her fork on her plate, dabbed at her face with her napkin, and stole a brief glance left and right at Annelle and Hanshaw.

Lorric frowned; Prenna *hated* the idea.

"Perhaps we should discuss the matter in private," Prenna said. She gave Lorric a pleasant smile, as cheerful as her yellow dress. It bore no trace of the argument this would brew into if he allowed "the matter" to be dragged off into their bedroom. She was already picking her fork back up, as if things were settled.

"I don't know," Lorric had said yesterday, when the subject first came up. "I don't think Prenna is going to agree to it."

Praine rolled his eyes. "So you're just going to do whatever she says? A woman? What does she know of business?"

"Well . . . she is *in charge of the books."*

"Which means she has a head for numbers. Men *make the actual decisions that guide those numbers."*

"I don't—"

"Do you think Prawl *would let himself be dictated to?"*

"I . . . well, no, probably not . . ."

"Of course not. He's proven himself as a force to be reckoned with. That's why he's been able to keep hold of this company for so long. The next leader— whoever he may be—is going to have *to do the same." Praine shrugged. "But if you can't handle something like that . . ."*

"No, I can . . . I . . . I can."

I can, Lorric thought to himself now. "No," he said, watching as Prenna raised her eyebrow and then her gaze, as if one was drawn along by the other. Lorric straightened up. He brushed down the length of his own fur coat, hoping to appear commanding. "There's nothing to discuss. I've made up my mind. I'm going to put in a bid for control of the company."

Prenna stared at him for a moment. Annelle and Hanshaw, previously engrossed in their own meals, stared at him for a moment.

Prenna smiled. "Children, can you excuse us, please?"

"No," Lorric said again. "Stay." He leveled what he hoped was an authoritative glare at each of them in turn: Annelle, not even really a child anymore, already so refined, held herself poised and controlled—a perfect mirror of her mother; while Hanshaw, still just ten, stared up at Lorric with wide eyes. This was important, Lorric knew. This was a moment that Hanshaw would remember, that would shape the way he looked at his father from now on.

Lorric returned his attention to his wife, still holding the same stern expression he'd been wearing. *I can.* He shook his head. "It's going to be common knowledge soon enough—they might as well hear about it directly from me. I'm going to bid, and fates willing, I am going to win."

"And you think this is a good idea, do you?"

Lorric sat back. He honestly would not have been more surprised if Prenna had reached across the table and slapped him. Prenna Fellows had never questioned or argued against her husband in front of her children, not once in all the time that Lorric could remember.

Of course, Lorric thought bitterly, *she* was usually the one calling all the shots before.

I can.

"I do think it's a good idea," Lorric said slowly. Deliberately. "And not just me. Praine has already given me his full support."

At the mention of her older brother, Prenna flinched. Almost imperceptibly, except that Lorric had been witnessing these tiny contractions of her facial muscles every time Praine's name arose for just over twenty years, and if he hadn't noticed the pattern by now, he'd *really* be an idiot.

"Oh, well," Prenna said, her voice as icy as the room, "if *Praine* thinks it's a good idea . . ."

"I don't know what you have against him, Prenna. He's a good man. He's been a good boss to me for a long time."

It was true: Praine had never been anything other than friendly and helpful to Lorric. Years ago, when Lorric was first married to Prenna, Praine had been kind enough to use his position as the head of staff to make sure Lorric got a job in the Fellows financial empire. He'd helped Lorric to achieve promotions, clued him in to various opportunities that arose. Trusted Lorric with important errands. Why, on numerous occasions, Praine had even offered to watch the children when they were small, saying that he'd be delighted to take the girls off of Prenna's hands for an afternoon or two here and there. Prenna had never allowed it—not *once*, no matter how busy she was—and Lorric had never understood her stubbornness. When he would ask, Prenna would always shut the subject down. A shake of her head, her lips set firm. Never a word spoken against her brother, and yet . . .

Prenna stabbed at her toothfish with more force than was strictly necessary. "This is a mistake," she said, speaking more to the meal than to her husband.

Lorric's fist snapped tightly over his own fork. "I wasn't asking for your *opinion*."

The silence that followed was absolute. No one was looking at Lorric, and for a moment it didn't seem like anyone was even *breathing*. The air of the dining room felt colder than normal, nipping at the exposed skin of Lorric's hands and flushed cheeks.

Prenna let her fork drop. It clattered down, silver against porcelain, as she looked up. Never had she looked more like her mother, her soft face gone hard, framed by the ostentation of the collar fanning behind her head.

"Very well," Prenna started. "You don't want my opinion, and so you will not have it, my 'dear.' I will only tell you what I know to be a *fact*: whatever it is you think you're getting from Praine in this deal, I promise you he will not deliver it. He is using you, although for what ends I cannot say yet. Furthermore," she said, raising her voice to barrel right over the beginning of Lorric's objections, "in the future, if you cannot do me the courtesy of discussing these types of decisions beforehand, then don't bother to tell me at all."

Prenna paused. She took a deep, steadying breath.

"Now," she continued, drawing herself to her feet, "if you'll excuse me, I have a headache. I believe I'll go back to work early, if it's all the same to the rest of you."

No one made a move to stop her. Lorric frowned at his plate, the once-inviting meal now holding the exact same appeal as if he'd been served his own waste. He stole a glance at Hanshaw, but the boy wasn't looking at him anymore, instead squirming in his chair and poking idly at the remains of his own lunch.

The door to Prenna's office slammed shut behind her.

Lorric's shoulders slumped.

IT WAS HOURS before Praxis finally left Bolt.

Well, she wasn't going to waste the effort it took to make the trip. She'd come on foot, not wanting to make a spectacle, and she wasn't exactly looking forward to the walk back. So after Praxis had left Lexthur's office, she'd returned to the doctor that she'd spoken with the other day. Unfortunately, he was still just as baffled as he'd been when he first examined her.

"I'm sorry, Miss Fel—Miss P," he quickly corrected himself. So he'd figured it out. He flushed slightly at his error, clearing his throat for cover. "There doesn't seem to be anything modern science can do for you. The system you've rigged up appears to be as good of a solution as you're going to get."

"But it doesn't solve the problem," Praxis had said. "And you still haven't explained why there's suddenly pain."

The doctor shrugged.

Useless.

Anger at that had propelled her to a rival doctor, who had been fasci-
nated in the way of a nerdy child presented with a new puzzle to solve,
but he wouldn't have anything in the way of answers for her *yet*, oh no,
surely not. "I will not be rushed into making a false conclusion," he'd
said, bristling at the very idea.

Praxis had rolled her eyes. Well, fine.

Not wanting to waste her time, she'd stopped by two more doctors,
just to get the process started in as many different places at once. If she
was going to be kept hanging, she figured, she might as well spread the
likelihood that *someone* would come back with answers.

This left only one last errand.

Praxis had put it off as long as she could, but ultimately there was only
so long she could keep dodging Kaedrich's questions. Really, it had been
a minor miracle that it hadn't become a problem yet.

"Is that it?" Praxis asked. She stood in a parlor, in the home of her
family's former jeweler. In front of her was a simple whale-bone end
table, a hinged white box resting on top. Without waiting to be told, she
reached out and ran her finger along the length of the box. Just longer
than her hand from wrist to fingertips, but only about three fingers wide,
the box certainly looked as if it would house the piece that Praxis had
commissioned from Mr. Brenner the last time she was in Bolt.

Mr. Brenner offered a reserved smile. "That's it," he confirmed.

He stood slightly behind and just to the side of Praxis. He was a tall
man, quiet and focused. Everything about him was styled just so, from
his shorthaired fur coat to the gloriously elaborate mustache that swept
from one ear to the other. Praxis knew he'd been disappointed by the
austere nature of the design she'd commissioned, that he viewed himself
as an artist first and a craftsman second. Still, there was no one else that
she trusted to be this exact, or keep this silent. In return for his discretion,
she'd bestowed upon him the one thing he'd never be able to resist: one of
the shifting-color Fellows gemstones, reserved for only family members.
They were never sold, never gifted, never bartered. As the former master
jeweler of the family, he'd spent his whole life working with these, but
never for his own design, never allowed to keep one for himself.

Praxis took a breath as she drew the box toward her. She undid the
latch.

"I hope it's to your satisfaction," Mr. Brenner said. "Your designs were
not as precise as I'd have liked, and the glassblower did face some challenge
in matching the specifications. Still, if I may be so bold—"

"It's perfect," Praxis said, and it was. Her gloved fingers tangled in the heavy chain as she raised it up. The right weight, the right swing to it when she swayed the pendant back and forth. If it wasn't for the lack of a writhing, shifting light nestled within the glass orb, Praxis would have believed that she actually *was* holding the pendant for the Beacon of Souls again—and her magic would take care of that soon enough. Praxis had worked for weeks on the calculations, testing out spells while Kaedrich slept. The magic would need to be refreshed every day, possibly more than once, but it would be worth it. Anything that kept her secret would be worth it.

Probably, Praxis should have just made up some other lie, one that was truthful enough about the fact that she'd been stripped of her power as Lady of Souls, without being honest about *why*. It certainly would have been easier than this, but by the time she'd thought of it, it had already been so long that it felt awkward mentioning it now.

So this would do.

Without ceremony, Praxis tucked the fake Beacon into her pocket. She drew out Mr. Brenner's payment in its place, flipping it through the air between them. He caught it with deft fingers, his eyes shining almost as brightly as the gem he cradled. It was a fair-sized stone, raw and uncut as he'd requested.

She said nothing else as she let herself out.

In the tunnel outside, a heavy flow of traffic streamed past. Mr. Brenner lived in a branch-off about halfway up the great spiral, in an offshoot of an offshoot, about two miles from the main trunk. A densely populated branch of the city, the home of artisans and museum curators and stockbrokers. Praxis kept her collar flipped up, her coat snug around her. It's not that a Fellows couldn't be seen in a place like this, *exactly*, but Praxis would rather not leave a trail of questions in her wake. She gritted her teeth, setting off.

Her leg was killing her. By the time she'd made it to the first junction, shooting pain, like hot needles driven through her skin, spiked both up and down from her knee each time she put pressure on her foot. She considered stopping for a bit, trying to find a place to catch her breath, but there were no shops or businesses to stop at, and she didn't want to draw attention by just sitting down in the middle of the street. Praxis made her way over to the edge, leaning against the wall with her free hand as she maneuvered herself along. It was the best she could do.

It wasn't enough. Halfway down the next tunnel, the corner now visible in the distance, Praxis collapsed. She'd timed her motions poorly, her fingers curling at the wrong point, and this threw off her entire balance.

Her fall startled her. She yelped without thinking. Her face slammed into the ice of the floor, fresh pain flaring in her cheek and along the palm of her hand. Her wrist had twisted awkwardly, her knee caught in a tangle behind her back. When she managed to turn a little, she found her leg was wrenched up in the air, flopping around like a broken marionette.

People were rushing over, damn their good intentions. Praxis tried to push herself up, but something in her gears had gotten stuck, and she fell forward again. She ground her teeth together, cursing herself, cursing Yandosia, cursing everything that had led her back here, to this. A pair of hands had settled on her, trying to help her up, and Praxis threw them off with somewhat more force than strictly necessary.

"All right, people, that's enough," a familiar voice said. It boomed in from the distance, polished and commanding. "Give the lady some space, now. Let me handle this."

The tiny crowd around her shuffled back, automatically making room, and Lexthur's polished white shoes filled Praxis's vision.

Damn it.

Praxis shifted her thumb, and a soft *click* told her that the tension system of her gears had been temporarily cut off. Her leg flopped down, landing hard against the ice. Lexthur was still gently sweeping people away, assuring them that there was nothing to see here, and Praxis fought hard against the impulse to be grateful for his help. She managed to push herself into a sitting position, at which point Lexthur crouched down beside her. "Ready?" he asked, his arm already slipping around her waist. As if there was no doubt he'd be there for her, as if it was as natural as breathing.

He hauled her up. Praxis nodded, the closest she could come to saying "thank you." Lexthur let her go, standing by in case she had any further trouble. Praxis clicked the mechanism by her thumb, reengaging the system. She curled her finger, but . . . she frowned as nothing happened.

Praxis swore under her breath. She'd have to take the time to inspect the network of gears and harness, to find where something had gone wrong.

"Come on," Lexthur said. He put her arm over his shoulder for support, and Praxis did not argue as he led her across the street, where a sleigh stood waiting. The driver glanced curiously at them as he helped Praxis inside, but Praxis no longer had the luxury of worrying about her image. Besides, a Fellows accepting a ride from the Archon—there was far worse gossip to be had. Like a Fellows lying helpless, or futzing with a complicated device all along her leg, in the middle of the street for anyone to gawp at.

"This doesn't mean I'm grateful," Praxis said as soon as they were settled. She felt the familiar pull as the sleigh started up, jerking her slightly in her seat.

Lexthur sat across from her. Smiling pleasantly, as always. "I would never presume such a thing."

"Hmph." Praxis ignored him. She pulled off her glove, examining what little bit of the mechanism could be seen along her hand.

They rode in silence, and for nowhere near as long as Praxis expected. When they came to a stop a short while later, she glanced out of the window.

They were not at the Fellows' gates.

"I didn't think you'd want to make an appearance at home quite yet," Lexthur said, answering Praxis's unspoken question. He shrugged. "Of course, if I'm wrong . . ."

Praxis scowled. "No. You're not."

Lexthur nodded. "Shall we, then?"

Praxis heaved a weary sigh. But she accepted his outstretched arm, and she let herself be shuffled slowly inside of the dwelling before her. It was significantly smaller than her family's, of course, more equivalent to a Durlish townhouse as opposed to her family's sprawling manor. Lexthur led her down a main hall, to a quiet study not far into the home.

She didn't need to be told that this place belonged to him. That this was his study, in his private halls. Despite herself, Praxis looked around with more interest than she cared to admit. There was a comfortable-looking sofa, which is where he guided Praxis, and a couple of chairs sitting nearby. A pale desk along the side, a bookshelf brimming with volumes in what looked like at least four languages. A globe of the world, as well as a map tacked up along the wall. A gilded mirror overlooked the room, and another obviously magical painting stood opposite; this one was an abstract design, but the colors shifted like lazy pools, bubbling up and falling down in gentle rhythms.

"Thanks," Praxis forced herself to mutter.

Lexthur nodded, like it didn't even matter. "Is there anything I can do?"

"No," Praxis snapped. Then she made herself take a calming breath, trying to settle her temper. "That is, I'm fine now. I'll manage from here."

"As you wish." Lexthur pointed at her face. "Though that looks somewhat painful. You might want to tend to it first."

Praxis flushed. In the commotion, she'd almost forgotten about landing on her face. She hadn't taken the time to heal it up, so she tugged off one of her gloves and cupped her cheek, her skin warming and then cooling underneath her healing spell.

"You make that look so easy."

"It *is* easy," Praxis said. "If you're a wizard, anyway."

"Must be nice," Lexthur said. "Not to have to worry about getting hurt."

Praxis grimaced. "It's not *quite* that simple. Some things . . ." But she trailed off, shaking her head. She shifted, trying to turn so that she could get her leg up onto the sofa with her. Lexthur, to his credit, did not rush forward to help her with this part. Praxis's knee flared, pain driving itself even farther into the rest of her leg, and she fought hard to bite down on the cry trying to work itself up her throat.

"Gods," Lexthur said. "It's that bad?"

Praxis shook her head. "It's fine."

Instantly, Lexthur was on the move. He rounded to the far side of his desk, and began to rummage through a drawer. Praxis ignored him, waiting for him to leave—there were some things she wasn't willing to do in front of him, and unbuttoning the side of her pants to gain access to her leg harness was very clearly in the "no" camp—but instead, he withdrew a small leather case. He came back around, opening it up and holding it out to Praxis.

Praxis raised an eyebrow. "Um . . . ?"

Five purple vials sat in velvet padding, a long syringe sitting beside them.

"They call it 'glee,'" Lexthur said. "Though there's a long, proper name for it as well that I can never remember."

"Yeah, I know what it is."

Lexthur laughed under his breath. "I promise, it's not what people say. Well—okay, I suppose it *is*. But there's a medicinal purpose to it, as well. When used in moderation, it dulls most pain to a low ache, and is quite safe. I have it for an old sporting injury."

"Thanks, but . . . I'll be fine," Praxis said.

Lexthur shrugged. "Suit yourself." He rested the case on an end table beside the couch, leaving it open. "I'll be in the hall. Just shout if you need anything."

Praxis nodded. Lexthur let himself out, the door shutting quietly behind him. And so there was nothing to do now, but to see what had gone wrong. Praxis began to undo the row of buttons, fixedly keeping her attention turned *away* from the vials.

She would not accept still *more* of Lexthur's help. Not today.

LEXTHUR RETREATED TO the hallway, shutting the door quietly behind him. It would not due to hover over Praxis, to make her feel watched, rushed. There was a padded bench not far away, and Lexthur sat down on it, leaning his head against the cold wall. He kept half an eye on the door to his study, and the other half on a clock molded into the ice across from him. It was ironic, he thought, that everything had started in that very room.

He had heard the rumors of Praxis's return days before she actually showed up at the Fellows' doorstep, but at the time it had meant nothing to him. The network of idle gossip relayed the information, and Lexthur had filed it away in his mind as an interesting tidbit—nothing more. He suspected that her return would mean his social ban from the Fellows' parties would be lifted, and there it was, right on time. The messenger was a young man, barely old enough for his voice to start cracking, and it had taken all of Lexthur's self-control not to laugh in the boy's face. The party began in an hour. What had they expected, that Lexthur would simply up and follow the messenger back right then and there? He had sent Huxley in his place to relay his regrets properly. Quite apart from the fact that he'd long since buried away his affections for Praxis, Lexthur already had other plans for the evening.

What he hadn't expected was the mother.

Prestina Fellows. By all accounts, the ruthless matriarch of the family; technically subservient to Prawl in business matters, she nonetheless ruled every inch of her domain with an iron fist. Lexthur knew her some. They'd gotten to know each other a little when he was still young and foolish, besotted with the youngest daughter, and of course they'd brushed through each other's lives at political events and parties ever since. But most of their business operated in separate circles, their lives reaching each other by proxy, rarely overlapping.

Until that night.

He didn't question how she managed to gain entrance to his home. No doubt his staff would have opened the doors gladly, would have let her roam free as if she owned the place. It used to bother Lexthur, the effect the Fellows had on people. Rules did not apply to them. Doors were never locked. If one of them had wanted to come into his *office* and rifle directly through his paperwork, he doubted they'd be told "no." So the fact that she'd been allowed in wasn't so much the shock, as the fact that she'd chosen to do it in the first place.

His first glimpse of her was upside-down. For anyone else, perhaps, this would have been a shameful memory, a moment where, looking back, he'd cringe as he watched the ghost of his past scramble madly to his feet, covering himself in haste. And if all of this had happened a few years earlier, Lexthur might have done just that. But he was too far beyond such concerns these days—and, at the time, too stoned to give a single fart's worth of care.

He looked at her, instead. He was sprawled across his sofa (the very same sofa, he noted with amusement, that Praxis was resting on now), his feet thrown over the back and his head lolling off of the front, as if he was sitting in it, only upside down. He was still wearing his silk shirt, but looking back, he had to admit that he probably did not have pants.

Lexthur hadn't noticed this at the time, however, and even if he had, he wouldn't have cared. His party guests were still scattered all over the house, and the ones that were in the study with him immediately began to shriek and stumble over themselves at the sight of her. They raced to their feet, grabbing clothes at random from the backs of chairs and the top of Lexthur's desk. Prestina hadn't told them to leave—he didn't think so, anyway—but leave they did, and with no small amount of haste. Lexthur started laughing, watching all of those naked asses flutter past him one by one, tits and pricks bouncing in equal measure. He reached up and slapped at one or two as they passed.

"You didn't come to my party tonight," Prestina said once they were alone.

Lexthur looked up at her, inverted. From his angle he could see up her nose. He was surprised that her nostrils weren't flaring in disgust or alarm, and the fact that she didn't appear ruffled was a small jab at his pride.

"I already had a party of my own," Lexthur said. He swung his legs, toppling to the floor for a moment before pulling himself into a proper sitting position. Something poked at his thigh, and he found himself holding one of his syringes, the inside stained deep purple from frequent use. Lexthur frowned, disappointed that it was empty, and set it aside. Once settled, he rested one leg widely on the other, motioning for Prestina to take a seat in the chair opposite him. It was tipped on its side, but he sure as hell wasn't going to get up to neaten it. He was the Archon. She was a private citizen.

Besides, he doubted that he could stand straight, at the moment. The room hung thickly around him, hazy even without the thin layer of smoke lingering behind. Lexthur didn't like smoking, himself, but he made no protests as to the pleasures of his guests, so long as they made no protests to his.

To his surprise, Prestina did right the chair, and settled in it comfortably. She folded her hands in her lap.

"You really should have come," Prestina said. "Oh, I know that my modest little gatherings are not as"—she glanced around, taking in the bits of clothing still strewn around the room, the syringes and bottles littering the floor—"colorful . . . as the ones you're throwing these days. Still, I think you would have found it worth your while. My daughter was there, you know."

Lexthur huffed. "I know. I sent a meaningless counterinvitation."

"I know," Prestina said. "I'm surprised that even you would put carnal pleasures over such a ripe personal opportunity."

Lexthur frowned, certain that he'd just been insulted but not quite able, in his fuzzy mental state, to figure out exactly where. He squinted at Prestina, blurring her image until the years seemed to wash from her face. He was trying to see her daughter in her; everyone was always saying how much they looked the same, and rumor had it that the physical resemblance had only grown stronger in Praxis's absence.

He couldn't see it, and he shook his head in dismissal.

What had they been talking about?

Oh.

Lexthur waved his hand. "Your daughter has nothing to offer me these days."

"That's very small-minded of you."

"What do you *want*, Prestina?"

Prestina bristled slightly at the casual use of her name. No doubt even Lexthur, if he'd been sober, would never have dared to cross the borders of formality like that. You did not show disrespect to a Fellows, not if you knew what was smart for you.

Tightfisted, prissy-ass bitches, Lexthur thought to himself. Though Prett Fellows, he had to admit, had been a good friend to him over the years.

Prestina brushed her skirt, as if something as prosaic as dust or debris would ever have the audacity to land upon her person. "What I want isn't really important," she said. "Let's talk about what you want."

"I have what I want."

"Do you really?" Prestina raised an eyebrow. "Because I always thought you wanted power, Mr. Delford. Or was I mistaken?"

"I'm the *fucking* Archon," Lexthur spat back. "How much more power could I get?"

"Yes," Prestina said with a smile. The laugh that she *didn't* offer rang somehow louder than if she actually had. Lexthur felt it rippling through the room, drumming into him, pounding against the walls.

He shoved himself to his feet. He didn't really have a destination in mind, he just knew that he wasn't going to sit there and look into the smug face of the woman that had rejected him—or the closest thing to it that he was ever likely to see, anyway. Lexthur was an idiot, before: they looked exactly the same.

He veered over to his desk, where a case of purple vials lay open and inviting. Most of them were gone by this point, used up by either him or his guests, but a few of them still lay there in their velvet beds. They glimmered in the light of the lapus lumeni, as beautiful as any gem.

"Did you know that my daughter is still unmarried?" Prestina asked from behind him.

"Don't care."

"You should. Especially if you'd like to become the first person in the history of Bolt to claim the title of both Archon *and* Fellows at the same time."

Lexthur stilled. Unlike in other cultures, a newly married couple assumed the last name of the most financially successful individual. "Fellows," over the years, had taken on a near god-like status within Bolt. They wore their name like the jewels upon their fingers. It was a prize too tempting to ignore, and Prestina knew that, but . . . Lexthur looked up. There was a mirror hanging on the wall, some meaningless decorative frill, and he caught Prestina's eye in the reflection. "She wouldn't want me."

"What makes you so sure?"

"She *wouldn't* want me," Lexthur repeated.

This was the one thing he knew for sure, in all the world. Even if everything were to turn inside out again, the ghosts of the dead breaking free and yanking down the souls of the living, just like they'd done before; even if the sky inverted, up became down, and humans sprouted wings; even if time itself reversed, and Lexthur could go back to the days when he'd been courting Praxis, and he had the opportunity to do it all over again, different, better, this would never change: Praxis wouldn't want him. He didn't know why, but that didn't mean it wasn't true.

Prestina gave a dismissive half-shrug. "That may be true. However, she really doesn't need to want *you*, so much as what you can offer her. Something you didn't have last time."

Lexthur huffed. "I doubt she's interested in politics."

"Nor should she be," Prestina said, a twist of offense lining her voice. "I'm talking about something much more important."

"Which is?"

"Control of the company."

There was no question as to which company she meant. Lexthur was quiet for a long second, then he burst out laughing. He grabbed a new vial from the case on his desk and threw himself back at the couch, slumping his ass deep into the plush cushions. He was still laughing as he picked up the syringe from the end table. However, as he pierced the vial and began to sucker out the purple liquid, he realized with a cold horror that Prestina did not *have* a sense of humor—not if any of his reports were to be believed.

His laughter dried up, and he rested the syringe and the vial in his lap, still together and half-filled. "You can't be serious."

"Can't I? Let's not play coy: I know the oversight committee is eager to take it away from Prawl. Praxis—"

"Is a woman."

"—is a *wizard*. Openly, and internationally respected for her contributions to the field. There can be no question as to her legality." Prestina sat back, striking a remarkably casual pose for someone of her status. "You're not an idiot, Lexthur. Picture what it would look like, her power combined with your influence. Imagine the bid that would make."

Lexthur pictured it. Something had snapped in his mind, the haze of his thoughts blowing away, and in their place was a sharp and perfect image: the combined respect that his own achievements and connections would merit when stacked beside a *Fellows*. The way that such a marriage would transform him overnight, granting him access to Bolt's most coveted status. Lexthur Fellows.

He had wanted it once.

"I want to be perfectly clear here," Prestina went on. "If you're successful, *you* would have no say over what happens in the company. Praxis is the true Fellows, and Praxis is the one that would have ownership over the mining operations. You will make no attempts to influence her business decisions, nor will you attempt to brag of higher status than you'd actually have. You would, of course, be afforded all courtesy that a Fellows deserves, and in fact you would be in *my* place, essentially, and that's not a bad lot in life. However, should you attempt to upset that balance . . . well, let's just say it would be in your own best interest not to. Do we understand each other?"

Lexthur frowned. For one wild, irrational second, he considered arguing with Prestina—but he quickly realized that her terms still offered him vastly more power and influence than he'd ever achieve under his own family name. What difference did it make to him, really, how mining operations were handled? Leaving it under Praxis's hands cleared him up to reap the rewards without doing the actual work. He wiped the frown from his face and nodded at her instead.

"I understand," Lexthur said.

"Good."

"This still doesn't mean that *Praxis* will agree."

Prestina waved her hand in dismissal. "She's a Fellows. She'll agree."

"But if she doesn't?"

"Then you must *convince* her, my dear boy," Prestina said. "That is what you politicians do, isn't it? Convince people?"

Lexthur scowled. Prestina made his job sound so dirty, although he couldn't bring himself to outright argue the point. "I suppose I could try."

"Wonderful," Prestina said. She was smiling broadly as she got to her feet. "I look forward to hearing of your success."

Chapter Sixteen

Praxis had barely gotten twenty feet inside of her family's dwelling when her father set upon her.

"*There* you are!"

"I did say that I was going out," Praxis said. She brushed past him. Though she'd managed to repair her brace, her leg was still killing her, and she wanted nothing more than to retreat to her bedroom and lie down.

She rounded a corner, but Prawl was still keeping up with her. Praxis ignored him. "Where's Kaedrich?" Her sense was muddied at the moment, the pain from her leg flaring up and distracting her every time she tried to reach out farther than a room or two.

"Busy with his work, little opal—which is perfect, because it means you'll have time to attend to your own."

Praxis groaned. "Really, Daddy? You're not even going to give me the day?"

"Praxis, I'm not going to pretend to be an expert for how they do things in Durland, but here, we do not *waste time*. Especially when there are pressing deadlines to be met."

"I'm not—" Praxis started, but cut herself off. Pain spiked up from her knee, driving in so sharply that it seemed to spread to her entire body all at once. She caught herself against the nearest wall, pressing her forehead against the ice. Cold leached into her skin, numbing her skull, but it wasn't enough. She felt her fingers involuntarily curl into fists, felt her leg jerk out at the confused jumble of instructions she'd inadvertently sent it. It was all she could do to click her thumb, disengaging the system. She heard her foot *thump* back to the floor as she rode out another wave of nauseating pain.

"*Praxis!*"

Her father's voice cut in, temporarily elbowing the pain aside. Praxis shook him off, trying to find her balance. "I'm fine," she said, answering his question before he even asked it. "I'm fine."

Her father didn't believe her. Genuine concern twisted up his face. "You know, maybe you're right. If you need some time—"

"No." Praxis pushed herself off from the wall, clicking her thumb back. She curled her fingers in her familiar dance as she set off again— turning left, this time, instead of the right that she was planning to make before. It felt vitally important to distract him now, to get things back on track. "Let's get to work. What did you have in mind?"

They let themselves down the main staircase. Though Prawl was reluctant to move on from his daughter's incident, the work he had planned was obviously important to him. And so, slowly, as they made their way into the family's business branch, as they wound deeper and deeper toward the lapus lumeni division, Prawl explained his idea.

Essentially, he said, he was hoping Praxis could find a way to alter the lapus lumeni, so that the magical energy that was poured into them could be *stored*, rather than slowly converted into the bright blue light they were known for.

"Stored for *what*?" Praxis asked as they walked.

Prawl shrugged. "Later use, of course. At the moment, as I understand it, once the power enters the lapus lumeni, it becomes unstable. Even if someone wanted to drain it prematurely, the result wouldn't be worth more than a tiny spark. Isn't that right?"

"Essentially, yes . . . but since when did you have an interest in this? I'm the wizard, and even *I* find it boring."

"It's my *business*, Praxis," Prawl snapped. "I have to be interested. And just think of the potential!"

Praxis shook her head. "I admit: offhand, I can't think of any."

"Don't play stupid with me. You've seen the world. Every other developed country has been branching into electricity lately, except us."

"Because we don't *let* them," Praxis said. "Because it would cut into our bottom line, if people didn't need us to light their homes."

Prawl waved his hand in dismissal. "It's going to happen eventually—

even I can only hold back progress for so long. Is it really so hard to imagine that I want to find a way to capitalize on it, before I am forced to abandon everything I know when it turns outdated?"

"If that's what you're going for, this isn't going to help," Praxis said. "We *call* them both 'energy,' but they're really very different things."

"But the potential for use remains."

"Perhaps."

"Then it's worth exploring," Prawl said. He clapped his arm around Praxis's shoulders, bolstered by enthusiasm. "And who better to make this great discovery than my daughter!"

Praxis shook her head. Unfortunately, her doubts about the idea didn't matter. What mattered, Praxis told herself, was her father's salesmanship—and *that*, she had full confidence in. So what if there was never any practical application of these modified crystals, assuming that Praxis could get it to work at all? All Prawl had to do, Praxis told herself, was convince the Minor Conclave that it had enough earnings potential, and they would be obligated to freeze the bidding process. Then he would approve the patronage of an army, and Praxis could take down Lanali. What difference did it make, if everything fell apart after that? All Praxis had to do was prop things up long enough to get what she needed.

She could do that. *And you will do that,* said a voice in her head, an odd little rush of confidence. Praxis brushed it off, as easily as brushing the dirt from her coat. The first thing she needed was space to think. Which meant that she needed the pain in her leg to subside, at least a little.

Which meant that she needed her father to leave.

They had reached the lab by this point. Praxis took it all in with detached interest, assessing the equipment, the workspace. She would have been more engaged, if it wasn't for the knot of agony growing in her leg. It wasn't enough yet to flare up again and risk another collapse, but it was getting there. Praxis kept clenching and unclenching her teeth, riding out waves of pain that built like an incoming tide.

When at last Prawl left, Praxis did not waste any time. She all but ripped off the buttons running up the side of her trousers, and then, with shaking hands, she drew out the leather carrying case that she'd buried deep in her coat. Praxis had pointedly given it back to Lexthur when he'd reentered the room, only to steal it later while his back was turned—thus, she reasoned, she had not accepted his gift, and therefore she owed him nothing.

The purple vials glinted up at her, their lush color as inviting as a queen's bed. Praxis gathered up one of them, along with the syringe, and stuffed the rest of it back into her coat. She had to steady herself against one of the large slab-tables that took up most of the lab's floor space as another wave of pain crashed over her. When it was done, she did not think—she jabbed the needle into the flesh above her knee, pressing the end of the syringe down.

Instantly, relief began to flood through her. Praxis almost cried as the pain fled back into the core of her knee, like a retreating army. She stood there for a moment, just breathing in the cold air.

"You certainly don't waste time, do you?"

Praxis jumped at the voice. She dropped the syringe into the nearest drawer, slamming it shut. Her eyes were already narrowing as she turned around.

"What are *you* doing here?" she asked. Carefully, Praxis arranged her long coat to cover the exposed portion of her leg.

"Thank you, little sister," Praine said as he strolled casually into the lab. "It's nice to see you, too."

"I asked you a question."

Praine held out his open hand. Resting in the middle of his palm was a silver bell with a crystal handle, a traditional symbol of friendship and good fortune that was often given out for weddings, coming-of-age celebrations . . . new jobs.

He smiled at her. "I came to wish you well. I know you'll make Father very proud."

Praxis regarded the bell for a moment. The base swept gracefully down like a ballgown, and the silver was carved with patterns of frost and tundra lilies. She hated the idea of accepting anything from Praine. She snatched it out of his hand and tossed it into a wastepaper basket sitting in the corner, where it landed with a melodic crash, the handle shattering on impact.

"Thank you."

Praine continued to smile benignly, as if none of this was the slightest bit offensive. He tucked his hands into the pockets of his rippling green coat, far more vibrant than anything nature could provide. He strolled around one of the lab's many worktables, looking about the room as if he'd never had a chance to examine it before. "So! You've decided to join us after all."

"Temporarily," Praxis said.

"Of course. And might I say, we couldn't be luckier than to have a wizard of your skill taking up the mantle of this department—for however long you might grace us with your talents."

"I don't have time for games, Praine. Either say what you came here to say, or leave me alone."

Praine shook his head. "You might not believe this, but I really have missed you, Praxis. You bring such *spark* to our family dynamic. It's a quality many of the rest of us are sadly lacking."

"Uh-huh. Is that all?"

"No," Praine said. He moved a few steps closer, and Praxis had to resist the urge to move a few steps back. They were on the same side of the worktable, now, and Praine's smile was so earnest that his teeth shone in the light of the lapus lumeni overhead.

A spark of magic was fighting to snap to life behind her eyes. Praxis did her best to tamp it down, lest stray bursts of flame start spitting forth from her fingertips. If he took *one step* closer . . .

He didn't.

"If you think you can keep it a secret, you're wrong," Praine said, instead. He leaned in, just enough to lower his voice to a stage whisper. *"I know."*

Praxis blinked. A parade of her secrets danced on the back of her eyelids: her attraction to women, her disabled leg, Kaedrich's identity, the trip that Praxis had made to the former family jeweler, the leather case sticking half-out of her pocket. Any one of these had the potential to destroy something dear to her, if placed in the wrong hands.

She said nothing. Watched as her brother spread his hands, his rings catching in the light. He shrugged, exaggerated like a pantomime, his palms upturned. "Sorry."

"I doubt that."

Praine laughed. "Praxis, relax. I'm joking with you. Though, honestly, if you thought you could keep your deal with Father a secret, you're delusional. It's all he can talk about. To hear *him* tell it, he's already won back control of the company."

"Oh," Praxis said. She tried not to let her relief out all at once. "Well . . . maybe he has."

Praine shook his head. "No. Though I do applaud his efforts—it's nice to see the old man still cares enough to fight for what he believes in. I have to admit, his heart hasn't seemed to be in it these last few years."

"What do you mean?"

"Just a feeling," Praine said. "It might be nothing . . . but it seems like he's been more withdrawn lately. Distracted." He grinned. "It's kind of you to help him out. It seems to be really lifting his spirits."

Praxis grimaced. "Oh *please*. If you think I'm doing this out of the *goodness of my heart*—"

"So there is a price."

Praxis cut herself off. She shut her mouth, cursing her loose tongue. What was it, she wondered, about family? So easily able to worm themselves underneath her skin, so easily able to get her to speak without thought.

Then again, it's not like her terms with her father were terribly confidential. If she was successful, they would all know soon enough.

A moment passed, two. Praine glanced at a scrap of crystal on the worktable, and he picked it up to examine. "Have you heard that Lorric is putting in a bid?"

If this was supposed to get a reaction out of Praxis, it didn't. "I'm not interested in family politics."

"I think it's a bit late to be claiming *that*, sweet sister. You've thrown your favor in Father's camp—unofficially. You might as well go ahead and take a proper stand."

"*This* isn't a proper stand?" Praxis asked. She swept her arm wide, to indicate the lab, the workshops, the entire lapus lumeni division spreading out around her like a nervous system.

Praine inclined his head. "Point. Though I think you and I both know I meant in the bidding."

"I'm not bidding."

Praine laughed. "No, I'd certainly hope not. Give the rest of us a chance." He set the crystal down, and now he took the step. "I'm talking about casting your support for someone that *is* bidding. Officially. Your favor would go a long way toward fattening someone else's bid."

"You mean *your* bid."

"Yes," Praine said.

Praxis laughed. She didn't really *mean* to, but it came out anyway. The rules of bidding were a complicated dance, and not one Praxis was terribly familiar with. She knew the prospective heir had to submit a proposal, a detailed summary of what they planned to do with their inheritance, if granted. She knew that family members as young as fifteen could cast their endorsements, on the record, and that *which* family members were on your side, and how many of them you had, could go a long way in swaying the oversight committee. She knew her endorsement was likely to be courted by each of her brothers, now that she was here, though she'd assumed they would do it out of a sense of *obligation*.

Now here Praine was, acting as if her voice actually mattered, as if she was someone of influence, as if—

Seven hells. Praxis stopped laughing.

Praine was acting as if Praxis was a respected wizard, recently made head of the lapus lumeni division.

A prickly sensation settled over her skin. Praxis was used to the idea of being separate from her family—and therefore, of her opinion carrying little weight.

Praxis shook her head. "No."

"You haven't even heard what I'm offering you."

"I don't need to," Praxis said. "I'm not endorsing you. I'm not endorsing *anyone*—and you're welcome to spread the word on that. I'm not getting involved."

She turned away, attempting to bury herself in her work. Unfortunately, she hadn't *started* anything yet, didn't even have any ideas where *to* start on the task her father had saddled her with. That didn't stop Praxis from moving things from one area to another, from lighting one of the fiddly little burners in the instruments strewn across her worktable, from stacking together some papers that may or may not be related into a single pile and tapping them twice against the tabletop to neaten them.

"If you're worried about offending Father—"

"I'm not."

"—then you should know that your endorsement has no impact on whether or not the oversight committee is going to rule in his favor. It's a completely separate process."

"Thanks for the civics lesson. Now, if you don't mind, I really do have to—"

"Praxis," Praine said, and something about his voice made her stop. She couldn't quite place what. "Praxis . . . I know we've never been the dearest of friends—but nor have we ever had cause to quarrel. This *looks* self-serving, and I'd be lying if I said I didn't have a lot to gain from your support. But really, this is in your own best interest, as well."

Praxis laughed under her breath. "Oh, I doubt that."

"Really? So if Father fails, you're not going to want to make sure that the person who takes over from him is going to be on your side?"

"He won't fail."

"But if he *does*," Praine said. He shook his head. "Purely for the sake of argument, let's say his efforts are for naught. You have a rare opportunity to protect yourself in the event of *either* outcome. There are some people that would kill for such a chance."

Praxis glanced up, eyes instantly narrowed. "Would they?"

Praine held up a hand. "A poor choice of words. My point is, you can win no matter how the game is settled. Surely Father has taught you enough Fiddler's Dash to appreciate the value of such a position."

Silence fell between them. Praxis was already turning away, trying not to listen. "I really am very busy."

"Whatever Father has promised you," Praine said, "I will give you the same thing, twice over."

Praxis laughed. "You don't even know what it *is*."

"That doesn't matter. If he's willing to buy it, then we can afford it. And if we can't . . . Let's just say that I always find a way to honor my debts, Praxis. Can any of our brothers offer you the same?"

Probably not, Praxis almost said, but didn't. She bit her tongue at the last moment, folding her face into a scowl. A half-laugh marred her voice as she asked, "Does my support really mean that much to you?"

"Yes," Praine said. His face was still and deadly serious, a high contrast to the bright, pluming display of his clothes. "And if anyone else tries to get your favor by offering less, then they're either a fool, or hoping *you* are."

Praxis stared. She hated that Praine was right, but that didn't make him wrong.

"Just think about it," Praine said. He reached out, patted Praxis's hand before she could stop him. He turned to go, but just as he was starting, he stopped again. "Oh, and I *do* hope that you and Kaedrich will be joining the family for dinner again soon. It was so enjoyable to have you both there last night."

Praxis snorted, turning back to her work. "Sure it was."

"I mean it," Praine said. He smiled. "I'm so pleased you've found someone that makes you as happy as Kaedrich does. And he's such a delightful young man. So . . ." Praine spun his hand in the air, as if trying to stir up the right word. He snapped his fingers. "Delicate. Yes. It's refreshing, don't you think? It's not a quality often found in men."

Praxis froze. It took every ounce of self-control not to instantly whirl around—but any immediate, startled reaction would speak louder than her silence. She made herself glance up casually, as if irritated that he hadn't left yet.

Praine was continuing to smile at her. Friendly, controlled . . . and deadly.

Oh gods. *He knew.*

Fear sent Praxis's thoughts bolting in a dozen directions, like frightened animals. Denying it felt naïve at this point, but nor could Praxis bring herself to confirm Praine's subtle accusation. She swallowed down the lump in her throat. In a family like hers, secrets were a powerful currency, and now Praine held one of the most precious of Praxis's in his slimy hands. Two, really: her own inclinations, and Kaedrich's true identity. Praxis did not even want to consider what he could buy with those—and then she realized that she didn't *have* to consider it. Praine had already told her what he was shopping for.

In the end, he did not acknowledge what he'd said. He didn't need to. He gave Praxis a little nod, tapped the table with his ring as a kind of nonverbal goodbye, and let himself out of the door as if he already owned the place.

Chapter Seventeen

"*I* WAS HOPING I'D been misinformed," Kaedrich said as she stood in the door of the lab, a sour feeling knitting her insides together.

Oh, how she'd wanted to be misinformed. She'd been having a bad enough day already—drifting from one Fellows' department to the next, taking notes and trying to look serious, ignoring the dirty glares being shot in her direction, hoping her every question didn't reveal the depths of her ignorance when it came to matters of the mining business. The *only* bright spot had been the two hours she'd gotten to spend in Prett's law office. More library than office, really, the room had been an expansive space of worktables, bookshelves, and reading alcoves, and Kaedrich could have easily wiled away the rest of the day there. It also didn't hurt that Prett had somehow managed to dig up Durlish translations of Yandosian newspapers. Kaedrich had gratefully retreated to one of the reading alcoves, pouring over the news of her homeland. Not that there was much news to be found, and not that the news she did have was *good*, by any stretch of the imagination—still, knowing was better than not knowing. That's what she told herself, anyway, as she hunted through one page and then the next, dread growing inside her like an oncoming storm. More than once, she'd nearly wrenched her pin from her jacket, from how hard she'd been rubbing at the metal as she read.

Still, nothing had compared to the moment when the rumor reached her: young Annelle, rushing into the law library with gossip that Praxis had accepted an offer within the company. Annelle told Prett first and

Prett, warily watching Kaedrich for her reaction, had told Kaedrich himself. Kaedrich had listened, rolling and unrolling the corner of one of
her newspapers as she did. "Excuse me," she'd said, rising to her feet and
tucking the pages into the breast pocket of her jacket. She'd held out hope
for as long as she could as she returned to the very same lab they'd all
gathered in that morning, a dead body at their feet. She *had* to have been
misinformed.

But now the door slipped from her cold fingers, the truth revealed.

She wasn't misinformed.

Praxis was seated at a high table, a mess of papers stacked around her,
pale blue gems dotting the tabletop and holding the pages down like
paperweights. She wore no gloves as she worked, her fingers stained with
ink and singed with red patches. Her hair stood up in the middle, as if
she'd been running her hands through it and tugging in frustration.

She looked up now, at the sound of Kaedrich's entrance—but only
long enough to be dismissive as she turned away once more.

"I'm busy, Kaedrich."

"Yeah, I can see that," Kaedrich said as she stepped farther into the
lab. "I thought we weren't going to get involved."

Praxis said nothing, just scribbled some more notes on a spare bit of
paper near her elbow.

Kaedrich sighed. Without a word, she walked over to the table and
picked up one of the gemstones. It was a chunk about the size of her fist,
raw and unpolished. Its cloudy surface glowed faintly against her skin,
turning it chalky.

"Is this lapus lumeni?" Kaedrich asked. She'd never seen it in its natural
state, and this question, while meaningless, was the closest Kaedrich could
make herself toe to the truth.

Praxis nodded, distracted. She flipped one paper over, reading the
back. Handwritten notes, complete with sprawling calculations and dia-
grams, stared back at her. Praxis chewed her bottom lip as she read through
it all.

"Praxis, you've never wanted anything to do with the company,"
Kaedrich said finally, after several long moments of watching Praxis ignore
her.

Praxis shrugged. She tucked a stub of hair behind her ear, and it instantly fell forward again. "Times change."

"You don't. Not like this. What's happened?"

"Nothing," Praxis said. She bent farther over her work, resting her
head on her fist to avoid looking at Kaedrich.

"Really? So you expect me to believe that you just *suddenly*, for no reason, decided you wanted to embroil yourself in your family's business?"

A dismissive shrug. "Looks that way."

Kaedrich sighed. "You know, you're really not as good of a liar as you like to think you are. Not to me, anyway."

"I'm not *lying*," Praxis snapped. She flipped another page. "It just seemed like the right course of action. I think we need to."

"No—what we *need* is to keep our distance. That's what we agreed to, remember?"

Praxis slammed the paper down, finally turning to scowl at Kaedrich. "It's a bit late for *that*, don't you think?"

Kaedrich's thumb found Prawl Fellows's ring as memories of her morning swirled around her. Kaedrich swallowed. "I didn't have a choice. You know that."

"That's convenient."

"Look, *you're* the one who's always insisting we need your family's help to defeat Lanali! You want me to tell your father 'no,' and walk away from all this? Because I'll do it. I'll do it *right now*, and we can leave by tonight."

Praxis rolled her eyes. "Don't be stupid."

"I'm not! In fact, for the first time since arriving, I think I'm actually seeing things clearly."

It was true. Seeing Praxis here, absorbed in her work, suddenly it felt as if everything that had happened since coming to Yandosia was as clear as the diamonds embedded in the walls. Kaedrich had suggested leaving before, but now—now she knew they had to. The certainty of it settled firmly in her gut, an ancient and primal need to retreat from this place of danger. She'd been stupid to agree to any of it in the first place. Kaedrich came around the table, but when she reached for Praxis, Praxis shifted away.

"I know you think we need some kind of support," Kaedrich said, her voice soft, "but Praxis, *we don't*. We can figure this out on our own, I promise. After everything we've been through—"

"That's exactly why we *can't* do it alone," Praxis said. She looked up, her brow and her voice both leveling. "Or did you forget what happened, the last time we tried that?"

Praxis searched Kaedrich's face, naked fear clearly visible in her eyes. Her eyes, which darted from point to point across Kaedrich's cheekbones and brow, her lips, her nose, as if grounding herself against each familiar feature.

Kaedrich looked down. The raw lapus lumeni was still in her hand, and she ran her finger along the rough edge.

Of course she hadn't forgotten. You don't forget the moment when you're convinced you're going to die. That moment haunted her, every day, every breath. The time she'd bargained for had finally arrived—Kaedrich had known that, had *known* that, seared into her soul, more certain than anything she'd ever felt before or since. That this was *it*. The moment was *here*. Kaedrich had stepped forward, knowing full well what was about to happen.

But then . . . Kaedrich frowned as she turned the lapus lumeni over in her hands. Her memory of what happened next was tattered, like a battle-scarred banner. Strips slid through her fingers whenever she tried to pick it up. Something had *happened*, though. Something to save her life.

She'd come so close to death, closer than she'd ever thought possible, and fate had given her a second chance.

Kaedrich raised her head. Her shoulders squared.

"But that's the point," Kaedrich said. "I *didn't* die, Praxis. We survived, both of us. We can survive again. I know we can."

Praxis's face iced over. "You don't *know* anything."

"*Yes*, I do. I know it's going to be hard. I know we're going up against odds that don't exactly run in favor of us having a nice old age together. I know we should get help, and I know your family is *capable* of providing it, but love, they're *not going to*. Don't you get that, by now? We're wasting our *time* here!"

"It's not a waste! It's *tactical*. It's *safe*. For sanity's sake, Ella, what do you expect us to do without it? Storm the palace? Sit Lanali down, and hash it out over a cup of coffee?" Praxis snorted—a messy, ugly sound. "Going up there now is a death wish."

"Better than sitting here doing nothing! Don't you get that? I *can't* ignore it any longer. She's up there right now, doing Perlandra-only-knows-what with my country, and I *have* to try to stop her. I have to. And maybe . . . maybe you're right, maybe there's nothing I can do, maybe I'll die in a pointless effort, but at least I'll be *trying*. Don't you understand? I just . . . I just want us to go *home*."

"I *am* home."

Kaedrich took a step back. Her whole body was cold, as if she'd just plunged into the seas around Yandosia.

Instantly, Praxis was deflating. The fight had left her face as her shoulders slumped, as she tried to reach out to Kaedrich—only this time it was

Kaedrich's turn, to step back even farther, cold air rushing in to fill the
void.

Praxis's hand fell, useless, between them.

"Ella, I'm sorry. I didn't mean it like that."

"I think you did."

It was the wrong thing to say, for both of them. Praxis hardened, her
whole body growing tense. She turned away, back to her work. "Fine. If
that's what you think, then maybe you should just go," Praxis said. "I
have a lot of work to do."

"Yeah," Kaedrich said. She set the lapus lumeni down, the gem settling
with a heavy *thunk* on the table. "You certainly do."

Kaedrich's anger propelled her before she could question herself. She
thought she heard a sharp breath, the beginning of a "Kaed—", but the
door was already swinging shut behind her.

THE FACT THAT foreign newspapers had nothing of substance to report coming out of Durland did not, however, mean that nothing was
happening in Durland.

On the contrary, there was a lot happening. Durland's borders were
under lockdown, with only the most essential traffic being allowed to
pass through; incoming carriages and cargo were thoroughly searched,
motives questioned, crossers detained. It was, Lanali freely admitted, a
much unpleasant but sadly necessary byproduct of the dangerous times
they were living in. Their long border with Rolmstan, a land where magic
still ran free and unchecked, made them vulnerable; the attack on Lanali's
life, which had precipitated her move to the palace, only proved that
point.

Closer to home, in the capital city of Monfort, the changes were
more popular. Sweeping reconstruction efforts had been set to work
repairing the damage that the last few years of economic suffering had
wrought upon the city. The availability of electricity was being expanded,
lines installed in crisscrossing segments over most of the districts. Roads
and buildings, long since fallen into disrepair, were being torn up and
torn down and rebuilt stronger than ever before. Granted, there were a
few grumbles about the smog beginning to creep into the city, but that
couldn't be helped. And look! Gleaming new construction peppered the
streets all up and down the slopes of Monfort—along with the ubiquitous presence of the blue-and-white uniform of the reorganized and
restructured Durlish Authority.

It was good work, solid and well-paid: every volunteer to the army was set up with a job rebuilding the city, provided fresh food, clean housing, sturdy clothes. The poor had signed up in droves, the moment the reconstruction efforts were announced. There were to be no combat duties required, all of the town criers were singing. All the Pon asked for was hard work, an honest heart, a pair of strong hands. Fresh recruits set about the tasks, while officers patrolled the streets to ensure that indolence did not win out among the new ranks.

And from the top of the city, perched high in the clutches of the royal palace, the great and venerated Pon Lanali surveyed it all.

Sometimes, she still had difficulty believing it.

Not that she didn't feel she deserved her success, but Lanali knew well that *deserving* something did not necessarily mean you would *get* it. The world was cruel like that.

Not this time, though. This time, she had won. Lanali would wake up in the morning in a canopy bed ten times too large for her, surrounded by silks and satin and feather pillows; she ate breakfast at the same table that a high king of old would have used, the weight of power and history nudging her spine straighter; she had multiple teams of advisers, on everything from military readiness to internal revenue to the state of housing values in the heart of Monfort. It was a lot of work, far more than Lanali had ever anticipated, but she was managing. For now.

And now, finally, it was almost time. The cumulative result of years of hard toil and careful manipulations were nearly upon them— all Lanali had to do now was stay strong, stay steady. *Almost,* fate whispered into her ear constantly now. *Almost time, almost time, almost . . .*

There was really only one thing left standing in her way.

Well, sitting. Slumped, really, if Lanali was being honest. It was a pitiful sight, an unworthy block to a great and epic goal. An insult to the strength of Lanali's power and the breadth of her designs.

Nonetheless: Lord Redly Madgar, bound in irons, reduced to bones and rags, was the last knot that needed to be ripped out before the tapestry of Lanali's dreams could be completed.

There he sat, tied to a heavy chair, which was itself bolted to the stone floor of the dungeons deep in the belly of the great palace. His hair had grown unruly, falling in unrefined clumps across his dirt-smeared forehead. A thick beard floofed out from his cheeks and chin, dotted with flecks of dried blood and old food.

Traditional torture hadn't worked. Attempting to use magic to force-convert him into a loyal follower hadn't worked. Starvation hadn't worked. Bribery hadn't worked. Threats hadn't worked. Even her first attempt, appealing to his base need for bloodthirsty vengeance—that hadn't worked.

That one had come as something of a surprise. When he'd first been found in the ruined corner of the Council's Crescent, broken and abandoned by his so-called friends, Lanali was sure she could turn him toward bitterness. She saw the seed of it already, deep in his eyes, and every time Praxis Fellows's name came up, that seed had jittered, as if *waiting* to burst forth sprouts of hatred and revenge. Lanali still did not know the how or why or when, but one thing was clear: Lord Madgar hated Praxis now, almost as much as Lanali did.

And yet. No matter how hard Lanali had tried, no matter what logic she'd used to convince him, no matter what promises she made—did he want to kill Praxis himself, did he want to see her broken, did he wish a public execution?—nothing Lanali said had moved Lord Madgar's resolve. He would not help the Pon.

It would have been an impressive display of stubbornness and willpower, if it wasn't impeding Lanali's own plans so damned much.

Somehow, though, Lanali suspected this wouldn't be a problem for much longer.

Lanali folded her hands demurely in front of her. "Lord Madgar, I feel I owe you an apology."

Nothing.

He did not answer, did not raise his head. Did not even snort in derision. His chest breathed in and out, his eyes stayed open and unfixed on a point of the floor somewhere behind Lanali's skirts.

That was fine. Lanali did not need him to speak—yet.

"I believe we got off on the wrong foot," Lanali continued. "It's clear you don't want to help me, and I understand that. I even respect it, in a way. You're a man of principle—of rules, you might say. I have rules, too. Would you like to know one of my favorites?"

Lord Madgar continued to ignore her.

Lanali gave him a full thirty seconds, counted out in her head. Long enough for the pause to be noticed, to border on uncomfortable.

She reached into the pocket of her skirts.

"Never be afraid to capture a pawn," she said.

The soft *shink* of a chain. Lanali let the weight fall from her palm, catching it just before the last of the necklace slipped from her grasp. She held it out toward Lord Madgar. The end of the necklace swung down from her fist, just within his peripheral vision. Light from the high slit window caught the gentle curves of blue glass.

Lord Madgar jerked as it snared his attention. His eyes went wide, his face went pale. He opened his mouth to say something, but all that came out was a dry creak.

Lanali looked at the necklace. It was a delicate little thing, pale glass folded to resemble a bluebell.

"Your girls were most reluctant to part with it," Lanali said. She shifted her hand, letting each petal of the necklace catch the light. "Since they only had the one of these between them, I assume it used to belong to their mother?"

Lord Madgar wet his lips. "This is a trick."

"No."

"It is," Lord Madgar said, though his tone sounded more like he was trying to convince himself. "You couldn't have found them."

"Heathview School for Girls?" Lanali snorted. "You weren't even *trying* to hide them."

A strangled wheeze escaped Lord Madgar. "Pon, please—they're innocent."

Lanali made a noncommittal *hmm* as she disappeared the necklace back into the pocket of her skirt. Lord Madgar's wild eyes tracked the movement in jerky bursts.

"And yet," Lanali said, patting the pocket, "they're the ones who will suffer if you should continue to prove obstinate. It's a pity."

"I *don't know* where Praxis is!" Lord Madgar shouted. He strained against the irons that pinned him to his chair, his face stretched tight with fear and effort. "Dammit, woman, you think she would have *told me*? She left me for dead!"

"Then I suggest you get creative—because I promise you, that answer will not satisfy me much longer." She leaned in, cupping his filthy cheek in her hand. "You were her best friend, Lord Madgar. By all accounts, one of her only friends. Now, I think if you really put your mind to the task, you can surely think of one or two places she might be hiding. And if not . . ."

Her voice trailed off. Lanali smiled. Patted Lord Madgar's bearded cheek once, twice, as she straightened up.

The silence of the cells was interrupted by the loud *bang!* of a door slamming open somewhere above them. Lanali's jaw twitched as her teeth ground together. Footsteps slapped down the stone stairs, and soon the impression of Tol entered Lanali's periphery.

Lanali forced a cool smile. "Think about it," she said to Lord Madgar as she turned toward the door. As if this interruption was her idea, as if she was planning to be done.

She met up with Tol four steps from the bottom of the stairwell.

The Pon threw her hand up. "Whatever it is that you have to say, I don't want to hear it." She continued up the stairs, marching past him, her thick skirts brushing the filth of the walls.

"Good," Tol said, "because I came here so *you* could do the talking. How could you be so foolish?"

Lanali ignored him. The stairwell rang with nothing but the bitter heave of her breath and the clack of their shoes.

It wasn't until they reached the top that she spoke, and even then, all she said was, "I don't answer to you." She yanked the door open, storming out of the dungeons.

Twin guards snapped to attention as they passed. For a moment, Lanali considered stopping and reprimanding them for allowing Tol to pass—she had told them, very pointedly, *no interruptions*—but though it would make her feel a little better to blow off some steam, ultimately it would not help matters. Her staff had a way of treating Tol as the one exception to just about any rule Lanali laid down, and no amount of effort on her part had stamped that out.

It was probably her own fault. From the beginning, Tol had been there. Allowed access to the Pon when no one else was permitted, consulted on every detail of her ascent to power. He was not a public face, and had no legal standing in this new transitional government, but the inner circles still yielded him what they perceived to be his due deference.

She would have to do something about that. Soon.

"You're going to answer to somebody," Tol said. He did, at least, have the sense to switch his words to their native Aul, but his discretion did not stop him from seizing hold of her arm.

Lanali bristled. She stopped, only because if she didn't she would have tumbled forward in a graceless heap, and already there were witnesses to this confrontation. Footmen, guards, palace couriers. Tol had probably timed it such on purpose.

Every performer needs an audience. Rule eleven.

Lanali slapped him.

"How *dare* you question!" she shouted. She left her language such that their audience could understand her, tweaking her grammar just slightly. In the beginning of her great con, she'd affected a poor understanding of the Durlish language, and had been slowly scrubbing her speech "errors" one by one. Though she had sped up the process in recent months. "Unhand me! At once!"

Tol glanced briefly at the guards standing nearby. They'd turned, their hands shifting to the swords at their hips, though Lanali knew they were hesitating. *Damn them.* If Tol was anyone else, he would already be dead.

One by one, his fingers uncurled from her upper arm. He pulled his arm back, raising his hand wide so that everyone could see he'd really let her go.

"You should have involved me," Tol said. *"He can't be trusted with this much power."*

Lanali resisted the urge to roll her eyes.

The "he" in question was Lord Braynish, temporary minister of national defense. It was a new branch, overseeing what used to be the Department of Security, the royal guard, and the spymasters. It also positioned him as second-in-command of the armed forces, answering only to Lanali herself.

The appointment had gone through in that morning's session, which Tol had conveniently missed due to a trip to the city of Larnish to quell some pro-magic sentiments trying to take root.

True, it had been a risky move. Putting that much power in the hands of any one individual always was, but it was important for Lanali to have his complete support. And in order to do that, he needed rewards. Lavish rewards. Real power.

At least, as far as he knew.

"I know what I'm doing," Lanali said.

"Do you? I'm starting to wonder. This is breaking every rule we've lived by."

"It's one *appointment, Tol. I hardly think—"*

"I'm not talking about this one appointment," Tol said. *"Do you really not see the fragility you've surrounded yourself with? You're like a feather-glass spinner. And I fear what will happen when you lose hold of your thread."*

"I won't," Lanali said.

She let this hang in the air for a moment, as if daring Tol to challenge it.

He did not—or at least, not openly. There are some lines he still would not cross, but Lanali was beginning to see the struggle behind his mask. He had never supported this con, not really. Now look at him: every day, it seemed, he embraced still more signs of their backwater heritage, wearing them like badges of honor. The short-sleeved white suits, no ties, no adornments; his intricately braided hair had been growing longer and longer ever since the ghost incident; he'd even stopped trying to draw so much attention away from his few tattoos, the one he'd been given by his father, and the wave he'd stamped proudly across the back of his own hand three years ago.

It was pitiful. It was an insult to everything he and Lanali had worked for.

It would stop.

She smiled at him. A practiced smile, polished along every hard edge. *"You're right, though,"* she told him, extending her hand for him to take. *"I should have involved you, and I'm sorry. Come. I have a new task, and I believe it's one well-suited to your skills."*

Tol hesitated. Lanali could practically see the gears of his mind, over-taxed at trying to figure out what new angle Lanali was taking, what scheme she was concocting now. *Oh, Tol,* she thought wearily to herself. *When did we become like this?*

"What's wrong?" Lanali asked after a moment. *"Don't you trust me?"*

The smile that he gave her was one she'd taught him. *"Of course,"* his voice said, while his mouth itself said, *Of course not.*

Lanali only barely suppressed her smirk.

Almost time, almost time, almost . . .

Chapter Eighteen

KAEDRICH SPENT A good hour or more pacing the twisted halls of the Fellows household. Past rooms full of working servants, past empty corridors and lonely sitting rooms, past closed door after closed door. Remorse and the flat light of the lapus lumeni were combining to give her the mother of all headaches. Gods, what she wouldn't give to see *sunlight* about now. To stretch her limbs in the warm, open air, to breathe in the smell of trees and moss and damp soil! She missed *everything*. Her sense of home was buried so deeply into the core of her body that being apart from it was withering her, little by little. She needed to get back. Praxis had to understand that. She *had* to understand that. Kaedrich turned on the spot, suddenly determined to find her way back to the lab. To *make* Praxis understand, no matter what it took.

Although . . . what if Praxis already did? She'd said it herself, I *am* home, such conviction that it could have only slipped out from a place of truth. What if this was how Praxis had felt, every day she was in Durland? This restless twitch in her muscles, this unsettled tickle of her skin? Okay, so Praxis had rarely, if ever, talked about her homeland with anything less than disdain . . . it was still *home*, wasn't it?

Was it?

There was really only one way to find out—and though getting Praxis to talk about *anything* honestly wasn't an easy task, it was one that needed to be done. Apologies were already churning through Kaedrich's mind as she turned around and tried to reverse her path.

She checked the lab, but Praxis had already gone. A guilt swept up as Kaedrich let herself back out into the hall, but she certainly wasn't going to stay there alone. Besides, there was no guarantee Praxis would return any time soon. In fact, for all Kaedrich knew, Praxis might have been heading back to their suite even now, hoping to patch things up—and here Kaedrich was, looping them both in endless circles, wasting time.

She didn't remember, at the time, that if Praxis wanted to find her, surely her wizard's sense would have let her. Kaedrich wasn't thinking, reacting purely on impulse and instinct. Panic flared through her, and she traced her way back to Emerald Level as best as she could. She threw the door to their suite open, calling out, "Praxis?" as she entered—

But the rooms were cold and empty. Nothing but the small blip of Kaedrich's dark suit, in a sea of open blue.

Kaedrich sighed. She leaned back against a wall, head softly clonking the ice. The cold leached into her scalp, numbing her thoughts. Gods, she'd been so *stupid*, earlier. What she wouldn't give to go back and do things differently.

Regret wasn't going to help her, though. It was getting late, and the two of them had already made the mistake of agreeing to attend another dinner with the Fellows. Kaedrich had no idea what the reaction would be if Praxis chose not to show, but what Kaedrich *did* know is that she was not willing to risk the reaction of Prawl's generosity running out if *she* snubbed the family.

She entered the room alone twenty minutes later.

The sleeves of her newest suit were slightly too short, and the collar slightly too tight, but there was nothing Kaedrich could do about that. She tugged at the edges of her clothes, trying not to look too obvious about it, as she surveyed the room. All around her, Fellows spread like wild falcats, roving in packs. Kaedrich clung to the edges, hoping to minimize the need for interaction. Gods, where was Praxis? Without her, Kaedrich was a cart with only one wheel, lopsided, purposeless. Every time someone turned their head, Kaedrich looked away. She knew it was rude, but eye contact in these circumstances felt like a venomous bite, and Kaedrich wasn't willing to risk it. She shifted through the guests, hunting for a quiet space.

"Here," Prett said from behind her. Kaedrich turned, and found him holding a fresh glass for her. Kaedrich accepted it gladly for once.

"You looked like you could use the company," Prett said after a moment. He'd given Kaedrich long enough to take a drink or two, the wine already spreading warmth through her limbs.

Kaedrich tried to look more comfortable than she felt as she laughed off what Prett was saying. "Is it that obvious?"

"Not so bad, no," Prett said. "You hide it well. But I'm used to spotting discomfort. I work in law, remember?" He shrugged. "It comes in handy."

"You must also be used to hiding it, then," Kaedrich said. She nodded at the way he held his own glass with both hands, his fingers perfectly still. Not a single ripple disrupted the surface of the wine, even as they walked. "Praxis oversteadies herself when she's upset, too."

A single eyebrow quirked up. "You're good."

"Not really. You just happen to be a lot like your sister."

"I'll take that as a compliment," Prett said with a faint smile. He raised his glass in salute.

Kaedrich returned the toast. They drank in silence for a moment.

"Where is Praxis, by the way?" Prett asked finally. He brushed at the sleeve of his royal-blue suit, as if he didn't care, and so of course he did. "I don't believe I've seen her yet."

Kaedrich glanced at the drink. She swirled the golden liquid around the bottom of the glass. "Delayed. She'll be here . . . soon."

It was a terrible lie, and they both knew it. But Prett merely nodded, accepting the situation in silence.

When it felt like the air had hung long enough, Kaedrich cleared her throat. "Do you want to talk about it? What's bothering you, I mean."

Prett smirked. "Oh, I doubt you want to hear about it. It's just more family politics."

"Believe it or not, I could use something distracting right about now," Kaedrich said. She stared at her drink, trying not to think about their fight in the lab. "And trust me, nothing is more distracting than trying to untangle your family's conflicting loyalties."

Despite himself, a laugh escaped Prett. "I can't argue with that."

Kaedrich forced herself to look up. "So tell me."

Prett studied her for only a moment before he said, "Lorric has put in a bid."

Kaedrich frowned. She shut her eyes, dragging up a sprawling mental chart of the Fellows' faces. "Prenna's husband?" she said, taking a stab.

Prett raised his glass in a salute. "None other."

"Is he even allowed? I thought—"

"Only a direct heir can petition them to *open* the bidding," Prett said. "Once it's done . . . the net gets a lot wider."

"Perlandra's breath," Kaedrich muttered. "You people make every-thing so complicated."

"I suppose you prefer how the Durlish do things? Putting fortunes at the mercy of a fickle thing like *birth order*?"

"At least that's straightforward. Here, I feel like I need to study a primer just to know who's doing what."

Prett laughed as he brushed his overlong hair from his forehead. "Trust me, there is nothing *primary* about Yandosian inheritance law. It's a twisted game of favors and finances and popularity, and the rules are so technical that hardly anyone even knows it all. But at least it's based on merit." He paused, the furrow between his brow deepening. "Or it's supposed to be, anyway."

"Sounds like you have your doubts."

"No," Prett said, though he didn't sound certain of that. "It's just . . . unnerving, when something like this happens."

"How so?"

Kaedrich wasn't entirely sure that Prett was going to answer her, at first. He looked down, twisting the family ring around his finger with his thumb, then glanced about the room at large. He moved casually away from the other groups, and Kaedrich trailed after him. Soon they stood in a corner apart from everyone else, though Prett still lowered his voice.

"It's been, shall we say, something of an unwritten family rule that when the time finally came, it would end up being a contest between Prewish and Prommel," Prett started. "Truth be told, most of the family support has always gone to Prewish, but Prommel has a stronger pull with the Minor Conclave. They've probably both got strong proposals for how they want to use their position should they be granted control— I wouldn't know, but I assume they're both smart enough to do that—so *support* in this instance means everything."

Prett hesitated. He looked down at his hands, back up at the party. He squinted.

"Lorric's bid . . . I mean, it has no chance of winning, but now Prenna's going to need to pull her support from Prewish, to stand behind her husband. Their children, too. And Lorric's obviously not going to cast his support for a rival, so even assuming no one else is foolish enough to throw their weight behind him, that's *five* votes Prewish has lost in an instant."

"Forgive me, but that doesn't really sound like a lot," Kaedrich said. Even without trying, the parade of Fellows faces that she'd been speaking with lately felt endless, far more than enough to cover the loss.

"Maybe so. But anything that chips away at his strongest asset is . . .

disturbing." He glanced up—past Kaedrich, to the sea of his family's laughing, chattering faces.

Kaedrich turned, looking over her shoulder to follow the line of Prett's eye. She watched them all in turn, bedecked in shimmering dresses with high collars, thick fur suits of every shade and color. Prewish, in black, didn't appear ruffled by the news, but with his stern face it was impossible to tell his mood about anything. He was surrounded by his own family, his wife and one of his sons and his son's wife, a protective wall of support. His son, Tannem, had a young boy standing in front of him, his hands resting protectively on the lad's shoulders. The child was no more than four, but already he wore the Fellows face: impassive, disconnected, vaguely superior to the world around him.

Around the rest of the room, the family was more divided. Annelle spoke with Micadel. Pranders, portly and unremarkable, was studying a statue in the corner as if he hadn't grown up here and seen it every day. Prawl was at one end of the room, laughing at something Praine had said, while Prestina surveyed the room from the other end like a queen at court; a flock of her daughters-in-law and granddaughters surrounded her, hanging off of her every word. Lorric himself, man of the hour, sat on a sofa near the middle of the room, Prenna standing just behind and to his left; she kept smiling, answering questions put to her, though it was clear that she was keeping a watchful eye out as Prawl and Praine crossed the room, drawing nearer to Annelle.

It was all so much. Too much, really, for Kaedrich to fully understand yet. Unspoken loyalties wound like perfume through the air, a scent only the Fellows knew how to read.

When she finally turned back, Prett was watching her carefully. He looked so much like Praxis: a thin face, slightly effeminate now that Kaedrich took the time to study it; hair a little longer than the rest of his brothers, curling underneath the sweep of his ear; he had the same steady, unwavering gaze that Praxis used when she was sizing somebody up.

"You think someone did this on purpose," Kaedrich said. She didn't ask it. "That Lorric was *encouraged* to bid, so it would weaken Prewish's support."

"I think these are unbalanced times." Prett shrugged, a practiced indifference. "Anything is possible."

He smiled at Kaedrich now, but Kaedrich knew better. Prett wore his cheerful disposition as a well-tailored suit.

"But let's not talk about such ill topics right now," Prett said. As he clapped his hand on Kaedrich's shoulders, it forced Kaedrich to turn, and she spotted Praine making his way casually toward them.

"Prett," Praine said when he drew close enough. He nodded at Kaedrich. "Lord Mannly."

Kaedrich's cheeks warmed. She still wasn't used to the lie about her bloodline, and she doubted she ever would be. "Good evening, Praine." Hastily, Kaedrich remembered to tap her middle three fingers against her lips.

Praine grinned. He motioned grandly at Kaedrich, the purple fur of his coat outright *shimmering* in the light. "Such manners! I tell you, Prett, young people here could learn a thing or two about respect from the gentlemen of Durland."

"Oh, I don't know," Prett said. "I'd say for a generation that's already looked mortality square in the face, they're remarkably composed."

Kaedrich was confused for only the briefest of moments before understanding set in. Naturally, the whole *world* had suffered during the great ghost crisis three years ago—but there was something different about hearing someone talk about it from the perspective of another culture. Besides, it was hard to imagine *any* kind of crisis happening within these immaculate walls, never mind something of that magnitude.

"Yes, you would think so," Praine said. "But then, you're still half a child yourself, aren't you? Tell me, don't you ever get tired of the indulgence?"

"Obviously, if you'd been paying attention, you'd know I *have* gotten tired of it. I don't . . . go out like that anymore."

"True—though I hear from a reliable source that you haven't kicked quite *all* of your old habits, hmm?"

Prett flushed, just a little around the edges. "Where did you hear—?"

"Oh, just a rumor." Praine shrugged. "It could be nothing."

He flashed his grin again, and Kaedrich had the distinct impression of having spotted a wolf out in the middle of a quiet street somewhere. She only just repressed the urge to shudder at the sight of it.

Prett's eyes narrowed at his older brother. "You have no right to judge. If you had experienced it—"

"But I didn't," Praine said. He turned to Kaedrich, and laughed like he was trying to brush it off as nothing. "Ah, but we're boring our young guest here with all of this talk of the past. Tell me, Lord Mannly, were you lucky enough to escape the crisis up north?"

Kaedrich hesitated for a moment, her head throbbing with a renewed vigor. She had never felt an urge to lie about her experiences during the ghost crisis—indeed, for the first year or so, she'd taken almost any opportunity to tell people about how she and Praxis had plunged headfirst into the land of the dead on purpose, to try to stop Lanali from throwing the world into total chaos. But that was different: they'd been in Durland, where Kaedrich understood the rules, and she'd been using the story not to boost her own glory, but to illustrate the danger of the Pon, who'd been growing in influence every day since.

But in this case, it felt safer to keep her cards close to her chest.

"No," Kaedrich said, and left it at that. Though Praine waited for a moment longer, seeing if she would add anything to her story, and even Prett was watching her with an openly curious eye, she kept her silence.

Gods, Kaedrich thought to herself, *it's no wonder Praxis is such a liar.* Her chest ached, and the resolve she'd felt in the lab returned to her tenfold. If she'd ever harbored any doubts, it was clear to her now that she *needed* to leave, that they both needed to leave. Before the ice ensconced them both in the trap of their own falsehoods.

OF ALL THE changes since getting together with Kaedrich—and there were a lot of them, everything from the subtle nuances of learning to share her time and her life with somebody, all the daily habits that Praxis had only ever seen from afar now right in her face, to the familiarization she had joyfully undertaken to learning the topography of Kaedrich's body and all the unique little ways she preferred it stimulated, to the growing sense of rightness that nestled deeper into Praxis's chest whenever the two of them were together—perhaps the biggest change was simply this: Praxis didn't like to lie to her anymore.

Not that she'd ever relished it, before. There were people that Praxis took pleasure in lying to, and Kaedrich had never been one of them, not even in the very first days of their acquaintance, when Praxis didn't even know that Kaedrich was a woman. But . . . there were dangers in Praxis's life, and her cloak of lies had always kept her safe from harm. At times, it had kept Kaedrich safe from harm.

It was still keeping Praxis safe, though somehow that didn't help assuage the prickly feeling it left behind on her skin.

She kept noticing the lies now. The way they would pile up like dead leaves blown into the corners of her life. The biggest one, of course, was never far from her mind: that Kaedrich hadn't just come *close* to dying three months ago, but that she actually *had* died; that Praxis had used her power over the Beacon of Souls to bring Kaedrich back to life; that her actions had stripped her of her status as Lady of Souls, but also, oh, as if that wasn't enough, that the choice she made had also destroyed their one and only chance to *try* to stop Lanali from seizing power.

The guilt of that one struck her at the most random times. Not guilt over what Praxis had *done*—Praxis would never consider feeling guilt about *that*, and told herself constantly that she would make the same choice again if she had to—but rather the fact that she had to conceal something so enormous. Kaedrich was still laboring under the assumption that their plan had failed simply because they'd run out of time. If she ever knew the truth . . .

Well. That wasn't worth dwelling on.

But that lie was one thing. A burden that Praxis would have to bear for the rest of her life. It was difficult to accept, but that was just how it had to be.

It was all of these *other* lies that were truly beginning to gnaw on her: the details of her meeting with Lexthur; her *second*, unplanned, meeting with Lexthur, and the vials she'd stolen from him; the pain shooting through her knee; Praine's threat looming overhead; the pendant she'd commissioned, to look like the Beacon of Souls. All of it was too much to be borne, and so Praxis had done what she always did when faced with a difficult problem: she ran away from it.

This, too, she wasn't proud of, but there it was. Not even two minutes had passed since Kaedrich left the lab, when Praxis, too, walked through the door.

At first, she even lied to herself. Praxis told herself that she was going to catch up with Kaedrich, and attempt to clear the stale air that had settled between them. She had *tried*, after all, as Kaedrich was leaving—calling out, just as Kaedrich let the door slam shut behind her. Surely, then, it made sense for Praxis to go after her? Why, wasn't this even a positive step forward for Praxis, because look: personal growth! That was something, wasn't it?

This sense of superiority over her past self mingled with the increased sense of peace from the injection she'd taken, and it guided Praxis forward, all the way out of the business district. She slipped into the halls of Topaz Level, where the Fellows housed a collection of art galleries.

By the time she'd looped past the last painting, however, she could no longer lie to herself. Praxis wasn't even *trying* to find Kaedrich at this point. The movement was simply something to *do*, some way to stay

ahead of the guilt over what Praxis had said during their fight. *I am home.*
Gods, how could she have been so stupid? The ice had never been home,
not even while Praxis was growing up. How many times had she planned
her escape, during the endless stretch of her childhood?

The heat of Praxis's scar flared, so hot that she had to pause to clutch
it. The pain of it cut through even the haze from the injection, churning
just beneath the skin. Praxis's teeth ground together, and she leaned her
forehead against the cold of the ice. "Not now," she grumbled, trying the
sound of the words out like a mantra on her tongue.

The sound of approaching voices cut through, snaring Praxis's attention. Just servants, probably, but—gossip, in a place like this, could
be more deadly than the midnight vipers of Tjalava. Panicking, Praxis
shoved herself off the wall and began to lurch down the hallway. The pain
in her wrist made it difficult to concentrate on the curl of her fingers,
and twice Praxis stumbled forward and had to catch herself. Dammit,
she would never make it out of sight, not by the time the voices reached
her—already, they were drawing close.

But then, like a gift from the gods, there: up ahead, a familiar bookcase.
Built straight into the wall, one of hundreds like it sprinkled throughout
the Fellows household. It meant nothing to anyone—except, perhaps, a
wizard.

Praxis hurried over to it, muttering a passphrase as she reached up to
trace her finger along the edge of the shelves. The voices were nearly
to the corner now, almost within view, and Praxis cursed under her
breath as the bookcase slowly, *slowly*, turned on point, revealing a passage
beyond.

She darted into the space behind it, tucking herself out of sight just as
the voices came into the hallway. With a tap, the bookcase rotated back
into place and Praxis leaned against the backside of it, shutting her eyes.
She tried to focus her magic, but the pain in her leg was making it hard
to concentrate. Always, gnawing at her, distracting her, a constant jab
that set her teeth on edge and disrupted her senses. Praxis gritted her
teeth, trying to fight through it. There: an idea of her world resolved
around her, the servants breezing past her hiding spot with no apparent
interest.

Praxis let go of it with a sigh of relief. Her world shrank back down,
nothing but the tunnel all around her and the whale bone of the bookcase
at her back. She rubbed at her eyes, which had grown dry with the effort.
What are you even doing here? A whisper in the back of her mind, doubt-
ing herself, but it was right. There was still so much work to be done, and

brooding about Kaedrich wasn't going to help. Praxis needed purpose, yes, that much she could tell even without the cold voice in her mind. Perhaps that was all she'd *really* meant, when she said she was home; that now she had a task at hand.

It was a terrible lie, not enough to distract her from her discomfort. Still, any lie in the darkness . . .

This is when something brushed against her mind. In the darkness . . . Praxis had already turned back toward the bookcase, ready to leave, when something cold ran up her spine.

She couldn't quite put her finger on it at first, and she *should* have—that's the thing. She *should* have seen it immediately, because it's not like this was something that could be hidden. But she didn't, and her lack of seeing it, once she realized her mistake, is what sent a spark of magic down to her fingertips. Flames erupted from her fingers as she whirled around, as her eyes widened, as she took in the view of the secret passage trailing away from her, twisting and tantalizing like the perfume of an exotic beauty.

Praxis knew every inch of these passages. There were advantages, after all, to being a wizard, especially when you were a small and socially uncomfortable child, prone to rebellion. Praxis had spent a lot of time down here when she was young, one of the few places that felt truly *hers*. Even more than her bedroom suite. She found the first secret passage when she was just nine, a couple of months after Moc had come to live with them. It had been quite the shock, to touch a statue and have it move aside for her; Praxis nearly screamed, but it was a good thing she hadn't. Even then, something in her magic told her to stay quiet. Instead, she'd crept inside, the air stale, the lapus lumeni dim from lack of recharging. Praxis wasn't tall enough to reach the ceiling yet, and so her first exploration of them was in semidarkness. It had been such a novelty, so terrifying and delightful all at once, that she wasn't sure if she wanted to get them lit again.

Now here she stood, nearly twenty years since the last time she'd sought isolation within these frozen walls. Her breath hung as mist in front of her, cooling against her lips. Gods, how stupid was she, not to have noticed? It was obvious and everywhere, and yet so subtle that it blended into the background like camouflage.

Praxis let her gaze shift farther down the secret passage. The cold blue walls, the veins of brighter blue in the ceiling. Everything empty, even the shadows gone into hiding. The passage, lit all the way to the first bend, far in the distance.

The passage, *lit*.

Praxis's head tipped back, just enough to trace the path of the lapus lumeni overhead. She snuffed out the flames of one of her hands as she reached up, fingers brushing the rough veins. The last charge she'd given them should have faded long ago, but these were lapus lumeni with full bellies, the magic all but hanging glutenous from their middles.

Someone else had been here—another *wizard* had been here.

Recently.

Chapter Nineteen

THE DAY WAS not going especially well for Tannem Fellows.

This wasn't surprising. His entire week had been filled with one fiasco or another—at work, the markets were shaky, news of the Fellows' inheritance bidding having broken a few days earlier, and this was driving everyone to the brink with frustration and exhaustion and panic. Tannem himself probably hadn't slept properly since, though he was so tired that he couldn't quite recall.

Everyone at the markets expected *him* to have some inside edge, that was the real problem. As if, by being the third child of Prewish Fellows, his knowledge of the family dynamics could help them predict the uncertain financial future of the Fellows dynasty. Tannem didn't exactly *blame* them for this. Fellows' stock, while having taken a small beating in recent years, was still one of the cornerstones of the whole market. If it were to suddenly plunge . . .

But that wasn't going to happen, Tannem told himself. Yes, his uncle Lorric's bid had taken away some of his father's support, but Prewish was still more than secure. They just needed to be patient. Bide their time, attempt to shore up the loyalty of the rest of their family.

Which is what Tannem had been doing all night. All throughout dinner, all throughout drinks, all throughout Fiddler's Dash and Sailor's Choice, Tannem had been talking up his father's merits. His years of service to the company. His extensive knowledge of both the mines, and the physical gems themselves. His plans for expansion and company growth.

"And did I mention my father's meticulously trimmed beard?" Tannem said—slurred, really—as he finally sank into the depths of a sofa at the end of a long and grueling day. He held his glass up, half-empty, and pointed it at the woman he was speaking to. "A good beard is not to be taken lightly."

Jadie giggled. She skipped across the remaining space between them and, hitching up the skirts of her maid's uniform, climbed onto Tannem's lap. "Is that why yours is so *lush*?" she asked, her voice dipping low. She raked her fingers through the hairs of Tannem's face.

Tannem grinned. "It is." He reached up, cupping the back of Jadie's head, and pulled her mouth to his. Her hands left his face, dancing nimbly down the length of his chest, slipping around his belt.

Someone cleared their throat.

A groan of frustration escaped Tannem as Jadie sat up, pulling back from him. He kept his hand locked around her hip, holding her in place, a clear command that whatever this interruption was, they were not finished. Jadie responded by biting her lip in a devious way, and rocking once against the hardening swell in Tannem's trousers.

A sloppy smile laced Tannem's face as he leaned over to see around her, dragging his eyes away reluctantly. He was expecting, perhaps, his younger brother, come to interrupt Tannem on purpose. He was expecting, perhaps, another servant, come to whisk Jadie away to attend to Prestina's hair or something. He was expecting, perhaps, his wife, with news from her doctor.

He was not expecting Praine.

His smile disappeared.

"Uncle," Tannem said in surprise. He shifted higher, straighter, in the sofa, nudging Jadie until she slithered off of his lap and stood back, hands folded, head demurely downcast like a good servant. Tannem started to stand up out of respect, realized the obvious state of his trousers, and thought better of it. He motioned instead at a nearby chair. "Won't you have a seat?"

Praine. He was, of course, welcome in the halls of Prewish and his family, although the two brothers had never particularly gotten along. Praine regarded the sitting room from the door for a moment, biding his time. As both an older generation, and a family member working *for* the company, Praine's status was significantly higher than Tannem's, and the social dance of rank and importance must be preserved. Like brusker dogs pissing on each other to mark their dominance, Praine waited in the doorway until he was good and ready to enter.

"Forgive the intrusion," Praine said as he finally strode forward. "I was actually looking for your father."

Tannem frowned. His head was murky from drink and lust, and soured by the jarring change of his evening's trajectory. Thoughts came slowly, picked as if they were bits stuck in taffy.

"Oh," Tannem said. "I . . . He's gone to bed. Just a while ago."

"So soon?" Praine asked. He sat down across from Tannem. "I suppose a man his age does need the extra sleep."

"Yes . . . I mean, no. I mean . . . It's been a long day."

"Indeed. I understand you've been pushing quite hard, trying to shore up your father's support."

"I do what I can."

Praine smiled. "Just so. What a good son you are, to be so loyal. Well, you can tell your father that he still has *my* support, and that I'll do whatever I can to make sure everyone else stays in line."

"I see," Tannem said. "Um. Thank you. I'm sure that'll mean a lot to him."

"Not that he needs to worry," Praine went on. "The oversight committee would be fools to think anyone else could run this company better than Prewish. I mean, who else has the hands-on experience that he does? The many, *many* years of diving quite literally headfirst into the mines?"

Tannem nodded. "Exactly."

He was, he admitted to himself, slightly surprised to hear Praine speak like this. Though Tannem didn't know his uncle Praine as well as some of his other family, he had half expected that Praine might attempt to challenge Prewish in a direct bid for the company. Knowing that he wasn't came as something of a relief.

At least that's one we don't need to worry about, Tannem thought.

"And you can't fault his plans for the company," Praine said. "Why, expanding into the Foreshaw region alone is sure to double our output—if not more."

Tannem flinched before he could stop himself. He tried to cover by raising his glass to his lips. Of all the topics Praine could have chosen . . .

This was, perhaps, the one strong point of contention between Tannem and his father. Prewish had released his company plan that morning per the rules of bidding, and Tannem had been surprised to see this item on the list. It was a thought the family had bandied about briefly, a year or two before, but that Prawl had ignored in favor of expanding operations near Drift. Tannem had always thought his grandfather had made the right call—the deep seaside caves near the coastline at Foreshaw were too far away, small and remote, too hard to maintain a strong company presence without relocating a significant portion of trusted staff. Not to mention the danger, where erosion and washouts were commonplace. Prewish insisted the mining output there would be worth the extra cost and difficulty, citing the rarity of the minerals taken out of it in recent years. Tannem had managed to avoid the subject completely with the rest of his family, but it seemed his luck here had finally run out.

"Well," Tannem said. He studied the glass in his hands. "They *are* just proposals at this point. I wouldn't assume anything too far ahead yet."

Praine scoffed. "Oh, come now. You can't mean to tell me that you have reservations about the project?"

Tannem looked up. "If I do, it's only because I have a strong love for this company. But . . . I trust my father to see reason, when the time finally comes. He's a good leader. He'll listen to what people have to say."

"Which is precisely why the expansion will go through," Praine said. He gave Tannem a condescending smile. "Oh, I don't expect someone your age to understand the nuances. Believe me, your father is making the right call on this."

Heat flared in Tannem's chest. "My *age* is irrelevant. Grandfather himself was younger than me when he turned this company into what it is. I'm telling you, it's a bad idea. The costs are too high."

"In your opinion."

"In *any* reasoned opinion," Tannem snapped. "Figures speak for themselves."

"Your father disagrees."

"My *father* doesn't know everything!"

A heavy silence rang through the room. Tannem's face flushed, embarrassed and angry and righteous all at once. His drink had loosened his tongue, but dammit if this hadn't been building all day. Every time Tannem had to sing of Prewish's praises, again and again and again. Yes, Prewish was a good man, and a good choice to take over the company— but, for sanity's sake, the man wasn't *perfect*.

Tannem grunted and he leaned forward, grabbing a decanter off of a nearby table and sloshing a little more liquid into his glass. It burned on its way down, all in one gulp, and then he closed his eyes, biting down on his tongue to steady himself.

"My apologies, Uncle."

Praine waved this off. "No, no, it's all right. I'm glad to see you're taking such a strong interest in the company lately—even if you are somewhat misguided as to its operations." Praine chuckled to himself. "Still, it's a good thing for us that your father doesn't *actually* need to listen to you. No offense."

Tannem frowned. "I'll take a little, if it's all the same with you."

Another chuckle. "Oh, come now, boy. You really think that Prewish hasn't thought his position through? That he hasn't considered your figures, your perspective on the matter? It's a complicated business, running an operation like this."

"I understand that," Tannem said. "I just think . . . in this one matter . . . that there needs to be some further discussion before we move forward."

"Oh, I see." Praine snorted. "So you're smarter than your father now, is that it? More educated? More experienced?"

Tannem sat up, shaking his head. Dammit, this whole conversation had spun so far out of control. "No, I didn't say th—"

"And I suppose now you're going to tell me that you think *you* could do better?"

Tannem blinked. "N-no . . . ," he said slowly. "No, I . . . I'm not saying *that* . . ."

"Good," Praine said. "Because the last thing we need is some young upstart getting big ideas about how his generation could do things better. Trust me, things will be much safer in your father's hands for a few decades."

Tannem nodded numbly. "Yes . . . yes, of course."

"Well," Praine said as he stood up. "Not that this hasn't been lovely, but I think I'd best be following in Prewish's example and turn in, myself. Do please let your father know I was here, won't you?"

"I will," Tannem said. He looked up at his uncle. Praine was only slightly younger than Prewish, though he wasn't showing quite as much of his age yet. Still: there was a slight paunch about the middle, the faintest trace of lines mostly hidden by the wash of the lapus lumeni's glow. They were not young, anymore, these men.

Praine inclined his head. "Goodnight then, Tannem."

Tannem shifted a little straighter in his seat, tapping his middle three fingers against his lips. "Goodnight, Uncle. And . . . thank you. You've given me a lot to think about."

It's worth noting, of course, that up until recently there *was* another wizard roaming around the Fellows' tunnels.

Praxis realized this about ten feet down the length of the secret passage, her defensive flames sputtering with embarrassment. True, Trendall should never have been roaming the private halls of the family branches, his business keeping him solely in the lapus lumeni division, but that did not mean he *couldn't* sneak in. Praxis was the last person to have right to judge someone for nosing around where they didn't belong.

She snapped her hand shut, feeling ridiculous. What did she think, that somehow a wizard had snuck into her parents' dwelling without their knowledge, and been skittering about the secret passages like a rat in the walls? And for what purpose? The idea was ridiculous, born of a mind so riddled with paranoia and conspiracy that she couldn't see a simple situation for what it was: the snooping of one man, already dead. Even if the trespass *had* been for nefarious purposes, the deed had long been done. Praxis moved down the length of the secret passage, the ghost of Trendall's memory hovering in the back of her mind. Never mind that she had never known the man in life. He took on a shape in her perception, now: slippery and arrogant, never quite to be trusted. Prowling through the back passages of the Fellows' private living area, snooping on them as they went about their lives.

Nothing to see here.

The thought entered Praxis's mind without preamble, without ceremony. Annoyance and curiosity bubbled through her one moment, and then they did not. Praxis stood in the tunnel, blinking, shaking her head. What was she even doing down here, really? There was nothing to see, nothing to discover. She knew what she *should* be doing: getting back to work, trying to retrieve the line of thinking she'd begun to have about the puzzle her father had left her. The surety of this seized Praxis, a whisper through her mind.

She almost turned around. Maybe, if she'd been a little faster, she might have gotten out of there without incident. She was already curling her finger, already turning her head. But then a sigh of the ice brushed by her, a draft from the ventilation, and the hair on the back of Praxis's neck pricked with awareness.

Nothing.

It wasn't nothing. A trace of residual magic, drifting through the air. Something powerful and sloppy, something that had been cast in haste and without the proper skill needed to manipulate it. Excess energy teased at Praxis, something from farther down the corridor. It snared at her, drawing her along, her fingers dancing to carry her in haste down the secret passage. The image of Kaedrich's hurt face drifted through

Praxis's mind, but she shoved it aside, because this was too important, suddenly, she knew that now. This was . . . wrong. The magic led her forward, growing stronger, and Praxis's pulse kicked up the closer she got, the faster she moved. Another tunnel branched off just ahead, and Praxis threw herself around the corner, a blast of residual magic hitting her full in the face. Whatever had happened, it had happened here.

The corridor was empty.

But the magic that filled it, saturating the air around her, pouring against her, twisting into the fiber of her senses . . . the magic could not be ignored, or denied.

The magic left the taste of death on the back of her tongue.

PROMMEL FELLOWS'S OFFICE was a model of efficiency.

He would have it no other way. From the pencils spaced a quarter inch apart in his desk drawer, to the framed maps of all of the Fellows' tunnels that covered one entire wall, to the no-nonsense grid pattern of lapus lumeni veins in his ceiling, every bit of space had a purpose, and every object sat in a meticulously considered location. And it certainly cannot be said that the rest of the Fellows' tunnels were disorderly, no, not ever, but . . . there was a degree of *organic* arrangement to Prestina's decorating tastes. Rooms were plushly appointed, designed to make people feel *at home*. Even the opulence of the dining rooms or ballrooms, while never anything less than perfect, were about style, framed to display the Fellows' power to all who would behold it.

There was nothing powerful about Prommel's office, except for the power that it took for him to maintain such a utilitarian state, when opulence threatened to overwhelm him at every turn. But it had always been perfect, the exact respite Prommel needed after dealing with his family, the one place that was wholly his to control as he wished.

It was this sense of control that emboldened him enough to take his next move.

A knock sounded on Prommel's door, precisely on time.

"Enter," Prommel called. He sat at his desk, hands folded exactly in the middle of the open surface, face held patient. Behind him, he knew, his maps framed the view of him, the tunnels seeming to branch from his shoulders. His suit, steely gray, was the perfect match to his face.

Kaedrich's hand appeared first, curled around the edge of the door as he eased it open. The ring that Prawl had bestowed upon the young lord glinted, colors shifting, as the rest of his dark shape came into view.

"You asked to see me?"

Prommel gestured for Kaedrich to sit. There was a chair across from Prommel, brought in especially for this meeting—normally, Prommel did not provide one. Normally, there was no need.

But this meeting was different. This meeting needed to be handled with a great deal of consideration, and one of those considerations was with respect to the customs of Kaedrich's homeland. So they would sit.

Kaedrich took the time to shut the door behind him, before coming over and taking his proffered seat. He was still dressed from dinner, despite it letting out over an hour ago. Most of the rest of the household had drifted off to their separate corners by now, and it was this lull that Prommel was hoping to take advantage of.

Prommel wasted no time. "Where were you last night, around two in the morning?"

Kaedrich blinked. "Excuse me?"

"Last night. Two o'clock. Your location, please."

"Why do you want to know?"

A valid enough question, Prommel had to concede, but not one he was comfortable answering. *Because I'm not entirely convinced the wizard's death was natural,* he could have said, or *Because I can't rule out the idea that you had anything to do with it,* or even *Because I don't trust anyone to tell me the truth right now.* Each of these would have been perfectly true, but none really gave the full picture.

Because *if* the wizard's death wasn't an accident, then it had to have been an inside job. And this, Prommel suspected, was the real reason why Prawl and Prestina had not wanted to entertain the possibility, nor wished it investigated. Because to suggest such a thing would surely be the death of the company.

Prommel said none of this, however. Even when they'd discovered the body, he'd been careful to dismiss Prewish's concerns, when he'd spoken the same worry that had slipped inside Prommel's mind. Instead, now he opened his desk drawer and took out a couple of papers, white and clean, and spread them on his desk. "It's just routine," he said. "There have been a few security concerns lately, and I never did receive your credentials when you arrived. You understand."

Kaedrich's eyebrow raised up. "My 'credentials'? What is this, the army?"

"Hardly," Prommel said. "Their standards are far more lax than mine."

"You're serious?"

"As the sky," Prommel said. He picked up a pen, dipped it. Held it above the paper. "So last night?"

"Praxis trusts me," Kaedrich said instead. He raised his hand, his ring glaring in contrast against his skin. "And for that matter, so does your father."

"My father is not in charge of company security—*I* am. Now, I'm going to ask you for the last time: where were you last night, around—"

"All right, all right," Kaedrich snapped. He sighed. "I'm not entirely sure. I don't exactly know how to read your clocks, now, do I? But I was either playing cards with your father, or else I was asleep. Because that's *all I did.*"

"So you're saying you went straight from one to the other?"

"Yes."

Prommel nodded. He withdrew a little notebook from his suit jacket, flipping it open. "It takes you thirty-three minutes to get from my father's parlor to Emerald Level?"

Kaedrich narrowed her eyes. "How do you know how long it took me?"

"It's my job to know." Prommel shrugged. "And I have the guards tracking your movements."

"You *what*?"

Prommel leveled a heavy look at Kaedrich. "I'll not apologize to an outsider for doing my job. The guard outside of my father's parlor logged your departure at a quarter to two. The guard outside of *your* rooms didn't admit you until two seventeen." He flipped his notebook shut, tucking it away again. "You care to explain the delay?"

There was a pause as Kaedrich absorbed this. It was obvious that he wasn't pleased, but what could the young man do, exactly? Prommel watched as an argument churned back and forth in Kaedrich's mind, until at last Kaedrich's shoulders slumped.

"Well?" Prommel said.

"I get lost," Kaedrich said, his voice stained with defeat. "A lot. Okay? This place could be used as a torture chamber, just trying to find your way out of it."

Prommel raised an eyebrow. "Is that so?"

"Look, I don't know what you think you're trying to find out here, but all I've done since coming here is do what I'm told. And frankly, I don't know enough about the company to sabotage it even if I wanted to. Which I don't. Because I'm not a criminal."

"So you say. Convenient, though, that nobody else knows anything of your personal background, and that your homeland is not only too far away to check, but currently too unstable to be relied upon for information extraction."

"*Praxis* knows."

"That's true," Prommel said. He nodded slowly. "Praxis knows. And could easily be exploiting that knowledge for her own personal gain."

"Like *what*?"

"Control of the company."

Kaedrich groaned. "Look, Prommel . . . I promise you, Praxis has no interest in that."

"So you both keep insisting. And yet, within a week of her arrival, the inheritance bidding has opened, you've been appointed as Father's personal assistant, and Praxis herself has just taken control of the single most valuable division in the entire operation. It's a tidy takeover, don't you think?"

"You're insane!" Kaedrich said. "I'm not—She's not . . ."

Prommel let him sputter out. He could see a cloud of disbelief cross Kaedrich's face, and though it was far from an indication of guilt on either his part or Praxis's, it was enough for now. Prommel got to his feet.

"I'm going to need to ask you to stay here, for the time being," Prommel said. "Just until I can rule out a few things."

"*What?* No! I'm not . . ." Kaedrich shook his head. "Are you trying to *arrest* me?"

"That's a somewhat crude understanding of the situation," Prommel said as he rounded the desk and rapped twice on the door. He gave a little shrug. "But if you like."

"You can't do that!" Kaedrich said, though a hint of uncertainty damped his conviction.

In fact he was right—Prommel couldn't arrest Kaedrich, not really, not formally—but what would this man know of such matters? A Durlish lord, out of his element. Who could he even check with, if he suspected? As far as he was concerned, if Prommel said it, that made it true.

An instant later, Micadel opened the door. He glanced at Kaedrich, then Prommel. "Father?"

Prommel jerked his head, and Micadel made for Kaedrich.

Kaedrich leaped to his feet.

"No, wait! Hang on. Does Prawl know you're doing this?"

Micadel shot a nervous look at Prommel, but Prommel did not return it.

"My authority supersedes his, in cases of company security," Prommel said.

Another blatant lie. Prommel saw, out of the corner of his eye, as Micadel stiffened slightly at this statement. In truth, Prommel wouldn't dare risk offending his father in this manner, not if these were ordinary circumstances. But that was the key, now, wasn't it? Ordinary circumstances. You could say a lot about the events of late, but one thing you couldn't accuse them of being was *ordinary*. Not when the fate of the company was at stake.

Not when there was so much to prove. So much to lose.

So much to win.

"What's it to be, then, Lord Mannly?" Prommel said, holding his gaze and his voice level. "Are you going to cooperate with civility? Or are you going to allow this to get ugly?"

Chapter Twenty

THE MAGIC SENT Praxis's head reeling, bone-chilling terror and steely determination coursing in equal measures through her soul. Traces of what had happened hovered just beyond her perceptions, leaving behind only an empty ringing that crashed back and forth between her ears for several long seconds. Praxis staggered away from it, moving just outside of range of the worst traces left to linger. She leaned against the wall, gulping in the frozen air as she tried to calm her racing heart.

"What the hells?" she whispered to herself. She had never encountered anything quite like that before, that was for sure. Whatever had happened here . . . it wasn't normal. This magic was *powerful*, weighed down with its own importance, and thick as if choked on ancient dust. Why, if Praxis didn't know any better . . .

The first prickles of an idea began to cling to her—she clutched at the front of her shirt, instinctively reaching for the pendant of the Beacon of Souls for a moment, before remembering that the orb nestled there now was just a fake. Scowling, Praxis smoothed her shirt out, feeling silly. Of course it was impossible for a Beacon to have had anything to do with this. Whatever *this* was. Instantly, Praxis remembered the way it had felt, to let the weight of the pendant of the Beacon of Souls slip from her grasp, to watch it hit the waves of the ocean far below the deck where she stood. It was *gone*, she told herself, it would never be found. And okay, sure, *technically* maybe there were others, but what were the odds of that?

They'd been lost so long as to have fallen into myth and then very nearly forgotten. The odds of the Beacon of Souls being found originally, more than three years ago, had been extraordinary enough. There was *no way* a second would ever turn up.

No way, she told herself, as she turned back around, to face the tunnel, the mystery before her. None at all. Praxis pushed the idea forcibly from her mind, and stepped back into the fray of the residual magic.

She knew what to expect this time, and so the feeling was somewhat easier to deal with. Praxis let it hit her like a wave coming into shore: she faced it head-on, feet planted firm to steady herself. Just as before, shades of what had happened swept through her. Madness and fear. Desperation and need. A cold, steady rage, so well-controlled as to be smoothed into something that could almost be called peace. There was something familiar about it, in the way of a well-worn coat. Praxis shut her eyes, trying to step into it. If she focused . . .

There. A single image, faded as a memory half-forgotten. Trendall, huddled in the hallway, oblivious to the presence hovering at the place where Praxis stood. Praxis grasped at the image, clawing to draw it closer. Her perception of Trendall bloomed clearer, colors popping into sharp relief in her mind. The jut of his shoulders as he cradled something against himself. The skewed mop of his hair, unwashed for days. The glint of a knife by his feet, a thin slice of blood along the blade. One of his hands, stained a dried and crusty red, reached out to steady him against the ice, his fingers tracing the jagged groove of letters carved into the wall. The motion turned him, just enough, for a pale and otherworldly glow to creep up from where he held its source against his chest. Praxis felt a hitch in her own chest, someone else's excitement coursing through her, as a jolt of recognition struck her in reality. Praxis opened her eyes with a gasp, and in the memory that she'd plucked, Trendall whirled, his own eyes popping as wide and round as the Beacon that he cradled fiercely against himself.

"Two invitations within two days," Prett said as he strode up behind the stack of enormous pillows. "You'll want to be careful, Lexthur. Someone might get the impression that I *don't* loathe you entirely."

Lexthur's head tipped back, so far across his shoulders that his mouth had difficulty staying closed. His glassy eyes, not quite blue, stared up as he grinned.

"And yet, you're the one who keeps accepting."

"Do I have a choice?"

"We all have choices, Prett," Lexthur said as he righted his head. The back of Lexthur's lanky white-blond hair swung as he shifted upon the pillows, making room beside him.

Prett rounded the stack of pillows, his fists clenching and unclenching as he walked.

That was a lie, and both men knew it. Prett had been *summoned*; there was no other word for it. Two times in as many days, Lexthur had snapped his fingers, and Prett had come running like a brusker dog, and there was *nothing* he could do about it.

He remembered the first one as he looked down at Lexthur. There, at least, Lexthur had the decency to meet with Prett in his office. It was the day after Praxis had returned, the day after she'd rejected Lexthur's invitation. How delighted Prett had been, to see his sister snub her ex-lover so publicly as that. When Lexthur's man had arrived in Prett's law office the following morning, Prett had almost been *pleased* for the excuse to see him. It had been about two years—ignoring the odd passing at formal parties, the polite nods when seen in the street—and Prett was deeply looking forward to rubbing Lexthur's nose in Praxis's rejection of him.

Except that when Prett had arrived, a plate of zesty piconda had been sitting out on a table in Lexthur's office. Prett's face instantly soured, his joy replaced with bitter indignation; Praxis had accepted after all.

Worse, her visit had been the precipitating cause to Prett's summons. And though it had delighted Prett to learn that she'd rejected Lexthur once more, his new joy was again short-lived when Lexthur got to the heart of the matter: he needed Prett's help, in order for his plan to sway Praxis's decision to work.

"Fuck off," Prett remembered saying. His first impulse, and judging from Lexthur's blank expression, exactly what he'd been expecting. A quick tongue was a well-known vice of certain branches of the Fellows family, after all.

"Your sister's been gone a long time," Lexthur had said as he swirled the drink in his hands. "Perhaps she's ready to settle down now."

Prett had inclined his head, thinking of Kaedrich, and of Praxis's declaration in her mother's office. "Perhaps. But not with you."

A smile. Lexthur's smile, one Prett had seen too often to trust anymore.

"Even if it means she gets control of the company?"

This had gotten a laugh. The memory of it still echoed strongly in Prett's mind, sharp and cutting as it stretched out beyond the confines of Lexthur's towering office.

"Praxis doesn't care about that," he'd said.

Lexthur had taken his time, finished off his drink. Poured himself another. When he did start to talk again he spoke slowly, deliberately, laying out the benefits to Praxis, as if Prett couldn't figure them out for himself.

Prett shook his head. "That won't matter to her."

"You have to know that the bidding is coming soon, Prett," Lexthur said, ignoring Prett's argument, "whether any of you like it or not. My ministers are getting restless. Eventually, they'll work up the courage to open up the bidding process even if none of you request it. The only thing is . . . if they wait until Praxis *leaves*—and we both know she will—then you're going to get bogged down in the legal disputes. The *endless* legal disputes. As the winner is contested, and then contested again, and you, stuck to bear the brunt of this petty bickering."

Prett frowned. This was, perhaps, the first true thing that Lexthur had said since Prett arrived.

He'd stared down at his drink, so far untouched in his hand.

"Whereas," Lexthur continued, "if Praxis is here, and she *wins*—"

"Hers would be the most contested of all," Prett said.

Lexthur raised his glass. "True. But before that gets started, the very first thing she'll do with her newfound power is to fund an invasion of Durland. That's why she's here, you know. She wishes to use it to fight against this . . . Pon, or whoever, that we've read about."

Prett stared, dumbfounded. "She told you this?"

"She wanted my help."

"And you said no."

"On the contrary," Lexthur said. "But you're missing the bigger picture. An invasion of that size, it's not just going to require foot soldiers. She'll need navy men, wizards, gunners . . . and *diplomats*." Lexthur smiled. "You're a Fellows with a specialty in international law. It really wouldn't be hard for me to arrange a posting for you. And once you're out . . . there's no reason why I couldn't find plenty of other venues where you'd be useful. Why, these sorts of things can keep people busy for a *lifetime*."

A lifetime. The idea had rushed Prett, hitting him like a shot of glee straight to his veins.

Damn Lexthur, Prett thought now, as he stood before him for a second time. Though it was really as much Prett's own fault as Lexthur's. He's the one that had allowed Lexthur to be such a close and trusted friend for so many years. He's the one who had confessed his desire to leave Yandosia, years ago. He's the one who admitted that the only reason he hadn't was because Praxis had just left—abruptly, with no explanation— and that the family was still reeling from the loss of her. What kind of son would Prett have been, then, to abandon his parents so soon?

So why haven't you left since? was the first question out of Lexthur's mouth. It had been almost a decade by then, surely that was long enough?

Prett didn't have a good answer. He still didn't, except that by now he had so many responsibilities within the company that the idea of asking for a replacement felt like more of a burden than his original departure might have been all of those years ago.

But if *Praxis* was in charge . . .

Of course, that didn't seem very likely to happen anymore. Prett had done his part, he'd opened the bidding process as Lexthur had requested. But in the days since their first meeting, Prett knew that Lexthur's repeated efforts had been met with nothing but the sharpest refusal.

Which is why it had been such a surprise when Lexthur's man showed up once more, summoning Prett in. A thick knot of dread had accompanied Prett all the way out of his family's dwelling, had ridden alongside him in the sleigh to Lexthur's home. Had walked hand-in-hand as Prett was shown inside.

"What do you *want*?" Prett asked now, disgust lacing his voice.

Lexthur glanced up from his spot on the pillows. He was sprawled to the point of nearly lying down, barefoot, shirtless, a thick fur blanket draped across the back of his shoulders. Under one arm was a sleeping woman—or perhaps merely succumbed to such stupor that she may as well have been asleep, it was hard to tell—and under the other, a man, his pale skin stripped of hair and oiled. Both of his companions were in as equally casual states of undress as Lexthur.

None of this shocked Prett. Lexthur had started throwing these "parties" years ago, shortly after the ghosts had broken free and swept through the frozen tunnels of Yandosia. He and a number of Yandosia's elite, mostly those under the age of forty or so, had taken the crisis rather hard. What good was their wealth, they decried, if death could snatch them from their beds so easily? Everything they'd worked for, everything they'd built—gone in the blink of an eye.

At the time, Prett had been one of Lexthur's right-hand men. They'd just won the election, just stepped into the Archon's office. Prett was juggling both his family's legal business and Lexthur's political staff, and the strain of it had nearly broken him *before* the ghosts had even shown up.

These parties, then . . . they'd provided Prett with the respite he'd so desperately needed.

For a while.

Now he just found them tedious. It was nothing Lexthur and his companions hadn't done a thousand times before, and no matter how much they dressed it up—this time, with several acrobats hanging from velvet drapes in the ceiling, contorting their bodies into increasingly lewd and interactive displays—it was still just sex. Get high, get fucked, get a headache the next morning.

Prett had no patience for it anymore.

He kicked Lexthur's leg, sharper than was perhaps necessary. Lexthur's attention had started to drift, to a point beyond Prett where the acrobats were twisting themselves into a human knot.

Lexthur frowned as he returned his gaze. "That's not a very nice way to treat a brother."

"You're *not* my brother," Prett said.

"I will be."

"That's not what Praxis says."

Discontent twisted Lexthur's face. "We'll see." He leaned over, kissing the bald head of the man curled up underneath his arm. "Scoot," Lexthur whispered to him.

The man sighed, but drew himself languidly to his feet. Prett averted his gaze as the man shuffled past, finding himself a new nest of flesh to settle into.

Lexthur patted the empty spot beside him.

Prett crossed his arms. "No."

"These things are best not discussed at volume," Lexthur said, his voice echoing through the large room. And though nobody appeared to be paying them any attention, Prett knew that Lexthur was right.

Prett jerked his chin toward the maybe-maybe-not sleeping woman. "What about her?"

Lexthur glanced down, almost as if he'd forgotten she was there. He propped open the woman's eyelids, but the pupils that stared back were so small, lost in a sea of frozen ice. Lexthur shrugged. "Not a concern."

With a sigh, Prett grudgingly sat down. Not *right* beside Lexthur, instead perched on the edge of one of the massive, feather-stuffed pillows that made up the perimeter of his stack.

"What do you *want*?" he asked again. He made sure to keep his voice low enough to hide among the notes of the lone violin playing mournfully in the corner of the grand room. At another corner, a group was gathered around a smoking tower, drawing puffs and chanting as they tried to contact the dead. Praxis, of course, insisted that such things were impossible, though Prett still sometimes wondered.

Lexthur sighed. "Our plan isn't working."

"You mean *your* plan," Prett said. "I've done what you asked. I opened the bidding process."

"Yes," Lexthur said, frowning. "And as much as I wish that was enough, I'm afraid it isn't. Praxis has been . . . more stubborn than I've anticipated."

"You mean your 'charm' hasn't won her over yet?"

"Mock me all you want. But if this fails, you will have lost perhaps your only viable way out of this frozen hell. And, I might add, away from me."

Prett sighed. He ran his hands across his face. Stubble from a long day raked against his fingers. "I don't know what you expect me to do about it."

"Talk to your sister," Lexthur said. "See what her reluctance is really about."

"And if her 'reluctance' is you?"

Lexthur turned away. Idly, he lifted the edge of the unconscious woman's hair, splaying the ends apart in the grip of his fingers. "Let me put it this way: you know better than most people that I will always get what I want in the end." Lexthur glanced back, cutting Prett with a heavy look.

Prett shifted, suddenly uncomfortable. The final days of his time working for Lexthur were not something they'd ever discussed, not once. The real circumstances of Lexthur's ascent to power had been creeping nearer and nearer to the surface, as investigators from the Major Conclave circled ever closer to the truth. *Something* had to be done, and when Lexthur had finally done it . . .

Lexthur was still toying with the ends of the woman's hair. He wasn't even looking at Prett now, but Prett understood well enough what the man was capable of.

"What's it going to be, Prett?" Lexthur asked. His thumb ran across the fanned edges of the woman's hair, and a soft raking sound, like sand falling through an hourglass, drifted between them. Prett flinched, but Lexthur didn't even seem to notice as he turned back to Prett. "Like I said, we all have choices. So tell me . . . are you going to choose to have me in your debt, once it's done?"

No no no no, not a Beacon, never another Beacon.

Denial, Praxis's old friend, swept in and she moved out of the haze of residual magic. "Okay, okay," she told herself, listening to that voice, "breathe." The whole thing was ridiculous, surely. There had to have been some sort of misunderstanding. Trendall could not have been holding a Beacon, in the moments before this deadly magic had been cast so haphazardly in the secret passage, staining the walls as surely as a spray of blood. There was simply *no way*. No way that another Beacon could have been found now, after so many years and so soon on the heels of the last one. No way that it would have ended up in Yandosia, in the hands of the Fellows. What were the odds? Why, the whole idea was laughable, look, hahahaha . . . ha . . .

Praxis's mouth twisted up. She wasn't laughing.

She hadn't misunderstood.

Somehow, somewhere, despite all odds and against the very nature of fate itself . . . somehow, a Beacon had ended up in the Fellows' tunnels.

The question, then, was simple: where was it *now*?

Praxis's head snapped back up, her eyes instantly narrowing in on the place where Trendall had apparently met his ill-fated end. Never mind, for the moment, how he had come to be discovered in his lab, if he'd died here instead. Never mind, for the moment, who may have killed him— though that question settled as thick sludge in Praxis's heart, because unless Trendall had opened the secret passage to his murderer *himself*, then . . . Well, Praxis wasn't ready to think about *then*, not yet. Those were both important questions to be settled, but when stacked against the prospect of a Beacon loose somewhere in Yandosia, those questions could stuff themselves in a box and wait for another time, as far as Praxis was concerned.

She reached back out, but now the magic that Praxis had encountered was fading, as if, by having been disturbed, the cloud was breaking up. Praxis shut her eyes, trying to grab back even as much memory as she'd found a moment ago, but the images were fading fast. She cursed under her breath, trying to dredge it back up, in her own mind if nothing else. Trendall, huddled. The glow, peeking out from around his shoulders. His hand, stretched across the walls.

The walls! Praxis's attention sprang to the walls, and she actually slapped her forehead for not having noticed it sooner. In the memory she'd found, the walls were covered with carvings, probably etched in by Trendall himself, if the knife was any indication. But looking at them now, their surface gleamed as smooth and perfect as if they'd just been carved. Perfect, polished . . . a far cry from the somewhat dulled sheen of the rest of the tunnel.

A pressure built at the back of Praxis's mind, an angry buzz like a frenzied whisper, but Praxis clamped down on it, shoving the sound aside. She tugged her glove off and stretched her hand out, running her fingers across the walls. They were so bright, nearly mirrored—a faint reflection of her palm winked back at her, and Praxis watched the reflection, waiting . . .

There. A ripple, hardly worth noticing, but the reflection definitely *wavered*, just there.

Praxis grinned. Magic sparked to life behind her eyes and she threaded it down, letting it seep into the new ice of the walls. Water met her fingertips, the first of the lines beginning to melt out.

"Let's see what you've been hiding, shall we?" she said to herself as the sharp slant of a letter began to take shape beneath her touch.

Chapter Twenty-One

TRENDALL'S NOTES FILLED the entire corridor. Spilling around the corner, stretched up to the ceiling, even scrawled across the floor in some places. Whoever had filled them in had been meticulous, scrubbing down and reforming the walls until only the faintest traces remained, almost imperceptible. Praxis spent the entire night uncovering them, teasing out the new ice from each groove. She'd hoped that, whatever they contained, it would provide some clue as to where she should search next—ideally, it would give her a solid idea about who might have been nosing about in Trendall's business, and therefore, who might have known enough to seek him out and kill him.

In the end, it didn't, but that didn't mean the night had been wasted. Even if Praxis couldn't track down who had taken the Beacon, there was, at least, copious amounts of information on the Beacon itself. Well, as far as Trendall understood it, anyway, which wasn't as much as Praxis would have liked, but at least it was something.

At one point, she even found a notebook Trendall had started before he'd begun his mad carvings, hidden in a chunk he'd carved out of the wall. It had been sealed over, and probably gone unnoticed by whoever had killed him, whoever had filled in the rest of his notes, but Praxis found it. She pulled the notebook out and flipped it open with trembling fingers, the rest of the story filling itself in for her.

So that's what Prewish had been up to, when Praxis had first arrived at the gate. Praxis should have known he was up to something, never should have accepted his story at face value. Annoyance burned through her, that she'd been so wrapped up in the emotions of her homecoming that she hadn't taken the time to be more nosy, to snoop into his business. If she *had*, if she'd gotten involved days ago . . . would Trendall still be alive? Moreover, Praxis felt certain she'd have been able to suss this out, to seize the Beacon herself. Praxis shuddered just thinking about what could happen, the Beacon in someone else's hands. She remembered the twist of victory she'd picked up from the memory, the *hunger* that had filled the soul of . . . whoever it was that had set the magic off.

Praxis still wasn't ready to contemplate who *that* might be, though the not-knowing hung forever in the back of her thoughts, a dark cloud looming just over the horizon. That storm would be here before she knew it, that much was certain.

She turned, taking one last look at the madness that spread across the walls like a creeping rot. You could *see* the deterioration of the man, his thoughts and his letters morphing and twisting the longer the Beacon had sat with him. Just looking at it sent a cringe over Praxis's skin. For a moment, she considered taking the time to wipe it clean again—what would happen, if whoever killed him came back, and realized that someone else had discovered this place?—but in the end, it wasn't worth taking the time. Already, she'd wasted the entire night on this project, and in the morning the weight of all the time that had passed between Trendall's death and now dropped heavily on Praxis's shoulders. There was none left to waste on tidying up. Praxis needed to act, she needed allies, she needed . . .

Her wizard's sense stretched out, without her consciously meaning it to. It found Kaedrich, first and instantly, but Praxis's brow wrinkled as she realized where Kaedrich was.

Well. They *did* need allies, and Prommel seemed as good of an ally as they were likely to get. How convenient, really, that Kaedrich's audits had brought her there this morning.

Praxis didn't pay much attention as she made the snaking walk up to Prommel's offices. All her thoughts were swirling toward the Beacon like a vortex, the mere idea of it drawing her in again and again. So she didn't even really notice Micadel, in the outer offices of Prommel's territory, until he sprang to his feet, eyes popping wide.

"It's not my fault!" Micadel said, rushing forward. Guilt radiated off the young man as he scrambled to block Praxis's path through the outer office. "I tried to tell him it was a bad idea, but—"

"Tried to tell *who* that *what* was a bad idea?"

The question, Praxis felt, had not been asked with any great degree of antagonism or threat in her voice, and yet Micadel paled just the same. His great frame sagged, the wide plane of his shoulders tipping as off-balance as his mood. He gripped one of his fingers in his opposite hand, twisting them around in a nervous expression that was entirely at odds with the size and scale of the man. He looked like nothing so much as a little boy, trying not to admit to having wet the bed the night before.

"It's just, Prommel thought it would be a good idea if we kept an eye on him?" Micadel said, his voice turning up at the end. "Just—just for now! Just to rule out the possibility!"

"Kept an eye on him?" Praxis asked. "An eye on—?"

But the answer revealed itself, her wizard's sense filling in the blanks for her. Earlier, Praxis had thought Kaedrich was actually *in* Prommel's office, as part of the audits, but no—she was in a room *just off* of Prommel's office, someplace small and cramped, cut off from the rest of the household.

The warmth of flames felt good, hovering above Praxis's palm. She snapped it into being as she stormed past Micadel, cupping the flame protectively in the curl of her hand. No one stopped her as she stormed through the outer offices, and when she reached the door to Prommel's private office, she did not even stop to tell the guards to get out of the way—if they were not smart enough to recognize the look on her face as warning enough, then let them be singed.

They dove to the side as Praxis's flames expanded in midair. The fire hit the door with enough force to send it bursting open. Hinges twisted, wrenched out of place, whale bone shattered, and the first traces of ceiling and doorframe melted and dripped across Praxis's head as she tore into the room.

"Have you lost your damned mind?!"

Prommel scrambled back from his desk, his chair knocked aside in his haste. His eyes sprang wide in a manner to indicate that he *might* have just pissed himself in shock and fear. The light of fresh flames, newly conjured, danced off of his face, sending wild shadows up from his cheeks, his nose, his brow.

"P-Praxis, I didn't—"

"Didn't *what*? Didn't unjustly lock up the *sare l' dell* of the head of the lapus lumeni division? Or are you going to tell me I'm wrong?"

"I had no choice! There are significant security concerns here, and I—"

"I don't give a flying shit," Praxis snarled. "You've got no grounds to hold anyone, and you know it. Now, you let him go *this instant*, or you'll find out exactly how well-deserved the reputation of my temper really is these days."

Prommel held up his hands, in what he probably hoped was a supplicating gesture. "Praxis, please—"

Unfortunately for him, Praxis was in no mood to be supplicated. Not now, after all she'd learned overnight, and certainly not about *this*. Already, the familiar coil of guilt was beginning to snake itself around Praxis's heart, squeezing tight. Her scar flared, hot and angry. If she hadn't been so lost in her investigations, would she have noticed Kaedrich's location earlier, would she have been able to prevent this from happening at all? The thought of Kaedrich, locked up like a common criminal, wondering where in the hells Praxis *was* . . . it was almost more than Praxis could bear.

And now here Prommel was—Prommel, who Praxis had actually thought might be trusted to *help*, what a lark!—trying to calm Praxis down, trying to *justify* what he had done in her absence. The flames in Praxis's hand flared, so suddenly that Prommel had to leap back to avoid being singed.

"*I said now!*" Praxis screamed, louder even than the cry that escaped Prommel as he slapped out the fire that had caught the sleeve of his gray fur coat.

"Fine!" Prommel said. He raised his hands, trying to still her, and Praxis allowed him this. She closed her grip in his face, her fingers curling shut one by one, tamping out the flames until nothing but the lingering smell of smoke drifted up from them. Prommel gulped. He scrambled past Praxis, calling for Micadel.

There was no need: Micadel had toed in through the outer offices, standing just outside of the broken door. He was already leaning his head in, his eyes wide as they took in the situation. "Father?"

Prommel dug out a key from his pocket and tossed it into the waiting hands of his stepson. "Let Kaedrich out. Quickly."

A fast nod, and Micadel turned away.

Even so, Prommel was apparently unwilling to concede his loss quite yet. He scowled, Praxis's scowl mirrored back at her, as he said, "But I'm telling you, there are *serious* security concerns in this household right now, and *he* is the only unknown element at play. Honestly, Praxis. What conclusion would *you* draw?"

"That you're a contortionist," Praxis said. "To be able to shove your head so very far up your own ass."

"Your wit is as charming as always, sister dear, but that doesn't negate my point."

"Because there is no 'point'!" Praxis said. Flames spat, unbidden, from her fingers as she reached up to rake her hand through her hair, snuffing just before she lit her head on fire. "Look, Kaedrich is the single most upstanding person I've ever met in my *life*. He's the *last* person you should be investigating."

"According to you! The rest of us know nothing about him!"

"You know *me*."

"Do we?"

Praxis jerked back. She would not have been more surprised if Prommel had reached out and struck her. The urge to argue his point rushed up the back of her throat—gods, they were her *family*, of *course* they knew her—but something lodged her words in place before they actually made it out.

Did they know her? Suddenly, Praxis wasn't so sure. Years abroad had changed Praxis, sure, but even before that, she'd always been so private, so secretive. She never told anyone what had happened on her Qol Nar, never told anyone her reasons for giving up magic. And then, when she left, she hadn't taken the time to even say goodbye, much less explain her change of heart. Why *wouldn't* Prommel suspect her? What time had she ever spent with him, really? What chance had she ever given him, to see her for herself?

Praxis steadied herself against the edge of Prommel's desk, each of her ten fingers a tentpole to the circus of her roiling emotions. In the back of her mind, her wizard's sense tracked Kaedrich, moving alongside Micadel now, coming back to the office. If Praxis *was* going to talk to Prommel, if she had a wish to loop him in to the situation she'd discovered, the threat of the Beacons, the time was now. It would not last long.

She gritted her teeth. Tried to shove aside her righteous anger, her wounded pride. "Look, you don't have to trust me, all right? I get it, I really do. But whether you *believe* me or not, I am on your side. Perhaps more than you realize."

Prommel snorted. "Uh-huh."

"These 'security concerns' you mentioned: you're investigating the death of the wizard, aren't you? Because something's just not quite settling with you about it—something you can't quite put your finger on. It's like there's this haze around his death, and you're trying to squint through it, but you can't."

Prommel said nothing, but that was just as well. His face was the perfect mask of Fellows reserve. Unfortunately, most of the siblings were as well-versed in reading these silences as they were in speaking them. He may as well have shouted his agreement, for this confirmed Praxis's suspicions as well as if he had.

Praxis reached into her coat pocket, drawing out a folded slip of paper. One edge ran ragged from where she'd torn it from Trendall's notebook. She held it out to her brother, before she had a chance to change her mind. Shook it slightly.

"Go on. Take it."

She watched his face as he took the paper from her hands and flipped it open. Uncertainty to skepticism to confusion. Distrust, as if he wasn't sure whether he was being played a fool. When he looked back up at her own face, his eyes had turned wary at the edges.

"Where did you get this?"

"It belonged to Trendall," Praxis said, not exactly an answer. "You're right. Nothing about his death was natural. And that"—Praxis nodded at the paper in his hands—"is very likely the reason someone killed him."

"What is it?"

"That's not really the primary concern right now. What we need to do is *find* it. I don't suppose it was on his body?"

"No," Prommel said.

"No, I didn't expect it would be that easy." Praxis nodded. "Very well, then. We'll just need to start at the beginning."

"The beginning?" Prommel asked, but Praxis didn't answer. She'd already turned away, arms spread to wrap Kaedrich in a hug before she'd even fully entered the room.

"Are you okay?" Praxis whispered, and the nod that slid against her cheek sent a jolt of relief coursing through Praxis. Kaedrich's arms were slightly stiff against her, though, her muscles tense even as she returned the squeeze Praxis gave her. A brief flutter of panic passed over Praxis, until it hit her: their stupid fight in the lab, the way Praxis had so utterly botched things.

Praxis slithered back, suddenly embarrassed. She scowled, hoping to cover for it—not that she *really* expected to fool Kaedrich with this display, but . . . trying, at least, was better for her rattled nerves.

She made herself turn away. Prommel had folded the torn-out page back up, the Beacon tucked out of sight. He was just watching Praxis, a vague twist of annoyance on his otherwise smooth face.

"If you're quite done with sentimentality," he said, making no effort to keep the sneer from his voice, "can we return to more pressing business? I believe you said something about starting at the beginning?"

Praxis cut him a sharp look. "You're the last one that should be lecturing me on *sentimentality*, Prommel."

The barb barely phased him—a twitch of the cheek, easily mistaken for an itch. "I've learned from my mistakes."

"I sincerely hope not," Praxis said. "Because our first order of business should probably be to question the grubs. That thing was dug out of the mines, and if anyone knows what's been going on down there . . ."

"The grubs?" Prommel snorted. "Oh, sweet sister. You really have been gone. They'll never talk; not to us. Praine's gotten them so scared they've gone loyal."

"They can't *all* have."

Prommel shrugged as he crossed his arms. "You want to waste your time, you're welcome to try. I'd enjoy the show. But I'm telling you: it's not going to help. You'll get nothing."

"We'll see about that."

Another shrug, rolling off him with dismissal.

The sound of someone clearing their throat cut in from behind Praxis. "Hang on," Kaedrich said. "I think I missed something. What's going on? What are the 'grubs'?"

Praxis glanced at Prommel, but Prommel wouldn't meet her eye. *I knew you hadn't changed,* Praxis thought, but even so, he wasn't going to risk exposing his sentiment to anyone else, by helping Praxis out with this question.

Praxis turned around. Kaedrich was just watching, curious but not yet concerned. Praxis's heart twisted up, seeing the innocence, knowing that it was about to be shattered. There was no way Kaedrich would understand, if she saw it. There was no way to keep her from seeing it, though, not now, not anymore. Praxis knew, even without being told, that Kaedrich would follow them, that no distraction Praxis offered up now would divert her. She swallowed, her mouth suddenly dry. "It's . . . complicated," she said. No getting out of it now. "It's probably better if we just show you."

THE SMELL OF it hit Kaedrich first: the unmistakable stench of filth and misery, of decay and human waste. It was every poor quarter of every major city, it was the underbelly of a barge, it was the signature of a life deemed meaningless by those in power.

Prommel pushed open the door. The wail of a baby escaped.

They stepped through, into the realm of the "grubs."

When Praxis had explained that they were going to the mineworkers' living quarters, Kaedrich never would have guessed this is what it would look like. *Living quarters.* The term could not have been more misleading: a single massive cavern opened up before them, low-slung ceilings creating a sense of claustrophobia despite the sheer size of the room. The space was divided up by poorly strung blankets, or small tents pitched together for the illusion of privacy. Here the lapus lumeni blared strong, washing aside every hidden secret, every potential moment of peace. Blankets and bedrolls lay on the floor in haphazard rows, and everywhere Kaedrich looked, people were slumped, huddled, and collapsed. Even the children, even the babies, lay across the laps of adults with a sense of bone-deep weariness.

Prommel led the way, cutting straight through the middle.

"Who *are* these people?" Kaedrich asked, even as she feared the answer.

Praxis picked her way through the narrow path. She glanced once over her shoulder, but couldn't seem to hold Kaedrich's eye. "There's not really a proper translation," she said finally. "Though I suppose you could say they're Yandosians."

"*Yandosians?*" Kaedrich looked at the workers again; at the sallow skin, like someone had poorly bleached a tone that was naturally much darker than this; at the narrow gap of the eyes, upturned at the edges. Black and brown hair hung in stringy clumps beside their faces.

"They don't look like any Yandosians I've ever met," Kaedrich said.

She didn't just mean the genetic differences. Not once since arriving had Kaedrich seen anything less than affluence and wealth. A sour knot tightened in her stomach as she realized that she should have known there was an ugly underbelly to the society *somewhere*—but she had never expected it to be this bad, and she'd never expected it *here*. Rashes and welts littered these people's skin. Patches of their hair was missing. One of them had a scar running over an empty eye socket, and another had three bent fingers sticking out an angle that would never be useful again. Kaedrich fought hard not to shudder as a child—a girl?—lifted her arms and her shirt slid up enough to reveal the hollow dip of her stomach, the sharp line of each of her ribs.

Praxis's face was carefully impassive as she strode by them. "Yandosians —what you know us to be—didn't always live here," she said. She spoke with cold indifference, as if she was a bored tour guide. "Our ancestors came to the ice in search of a better life. We found it, but there were already people living here, on the surface." She shrugged. "We conquered them."

"You mean you *enslaved* them."

The words escaped Kaedrich before she'd realized she was saying them, tasting like ash and iron on her tongue.

"No," Praxis snapped.

She stopped walking, just for a moment. Long enough to glance at Kaedrich, and then at the back of Prommel's head, several feet ahead of them.

As she started up again she lowered her voice and said, ". . . Yes, okay, at first. But that was hundreds of years ago. I know what you're thinking, but they won their freedom generations before my family became what they are today."

"You call *this* freedom?" Kaedrich's hand swept wide, gesturing at the room at large. Several heads swung in their direction, hungry eyes drinking in the sight of Kaedrich as fast as they could before they hastily turned away.

Kaedrich's skin was crawling now. Not so much from the horror around her, or the scrutiny she was receiving as she made her way through the crowd, no—she realized with a sudden chill that what she was reacting to was her position within the room. Standing next to a *Fellows*. Dressed like one of them, wearing their gems.

It should have helped that the Fellows beside her was Praxis. But looking at her, the way Praxis barely even seemed to see them, it didn't.

"You don't understand," Praxis said. "It's not—"

"Enough," Prommel said. He'd stopped and turned, and now his hardened stare was leveled at Kaedrich, just as steady as it had been when he'd dragged Kaedrich into his office. "We don't need to explain our politics or our business practices—least of all to the likes of you."

The heat of indignance flared up to Kaedrich's cheeks, but it was Praxis that reacted first; she whirled to face Prommel, and a tiny flame sprang to life in her palm, inches from Prommel's face. He flinched back as Praxis said, "I will explain what I please."

Prommel's jaw tightened. He shot a fast glare at Kaedrich, but then he nodded once—reluctantly—at his sister.

Praxis snapped her hand shut. The flames doused, nothing left but faint wisps of smoke curling up from her fingers.

Prommel turned, marching off through the sea of despair. Kaedrich expected Praxis to set off after him, but instead she was just standing there, looking up at Kaedrich.

"Ella," Praxis said, her voice so soft that it barely carried the narrow distance between them. "I promise, it's not what it looks like. These people are here to work off the value of a criminal fee, not just as a matter of course."

"And the children?"

Praxis frowned, confused. "We would never be so cruel as to separate them from their children."

"Perlandra's breath," Kaedrich muttered. "You actually *believe* that, don't you?"

Praxis's mouth pinched tight. "If we didn't employ them, then someone else would—probably someone worse. I don't make the rules, Kaedrich. It's just how it is."

And with that, she turned back to Prommel, jerking her chin to indicate she was ready to move on. A wall of cold air rushed between them as Kaedrich watched Praxis's retreating back, nipping at Kaedrich's cheeks as sure as the bitter surface winds.

Chapter Twenty-Two

THERE WAS NO time to talk between them, not really. Not properly.

This was just as well, as far as Praxis was concerned. Kaedrich's jaw was set, her teeth grinding together in a way to indicate she had a *lot* of things to say, none of which Praxis was going to like. Which meant that once the conversation was uncorked, waves upon waves of alternating guilt and shame and self-doubt would come crashing over Praxis's head; which meant, inevitably, that Praxis would shut down all rational thought and operate on instinct, lashing out at anything she didn't like to hear as if she was a cornered animal. And Kaedrich would accept this gracefully, her controlled expression hiding a smugness as she *knew* that Praxis didn't really mean what she was saying, which would in turn enrage Praxis more. Until, finally, the whole thing would end in Praxis stalking off, shutting down the conversation completely and probably leaving the room until she could process it.

At best. At worst, Kaedrich would be so frustrated herself that she wouldn't be able to stand there and take Praxis's bullshit, and the two of them would end up shouting—again, until Praxis stalked off in a childish fit of *enough*.

At least, that's how it always used to go, back in the days when they worked together. Knowing that her behavior was petty and irrational had not, insofar, ever helped Praxis to prevent it, and since Praxis hadn't yet had cause to test if the pattern held true in their new relationship, she threw herself into the task at hand. Maybe it didn't help, maybe putting it off would only make things worse. But for now, at least, it was better than going through the terrible motions.

They were shown to Praine's office. It was the only one the grubs were allowed anywhere near, Prommel said, so it would have to do. Praine was in charge of "staff," putting the whole of the grubs' lives in his moisturized, well-manicured hands. The front entrance to his office, the main one, was tucked into the immaculate tunnels of the Fellows' business operations, but the one that they used, because it was closer and more convenient, lay beyond a balcony that overlooked the whole of their living quarters, like a king's balcony overlooking the peasants' square. Praxis wasn't looking at Kaedrich, but her wizard's sense *felt* Kaedrich's body convulsing as she noticed it. They ducked through a well-guarded door nearby, a set of stairs beyond them.

Praine had sent his private secretary to greet them at the top, as if he was expecting the visit. Praxis blinked slightly in surprise as she found herself acknowledging the lip-tap of Praine's only son. Being handed such a prestigious job before he'd even had his coming-of-age ball was . . . not *quite* so far beyond normal as to be called scandalous, though it skirted damned close.

"Uncle, Aunt," the boy intoned, his voice as polished as the ice. He did not even acknowledge Kaedrich's presence. "This way, please."

Praxis had never really paid him much attention before, at the various family dinners and parties she'd drifted through since her homecoming. He'd been introduced, alongside his twin sister, but all Praxis remembered from their initial meeting was the sheer number of faces that had been paraded in front of her. She would not have been able to pick him out of a crowd, or so she believed.

But now, she had no doubt. Oh, this was Praine's child, all right. He had the same disconnected smile, the same piercing eyes. He held his hands loosely behind his back as he led them through the antechamber of his father's office, his shoulders a level, controlled plane. When he opened the door and stepped aside, motioned for them to enter, his head was bowed in a careful façade of politeness.

Praxis had managed to avoid Praine's office when she was growing up, so she'd only ever been in it once before in her life. Sixteen years old, her own coming-of-age ball looming directly before her. Prenna had insisted upon accompanying her, her grip tight on Praxis's elbow the entire time. The meeting was perfunctory, an interview arranged by Prawl in an effort to see if there was anything Praxis might find interesting in the company's offer.

The office *itself* hadn't changed from Praxis's memory—but her perception of it had. She came to a sudden stop in the doorway as she took it in. Color flooded the room. The walls were covered in paintings, every square inch filled by canvas and gilt frames. But whereas the rest of the household was overseen by Prestina's ostentatious taste, Praine's choices were more . . . cosmopolitan, and far more disturbing.

Some of the paintings she recognized. Re-creations, she supposed, although with her family you never knew. There was a piece by Ducabrum, and another by Turelli. Another one she couldn't place immediately, though she thought it was from Rolmstan. On first glance, there was nothing particularly troubling about any of them. It wasn't until you took in the sheer number of them, and the number of them that featured young, *young* women—girls, really—and the number of *those* where the artist had found convenient excuses to reduce their amount of clothing, that it became . . . unsettling.

Praxis forced herself to look away.

And there he was: Praine sat in the middle of it all, the king of his own private kingdom. He had no desk, that much Praxis remembered from the last time. Instead, a comfortable armchair dominated one side of the room, high-backed, and so ornate that it could be called a throne. A handful of smaller chairs faced it in two semicircles, end tables dotting the gaps, and decanters dotting the tabletops.

He looked up as soon as they entered. Smiled at them, as if their visit was the most pleasant thing that could have happened that afternoon.

"Ah! Praxis, Prommel . . . Kaedrich. Do come in, do. Have a seat."

For a minute, Praxis considered asking Kaedrich to wait somewhere else. There had to be other things Kaedrich could be doing, surely? But that idea fell as Kaedrich strode right into the thick of Praine's office, and parked herself in one of the chairs as surely as if she belonged there. She cut Praxis a look, heavy with meaning that Praxis couldn't quite settle yet.

Praxis sat. Prommel was beside her, with Kaedrich across from them. Praine took casual note of this as he motioned for his son, standing in the doorway, to leave them be.

"So," Praine said. He crossed his legs at the knees, wrapping his grip around the hook of his kneecap. "I understand that you wish to speak to some of my grubs."

"Your *workers*," Kaedrich said, while Prommel said, over him, "Technically, they belong to Father."

Praxis said nothing. Not to Praine, not yet. Praine glanced, briefly, at Kaedrich's rigid indignation, before turning the bulk of his attention on Prommel and Praxis. "You have to admit, though, it's an unusual request," Praine said. He tipped his head. The shift was just enough to narrow his focus from the both of them down to Praxis. "Care to tell me why?"

She did not need to be told that he expected an answer. The weight of his gaze, pinning her in her chair, the way that he was not looking at Kaedrich, even as Kaedrich shifted in her own seat. Praxis remembered, vividly, the last time he'd leveled her with that look. *He's such a delightful young man. So . . . delicate.*

Would it really hurt matters, to tell Praine a fragment of the truth? After all, it's not like he killed Trendall. Praine wasn't a wizard—Praxis would be able to tell, surely.

But could she trust that? With her wizard's sense dulled by the pain in her leg, her thoughts muddied from the cold and the constant onslaught of memories, the vague whisper that cluttered her mind even now. Praxis thought about her family: her siblings and their spouses and all of those endless children. Granted, the younger generation seemed much more likely to be harboring a secret wizard than any of Praxis's peers, but seven hells, what did Praxis really know of her family anymore? *Someone* killed Trendall. If it wasn't a member of staff, and there were no visitors beyond her and Kaedrich . . .

Praxis swallowed. She took a breath.

"We can't tell you," Prommel said, speaking for her. He offered Praine a cold smile to rival his own. "Security matters. You understand."

Praine's attention broke. "Of course," he said, turning from Praxis as he rose to his feet. "Well. I'll just go and get them for you, then."

"PRENNA, I'M *FINE*, I can handle this on my own," Praxis had said, just before the last and only time she'd seen Praine's office.

Prenna nodded, but her grip on Praxis's elbow did not loosen. If she kept it up, Praxis was sure she was going to lose all feeling in her fingers.

"I know you are. It's just my job to make sure that you *stay* fine."

"What's *that* supposed to mean?" Praxis asked, frowning. After all, what possible danger could Praxis face that she hadn't faced worse already? The fire of her scar, tucked out of sight beneath layers of sleeves, rolled over underneath her skin, making Praxis flinch. Not to mention that, should worse come to worst, what good was *Prenna* going to do? Nearly to term with her third child, her stomach was a constant reminder that Praxis noticeably did not point out.

Prenna didn't say anything else as she led Praxis forward. She never said anything, not where Praine was concerned. She guided Praxis in cold silence down the tunnels of the business division, until finally they had arrived.

Praxis tried not to roll her eyes at her sister's protectiveness. Her presence was making Praxis feel like a baby, and this was supposed to be a moment of independence and adulthood. Not that Praxis particularly *wanted* this meeting—she hadn't wanted anything to do with the company when she was slated to take over the lapus lumeni division, and now that she'd sworn off her magic and closed the door on that opportunity . . . well, she certainly hadn't changed her mind about working for the company, that much was for sure. But her father had arranged it, smiling like this was some great birthday gift, and what was Praxis supposed to say? Besides, Prawl had said, sensing his daughter's hesitation, it's not like she had to accept anything. Just see what her options were.

Her options.

Praxis didn't like to think about her options.

In truth, she didn't know *what* she wanted from her future. For someone that had spent the last year trying to move forward, Praxis realized she had a remarkably uncertain view of what exactly it was she was moving *toward*. Mostly, she had been moving *away*: away from her magic, away from her memory of the Qol Nar, away from the roiling fog of guilt that hung forever over her shoulders.

They stopped in the antechamber to Praine's office, just as Merylda was leaving. Praine stood in the open doorway; he had his hands around Merylda's shoulders from behind, giving her a protective squeeze as he kissed her cheek. Merylda giggled at his affections—he was being extra indulgent of her as her time grew closer and her belly seemed to swell larger by the day. Gods, there were so many babies in the Fellows' halls these days. Too many, as far as Praxis was concerned.

"Ow," Praxis muttered, because Prenna's grip had tightened sharply at the sight of Praine and Merylda.

Praine and Merylda glanced up in unison. Matching smiles. Not quite matching—Praine's was always just a little too polished by Praxis's standards, the stretch of his lips unnervingly wide. Merylda's, meanwhile, was young and girlish, which was to be expected; she was only a few months older than Praxis, married just before she came of age due to permission from her father. The pregnancy had been announced exactly three weeks later.

"Ah! Prenna, Praxis!" Praine said, grinning. "Doesn't she just look wonderful?" He motioned at Merylda, who blushed but didn't stop smiling.

Praxis forced a smile in return. Prenna's was much more practiced.

"You're certainly coming along," Prenna said. Instinctively, her hand rubbed at her own, even as she regarded Merylda. "He's going to be a big one, that's for sure."

Merylda wrapped her arms around her stomach, hugging herself and her baby all in one. "Not *too* big, I hope."

"Nonsense," Praine said. "A strapping young boy is just the thing."

"It's not *one* baby," Praxis said. "It's twins. A boy and a girl."

It was only as the room fell silent that Praxis realized what she'd done. She cleared her throat uncomfortably. "I didn't—"

"Twins!" Praine said, turning to his wife. "Even better!"

They laughed as he kissed her again, pride and pleasure flushing their cheeks. Praxis's blunder fell by the wayside, though she did not forget it so easily.

It didn't *feel* like magic. That was the problem, in cases like this. It kicked in, reflexive, before she could even realize she'd done it, and by then it was too late, the damage done. Still: it had been more than a year since she'd sworn off using magic. Shouldn't that be long enough to learn control?

Praxis sighed as Praine showed Merylda out. It wasn't so much about the occasional slip of her tongue. Lately—and she didn't really know why—it was getting harder to control her magic. It kept building, crackling always as a spark behind her eyes. She did her best to suppress it, but little bits kept slipping out. A spark of flames dancing between her fingers before she could tamp it down. A gust of wind when someone irritated her. Last week, Praxis had gotten so bored listening to options for her dress that she'd fallen asleep, and when they'd woken her up she'd been so startled that her magic had lashed out, sending the dressmaker flying across the room. Praxis had screamed in terror—it had been so much like Moc's death, too much like Moc's death—but the woman was fine, merely rattled.

Even just thinking about it brought a stir to her mind. Pain flared in the scar on her wrist, so hot that not even the ice of Yandosia could help it. Praxis gritted her teeth, trying to focus. She was grateful, for once, for Prenna's strong grip, the way it cut some of the circulation off from Praxis's wrist.

They settled in Praine's office. Praxis had barely even noticed as Prenna guided her inside, as they picked the seat nearest to the door, farthest from Praine. She looked at him and her magic swirled, protective, through her veins.

Stop it, Praxis thought, willing it back.

Praine cleared his throat. "So!" he said brightly. "You're here to see if there's a place for you in the company."

"I guess," Praxis said.

Praine raised an eyebrow. "You 'guess'? Sister dear, the company is not a charity. If you're not seriously interested in this opportunity, I assure you that I have plenty of other applicants who would jump at any of the valuable postings I have on offer."

Praxis's cheeks burned. "No, that's—that's not what I meant. I—"

Prenna's hand rested gently across the back of Praxis, quieting her.

"Other applicants or not," Prenna said, her voice steady and just a little dangerous, "a Fellows will always have a place within this company. That's what Father always says. Praxis doesn't need to show enthusiasm in order to be welcome in her own family."

The corner of Praine's mouth quirked up. "Of course. Forgive me, my sisters, I meant no disrespect."

"No, I'm sure you didn't," Prenna said, though her tone did not share the meaning of her words.

Praine shrugged it off. "Now then." He sat back comfortably in his chair, twirling one hand lazily beside him. "Let us begin, then. What is it you *want* from life, Praxis?"

Praxis blinked, oddly startled. What did she *want*? She wasn't sure that anyone had ever asked her that before. She wasn't sure *she* had ever asked that before. To be a Fellows wasn't about what you *wanted*.

Except . . . that wasn't entirely right, either, Praxis realized. Looking across at him, Praine clearly had what he *wanted*. Prewish, too. And Prommel, more or less, and probably Pranders, and Prett had a solid plan in place for where he would go after leaving here. Previn . . . well, who could even tell what a person in his condition wanted?

In fact, looking on it, the only sibling that Praxis wasn't sure had gotten what she wanted was . . .

She stole a glance to the side. Prenna sat in her chair, hands folded serenely over her stomach, hair twisted into the latest style. Her head was framed by the ornate collar sticking up behind her, by the sparkle of the gems hanging from her ears and around her neck. To the outside world, Praxis's older sister appeared to have everything—looks, money, two children and one more on the way, a husband—and yet, had she ever expressed a true longing for any of it? Looking back, the only true passion that Praxis could remember in her was for numbers, and while she had managed to wedge herself a spot in the company, how often did those duties take a backseat, even now, to her other obligations?

What did she *want*?

What did any of the women she knew want? Self-determination, autonomy. The freedom to speak out, to choose her fate, to set their own rules. Praxis used to have those things, once, when she was an open wizard and the world was full of endless possibilities.

And look where that had gotten her.

The heat in Praxis's scar flared. She bit her lip, turning back to Praine, who was still watching, waiting patiently. The question hung stale in the air between them. *What is it you* want *from life, Praxis?*

What she wanted, right now, was to be ignored. To have her life set out, and follow it without thought. Dull, disappointing—safe, for everyone around her. That kind of question had no place for someone like her, whose power rippled just beneath the surface. Maybe, once, it used to. But not anymore. Not since she'd proven how terrible her choices could be.

"I want something safe," Praxis found herself saying, before she could think better of it.

Praine smiled, and Praxis was unable to hold his gaze. She turned to her sister instead, whose expression blanked almost as soon as Praxis found it, but not quite fast enough. Disappointment hid in Prenna's eyes as she made herself nod encouragingly at Praxis.

Praine cleared his throat. "That I can do," he said, and Praxis closed her eyes, feeling the cold air around her brush like shackles against her skin. There it was, then.

There was no backing out now.

THEY DIDN'T TALK.

At first, it was a matter of logistics: there was no way Kaedrich could say what she wanted to underneath the watchful gaze of Prommel, and certainly not *Praine*—there was something deeply unsettling about that man, made all the more obvious when she'd found out what, exactly, it meant to be in charge of "staff."

Staff, sure. Kaedrich hated herself for even calling it that inside of her head. Call a broom a broom, her mother always used to say; they were slaves, no matter what legal quibbles the Yandosians put forth in an effort to create a comfortable distinction that didn't exist in reality.

She still felt queasy every time she thought about it. Every jeweled mosaic decorating the walls, every lapus lumeni chandelier hanging from the ceiling, every hair of their fur suits and the leather of their dresses—every bite of the elaborate food they ate, every book in that marvelous library, every creature comfort fitted into these tunnels carved from the ice (probably every tunnel carved from the ice)—every *everything* in the Fellows' sprawling domain, from the largest piece of ostentation to the smallest tool of their household staff, *all* of it was built on exploiting the blood and sweat and broken lives of innocent people.

But it didn't stop there. All her life, Praxis had been benefiting from slave labor. Even after leaving Yandosia, she'd sustained herself on her hefty bank account. Her ratty clothes, Brex's food—gods, Kaedrich's emerald *cufflinks*.

Falconridge.

Praxis had paid for all of Kaedrich's enormous tuition, more than a year of Kaedrich's training at the most elite defense academy in Durland.

The thought hit Kaedrich like a punch to the gut about twenty minutes into Praxis's interview with the workers. Slaves. The conversation itself was taking place in Yandosian, so Kaedrich's thoughts had largely just been swirling deeper and deeper into a pit of discomfort and horror. Mostly, she was there just to make sure that the men were being treated all right, however temporarily. To witness, and speak out if anyone tried to make a violent move. Normally, this was something she trusted Praxis to do on her own, but . . . Kaedrich wasn't sure, anymore, if Praxis would necessarily notice, if she would register the act as proper violence.

The idea was making Kaedrich sick, but Perlandra help her, it was the unvarnished truth. Kaedrich reached up, touching the pin on her lapel in an effort to ground herself, as Praxis asked another question, her brow furrowed in concentration. Only once did Praxis look up, her eyes flitting to Kaedrich as if she'd sensed Kaedrich's thoughts. Kaedrich had hurriedly looked away. She didn't make eye contact with the men Praxis was speaking to at all.

So they didn't talk. Not at first.

It was easier to not talk. After an eternal agony, Praxis finished her questions, and the men were escorted from the office with (Kaedrich was sure) much more care and grace than they would have normally been treated with, and probably much more than they would be receiving later as compensation. Briefly, Kaedrich wondered if maybe it would have been better if she *hadn't* been there, if they'd been subjected to their usual level of mistreatment, rather than whatever sick revenge they'd be subjected to as punishment for their handlers having to hold back. But maybe that wasn't fair, maybe nothing retaliatory would happen. And even if it did . . . was it better to prevent cruelty in the moment, even if there would be worse later? She couldn't decide. How much was a stand on principle worth? How much did acting moral in the moment balance out against future evil?

The whole situation was making her head hurt. She didn't want to think about any of it—not the Fellows or their blood money, not the moral implications of having accepted gifts paid for with said wealth, not the lack of emotion crossing Praxis's face as they'd entered and left the business trunk of the Fellows' tunnels. They'd left Praine's office in silence, went back to their separate jobs in silence. Even coming back together at the end of the day, ordering a private dinner, reading for a short while, getting ready for bed, all of it had been in careful silence. Controlled silence. Safe silence.

Too much silence.

"Praxis?" Kaedrich whispered, hours later. It had to be the middle of the night, if you could call it "night" in a place where the lights remained constant, where the family and the servants operated on an arbitrary schedule Kaedrich still didn't understand.

Call it the middle of what was supposed to have been sleep, then. Kaedrich lay there, a mask over her eyes that never completely blocked out the light. She was facing away from Praxis, though Praxis's arm was slung casually over Kaedrich's hip, Praxis's warm breath against the back of Kaedrich's neck. It was close enough for Praxis to hear.

Praxis didn't answer. Her breathing remained steady and deep. It was possible—even probable—that Praxis was long-since asleep, and Kaedrich wasn't going to purposefully try to wake her up by repeating herself.

Kaedrich bit her lip, listening. Waiting. Her eyes were open, just a little, behind her mask, and she watched through the narrow gap at the bottom as Praxis's hand didn't even twitch, where it lay on the blanket, out in the cold.

"What?" Praxis said finally. So long after the initial query that Kaedrich had given up hope, closed her eyes, tried to go to sleep herself.

She jerked back to alertness now, though. Rolled over onto her back, Praxis's arm readjusting itself across Kaedrich's stomach. Kaedrich slid the mask up her face, squinting.

Praxis pulled the blankets up. Just the one layer, right up over their heads. Enough to block out the light, mostly, though Kaedrich could still see Praxis's face. Closed eyes, one hand tucked under her like a pillow. The pillow itself was pushed so far up the bed that Praxis was only half on it. Her other hand, the one she'd used to pull the covers up, slid back down and settled once more over Kaedrich.

"I need to start paying you back," Kaedrich said. "For—for Falconridge. And . . . everything. I don't know. It's probably going to take me forever, I realize that, but—"

"Okay."

"What, just like that? You . . . you're all right with it?"

Praxis's eyes slid open. She fixed them on Kaedrich, so little space separating the two of them.

"Of course I'm all right with it. If that's what you need to do, then that's what you should do."

"Oh . . . okay, great. I mean, thank you. I mean . . . I don't know, I guess . . . I just didn't think—"

"You didn't think I would understand."

Kaedrich winced. "No. I mean, yes. I mean . . . you're right, I didn't."

The hurt was plain enough on her face. In here, blocked off from the rest of her family, a trace of the Praxis that had made the journey down to Yandosia had resurfaced. The one that actually *talked* to Kaedrich, the one that tried to open up that scared, vulnerable part of herself. The one that Kaedrich had almost forgotten existed, underneath all of that ice and control.

"I'm sorry," Kaedrich said. She didn't elaborate; she probably didn't need to.

Praxis sighed. Her eyes had shifted, her attention no longer fixed on Kaedrich, but rather turned inward toward her own thoughts. Her finger traced patterns absently on Kaedrich's hip.

"I knew where it came from," Praxis said after a moment. "Obviously. I'm not going to try to pretend like I don't know the history of my people, or my family. I could tell you it doesn't feel like cruelty, or that it's just normal here, but I know that won't change things in your eyes. Maybe you're right."

Kaedrich just laid there, holding her breath. Introspection, she knew, did not come easily to Praxis, especially if it meant admitting something ugly about herself. Not that Praxis's role in this had been large—the benefactor of a crime, not the direct perpetrator—but Kaedrich would never be able to draw the clean distinction that Praxis herself no doubt would.

"They really are criminals, though. We don't just go grabbing people off the street and force them to work for us, or something. They've had a trial."

"Then why aren't they in prison?"

Praxis shook her head. "It doesn't work that way here. People pay back their debt to society quite literally—criminal fees are the cost of breaking the law, and if you can't pay back the state, well . . . you're allowed to work for a company that will put your wages toward your debt."

"In other words, if you're rich, you can get away with whatever you want. Don't try to deny it," Kaedrich added as Praxis took a sharp, defensive breath, "because you know I'm right."

Praxis's face scrunched up. Kaedrich could see the desire to argue the point, could see Praxis quite literally biting in her lips to hold the words back.

"It's not quite that simple," she said eventually, the closest thing to an agreement Kaedrich was going to get from her right now.

"What ever is?"

There. A truce of sorts lay between them. It could be raised again later—it would be raised again later—but for now, it was a silence they could live with.

"So are you going to tell me what's really going on, now?" Kaedrich asked. "And before you try to play dumb, don't bother. I heard you say something was dug out of the mines. What was it?"

Kaedrich watched the war play out in Praxis's eyes. The desire to clutch her secrets close, against the need to be loyal to Kaedrich. Kaedrich didn't push her—yet. Praxis had been making so much progress, on the journey down here, but being back home . . .

The secrets were winning, and so Kaedrich took Praxis's hand in hers, kissing the back of Praxis's fingers. "Please just tell me. Please."

Praxis's words came out fast, before she could change her mind. "My family found a Beacon."

It was not even remotely the answer Kaedrich was expecting. Which was more shocking: the sudden influx of cold and bright light as Kaedrich sat up wildly in bed, the covers flying off of her, or the news itself that had propelled her upright? She was up, blinking in the light and scrambling to her knees on the mattress, before she even realized what she was doing. Her gasp of alarm and sputtering cries of *"What?"* and *"How?"* and *"But—!"* covered the shriek from Praxis as the cold air hit her. Kaedrich shut up only when Praxis ripped a pillow from the stack and pummeled it against Kaedrich's shoulder.

"It's cold!" Praxis shouted.

"But—but—*how*? Praxis, a *Beacon*, I—I don't even know what to—"

"I know," Praxis said. She dropped the pillow, squinting now as she peered up at Kaedrich. "Are you going to sit back down?"

Kaedrich did not sit back down, not properly. She knelt on the mattress, running her hands over her hair. "How did they even *find* it?" she asked.

"How do you think? Like you said, they dug it out of the mines."

"And you're just going to let them *keep* it?!"

"If that was still an option anymore, I might consider it."

"What do you mean?"

Praxis squirmed. Discomfort radiated off of her. A truth was burrowed just underneath the surface of her mind, and Kaedrich could practically see it, wrestling against Praxis's stubborn, secretive nature as it tried to free itself.

"Oh, for Perlandra's sake," Kaedrich said in a huff. "Just *tell* me."

"It was with Trendall when he died. I found the tunnel where it happened—he didn't die in the lab. I . . . well, it's a long story, but his death wasn't what it appeared to be, and apparently whoever killed him . . . they also stole the Beacon."

"I see," Kaedrich said. What more was there to say? Such a rush of information, and there was no time to process it. Kaedrich cupped her head as a great wave of shame crashed over her. Because okay, yes, this was undoubtedly terrible news, and she felt awful about the death of Trendall, though . . . Kaedrich did have to admit, the news was not quite as much of a shock as it should have been. Had she always known, on some level, that his death wasn't quite *right*? And of course all of this cooked together into a dangerous development that would need to be dealt with as soon as possible—but that was kind of the problem. Here Kaedrich was looking for excuses to get *out* of Yandosia, and now . . .

Now they were stuck. For as long as it took to track down the fate of this new Beacon, and determine who had killed Trendall. And it was going to be dangerous, and complicated, and fraught, and blast it, hadn't Kaedrich earned a *break* from this kind of nonsense by now? Hadn't she already proven herself as reliable, noble, and true? What more did the gods want from her? Must she and Praxis fix *every* crisis, plunge into *every* danger? Why did it always fall to *them* to clean up others' messes?

She knew this reaction was immature, though, and it was the knowing that tore at her insides. It did no good to call yourself noble, if you were willing to sit the next one out.

Kaedrich reached down, wrapping her hand around Praxis's, their fingers tightly locked. "All right," she said finally. She tried not to sigh as she spoke, though a little might have slipped out in the shape of her breath. "Where are we going to start?"

"I don't know," Praxis said. "Prommel was right, the gru—workers wouldn't talk. Without knowing where it was found, I'm not sure I can do much to identify which one it was, and without *that*, I can only really guess who might have wanted it, or why. I think . . . I think we're just going to have to wait. See who might be hiding something."

Kaedrich frowned. "You realize that could take forever, right? I mean, Praxis . . . everyone here is hiding something."

"True." Praxis sighed, weary as the breath of the mines. "But only one of them is hiding magic."

Chapter Twenty-Three

WHEN BAD NEWS hits, it rarely hits alone.

This is a lesson Prewish Fellows had learned a long time ago, and not one he'd learned easily. For so much of his life, everything had gone exactly the way it was supposed to. He came from a powerful family. His interest in gems and caves made him the easy choice to apprentice with their head geologist, and the timing couldn't have worked out better: by the time Prewish came of age, the old man was ready to retire. He met and married a woman who brought with her the rights to expand into the city-state of Harken. His children were all born healthy. He was the easy choice to succeed his father when the time finally came, but that time could wait a long while, as far as the younger Prewish was concerned. For now, he had it all—family and mistress and work and wealth and respect.

Ten years ago, all that changed. Because ten years ago, his oldest son died.

It was Prewish's fault.

Not officially, of course. Investigations revealed a flaw in the safety harness Anthon had been using, a defect in the metal that held the braces together. There was no way to tell beforehand, they said. It was only a matter of time, they said.

Saying something didn't make it true.

Prewish knew the truth. Knew it in a way only a father could. He'd taken the boy down into the depths so many times—taught him every-thing he knew. They'd gone over safety procedures until they were blue in the face. Every morning, before setting out, they did a check of all of their equipment. Didn't matter if they were just starting out. Didn't matter if they'd already spent days climbing deeper and deeper into the ground, the darkness howling around them as the breath of the world ruffled their hair, their clothes. Safety checks, every morning, without fail. Prewish and Anthon and the entire expedition team.

Until that morning.

Gods, but if Prewish could do it all over again. He'd replayed the scene to himself over and over in his mind, so many times now that it was soft around the edges, like a book that's been read so much it's falling apart. A night spent on a narrow shelf, their bodies strapped down to drilled platforms to avoid rolling over in their sleep. Anthon was awake first, already unbuckled and scrambling across the rest of them as he prepped and packed his gear for the day ahead.

They were getting close to a new cavern. Anthon could feel it, Prewish could feel it. A caver's instinct, a combination of air pressure and smell and the feel of the rocks beneath their hands. New caverns could easily mean new caches for mining, but even more than that—they were *deep* by this point, deeper than most men had ever gone. A cavern could mean a swift descent, depth easily spooling out to add to their already impressive trek. Was this to be the one? The record breaker?

Only pressing forward would answer that.

Prewish hated pressing forward these days, a decade later, but what other choice did he have? Fate was a downward pull, like gravity, and the only thing you could do was try to navigate your footing as well as you were able on the steep slope down. If you were lucky, you avoided losing hold completely. If you were lucky, the nicks and jabs of the rocks were minor.

This was minor, Prewish tried to tell himself as he straightened the rich black jacket of his suit, though it was certainly a jab at his heart. The sounds of the ball already filtered out, music and laughter pricking at Prewish with every step closer that he took. Still, Prewish put on a good face. It was important he be seen as strong and capable—especially tonight. A coming-of-age ball was far more than a celebration of a youth now entering the world of adulthood. For a Fellows, it was always an *opportunity*. Members of the Minor Conclave's oversight committee would be in attendance, with their families, and the time could not be wasted.

Even if it killed Prewish to face it. Even if all the what-ifs billowed up like a gas spill from the mines, threatening to choke him. What if he hadn't taken Anthon on that particular trip? What if Prewish had used that harness instead? What if Prewish had been a little faster, a little stronger? What if his grip had held? Anthon was sixteen when he died, just a year away from his coming-of-age ball. He'd already talked about it, a little. What he wanted to achieve with it, where he hoped to go from there. He'd wanted to work alongside his father, properly and truly a member of the expeditions.

Anthon always had been the ambitious one. Of all Prewish's children, he was the one they expected great things from.

Which is what made it extra cruel, that *Tannem* was the one putting in an inheritance bid now. The news had broken that morning, along with the announcement of his wife's pregnancy, as if somehow the latter would help the former. Prewish snorted now, just thinking about it. What did Tannem know about running the company? Tannem, who'd been purposefully kept *away* from the mines, and therefore didn't understand a single thing about what it was truly like down there. Tannem was . . . gods, Tannem was nothing. Oh, he may call himself a businessman, may work in finances—there was so much more to it than that. Tannem worked in abstracts, in the *idea* of business. He had never been to the depths, never seen the raw power of the world. The *heart* of it. That's what no one else in the family understood—the mines were alive, in their own way. They had personalities, moods . . . tempers. They needed care and respect, careful tending. Not to be used up like the only whore at a party.

Prewish could have stood it, he thought, to have Anthon live, to have Anthon challenge Prewish's claim. But *Tannem*?

That was just insulting. And the longer he stewed in it, the more insulted he got. Not to mention the strategic blow, still *more* family support siphoned off, each lost vote slowly chipping away at Prewish's strongest asset.

What he'd *thought* was his strongest asset.

He needed a way to repair the damage, to shore up support, and he needed it *now*.

Which is the second reason why he was making himself go to this ball, despite everything. And the reason why, despite everything, his mood actually lightened at the sight of Prommel coming down the hall toward him.

Prewish slowed his pace, hovering just outside of the archway to the ballroom. A handful of family members milled about outside, waiting to be announced to the assembled crowds—Prewish's wife was among them, and so he caught her eye and gave her a brief *wait* look as he returned his attention to his brother.

He caught Prommel by the sleeve. Prommel hadn't even bothered to dress for the occasion, not really, his usual steel gray suit and white furs only grudgingly accented by the addition of a heavy pin on his fur coat.

Prommel cut Prewish a disapproving look, as if somehow Prewish's more obvious adherence to formality—the black brocade jacket, polished boots, the silver circlet across his forehead—was the insult. "What do you want, Prewish?"

"Have you given any thought to my offer?" Prewish asked. He led them away from the rest of the crowd, to a small alcove where their voices wouldn't carry.

Prommel's mouth went flat. "You mean the ridiculous suggestion that I would offer you *my* vote?"

"That we'd offer *each other's*, yes," Prewish said. "And I resent your tone. Neither of us can vote for ourselves. Abstaining to cast a ballot at all—"

"Is customary."

"—is *absurd*. Why should we waste the opportunity?"

"Because, mathematically, it doesn't actually help either of us? Because it shows a lack of confidence in my own chances? Because—"

"Actually, I think you'll find that it demonstrates to the oversight committee a willingness to look at the greater good of the company, as opposed to being solely concerned with your own ambitions," Prewish said. He shrugged. "And as for mathematics, it may not help either of us *directly*, but it does help to ensure that no one else gets control. Think about it: do you really want a man like *Lorric* to control our fate? Or Tannem? And what about when Praine—"

"Stop," Prommel said. He glanced over Prewish's shoulder, down the length of the hall behind him, and then turned to look the other direction as well. When he turned back, he lowered his voice. "All this nonsense aside, the answer is still 'no.'"

Prewish clenched his teeth, just for a moment, before he was able to control it. "I see. Care to tell me why?"

"Because I *know* what was stolen from the labs," Prommel said, still talking softly. "And moreover, I know that it wasn't just stolen; someone *murdered* Trendall for it, and *you* decided to keep quiet about it. You knew—"

"I didn't *know* anything!"

Prommel scoffed. "Don't play dumb. You tried to hide this from the rest of us."

Rage coursed through Prewish, hot and sudden. He grabbed his brother's arm, gripping down hard. "I was doing you a *favor*. How do you think it would have looked, to have a security breach of this magnitude *now*, of all times? That *you* let someone get *murdered*, right under your nose?"

"Am I supposed to thank you?" Prommel asked. "You've let a murderer wander free for *days* now, Prewish. This is bigger than my bid. It's bigger than yours. We need to think about what's best for the company—for the *family*."

"Really?" Prewish asked. He smirked. "Then how come *you* haven't told anyone about this? How come you haven't locked down the household? Questioned everyone? Seven hells, this ball is a huge security risk—all these people, coming and going . . . Preparations have been underway for *weeks* now, what makes you think one of *them* wasn't responsible?"

Prommel frowned.

"I'll tell you why," Prewish continued. "It's because you don't want this coming to light any more than I do, and you know it. So don't play the morally superior one with me, Prommel. I'm not buying it."

"Praxis knows."

Two words. Hardly a sentence at all, really, and yet they landed as hard as a fall in the mines.

Prewish blanched, not even trying to rein in his emotions. "You *told* her?"

Prommel shook his head. "She worked it out on her own."

"How—?"

"I don't know. Not exactly. But she had a drawing from Trendall's notebook. She knows what it is. More than she'll say."

Prommel took a step closer, until he was nearly nose-to-nose with his brother. Gods, but Prewish hated when he did that—Prommel's size, trained in combat, reducing Prewish to the proportions of a child.

"The point is," Prommel said, "*she's* not likely to keep her mouth shut. So unless you want *your* involvement in keeping this quiet to come to light, I'd suggest you tread carefully around our dear sister. As for your request, that information should be worth more to you than *one* measly vote, shouldn't it?" He cut one last look down at his brother, dismissal written clearly across his face. "We're even, Prewish. Don't threaten me again."

"SHOULD WE REALLY be wasting time with something like this?" Kaedrich asked as they stood outside the doors of the ballroom, waiting to be announced. They were the last to arrive, the antechamber already empty save for the one servant by the door, awaiting word that it was time to proceed.

Praxis glanced at Kaedrich, eyebrow raised, and Kaedrich understood why: what she'd just said was a fairly un-Kaedrich-like comment, after all. She knew how important these coming-of-age balls were, to the family and the individuals both, and ordinarily she wouldn't let something distract her from doing her duty toward these kinds of rituals, these markings of the passage of life. Ordinarily, Kaedrich even kind of liked them. Birthdays and weddings and new babies—celebrations of a life well lived, of achievements checked off.

But with the threat of a Beacon hanging over their heads, even Kaedrich had to admit that such concerns seemed a little trivial. And if *she* was feeling that way, there was no chance Praxis actually wanted to be here, not for its own sake. They should be out there right now, doing . . . something.

That was the problem, though. In the days since Praxis had found out about the Beacon, all they'd managed to do was descend further and further into paranoia. Sometimes, Kaedrich found it difficult to figure out who was more obsessed: Praxis, staring hard at everyone she passed, trying to suss out a hint of magic or guilt; or Prawl, still sending Kaedrich daily to this or that department of his children, hunting for clues about who might have "betrayed" him.

Was it any wonder, then, that Kaedrich had no enthusiasm left for this evening? It didn't help that this ball was for Praine's children. A dual event, nearly unprecedented, or so was the word swirling eagerly throughout the household. Servants and family alike had been talking about it for days now. No one knew exactly what to expect beyond these ballroom doors, for all the planning had been done in almost complete secrecy.

Too much secrecy? Kaedrich frowned, considering it.

Good gods, she was getting as bad as Praxis.

A gentle cough brought Kaedrich back to herself. The waiting servant, getting their attention at last. He'd been standing near the entrance, listening for his signal, as Praxis and Kaedrich stood quietly to the side. He tapped his lips now.

"Forgive me, ma'am. They're ready to announce you."

"You know, this fuss really isn't necessary," Praxis said, but the servant shook his head.

"I'm afraid it is, ma'am. Special orders from Praine. You're to be afforded every courtesy." He glanced at Kaedrich, just for a second. "As is your . . . companion."

Companion. As far as phrases go, there were far worse—certainly, worse had already been thrown in Kaedrich's face on this trip. And yet, as Praxis nodded an acknowledgment, as they stepped up toward the doors, as the servant moved through and called out their names to the assembled crowd, a fierce burning bloomed in Kaedrich's cheeks. Is that really all they'd ever be, here? What was it going to take, to get even the slightest bit of recognition in their eyes?

Kaedrich stepped through, trying to ignore the curious glances thrown her direction. She turned her attention past the crowd, to the room itself, and drew to a sudden halt in the doorway, her embarrassment and annoyance blown away by the sight in front of her.

The only word that Kaedrich could think of was "spectacle."

"Oh, for sanity's sake," Praxis muttered beside her—so at least it wasn't just Kaedrich, then.

It didn't take an intimate familiarity with the Fellows family to understand that this was *not* their average party. Kaedrich supposed she should have taken a cue from the music that had drifted out into the hall—faster and more discordant than the sedate waltzes she'd come to expect—but for some reason, she hadn't given it much thought.

The room was packed with color. Banners hung from the ceiling, acrobats twisting up and through them as they leaped from banner to banner, in pairs or by themselves. The walls were splashed with light that had been shone through various gems, creating twisting patterns that seemed to dance around the perimeter of the room as vibrant shadow plays. Performers in elaborate costumes skated seamlessly through the crowd, transforming themselves into mythic figures, animals, ghouls. Despite Praxis's scoffing, Kaedrich spotted a fortune-telling station set up along one wall, and a long trail of young Yandosian men and women stood in line. Beside that, a performance wizard stood drawing shapes and letters through the air, and then next in line, another performer threw carefully controlled flames *just* low enough to avoid brushing the ice of the ceiling.

"*That's* going to be hell to shore up later," Praxis said, her gaze following Kaedrich's as they took it all in. "Come on," she said. "I don't know about you, but I need a *drink.*"

Kaedrich nodded, the most that she could muster. They pushed their way through the crowd. They'd both forgone the usual skating blades—

Kaedrich, because she'd never learned how, and Praxis, for reasons of her leg—and Kaedrich fought hard to keep her shoulders straight and purposeful, like this was all perfectly ordinary. Like she knew exactly what she was doing. Like she wasn't drawing curious stares, both from the myriad of Fellows that she was familiar with and the invited dignitaries that she wasn't.

It wasn't hard to find refreshments. Within moments, a server had appeared at Praxis's elbow, and she took two glasses, downing the first one instantly and dropping it back on his tray as she cradled the second.

"Get some more," she told the server, and he tapped his lips and pushed off, skating toward the edges of the room.

"Praxis," Kaedrich said, "don't you think you should—"

Praxis raised a hand. "Don't start. Not tonight."

Kaedrich sighed, defeated, because the truth is she couldn't really blame Praxis. Kaedrich turned as still more details of the party caught her attention, one after another. She looked one way, looked the other—then did a double-take, whipping her head back, her eyes popping wide.

"Wait a second, is that . . . is that a *giraffe*? How in the world did they manage to get a *giraffe* down here?"

Praxis shrugged. "Money?" she said, as if it was obvious.

"Perlandra's breath. If this is how you people throw a *birthday party*, I'd hate to see a Yandosian *wedding*."

"Would you?" Praxis gave a fast shrug, dismissive, as she turned to the drink in her hand. As if she hadn't said anything at all.

Kaedrich froze. Even her heart had stopped—just for a moment, just long enough to startle her, as she realized what she'd said.

"It's . . . I . . . No, that's not what I—"

"You wouldn't be missing much, though," Praxis said, talking quickly. "It's not like in Durland. Trust me, *this* is the bigger deal, here. By the time a marriage is finalized, there's much better things to spend a merged couple's money on than a party. I mean, they usually only get married in the first place because they have a business expansion in mind, so unless they're trying to woo a potential investor or something . . ." Another shrug, like that explained everything.

Kaedrich watched Praxis carefully. She had gone back to scanning the room, studying the faces gathered around them.

Surely, Kaedrich must be reading too much into this. Surely, she couldn't have accidentally offended Praxis. Because it's not like Praxis had a lot of pride in her homeland or its customs, so the only reason why she'd have been uncomfortable by Kaedrich's dismissal . . .

Well. That wasn't worth thinking about. Certainly not here, anyway, while they were trapped under the ice. Besides, Praxis had managed to make her feelings on *that* whole subject pretty clear, the last time it had accidentally come up between them.

"I didn't mean that I was *opposed* to them," Kaedrich said. The words were out before she realized it, and now her cheeks *really* grew hot. Kaedrich bit her lips shut, to keep from digging herself an even deeper hole.

But if Praxis was at all picking up on the undertones of this conversation, she wasn't showing it anymore. She blinked at Kaedrich, her expression blank. "Okay."

It was almost a relief, then, when Prewish skated up to them next. He appeared suddenly, a dark shadow slipping out of the crowd.

"Enjoying the party?" he asked, though he didn't sound like he honestly cared one way or another. He was looking at Praxis as if she was something vaguely distasteful, though Kaedrich couldn't imagine why. For that matter, though, she couldn't imagine why Prewish even bothered to ask in the first place—it's not as if the party was for *his* children, and Kaedrich had never seen any sign that Prewish liked Praine at all.

Praxis shrugged. "Not really."

Prewish nodded. Why? Kaedrich couldn't quite figure out. He seemed to be struggling with his thoughts, rubbing his thumb against the pointed nub of his beard, like there was something he wanted to say, but didn't want to say. Praxis, meanwhile, was ignoring him, but Kaedrich's heart twisted up. Even though Prewish wasn't her favorite, the awkward silence was almost unbearable, even for her.

So she cleared her throat.

"Congratulations, by the way," Kaedrich said. Prewish glanced over, a puzzled frown marring his face, as Kaedrich added, "About the grandchild? It must be exciting."

Prewish raised a single eyebrow. "Must it? My own son is bidding against me, and using his expanding family as leverage for sympathy votes. You have a strange definition of 'exciting,' Mannly."

"That's . . . not what I was saying. It's just—I mean, a new grandchild. Isn't that something to be happy about?"

Prewish looked from Kaedrich to Praxis. "I assume this is a cultural misunderstanding?"

Praxis shrugged. "Some people like babies."

"Really?" Prewish asked. He glanced at Kaedrich, confusion splitting his face. "What are you, a woman or something?"

Kaedrich flushed. "I—no, I just—I only—"

"I resent that," Praxis cut in. "*I'm* a woman, and I can't stand the things."

Prewish tipped his head. "True, but . . . you were never exactly 'womanly' to begin with."

"*Fuck you,*" Praxis said, one of the few Yandosian phrases that Kaedrich was fluent with.

The tips of Prewish's cheeks tinted. "I just meant—"

"I don't care what you meant."

"Dammit, Praxis," Prewish said, sighing. "Why do you need to be like this? Can't you see that I'm on your side?"

"I wasn't aware that I *was* a side."

Prewish scoffed. He leaned in closer, lowering his voice. His body was turned to block Kaedrich out of the conversation, but Kaedrich could still hear as Prewish said, "Don't play coy. We both want the same thing here. The only difference is that I'm not so stupid as to go announcing the danger to others."

"Maybe they have a right to know," Praxis said. She pulled herself back from him, just a little, just enough. She did not look over at Kaedrich, but Kaedrich could see the way Praxis's attention had shifted, a cool indifference to cover up her curiosity.

"Don't be stupid, little sister," Prewish said. "Do you want the whole household to descend into panic? At a time like this, of all moments? If I hadn't quarantined the grubs, the person who stole the artifact might already have gotten to them, and *then* what do you think would happen? Honestly." He shook his head, as if Praxis's stupidity knew no bounds.

Kaedrich watched as Praxis held Prewish's gaze for a moment. Just long enough to make it look like she was being stubborn, but losing. Her eyes cast downward, in false shame and humility, as she mumbled, "No, of course you're right."

When Prewish smirked, triumphant, Kaedrich almost laughed. Gods, was he really so convinced of his own intellectual superiority that he would believe he'd convinced Praxis to *back down* from something?

It did not take Praxis long to extricate herself after that. A brief flutter of *excuse me*, and *so sorry*, a hard grip on Kaedrich's elbow as she led them off to an isolated corner. Praxis held her face remarkably still, remarkably calm, but Kaedrich could see the sparkle of glee flitting in her eyes, in the moments when her control slipped.

"What was *that* about?"

Praxis smirked. "That, my dear, was my brother being stupid enough to give us exactly what we needed. I don't know how he learned that I knew about the Beacon, but it doesn't matter now. He must have assumed that I already knew he'd quarantined those grubs, as well, which is lucky for us. So here's the new plan."

"Wait, we had an old plan?"

Praxis frowned. "Of course we did, I just said we did. Now listen: I'm going to find Praine. You need to run interference—don't let Prewish, or anyone else, come over to see what we're talking about. I mean *anyone*, but especially Prewish. He's not going to like what I'm asking for."

"The way you're talking about it, I'm not sure I will, either."

Praxis shrugged. "Yeah, you probably won't. The difference is that you'll at least understand it."

"I'm not sure I will, if it involves Praine. Praxis . . . are you sure you want to involve him in this? He's *evil*."

Praxis rolled her eyes. "He's a creep and a jerk, yes, but I don't know if I would go so far as—"

"Yes, you would."

"Okay, fine," Praxis said with a sigh. "So he's 'evil.' He's still the one we need, if we're going to get to the source of this."

"I thought you said the workers wouldn't talk to you."

"They wouldn't—but now I know what I'm looking for." She glanced around, lowered her voice. "Don't you see? Prewish ordered the quarantine to keep the grubs from talking."

Kaedrich flinched. "Can we *please* not call them that?"

"Yes, yes," Praxis said, waving it off. "The workers, whatever. The point is, we know which ones found the Beacon."

"Okay, great, but what makes you think they'll be any more willing to talk to us than the last ones?"

Praxis shrugged. "They might not be. But this time, I'm not going to give them a choice. This time . . . we're going to go to the mines ourselves."

"You really think that's going to work?"

"I . . . don't know. I'm working without a map here, Kaedrich. I have to think that examining *where* the Beacon was found will lead to something, though, because otherwise . . ." She shrugged. "What else is there to do?"

Kaedrich raised her eyebrow. A thousand doubts danced through her mind, swirling past as endlessly as the string of Yandosians surrounding them. But before she could voice any of them, before she could even begin to separate one from another, a high note pierced the room. The music swelled, stopped.

At the far end of the ballroom, a platform had been erected on the ice. Performers had been positioned on it a few moments ago, but now it had been cleared, and lights had been turned to draw the eye as Praine bounded up the few steps toward an impromptu podium.

"Shit," Praxis muttered as Praine looked out over the sea of upturned faces that acknowledged him. "This isn't going to be good."

Chapter Twenty-Four

Praine's suit was gold, because of course it was. His jacket hung down to his knees, cinched together with a belt studded with diamonds and the occasional Fellows family gem, shifting colors as he waved at the assembled guests. White boots caught light from the projections, lending his whole appearance a shimmering, ethereal quality as he stood above them.

Blah blah blah, he started, or at least that's how Praxis heard him in her head. His opening remarks were unremarkable. He went on about how thrilled he was, how proud of his children, how pleased to see his family coming together for such an important moment.

This is when Praxis's skin had gone cold. Could she tell what was coming, even then?

"And of course," Praine said, his voice booming out through the ballroom, "how fortuitous the timing, that my dear sister should have returned to us from so many years abroad, just in time to attend!"

Praxis gritted her teeth, shaking her head as subtly as she could at Praine, but he only beamed and thrust his hand in her direction.

"Praxis Fellows, everyone! New head of the lapus lumeni division! Let's make sure to give her a warm welcome."

Polite applause washed the room as attention shifted, trying to spot her. Praxis gritted her teeth, nodding at those closest to where she stood.

Gods help her, she was going to kill him.

"You know," Praine said, chuckling slightly as he looked out at the crowd, "it was Praxis who first told me that my wife was having twins. I'll never forget the joy I felt at that moment. I don't think I've ever thanked her for that, so I'm going to now. Praxis: you may not have children of your own, but I want you to know, the gift you gave me, well . . . it's been indescribable. You will always be a part of my family—not just my sister, and a dear aunt to my children. You're in my heart."

Several *awww*s rippled through the crowd. Praxis glanced awkwardly at Kaedrich, who couldn't understand a word Praine was saying and that was probably just as well. But oh, what must she be thinking, right now? What did she assume was going on? Her blank expression conveyed nothing.

"Of course," Praine continued, drawing everyone's attention back to where it belonged, "it gives me extra pleasure that my sister has chosen to attend *tonight*, because tonight is not just a special night for my beloved children, oh no. Honored guests . . . it is with extra delight that I announce to you that I have put in a bid for the inheritance of my father's company!"

And there it was, Praxis thought. Not a hint of surprise jolted through her, but *now* she understood the point of Praine's false praises. Praxis gripped her fists, sparks kicking to life behind her eyes.

She held herself back—barely—as Praine finished his speech. She didn't even listen to the rest of it. He spoke for only a few more minutes, before finally waving to the crowd and slipping back down to the dance floor. Praxis was already moving by the time the music started up again, lively and joyful.

Well. She'd wanted an excuse to talk to him, all right.

Praine had just straightened up from reattaching his skating blades when Praxis stormed up to him. Sparks flicked from finger to finger, and it was all Praxis could do not to lash out at him right then, right there. At the very *least* her arm ached to throw a punch straight for that smug, smarmy face of his.

Which lit up now as he turned toward Praxis.

"Ah! There you are! So happy you—"

"Cut the shit," Praxis snapped. "You bastard. You planned that, didn't you? That's why you *insisted* on making sure I was announced—so you would know if I turned up. Don't try to deny it."

Praine laughed lightly as he shook his head. "My dear Praxis. You do say the most outlandish things sometimes."

"Fuck off. I know what that was about," Praxis said. "Trying to make it seem as if I endorse your bid. Like we're *so* close."

"Oh, but we are close," Praine said. He skated over, and before Praxis could stop him, he'd wormed his arm around her shoulder, hooking her in place. "Why, we share all *sorts* of secrets, Praxis. I'd call that close, wouldn't you?"

Praxis raised her hand. A tiny burst of flame jumped up from where she snapped her fingers, flaring and dying just long enough for the reflection to catch in Praine's eyes. "You have two seconds to get your arm off of me."

Praine smiled as he backed off, raising his hands in supplication. "Whatever makes you happy, sister dear. Whatever makes you happy."

"This doesn't change anything, you know," Praxis said. "And you're a fool if you think that it does. I'm *never* going to endorse you. Whatever people think—"

"Is whatever they're going to think." Praine shrugged. "It makes no difference to me. My bid will stand on its own merits, and you must do what you feel is best, in your heart. I understand that."

Praxis's whole face wrinkled in disgust. "Gods, is there no sentiment that you can't make sound vile?"

Praine laughed. "You always think so cheaply of me, Praxis. I'm trying not to read too much into that, I really am. Do you really believe my motives are always self-serving?"

"Yes."

"I'll be honest, Praxis: that hurts me to hear. I've always wanted us to have a *healthy* working relationship, based on mutual respect and honesty, and I'm sorry I've done a poor job getting you to understand that."

"Okay, you know what, just *stop*," Praxis said. "Honestly, this whole false-humble routine might work on other people, but it's not working on me. You're not sorry. You've never been sorry a day in your life. *I'm* the one who's sorry—to think that I could have ever considered asking a favor from someone as—"

"A *favor*?" Praine grinned. "Oh, now this I like."

"Yeah, well, you can just forget it," Praxis said. Though she knew he wouldn't. Is that why she'd said it, then? It seemed, at the time, to be just a slip of her tongue, an ill-advised thought, but what if a part of her had known he'd latch on to it? And so, look:

"No no," Praine said. He crossed his arms over his chest. "Go on. Try me. What do you need?"

Praxis scowled. Swears danced on the end of her tongue, itching her to spit them into his face. She knew she should just let loose, cuss him out to within an inch of his life—of course she should, for how could she even *consider* asking him for anything now? A whisper in her mind agreed with this, so readily, yes yes, stoking her righteous anger. Don't play Praine's game. And yet, *something* kept her jaw clenched tight, *something* forced her breath in, out, trying to calm her temper. Praxis turned, looking out across the ballroom for signs of Kaedrich, but Kaedrich was nowhere to be seen. Hopefully, she was doing as Praxis had asked, and keeping her family away from Praxis. Praxis's sense reached out, finding her without being asked to, drawing strength just from her proximity in the sea of dancing Yandosians. *Where do we start?* Kaedrich would do whatever was necessary, no matter how distasteful, to find the Beacon. To stop whatever was being planned for it. Whatever *it* might be planning.

Praxis kept her scowl firmly in place as she turned back to Praine.

"I need use of a few of the . . . grubs," she said, finally. "To go into the mines. But *don't* for a second think that I am willing to give you my endorsement in exchange, because that simply *is not happening*, Praine. Not *ever*."

"And I would never ask it," Praine said. "In fact . . . I'm going to *give* you the grubs, Praxis, and I'm not asking anything from you in return. Why, you can even pick out which ones you'd like to use, if it makes a difference."

Praxis snorted. She knew his generosity was not, in fact, without a price—though exactly what he was thinking he'd gain from it, Praxis wasn't sure yet. Still.

"In that case, I'll take the ones in quarantine," Praxis said, before either she or Praine could change their minds.

One of Praine's eyebrows ticked up. "You want . . . *infected* grubs?"

Praxis shrugged. "You said it was my choice. Have them meet me by their gate tomorrow morning, an hour before first breakfast."

"As you wish," Praine said as Praxis turned away. "Oh, and Praxis? Do enjoy the rest of the party, won't you?"

But a rude gesture is all he got in reply.

ANNELLE WAS STANDING next to her father when the news broke.

For a while, Lorric just stood there. All throughout Uncle Praine's speech, frozen in silence, his jaw grinding together, shifting back and forth, back and forth. Annelle watched it, transfixed. Lorric was normally such an amiable person that Annelle could probably count on one hand the number of times she'd seen him truly angry.

He was angry now. Spitting angry. Raging angry. The kind of angry that Annelle was used to from her grandmother, from her uncles—even from her mother, on rare occasions. The kind of angry that, in the Fellows household, usually resulted in screaming matches, doors slammed so hard the ice frames cracked. The kind of angry that had toppled schemes, and frozen relationships, and overturned appointments on the Minor Conclave.

She did not expect it from her father, and a twisted pride filled Annelle's chest as she watched it now. "How . . . how *dare* he!" Lorric sputtered as Uncle Praine finished his announcement with a wink and a wave to the crowded ballroom.

"I'm sorry, Father," Annelle said, and she meant it. Just because she hadn't been in favor of Lorric putting in a bid, that didn't mean she was happy now to see his hopes dashed. For they were well and truly dashed now—what little chance he'd had, had all been built upon Praine's support. Now Lorric's choices were reduced to either withdrawing his bid, thus admitting he'd made a mistake to do so in the first place . . . or face a humiliating failure, when literally his only support came from his wife and children, out of loyalty and pity more than anything else.

It was a crushing blow and a terrible betrayal, especially after Lorric had worked so hard to help Praine put together this very ball. It had concerned Annelle at first, the time and money he was investing in what could be viewed as a rival ball to the one she was planning, but . . . he still didn't deserve this kind of treatment. Not from his own *brother*.

Even if that brother *was* Praine. And even if this wasn't *entirely* surprising, given the circumstances.

Lorric's fists clenched and unclenched and clenched, held fast by his sides. Annelle reached out, running a hand up and down his shoulder. "I'm sorry," she said again, because what else was there to say?

"I'm going to have it out with him," Lorric said. He nodded, not looking at his daughter, as if he was trying to convince himself of the soundness of his decision. "Right now. You just watch. Praine has *no idea* what he's just opened himself up to."

"Good," Annelle said. "He needs to hear it."

Another nod. "Yes. I'm going to do it. I'm going to do it!"

With that, he pushed off, skating an angry line through the swirl of dancing that had resumed at the conclusion of Praine's speech.

Annelle did not hesitate. She gathered up her skirts, following suit. They'd been standing on the far side of the ballroom when the announcement happened, so it was a fair bit of navigating as father and daughter cut between couples and groups, the music bouncing loudly around them.

Annelle's heart raced, so thrilled at the prospect of seeing Praine taken down a peg, that she barely watched where she was going, and so when Lorric stopped abruptly in front of her, she crashed right into his back.

There was Praine, not far off—and there was Praxis.

All they could see of her was her back, her head partially obscured by the large fan of her collar, but it was enough. Praine was grinning at her, so pleased, and the weight of disappointment crashed hard onto Annelle's shoulders. She'd thought all of Praine's bluster about his relationship to Praxis was just that, but now . . .

She watched as her father's whole body slumped, like the puppets at the end of the shows that some of Annelle's cousins' nannies used to perform for the children.

It's not that Annelle didn't understand, because she did. She did. True, Fellows blood flowed through her veins, strong and determined—but so did *Lorric's*, and though she tried hard to fight against it sometimes, the timidity of that half of her heritage was hard to overcome.

"Don't give up," Annelle said, but her father shook his head at her, annoyance carved into his face as sure as if it was an ice block.

"Forget it," Lorric said. He shoved past her, muttering, "If he's already got *Praxis's* support . . ."

She watched him go, wanting to call after him, to tell him to stand his ground, but . . . what more was there to be done? Maybe her father was right, maybe it was really over.

No, Annelle thought as she squared her shoulders. If her father would not defend himself, then she *would*. She turned back, but Praine had already moved off, swallowed into the crowd. Praxis was cutting a fast track back to Kaedrich's side, but to the depths with *her*—Annelle would deal with *her* later, maybe, unless her courage failed her. She turned her attention to smaller targets first, gnawing her lip as she surveyed the ballroom.

There he was. Annelle pushed off, determination lending her speed.

Only, the closer she got to him, the more her certainty began to waver. The realization began to catch up with her. Her Uncle Praine: there he was, in conversation with several members of the Minor Conclave, and even just the look of him, so slippery, so deceitful, was enough to turn Annelle's stomach. Years of stern warnings went ringing through her mind all at once: do not talk to Uncle Praine, do not let yourself be alone with Uncle Praine, do not smile at Uncle Praine. A drumbeat from her mother, that ran as an undercurrent through Annelle's entire childhood. Just looking at him, it began to ring loudly in her mind, danger

danger danger. Her father had never understood, but Prenna made certain that her daughters did. Annelle still remembered with perfect clarity the afternoon when her mother had finally sat her down, told her she was old enough to hear the truth.

She cringed now, just thinking about it. *This* was the man Annelle was so determined to give a telling off to? The conversation with her mother billowed up fast in her mind, the fear and disgust that had gripped her to the core. *How could they let him get* away *with it?* Annelle had asked, shaking as she sat by her mother, but Prenna had merely rubbed Annelle's back. *They put a stop to it,* Prenna said. *That's all you need to know for now.*

Maybe so, but Annelle still hadn't been able to look either of her grandparents in the eyes for a year after that.

Seven hells, Annelle's mother was going to *kill* her when she found out what Annelle was about to do. Annelle told herself that it was worth it, that Praine had wronged her father, that *someone* needed to stand up to him, to call him out on his behavior, and if no one else was willing to do so . . .

She told herself that, and yet she still veered off course, just before she drew close enough to be spotted. She ducked behind an ice sculpture that had been brought into the ballroom, shaped like some type of large bird with a long, curved neck, and there she tried to recover her shuddered breath.

Praine's laughter reached her, even there. Safe, but still too close for Annelle's taste, and now a couple, moving slowly, shifted their dance and blocked her escape. Annelle bit her lip, cursing her earlier bravado. Look at where it had gotten her—just look!

"—been an interesting year for your family, I must say," one of the ministers was saying to Praine now. "I admit, a few of us weren't sure if you were going to make it through to the other side."

"Of course," a second minister added, "none of us could have predicted the cash flow from the Hern family."

Annelle peeked around the sculpture in time to see Praine nodding.

"Yes, Prommel's marriage was certainly a joy to us all—and I mean this not just from a business perspective. We've been very fortunate, in Sharmity and Micadel. I dare say that these days, it would be difficult to imagine the household without them."

"You're not threatened by it, then?" the first minister asked. "Forgive me for being blunt, but your own bid hardly stands the chance it might once have. Not with the support the Herns have within the Conclave."

Praine shrugged, unconcerned. "Not particularly. I hope the strength of my bid will speak for itself, once it reaches your hands. Still, if I'm to lose, I will lose gracefully, and in full support of the new inheritor. Whoever he may be."

The second minister raised a thick eyebrow. "That's very gracious of you."

"Well, Prommel is extremely worthy. Though he'd *have* to be, I suppose, for the auditors to overlook his criminal fee when they approved his marriage to a Hern."

"*Criminal* fee?"

This was Annelle's reaction, too, though at first she'd just assumed that she misheard what Praine had said. She'd never heard of such a thing— not that the idea of a Fellows breaking the law was so unimaginable, she thought with a sour twist of her mouth—but rather the idea of them allowing it to go so far as to pay the *fine*. Surely, if Prawl and Prestina could have covered for Praine, all those years ago . . .

What could Prommel have done, what could possibly have been so terrible that they wouldn't come to his aid?

"Why, yes," Praine said. He took a drink, then raised his eyebrow. "Surely he disclosed that, in his bidding application? Oh, but don't hold it against him—I'm sure it was an oversight. He certainly wasn't trying to hide anything, and it was all so minor, really, and such a long time ago. And who can blame a young man, after all, for having a *bit* of sentiment. He'd never do something like that *now*."

"Something like *what*?"

"Ah." Praine paused, looking slightly sheepish. "That, I'm afraid, I really shouldn't say. I'm sure it's all in the court records, if you really must look into it, but trust me—it's nothing that should factor into your considerations. As I said, if his ledger was good enough for the Hern family . . ."

"Yes," the first minister said, though he sounded just a little unsure. "Yes, of course."

Annelle's fists tightened. A fresh surge of determination coursed through her. Why, that filthy, rotten, scheming—!

A firm grip found Annelle's elbow, so suddenly that she actually yelped as she whirled around.

The stern eyes of Prenna Fellows glowered down at her. Gods, but that look—like she could peer straight through Annelle, see everything she'd been thinking, everything she'd been planning. Annelle shrank back against the statue. "It's . . . I'm not—"

"No," Prenna said, sounding and looking so much like Grandmother that a chill went straight down Annelle's spine. "No, you most certainly are *not*. Come. Your evening is *over*, young lady."

What other choice was there, under that glare? Annelle crumpled, as surely as her father had before her. "Yes, Mother," she muttered, hating herself even as she dutifully skated off behind Prenna.

Oh, but one day, Annelle told herself, her teeth grinding together. One day . . .

Chapter Twenty-Five

THE WORKERS HAD to be signed out, as if they were parcels that Praxis might lose en route.

She decided not to tell Kaedrich this as she signed her name where the overseer indicated, his pale finger so thin that Praxis worried it might snap as he shut the ledger around it once she was done. Several feet behind Praxis, a sleigh stood waiting, Kaedrich beside it with her hand extended for the bruskers to lick with gleeful abandon. Praxis could see, when she turned around, Kaedrich's shoulders shaking as she tried not to giggle at the slobbery tongue against her skin. There was no way she would appreciate knowing something like this, the weight that Praxis had just accepted upon their heads.

"You'll need this," the overseer said next. He reached underneath a counter that divided the workers' section from the outside tunnels. Steel bars cut from the counter to the ceiling, and a door like a jail cell stood rooted beside him. The ledger, and the keys the man produced next, were handed through the bars like contraband.

Praxis wrapped her fingers around them, suddenly unsure. The keys were cold, old, the tines of their blades worn to soft nubs. She tried not to think about how many times they'd have had to have been used, to be this spent, but the weight of *not* thinking about it was somehow almost worse. She thought back to the few times that she'd accompanied Prewish when she was a child, wondering, had this been part of the process all along? Surely, she'd have noticed something like that . . . right?

"Out of curiosity," Praxis said a moment later, because it was less uncomfortable to question the overseer than to question herself, "I don't suppose you could tell me the last place these particular wor—*grubs* . . . were assigned, can you?"

The overseer looked up. He was old, Praxis tried to tell herself, and just doing his job, just trying to support himself and his family. Could she blame him, for working for the Fellows? Could she blame any of them, any of the faces she'd passed that morning—the maids, scurrying to right the Fellows' world before the rest of them would rise; the cook, gruff at having his work interrupted this early; the driver, who'd hauled the dogs out with the bribe of a fresh seal steak swinging in front of their noses? This man worked more directly for the underbelly that Praxis herself felt like she was only just now discovering, despite knowing of its existence all her life, but did that *really* make him somehow more complicit than any of the rest of them? If not this man, then another. If not the Fellows, then another.

It was the way of things. Who was Praxis, to judge the system? She could do nothing about it.

With a brief grumble, the overseer retrieved his book again, flipping back through the pages as he muttered a worker identification code to himself. HXQ3RT, over and over, like some kind of enchantment. And what a trick of magic it was, Praxis thought to herself, to convert a person into a code. Even she could not manage such a feat.

"Ah," he said finally, with a dry smack of his lips. His frail finger jabbed the page again. Then he looked a little closer, bending in, and then his eyes popped open, and then he leaned back as if he'd seen something truly disturbing. He cut Praxis a look, side-eyed, tipping his head to study the image she made before him. Praxis put her hand on her hip, trying to look as impatient as possible.

"Problem?" Praxis asked. She kept her voice level, unconcerned, loaded with the boredom only someone of the Fellows' authority could afford. What did it matter to someone like her, if there was a problem? It would be someone else's problem, in a moment.

The overseer's eyes skittered away from her, as sure as if she'd slapped him. "No . . . ," he said, slowly, "no problem . . . It's just . . . These grubs . . . You are aware, miss, that you're breaking quarantine, to take them out . . . don't you?"

Doubt whispered in the back of her mind. What if she was wrong? What if they really were infected, what if Prewish was lying, or she'd misunderstood? What if she was going to get sick, get Kaedrich sick? But

Praxis rolled her eyes, determination and arrogance carrying her forward. "Of *course* I realize, you fool. Do you think I would be taking out *infected* grubs, if I didn't have a good reason for doing so?"

"No, ma'am!" the overseer said. He snapped to attention, as if he was a soldier and she his commander. His chin thrust forward, proud and true. Nothing to be offended by here, nope, look, a loyal agent to the crown that her family may as well wear.

It was in this moment, Praxis's spine haughty, the overseer's so straight it threatened to bend itself backwards, the perfect sheet of ice over Praxis's expression, that the workers were led out.

Their faces registered nothing as they saw her. And why would they, Praxis realized with a kick to the guts—it's not as if she wasn't anything they weren't expecting to see. An expensive Yandosian, Fellows brow and disdain on full display, waiting to accept their charge. She wanted to do . . . something. Say something, show some display as a means to indicate that there was a difference, that she was different, but what could she possibly show them? Even the mark on her wrist, the tattoo that reminded her of herself, would mean nothing to these people. They just stared at her, seeing only a Fellows. Four workers, three men and a woman, she *thought*, though it was hard to tell with their hair shorn close to the scalp, their bodies worked down to the bone. There was something hard and glinting in each of their eyes, though, a scrap of proud defiance even as they shuffled where they were told to shuffle, stood where they were told to stand. Chains bound together their wrists, ankles, and neck, while another length strung them all together like popcorn threaded into a garland, the end in the hands of a guard no older than Micadel. It was he that opened the gate, and he that tapped his fingers to his lips as he acknowledged Praxis.

But if he was expecting any of Praxis's attention, he would be sorely disappointed. As soon as they were through the gate, Praxis clicked her thumb, moving over to stand directly before the workers. She felt Kaedrich's attention on her back, and Praxis let that moral compass prod her forward, even as her own needle spun around on point, uncertain where to settle. She folded her hands in front of her, hoping to appear less threatening.

"Hello," she said to them. All the workers spoke Yandosian, though they did have a native language among them that refused to be stamped out, no matter how hard the rest of her society might try, no matter how harsh the punishment was for being caught speaking it. Praxis imagined, for a brief but satisfying moment, the horror that would appear on the guard's face if she addressed them in it now, but of course, she had never taken the time to learn it.

The workers did not react to her greeting. They watched her with blank expressions to rival those of the Fellows. Praxis cleared her throat. Tried again.

"I'm Praxis." She held her hand against her chest, as if there was any doubt. "I know that you found something in the mines. I know that's the real reason you were quarantined. We're going to head back there, and I was hoping that you four would show me the exact spot where you found it."

For a second, nothing. Then one of them, the third in the row, drew his mouth up into a smirk. "Were you, now?"

The guard beside Praxis took a fast, threatening step forward, but Praxis raised her hand to still him. She felt the guard's irritation with her, pooling off him like steam, but she did not bother to turn her head in his direction.

"That's right," Praxis said. "And I'd be very much interested in hearing anything you might know about it, as well. I'll pay handsomely for whatever information you feel like sharing."

This, Praxis was sure, would convince them. Their criminal fees were the only thing holding them here, after all—why wouldn't they jump at the opportunity to reduce them, and for no effort at that?

But no—instead, the third worker was continuing to smirk at her in open defiance of the death-glare being cast by the guard, and even the other three were biting down on their own amused smiles.

"Yeah, sure, I've got some information," the third worker said. "You can take your offer and shove it right up your pompous little—"

The guard struck him hard across the jaw before Praxis could stop him. During the brief but savage beating that ensued, she could only stand there, in open shock. Kaedrich shouted, rushing forward, but by the time she'd arrived the punishment had already been carried out. The guard glowered at Kaedrich, as if daring her to question his methods, but Kaedrich ignored him, rushing to crouch beside the third worker, to see if he was all right, could he still open his eyes, still speak, still stand? When the guard lurched forward to drag Kaedrich back, perhaps, Praxis stopped him with a single look.

Meanwhile, a sick prickle had begun to spread across Praxis's skin as the rapid scene had unfolded before her. Because a knee-jerk understanding of the guard's actions had sprung up inside of Praxis, buried from deep within the box of conditioning her parents had saddled her with when they raised her. *Of course,* a part of her had thought, as the guard had laid into the third worker, of course he shouldn't have dared to speak to a *Fellows* with such a tone.

Now Praxis's skin crawled, disgusted with herself, with the world, as she crouched down beside Kaedrich. Kaedrich, who hadn't exactly heard the conversation, but language barriers would have only shielded her from so much understanding of what had just happened. Praxis steadied herself against Kaedrich's shoulder as she regarded the battered worker. Would he allow her to reach out, to heal the bruises blooming fresh over his face, stanch the trail of blood that trickled from his nose down over his chin? But if she forced her magic upon him, was that really better?

Praxis shouldn't have tried talking to them herself. She realized this as she looked at his face, the way that even now he was cutting a glare sharply through his swelling eyelids. She could have used Kaedrich, could have acted as mere translator and stayed out of the whole thing. In retrospect, this option seemed glaring and obvious, the most obvious answer in the universe.

Retrospect, Praxis decided, was a bitch.

"If you don't want to help me, that's fine," Praxis said, keeping herself to herself. It was better to move on than to try the impossible task of going back to fix her past mistakes. "I understand. But we're going anyway, so enjoy the change of scenery, and if you decide there's anything you want to tell me, I'm still interested in hearing it. And . . . I'll still pay you for your time, regardless. I just want you to know that."

The worker's expression didn't change. Praxis's words made no difference, they would never make a difference. But maybe that wasn't the point. Praxis glanced at Kaedrich, still trying to assess the worker's injuries. Maybe, sometimes, you had to do what was right, even if it wouldn't change matters.

She reached out, running a healing touch across the worker's battered eye, before she had a chance to change her mind.

"THEY'RE NOT GOING to ride with us?" Kaedrich asked as Praxis hauled herself into the waiting sleigh, and the workers were led away down the tunnel, on foot.

"Somehow, I doubt they'd be interested in spending that much time in an enclosed space with me," Praxis said. She sat down, a visible sense of relief radiating off of her as she took the pressure from her legs. Praxis shrugged it off. "Besides, it would never be allowed. There are protocols."

Kaedrich glanced uncomfortably over her shoulder. "Yeah, but . . ."

"Look, I can only fight so many battles at once, okay? If it makes you feel any better, I swear they're not going to be made to walk. There are other sleighs used for this. It's not as *comfortable* as this one, no, but it'll do. Can we please go now?"

"All right, all right," Kaedrich muttered. She climbed in after, sitting across from Praxis.

"For what it's worth, I *am* trying," Praxis said a few moments later. "It's just . . . there's so much I can't control about the way things are, and I'm not saying they're good, but I'm *one person*. How do you even start dismantling something that's been in place for hundreds of years?"

"If there was a simple answer to that, I think the world would be a lot better place," Kaedrich said. Her voice softened. "But . . . I'm glad that you're trying. That you're caring. It means a lot to me."

The flush that hit Praxis's cheeks was sudden and intense, blooming up from her neck before she could cover it. Kaedrich watched it, even as Praxis ducked her head, even as she reached up in a pitiful attempt to make it look like she *wasn't* hiding her face, no, she just had an itch that suddenly needed scratching.

"By the way," Kaedrich said, leaning back in her seat, "I am officially apologizing for every time I thought you were unimaginably rude and insensitive. Compared to the rest of your family, you're a Sister of Perlandra."

Praxis's flush deepened, but she risked a quick glance up, eyebrow cocked. "There were a lot of those times, were there?"

Kaedrich tossed Praxis a smile, half sheepish and half coy. "*That* I'll never say. Still . . . when you consider the environment you were raised in . . ."

Praxis shrugged. She reached into the bag beside her, rummaging. She was obviously fighting the color in her cheeks, though it wasn't clear yet which would win in the end. "I don't know. I mean, apart from the situation with the workers, which is more cultural than personal, they're not *that* bad. Not really."

"*Seriously?*"

"Fine, maybe some of them," Praxis said. She rummaged for another few moments, finally drawing out a slim book bound in red leather, and then reached back and knocked on the wall behind her to signal they were ready. By now, at least, her face was regaining its normal composure. "But you make it sound like they're universally insufferable."

The sleigh jostled slightly underneath them, setting off, and Kaedrich quirked an eyebrow. "And you think they're not?" She raised her hand, ticking up her fingers one by one. "Praine is the slimiest man I've ever met. Your mother is trying to break us up at every possible opportunity, for no reason other than her own bigotry. Your father *acts* nice enough, but he's not above threatening people to get what he wants. Prewish doesn't even care about his own *grandchild*—"

"Now, *that* one you really can't hold against him," Praxis cut in. "I mean, he's not *wrong*. Tannem's bid isn't actually going to win, so the only effect it will have is to damage Prewish's odds."

"Yeah, and I'm not unsympathetic toward him. But . . . it's family. He's going to be a *grandfather* again. Doesn't that have to count for something?"

"You're asking the wrong person," Praxis said. She opened the book, spreading it across her knees as if the subject didn't matter at all.

"Oh, come on. You can't mean to tell me you're not at least a little happy for them. He's your nephew."

A rough laugh escaped Praxis's chest as she looked back up. She set the book down and folded her hands across the open pages. "Happy, sure. Whatever. Happy for what? They'll foist it off on the nanny, which is great for their sleep and their sanity, but means they're barely going to see the child, which means that the biggest impact it's going to have on their lives is his wife has to go through pregnancy again—and why anyone who's gone through that once ever chooses to repeat the experience, I have no idea."

Kaedrich's throat tightened up. "I don't know," she said, trying hard to keep her voice light. "It can't be all bad."

"No, trust me—it can."

"Sure, like *you* would know."

"Better than you would," Praxis said.

"What?"

There are moments that shift the world underneath you. Most of these are large—the start of something new, or the end of something old, a change that will forever redirect the course of your life. But occasionally there is one like this. Something small, a sliver of knowledge that lodges itself just underneath the skin. Something that you can never quite manage to pick out again, no matter how much you might want to.

Kaedrich took one deep, steadying breath, and then another. Maybe she was wrong, she told herself. Maybe Praxis hadn't really meant what it sounded like she'd meant. She clung to this option, despite knowing on some instinctual level that her hope was misplaced.

"You—?" Kaedrich started, but then she had to pause and collect herself again. Praxis was just sitting there, already bored, staring at the open book in her lap. Kaedrich made herself look straight at Praxis, level and steady. "You have a *child*?"

"*What?*" Praxis asked. She looked up, her stricken face contorting into shifting horror and shock and revulsion. "No! Gods, why would you ever—? Oh. Oh, no, Kaedrich, it's not . . . No"—she stopped, cleared her throat—"That is, it didn't last."

"But you were . . . ? I mean, you did . . . ?" Kaedrich waved her hands, hoping she wouldn't need to finish that sentence.

How could she even consider finishing that sentence?

Praxis's cheeks turned pink as she studied her fingernails. "I was . . . Yes . . . for a little while. Once. But like I said, it didn't last. And it was so long ago now. Just after I left home, in fact."

Kaedrich bit down on this, physically pinching her lip between her teeth. She didn't trust herself to say anything, not right now. She didn't even really know, *exactly*, what was bothering her so badly about it. It's not as if she hadn't already been surprised by Praxis's history, but this was . . . different, somehow. This was . . .

She didn't really know what this was.

Kaedrich didn't notice Praxis's approach. "Hey," Praxis said. She scooted forward, until she could reach across the space between them and cup Kaedrich's cheek. "Ella. Listen to me: I wasn't trying to keep this from you. It just . . . it didn't come up before."

"You could have brought it up."

The truth of this twisted Kaedrich's lips in a bitter sneer. Praxis *could* have brought it up. In all of those long conversations, sprawled on the bed in their shared cabin on the voyage down here . . . They'd talked about everything, or at least it had felt like it at the time.

Praxis retreated to her own seat. "I'm sorry," she said, and Kaedrich supposed that should have helped. Instead, all it did was bring to mind everything *else* Praxis hadn't talked about. How much more was she keeping to herself? Finding out about Lexthur had been bad enough, but—

Kaedrich's eyes widened. *Blast.* Her head snapped up. "Oh gods, Praxis . . . is this why you didn't want to see him? Lexthur, I mean?"

"What?" Praxis frowned. "No . . . why would I care about seeing Lexthur?"

"Because . . . well, because . . ." Gods, was Praxis really going to make her say it? "I'm sorry, it's just—Praxis, I thought you were saying that you had . . . I mean, it sounded like . . . like you said that you were pregnant."

"Yeah, I was . . . ?" Praxis said, although slowly, and like she wasn't really sure what the problem was.

"Right, so . . . it's just . . . That is, I just assumed he—"

"Ugh, gods, no!" Praxis said. Her whole face contorted in disgust, and she actually reeled back, looking at Kaedrich as if she'd handed Praxis something offensive. "Seven hells, don't be disgusting. I never slept with Lexthur."

"Okay, but if it wasn't him—"

Praxis raised her hand, cutting Kaedrich off. "There wasn't . . ." She cleared her throat. "That is, her name was Rinn."

"Her."

For a moment, Kaedrich could only stare. She opened her mouth, and then closed it again. Words tumbled through her, but kept collapsing before they had a chance to fully develop. Kaedrich was hardly naïve these days—she knew the world was a vast, diverse place, full of all kinds of different people. She'd even met a woman back in Monfort, a friend of and fellow performer with Kaedrich's friend Tristy, who struggled to be accepted because people had misidentified her as a boy when she'd been born. But somehow . . . somehow Kaedrich didn't think that was the case for Praxis's former lover. Kaedrich didn't have anything to directly point to, but she got the distinct impression Praxis wouldn't have "approved" of that sort of identity; as if a person's sense of self was a thing that someone else got to decide on. This feeling lodged itself, prickly and uncomfortable, beneath Kaedrich's skin, but that was probably a topic best left for another time.

"Um . . . Praxis, I don't mean to be insensitive, but . . . how did—?"

Praxis waved off the question before Kaedrich could even finish. "There's an Aul spell that allows conception between women. It's . . . useful, in a place like that. They have no social barriers defining who you can fall in love with there."

"You're kidding."

"Why would I make something like that up?"

"I don't know," Kaedrich said. Her head was spinning, thoughts colliding and sparking and dying out faster than she could keep up with them. "I mean, I guess you wouldn't, obviously. It's just . . . wow. There's really a spell like that?"

Praxis didn't answer, although Kaedrich didn't notice—not at first. She was too lost in trying to sort out the explosion of ideas swirling through her mind.

Ignore for a moment the logistical questions of *how*, though that was certainly a heavy curiosity for her. The idea that there was a place where women were able to live openly together without fear of reprisal, where they could have a normal life as themselves, where they could *raise a family*, where the choice to pursue their hearts' desire did not mean trading away the option of motherhood . . . Kaedrich could barely even imagine what that would look like. She tried to picture Aul, from what little she knew of it. Praxis had lived there once. What would it be like for her, to live there again? What would it mean for the two of them, if they did?

She did not realize, until she looked up and saw Praxis's face, that while she'd been thinking, Kaedrich's hand had inadvertently come to rest on the lower portion of her own abdomen, cradling it like it was something precious.

A blush burned fast over Kaedrich's face as she whipped her hand away and tucked them both beneath her legs. Neither she nor Praxis said anything as the two of them fastidiously tried to avoid making eye contact with each other. Kaedrich shut her eyes, wincing, but it wasn't the escape she'd hoped for. Praxis's expression followed her, scared and unsettled and . . . haunted? It was more than just her usual aversion to children, that much was clear.

Gods, what had happened to her? Kaedrich made herself look back up, but by now Praxis had managed to smooth herself out, lock everything down again. She was back to her book, staring at the pages with an indifference so well-rehearsed that anyone else might have had a difficult time spotting it.

Praxis didn't look back up for hours, and neither of them spoke again until the sleigh had stopped.

Chapter Twenty-Six

THEY HEARD THE mine long before they saw it. A low rumble that led way to a metallic howl, as if they were approaching the underworlds and the churning of a demonic beast was rising up to greet them. It reverberated through the ice, and permeated the air, and pounded against the sleigh. It shook beneath their feet as they stepped out.

It had taken a full four days to reach this particular mine. Sometimes, it felt as if they'd never make it. Between the bruskers getting spooked just ten miles outside of Bolt, to the driver's inexplicable memory trouble when he tried to figure out where to exit the first major junction, to the misplaced set of keys that kept them from using the Fellows' stop-off lodges, the whole thing reeked of disaster by the time they arrived. It was a wonder, Praxis decided, that the workers had managed to make it there beside them. Rarely, in all of her years of travel, had she been more grateful to finally arrive at her destination.

Unfortunately, the final tunnel had to be traversed by foot. The workers and their handler led the way down a set of crude steps carved out of the ice, so steep and narrow that it felt more like scrambling down a cliff face than walking. Praxis took the stairs two feet at a time, wincing each time she had to put weight on her braced leg. Pain flared out from her knee, hot and fierce. Dammit, Praxis thought, not here, and not now—she had left behind the one remaining vial she'd stolen from Lexthur, uncertain as to how she would hide it from Kaedrich on such a journey.

It was a decision Praxis had made from a more confident time, cocky on the effects of her last dose of glee. It was a decision she was now deeply regretting as she maneuvered each terrible step down into her family's mine.

About halfway down, the stairs turned from ice to stone, and at the bottom a cavern opened up around them. Nothing like the carefully carved ice caverns of the rest of Yandosia; this one was raw and wild, a gap in the underbelly of the world. A stone floor slanted down toward the middle of the open space, while a rough ceiling cut a jagged path over their heads. Stalactites and stalagmites raced back-and-forth contests throughout, meeting occasionally in the middle as a bulbous column. Traces of raw lapus lumeni veined the ceiling—it was said they were powered by the heart of the world, magic leaking up from far, far below. The place was magnificent and dizzying in the way only pure nature could be, but there wasn't time to properly absorb it. In the open stretch of the cavern, a sea of activity was raging like a hurricane. A series of wide tunnels branched off in all directions, each one gagging up a set of tracks that hauled whale-bone carts overwhelmed by ore and rocks dotted with the dull sheen of unprocessed gemstones. These carts were then sorted by the curling backs of the workers, their contents divided and crated into dozens of separate categories.

And everywhere you looked, a sea of bronze faces, dulled by darkness and centuries of hard labor. Only the pale faces and gleaming uniforms of guards and foremen, popped up in the middle of the mass like overgrown weeds, stood out among the ubiquitous wash of servitude and sweat.

"Still think this is a just punishment for their crimes?" Kaedrich asked softly, but Praxis couldn't bring herself to answer. Nearby, the workers they'd brought with them were being unchained, additional guards already breaking off from the main pack of the room and coming over to assist.

It was the guards that led them to the foreman, a woman standing central to the whole operation. Her back was to them, and her head was bent as she listened to something someone else was telling her, and so at first all you could see of her was a white braid trailing midway down her spine, but already a queasy little feeling of familiarity was sneaking up on Praxis. Surely it couldn't be, though . . . ?

The guards reached her first, saying something too low for Praxis to hear. And then the foreman turned around, and Praxis's stomach plunged toward her ankles.

Oh, of all the workers the Fellows employed, of all the mines they owned scattered all over Yandosia, of all the assignments and schedules and overlapping duties that the dozens—hundreds—of foremen had to juggle, fate had landed this one, on this day, at this mine, in *her* hands.

Nellen gave Praxis a polite smile, and tapped her lips respectfully. "Miss Fellows," she said, crisp and professional. "It's an honor. How can I assist you today?"

Praxis forced herself to swallow down the cotton in her throat. She told herself this meant nothing, because of course it was the truth. There was no reason to panic, and there *certainly* was no reason to feel slighted by Nellen's collected poise, her lack of reaction at seeing Praxis again.

After all, their love affair had only ever existed in Praxis's imagination. But oh, what an imagination. Fourteen years old, flush with the throes of her first proper crush; Praxis had harbored her daydream for months, nurturing and protecting it from the harsh cold of reality.

Praxis's cheeks heated involuntarily as Nellen regarded her with polite interest.

In truth, the two of them should never have met in the first place, all those years ago. Nellen was still just a junior supervisor in those days, overseeing a small group of miners in the processing centers. The spoiled youngest daughter of the Fellows family had no business running into her—until there was a problem, something with the lapus lumeni Nellen's team had been separating from the rest of the gems. The wizard employed as head of the division had been called in and then, when he couldn't figure out the problem, Moc was asked to take a look. By that point, young Praxis trailed Moc everywhere. Praxis was well-versed in the magic involved in lapus lumeni—really, she thought, it wasn't that hard—and a part of her was curious what kind of problem could have possibly arisen.

She never did find out. Because the moment they were led into the processing center, Nellen was there to greet them, and suddenly all thought of business tumbled down into the depths of the mines.

Nellen was, at the time, by far the most beautiful woman the teenage Praxis had ever seen. If Praxis hadn't been aware of her own leanings by that point, she sure as hell would be now. Praxis's heart nearly stopped, just to look upon her.

Nellen, meanwhile, was not as thrilled. It was clear, in the press of her lips and the critical squint in her eyes. Young Praxis remained undaunted. She did not take it personally. After all, it made sense: Nellen had only been hired due to the fact that the Fellows had just recently absorbed her own family's company, and some bitterness was to be expected. Praxis stood rooted beside Moc, towering over him, as Nellen gruffly introduced herself and laid out the situation at hand, but all Praxis heard was the relentless rush of blood in her ears. It was, she decided at that moment, the sound of determination—and possibly destiny, though it was hard to say right then.

Praxis nodded along, pretending like she was listening. She wanted to look smart. Also older, and more worldly. Ideally, a little more attractive herself—she remembered, with a cringe, the spread of blemishes that had crept up overnight onto her forehead and one on her chin, and she tried to angle her face in a way she hoped would keep them from Nellen's view. Praxis was smitten, but only *mostly* stupid in the heat of it: she knew that Nellen was much older, six years at least, and she needed, above all, not to look like a dumb little girl.

She was focusing so hard on all of this that she didn't even realize as Nellen turned away, going to retrieve something or other, Praxis had no idea, and Praxis took a step to follow, but then Moc took Praxis by the elbow. "Young thing," he said, and Praxis barely heard him, so Moc coughed, and tugged harder on her elbow. *"Praxis."*

This, finally, had gotten Praxis's attention. She could not even remember the last time Moc had addressed her by name. She blinked, surprised to find herself in an office. She didn't remember coming in here. She would have followed Nellen anywhere.

Moc's face, as he looked up at Praxis, was soft and sad. His age seemed to wear on him like an old coat, dragging down his shoulders. "Might I give you a piece of advice that has nothing to do with your studies, young thing?"

"Of course," Praxis said, already nodding. Of course Moc was welcome to share his wisdom with her, guide her, counsel her. Goodness, did he really need to ask, after all this time? Of course.

Moc's cheek twitched, like he wasn't quite sure he believed her, but he took a breath and pressed on anyway.

"I understand that, at your age, certain . . . impulses are difficult to control," he started, "but between you and me, you're going to need to learn to master yourself around the pretty girls."

Praxis froze. She stared down at him, suddenly somehow both cold and hot at the same time, as her dread and embarrassment raged a battle inside of her. She knew she had to defend herself, to deny what Moc was saying, now, quickly, with as much vehemence as she could muster, but when she opened her mouth to try, the only thing that came out was a squeak.

"It's all right," Moc said, reaching out to rest a hand on her upper arm. Praxis's eyes slid to his hand, the only thing she could focus on at the moment. Moc squeezed. "I'll not tell anyone, and I'm not judging you. In my homeland . . . things are different. We don't have walls around attraction. But here . . ."

Praxis forced a nod. *I understand,* she wanted to say, but the words lodged in her throat. Gods, but how could she ever speak again? How could she ever look Moc in the eyes again? She watched as his hand pulled away, the fading lines of his tattoos disappearing from view.

She thought she'd been so careful, that was the thing. Okay, so . . . looking at it, she did have to admit that her actions around Nellen hadn't been anywhere near as "mastered" as they should have been, but something in Moc's tone told Praxis that his advice had come from a deeper place than just this one incident. How long had he known? How long had he been watching over her as she studied girls out of the corner of her eye and pretended to be interested only in their dresses or their hairstyles? And no sooner had she wondered than the next question rushed in, hot on its heels: who *else* had figured it out?

Moc's mild chuckle brought her back to herself with a start. He patted her arm. "It's all right, young thing. I'm sure you'll find your footing eventually."

He was right, of course, but now, years and years later, Praxis felt herself reverting back into her childhood self. Time collapsed, and it felt as if she'd never left this spot. Moc may as well have still been standing beside her. Nellen was still beautiful. Somehow—was it possible?—even more so, her years lending her a stately quality as she tipped into middle age. Nellen asked a question, her face warm and open, and Praxis nodded without hearing it.

A disgusted huff, from somewhere beside Praxis. Praxis turned, a trace of annoyance knitting her face together, to find Kaedrich reaching forward, hand extended Durn-style.

"Lord Mannly," Kaedrich said, "from Durland. Pleased to meet you. Forgive my companion—she's had a long trip."

Nellen laughed, and it was the sound of glass shattering. Praxis shook her head, the shards of memory raining off her shoulders. She looked at Kaedrich, her heart twisting, disgusted by her own behavior, and then, when she looked back at Nellen, a harsh edge lingered on her face that wasn't there before. Praxis didn't know why she hadn't noticed it a moment ago, because now that she looked again, time and bitterness had not in fact helped her; and even though she was nothing but the model of professional, giving both Praxis and Kaedrich their due deference, there was a tiny cringe in the nose, when she looked at Kaedrich. And so Praxis was wrong: Nellen wasn't the great beauty she'd always remembered her as.

"Right, well, unfortunately that's going to be a problem," Nellen was saying to Kaedrich now. She had her hands folded placidly in front of her, as if she was explaining a very simple concept to a very slow individual. Even her tone was elongated, the words distinct for ease of understanding. "You see, those tunnels are closed off."

Praxis snapped back to herself as she put her hands on her hips. "So? Consider them reopened."

A patient smile met Praxis. "I'm afraid I can't do that, ma'am. I have specific orders."

"From whom?"

"Prewish Fellows himself, ma'am. Safety concerns. You understand."

Praxis nodded. "Oh, I do. I absolutely understand." She narrowed her eyes. "It's *you* that's having trouble comprehending this situation. You may not have gotten word, this far out in the backwater depths . . . but I'm in charge of the lapus lumeni division now. That means I have cause to inspect any mines which I suspect might have untapped veins inside of them, regardless of what operations Prewish has going on."

Nellen frowned. "With respect? There are no lumeni veins in that section. We were about to give up on it, anyway."

"Are you questioning my sense as a wizard?"

"Not at all," Nellen said. "But I do think you're lying, and using your authority as a means of bullying your way through Prewish's orders, and I don't appreciate you jeopardizing the safety of our workers for your own purposes. Ma'am."

Praxis smiled. "And you know what? You may well be right. Here's the thing, though . . ." She leaned in, curling her finger to encourage Nellen to lean in as if they were sharing secrets. She did—reluctantly— and Praxis lowered her voice to a stage whisper. "Truth is, sweetie, even if that were the case, you have no grounds to stop me." Praxis straightened up, waggling her eyebrows. "So the choice is yours. Are you going to get us use of a cart . . . or do I need to report your insubordination to Praine? You know how much he 'hates' having to call people in for a scolding."

Nellen scowled. "Wait here," she snarled.

"I knew you'd see things my way!" Praxis called, waving merrily as Nellen turned on her heel.

"Wow," Kaedrich said, laughing from beside Praxis. "Sometimes I really love you."

Praxis flashed her a grin. "Only sometimes?"

"Weeeeeell, you do still have a tendency to snore."

Praxis stuck her tongue out. "Shut up."

"Never," Kaedrich said, smiling as she leaned in to kiss Praxis's cheek.

SO THAT WAS the first delay, but it was far from the last. As they were led into the depths of the mines, it seemed as if everything that could go wrong, did. First the cart they were going to ride was missing a wheel, because one of the workers hadn't gotten the message and thought he was supposed to perform a routine maintenance check on all the transports. Then the replacement wheel they were going to use was dropped, and cracked right down the middle. Then the appropriate tool to reattach the *next* one—not quite the right size, but it would do in a pinch, and Praxis's patience was fast running out—couldn't be found; turns out, it was left on the wrong tool bench that morning. By the time the cart was finally rolled up, a wide platform with a pump-motion handle to propel them along the miniature, train-like tracks, Kaedrich was beginning to question the whole trip.

It wasn't just that everything kept going wrong, though that was reason enough to doubt the conviction with which they'd been pressing on, and more than once Kaedrich had wondered if Perlandra, or some other outside force, was trying to keep them from reaching the place where the Beacon had been found. In which case . . . was it even wise to continue? What awaited them, if they dared to challenge such an influence?

And, of course, there was Praxis.

Nothing about her behavior lately was right. True, she'd been acting *off* ever since they'd arrived in Yandosia, but it had only gotten worse since setting off for the mines. Kaedrich had thought, perhaps naïvely, that getting some distance between Praxis and her family would help matters, but that didn't seem to be the case so far. She'd spent most of the trip in silence, grunting or nodding whenever Kaedrich asked a question, and even Kaedrich's few attempts at proper conversation or flirting, while responded to, felt forced.

Not to mention the way Praxis had made a spectacle of herself over the foreman. Stumbling and all but drooling over herself—why, Kaedrich had practically expected her heart to shoot forward from her chest, punching at the front of her shirt like in the comedy skits Kaedrich used to catch during jesters' hour back in Monfort's theater district. Irritation had flooded Kaedrich, but thankfully once she'd stepped in, Praxis seemed to come back to herself. Kaedrich's spirits had soared, watching Praxis eviscerate the foreman's objections. Even threatening her with Praine . . . Kaedrich knew Praxis would never *honestly* follow through with that, so Kaedrich had enjoyed watching the foreman squirm, the twist of her face as she turned to make arrangements. And it was true that Praxis hadn't so much as glanced at the foreman since. Still . . . Kaedrich found herself studying Nellen, now, wondering: what was it about her that had ensnared Praxis, if only for a moment? Kaedrich had spent years trying to gain Praxis's attention. Was this what it took, then, to gain it quickly? She didn't like to think about it, but not thinking about it was burning a hole in her chest, and so she could not deny the relief that poured over her when their cart rounded a corner, the tracks sharply descending in front of them, and the foreman called back, "Almost there now."

But then they heard the shouts.

Then they plunged into a haze of rock dust.

Then all of Kaedrich's relief crumbled, swirling up to match the cloud that rushed to greet them.

At the bottom of the slope, a kind of organized chaos was unfolding, a clamor of inquiries and orders, barked suggestions and snapped responses, the percussion of panic as recognizable as the taste of blood, and Kaedrich's tongue soured as she took it all in. Words darted through the clouds of choking dust, abrasive, aggressive, unidentifiable to Kaedrich; but as their driver set the brake on their rickety little cart, the whole thing squealing and lurching to a stop in the cacophony of the tunnel, a kind of quiet understanding had begun to settle in Kaedrich's mind. By the time news of the disaster had been relayed to the foreman, and then translated by Praxis for Kaedrich's benefit—almost as an afterthought, as if it didn't quite even matter, a shrug of Praxis's shoulder—the idea of a cave-in was so assumed that it came as no surprise at all.

"Was anyone hurt?" Kaedrich asked, talking to Praxis but already looking around for the answer. A handful of the workers were rushing by with cuts on their faces or arms, but never stopping, not bothering to attend to themselves, instead racing for pickaxes and shovels. Kaedrich did not even wait for an answer; she drew out a handkerchief and attempted to tie a crude sort of mask around her face, then quickly peeled off the outermost, warmest, most lavish and useless layers of her outfit and laid them over the filthy lip of a nearby supply cart. She undid her cufflinks, pocketing them for safekeeping, and was already halfway through rolling up her sleeve when a hand found Kaedrich's elbow.

"Kaedrich," Praxis said.

A name can mean a lot of things. Said by a boss, it can be praise or admonishment. Said by a priest, it can be a sacred oath, a bond that can never be broken. Said by yourself, it can be a declaration of purpose, a dare to those who might doubt your sincerity. Said by a lover . . .

There were a thousand shades that Praxis could have colored Kaedrich's name with. Love or support, or joy or relief. Ecstasy or anguish. Fear or delight. It could be a plea, or a question, or a promise.

Or it could be weary.

Kaedrich stepped back, her name grazing her like a bullet. "You don't think we should help them." It wasn't a question—there was no need for it to be a question, no up-turn necessary at the end, leaving things just a little uncertain. Instead, her voice flattened itself as her breath escaped her, the finality of her understanding of what Praxis meant knocking the wind out of her. "How . . . Praxis, how can you *not* think we should help?"

"We have important things to do," Praxis said, and Kaedrich almost laughed in her face, at the absurdity of it.

"'Important things'? There are *people* trapped in there!"

Kaedrich did not need translation to know this. The bustle of the tunnel, the severity and swiftness with which they worked. Even Nellen had plunged into the situation, taking charge of the efforts without a backward glance at her distinguished guests.

But Praxis just squirmed, a child caught out in a lie. "There's no guarantee they're even still alive. My sense—"

"Isn't always perfect. You've told me yourself. There's no guarantee that they're dead."

"But if they *are*?" Praxis said. She spoke quickly, perhaps hoping to outrun Kaedrich's compassion. "Do you really want to risk delaying, when a Beacon is loose, in the hands of who-even-knows? Kaedrich, every minute we delay is another minute for them to *act*. I don't need to remind you what happened, the last time someone got their hands on—"

"No," Kaedrich said. "In fact, you don't need to remind me."

For Kaedrich remembered, oh, she remembered. Their trip into the land of the dead, the start of everything terrible that had destroyed the peace of her homeland. She remembered, perhaps better even than Praxis, because it was this action that sealed the fate of Kaedrich's death forever, this action that led her to believe the moment had come, finally, in the halls of the Council's Crescent, on the day Lanali took power and they had to flee Monfort. Never mind that she'd been mistaken, somehow— the day still loomed for her, somewhere in the future. It was never far from Kaedrich's mind, not any of it.

"Then you know what's at stake," Praxis said, lowering her voice. "The workers can take care of themselves—they deal with cave-ins, they know how to handle it."

"But surely you know some magic that can speed things up! Praxis, please . . . if we do nothing, they could *die*."

"And if we stay, whoever has the Beacon could rip a piece of the *world* apart." Praxis shook her head. "It's not worth the risk. I'm sorry, but it's settled—we're leaving. We'll backtrack up the tunnel, and find another way around."

Kaedrich's mouth dropped open behind her makeshift mask. Praxis turned away; she started to weave through the chaos, past streaming lines of workers already attempting to pull rocks out of the thick pile that had cut off a pocket of their compatriots. She did not even seem to see the workers, the tension and worry that lined their faces and lent strength to their roped muscles. She was trying to find the workers that had led them here, though did she even remember what they looked like, did she even *care*? Vertigo seized Kaedrich and she actually had to lean over and rest her hands on her knees for a second because, gods, maybe Praxis *didn't* care about it. Was she actually any better than her family, after all?

There was, perhaps, one way to find out. Kaedrich's fists curled up against her thighs. She pushed herself upright, squaring her shoulders. Then she pulled down her handkerchief from in front of her face, the better to ensure that her next words weren't muffled in the choked air.

"No."

For half an instant, Kaedrich was worried that Praxis hadn't heard her. It wouldn't have been a surprise—between the scraping of the rocks as the workers began to haul away the outermost layer of rubble, between the grunts and heavy breaths of exertion, between the questions and orders still flying from one end of their cramped tunnel to the next, between the crunch of rock underfoot as people shifted from place to place, between the ping of several pickaxes, it would have been easy for Kaedrich's declaration to have gotten lost. *No.* For a word with such a huge meaning, it had such a tiny body, as small as a baby bird just trying to take flight. Kaedrich was prepared for it to fall to the ground on its first attempt, but she saw it reach Praxis instead. The jerk of Praxis's shoulders, where it hit her from behind; she shuddered on impact, as if Kaedrich's word had physical weight to it.

When Praxis turned, her eyes were already narrowed, and they found Kaedrich instantly. It reminded Kaedrich of a look Praxis had given her once, years ago, when they'd first met. That time, the air had seemed to disappear from Kaedrich's lungs, her chest squeezing down—she'd actually staggered to the ground, gasping for breath, before Praxis had ripped her gaze away, and the air came freely once more.

Not that Praxis would ever actually *use* a spell like that against Kaedrich, certainly not anymore (and, in point of fact, Kaedrich often felt like Praxis hadn't really meant to that first time, either). Even without the potency of Praxis's magic behind it, though, a look like that, from a face like hers—it wasn't something you'd want to cross. It was designed to cut through ice, to crush hearts. To win.

"Excuse me?" Praxis said.

The jut of Kaedrich's chin spoke at least as loudly as her voice. "You heard me. I said 'no.' I put up with a lot of your shit, Praxis, because frankly it's easier that way, but *not this*. I'm not going anywhere, not until this cave-in is cleared and we know if the workers are safe." Kaedrich paused—not long enough for an argument, just enough to gather her words, and her courage. "It's the right thing to do. And Perlandra knows I can't force you to stay here and help, but I'm telling you . . . if you walk away now, you're going to be leaving a lot more than just these miners."

Finally, at last, here was something that could pierce the impenetrability of the Fellows emotional armor. Praxis's face blanched as the muscles of her jaw went slack. Her lips parted an infinitesimal amount before they caught themselves. One hand reached out, unthinking, to steady herself against the ragged wall beside her.

"You wouldn't."

"To help save innocent lives?" Kaedrich shook her head. "You know I would."

"No," Praxis said. She pushed herself straight, the ice reasserting itself across her heart. "No, I refuse to believe you would throw away everything we have, not for something like this. It matters too much to you, and I *don't appreciate* you using such a cheap tactic to try to manipulate me!" And now, here, her face turned sour, an old bitterness contorting her expression. "I thought you were better than that."

"And *I* refuse to believe you would really do nothing!" Kaedrich said. "People's *lives* are at stake, Praxis! I don't care if there's a chance they're already dead, you would *really* walk away from them? If there was anything you could do to help, if there was *any chance* you could prevent tragedy, you would really turn away? *Really?*"

Praxis's face blanked out, her reaction wiped clean so fast that it could have only been a practiced maneuver—but not before a trace of horror had already dashed across her eyes, and so Kaedrich breathed a little easier, the knot in her chest loosening just a fraction. Kaedrich did not even bother waiting for Praxis to make the right decision; she turned away, pulling her handkerchief back up, making herself useful, sure in the faith that Praxis would follow suit in the end. When even the *idea* of doing nothing was enough to scare her that deeply . . . there was no doubt the path she would take. A flare of shame cut through Kaedrich as Praxis caught back up with her, that Kaedrich had ever doubted Praxis's good intention. Kaedrich squeezed Praxis's shoulder as she passed.

"I knew you would do what's right," she whispered, but Praxis didn't react, her face set in stone, her eyes already cutting up the blockade of rubble before her, and so there was nothing more to say.

They got to work.

CLEARING THE BLOCKAGE in the tunnel took a long time, longer even than Praxis feared it would. Even with her magic, her hands softening the rocks one by one until they were first supple and then fragile and then, finally, crumbling beneath her touch like wet sand sculptures upon a beach. The workers labored alongside her, shoveling and hauling. They looked upon her first with an affronted air, and then shock, and then a kind of fierce curiosity, studying the way her fingers stroked the stubborn rocks, the subtle muttering beneath her breath.

And then, about twenty minutes into the process, one of them surprised Praxis by laying his own hands beside hers on a particularly large stone. The words that whispered out of him were not the same, no, but close enough, and even then Praxis could feel the greater softening of the stone beneath her hands, crumbling at the combined effects of the magic. It was well known that the natives of Yandosia had a higher magical propensity than those of Praxis's people, but to act upon their natural instincts was a sternly punishable offense, and so Praxis had never seen it for herself. Shock turned her head toward his, that he would so openly defy such a stern edict, and in front of a Fellows no less, and she found herself looking at the face of one of the workers she'd brought with her, the face that she'd healed before they'd even left Bolt. He was staring at her with much the same quiet swagger he'd held even then, even when he was in chains; and when Nellen rushed forward a moment later, as she was supposed to, a baton already raised to punish him, Praxis stilled her with barely more than a look.

Thus it was that a silent revolution took place. Oh, surely it would amount to nothing once the crisis was over, surely it would soften neither

Nellen's, nor the Fellows', nor Yandosia's attitudes as a whole. But it was, for this moment anyway, a tiny but measurable victory, as at least half of the workers who'd been helping to clear the tunnel stepped forward, trying out this new spell. As the rest of them, including Kaedrich, and even, finally, reluctantly, Nellen herself, grabbed shovels and buckets and their bare hands, pawing sand away almost as fast as the workers could generate it.

Still, the process was neither swift nor without setback. Twice, a portion of their work collapsed underneath them—staggering several workers, only narrowly avoiding additional rocks that tumbled forth from the ceiling now that the weight that had previously held it had disappeared. Bits of broken whale-bone supports needed to be carefully removed, so as not to spear the very workers trying to dig through the rubble. The cave-in was also deeper, thicker, more tangled than Praxis had at first believed, and a part of her wondered if there was ever an end to it. Surely, she thought, anyone who was unfortunate enough to have been caught up in the disaster had been crushed in the first moments of collapse? Indeed, in their work they did unbury a handful of unfortunate victims, those who'd been too slow or inattentive to avoid their inevitable fate. But whenever Praxis began to consider calling the operation off, or simply walking away from it, abandoning the workers to their own fate, a flash of Kaedrich's eyes would flare in Praxis's mind, stern and cutting and achingly *disappointed*, and this would, if not exactly spur Praxis onward, at least get her to grit her teeth and keep going.

It was impossible, of course, for Kaedrich to have *known*. Her memories of that afternoon in the Council's Crescent were scattered and incomplete, and Praxis took comfort in this every day. The fact that Kaedrich had actually died, that Praxis had used the Beacon of Souls to bring her back, that she'd willingly given up their only chance to try to stop Lanali's rise to power, this was a secret that Praxis would take to her grave. But still, Kaedrich's words had cut a little too close for Praxis's liking. *You would really turn away? If there was any chance?*

What Praxis couldn't say, what she would never say, was the truth. *Yes, my love, I really would. I already did.* And she would have turned away today, too, was in fact already turning away, but what other choice did Praxis have now? To leave in the face of that would be almost as bad as confessing, the two choices mingled up in her mind and her heart, and there was only one thing she *could* do, anymore.

So it was that Praxis and Kaedrich stayed, and so it was that in the end they and the rest of the workers rescued thirteen more of their compatriots from deeper in the tunnel. They stumbled out, legs shaking beneath them and blinking in the light like newborn foals, into the welcoming arms of the workers, who guided them and assessed them and openly healed their wounds, even under the disapproving eyes of Nellen.

More importantly to Praxis, though, than their rescue itself, was that the tunnel beyond them lay open and unobstructed, and so she was able to scramble through the *other* direction, after the workers had been pulled to safety, not bothering to wait around to see how it all shook out. For it turned out there was no work-around path to where she wanted to go after all, and so staying and clearing the blockage was the correct course of action, the only course of action—not that Praxis was particularly inclined to share this with Kaedrich. She wasn't inclined to share much of anything with Kaedrich, not right now, and so she pushed her way through as if escaping, running away from the truth of what she'd done, again, what she'd almost done again. Kaedrich would follow, of course. She would always follow, when the cause was true.

That's what made it worse.

In the tunnels beyond, they were greeted by darkness, the first proper darkness they'd encountered since arriving in Yandosia. Even on the surface, traveling in the caravan through the endless stretch of night that glittered high above them, there had been a kind of ethereal glow: between the moonlight and the stars, between the swirls of green and pink and blue that spread like a painter's palette in the sky, between the way the snow reflected everything so brightly that at times it hurt to look at it, there had never been a proper darkness. Not like you'd find in a Durlish night, and not anywhere *near* like the abyss of the mines.

In the darkness, the air felt colder. A sense of weightlessness descended over Praxis, a dizzying rush in which there was no up or down, in which she was simultaneously trapped as if in her mother's womb and flung free into the endless expanse of infinity. Praxis couldn't tell if the rushing in her ears was the sound of her own breath, or a whisper just out of hearing range, or the stale breathing of the cave itself, the way the air continually cycled and shifted as it led miners and explorers into ever-deeper depths with its temptress melody. Quiet panic crept up her throat, the cold hand of dread wrapping itself over the skin of her neck.

And then, like a spring breeze, Kaedrich's hand brushed over Praxis's back. The panic melted off. Praxis shook herself off, squared her shoulders. She snapped her fingers and cupped a flame over her palm, the light sparking so brightly that it left spots across her vision.

Praxis had been worried that it would be difficult to find the spot where the Beacon had been found. Would the workers even remember the exact place where it had tumbled out of the rock face? *The whispers,* they'd finally told her, somewhere between shifting and hauling, somewhere after the first shouts of help were heard through the rock, somewhere after the first battered arm had thrust itself out, pleading, imploring, through the gap. They'd followed the whispers, as if the mine itself was guiding them forward.

In the tunnels now, it wasn't so much whispers Praxis heard, but she did pick up a trail of . . . something. Some lingering magic, buzzing in the air just enough to raise the hairs on her arms. She followed it, instinct and impulse and maybe something like faith guiding her forward, deeper into the twisting maze of her family's mine. Into an offshoot of an offshoot of a smaller access tunnel. This was clearly more of an exploratory branch, rather than a fully equipped mining setup. At one point, she was worried she wouldn't be able to track it farther, the tunnel both shortening and narrowing so that she had to maneuver down and wriggle through. She actually disconnected the tension to her harness at one point, squeezing herself in and then dragging her leg up behind her, but in the end she was rewarded, for look, here: she had found it.

She did not need confirmation to know this was the place. Loose magic swirled in the air like stale smoke, and in one corner, a portion of the wall had been hacked at so inexpertly that it could have only been a kind of delirium driving them forward. Praxis actually reeled back from the force of the magic, letting it wash around her, embrace her. It was no wonder the workers had been so drawn here, so desperate to keep moving deeper into the ground. "What's wrong?" Kaedrich asked from behind her, but Praxis could not answer. Instead, she moved forward in silence, laying her hand with gentle reverence on the concave arch just inside of the hacked apart wall, the spot where the Beacon had popped out.

A swarm of impressions swallowed Praxis whole, half from the workers, and half from something else, something nameless, something ancient, something unimaginably weary. She saw the workers, hacking at the wall as if in a fever dream, and tasted the determination on the back of their tongues. The first hints of the Beacon's light pouring through the crack in the wall, spurring them on, and then the sight of it as the rocks fell away, the pureness of it, the glory, like staring into the face of their god. The hitch in the workers' chests as they realized what they'd found, and the soft weight of it falling into the supplicant cup of their cracked palms. An intoxicating burst of glorious freedom gushed off it, the Beacon's pleasure gutting them like a hundred orgasms. So long it had languished in its prison, cold and dark and utterly alone, so alone, not even its tether and influence on the world providing comfort. So long that it had become complacent, lulled, numbed. So long that it had, perhaps, begun to die, if such a thing were even possible. What had awoken it? It was difficult, even for the Beacon, to figure that out. In terms of its lifespan it had been mere moments, and yet, to be awake for the first time in eons, each second became its own eternity. Mortals might have called it years—not many, but some. It had awoken, and it had seen itself, seen its circumstances, felt its loss, and it began to scream. So long had it been screaming now, begging to be found.

These thoughts found Praxis all at once, an understanding drilling itself into her temples like the sharpest headache. For a second she could barely breathe, her chest constricted, her mouth dry. This was worse than she'd been imagining—forget this one Beacon, forget this one problem, the sensation Praxis picked up now was one that had thrummed straight through the heart of the world, reaching every corner at once, a *jostle* that had roused not just one, not just some . . . She had no actual, tangible proof, nothing to grasp onto, not really, but as Praxis stood there, terror rooting her in place, she was suddenly convinced that, whatever had woken this one up, it had touched every Beacon in the world.

A whisper crawled up behind her, crouching as carefully as a scorpion on her shoulder. *Nonsense,* it whispered to her, not so much a word as a feeling, a truth that seemed to vibrate at the same frequency as her soul. *Nonsense, you're being silly. Forget this. Forget this.*

A layer of doubt, just enough, fell over Praxis like a light dusting of snow. Maybe . . . but no, she told herself, she had been sure of it. Sure of what?

Forget this.

This. The Beacon, its awakening, its discovery. Panic seized at Praxis, and she grabbed hold of the certainty while she still could, but even then, she could feel it slipping. *Forget this,* and Praxis found it harder to remember, exactly, what had she seen, what had she felt? "They're awake," she said, aloud, trying to ground herself in the truth that now slipped another measure beneath her feet, like walking on the shifting sand of a tide. *Forget this.* Praxis didn't want to forget this, but she was losing hold of it fast—alone, so alone, and then, and then, then what? Then something, *something*—*Forget this*—The sight of the Beacon, so pure, so perfect, falling as a newborn babe into the cradle of their hands—*Forget this*—The sliver of light, as nourishing as mother's milk, barely hidden now, almost within their reach—*Forget this*—The need, as it pulled the workers forward, the scream and the song that they couldn't so much hear as feel—*Forget this*—eternity and destiny and screaming and pain and unspeakable bliss and don't forget don't forget this is important and the Beacon so old and angry and lost and found and alone and—*Forget this.*

"Praxis?"

Praxis forgot. She blinked, stepping back, as Kaedrich placed her hand on Praxis's arm. When she turned, she felt something slide off her, like a blanket falling from her shoulders, but even that, too, was fleeting, and there was nothing now, a sleepless sort of confusion like waking up from a dream. She looked at Kaedrich, and Kaedrich asked, "Are you all right?" and Praxis nodded. She was almost startled to find a flame still caught in her palm, the only light between her and Kaedrich. Shadows danced like satisfied laughter across both of their faces.

"What did you find?" Kaedrich asked, but Praxis could only frown. Because she'd found nothing, not a single damned thing, but admitting that felt like one failure too many. The rocks had been as lifeless as anything, the cavern nothing more than an empty pit in the bottom of a hole in the ground. They shouldn't have come here at all, shouldn't have wasted so much time—time they could have spent searching the Fellows household, asking uncomfortable questions, being nosy and invasive and obnoxious in her search.

Do you really need to look, though?

The question posed itself in Praxis's head without her thinking it, but now that it was there, perhaps it was right. What was she hoping to find, anyway? There were so many immediate concerns, so much to occupy her attention, yes. She still owed her father a modified lapus lumeni, the fate of the company still hung in the balance. *What are you even doing here?* What *was* she doing here? They needed to get back, she needed to forget this.

"We have to go," Praxis said. She was already moving, already escaping the questions Kaedrich wanted to ask.

"Praxis—wait. What did you find? What did you mean, 'they're awake'?"

Praxis frowned, but she did not stop walking. Kaedrich hung at her back, and Praxis tried not to pay attention, even as she said, "I don't know. I said that? I don't remember saying that."

"You said that."

"It doesn't matter," Praxis said. "Forget this. It was a waste of time to come here, anyway."

"But—"

"I said it doesn't matter," Praxis snapped. She wedged herself sideways, her skin crawling with the need to leave, hurry, now, get out of here. "I was wrong, all right? There's nothing here. We're going home."

And maybe Kaedrich didn't believe her—probably Kaedrich didn't believe her—but for once, she didn't try to argue. Praxis lurched forward, fingers flexing madly, scrambling to get away, to leave it all behind. She had to get home.

She had to forget this.

Chapter Twenty-Seven

THERE WERE EIGHT Fellows children. In a large family especially, every child has their role. So it was with the sons and daughters of Prawl and Prestina.

There was Prewish, the oldest. His job was to always be right. It was a heavy burden, and one he did not shirk, even when lesser men might cave under pressure. He worked right. He married right. He bore the right children. Even in his darkest depths—even under the most diamond-hard scrutiny—even when his son died, in his care, on his watch, Prewish was not to be blamed. He mourned, as a good father should. And then he showed them all how to move on, as a good father should. He would lead them all, eventually—of that, there was really no doubt.

Previn, of course, was the object of pity. The one that was hidden away for safekeeping, brought out only when the rest of them needed a reminder about how lucky they really were, how lucky they all were, to be graced with this life, blessed with this family. When the bickering got to be too much, when the infighting threatened to turn dangerous, when the other children's self-destructive tendencies of drink or drug or lust or magic or ego threatened to consume them, there would be Previn. Poor, sweet Previn.

In Praine, the family was graced with charm. His father wielded him like a weapon. It was said, in the whispers, that no deal could not be bargained, no fight could not be won, no mind could not be turned, when Praine's cutting smile was put on full display. The others could tell in a glance when a negotiation was growing tense, for there he would be—no need for summons, no reason to ask. A rival family would come to dinner, and the sons would grow fat with promises, while the objections of the daughters died in their throats.

They had Prenna for the nurturing of a mother. No need to bother their own. Her song could soothe every heartache, her hugs could mend every wound. She was the perfect woman: selfless, compassionate, tender, respectable—tamed, or so they believed. Only a few saw the puppet strings attached to her husband, and fewer still understood the danger therein. Sweet Prenna, kind Prenna. Who better to bare your soul to, if not she?

For Prommel, the role was simple: protector of them all. In another time and place, he would have been the mightiest and most feared warrior in all the lands—as it was, he had to content himself with smaller chances for glory. Still, his heart was pure, as any good knight's. His job consumed him. Ignore the woman who finally stood beside him; the work was his true mistress.

Every family needs a jester.

Prett was well-suited for the task. Do not ask whether he wanted it—it was his, from the moment he first stepped out of the cradle. Any trouble underfoot, any prank needing a party to blame it on, any mischief discovered without a single culprit to be found—they knew where to look. His smiles and laughter infected those around him, protecting him from the potential of their wrath. Who would dare to blame him, their shining son, the one whose merriment filled the tunnels of the household as if every day was a holiday?

And Praxis.

What need be said of Praxis? The outcast. The black mark. The dream turned into a nightmare. It would be better not to speak of her at all.

This left, of course, still one.

Did you miss him? You wouldn't be the first. Countless times a tally has been made, and countless times a name left off. A vague wrinkle of the forehead, as if the speaker couldn't quite remember. *Wait,* the words would come next, *were there . . . eight of them? Or just seven?* Fingers counted, numbers double-checked. Eventually, a shrug. *Oh, well. Who even knows?*

Pranders, the forgotten.

It was never out of malice. Or spite, or shame, or hatred. The boy was simply . . . well, dull, in comparison to the rest of them. A pale shadow, blending into the ice, in contrast to all the glittering gems of the others. Therein was his curse. And therein was his greatest gift.

For you see, a forgotten child is not looked for. A forgotten child can wander. A forgotten child can get lost, pop up again, lost once more, and you'd never think to wonder where he'd gone. You'd never think to ask what he'd seen. What he'd heard.

He heard so much.

He heard Prewish, talking to the wizard about the mighty treasure that had entered the household. He heard Prommel's uncertainty, his doubts about the nature of the man's death. He heard maids whispering among themselves, fear bleeding through the frozen walls—if death could strike a *wizard* like that, then what was to protect them? How long would *they* be safe? He heard the whisper of footsteps. He heard the tumbling of a lock, the careful, subtle shift as the numbers slipped by.

He did not, however, hear the cry being emitted from the object that he now held in the palm of his hand.

It truly was a thing of beauty—every bit as amazing as the grubs who found it had said. The light of it filled the room, bathing Pranders in an otherworldly glow. The point of light that writhed in the middle reflected back at itself in Pranders's eyes, twin points creating, for a moment, a triangle of staggering beauty and power.

"How in the depths did you get in here?"

The voice was as Pranders expected, though he'd hoped to delay this conversation. Ideally, it would never have happened, but then, Pranders never was the one blessed with luck. If he was, he'd be living quite a different life right now—married to the only woman he'd ever loved, somewhere undefined but far from here, basking in the glow of his own family.

That was not his fate.

This was.

Pranders turned around. The orb was still in his open palm, his fingers barely curved up at all to ensure it did not roll off.

Two more eyes reflected the glow of the orb. Wide and angry. The point of light flashed, its eternal frenzy whipped into even more agitation. Four mirrors now bounced the image back and forth between them, building like a storm on the horizon. Or so Pranders imagined—he'd never seen a storm, not for real anyway.

He'd liked to have.

But now he never would. Pranders saw the moment happen, the sealing of his fate. In the eyes across from him, shock turned to anger turned to rage turned to a sadness so deep, not even the mines of the Fellows' fortune could find the bottom. Pranders understood it, though he wished he didn't. Finally, he had gone too far. Finally, he had pushed his luck to the breaking point. Finally, he had witnessed something he shouldn't, something he *mustn't*. Finally, he was seen.

I'm sorry. The apology was spoken in the turn of the eyes watching him. No words were uttered.

Pranders shut his own eyes. He did not want to see his death coming. He was not the brave one. But just before the end came for him, just as panic began to seize his heart, the tiniest flutter of peace entered his mind: they would never forget him again.

Finally, at last, Pranders Fellows would be remembered.

KAEDRICH SAW THE banners before anyone else.

Not that it meant anything to her. Slate-blue, nearly the same color as Praxis's battered old coat, they hung, bunting-style, along the tunnels leading up toward the entrance of the Fellows household. More of them wrapped the bars of the gates. They were gauzy and delicate, fluttering slightly at the subtle breezes of breath and movement, and Kaedrich's first impression was that they must have been put up for the next coming-of-age ball. She tried to remember the date in her head, but—surely, that must be soon? Annelle had certainly been fixated on her preparations, when they'd left.

"Oh gods," Praxis breathed as she exited the sleigh behind Kaedrich. Her face was horror-struck when Kaedrich turned around, her hand at her mouth in disbelief.

"What?" Kaedrich asked, but Praxis couldn't answer. She was already racing forward, the click of gears churning furiously with her footsteps.

Micadel was at the gates, and his sad eyes met her as they approached. He did not need to say anything, though—before he even could, Praxis held up a hand to stop him. Her face was still, her gaze turned inward in a way that Kaedrich recognized as concentrating on her wizard's sense.

After only a moment, her expression crumpled. "Pranders?" she asked, and Micadel gave a solemn nod. Praxis made a quiet "huh" sound. She linked arms with Kaedrich, and the two of them passed through the gates without another word.

Inside, more slate-blue drapery. Several of the pieces of art and opulence had been taken down, and it was this subduing of the usual standards that finally began to click the pieces together for Kaedrich.

"Praxis . . . ," Kaedrich asked slowly, keeping her voice down to avoid the ducked heads of the servants moving numbly past. "Has . . . has someone *died*?"

A subtle nod.

"Pranders," Praxis said under her breath. "And before you ask, no, I don't know what's happened yet. I only figured it out because he's the one who's missing."

"Pranders," Kaedrich repeated. She frowned in concentration, running down the list of Fellows. "He's . . ."

"Sixth," Praxis said. "Just above Prett and me. It doesn't make sense . . . Pranders was so young, I don't—"

She broke off, turning away. Her fingers dug at the ice as she caught herself against the wall.

Kaedrich's heart twisted up, seeing her. "Oh, Praxis—"

"I'm fine," Praxis said. She straightened up, squaring her shoulders. Her face, when she turned back, was as impassive as ever. "Really." She shrugged. "I barely knew him."

Kaedrich raised a disbelieving eyebrow. "He was your *brother.*"

"And?" Praxis was already moving off, leaving Kaedrich to catch up. Praxis sighed. "Look, I know you think this is heartless, but when you have a family as large as ours, well . . . there are siblings you care about, and there are ones you don't. Pranders and I never spent time together, not really. Certainly not by ourselves. He was . . . quiet, and really more of Praine's bootlicker than anything else, which frankly wasn't the key to popularity in my book."

"Still . . . ," Kaedrich said, not ready to be convinced. "You have to have cared something for him. I won't believe that you didn't. You're not *that* cold, Praxis. I know you're not."

"Then you have more faith in my humanity than I do."

Kaedrich huffed lightly under her breath. "I think we all knew *that.*"

She'd said it as a joke, a feeble attempt to lessen some of the shroud that had enveloped them at the Fellows' doorstep—yet as soon as it was out of her mouth, she knew it was a mistake. Praxis's pace faltered, and though she'd covered it almost instantly, Kaedrich had seen. A subtle tightening of her face, the smallest flinch of her shoulders.

"I'm sorry," Kaedrich said. "I didn't mean it."

Praxis waved the apology off. "It's fine if you did. You're right—you're the one with the heart. You always have been."

"Careful," Kaedrich said. "If you tell yourself that long enough, you might just start to believe it."

Praxis drew to a stop as a bitter laugh escaped her. "And why shouldn't I believe it?" Praxis asked. She threw her arms wide. "Look at me,

Kaedrich. My own brother is dead, and I can't bring myself to care. You, on the other hand—"

"You're in shock, that's all." Kaedrich reached out, going for Praxis's shoulder, but Praxis slid from the touch.

Praxis shook her head. "I really don't think I am. I mean, I'm *surprised*, obviously. It's not like I was expecting to come home to find somebody dead. But shock?" A sad look softened her otherwise stoic face. "The truth is I'm more upset about you seeing my lack of grief."

This was probably the kind of statement Kaedrich should argue with, but the way Praxis said it rang with too much naked honesty, a thought slipped free when she'd meant to keep it private. Perhaps Praxis hadn't even realized she'd felt that way, much less that she was going to *say* it, because now her cheeks flushed a deep pink, and she looked away.

She set off again, fingers flexing, leaving Kaedrich to keep up, or not.

"Where are we going?"

"*I'm* going to see how my parents are doing," Praxis said. She did not look behind her, merely tossed out a casual shrug that Kaedrich watched from behind. "What you'd like to do is your choice."

The barb stung as it flew past, nicking heat into Kaedrich's cheeks.

"I guess I'll go catch Prommel up, then, on how the trip went," she said—though, could Praxis even hear her by that point? Already, she was retreating from view, the hem of her coat waving a disinterested goodbye.

It's nothing, Kaedrich told herself. Praxis was just . . . Praxis, and hurt by the loss of her brother, whether she would admit it or not. Kaedrich clung to this, holding it like a poultice against the burn, as she turned and set off for Prommel's office. Besides, Praxis had been acting strange for days now, the whole time back to the Fellows household; and all that would need to be addressed, certainly, but for now . . . for now, there were larger issues at stake, and maybe Prommel would have had better luck at fixing them than Praxis had.

WHEN PRAXIS HAD said she was going to see her parents, she wasn't exactly *lying*—but she wasn't exactly telling the truth, either. After all, she did fully intend to seek out Prawl and Prestina, to report home and express her sympathies, to see if there was anything she could do for them. To . . . try, at least, to be something of a good daughter, in this moment of need. It wasn't familiar territory for her, but surely if Praxis was ever going to make the effort, the time should be now, right?

But first, she had a stop to make. The pain in Praxis's knee had bloomed to an unimaginable proportion during the ride back, making conversation between her and Kaedrich nearly impossible. Probably, it was muddying Praxis's thoughts—it felt as if she'd behaved badly, in the wake of their return, though it was difficult to figure out the exact hows and whys. Certainly, it was affecting her magic. The world around Praxis closed in, an ever-tightening sphere of awareness that muddied even the shining impression of Kaedrich; already, not even two floors between them, and Praxis was losing her mental impression of her. Not just once, but three times on Praxis's way to her lab, she lost track of where she was going, her perception of her parents' dwelling getting jumbled up or outright blocked by the pain flaring through her entire body. If Praxis had any hope of handling this with even the slightest bit of grace or sanity, if she was going to face talking to her parents in the wake of such a loss, if she was going to try to piece back together whatever was going wrong between her and Kaedrich, she needed her mental stability back. In Praxis's case, that meant a clear head and a strong touch on her magic—and to regain *that* . . .

Even she didn't exactly relish the way her body lurched forward, the pure, animalistic *need* that drew her toward the lab, but that didn't change facts. That didn't scrub from her mind the image of the last vial Praxis had stolen, the glorious, deep hue to the purple liquid trapped inside, the color of Durlish wine. That didn't calm her racing heart, or return saliva to her mouth. All Praxis could think about was the sweet, cool relief waiting for her just inside of her lab, the comfort of plunging into its embrace as it stole the pain away.

She didn't pay attention as she slipped past the guards protecting the entrance of the lapus lumeni division. She didn't pay attention as her fingers fumbled over the lock, her magic threading down to the tumblers. She didn't pay attention as she let herself inside. All she could focus on, as she threw herself into the room, was the pain, and the promise of relief.

On the other side of the door, Praxis slammed into her father.

They bounced off each other, a shriek escaping either one or both of them. For the briefest instant, he looked as startled as she did. "Praxis!" he said, while she called out, "Daddy!", and then the two of them flushed and looked in opposite directions.

Praxis's thoughts scattered to the floor as the mood of the room tipped suddenly from surprised to awkward. For the life of her, Praxis could not imagine what her father was doing here. His presence in her lab made absolutely no sense, like a flame burning atop the waves of the open sea, and the not knowing, combined with the obstacle he was presenting to the time it would take to reach her relief, turned to hot resentment. Praxis's fingers twitched, wisps of smoke drifting up. She was, perhaps, thinking about asking him just what in the seven hells he was doing here, demanding that he account for himself, when she spotted the rolled-up cuff of his sleeve, his jacket and fox fur coat discarded carelessly on the floor, the glint of Praxis's own needle sticking out from the clench of his fist.

Prawl saw her see these things. One tick forward, and then two, as a quiet understanding set thick in the air between father and daughter. It was clear, in the twitch of his beard, that a decision was being made: did he even attempt to hide the truth, lie his way out, sweep the evidence aside; or did he buckle down, take a stand in what he'd been caught doing, let his authority give weight to whatever action he took?

Did it make any difference, in the end? In the heartbeat that he had to decide, a fresh course of pain jolted through Praxis, as bitter and resentful as she was, and the realization that her last relief was simply *gone*, that it had been *stolen* from her when she'd needed it most, shot her forward before she could realize what she was doing, certainly well before Prawl could make up his mind. She lashed out, her hand flying, a cut blooming across Prawl's face without the slightest contact between them. It ran a jagged, ugly line starting just above his beard, jutting across his nose, stopping short of his opposite eye. Prawl cried out, clutching his face, the syringe clattering to the floor. His knees collapsed beneath him, and a swell of guilt lurched up into Praxis's throat. She found herself crouching down, all but blubbering apologies, her fingers wrenching themselves as she attempted to huddle over her father, even as he waved her off.

"No, Praxis—Praxis, *enough!*"

He shoved her back, the force of it nearly toppling them both. Shame and anger simmered the air between them, all but crackling with raw sparks. It was difficult to tell, for a moment, which of them the tangle of each emotion was coming from.

"Daddy, I . . . I'm so s—"

Prawl shook his head. Blood trailed like tears down his face, smeared beneath his fingers. He wasn't even really trying to stanch it, and now his shoulders shook, and before Praxis knew it he was laughing, and crying, and laughing and crying, and the small bit of support that he had beneath him gave out, his ass hitting the floor and his shoulder collapsing against the side of the counter.

"Sorry, I'm sorry," he was saying, whimpering, gasping out in the space between his twisted grief, Praxis's own sentiment reflected back at her. He could not bring himself to look at his daughter, and Praxis couldn't blame him. In all her years, had she ever seen him cry? Prawl Fellows had been a towering figure, once, a powerful force of nature that billowed out to fill the space of every tunnel under the Fellows name. In the beginning, the very idea that someone might try to take that power away from him was preposterous, but now look: on the floor, wracked with emotion, high as the stars above, he was *old*, in a way that made Praxis both sympathetic and disgusted.

Praxis gritted her teeth against the pain and twisted her fingers until she could sit down as well, the two of them facing each other, there down on the frozen floor. Prawl's gallows mirth had dried up by now, and he just slumped there, against the counter, blood seeping into the thick forest of his beard. Praxis ached to reach out, to heal up the damage she'd done, but she didn't dare. Not this time. Instead, she rummaged in her pockets until she found a battered handkerchief, stolen from Kaedrich's stash, and pressed it into her father's shaking hands.

He did not raise it to his face, not at first. The very gesture sent a fresh ripple through his chest, a fresh round of tears to fight against the crimson tide on his cheeks. It took Praxis, guiding his hand up, before he finally began to press at the mess of his face, before he finally began to take a few gulping breaths, before he dared to blink his eyes open. They slid from Praxis to the floor, dull, unfocused, his pupils reduced.

"How did you know?" Praxis asked, finally, after several long minutes of silence had passed between them. She did not need to clarify that she'd been talking about the vial of glee—her possession of it, where to find it. They both knew what she meant. The needle itself lay not far away, though both of them were studiously avoiding looking at it, their shared secret curdling the air of the lab.

Prawl didn't answer her, not directly anyway. "I had to take it," he said instead. His voice, like his gaze, was deadened, though by grief or by the drug itself, Praxis couldn't say. "I had to."

If she was being honest, Praxis wouldn't have thought the death of Pranders would hit her father this hard. Not that she didn't expect him to love each of his children, not that she would have ever imagined him to be unaffected by the loss, not that she didn't think he would mourn her brother as she herself never would . . . but there was something raw and broken and unflinchingly *honest* in the way he sat crumpled on her floor, unable to bear the weight of life, even if just for a moment. It scared Praxis, perhaps even more so than the Beacon's discovery and subsequent disappearance. It was no wonder Prawl felt he had to indulge in the glee in Praxis's vial, to numb some of his pain away. Looking at him, Praxis was forced to wonder just how deeply it ran—was it possible that it had even turned physical, hurting as real as a gouge carved out of his middle? Praxis would never ask. But the question would haunt her, forever teasing the edges of the way she understood her father.

Pain flared out from her leg, blinding hot, and Praxis grimaced as she turned away from Prawl. Seven hells, though, why did he need to steal from her *now*? If she'd had more, she'd have been—well, not exactly *happy* to share, not this, but—at least less vexed. Her mind was already spinning ahead, trying to determine the best means of replenishing her stock. Going to Lexthur was absolutely off the table, regardless of whether she asked or just took. But that left . . . what, exactly? She supposed she might be able to approach some of the doctors she'd been seeing, but it was bad enough to have them gossiping all over Bolt about the state of her knee; the last thing she needed was to give them even more fuel. Especially now, with the family so scrutinized by the oversight committee. Praxis gritted her already tightened teeth, disgusted by herself for caring about something like that, but . . . dammit, she *did*. Somehow, and against all better judgment, she did not want to tarnish her family's reputation— and by extension, she told herself, her father's as well—when faced with the decision the Minor Conclave would be making soon.

"Will you perform the encasing?" Prawl asked.

Praxis jerked, her head whipping up as if she'd been bitten. *"Me?"*

Prawl nodded. He was watching her steadily, more composed than he had any right to be, the Fellows stoicism taking hold once more. Only the rashy red of his eyes betrayed his earlier fall from grace. He was even dabbing at his cut now, frowning at the bloodstains as if he wasn't entirely sure how they'd come to soak the cloth in his hands. "I'd appreciate it. I think your mother would, too."

"Is she all right?"

A messy huff escaped Prawl's chest. "She's sitting with him now, but . . . yes. Your mother is always all right."

This was true, so Praxis didn't bother arguing with it. Tentatively, she reached out, but her father did not try to stop her as she touched her fingers against his face, tracing the line she'd inflicted upon him earlier.

"You know, I might have said the same thing about you too, once."

Prawl shut his eyes. For a moment, Praxis feared he would start crying again, but he was only wincing as the skin beneath Praxis's touch first warmed and then cooled in the face of her healing magic. When he opened his eyes again, they weren't exactly *clear*, but they were at least dry.

Praxis pulled her hand away, her work done. Prawl's beard was still a mess, but that, at least, he could clean up on his own. On cue, the two of them began to drag themselves to their feet, each hauling up against the counters for support. Once standing, Prawl glanced down at the mess that had dribbled onto his shirt, scowling a familiar Fellows scowl.

"If you think it'll help," Praxis said finally, "then yes. I'll perform the encasing."

She didn't even know she was going to agree, until she'd already done it. Her easy acceptance surprised both of them—Prawl glanced up, sidelong, almost as if he was uncertain that his daughter was telling the truth. Praxis found herself straightening up, the idea of backing out somehow not even occurring to her; turning, in truth, almost offensive once it did. She waited for her father to say something, and he waited for her to change her mind, and when neither happened, he nodded.

"Okay," he said.

"Okay," Praxis agreed.

They said nothing more about her brother, the needle, Prawl's breakdown. They said nothing more at all. Prawl wiped at his face one more time before passing the handkerchief back to Praxis, and then Praxis picked up the syringe and found and disposed of the empty vial while Prawl gathered up his jacket and coat, and by the time she turned back, a minute or two later, he was gone, and the lab was empty save for her.

IT WAS OBVIOUS that something was wrong from the minute Kaedrich walked through the door. In the outer office, she did not find the serene order of Prommel's staff—each person working like clockwork, an intricate piece in the larger structure of his department, their coats crisp and perfect, their movements so precisely timed that it made its own kind of music. Instead, a scene unfolded before her that could have only been called a *bustle*: people moving hither and thither, carrying chairs and paintings and swords and whale-bone crates, the shouts of confusion and misdirection echoing throughout the room as their paths crossed and uncrossed with all the grace of a dancing elephant. Kaedrich dodged to the side as two men swept past with a heavy crate slung between them, their faces red with the effort. She craned her neck, trying to spot Micadel somewhere in the swirling sea, but his familiar face was either absent, or hidden like a single fish in a shifting school. "Excuse me," Kaedrich tried asking someone at random, anyone at random, grabbing a guard by the elbow, but all she was met with was a nasty look and a fast curse as they jerked out of her grip and hurried onward.

Kaedrich swallowed down the dry lump in her throat. She was hoping the chaos was simply a result of the upended nature of the Fellows household right now, given recent circumstances, though even as the thought formed, she recognized it for the comforting lie that it was.

She darted through the outer office, finding whatever gaps she could. Under a reaching arm, around a load of shields, stepping wide over a box as it was set on the floor. No one stopped to help her, but then, no one tried to stop her, either, so she was prepared to count that as a win. She made her way to Prommel's inner office, her mind swirling with questions, which all fell to the ground the moment she stepped inside.

Praine stood in the middle of the room, one hand on his hips, the other holding his chin as he regarded the levelness of a painting being affixed to the wall before him. His back was to Kaedrich, though something must have caught his attention, for he turned almost immediately, before the contempt could even slide its way up Kaedrich's throat. His attention landed on her, and he smiled, grinned really, his mouth stretched almost reptilian wide, and Kaedrich swallowed down the sour taste that rode up into her mouth.

"Ah, Kaedrich. You and my sister must be back, I see."

"What in the darkness are you doing here, Praine? Where's Prommel?"

She hadn't really *intended* to start out so aggressive, and a part of Kaedrich wished she could take it back. True, she hated Praine—that didn't mean it was a good idea to antagonize him.

But if Praine was at all offended, he didn't show it. His smile toned itself down to a patient curve, and he sighed lightly, as if he was addressing someone very naïve, or very thick. "I'm afraid there's been some restructuring while you've been away. Prommel has been let go."

Kaedrich actually took a step back, so unsettled by this declaration that she didn't know how to process it. "Let go?" she asked. Her skin was already crawling at the news, even as she asked, "How could that have happened? And . . . and who would have done that? Who *could* have? I mean, Prawl—"

"Had no choice, I'm afraid. It seems a rather nasty rumor about my brother's past made its way to the Minor Conclave. You wouldn't think they'd have cared about something from so long ago, but . . ." Praine shrugged. "These are delicate times, I suppose. One never knows what kind of things might set them off."

"What did he *do*?"

Already, Kaedrich's mind was whirling, scenarios running rampant. What *could* he have done, to have warranted such a strong reaction, and so swiftly handed down? True, Kaedrich didn't know any of the Fellows that well, but Prommel . . . well, she didn't know if she'd go so far as to say she *liked* Prommel, not after the business of her sort-of-arrest, but he seemed honest, and generally good. Certainly better than a lot of the others, at any rate. Certainly better than *Praine*. Perlandra's breath, if Prawl was willing to let *Praine* keep his position within the company, but not *Prommel*—

"I suppose I shouldn't really say," Praine began, "but then, it's no doubt already flying through the gossip circles, and I'd wager you have a right to know, being practically family yourself."

Kaedrich's cheeks burned at Praine's words. It could only have been a calculated move, designed to throw her off-balance.

Praine continued, as if there was nothing to it, as if what he'd said was so insignificant as to be unnoticed. "Many years ago—like I said, it's so old I'm surprised they even care anymore—but many years ago, Prommel was caught slipping extra company scrip to a number of the grubs."

It took a moment before the full impact of Praine's words settled on Kaedrich. "Company scrip" was not a phrase she was used to hearing, but she did not want to appear the ignorant Durn by asking. And it *was* a familiar phrase, it just took her a second to remember: even in her own home country, companies had once gotten into trouble by paying employees with currency, or "scrip," printed up by the company itself, redeemable only at company-operated stores. The idea was to keep employees wholly dependent on the company they worked for, and it wasn't until labor revolts and unionization a couple of decades ago that they'd finally gotten laws in place to prevent such mistreatment. The taste of ash filled Kaedrich's mouth now, because of course such a system would still be in place here. Really, she should have expected as much.

A light chuckle from Praine broke throughout the room. "You disapprove."

"Of *slavery*?" Kaedrich scoffed. "I don't exactly have a good history with the subject."

She was expecting a sneer, an eye roll, contempt. She was expecting Praine's words to be dismissive. She was expecting him to lash out, wave her off. She was *not* expecting a gentle, almost thoughtful tilt of Praine's head. He leaned back against the desk that used to belong to Prommel, folding his hands neatly in front of his suit, the colors far more muted than Kaedrich was used to for Praine.

"Do you think we enjoy our role?"

Kaedrich blinked, thrown off-balance. "What?"

"Our role," Praine said. "You think we want to be the sole teat these people depend on just to live? Believe me, I would love for them to be their own charges, but these people are *criminals*, and like it or not, they rely on us for support as they pay back their debts to society. The Fellows family provides them with scrip to give them some measure of independence back, but it doesn't come cheap—and Prommel's little *stunt* all those years ago blew through a quarter of their annual feeding budget in a matter of weeks. If Prenna hadn't tracked down the source of it when she did—"

"Stop," Kaedrich said. She couldn't listen to any more of this. "Look, I know you *think* you're being all benevolent, but the truth is if you can't afford to even feed these people enough to be healthy, then you don't deserve to benefit from their labor. What Prommel did was . . . frankly heroic, given the circumstances. And you're telling me not only was it a *crime*, but now he's lost everything because of it."

Praine smiled, brittle as feather-glass. It was a strange look on him, when he was normally so polished and controlled. But then . . . now that Kaedrich looked, everything about him was just a bit off. His muted coat, the slightly rumpled bit of his hair, a certain spark gone from his eyes. It chilled Kaedrich, more so than his usual sleaze.

"You know, this is the one argument that Pranders and I used to have, sometimes," Praine said finally. He shrugged. "He didn't really take much of a stance on things. I'm sure that's why I liked him. But he agreed with you, on this. He was glad, when Prommel's criminal fee was paid in silence, when it all just . . . went away. I told him, there should have been more for it. I told him . . ."

A fragile silence fell. Praine studied the rings on his hands, the gems shifting as if in thought.

Kaedrich held herself perfectly still, even though she wanted to squirm beneath the weight of what Praine was telling her. It didn't sit well with her, none of it. Praine was a monster, and nothing he said in regret was going to change that, and it just felt *wrong* to stand there and listen to something that sounded almost sincere, coming from his cold lips.

Finally, Praine shook his head. "It doesn't matter now." He pushed himself off the desk. He did not look at Kaedrich as he smoothed out the fur of his coat. "I should get ready. Now that the two of you are back . . . I suppose we'll be burying my brother today."

Chapter Twenty-Eight

THE ROOM WAS small and cold, surrounding Kaedrich like a coffin. Even the thick fur of her coat and the fine lining of her gloves did nothing to dull the cold as it burrowed beneath Kaedrich's skin, freezing her bones. She stood shivering, clutching the length of a string of bells she'd been given, to keep them from chiming. They still rattled against themselves, chattering like teeth, and Kaedrich knew—she *knew*—that the Fellows could hear it, but was putting them down somehow more disrespectful than this? Already, she trod a fine line.

Not that she entirely understood what it was she had done, but she knew in the way of snooping children that she wasn't supposed to be here. She had only come at all because she'd been summoned, a tight-faced servant ushering her down here, handing her the chimes, leaving her to figure it out on her own. She couldn't figure it out, though. Fleetingly, Kaedrich wondered if she'd been summoned in error, or as a prank to make Praxis looked bad; but if that were so, she doubted she'd have been allowed to enter this place. The guards at the doors hadn't exactly been happy to see her, but nor were they surprised as they allowed her entry.

So that was something, Kaedrich supposed.

One other small mercy: Prommel's wife, Sharmity, was there beside her. And while she wasn't exactly *friendly* toward Kaedrich—none of them were, really, except for maybe Prett—she at least did not look upon her like something found on the bottom of a shoe.

The two of them stood together in a little pocket of a viewing room. Across from them, Lorric and Maylin shared a similar space, while a third stood empty off to Kaedrich's right. These viewing rooms ringed a central chamber, smaller than Kaedrich would have expected, and it was here the rest of the family had gathered. Pranders's body was laid out in the middle of the central chamber, beneath a vent that spilled cold straight down at him, a breath that flooded the room and spilled over the lip to where Kaedrich and Sharmity stood waiting. In death, he was surrounded by the family that had ignored him in life: his parents, his sisters, a ring of living brothers, all dressed in dusky, slate-blue robes, all laying a single hand upon his still body. Only Previn was missing, and Kaedrich was forced to wonder if it wasn't *her* presence that had led to his exclusion. There really was no particular reason for this suspicion, just a small slip of Prawl's face as he regarded his remaining children, his attention lingering for only a moment in the almost infinitesimal gap between where Prewish and Praine were standing; a slight look, exchanged between Prawl and Prestina. It may have been nothing, just Kaedrich projecting her own insecurities onto what she was witnessing, but she felt the truth of it, even if the meaning itself didn't match. She wasn't supposed to be here.

"It's starting," Sharmity whispered beside her as a long, mournful note, maybe something from a deep-bellied wind instrument, swept through the edges of the room. It raised the hairs on Kaedrich's arms, even more than the cold. Somehow, it was the exact sound of grief, like the feeling of weeping hopelessly, not even bothering to wipe your face or hide your eyes, just tears pooling endlessly down cheeks, the shuddered hitch of your chest as you gulped down only enough strength to keep crying. In the wake of it, Kaedrich felt breathless and spent. Sharmity raised her own string of bells, along with the rest of the observers outside of the inner circle, and Kaedrich hurried to follow suit.

In the middle, Praxis and her parents and her siblings began to peel back the layers of clothes that Pranders had been wearing upon the event of his death. Coat and jacket and shirt and undershirts and boots and pants and leggings and socks. His jewelry, what little he wore, was laid into a glass bowl beside his head, while his clothes were passed to Prenna and folded with all the loving care one might show to an infant. The family worked in silence, somehow a seamless unit. They turned and lifted, one brother tugging down the length of a sleeve, the other gently working the elbow through. Praxis undid the row of buttons down the front of Pranders's shirt, and Prestina slipped a ring off her dead son's fingers. The mournful note had only rung once, but the shuffle of tiny bells filled the space, like a winter breeze toying through frozen leaves.

Kaedrich almost couldn't bear to watch. She tried not to let her own culture color the proceedings, but she couldn't keep her skin from crawling with embarrassment for Pranders as his form was slowly revealed to everyone around him. It felt undignified, somehow, and vaguely vulgar, to reduce a person to their naked form with so many eyes watching. Is this what awaited all of the Fellows, one day? Their secrets laid bare, their truths exposed. And if Kaedrich stayed, if somehow she died in this tomb of ice, is that what would await her? Praxis, standing alone, unwrapping her in silence. Kaedrich bit her lip. She wasn't supposed to be here. Why had she been summoned here? Anyone could see that Kaedrich didn't belong, that this ceremony was too intimate to include the likes of her. Had she even said two words to Pranders? Now here she was, and his bare torso sprawled like a plucked chicken before her, and what *right* did Kaedrich have to witness this?

They stripped him down to nothing, not even a loincloth or a towel draped over his middle. Kaedrich tried to avert her eyes, but—his doughy form, the paunch now out on full display, the trail of his shapeless legs running down the length of the pale table. It wasn't possible to avoid looking at him completely. A scar cut up the side of his thigh, a jagged slash, so old that it was nothing more than a whisper of white on white. A spray of hair curled rigidly from his chest, and his arms were sprinkled with a handful of pale moles. Prenna swept away the piles of clothes, and unseen hands passed a tray back to her, jars of oil gleaming brightly beneath the ring of lapus lumeni in the dome. The family each accepted one, tapping their middle three fingers to their lips before dipping them into the oil before them. They swept the oil across Pranders's skin like the brushstrokes of a master painter, across the empty expanse of stomach, up into the roots of his hair, under the folds of his skin and the crook of his armpit. When his front had been coated, they turned him with reverence, and gave the same treatment to his back, before righting him once more. The final two sweeps, one across each of his closed eyelids, were drawn along his skin by Prawl and Prestina, respectively, and then they each bent in unison and kissed the sides of their son's face at once.

Kaedrich looked away. Sometime during the proceedings, the bells in her hand had gone still, and she flicked her wrist to set them ringing once more. When she looked back up, the family was wiping down their hands and waiting as Prenna swapped out the tray of oils for a change of fine clothes. Only Praxis remained stationary, staring across the body at Kaedrich, her face carefully blank.

A flush began to creep across Kaedrich's cheeks, burning hot in the extra cold of the room. She tried to offer up a reassuring smile, but it dried out, brittle on her lips, and blew away in the frozen breeze. Praxis turned away, back to her business, as Prommel passed her a folded silk shirt, deep blue moving from hand to hand, and the act was so small and yet so *meaningful* that it sent a shot of remorse deep into the beating recesses of Kaedrich's heart. She was not supposed to be here.

She was never supposed to be here.

HAD PRANDERS EVER looked this good in life?

This is probably the kind of thought that Kaedrich would have reprimanded her for, but Praxis couldn't help but wonder as she looked down at the trussed-up lump of flesh and bone that used to be her brother. Fellows were always buried in lavish outfits—Praxis remembered going to the crypts as a child, staring at the long lines of faces frozen into the ice, the preserved gowns and coats like something out of a tale of kingdoms gone by—but this was excessive, bordering on obscene. With no practical considerations like comfort or movement to consider, Pranders had been all but *sculpted* into a suit of gemstones. Tendrils of sapphires, so fine as to look like strands of hair, had been woven to approximate the aesthetic of a fur cloak. Beneath that, a jacket inlaid with emeralds, paneled like glass. His hands were dotted with rings that he'd never worn in life, his head ensconced in a circlet of pure diamonds. Praxis stared at her brother, transformed, and she did not recognize him at all.

The two of them were alone now, the rest of Praxis's family having retreated to prepare for the main ceremony. Praxis wished she was able to do the same, but her role as the wizard overseeing Pranders's encasing meant she was required to stay close. Her ceremonial robe, the neck high and choking, the collar behind her head for once absent, was somehow both stifling and entirely too cold. Praxis clicked a spark of magic to life behind her eyes, threading the power down until it began to warm her whole body. Technically, it was a waste of magical energy, burning off with no outlet to be funneled through, but it was the magic that had saved her life when she was a teenager out on her Qol Nar, and it would serve her needs here too. Deeper heat rolled beneath the surface of Praxis's wrist, running through her scar, and Praxis gritted her teeth against the pain.

She told herself that the presence of a dead body shouldn't bother her so much. After all, she'd handled more than enough of them in her time. What was one more, really? And yet, the effect it was having on her was undeniable. Praxis found her skin crawling, her stomach jumping. She couldn't bring herself to keep looking at him, but neither could she entirely pull her eyes away.

The start of the ceremony itself couldn't come fast enough, as far as Praxis was concerned, and it didn't—not anywhere near fast enough—but it did start, finally, eventually, a deep-bellied chime ringing out through the ice as Praxis's signal. She all but threw open the doors, where two servants stood waiting, ready to transport Pranders's carefully attended body. Praxis only just managed to affix an expression of solemnity, and was for once glad she did, for the hallway outside was already lined with mourners.

Though very few of them were probably, in fact, *mourning*, Praxis decided. Pranders had barely been noticed within the family—she could not imagine that he'd found this much support outside of it. Still, the hall was lined with friends of the family, with dignitaries from the Minor Conclave's oversight committee and the trades commission, with business partners. Each of them dressed in respectful slate blue, like stale ice. They gave their mourner's charms gentle shakes, filling the path with the whisper of death.

It was up to Praxis to lead the way. Ordinarily, she was supposed to carry a ceremonial lapus lumeni cupped in both hands, but the brace on her leg made that impossible. She picked up the crystal in just one hand instead, feeling the grooves of the carving with her thumb. For practical purposes, she'd removed the glove of her free hand during the ceremony, and she kept it that way now as she rubbed the line of the smoothed-over crystal. The fingers on her other hand flexed, setting the whole ceremony in motion.

This particular hallway required no insider knowledge to know how to navigate it; it only went to one place. Praxis kept a steady, deliberate pace as she passed by the watchful eyes of the mourners. The sound of their chimes washed over her, raising the hairs on the back of Praxis's neck. She'd managed to ignore it, when they'd been dressing Pranders's body, but now the sound was ushering Praxis forward, and all she could feel was that she was being led, somehow, to her own icy grave.

At the end of the hall, a hexagonal cavern opened up: the central hub of the Fellows' crypts. Spokes led off to various subcorridors, where the actual tombs were located, and Praxis couldn't help but notice the

similarities now, between these crypts and the main chamber of the land
of the dead. She wondered, was it purely a coincidence? Or did, somehow,
this image of death leach through the worlds, whispering in the minds of
the people who had originally carved them out of the ice?

There wasn't much time for contemplation, however. Praxis was
guided quickly down one of the branch-offs, and she tried not to look at
the frozen faces encased in the ice beside her. Thankfully, this was a newer
branch, and so the bodies they passed were not yet mummified behind
the ice, their flesh still *reasonably* whole—still, Praxis kept her gaze fixed
straight ahead of her. It was a familiar tunnel, the same one where her
grandparents were buried; a place of honor, and now a cold sweat broke
out across Praxis's skin.

The line of mourners ended about twenty slots in, replaced by the
faces that Praxis was most familiar with: her parents, Prenna, her remaining brothers, the spouses and children they'd attached themselves to . . .
Kaedrich. Praxis tried to force a soft smile at Kaedrich, stuck at the end
to make it clear that she'd been very nearly forgotten, but *there*.

Praxis drew their tiny procession to a halt in front of a slab of ice that
had been specially polished, the participants respectfully keeping their
distance. And now the chimes fell silent as all attention fixed on her.

When Praxis had agreed to do this, it seemed impossible to say no.
Her father was nearly destroyed, her mother probably not in much better
shape; of *course* Praxis would agree. What kind of a monster would she
be, to refuse? This needed to be done by a wizard, and they happened
to have a wizard right in the family, no need to loop in anyone else. Of
course. It was the least Praxis could do, to honor the brother in death that
she'd barely paid attention to in life.

Of course.

Now, though, the prospect became something . . . else. Praxis stood in
front of the wall of ice, a single occupancy's worth polished to a high sheen,
so strong that a ghost of her reflection stared back at her, mimicking her
hesitation. It's not that the magic itself was terribly complex; nor even that
she wasn't familiar with the ceremonial aspects. It's just . . . the prospect
of being the one to actually *do it*, to commit Pranders to the ice for all
eternity . . . Sure, he'd already been dead for a while, but there was a finality
here that Praxis couldn't shake. It felt like killing him.

Another chime rang out, low and thrumming. It resonated deep in
Praxis's chest, and she took a long breath to steady herself as a slow chorus
of tender voices welled up through the hallway. Praxis put her hands on
the wall, bare skin to solid ice, and clicked a spark of magic alive behind

her eyes. The process was straightforward: melt out an alcove large enough to position the body inside, wait for people to arrange him and bequeath their tokens to his memory, then gather up the water and mold it back into place around him. It was straightforward, sure, and yet. A searing heat tore through Praxis's chest as rivers wept across the back of her hands. The song was building now, everyone save for Kaedrich joining in as best as their grief allowed. Even Praxis was supposed to be joining in, except that she couldn't, not now. She watched the water pool beneath her, guiding it with her magic to a special reservoir by her feet. It wasn't that it took much concentration. It's just . . .

Praxis didn't really know, to be honest. Just that her eyes were dry, her voice was stone-silent, her chest an empty hollow. If she joined in now, it would ring with falsehood, a misplaced flat to pierce the melody of mourning.

The process took several minutes and by the time it was done, Praxis herself stood in the empty tomb, her arms outstretched above her as she melted the last curve of the arched ceiling. She knew she was supposed to say something now—her choice, perhaps a speech about the departed, or a ceremonial poem that wasn't quite a prayer but wasn't quite *not*, or a recitation of something that Pranders would have found meaningful. Any number of options, really, and all of them wrong. Praxis stood there, arms raised, ice brushing her fingertips, mourners at her back. She shut her eyes, feeling the chill seep in from all around her, the way that it froze her breath into place. If she could stay here, just for a moment . . .

But the world ticks on. Always, it ticks on. Someone cleared their throat, and Praxis came back to herself, her limbs retreating. She scurried backward from the alcove she'd cleared, the silence of the speech that she should have given now lingering in the air like a bad odor as Pranders's body was moved into position. Someone slid a chair in, and Praxis almost laughed, as if Pranders would somehow tire in the afterlife. Then she caught her mother glaring at her, as if she'd heard the unsung laughter, and Praxis's cheeks flushed as she remembered; how could she ever forget? There was nothing funny about a chair, the symbol of a life only half-lived, the seated body forever trapped from rising to its full potential. Praxis looked away, abashed. Had she really been gone so long that she'd forget such a thing, even if only for a moment?

It struck Praxis, then: she really didn't belong here anymore. So many years spent studying death rituals and the dead, so many cultures and beliefs passing through her hands and mind and heart. She'd allowed herself to forget about home. And it *was* home, or at least it had been once. Hadn't this ice once been meant for her, too? Hadn't her parents chosen a place for her, somewhere in this very hall, a spot reserved for each of their children? Praxis stole a sidelong glance, left and then right, wondering where exactly it was. Who it would hold, now that her future lay elsewhere?

Because she had escaped once, and depths help her, she would do so again. All she had to do was get back to work on the job her father had given her, help him reclaim the company for his own. A gentle tug drew at Praxis's stomach, a whisper in her ears. She bit her lip to keep herself from racing away from this ceremony right here, right now. What did it matter, really, all of these rituals and ceremonies for the dead? Pranders was gone—there was nothing more that could save him. What mattered was the living. What mattered was that Praxis still had the opportunity to dig herself out from the ice, if she was fast, if she was clever, if she was careful. The last of the tokens was laid at Pranders's feet, the last kiss bestowed upon his forehead, and Praxis hurried forward, eager to complete the task. She sealed him in with all the solemnity she could muster, but all the while her mind was whirring, searching for the formula that would help her father. That would allow her, and Kaedrich, to finally escape for good.

Chapter Twenty-Nine

THERE WERE NO two ways about it: the investigation was stalled.

Kaedrich knew this, even if Praxis still wasn't ready to admit it. But *five days*. Five days since the funeral, five days of nothing. Prommel refused to get involved, now that he was no longer in charge of company security, and no amount of wheedling or bribing or begging from Kaedrich had swayed his mind. Which, okay, Kaedrich knew better than anyone that Fellows were stubborn once they'd decided on something—but she'd never expected a Fellows to be stubborn about *following* the rules.

Apparently, getting burned once was enough for Prommel. His bid had been frozen before Praxis and Kaedrich had even gotten back, and though Micadel was fighting hard to get it reinstated, rumors were that Sharmity had already cast her support behind Prewish. This had delighted Prewish, of course, though the general feeling was that it was still too little too late, especially with the younger generation continuing to shift toward Tannem's camp; at times it felt as if the destruction of Prommel's bid had, in some ways, only accelerated the shift. The fact that Prommel wasn't fighting it, was barely acknowledging it, surely didn't help. It still seemed absurd to Kaedrich that something as simple as a *kindness* could be the cause of someone's downfall, but there you had it, and Kaedrich's disapproval didn't change matters. Prommel, Sharmity, and their children had gone into a kind of seclusion in the Fellows household while Kaedrich had been gone: eating in their own tunnels, ignoring the family dinners and routine parties that Prestina threw at least once a week, staying home even when invited out. The only exception they'd made had been Pranders's burial. The few times Kaedrich *did* see them, they spoke little, and made eye contact even less.

So fine, they'd lost an ally in the search for the Beacon—that was a setback, no doubt, but it didn't mean *they* had to give up. Wasn't nosing around, asking uncomfortable questions, and generally involving herself where she wasn't wanted basically Praxis's whole purpose in life?

Except that Praxis herself had barely left the lab in those five days. Since their return, she'd thrown herself into the work her father had asked to do, with a zeal Kaedrich hadn't seen from her in . . . well, maybe *ever*. True, Kaedrich was used to Praxis working long hours when she found a project to sink her teeth into, but this was ridiculous. Not sleeping, barely eating, testy to the point where she'd actually locked the door to her lab and refused Kaedrich entry on more than one occasion. The few times they'd passed each other were brusque and businesslike, Kaedrich making suggestions for what they might do next, Praxis insisting she had to focus, that there was nothing new, that they didn't have any reasonable way to proceed from here. Five days. Five days, Kaedrich had been holding back, waiting for someone else to take action, to stand up and *do* something.

She woke up the morning of the sixth day with a grit in her teeth and a fire in her chest. The space in bed beside her was empty, the sheets cold. Kaedrich threw the covers off and launched herself to her feet. Screw that. She had held back, she realized, because this wasn't her home, because she was afraid of stepping on people's toes, because she didn't know the rules.

No more. Kaedrich still had Prawl's ring, though even he seemed to have forgotten about the question of who had betrayed him—ever since his son's death, he'd been sullen and withdrawn, hiding out in his office, a mirror image of Praxis. Everyone knew that, and so Kaedrich was prepared to face some backlash to her investigations, but she would fight through them. No one would stand in her way. No one.

The ring was the final piece she donned that morning, sliding it purposefully into place. She looked at herself in the mirror, taking stock: a fine suit of alternating shades of green, cut in a Durlish style, a Yandosian coat of silver fur cascading over her shoulders and flowing with the broad sweep of a cloak. Thick boots, her trusty emerald cufflinks, a crisp white shirt. Her hand made a fist in front of her, the shifting color of the Fellows gemstone catching the light. It may not be traditional armor, but Kaedrich felt as sturdy as a battle-ready general.

She turned to go, her back straight, her stride long. Because if there was one thing Kaedrich knew for certain, it was this: she did not ignore a crisis, and if that meant going it alone, then so be it. If Kaedrich was going to be trapped here, below the ice, unable to help her homeland, then she'd be damned if she sat around doing nothing. Not anymore.

THE DEN WAS kept dim and, by Yandosian standards, excessively warm. Strips of lapus lumeni, barely charged, ran like rivers in the space between the stones that the den had been constructed out of. The stone floor was covered in furs, blankets, and bedding. The ceiling was low, requiring Prestina to stoop when she moved about, and domed overhead; the overall effect, she often thought, was very much like crawling into a giant oven. Not that Prestina had experience with ovens, but—she'd been to the kitchens plenty of times, to observe and to issue her orders, and to inspect the progress of the chefs and underchefs and kitchen maids.

By rights, most people would think she didn't have any business being in the den, either, but the truth is that Prestina had never been good at living by other people's rules.

The brusker in the den with her whined, and Prestina leaned a little closer, shushing the creature as she stroked it. Her fingers tangled in the thick fur of the dog's neck. Its head was resting in Prestina's lap, filling it entirely, a puddle of drool staining through the sturdy fabric of her skirt. This is the one dress Prestina owned that she did reuse, and reuse often— a common laborer's dress, the collar only medium-high behind her head, the color of rust and brick and dried blood. Most people were entirely unaware that she even owned it, and indeed that was the point. Prestina, like the dogs she whelped, liked her solitude in this endeavor.

It spoke volumes to the seriousness of her business, then, that she'd allowed this moment to be intruded upon. Prestina scowled as she heard his footsteps, but she made shushing, soothing noises at the dog in her lap; the girl was an old breeding pro, and no doubt was unsettled by the disruption to her and Prestina's routine. "I know," Prestina murmured to her as she ruffled the dog's fur again. "I know, I'm sorry. Just this once, I promise."

"Well," Lexthur said, from his place in the doorway. "This is . . . interesting."

Prestina glanced up, squinting at the bright light leaching in around him. "Get inside and shut that thing, will you? You're disturbing her."

Lexthur hesitated, just for a second. No doubt, he was trying to reconcile the image in front of him with his understanding of the great Prestina Fellows. Prestina didn't entirely blame him; after all, she worked hard to maintain her image. But then, like a consummate professional, he composed himself and shuffled inside, hunched over as he maneuvered to a corner far away from Prestina and the dog. So at least he had that much sense. The dog whined, once more, in Prestina's lap, but Prestina rubbed at the girl's ears, and the dog began to settle.

"I assume it goes without saying that if you tell anyone what you see here today, I will ruin you," Prestina began.

Lexthur made a noise, halfway between a grunt and a chuckle. In the world of the den, it sounded almost normal. "Would I really be so indiscreet?"

Prestina shrugged. "Probably not, but it's important we be upfront about this. I didn't summon you here because I trust you, Lexthur—make no mistake of that."

"The thought never once crossed my mind."

"Good." Prestina nodded, and stroked the dog's fur absently. "Good. Now then, to business: I have it on good authority that the oversight committee is close to moving forward on the inheritance. We're running out of time, and you haven't gotten the job done."

"I'm working on it."

"Working?" Prestina laughed under her breath—not so loud as to disturb the dog, but more than enough to cut his feeble excuse to pieces. "Yes, and if I wanted you to be *working on it*, I would have simply paid you off to do so. Did I not make myself clear, when we last spoke? I want a *result*."

"Prestina, you know full well that your daughter—"

"Is not the one I am talking to at the moment. *My daughter*, like all natural forces, has to adapt to the world around her as it presents itself. What *you* need to do, is to make sure that the world presents itself in a way that will guide her toward the correct path."

"You mean your path."

"It's the same thing."

"Is it?"

A smile twitched at the corner of Prestina's lips. "I don't expect you to understand," she said. "You don't have children."

This was true, and so Lexthur wisely said nothing.

The dog, meanwhile, jerked her head and dragged herself to her feet. Heavy canine panting filled the den, and Prestina leaned back as the girl lumbered past her. Standing, the dog's back easily raised above where

Prestina sat. Her belly hung fat and heavy below her, nearly knocking against Prestina, as the girl began to pace, restless and impatient.

Prestina drew herself up to a crouch, gripping the long fur of the dog's back to haul herself up. No one else could get away with being so close to the girl, not in this state, but Prestina had always had a special connection with the bruskers. "Easy, girl, it's okay," Prestina said to her now, her voice light and encouraging in all the right ways that it never was with her children. She leaned around, checking how far along the dog was, and then glanced up at Lexthur. "She's ready. Hand me some of those towels, would you?"

Lexthur looked vaguely queasy at the thought, a faint sheen of sweat pricking his forehead, but he dutifully removed two folded towels from a pile where they'd been kept warm in a heavy stone basin. Prestina grabbed them and stretched over the back of the dog just as the dog gave a heavy, grunting whine. Her back legs bowed, and she shuddered, and Prestina shuffled fast to position herself behind the girl.

At this point, there really wasn't much for Prestina to do. The first pup could come along in seconds, or minutes—possibly, it wouldn't be along for a half hour or more, but Prestina doubted it. This particular girl tended to be fast, popping out her pups with an almost businesslike efficiency. Prestina knew, because she knew them all, every last dog in the packs that the Fellows housed. She'd helped to whelp them all, including this one, though she harbored no particular memory of any one birth or another. After a while, at least if you were lucky, they all blended together into routine.

Though Prestina had to admit, it *felt* different this time. Rarely did Prestina ever feel a connection to what the dogs were going through, but now she couldn't help but remember the long string of her own pregnancies. The situation couldn't have looked more different, of course, but this time . . . this time, there was a universality to the birthing experience that resonated deep in Prestina's chest. As the bubble of the first pup began to emerge, Prestina remembered, with painfully sharp clarity, the moment when each of her children had been cleaned up and laid upon her chest for the first time. Most of them had been wailing, red faces scrunched at the harsh indignity of the world, like they already understood on some fundamental level what travesties awaited them. But Pranders . . . Pranders's vocalizations were more reserved. It felt as if he was testing out the act of breathing and crying, and his eyes were flinching as they tried to open to the sharp light of the lapus lumeni, as if he couldn't wait to see what was around him, couldn't wait to get started.

And now he was gone. He'd slipped from the world with the same lack of fuss that he'd made entering it. In the last few days, Prestina had gone through both his rooms and her own mementos, trying to find tangible signs of him, proof beyond just the searing loss in her heart that he'd been there at all, that he'd lived a rich life, that he'd been happy and loved. She'd come up disturbingly empty-handed. Each of her other children had left such a hard stamp upon the Fellows' lives, but Pranders had barely been a whisper, and now his frozen presence in the crypts took up more space in their household than he ever had while he was still here.

The first puppy dropped, a messy lump on the pile of furs on the floor, and Prestina snapped back to the present reality. She leaned over, breaking the membrane that surrounded it, vigorously rubbing the pup down with the warm, damp cloth. The mother dog curled around, her snout in Prestina's way, licking the mess of her child as the puppy began to yip and wail. Another success, the first of several. Prestina let the dog work, keeping a close eye on just how vigorously she groomed at her pup.

In the meantime, Lexthur had edged slightly closer, curiosity drawing him onward. He watched the process, his face still somewhat contorted. "Is it always like this?"

"Mostly," Prestina said. She edged the dog's nose back, sticking her towel in to clean off the puppy herself.

"What are you doing?"

"Just keeping an eye on things. Bruskers were bred for their size, but I think we grew them a little too quickly. They don't always realize their own strength. New mothers have been known to accidentally chew up their newborns, in their enthusiasm to get them clean."

"No wonder you get along with them so well."

Prestina did not rise to Lexthur's bait. The pup was tidy now, tidy enough anyway, and the mother was lying down again, regaining her strength. Prestina scooped the puppy, cradling it in both hands despite the fact that it could easily fit in one, and deposited it into a warm box beside her, where it could stay safely out of the way as it waited for its brothers and sisters. It nuzzled down against the blankets that lined its box, nosing into the folds of the fabric.

"It'll be a while before the next one," Prestina said. She turned back to Lexthur, smoothing out the front of her dress. "I've given our predicament thought, and I believe I know how to get Praxis to come around."

Lexthur's mouth slid into a tilt, like he wasn't entirely sure he believed such a thing were possible. But he waved his hand, saying, "Do go on," and so Prestina did.

"I know that you've given Praxis several vials of . . . 'glee.'" Prestina's mouth twisted up. She hated even stooping to that level, calling it by the name that it made its party rounds as. But somehow she doubted Lexthur knew it by any other name. Did the bastard even know that doctors called it something else? Previn was regularly dosed with it, whenever his fits got to be too much, and Prestina hated it even then, even when it was necessary.

Even now. Especially now.

Whatever Lexthur might have been expecting, this wasn't it. He went still, studying Prestina as if he wasn't entirely sure whether or not he should own up to his actions. She could see it, the question, in the way his eyes stayed locked in with hers: did she approve, or not?

In truth, she did not, but that wasn't going to stop her from taking advantage of the situation.

Lexthur stayed silent for another long moment before he asked, carefully, "And how exactly did this come to your attention?"

The answer to that one was simple: Prestina had recognized the signs of its use in Prawl as soon as he'd arrived with Praxis to prepare Pranders's body for burial. At the time, Prestina had gritted her teeth, keeping things together throughout the preparations for the burial itself, but then, the two of them alone in their rooms afterward, she couldn't contain her anger for a second longer. The fight that erupted between them was quiet but vicious, and in fact Prestina's shoulder still hurt when she lifted her arm all the way up. Later, it hadn't been difficult to snoop through Praxis's rooms and lab, until she'd found the leather case. Even empty, Prestina had recognized it as the same kind Lexthur had kept in his private office, the night Prestina had first gone to speak with him about her daughter.

She wasn't about to admit to any of this, however, and so Prestina just looked at Lexthur, face neutral, until Lexthur finally sighed and leaned back against the wall of the den.

"Fine," he said. "You're right, of course. What of it?"

"Can you get her more?"

Again, not the words Lexthur was expecting. He tipped his head. "I don't know. I doubt she would come to me for it."

"That's not what I asked."

No, it wasn't, but Lexthur didn't seem particularly interested in answering what she'd actually asked. Was it possible, Prestina wondered, that he was losing his nerve for the endeavor? True, the offer she'd presented him with—the promise of a Fellows title to claim for his very own—should be irresistible.

Should be.

Prestina had seen "should be" fail her before, though, too many times to lay her trust in it completely. She began to run through her other options, just in case; the threats she could level, the offers that might prove more pressing, the reasons why he should buckle down and commit to what he was already being handed. There was no limit to how far Prestina would go, to achieve her ends. She'd proven that, when she came up with the plan that had brought Lexthur to her today. She'd prove it again, before this was over.

In the end, she did not wait for him to answer. There was a vial in her pocket, already prepared. If he would not make up his mind, she would make it up for him. Prestina drew the vial out and held it in her upturned palm. She did not need to tell him that it was special; he understood. She did not need to tell him to be careful; she did not care if he was careful, so long as he succeeded. She did not need to tell him that time was of the essence, that they were running out, that this may, perhaps, be their last shot at getting Praxis to agree, at securing the future they both still dreamed of, even if only a little. Lexthur took the vial, tucking it into his breast pocket, then patted the fabric above. And so the deal was set, the promise made in silence.

What else was there to say? There was nothing. Lexthur would find a way to make this work, somehow, would deliver the vial to Praxis's clutching hands, somehow, and from there his role would be superfluous. That was the true beauty of Prestina's plan this time, so simple and so elegant, as pure as motherhood itself. A start, a spark, that's all it took, and then nature would take over the rest.

All Prestina had to do was be patient.

THE QUESTION, KAEDRICH decided, wasn't *Where is the Beacon?* or *What are they planning for it?* or even, on the surface, *Who would do such a thing?*, because those questions, while valid, were wholly unanswerable. No, the much more reasonable place to start was simple, because it was sitting right in front of her: *Who was benefiting?*

That, at least, she could puzzle her way through, for it surely wasn't Pranders, and it surely wasn't Prommel, and it surely wasn't Prewish. It surely wasn't Previn, or Prenna, or Prett. It surely wasn't Prawl or Prestina. It surely wasn't Praxis. Kaedrich did not really know all the names and personalities of the younger generations, the children and nieces and nephews, but she could rule out the babies, certainly, and it seemed unlikely that anyone earlier than their coming-of-age ball would have had the skills or resources necessary to steal a Beacon. Praxis had told her, finally, that the thing had been stolen from inside a secret passage, sealed off by magic—Praxis was convinced this meant the only person who could have taken the Beacon was another wizard, but Kaedrich wasn't so sure there couldn't be another explanation. All of the girls, after all, had been tested long ago by order of Prestina, and they'd all come up ordinary, nonmagical, mundane as soup. And of the boys? Again, Kaedrich was no expert, but—none seemed particularly suited.

Which left her with her original question, and as far as Kaedrich was concerned, there was only one answer to that. Who was benefiting?

At a subdued dinner, more than half of the usual faces absent from attending, Kaedrich found herself studying Praine out of the corner of her eye. It was not a comfortable premise to consider, but it was too serious to ignore. Anyone could see that his chances were improving rapidly, though he maintained a casual façade about the whole thing—oh, we'll see, he said; nothing is certain, he said. But every day the certainty was setting, like water slowly freezing into ice, and Kaedrich couldn't ignore the possibility.

This is how she found herself, about an hour later, letting herself into the staff offices of the Fellows financial empire—with a fire of pure purpose in her heart, and only the faintest cloud of doubt to obscure her otherwise righteous light. Fleetingly, she wondered: is this how Praxis felt, all those times that she frequently and flagrantly invaded people's privacy? The thought gave Kaedrich a vague sense of vertigo, but not enough to deter her.

Though Prawl's authority granted her every right to be here, Kaedrich still did not fancy the idea of anyone knowing what she was doing. So she told the guard at the entrance that she needed to inspect the "grubs," and then said that no, thank you, she did not need to be shown the way, she'd manage on her own. And then, at the corner, to the staff member walking the opposite direction: the lie that he was needed in the grubs' living quarters. To the next staff member, at the door to Praine's office: Praine was looking for him, and wasn't happy about it. Inside she found Praine's own son—Praine the Younger she'd heard him called—and he, too, received the lie that he was needed elsewhere; Kaedrich would follow, she'd said, but you mustn't wait around.

Though Praine the Younger, at least, appeared somewhat more hesitant to accept these orders, he did at least comply in the end. And so Kaedrich found herself, quite suddenly, alone in Praine's private office.

It was somehow worse than the last time. Alone, the paintings filled Kaedrich's perception, until it felt as if they were watching her, these pristine maidens with a vicious, hungry lust painted into their eyes. For a moment, Kaedrich could only stare, wondering, who were these women, who were the models, who were the stories based off, and how had it all gone so very, very wrong? For though Kaedrich recognized none of them—not the paintings, nor the women depicted in them from song or story—she knew without question that they had to have been the work of men. No woman would have painted one of her kin this way, as monster, whore, mother, meat.

Kaedrich ripped her attention away, the way she wanted to rip the paintings off the walls. She would not allow herself to get sidetracked. Praine's decorating was horrible, but it did not prove him complicit in any crime she was investigating. She stepped deeper into the room, and got to work.

There was no desk to rifle through, nor any apparent means of filing that Kaedrich could find. Papers did not appear to exist within this place. The few cabinets, sprinkled around the perimeter of the room, contained mostly bottles and glasses, their array of colors as dazzling as a gem display. There *was* a chest in the corner of the room, tucked away behind a sculpture, and it *was* locked, so that at least gave her an idea of a place to start, but—well, it was locked. And Kaedrich, for all of her skills, had never studied lock picking. Maybe, if she could convince Praxis to come back with her later . . .

The sound of a distant door made Kaedrich whirl. She'd left the one to the office opened just a crack, the better to hear when someone might be coming, and now footsteps echoed down like the beating of a drum before a firing squad. Panic seized her as she realized the carelessness of her plan. Fine, so she had an exit, but—the only place it led to was the hallway beyond. Indecision froze her because again, technically, no one had grounds to object to her being in here. This didn't offer as much comfort as it should have.

Kaedrich dove for cover. A heavy velvet curtain hung along one wall, what Kaedrich thought was just a kind of tapestry until she stepped behind it and there, like the guiding hand of Perlandra, an opportunity: a set of doors, concealed from sight. She stepped through them as the doors to the office opened and footsteps strode through. She did not care, at that moment, where this other door led, so long as it was *away*.

She found herself on the balcony that overlooked the workers' "living quarters." It appeared to be a rest period, the sprawl of human suffering all bundled down and lying there in resigned obedience, and though it was never technically dark under the ice of Yandosia, Kaedrich muttered a fast prayer of gratitude all the same. Fewer open eyes meant fewer people noticing her, or watching the botched attempt she made now as she slipped over the railing of the balcony and surveyed the distance.

It wasn't the worst drop ever. Especially not after Kaedrich crouched down, grabbed hold of the bars of the railing, dangled the length of her body. A minor twist of her ankle upon landing, a cry of pain that she bit down on fast. A few of the workers' heads raised at the commotion, one or two spotted her crouched there, but what was there for them to even report at that point, anyway? And would they even bother? With nothing of apparent interest to see, one by one they shut their eyes and laid their heads back down on the slim excuses for pillows and bedrolls that littered the ice floor.

Kaedrich stood up, straightened her suit jacket. Tried to pretend that she belonged here as she made her way out of the living quarters, past a handful of guards, through the passage to the main business trunk. But as soon as Kaedrich cleared the staff wing, she ran. Through twisting passages and endless stairs, up one level and then another, all the way back until she was almost where she'd started. Shortly before she actually reached the dining rooms, she veered left, and about halfway down that hall, she ducked through a familiar door.

She took a moment to steady herself, in the privacy of Prawl's . . . game room? Study? It was hard to say, but clearly the room meant *something* to him, because this is where he'd brought Kaedrich that first evening, when he'd wanted to be open about his knowledge of Kaedrich's gender, where they'd since wiled away several evenings over cards and drinks. It was one of the few places in the Fellows household where Kaedrich felt comfortable—perhaps even more so than their suite on Emerald Level, especially considering the fragile silence between her and Praxis. Kaedrich stepped forward, testing out her shaky legs. That had been *way* too close for Kaedrich's comfort. She couldn't shake the idea of Praine catching her. She just kept picturing what would have happened, if he'd been a little faster, if Kaedrich hadn't found another way out. She didn't know which was the worse outcome: for him to have seen her, and the ensuing dispute, or if he *hadn't* realized she was there, and had just . . . gone about his Praine-y business. Doing whatever Praine things that Praine did.

The very idea was enough to twist her stomach. It felt better to sit, and so Kaedrich sat. Not at the gaming table, but in an easy chair in the corner, beside a bookcase loaded with thick volumes. There was a comfort in their spines, the faint smell of them when she leaned over. Kaedrich reached for one, knowing it would be illegible to her but not caring, when she discovered that several of the books were not books at all.

It's true she'd heard of the *concept* of a hollowed-out book, but seeing it was something else entirely. As soon as she'd picked it off the shelf, she knew something about it was wrong; maybe the weight distribution was off, or the way the pages did not shift between the cover, or the particular stiffness of the spine, perhaps. Whatever the reason, she was unsurprised, even in her surprise at finding it, that when she opened the cover, she was met not with a title page, but a crevice containing a jeweled letter opener. Kaedrich lifted it out and turned it over in her hands.

Was it just that she was still in a snooping mindset, her previous attempt cut short, that made her investigate further? She would probably never know. But her curiosity had been piqued, and now she put the letter opener back and began to shift through the rest of the volumes, seeing what treasure lay buried on the shelves.

She found two more, in and among the actual books, and just as she was beginning to doubt herself, a prickle of guilt beginning to creep into the back of her mind, a third.

Inside, a packet. Prawl's tiny, meticulous handwriting spelled out a single word: *Praxis*.

Kaedrich lifted the packet out, setting it on an end table beside her chair. The packet was actually a large envelope, and Kaedrich reached in and carefully withdrew a fat stack of papers of various sizes. Beneath the packet was a leather-bound ledger, and Kaedrich set that aside for now, turning her attention to the papers in front of her. None of it appeared terribly unusual. Prawl had said it himself: he was a devoted father, and so it made perfect sense that he'd have collected things to remind him of his wayward daughter, the one lost to him somewhere out in the world. At first, Kaedrich was even a little touched, on Praxis's behalf. Though the papers she sifted through were written all in Yandosian, they were clearly letters, addressed to Prawl, and a handful of photographs of Praxis. Kaedrich smiled as she picked up a stack of them. Praxis had never said anything about having contact with her father after she'd left, but clearly she must have at least on occasion, and why not?

Kaedrich thumbed through them. One showed a young Praxis in a library somewhere, sitting at a table, hunched over as she read a book. One was just a building, a quiet country house somewhere Kaedrich didn't recognize. One had Praxis sitting on a pile of crates at a dock: she was clearly bored, her chin cupped in her hand while dockworkers blurred as unidentified streaks around her. One appeared to be from her days at the Royal Society of Magic, in Monfort: she'd cut her hair short by that point, adopted men's dress style; in the photograph, she was working a chalkboard, her arm and face a blur of motion, her back to the photographer.

It was at this point that a sense of unease began to prickle along Kaedrich's skin. It was probably nothing, she told herself, but . . .

Kaedrich flipped through a few more of the photographs: Praxis on a beach, a vibrantly young and attractive Aul woman tucked into the crook of her arm; Praxis at a museum, hunched over an artifact on display; Praxis at a party, the one sour person sulking darkly in the corner of an otherwise merry-looking gathering.

Not a single one of them was posed, like a typical photograph. And not a single one of them showed Praxis actually *looking* at the camera—on the contrary, it seemed as if every time the photograph was taken, Praxis was thoroughly absorbed in some other activity. As if she hadn't even noticed.

As if she wasn't *meant* to have noticed.

Unease made Kaedrich dizzy. She set the photographs aside, too disturbed by the implications to look at them anymore, and picked up a stack of letters instead. They were not, as she had at first assumed, written by Praxis. The handwriting was all wrong, as if a variety of people had penned them. Their postmarks came from all over the world, the signatures bore a variety of names—but each of them featured Praxis's name. The instances jumped out at Kaedrich, as if they'd been set alight.

The ledger that she'd set aside was no better. A bank account—Praxis's bank account—filled nearly the entire volume. Prawl's handwriting tracked the debits, with several enormous credits made periodically from his own accounts. Of course he'd *said*, when they'd first arrived, that he was responsible for refreshing her coffers now and then, but never had Kaedrich imagined that he'd kept such careful track of exactly *where* all the money was going. Kaedrich stared in horror at the endless list of business names, personal names, the running tally of amounts going in and out. Nearly everything Praxis had ever done, nearly everyone she'd ever conducted business with, laid out in orderly columns.

And then Kaedrich's blood turned to ice. She'd flipped far enough into the volume by now that the dates were drawing nearer and nearer to the present and there, in crisp ink: Falconridge Academy of Arms. Again and again, the entire year and a half Kaedrich had been attending.

Kaedrich abandoned all sense of discretion then. She pawed through the rest of the contents of the packet in a frenzy. She didn't even know what she was looking for, until she found it. A single sheet of paper, a single letter in Durlish. Kaedrich recognized Falconridge's crest along the top, recognized the name of Director Tarlock's secretary scrawled along the bottom, but all that she could really look at was her own name, and the address of the apartment she used to share with Marlick.

Prawl had known. All of this time, pretending to be surprised by the changes in Praxis's appearance, in her life—pretending to be surprised by Kaedrich's arrival.

She felt bitterly exposed, all of a sudden. Like she was caught out on the surface, pinned beneath the harsh sun and the cruel winds. Kaedrich flipped through several more pages, dreading what she might find. At first, the return to letters written in a language she couldn't translate was almost a comfort—she wasn't sure she *wanted* to know, anymore—but then the name "Quorral" caught her eye in the jumble of Yandosian.

It was too much to resist. Kaedrich slowed, but nothing else stood out; just "Quorral," the town she'd grown up in, repeated twice over. Enough to make Kaedrich's skin crawl, not enough to answer her questions. Kaedrich frowned at it, chewing her lip. A dark shape from below bled up through the thin paper, and Kaedrich flipped to the next page.

In the next instant, she wished she hadn't. Her breath escaped her, along with her strength. It was a good thing she was already sitting, because if she wasn't, she'd have surely collapsed.

Kaedrich could only stare. The page trembled in her hand.

No. She thought it, felt the weight of the word as it tried to smother and soothe her mind, but there was no denying black-and-white. The image and the truth mirrored her grief back at her, deep enough to carve the very heart from her chest.

She couldn't look at it anymore. Her eyes stung as she stuffed the letter into the pocket of her suit coat. One of the photographs, too, taken at random from the pile. The rest of it Kaedrich shoved hastily back into the packet, and the packet and the ledger back into the book, the book back onto the shelf. It would be obvious that someone had gone through it, but Kaedrich couldn't bring herself to put everything away properly. She couldn't bring herself to look at the contents more than she already had. She was terrified, by now, of what *else* she might find in it, what *other* secrets might be buried in there. There was already too much.

Abandoning her business, Kaedrich made a fast line out of the study. She didn't even know what she was doing anymore, because it's not like she would magically pop herself back to Durland, and even if she could . . .

even if she could, how could she ever walk away from the danger they'd found here? What would it say about her? Even so: Kaedrich's racing heart, breaking under the weight of her discovery, led her out, up, away, and it wasn't until she was almost there that she realized she'd known where she was going this whole time.

Kaedrich burst into Praxis's lab.

Chapter Thirty

"PACK YOUR BAGS," Kaedrich said as the door slammed against the wall from the force of her entrance. "We have to leave. Now. Today. This minute."

Praxis did not flinch at the sudden burst of the door, at the slight gust of wind that Kaedrich carried in with the force of her entrance. She did not flinch at the abrupt conversational opener, or the speed and intensity at which it was delivered. She kept her hands steady, her mind clear, as she tugged at the elements that made up the half-melted lapus lumeni sitting in front of her.

Magic could not change the fundamental essence of a thing, true—but *science* could. Heat and light and pressure. Breaking chunks of the world down to their constituent elements, and then building them back up into something new. Lapus lumeni already had the ability to preserve light inside of its molecular bindings, why *shouldn't* it be able to house magical energy?

Fine, so there were about a thousand reasons why not, and each more nuanced than the last. But the idea had begun to spark something, in the back of Praxis's brain, a frenzied whisper she couldn't ignore. The very last thing she wanted was to lose that train of thought.

"I'm busy."

"Not too busy for this." Kaedrich had not stopped, not even once, since entering the lab, and now she shoved a piece of paper right in front of Praxis, slapping it down across her work so that there was no choice but to see it.

The impression of a gravestone stared back at her. A charcoal rubbing, the letters hovering ghostly in the mist of the black powder. It had gotten smeared, slightly, somewhere in transport, but its meaning and message were still plain enough for all to see:

MANNLY
Kaedrich & Kaedriella
Keep Dancing, My Stars

Beneath that, a twin set of dates: one easily recognizable as Kaedriella's birthday, the other a seemingly random date, five and a half years old.

Praxis looked at the rubbing for a long time, a chill setting into her bones. Fine, so it wasn't a monument to the day Kaedriella had *actually* died, when Praxis had used her power as Lady of Souls to break a fundamental oath and bring her back—at least this wasn't *that* conversation, at least Praxis's secret was safe for another day. Her heart had beat wildly for a split second as she'd realized what she was seeing, but it had quickly settled out at this thought. It pounded steadily now, still thick in her throat, but at least the fear had abated. But if not that, then . . . what? This gravestone didn't seem to make any sense, not at first, though later Praxis would realize that the answer was obvious.

She looked up. Kaedrich was standing nearby, arms crossed tightly over her chest, as if that was the only thing holding her together. Kaedrich's whole body was shaking, though it was hard to tell from her eyes whether it was rage or fear or something . . . else, something darker, that fueled her. Her lips were pressed together so tightly that they disappeared. Her eyes were rimmed pink, as if she'd been crying.

Praxis held the rubbing aloft. "Where did you—?"

"Your *father* had it. He's been spying on you—and me, now—this whole time. Look." With jerky motions, Kaedrich managed to unfold her arms, long enough to throw something else, something smaller, in Praxis's direction, which Praxis then had to scramble to catch.

This time, it was not a shade of Kaedrich's past, but Praxis's. The memory of it struck her numb. A perfect tropical beach, the nose of a tiny sailboat piercing the corner of the photograph. Praxis herself, rendered in gray, settled in the curve of a dune. She looked so young, impossibly young, and practically glowed. Though she was small in the image, the photograph obviously taken at a distance, Praxis would have recognized it anywhere, just as she recognized the face of the woman that her ghost's arm was wrapped around. Praxis was facing away from the camera, watching the sea, but the woman had turned, and obviously held still long enough to be captured in perfect clarity. She seemed to gaze right into the camera, Rinn's eyes held fast, and looking at it now, so many years after it was taken, it felt as if she was studying *Praxis*.

"I don't understand," Praxis said, still staring at the photograph. Rinn's gaze, even in miniature, was cutting and calculated, vaguely disapproving. It seemed to reach into Praxis's chest and squeeze down hard. Her hand seized around the photograph, bending it as she steadied herself against the slab of the worktable. "I don't understand."

"Don't you?"

She supposed she did. Really, it shouldn't have been a surprise. Isn't this sort of thing exactly what Praxis would have done, if she was the head of a family and someone had slipped out from her grasp? And the ease with which he had accepted Kaedrich, as if it wasn't even a surprise—well, it wouldn't have been, would it? Praxis glanced once more at the rubbing that Kaedrich had presented to her, Kaedrich's real name alongside her dead brother's. Even in Praxis's discomfort, she had to admit that the level of snooping that would have been required to get this was impressive, especially given that Prawl had to have been working via proxies and agents, letters traded back and forth across the vast expanse of oceans and continents.

It struck Praxis then: if this wasn't a sign of love and devotion, then what was? A swell of affection for her father rose up in her chest, smothering whatever annoyance had still been left to linger.

"You see why we need to go, then."

Praxis looked up. Kaedrich was still clutching at herself, trembling underneath the weight of her discovery.

"I'm afraid I don't," Praxis said, and she watched as Kaedrich's mouth dropped open.

"How can you say that? Praxis, he was *spying* on you—on us! Who knows what else he's dug up! We can't stay here—it's not safe. I mean, we'll keep trying to find the Beacon, of course, but we can't stay *here*."

Praxis rolled her eyes. "Ella, I think you're exaggerating the situation. He was just doing what any father would have."

"No," Kaedrich said. "I'm not. Don't you understand? Your father has been lying to you. He's been lying to all of you. It wasn't just your bank account—which he kept a lot closer eye on than he's let on, by the way, I saw the ledger myself . . . He *knew* you weren't dead, because he knew *exactly where you were*. How can that not bother you?"

Praxis shrugged. "I'm sorry, I just don't see what all the fuss is about.

If anything, this only proves his good intentions toward us. But never mind that," Praxis said, talking over Kaedrich, "how did you manage to get your hands on this, anyway?"

Kaedrich squared her shoulders. "I found it."

An arched eyebrow. "Found it."

"Yes."

"And where, exactly, did you 'find' it?"

"Does it matter?"

She may as well have confirmed it. Praxis shut her eyes, gathering strength. She found herself holding the photograph to her chest; the corner of it was bent, and Praxis toyed at the point with her thumb, softening the crease. A part of Praxis couldn't believe Kaedrich had been snooping through Prawl's possessions—really, it was much more of a Praxis move—but another part of her wasn't surprised at all. Hadn't Kaedrich been pressing Praxis, these last few days, to continue "investigating"? And once Kaedrich got a bit between her teeth, boy . . .

"I'm not sorry," Kaedrich said, and a surge of annoyance coursed through Praxis.

Praxis snorted, opening her eyes. "No, of course you're not. That would mean admitting you did something wrong."

"Because I *didn't.*"

"Dammit, Kaedrich!" Praxis threw the photograph down. Her fingers mashed hard against her forehead. "You can't *do this.* Don't you understand how dangerous it is? Two people have already *died* in this household—and one of them was a trained wizard, I might add. If he couldn't protect himself—"

"I know what I'm doing."

"Do you? Because it doesn't look that way from where I'm standing."

"Because you're not trusting me! Because you've never trusted me. Perlandra's breath, Praxis, how many dangerous situations do I need to prove myself in, for you to realize that I know what I'm doing?"

Praxis scowled. This was an old argument, and not one she fancied reliving again. "That's not the point."

"I think it is," Kaedrich said. "Unless you'd rather tell me why *you're* not investigating. Why you won't even retreat to the land of the dead, to see who killed your own brother."

A well of silence dropped down between them. Praxis had only just managed to brush off this subject, when Kaedrich first brought it up after Pranders's funeral; Praxis didn't think she had it in her to avoid it again.

"I *told* you, there was nothing to see," Praxis said. "The displays were obscured."

"And so, what, that's just the end of it?"

"What would you have me do?" Praxis snapped. "Spy on my family? Snoop through their things, as if they were common criminals?"

"As if you have a problem with that sort of thing."

"I do when it's my *family*! Just . . . stop and *think* about what you're doing. Snooping around in my father's belongings is one thing—I mean, okay, his tracking me isn't great, but he's ultimately harmless. But what if you'd been going through the real killer's stuff? What if they'd found you? Did you even *think* about that—even once? For sanity's sake, this isn't a game!"

"I'm not saying it is."

"Then you've got to stop this nonsense. I'm serious. You can't keep spying on them—I . . . I forbid it."

Praxis knew she'd gone too far as soon as the words were out of her mouth. Probably, she'd even known a little before that, but the realization came too late, like knowing you were going to fall just after you'd lost your balance. Gravity did the rest, the words landing with the heavy clang of finality between them.

She couldn't look up, not after that, but she sensed as Kaedrich stepped back, tasted the need to put some minor distance between them.

"You *forbid* it?" Kaedrich's words sliced the air, hitting Praxis dead-on. Praxis winced. "That's not—I didn't—"

"Just who do you think you *are*?"

A valid question, one that Praxis wasn't prepared to handle. She closed her eyes and bit her lip, trying to gather the strength she needed to dig herself out of this mess. "Please," Praxis said. She looked back at Kaedrich. "Please, Ella, just let me handle this. I'll fix it, I promise, I just . . . I just need more time."

Kaedrich sighed, and for a moment a flicker of hope sparked to life in Praxis. Maybe, she thought, just maybe, Kaedrich would agree? But when Kaedrich met her eyes, her face deadened and level, that spark died, snuffed out under the cold breeze of Kaedrich's determination.

"My parents think I'm *dead*," Kaedrich said, her voice cracking. She took a breath. "I mean . . . I guess I always knew that, but they think I'm *dead*, and they put up a *gravestone* for me. You've seen what that kind of loss is doing to your parents—imagine mine, their only children gone for *years*. So if you think you're going to stop me from investigating literally the only thing important enough to keep me from going home *right now* . . . you're wrong."

Praxis scowled. She looked back down, at her work, at the photograph and the rubbing Kaedrich had given her. She shoved these aside, refocusing on the one thing she could control. "Fine," she snapped. "Then would you mind leaving me alone? I have a lot of work to do."

But by the time she finished saying it, Kaedrich was already gone.

PRAXIS FOUND HER father in the kitchen.

Two full days had passed since Kaedrich had announced her determination to bully forward, and Praxis hadn't left the lab since. She worked with an unnatural frenzy, the idea for how to make her lapus lumeni work so tangible that she felt she could reach out and touch it. Praxis had chased that idea, stalked it through the forest of calculations and beakers and singed fingertips, and now here, at last, she'd emerged. Transformed, triumphant. All that was left was to reap her glory.

But now the door slid from her fingers, and she came to a stop in the archway. "What's this?" Praxis asked. All the way down, she'd known where to find her father, and all the way down, her wizard's sense had told her that he was alone, but somehow, as the room opened up before her, this wasn't what she'd expected to find.

Prawl was bent over the great slab of a table in the center of the room, drizzling a layer of chocolate over trays of something small and freshly baked. The air was warmed with not just the residual heat of the ovens, but the comforting scents of sugar and chocolate and something else, something tangy and almost . . . citrus? Praxis sniffed, but it was hard to place, exactly.

Her father ignored her, long enough to finish drizzling, anyway. He studied the work before him as if it was his masterpiece, and he a legendary painter. When the last confection was covered, he lifted the pan with a flourish, setting it all down beside the trays. Only then did he look up, his face lighter and somehow far more cheerful than Praxis had seen it since the news of the inheritance bidding broke. Bits of sugar clung to his beard, sparkling white on white. He actually *smiled* at her, just for a moment, before a flare of grief seemed to drag the corners of his mouth back down. He motioned grandly at the spread before him. "What do you think?"

"Honestly, I don't know what to think," Praxis said. "Since when can you *cook*?"

A small laugh escaped under Prawl's breath. "It was my father's idea that I learn. When I was twelve, he hired only the best tutors."

"But . . . why?"

Prawl blinked, as if it was obvious. "Because I was supposed to become a chef. That was his plan for me, anyway." Prawl shrugged. "I wasn't considered to be good for much else."

It took a minute for Praxis to process this. True, she'd known that the Fellows' company had been inherited from her mother's side—the *true* Fellows, Prestina had never failed to remind Praxis—but beyond that, her parents had never really spoken to her about their respective histories. Never once had Praxis asked. What good would it have done? And why would she have ever thought to? Neither Prawl nor Prestina were much in the way of storytellers, each history lesson they did give being for the purpose of instruction, trying to mold her growing personality in one way or another. Now Praxis realized just how much she didn't know, how many hidden facets they must each have, never once brought to light before her. It was enough to make her dizzy. She actually took several steps into the kitchen, leaning against the edge of the table to steady herself.

"Praxis?" Prawl asked. He was already halfway around the table by the time she'd caught the edge. "Are you all right?"

Praxis made herself nod. "I'm fine," she said. "It's just . . . why didn't you ever tell me about any of this?"

Prawl's soft smile very nearly melted Praxis's heart. "Oh, my little opal. I don't know."

"Did you come down here often?" she asked. "Did I just never notice?"

Prawl laughed. "No. I don't think I've so much as set foot in a kitchen in forty years. Maybe longer."

"So why go back to it now?"

"Ah." Prawl's eyes shifted, his attention sliding from her and drifting somewhere beyond even the kitchen. "I think I wanted to see if it would be different. I thought, maybe . . ." He trailed off, shook his head. When he looked back at her, he gave her an unconvincing smile. "It doesn't matter. Did you want to try one?" He motioned at the trays, still spread in a wide display before them.

But Praxis shook her head. She did not wish to be unkind, but . . . it felt better, not knowing. What if he was terrible, his skills atrophied? Or, somehow worse, what if they weren't—what if he was skilled beyond Praxis's imagination, his true talents wasted all these years?

It felt strange to present him with her gift now, but the weight of the modified lapus lumeni crystal hung low in her coat pocket, and really, what point was there in putting it off? She'd worked hard to get this far, harder than she'd worked in years, and Prawl deserved to be rewarded with the fruits of the labor he'd set her up for.

She drew the crystal out, resting it gently on the table between them. They were standing side by side, and Praxis's fingers almost brushed Prawl's as she laid it down.

Instantly, whatever nostalgia or curiosity that had drawn Prawl down here was abandoned. His eyes alighted at the sight of it, and he snatched it up so fast that Praxis felt the cold breeze of his movements against her cheek. "You did it?"

Praxis nodded. "I did it."

She still couldn't accept the truth of this statement, but that didn't make it false. Praxis had done it, somehow, modified the lapus lumeni to store magical energies for later retrieval. She still wasn't sure what kind of application the crystal would have, but that was more Prawl's problem than hers—whatever he sold the Minor Conclave on, whatever promises he made, Praxis wouldn't be around to watch the fallout. She'd done her job, and now it was up to Prawl to do his. All she needed to focus on now was surviving until the oversight committee ruled—and the pain in Praxis's leg provided her with her priority. It shouldn't take too much effort, to nose around until she found where the social elite of Bolt acquired their . . . recreation.

But that could wait, for a few minutes anyway. In the warmth of the kitchen, Praxis felt the need to clear the air between her and her father, even if he didn't yet know what had soured between them. And so Praxis cleared her throat. "I know, by the way."

A stillness settled over Prawl, a momentary hitch in his exuberance. His eyes darted to Praxis and then away again, settling on the crystal that he clutched in his hand. He started to speak, then had to pause to dampen his throat. Try again. "'Know'?"

Praxis reached into her pocket, withdrawing a folded sheet of paper. She passed it to her father, who hesitated for just a moment before accepting it. Praxis watched, carefully, as he held the paper close, as he gingerly unfolded it, as he took in the sight of the gravestone rubbing. He studied it for a long moment, his face betraying nothing.

"I'm not upset," Praxis said. "In case you were worried about that. I mean, I was at first. I wish you'd have just *told* me you were keeping an eye on me, but I get why you didn't."

Prawl nodded. "Thank you," he said as he folded the paper back up.

He tucked it into the breast pocket of his jacket, but Praxis did not object, nor try to take it for herself. He glanced at her, once. "I'm glad there are no hard feelings."

Praxis shrugged. "You've always been good to me. I know that." She leaned over, resting her head on her father's shoulder. Fur from his coat brushed against her face, her nose, creating a forest of stalks through which to see the world. It was not a familiar gesture for either of them, and for a moment Praxis felt the stiffness of her father's muscles, the hesitation he had at accepting this kindness. But then, slowly, he took a breath, his own motions shifting her head as his chest rose and fell.

"Thank you," Prawl said a moment later. His voice was oddly quiet, the words nearly cracked. He clutched the modified lapus lumeni, his knuckles even whiter than usual. "I try. Gods, I try."

Tried and succeeded, as far as Praxis was concerned, but even this moment of calm sentimentality wasn't quite enough to get her to break the silence on that. Instead, she reached up and squeezed her father's arm, trying to convey her faith in him without needing to outright say it. Kaedrich was wrong—Prawl, at least, was not a reason to fear Yandosia. If anything, Praxis thought, he had been the one good reason for their return.

YEARS AGO, ON Praxis's seventeenth birthday, she had woken up late. She did not immediately remember what day it was, nor even that her birthday was approaching at all. The entire coming-of-age ball had receded back to the farthest corners of her mind, and so she yawned and stretched herself out, her toes and fingers fully extended and yet barely reaching the edges of her bed. No one had woken her earlier because, for once, there was nothing more for the hostess to do other than to attend. So Praxis just laid there for a while, staring up at the twisting patterns of lapus lumeni that cut through her ceiling, feeling . . . nothing.

She got up feeling nothing. She got dressed feeling nothing. She went to the dining room and the maids, already sensing her approach, had just finished laying out a fresh round of breakfast. Praxis sat down to eat, and felt nothing.

Even once she did remember, it made no impact. Prett came in, teasing her about something or other, and she nodded and laughed at what he said, and then two seconds after he left, she could not for the life of her remember what they had spoken about, if indeed they had spoken at all.

The ball wouldn't start for hours, and so Praxis filled her day with idle distractions. She might have read—it felt as if maybe she read for a while, though it was hard to say for sure. Everything about the day was slipping from her as soon as it had happened, like it was all just nothing more than a sound carried in by the surface winds, torn from her the instant that it struck.

It was therefore something of a surprise when she found herself dressed for the ball, hours later. Her dress was perfect: slate-blue seal leather, dotted with gemstones. Her hair tumbled loose around her shoulders, only sections of it pulled back to leave a good view of her face and her cleavage. Praxis looked at herself in the mirror, trying to commit every piece of it to memory, but the image looked like someone else, and it slipped through the sieve of her thoughts as easily as anything else from that day.

She walked to the ballroom. Music and laughter were already spilling out into the surrounding corridors. She smiled and nodded at some of the people as she passed, stopping long enough to accept a gushing compliment about either herself or the party. She was almost to the ballroom when her father appeared, as if out of nowhere, and yanked her sharply aside.

He drew her into a side room, and wrapped her in one of his enormous hugs before Praxis could even start to protest. The flare of irritation she'd had melted. She wrapped her arms around him, breathing in the scents of leather and ale and spiced cologne off of the fur of his coat. "Oh, my girl, my sweet girl," he kept whispering—she would have almost called it "blubbering" if it were anyone else, but this was Prawl Fellows, and Prawl Fellows, for all of his jovial nature, did not tend toward sentiment.

And yet, when Praxis finally did manage to pull out of his embrace, she could have sworn that Prawl's eyes were moister than they should have been. Which really didn't make much sense, because even if he was likely to get emotional over the coming of age of his children, he'd already *done* these things so many times over that surely the effect must have worn off by now?

Apparently not, though, because he cupped Praxis's cheeks, looking at her directly in the eyes. "My sweet, sweet girl," he said again. "My little opal."

Praxis forced a smile. She drew her father's hands away, embarrassed by the childhood nickname and suddenly uncomfortable about the whole encounter. "Oh, come on, now. There's no reason for this. Nothing is going to change."

Prawl smiled sadly, and shook his head. "Praxis, you know that you've always been my favorite, don't you?"

In fact she had not, or at least, not more than just the inkling of suspicion, which was really nothing at all like hearing it out loud. Praxis jerked back, startled, and Prawl took her shoulder to steady her.

"This is a very important day," he said, as if somehow Praxis had missed that from all of her months spent planning. She did not offer up that sarcastic remark, however, merely reached up and patted her father's hand.

"I know."

"No," Prawl said. "I really don't think you do. There are going to be a lot of decisions that you'll be making over the next few months and years, things that will shape the entire course of the rest of your life. And . . . Praxis, you *need* to make sure that you're making these choices based on what's true in your heart. Not what you think is 'best,' or what your mother and I would want. *Your* choices."

A nervous laugh escaped Praxis's chest before she could stop it. "I don't think Mother would agree."

"To the depths with your mother!" Prawl snapped, and Praxis reeled back.

Prawl's face softened as he drew a breath to continue. "I know you love your mother, but what I am talking about is more important. This isn't about pleasing her, or me, or anyone else. This is about doing what's right for *you*—the person you actually are, deep down, and not just the person everyone wants you to be. Do you understand what I'm saying?"

Praxis nodded, slowly, though she wasn't sure she actually did. It felt important to agree with her father, though, if only to appease him.

As if drawn by their conversation, the sound of Prestina's voice filtered in from somewhere out in the hall. It was clear from her tone that she was looking for Praxis, and Praxis, acting automatically, moved to obey.

"Just remember what I've said, little opal," Prawl said as Praxis moved to the door. "Can you do that for me?"

"I will," Praxis said, though she was already moving out into the hallway by that point, the conversation drifting easily from her mind. Even with Praxis's quick response, her mother had apparently already moved on, drifting into the ballroom somewhere and lost to the crowds. Praxis stood for a moment on the threshold, steeling herself against the inevitable crush of the dance floor. Her skates hung from her wrist, and she took a moment to untie them and snap them into place over her shoes.

The evening swirled around her, swallowing her whole. She accepted one dance after another, her skates cutting a perfect line across the room, the end digging just at the right moment to spin on point. Praxis had spent *weeks* practicing by herself, or dragging Prett in when she needed to rehearse a move that could only be practiced with a partner. She'd fallen more often than not whenever she'd tried to do anything more complicated than a straight line, but eventually, finally, she'd mastered enough of the basic routines to string them together with, well, not exactly *grace*, but a competent execution. A part of her had even been excited, mastering these skills, imagining the way that she would impress Lexthur with it. They hadn't danced together in ages, and she was sure he'd be pleased.

She did not see him for a long time, however. She split her attention as often as she could without falling down, a watchful eye spying all the odd corners of the room. But she did not see him, and she did not see him, and though this should have worried her, it really didn't. She was still wrapped in her bubble of nothing, going through all the correct motions. At one point she went looking for him, ignoring everyone as she skated by herself to the edges of the room. But she was soon drawn back into the party by Prett, who'd come over and wrapped her in one of his signature one-armed hugs. "You know that Mother hates it when you hide in the corner all evening," he'd said, and she did not bother to tell him the truth of her errand.

There was nothing else to do but dance, so she danced. When the song ended, Praxis's partner tapped his lips and moved off, and then Hudal's twelfth waltz started up, one of Praxis's favorites. She was turning her attentions to see who else might be approaching the woman of honor for the night, when the crowd parted and she spotted Lexthur at last.

He was talking to her father, right in the thick of the guests. He kept bobbing his knees, shuffling his skates nervously back and forth, so much that it was a wonder if he didn't gouge a dip into the ice. On cue, Lexthur looked up, smiling at Praxis.

Lexthur excused himself from Prawl's company and cut a straight line through the dance floor, gliding up to Praxis with ease. "Miss Fellows," he said, tapping his curling lips.

Praxis inclined her head. "Mr. Delford."

She was expecting him to ask her to dance, but he didn't. Instead, he suggested that they go to the sidelines and talk, and that was slightly disappointing, but fine. Praxis's earlier desire to impress him with her dancing was just as removed as anything else right now, and she felt nothing as he guided her toward a refreshment table. She did note with mild curiosity that he was holding something in his hands, though he tucked it quickly into the pocket of his fur coat just as Praxis noticed it. Her present, she assumed, though she really didn't care.

They found a relatively quiet corner. They took off their skating blades and stepped aside, leaving the dance behind them for the moment. The waltz drifted over them, along with the whisper of skates and the trill of laughter. Lexthur gave Praxis a quick, discreet kiss, and the heat trapped in the scar of her wrist flared. *Not now,* Praxis thought, clamping her hand on it as she tried to smile over the pain.

By the time the pain subsided enough for Praxis to concentrate, she found that Lexthur had already started talking. She tried to nod along, as if she'd been listening the entire time.

"—never thought I would ever get so lucky, *never.* The time I've spent with you . . ." He paused, reaching out to intertwine his fingers with hers. "I never want it to end, Praxis. So I thought, well, what do I have to lose?"

Praxis blinked. It still wasn't sinking in, though it probably should have. She watched with an odd detachment as he reached in and drew the present out of his pocket again. He flipped her hand over, and placed it in her palm with the reverence of a preacher handling a holy relic.

It was a silver disk, sort of like a coin but large enough to fill Praxis's entire hand. She stared at it, and stared at it, feeling nothing, because the sight refused to connect itself with the understanding of what it was.

It hit her in a rush: the seal of the auditors, silver for approval. Praxis's eyes widened, and suddenly Prett's teasing from that morning came back to her, something about a portfolio.

"They said 'yes,'" Lexthur said, so softly that it was almost a whisper. "So . . . do you accept?"

"Accept?" Praxis asked. She didn't know why, because it wasn't as if there was any doubt as to what the question was.

Lexthur, however, seemed to find her stunned reaction endearing, damn him. He clamped his hand over hers, the approval seal held tight between them. He smiled. "Will you accept my proposal? And marry me?"

A crashing sound split Praxis's mind, a sudden wave of vertigo seizing her, and in the time in took her to blink, she was no longer standing in the ball. She wasn't in her parents dwelling at all, or really any one particular place. Her life tore open, a flood of images stormed her, and suddenly she could see it all wrapped up in one: the future they'd have together, how she'd enter this loveless marriage with a man that she respected but didn't *want,* the way she would make herself share his bed and bear his children, a life surrounded by the ice, surrounded by society smiles and tedious parties, surrounded by dull business and her mother's approving smile, a life that made her want to scream at the tedium of it all. This, when the alternative was a world of literal magic, where all the secrets of the universe were hers for the taking, where she could rip open life and see what it was made of, where she'd be able to do whatever she wanted. Her magic cracked open inside of her, flooding her veins until she felt it through every square inch of her body.

She finished her blink, and found herself staring at Lexthur's expectant face. And suddenly she didn't feel nothing anymore. Suddenly she felt as if she'd just woken up from a dream, a horrible nightmare in which she'd already buried herself in the ice of her grave. She was supposed to be so much *more* than this. With all the magic of the universe surrounding her, pulsing with life, begging to be explored and discovered, teeming with wonders beyond her imagining, and she had been willing to give it *up*? For this? For the approval of people she didn't even *like*, didn't even *respect*?

What would Moc have thought of her, now?

Praxis looked down at herself, disgusted by what she had become. She ripped her hand free, the seal of the auditors' approval clattering to the floor between them. "No," she said. It was not her intention to be unkind, but she could not soften this, not when a restlessness was clawing at her throat, so smothering that she felt that she could barely breathe. "I can't. I can't do this."

Lexthur's face fell. "Praxis—"

"No! Get away from me! All of you, get—!" Praxis backed up, bumping into someone. She spun around, staring at all the faces that were openly gawping at her now. Without thinking, she ripped one of the shoes off of her feet—gods, what hideous shoes, so impractical and frilly—and hurled it at the wall. It struck with a delightfully satisfying *crack*, the heel wedging itself deep into the ice. "This is *not me*!" she shouted, to the bewilderment of her guests, and on that note, Praxis kicked her other shoe off and ran from the ballroom.

She did not know where she was supposed to go, either in the immediate future or in the broader sense, but the need to run propelled her through her parents' dwelling. Her stocking feet slipped and slid across the ice, but she made it back to her chambers without incident. When she was almost there she passed a maid, who she grabbed by the shoulders and ordered to retrieve a trunk—or no, a suitcase, much smaller, easier to handle on her own. She didn't need much anyway.

By the time her mother stormed in a few minutes later, Praxis had already ripped the ballgown from her body. It lay in shreds on the crystal floor, reduced to a heap of useless rags. She was wearing her plainest dress, dug out from the depths of her closet, the collar only medium-high. She didn't even know where it had come from, because she'd certainly never worn it before.

Prestina was screaming at her before the door was even open between them. Praxis wasn't listening. She continued to rip through her closet, pulling out anything that wasn't the height of ostentation. Where did she even *get* all of this junk, anyway? There was so little of it that she actually needed, so little she would keep.

She was just reaching for a pair of her most basic shoes when Prestina's grip found her, strong as iron. She whirled Praxis toward her, their matching faces set in ice. "If you do not put on something respectable and go back down there *right now*—!"

"I won't," Praxis said. "I'm leaving."

"*Leaving,*" Prestina sneered. "And where, my daughter, do you think you're going?"

"Aul."

As soon as she said it, she knew it was true. Of course she would go to Aul. Where else, but the home of her mentor, the land where magic was rumored to have first begun, the one place that Praxis knew for sure where it wouldn't matter if her eyes lingered on the women rather than the men? She would go to Aul and get a tattoo to remind her of everything she'd almost lost, everything she'd been willing to lose. She'd seek out Moc's family, try to finally release his ghost with her confession. Perhaps, then, she could finally begin her life in earnest. Perhaps then she'd finally be *free*. The idea of it seized Praxis, as intoxicating as any drink. She grinned. "Aul," she repeated, so lightheaded that she almost giggled her speech. "I'm going to Aul."

"You most certainly are *not*," Prestina said. "I am not going to just stand here and let you throw your entire life away, do you hear me?"

Praxis laughed once, bitter and high. "And how do you propose to stop me?"

"By force, if I have to." Her grip tightened, her nails digging into Praxis's skin.

Praxis did not even have to think. She opened her palms and flames sprang to life, hovering neatly just over her upturned hands; Prestina had to jump back, probably already scorched. The room darkened around Praxis, the lapus lumeni drained of most of their power. She let the magic lure her flames up, twisting into long tendrils that swirled around her like animals waiting for her command to strike. Praxis glowered at her mother, knowing that she looked like a beast of the deepest hell and loving every second of it. Loving the way that Prestina took a few steps back, the skittered look in her eyes as she took in the sight of her daughter.

"You go ahead and try it, Mother," Praxis said. "Try to stop me, if you really want to."

Prestina's hand flew to her chest. *"Praxis..."*

It occurred to Praxis then, had Prestina ever seen Praxis's magic? *Really* seen it? Okay, so she'd praised all of Praxis's creations, and preened when she showed Praxis's "party tricks" off to her guests—but it was one thing to witness smaller acts of magic, or see the results of magic, and it was another to witness it raw and crackling, to stare into the face of it as it loomed over her. Prestina would never fully understand the depth of Praxis's abilities, the sheer *power* in even her smallest finger. But Praxis suspected that her mother was coming close to it, now.

"I'm going to Aul," Praxis said again. "I am not going to get married. I am not going to stay here. I am not going to smile, and go to parties, and pretend like everything is just *so* witty. I am leaving, Mother, and I am *never* coming back. Do you understand me?"

"Yes," Prestina whispered. She spoke so softly that it was barely even a breath, and it was in this moment Praxis knew she had won. Finally, and completely, in a war that she did not even realize she'd been waging against her mother. But she had won. She was free.

She was leaving.

They did not say goodbye.

Chapter Thirty-One

ANNELLE FELLOWS STOOD on the threshold of destiny . . .

Okay, so perhaps that was a tad dramatic, but Annelle didn't care. Her coming-of-age ball was just beyond those doors, and her heart was drumming furiously in her chest. *On the threshold of destiny.* That was how she was going to describe this moment, she decided, when she was old and spent and finally sitting down to pen her memoirs. When she had wrung everything she could out of life. When her memories stacked to the ceiling like books in her grandparents' libraries. After she had gone out into the world, conquered one adventure after another. Here, Annelle was sure, is where it would all begin.

After all, she was an adult now. Annelle bit her lip; the idea still brought a flush to her cheeks, and a jolt of excitement to each end of her extremities. Yes. *Here I am, life,* she thought to herself. *I hope you're ready for me.*

She was certainly ready for it. Ready for excitement, for independence. For change. For, oh! Tonight would be about change. Annelle had been planning it for months. Not the ball, no—though that had taken a lot of work, too. The main event, however, was something no one else knew about. Just thinking about it brought a flutter of anticipation to her stomach.

Annelle smoothed out her lilac skirts one last time. They were the latest style, lighter and freer than the fashions favored by her mother and her grandmother. Perfect for dancing. Annelle's skates were already clipped to her purple-jeweled shoes.

"Ready, miss?" a footman asked her. He stood by the door, resplendent in a uniform of white and gold. Military-style epaulets lent an authority to his manner, which would in turn lend authority to Annelle herself, when he announced her to the assembled guests beyond. It was a detail Prestina had arranged, and Annelle had been shocked and touched by her grandmother's interest.

A steady nod. Annelle would hold herself with a regal grace tonight, even if her insides were squirming with nerves and excitement.

The music swelled and then paused as the doors swung open. Inside the ballroom, all eyes turned to her. The footman moved inside, raised his voice.

The threshold of destiny. Annelle put her skate forward at the sound of her name, gliding into the room with confidence.

KAEDRICH SIGHED AS she knocked harder on the door to their bedroom. "Praxis, come on! We're going to be late."

No answer. Not that Kaedrich was surprised—Praxis had shut herself inside an hour ago, claiming she needed space to get herself ready. Kaedrich was already dressed, in a finely tailored suit that had been delivered the previous day specially for this. Green fabric shimmered, lined with gold edging, as she raised her fist to the door. Her coat was brown fur, soft and naturally colored. She hated to admit how much she liked it.

Not that she could enjoy it. Kaedrich checked her pocket watch, which she'd finally managed to get set to Yandosian time last week. Blast it, they were *already* late. She gritted her teeth. Kaedrich knew how much Annelle looked up to her aunt, and she'd be damned if she let Praxis disappoint her completely.

Another knock, unanswered, and Kaedrich sighed as she leaned her forehead against the whale-bone slats. It wasn't surprising. She and Praxis had barely even spoken after Praxis had finally emerged from her lab. Two days she'd been locked away in there, futzing and refusing entry even to Kaedrich. When she finally *did* show up, Kaedrich had felt a jolt, sure things were going to finally be settled between them, but. Now this. Kaedrich gritted her teeth, *trying* not to be too annoyed, it's just . . . blast it, she was *tired* of having a door between them. It was impossible to fix things through a door. Kaedrich's mother had always told her, growing up, to never go to bed angry with the person you love, but that's exactly what Kaedrich had been reduced to doing lately. Finally, she'd thought, that could change, but apparently not.

Enough was enough.

Kaedrich straightened up. "Praxis!" She pounded on the door now, the whale bone quaking beneath her fist. "Blast it, will you at least *answer me*? We need to get moving."

But still, nothing but silence lay beyond the door.

A sense of unease gripped Kaedrich. She tried to shove it aside—after all, what could have possibly happened to Praxis in their *bedroom*, of all places?—but now the force of Kaedrich's knocks grew again. "Praxis! Look, if you need more time, that's fine, but can you please say something so I know you're all right?"

Still no answer.

Kaedrich gripped the doorknob—locked.

"Praxis! Praxis, do you hear me? Are you okay in there?"

Kaedrich ran her hands over her hair. She sucked in a breath of cold air, sharp in her lungs.

"Okay, okay," she muttered to herself. She spun around. What did she have to work with?

The first thing her eyes settled on was a sitting chair in the corner. That would do.

It was surprisingly heavy. Kaedrich grunted as she hauled it up. She hitched it around, the feet pointing out, and ran until it slammed into the ice of the doorframe. Fleetingly, the thought of a collapse came to mind, but to the darkness with that; if, somehow, Praxis was in trouble . . .

No, it was best not to think about that.

Kaedrich rammed the doorframe again. A chunk of ice broke off and fell to the floor, sliding to a stop by Kaedrich's feet. Was it enough? Kaedrich gave the doorframe one more *thwack*, just to be safe, and then threw the chair aside and wrenched the door open.

Their bedroom lay before her, resplendent as ever, cold and perfect—and empty. Only Praxis's dress, laid out on the bed as it had been left for her, remained behind.

Panic grabbed Kaedrich by the throat, but okay, okay, there had to be an explanation for this. There had to be. Kaedrich checked the dressing room beyond, the bathroom, the closets, but of course Praxis wasn't there. Really, Kaedrich hadn't even expected her to be. She pulled her watch back out, and bit her lip, but did it even matter anymore how late they were? Kaedrich swept out of the room, her fur coat trailing behind her like the robe of a king, with only one goal in mind.

She would find Praxis, and they would settle things between them. She would find her, if she had to loot through the whole of Yandosia to do it.

* * *

SOMETIMES, PRETT COULDN'T believe this used to be his life.

He slipped into the party like stepping into a cold bath. Not Annelle's ball, no—that would come later—but another one, nearby, and infinitely more familiar. Prett had dug out some of his old clothes, the more colorful options of his wardrobe. Once, he had read a book about a bird called a peacock, how it spread its colorful feathers as a display of sexual prowess. These parties, Prett mused, served much the same purpose. Flashes of wealth littered the room, men and women in glittering displays of gems, dyed furs, and enchanted hair colors. It was a far cry from the stately, demure galas he'd grown up around. There, under the watchful eye of his mother, the rooms had been appointed to reflect the glory of Yandosia: ice and jewels crafted the décor while the notes of the best Yandosian composers plucked and purred out from instruments of rare arctic wood and the finest whale bone. The guests were equally selected, pruned from party to party. Nothing was mismatched, no hair out of place.

But here, everything came from somewhere else: paintings from Tjalava, and tapestries from Rolmstan; furniture made of the black wood of Marcovalla; silks from a remote island near Syll. Even the magic— what they called magic, what Praxis called bullshit—was strange and experimental, as they fought to contact ghouls and demons, loved ones and other realms. Everything new, everything exotic. Everything, that is, except for the people: faces that never changed, the same wide eyes that he used to see, staring back at him as he slid between their groups. They traced his movements with languid interest, somehow both sparkling and dead-eyed all at once.

Smoke stung at Prett's eyes as he moved deeper into the party. He'd almost forgotten the sickly sweet smell, but now a thousand memories rushed him all at once. Overturned furniture, torn paintings, beads scattered on the floor. Lips—so many lips, mouths panting and tongues twisting in the most creative ways imaginable. Pale flesh, and colorful silks scattered on the floor. Dreams, and things that may as well have been from dreams, as the elixirs they'd used distorted sound and light and touch around them.

It was magic, as sure as anything that Praxis herself could conjure out of thin air. Magic in a bottle, magic in the needle, magic in smoke. Magic in the veins, shooting straight to the heart.

He used to need it. Now, it just turned his stomach.

Still, Prett had a job to do. Not one he wanted, granted, but a job nonetheless. When Lexthur had summoned him, *again*, told Prett that he had to do something for him, *again*, this time Prett almost refused. Once was enough, twice was enough. Three times? He should have refused, but—oh, the lure of freedom, of escape, of the endless open spaces of the world, or so he'd been told. The idea was as addictive as any drug, including the one Lexthur had handed to him, the purple vial glinting in the light.

Now Prett scrubbed the discontent from his face as he moved effortlessly through the crowd. The party had started several hours ago, so already the room was full of various states of undress. The host of this particular evening was a woman from a family that often dealt with the Fellows, in the private security industry. Their family dwelling was riddled with mounted weaponry, half of which was off the walls and being used for entirely different purposes.

Prett averted his eyes. Doubt began to gnaw at his mind as he surveyed the room—or maybe it was hope? How far was Praxis willing to go to obtain this drug? He couldn't imagine her here, among the sprawled and the sedate. Maybe . . . maybe Lexthur was wrong, Prett told himself. Maybe Praxis hadn't stolen the vials after all, or maybe she hadn't used them. Maybe she had a different source to obtain more.

The flutter of optimism withered and died as he spotted a messy mop of short white hair across the room. She was huddled in scowly conversation with a pair of men that did not look happy to be interrupted. They waved her off, again and again, their faces turning back toward each other only to be broken apart by Praxis's jabby finger.

Prett sighed, bone-weary. His baby sister. How had she come to this? How had *he*?

"Well, well," Prett said as he approached. "Prax. Imagine running into you here."

Praxis whirled, her eyes popping wide. "Prett! I . . . I'm not . . ."

"Of course not," Prett said. He leaned in, gracing her cheek with a familial kiss. "I won't tell Mother, if you don't."

The wink that he forced himself to spare her broke his heart.

Praxis's face contorted, half flush and half scowl. She tugged her battered coat tighter around herself, gripping it closed across her chest. With a curl of her fingers they set off, stepping away from the couple.

"It's really not what it looks like," she muttered.

"Really? So you're not avoiding Annelle's ball, too?"

Praxis's scowl deepened. "It's not about that," Praxis said, but her voice was somewhat disheartened. She spared him a fast glance, and at his smirk of disbelief, her spine straightened with all the haughtiness Prestina had drilled into her as a child. "If you must know," Praxis continued, brushing her hair off her forehead as if none of this mattered at all, "I'm looking for someone. I'll make my appearance at the ball later."

"Ah." Prett swirled his drink before taking a sip. He looked out over the crowd, packed in thick between the ornate walls. It was far more than his parents ever would have allowed in one place like this. The body heat alone would play hell on the walls later.

Stop it, Prett told himself. He forced his attention back to his sister, forced a grin. He had a job to do.

"Anyone I might know?"

Praxis huffed. "I doubt it."

"Try me," Prett said, still grinning. Gods, but his cheeks hurt from the effort. "You never know."

Praxis rolled her eyes. But she sighed, relenting. "He calls himself Mr. Shiny," she said, cringing even as the words came out of her mouth.

Prett's eyebrow ticked up, an amused smile on his face. "Mr. Shiny, eh?"

"I know, it's the stupidest name ever."

Prett flinched. "Hey, now—maybe he just likes making people say it."

"Maybe," Praxis said with a snort. She waved her hand dismissively. "But, see, I told you that you wouldn't have heard of him."

"Oh, I don't know about *that*." Prett took a careful sip of his drink, the better to cover for the effort it took to still his hand. "I think you'd be surprised how well I know him, in fact. The question is, do *you* know him? Because I find it hard to believe you'd be seeking out a man like that. Or am I wrong?"

Please be wrong, Prett thought, though he knew he wasn't. Despite his animosity toward Lexthur, Prett wouldn't be here right now if he honestly thought there was a chance his information was wrong.

Still, Prett needed to see it for himself. He stood perfectly steady as he watched his sister—as she registered what Prett had just told her, as she leaned back like the subject between them now was distasteful (well, it was), as she weighed just how damaging this new understanding between them could get if she went so far as to confirm it. Meanwhile, all Prett could do was play his role. The smirk he used to wear had come back to him like a reflex, the loping set of his shoulders worn as a familiar coat. He may not actually *be* Mr. Shiny anymore, no—and yes, the name had amused him, to watch people stumble over themselves trying not to say it—but the persona still fit just as well as it used to. From where he stood now, the last two years may as well not have even happened.

Praxis swallowed down an obvious lump in her throat, clearly uncertain. "It's . . . not what you think."

"Sure, sure."

"No," Praxis said. Panic skittered in the corners of her eyes, as if she was just barely holding herself from bolting like a scared ice rat. "It's medicinal. For my leg."

Prett's stomach twisted up as his cold smile snaked between them. "Praxis, Praxis, Praxis." He loped his arm around his sister's shoulder and flicked his hair back with a casual toss of the head. "Let me tell you something, just between us: people get glee from doctors, if it's medicinal. Only bored socialites or the very, very desperate seek it from me."

"You?"

Praxis jerked out from underneath his grasp, and Prett let her go. He didn't want to look at the way she was staring at him now—with horror, with revulsion, with shock, with the smallest bit of hopeful opportunity beginning to spark on her face—but selling his role depended on cocky surety.

"Prett . . . what would Mother say?"

Prett laughed. It tore out of him before he could stop it. He'd been prepared for a variety of reactions from Praxis, but this was new.

"As if you've ever cared about that," he said finally. He'd stopped laughing, his mirth drying up when he saw Praxis's expression. Her shock and horror were gone, and she stared at him now with nothing but concern and open *pity*.

Prett pulled a long swig of his drink. It did nothing to wash away the bitterness on his tongue.

"Look," Prett said, "if you're not interested in buying, there are plenty of others who are."

"No!"

The hand that found Prett's arm was familiar, though not from memories of his sister. Desperate claws sank themselves into the soft blue leather of his jacket, the kind of desperation found only when you combined the very, very bored with the very, very rich.

How many fingers had clutched Prett's arm, in that exact same manner? How many hollow eyes had stared up at him, pleading for relief from a life they couldn't imagine living? Too many to count.

Weariness crashed into Prett, knocking into his knees. He wasn't sure he could do it, anymore. Praxis's face, as she watched him now, looked more like it used to when they were kids, and she'd needed him to cover up for something troublesome she'd gotten herself into—a broken vase, perhaps, or a stolen book from Prawl's private library. His *baby sister*. For years, he thought he'd never see her again.

How could he do it? The question bubbled up inside of him, then just as quickly burst.

It did not matter *how*. This was his escape, his only escape. If he did not take it now . . .

Casually, Prett reached into the pocket of his silk jacket. A purple vial, the length of it wedging his fingers open. Praxis's eyes alighted, latching onto it. Their sparkle matched the shine of the glass, the pure glint of the seductive liquid.

She swallowed. Licked her dry lips. Pain and fear and need were tugging at the muscles of her face as she asked, "How much?"

Prett tipped his head, as if considering this. A tiny piece of his soul dried up and fell away, a petal drifting down from a nearly dead flower. "For you, sweet sister?" he said, drawing the words out. His lips ticked up. "You must pay the terrible cost of an evening of conversation with your brother. Come," he added, motioning to the side. "I know just the place."

Chapter Thirty-Two

PRAXIS LAUGHED. IT rolled out of her with an ease she hadn't felt in ages. Her shoulders shook where they leaned against Prett as the drink and the sweet haze of the room loosened both her muscles and her tongue. The vial she was saving for later, tucked away into the depths of her coat, but somehow even without it, her knee was feeling marginally better. At least it had retreated down to that one spot, and the absence of pain throughout the rest of her body was almost more intoxicating than any injection would have been.

For the first time since coming to Yandosia, everything else seemed to fall away. The funeral, and the guilt that had been clinging to Praxis as she donned the ceremonial robes. The nerves of what might happen, if her father wasn't able to maintain control of the company for himself. The pressure that her mother was putting on her, to marry Lexthur, to seize the company, to be a shining example of what women were capable of doing. The distance inching open between her and Kaedrich . . .

Praxis grabbed another drink off the table in front of them, downing it in one. She shut her eyes, letting the mood evaporate like the liquid on her tongue. Untouchable. Nothing else existed, except for this party, which Praxis hadn't even expected to find herself in, much less stay. Much less *enjoy*.

"Is that why you turned Lexthur down?" Prett said. Praxis turned, trying to remember what it was they'd been talking about. She hadn't been paying attention, her mouth apparently running free. Prett grinned at her. "Should I buy a silver bell? Or, no, what do the Durns do again? Throw seeds?"

"Rice," Praxis said. She squirmed in her seat as she realized what Prett had been referring to, so she ignored his actual question. Gods, what had she *said*? "It's a grain. Don't ask me what throwing it like that is supposed to mean, because I've never been able to figure it out."

Prett shook his head, baffled. He took a drink. "That makes no sense."

"Weddings are strange up north."

"So did you come here to do things the Yandosian way?"

"Why does everyone always assume I *want* to get married?" Praxis asked, harsher than she intended to. She shifted, just a little, away from Prett on the couch.

Prett gave a lazy shrug. "Because most people do? Because women usually want to? Because it's expected?"

Praxis snorted. "You know I don't care what's expected."

"True. But you seem happy together. And it's my understanding that social customs are a bit more . . . rigid, in Durland. I'd hate to think your man didn't have *gentlemanly* intentions toward you."

"Shut up," Praxis said. She smacked Prett's arm, and Prett laughed to himself.

"No," Prett said after a moment, "but seriously, Praxis . . . what's the problem? He's obviously in love with you. You're obviously in love with him. You've *declared* him, for sanity's sake! You can't mean to tell me this relationship doesn't matter to you."

Praxis went quiet. She leaned forward, swapping glasses. "No, it matters," she said, her voice soft.

"Then . . . ?"

She shut her eyes. Her throat burned with everything she knew she wouldn't say. Sounds of the party swirled around her, whispering against her ear. Praxis sighed, and then she felt more than heard as words tumbled out of her:

"I lied about something. Something important."

Her eyes snapped open. Praxis raised her head, looking desperately in Prett's direction, but Prett was just watching her, as if nothing had happened. For the briefest second, Praxis wondered if maybe it hadn't, if somehow it was all in her imagination, but then Prett looked away, just one fast glance to the side, and Praxis knew he'd heard after all.

"I don't know why I said that," Praxis said, quickly. "Forget I said that."

Prett's easy smile sent a nervous shiver up Praxis's spine. He reached out, patting her hand. "It's forgotten."

Forgotten. The word seemed to whisper through her mind, shifting between Prett and Praxis as both of their faces blanked out. Praxis leaned back again, casting her thoughts wide. A trace of fear and irritation lingered in her mind, but she couldn't quite remember *why*. What had they been talking about?

Right, weddings.

"Anyway," Praxis said, changing the subject, "I don't exactly see *you* lining up to take the plunge. What's the matter, Prett? Nobody pretty enough in Yandosia for you?"

"Har har," Prett said. He smacked Praxis's shoulder. "Come on, Prax. Didn't you come home to *enough* nieces and nephews? Do the rest of us really need to fill the halls for you?"

Praxis rolled her eyes. "Hardly. Gods, there's so many of them already."

"That there are," Prett said with a chuckle. He glanced at his glass, now empty, as he turned it around in his hands. "You know, Lexthur doesn't want children."

Praxis raised a warning finger. "Don't start."

Prett shrugged. "I'm just saying, he's not so bad. Your ambitions, at least, are perfectly matched."

"I don't have ambitions," Praxis said, and Prett burst out laughing.

"Please. You can't mean to tell me the company doesn't tempt you at least a *little*."

"Does it tempt *you*?"

"Sure," Prett said. He laughed. "Don't look shocked. Of course it does. Oh, I wouldn't actually *want* it, not really, not when it comes down to it. Too much responsibility. You, on the other hand—"

"—don't handle responsibility any better than you do," Praxis finished for him. She gave him a heavy look. "You know I'm right."

Prett's face turned thoughtful as he looked across at his sister. "I'm not sure you are, actually."

"Yeah, okay," Praxis said with a snort. She rolled her eyes.

"Praxis. I'm serious."

"You're *high*."

"Eh," Prett said, tipping his hand back and forth like the scales hadn't quite settled out yet. "Still, I think you'd be good at it. I think you'd surprise yourself."

Praxis looked down at her drink. The glass was nearly empty now, and she ran her finger along the rim. "I can't stay, though."

"I know," Prett said. He sighed, wearier than anything he'd expressed that whole evening. His face was twisted up, as if he was only just now realizing something disagreeable—but then he drained the last of his drink, setting the glass down with a heavy *thunk*, and suddenly his grin was back in place. He held his hand out, palm up, inviting. "We should probably head back, don't you think? Can't avoid the evening forever."

Praxis groaned. She ignored his gesture, purposefully holding her glass tighter against herself like a child's favorite blanket. "Are you sure? I don't mind trying."

Prett's expression next was withering, almost as good as one of Prestina's. "Prax."

Praxis squirmed farther down into her seat. "You go," she said. "I'll . . . I'll be along shortly."

"Promise?"

"What are we now, twelve?" Praxis snapped. "I'm not going to *promise* anything. Just trust me, all right? I'll get there. Soon."

She didn't know why she was so insistent that he leave before her— after all, it's not like she was planning to use the glee until she was safely back in the privacy of her lab. Still . . . something about the way that he was looking at her now, that he'd been looking at her since she'd said she couldn't stay. It felt like wind going out of a ship's sails, like the emptiness of a house after a party, like the sadness at the end of a really good book. Praxis scowled at it. Besides, the last thing she needed was an escort, as if she was a disobedient child that had to be brought home by her stern, concerned parents.

It was doubtful that Prett could read any of this on Praxis's face, but he did not argue. Like flicking a switch, he shrugged it off, as if it didn't matter at all. "All right, then. I'll see you at home."

Praxis flinched, the word "home" landing hard against her cheek. She actually reached up and wiped at her face, as if that would help. "Yeah," she said, choosing to ignore it. "Sure."

Prett waved, and Praxis clutched the vial, safe in her pocket, as he loped off through the party. No sooner had he disappeared, a slip of blue into a sea of color, than she dragged herself to her feet. *Soon,* she told herself, though what exactly she was referring to, even she did not know. Soon, the pain would recede? Soon, they would be free of this place? Soon, everything would go back to normal with Kaedrich?

Praxis was too old to believe any of these things, but the promise, the delusion, hung thick in the air around her anyway, a warm glow that made her capable of putting one foot in front of the other as she shuffled toward the door. Soon. Soon.

Soon.

* * *

A THICK SUMMER drizzle mingled unpleasantly with the omnipresent layer of soot that hung throughout the streets of Monfort.

Officially, the soot was a byproduct of all the rapid growth and industry that had swept the city in recent weeks. So much construction, so much careful demolition of old buildings, it was bound to kick up dust. Everything would settle out, once the renovation efforts were completed.

Lord-Commander Braynish knew better.

Really, he was surprised the line fed so easily to the people. Didn't anyone notice that the soot had already started creeping into the city *before* the construction began? That the air of Monfort used to be clear as crystal, the smell of the bay sweeping in like a spring breeze? That it was a slow but steady build to where they were today, and that it all began after the Royal Society of Magic was disbanded?

Nobody paid attention anymore, that was the problem as far as *he* was concerned. Braynish grunted to himself as he moved swiftly from carriage to front door. It was best to avoid excess time out-of-doors these days, especially if it was damp.

Despite his efforts, a layer of grime was already clinging to his coat and top hat as his butler let him into the foyer of his house. Braynish grimaced as he shed his outer layers like a crab whose shell had grown tight. It felt that way, sometimes—the growing filth of his clothes seeming to press in against him. Braynish handed over coat, hat, walking stick; and then he bent and undid the laces of his shoes. It may not be socially polite, but Braynish was alone in his home for the evening, no guests to entertain, no lords to impress. He'd be damned if he tracked in mud.

He slid his foot out, slid it back in, slid it out again. Three times, and then he was able to nudge them forward with his stockinged toe, where the butler attended to them as if this was nothing out of the ordinary at all.

It was one of the reasons why Braynish had hired the man. He ignored all of Braynish's "little quirks"—the turning of his hat before putting it on, the spinning of his pocket watch. The shoes. The endless supply of new pens with fresh nibs. The list went on, each year seeming to add another infuriating ritual that Braynish had to perform before he could do even the simplest everyday tasks. It used to drive Braynish's father crazy. More than once, the elder Lord Braynish had attempted to beat the habits out of his son; Braynish still had some of the scars. Even Braynish himself, once free of his father's rule, had sought out the finest doctors and the most learned wizards to account for his odd behavior. Nobody could explain it.

So Braynish had learned to live with it. Because he had to. Allotting himself extra time, screening his staff for discretion, avoiding some of the actions that would trigger the more egregious tics while he was out in public.

But now he was home. For a little while, anyway. He sighed in relief, like scratching an itch after a long time ignoring it, as he moved up the staircase, tapping and counting each post of the railing as he went. Fifteen, sixteen, seventeen, and he was on the second floor. He was grateful he hadn't miscounted, because he did not have time to go all the way back down and start over again.

He passed a guard in the hall. The guard nodded at Braynish, the only acknowledgment between them. Braynish employed two dozen men on a rotating schedule to guard his house, usually about six at a time, but tonight he'd ordered extra shifts. Perhaps it wasn't the smartest choice, perhaps it would draw attention, but he did not care. There was too much at stake this evening. Braynish caught the guard stifling a yawn as he passed, probably on duty outside of his normal rotation.

In his study, the fire was already crackling. A merry blaze shone behind the hearth, hissing and popping like the tune of a familiar song. Braynish only allowed a specific wood to be used in his study, one that he knew well how it burned.

He settled into his desk. Withdrew a folded paper from the breast pocket of his vest.

The letter was only half-finished, and he spread it out now, smoothing the creases under his thumb. Braynish wasn't really in the mood to write this evening, but if she didn't hear from him at least once a week or so, she started to worry. And even though he didn't bother to put anything of substance into her letters anymore, even though he normally dashed them out without a second thought, this one was . . . different. It was important that he get it right.

And yet, he was having trouble concentrating. He knew he had to play the part—return to his home, be seen relaxing as if his tasks for the day were finally done—but his mind kept whirring ahead. To the news that would be breaking soon, the hurried footsteps of a runner sent from the palace with an urgent message. To the elaborate operations being played out in tandem across the southeastern border of Durland. He'd selected each of the men personally, trained them and trusted them, but any number of things could go wrong tonight. What if one of their practiced Rolmish accents slipped? What if someone found the prepared corpses before they could be arranged?

Stop it, Braynish thought. He pressed his fingers against the desk, stabilizing himself. Pushed the worries forcibly from his mind.

He shut his eyes, listening to the sounds of the house.

Some other members of the Monfort elite had purchased phonographs in recent years. They liked to play music in the evenings while they worked or read or drank or fucked. Braynish had never understood the obsession. His home was like its own symphony, if one only had the presence of mind to listen for it: there was the pop of the fire, yes, and the whisper of the wind against the windows; but also the sigh of furniture underneath him, the creak of wood as servants moved about their business. The sound of his own breath. Faintly, if the night was quiet, there may even be a hint of clanking from the kitchen, or the click of his guards assembling and cleaning their guns. Once in a while, someone on his staff would sing to herself. Always quietly, always at night. The sound carried up through the pipes, to an ornate grating above Braynish's head.

No one was singing tonight. No idle sounds of work and the faint murmur of conversation.

Raised hairs prickled the back of Braynish's neck.

It was coincidence, he told himself, though he did not really believe in coincidences. He looked down at the letter on the desk, damning words staring up at him. Braynish folded it back up, tucking it near his heart, and then reached into his desk drawer for his pistol.

Outside, the tread of light footsteps had reached the top of the stairs, and was making its way toward the study. Braynish glanced at the clock on his mantel—right on time for his dinner to be delivered. Braynish had a standing order for a tray to be sent to his rooms on evenings when he wasn't scheduled to entertain. A young footman would bring it. He was relatively new to the staff, about six months in, but showing great promise. Braynish had hired him from the household of a friend of a friend, highly recommended, and he could see why: the man was nothing if not exact, the lines of his livery starched and ironed so sharply that it was a wonder it didn't cut his chin.

These were not his footsteps.

Heart pounding in his throat, Braynish made his way softly to the door. He pressed himself against the wall beside it, just as a knock rapped against the wood.

Too late, Braynish realized that his answer would be coming from far too close to the door to be normal, but there was nothing to be done now. "Come in," he called, hoping that whoever it was wouldn't be familiar enough with his normal habits to hear the difference.

The door opened. His tray appeared, carried low—a child's height, perhaps, or . . .

Braynish's blood froze.

. . . or an Aul's.

Without hesitation, Braynish cocked the hammer of his gun, but not fast enough. The tray rushed at him without warning, before the person was even fully into the room. Hot soup flew up, burning against Braynish's face and obscuring his vision. The tray itself knocked his gun aside—Braynish squeezed the trigger, but the sound that it made was a bullet striking wood, not flesh.

By the time his vision cleared, Braynish's attacker was no longer waiting in the doorway. Braynish whirled. It looked for a moment as if the room was empty, but no, there: in the chair facing the fireplace, a hand was draped lazily over the armrest. A tattoo stared up at Braynish, a simple line drawing of a curling wave.

It was as Braynish feared.

"Sorry about the suit," Tol said. His voice carried easily over the back of his chair.

Braynish glanced down. His dinner ran in trails down the front of his shirt and jacket, his tie sopping wet around his neck. Under ordinary circumstances, it would drive him crazy—even now, a part of him itched to rip the offending clothes free and find a wash basin for his face—and probably Tol knew this. Braynish had never been *close* to Tol, but in the few years they'd known each other, Braynish had learned that the games Tol liked to play with people's heads were a sick source of joy.

Braynish would not be so easily distracted. He rounded the chair, his weapon rearmed and raised.

Tol looked up with the ease of a man in his own study. A book from Braynish's shelves lay open in Tol's lap, and Tol actually took the time to slide the book's ribbon into place to mark his spot before laying it aside.

"Truly," Tol said, "I am sorry about the suit. It's going to ruin the whole aesthetic."

"What aesthetic?"

He probably shouldn't have asked, he knew that now, but the words were already free, like doves set loose at a funeral.

Tol hooked his hands around his knee, one leg crossed over the other. "You must have realized by now that you're going to die tonight."

Braynish gritted his teeth.

He pulled the trigger.

The *crack* of his gun split the room. Braynish was not an experienced arms-man, though he had fired guns before. But never, he realized now, in such an enclosed space as this—and never, in point of fact, at another man.

Still, his aim was not bad. The bullet struck Tol somewhere in the chest, causing the man to double over around his injury. Braynish fought against a knot of dread and bile as he stepped closer, his weapon still outstretched in his shaking hands.

Tol's fingers were digging madly at the wound, blood seeping freely over flesh and the crisp white of his suit. Wizards were, of course, capable of healing themselves if they could knit their own flesh together fast enough—unless the weapon had been treated with the appropriate coating. One that Tol himself had helped develop for Lanali, one that Braynish wasn't even supposed to *know* about, much less have access to.

Braynish sent a silent prayer of gratitude out to the forces of the universe. He didn't believe in a *god*, per se, certainly not Perlandra or Tarmal, but he did believe there were things working behind the scenes, guiding people from one place to the next to the next. And he believed in being prepared.

"Sorry about the suit," Braynish said as he stood over Tol.

It was a cheap shot, Braynish knew, one that made him sound more sure of himself than he felt. He had just shot a man. Tol was probably going to die soon. A certain solemnity was probably called for.

And yet: the remark made Tol laugh. It started low, just a quiet, unsettling chuckle that jostled his shoulders as he continued to prod at his torso. Braynish swallowed down a lump of uncertainty. His grip tightened around the gun. Tol's laugh continued to grow as he curled over himself, as he dug at his bleeding chest, as he slid from the chair, his feet hitting the floor with a stagger. All of the hairs on the back of Braynish's neck raised.

It must be madness. A dying man, mortality curling a cold grip around his throat. That was what Braynish told himself, repeatedly, as he kept the gun trained on Tol. It was what he told himself, and told himself, and told himself, until the moment Tol finally straightened up, one final *ha!* bursting in the air. A broad grin split the Aul man's face. In his bloody hand, a nub of something coated in red sat pinched between his fingers— the bullet that Braynish had shot him with. Beneath his tattered and soaked suit, a patch of clean, new skin seemed to wink out mischievously.

"Oh, I'm sorry," Tol said as he reached into the pocket of his suit jacket. "Were you looking for these?"

Five new bullets in his hand. The kind Braynish had stolen for himself, stocked in the guns in his study, his bedroom, his office. Braynish's throat went dry as he popped open his gun, and the copper butts of standard-issue bullets stared back at him.

If Braynish had been someone else, perhaps things would have worked out differently for him. If he was a skilled marksman, if he'd gone to the academy when he was a young man like his father had wanted him to, if he'd joined the army, if he'd even made a habit of going hunting with some of the other men in the Governance Council, perhaps his fate would be kinder. If he had, he might have been able to close the gun quickly enough, fire off a perfect shot. A wizard could not, for example, recover from the right kind of blow to the head.

But Braynish was not that kind of man. He knew it, Tol knew it. Even as the thought formed in Braynish's mind, so too did it collapse. Tol was right: he was going to die tonight. The only thing left to consider was how much damage Braynish could do on the way out.

Braynish lowered his gun. "I suppose I should have seen it coming. This would be the last detail the operation needs."

As he'd hoped, a flicker of curiosity crossed Tol's face. That confirmed it, then, what Braynish had been suspecting for weeks: Tol wasn't involved. He had, in fact, been purposefully cut out from Lanali's inner circle, something previously unheard of. Braynish fought to contain his smile.

"What's it going to be, then?" Braynish asked. "Are you to 'accidentally' drop a Rolmish prayer book on your way out? Or maybe you've hired someone, in Rolmish dress, to be seen running from my house tonight?"

Tol pocketed the bullets. "I considered it. I have to say, I'm impressed—your spies do you justice."

"Spies?" Braynish laughed. "I don't need *spies* to tell me that. You really don't know what's going on tonight, do you? Oh, she's played you well. Please do pass along my compliments. Tonight couldn't have been planned better."

"What are you talking about?"

Braynish smiled. "You'll find out soon enough." He tossed the gun aside, undid the button of his suit jacket. He spread his arms wide, his heart thundering wildly beneath his breastbone. "Go on, then. Do what you came here to do. Play your role like a good little pawn."

He shut his eyes. Counted his breaths as he waited for the end to come.

Surprisingly, he was not as scared as he expected to be. It was not bravery, he decided somewhere between breaths thirteen and fourteen—fourteen glorious breaths, at least a dozen more than he'd ever expected to have again! Rather, his acceptance came from a much deeper, and more primal source than bravery: he had won. Even in defeat, he had won. He started to laugh, reveling in the thought of what Tol might do next, after Braynish was dead. If Braynish was lucky, if he was very, very lucky, he may have just sparked the beginning of what would eventually unravel the Pon's delicate plans.

Truly, the gods had blessed him in the end.

The pain that struck him next was brutal, but swift. Braynish was dead before his body hit the floor.

WELL. TWO HOURS into her ball, Annelle had learned one thing: destiny was a fat crock of shit.

Oh, the party itself was fine. Splendid, even, at least by any measurable standard. The food was exquisite, the flowers and décor flawlessly arranged, the music sublime. Annelle endured a thousand compliments, for she truly had done a remarkable job, and her attention to detail had been second to none. Everyone agreed that the evening was the perfect balance between traditional and fresh. More than once, Annelle's mother had been caught dabbing her eyes at the sight of it all, and even stoic Grandmother had skated over to Annelle, at one point, the cut of her blade as she came to a stop as expertly performed as that of a girl at the height of her skills. "I'm very proud of you, my girl," Prestina had said, and Annelle's heart had nearly stopped in shock. She wondered, briefly, if her grandmother had ever paid her such a compliment in her life, and was quick to conclude that no, no she had not. The praises of the great and mighty Prestina Fellows did not flow freely, and so Annelle had smiled, just the right blend between demure and prideful, and tapped her middle three fingers to her curling lips.

"Thank you, Grandmother."

Prestina nodded in approval. She looked Annelle up and down. "Yes . . . I do believe you'll do great things for us," she said, and then with the faintest trace of a smile crinkling at her eyes, she turned and skated away once more.

So it's not that, objectively, Annelle could complain about the day—not really. She had pulled off a nearly impossible feat with this ball, even managing to upstage that of her cousins, whose own hung so recently in everyone's memory. She'd managed to bring light and laughter into a household of mourning. By all accounts, she should have been the queen of the day, and she was, she supposed, but—

He still hadn't made an appearance yet. Annelle knew for sure, not just because her eyes were constantly scanning the room for the bright flash of his smile, the shine of his suit, but because she had managed to make a number of increasingly less discreet inquiries, and no one had seen or heard the slightest sign of him.

And sure, yes, the celebration of Annelle's birthday, *the* birthday, that was great and all—but it would all be meaningless, all of it, if she didn't manage to finally use this energy as the nudge she needed to seize control of her life. To take action, make a stand, declare her feelings and her plans and see what happened next. The mere *idea* of it had driven her forward, these past few weeks as the preparations for the ball reached a frenzy, and now . . . Well, now, if it all came to *nothing*, if he didn't show, if she didn't even get the chance to *try* . . . Annelle really didn't know what she would do.

The night was dragging on now, each note that was played another petal plucked from her bouquet, and still he was not showing up. Annelle scowled, and helped herself to the drinks tray. She'd never been particularly fond of drinking before, but then she'd also never been allowed to partake freely, all of her experience either in the forced environment of family dinners or stolen away in secret. Now, though, it was different; now, she was finally a woman, free in the world.

Yeah, sure. Annelle snorted as she tipped her head back, feeling the burn slide down her throat. As if that were ever really true, for a woman of her station.

Well. She supposed it had been true once, for one woman, but how often could you get away with something like that? Even now, a lifetime later, people were still telling stories of Praxis's departure. If Annelle were to try something dramatic like that . . . She giggled, because gods, could you just imagine the shock it would send through her family? Like dropping a fire into the center of the icy ballroom.

It was almost worth trying, except that of course it wasn't, not really. She took another drink, and then, a moment later, a third. Besides, she told herself, wasn't her plan ambitious enough? Daring enough? She did not need to cause the kind of damage her aunt Praxis had.

Annelle sighed. Oh, but who was she kidding? What made her think she'd even be able to do that much? She sighed, putting her glass down, and turned from the drinks table.

And then.

It was one of those perfect moments, nearly enough to get Annelle to believe in the tales of the old Yandosian gods. The dancers parted, gliding out of the way to create an aisle that led straight from Annelle to the door. Their skirts swept in dreamy arcs behind him, time seeming to draw the whole room to the high point of a breath and holding it there, just for a moment. For there, in the doorway, his head ducked as he clipped a skate to his shoe, there he stood, with nothing but a straight and open line between him and Annelle. Even with his hair across his features—always kept just a little longer than fashion allowed—Annelle would have recognized him anywhere. She'd studied his face from every angle, followed every expression. She could spot him in any crowd.

Prett Fellows looked up, his attention landing immediately upon Annelle. He tossed her one of his easy grins, and Annelle's heart leaped to her throat.

Truly, she did not care what people would think. He was significantly older than she was, yes, but still young enough to be handsome, not yet succumbed to the weariness and tedium that so many others were prone to by his age. As for their relation, well—what of it, really? Annelle was cultured enough to understand that in some parts of the world arrangements between cousins, uncles, nieces, were sometimes *commonplace* for the royal families; and really, if the Fellows did not qualify, then what good was all of their wealth and power? Let them claim their ranks with pride, as far as Annelle was concerned. She would not go so far as to say that perhaps it was time for Yandosia to return to a proper monarchy, but neither could she think of any active reason to object. If anyone could do it, she felt, it would surely be Prett. Prett, so smart, so clever, so likable. So knowledgeable, in Yandosian laws and loopholes. He already had connections in the political landscape, so who was to say what kind of heights he might be capable of rising to, if only he had the proper woman by his side?

Annelle drew her shoulders back. The rush of her heart pounded fast in her ears, whispering, urging her forward. She had nothing to lose. She had everything to gain.

Oh, but she would make a fantastic queen.

She pushed off, straight down the aisle of dancers. Onward, toward her destiny.

Chapter Thirty-Three

O<small>KAY, SO HE</small> was significantly late to the ball, but at least he had finally made it. Prett would hear about it from his mother, no doubt before the night was even over, but he was *here*. Earlier, he still hadn't been sure he'd be able to pull that off. Trying to circle Praxis around to *any* particular point of conversation wasn't easy under the best of circumstances, but when you combined that with a topic she didn't want to discuss and the wandering effects that alcohol had on her line of thought? Prett considered himself lucky that he'd been able to extricate himself at all.

Not that the conversation had gone the way he'd wanted it to, and not that he'd been able to make any progress in getting Praxis to agree to Lexthur's proposal. Still—tonight, he'd settle for what he'd gotten. Though he still couldn't figure out how Lexthur knew that Praxis would be seeking out new vials of glee, or why he wanted to help her with such a nasty vice . . .

"Prett! You made it!"

The sound of his niece's voice snapped him out of his thoughts. Taking a breath, he mustered up one of his so-called "easy" smiles, his face brittle with the effort. "Annelle, congratulations," he said. He motioned around the ballroom. "You've done an amazing job."

It was true, though it hardly surprised Prett. In the time that Annelle had been working for him in the law offices, he'd found her organizational abilities to be exceptional, easily the best he'd ever worked with. Her dedication and attention to every minute detail made her a quiet force to be reckoned with. Little wonder that her coming-of-age ball was lavish without being overdone, organized without feeling stilted, elegant without being stodgy. Even Prett, who gave little thought to such matters as decorations and music selection, found himself impressed by the skill that had obviously gone into arranging it.

Annelle skated to a halt in front of him, a furious blush tinting her from her hairline to her neckline. "Thank you," she said. "That really means a lot to me." Her downcast eyes were demure, her voice velvety soft. It was a tone he was not used to hearing from her, and the presence of it now was disconcerting, in a way that Prett couldn't or didn't want to quite figure out.

Prett grimaced. He tugged at the jacket of his suit.

Annelle looked back up at him, a shy smile toying at her lips. "Prett, you know this means I'm an adult now."

"Aw, don't say that," Prett said. The discomfort took on a distinct squirm in his stomach, like he'd swallowed a live eel; he wanted, suddenly, to reach out and ruffle Annelle's hair, the way he used to with all his nieces and nephews. But he couldn't, of course, not here, and certainly not with the elaborate way she'd swept it up and arranged it, just a handful of soft curls landing on her shoulders, accenting the line of her neck. "Seriously, though, you'll make me feel old if you keep that up."

The playful jut of Annelle's lip, a fake pout. Prett wanted to physically recoil from it, like somehow putting distance between them would make the twist in his stomach go away. Annelle reached out, putting a hand on Prett's chest, her fingers slipping into the button line of his jacket.

"But you're not old."

"Annelle." Prett grabbed her wrist, perhaps harder than he'd meant to, as he jerked her hand away. A fast glance around the ballroom told him that at least they weren't drawing too much attention yet, but he was not willing to risk causing a scene. Not tonight. Not for her.

He drew her out into the hallway instead, not bothering to let either of them unclip their skates first. This would wreck the floors, but Prett couldn't take the time to care. He clomped across the hallway, nodding at guests, until he could draw Annelle into a quiet alcove, nothing but the bust of a long-dead relative to scrutinize them.

"Annelle, what are you *doing*?"

Annelle's coquettish smile sent a knife of ice straight through Prett. "I think you know what I'm doing."

He did. Depths help him, he did know—he'd known from the

moment their eyes had met across the ballroom, the way she'd lit up at the sight of him. Prett was not numb to the signals of women, but this . . . gods, his own niece?

Somehow, he was still holding her wrist. He dropped hold of her and stepped back, raising his hands to emphasize the space between them. "Annelle, you can't possibly—"

"Of course I can. You have to see what a force we'd make. We work so well together."

That was true enough. It felt safe to admit that to himself, because it couldn't reasonably be denied. Since she'd come on as his assistant, his office had become a finely sharpened blade. Sure, Prett had always been good at his job—what he lacked, he'd realized over time, was any kind of vision for himself and his career, any sense of what the purpose of it all was. For a while, perhaps, he'd managed to find that, and yes, Annelle was a large part of that process.

It seemed that she could read this all on his face, because immediately she stepped forward, pressing her point home. "Do you really mean to tell me that you want to work for your father forever?"

Your father. She did not, he noticed, call Prawl her grandfather, a move that had no doubt been calculated to avoid drawing attention to the thing she'd wanted him to ignore. He'd taught her that trick, early on.

"You know I could help you," Annelle said. "Just think about it, Prett. Imagine what you could do, with me by your side. As your wife."

His wife. Prett almost laughed in relief. Oh, sure, the idea was still ludicrous—unthinkable, really—but here he'd been concerned she was making some kind of *romantic* overture toward him, some thought of the two of them *together*. But a wife? That, at least, he could discuss with the rational reasons to dismiss the idea.

He shook his head. "You have to know the auditors would never approve."

"I don't care about the auditors," Annelle said. A fire colored her voice, lifting her up. Her flush was back, just a little, creeping in along the edges of her dress.

Did he see the kiss coming, before it happened? Certainly there had been warning signs: the tiniest intake of Annelle's breath, acting both as courage and the inhale before a diver submerges; the angle of her gaze, fixed firmly upon Prett's lips; the gentle part of her own. Probably, if he was being honest, he might have noticed, might have even been afforded enough time to prevent it. It was this question that would keep him up nights, disgusted with himself, the tangled memory of his drunken thoughts burning a hole of shame where his heart should have been. And then, of course, less clear but undeniable: he did not break himself off quite as fast as he should have.

But break it he did, and so soon after it had started that he could only hope Annelle would not have noticed his hesitation. His face burned, his hands shook. The tremor of his voice betrayed him. "Annelle, *stop it*! I won't stand for this."

He thought he was being assertive. He needed to be assertive—older, wiser, the clear voice that would cut through the fog of adolescent day-dreams. If Annelle had ever stopped to consider this properly, really con-sider this properly, she would never have allowed herself to go so far. All Prett needed to do was make her see this, and then she would be grateful for his kindness.

What he hadn't expected is that perhaps she *had* considered this, and therefore anticipated the resistance she was meeting now. Either that, or Prett just wasn't being as persuasive as he liked to credit himself. Do not underestimate the power of self-delusion; his niece was a gorgeous young woman, and knowing that he shouldn't notice something like that did not make the observations go away.

She had arguments, then. Researched and rehearsed, prepared the way that Prett had prepared so many arguments before he presented them to the magistrates. She laid them out quickly, brutally, pelting down on Prett until it felt as if he must buckle from the onslaught. And yet he could not listen to any of them, not a single one, because it did not matter in the end what she said, what he said, what she wanted, what he didn't want to want, or what he didn't want. It changed nothing. The answer was no. The answer would always be no.

"Enough!" He could stand it no longer. The breath that he took now, he should have taken from the beginning. Perhaps he should have taken it months ago. It was his fault—he knew this, on a deep, intrinsic level. "It doesn't matter. This is never going to happen. I don't want it. I'm not . . . I'm not the person you wish I was."

Finally, at last, an argument she wasn't expecting. Annelle stepped back, studying Prett as if he'd suddenly sprouted wings and started talking in Tjalavan. He could see her recalculating behind her eyes, a shaken look as she tried to get back to her feet. He was familiar enough with it, the same distant look that Prestina would get whenever Prawl decided against following her business advice.

He did not wait around to see what she decided. Decisive action was called for, so decisive action was taken. Prett shoved past her, rougher than he would normally, and clomped back across to the ballroom. He could take pride, at least, that he'd done the right thing in the end, even if the experience left him shaken and queasy.

The ball had continued on without them. An effortless machine, Annelle's groundwork laid so efficiently that the party did not even need her to function. Prett looked around, at the glamorous faces of his family, the guests, even the servants done up to perfection, and for a moment he had to wonder what, exactly, he had given up in the name of propriety. He wanted a way out; what if she had been that way?

But then, like glass breaking, raised voices shattered the illusion of perfection that Annelle had spun. Prett turned like the rest of them, his attention seeking out the disturbance. There—in the far corner of the ballroom, a sight Prett hadn't expected: Praine, conversationally trapped like an animal in a cage, as Kaedrich shouted something Prett couldn't quite make out.

For a moment, the sight of it struck Prett dumb. Had everyone gone crazy today? Or had Prett, perhaps, entered into a land of dreams made manifest, nightmares clawing at him from every direction? Perhaps he was high after all, and hadn't just faked the injections he'd taken at the party? Could he even have gotten intoxicated from the smoke, lingering in the air with its come-hither hooked fingers pawing at his smooth blue suit?

But no. As Prett watched—as everyone watched—Kaedrich lunged forward, grabbing Praine by his coat and slamming him against the wall. A collective gasp slipped from the crowd; the music of the orchestra faltered, notes falling like pin drops on the ice floor. The shocked hush that followed was filled instead by Kaedrich's voice, disproportionately loud: "What did you do with her?!"

Prett's skates carried him forward in an instant. Before the crowd could regain their senses, before shock could turn to indignation could turn to violence. "Kaedrich." His grip was on Kaedrich's arm, the muscles beneath Kaedrich's suit as solid and honed as a trained fighter. Prett knew in an instant that he could not force this young man to do anything, not really, and so he desperately hoped he could convince Kaedrich to see reason. *"Kaedrich."*

Kaedrich said nothing, did nothing. All his attention was fixed on Praine, who was pinned against the wall, and yet so serene that he may as well have been a Tjalavan Cloud Monk.

It was Praine that broke the silence. "I assure you, I don't have the faintest idea what you're talking about. If Praxis is indeed missing, it has nothing to do with me."

"You're lying." The words came out in a growl, caught low in Kaedrich's throat.

Guilt sluiced through Prett, so sudden that his knees nearly buckled.

"And what if I am?" Praine whispered. His voice was so polished that it could have decorated the walls. "What are you going to do about it?"

"All right, that's enough," Prett snapped. He tugged on Kaedrich's arm, even knowing that it would do no good. Only one of the Fellows brothers might be strong enough to force Kaedrich, and he wasn't here. "Come on. I'll help you look for her. She has to be around here somewhere."

Depths, Prett hoped she was around here somewhere, back from the party by now. How long had it been, anyway? Surely long enough. It had to have been long enough.

But Kaedrich didn't move, not yet anyway. His grip remained tight on Praine's fur coat, the rainbow hairs sticking out at odd angles through his fists.

Prett leaned in, lowered his voice. "Kaedrich, you're smarter than this."

It's true that Prett didn't really know Kaedrich well, but he did know this, at least. And so: Kaedrich took a breath, seeming to come back to himself. He glanced, briefly, at the crowd now pressing in tighter around them, eager for the juiciest gossip. And he stepped back, his fingers loosening and then releasing Praine's coat. Prett breathed a sigh of relief, clapping Kaedrich on the shoulder as he turned him away from Praine, away from the crowd.

"That's it," Prett said, keeping his voice nestled down between them. "Just come with me, pretend this never happened."

"I can't find Praxis." Kaedrich's words were fragile now, all of his bravado abandoned with the scene behind them.

"I know," Prett said. Kaedrich looked over sharply, and Prett cleared his throat. "You weren't exactly being subtle, back there."

Kaedrich nodded, because of course this made sense. Never mind that Prett had already known Praxis wasn't at the ball. Never mind that he knew she was trailing behind. As Prett led Kaedrich out of the ballroom, away from prying eyes, all that mattered was that Kaedrich accepted his explanation.

Prett gave Kaedrich's shoulder a squeeze. "We'll find her." He meant this, with every ounce of conviction that he pressed into his voice. Anything to keep moving, to avoid thinking about all that had happened tonight. They left the ball, making plans; where had Kaedrich already covered, where else might be checked? They would split up, the best to cover more ground; and also, though he said nothing, so that Prett might slip back to the party, find out if—and more importantly *when*—Praxis might have left. There was so little Prett could do, to unmake the mistakes that he'd allowed to befall the night, but he could do this. He could find his little sister.

He could set, at least, this one thing right.

THE NEWS WAS breaking by the time Tol reached the street corner.

He could feel it in the air, an undercurrent of panic that inhabited every person he passed, but which somehow existed outside of any one individual's body. A primal instinct raised the hairs on the back of Tol's neck. The herd was spooked, and Tol was caught right in the middle of it.

Gossip slipped through the city like the swirling smog, sliding down streets and pooling along the edge of the bay. Tol tried to pick their words out of the air, but panic made people tighten into clusters, the horrible truth shared only among themselves. Tol raced to the next block, where even the newsboy was silent, handing out his wares with an apologetic grimace. Tol all but threw his money at the boy as he ripped a paper from him. The ink was so fresh that it bled onto his hands, staining them in the way the crime he'd just committed never could.

He read the headlines.

His breath escaped him.

He read them again.

No, it wasn't possible. And yet there it was, in black and white. Shots fired against the Durlish Authority's border patrols; a bomb that destroyed a bridge in Styford; pro-magic leaflets jettisoned against Monfort's shores from darting ships near the harbor. Worst of all, and bloodiest still: an attack on a quiet border town, sixteen found dead in their beds.

To anyone else—to everyone else—the signs all pointed to one thing: increased anti-Durland sentiment from Rolmstan. Coordinated efforts to make their feelings known. Fears in Durland were already high, after all, since they were still embracing wizards despite the ghost crisis. Tensions between the two countries had frayed significantly in recent years. It didn't take a genius to work out that the people of Rolmstan, if not the government itself, would be motivated enough to begin taking aggressive action against Durland's citizens.

It was a neat package, a tidy explanation. Only Tol would see it for what it actually was: Lanali's handiwork.

The newspaper crunched in his fists. How *could* she? They were a *team*! Always had been, always would be. Okay, so Tol hadn't exactly agreed with some of her decisions lately, and sometimes those decisions were quite large, but that didn't mean he deserved to be *shut out*.

Except no, it was worse than that; as Tol tossed the newspaper aside, letting it catch in the wind, he realized his own actions that evening had played right into Lanali's narrative. The death of the minister of national defense, his body turned over to hang from the ceiling, suspended by magic. Tol had dragged the furniture out of the middle of the room, carved symbols and runes into the polished wood floor below Braynish's resting place. He'd even gone so far as to climb up and slice a tiny cut into Braynish's lip, so that a thin trail of blood would splash down and puddle in the center of the display. True, Tol had known that Lanali wanted the death to look as if it had come at the hand of a wizard; true, she had stressed this point; and true, Tol hadn't bothered to question her, to ask her for her reasons when he knew she would no longer give them. But he had no reason to suspect she'd been planning something like *this*! Tol had been used, as readily as they'd always used any of their pawns. As if he was beneath her consideration, as if he hadn't been there since the beginning. As if he didn't know the truth about her, as if he meant *nothing*.

Tol felt something tear asunder, buried deep inside of him. A pain so sharp it was almost physical, and with it, the release of a fury he did not know how to handle. It did not so much course through him as over and around him, a great tide that swept him up and crashed him, haphazard, stripped of identity, on a distant and unrecognizable shore. He very nearly collapsed under the force of it, right there on the street, and only the edge of a nearby flower stand caught his balance. A passing voice, full of sympathy, threw questions at him as he staggered back to his feet, but he barely heard it. The tide was pulling back, drawing Tol along with it, his head full of nothing but the thought of Lanali and the roar of the sea. Tol turned his face toward the glimmering palace, seated high over the evening smog of Monfort, and he followed the sound, up up up the slopes, the waves pounding as an angry hurricane across his heart.

FIRST PRAXIS, AND now Prett. Kaedrich was in the habit of losing people tonight.

No, she thought sharply to herself. *Not losing.* "Losing" had the discomforting aura of death and permanence about it, a tang that left a bitter taste in her mouth. She had not *lost* Praxis. Surely, as close as they were, Kaedrich would be able to tell if something terrible had happened . . .

right? Fine, so she didn't have magic—there were other senses. Intuition. Connection. Love. Things that ran deeper than magic, things that she clung to as she checked one room after another, one lonely hallway after another.

But it was true that she'd had no luck, and it was true that now Prett couldn't be found, either. He'd said he was going to check a few places on his own first, and then meet up with Kaedrich after, but Kaedrich had waited and waited, and he hadn't shown up, and then she couldn't bear to wait any longer. She'd resumed her search, frantic and fruitless.

Not in their rooms. Not in her lab. Not in the libraries, or at least not the ones Kaedrich knew about. Not at Annelle's ball. She could not check Prawl's study or Prestina's office, but considering both of them were soaking up the adulation of wealthy bootlickers at the party, Kaedrich doubted that Praxis was waiting for either of them there. So Kaedrich kept going. Sitting rooms and smaller studies, dining rooms and gaming rooms and wine rooms. She found a kitchen, and a storage room, and a room full of nothing but paintings. She asked everyone she passed, servants and guests and family alike, but anyone that could speak either Durlish or nervous gestures gave the same answer: no. No and no and no and a dozen shaken heads, over and over and over again.

By now, it was hard to ignore the flutter that tightened her stomach with each new room. Her breathing had gone fast and high, and it took all of her self-control to pause and force herself to suck down several lungfuls of cold air. She checked more rooms, and then she rechecked all the rooms she'd already checked.

Twice.

She finally lost it in the labs.

Several minutes of ugly crying. With the door shut behind her, Kaedrich slid to the floor and leaned her back against the wall as everything caught up with her at once. Not just Praxis's . . . disappearance, for lack of a better word, but *everything*. The barrage of dirty looks snuck in Kaedrich's direction every time she was around a Fellows. The constant lies, having to maintain a false biography of noble blood. The cold. Her near-death back in Durland, the faces of the men she'd had to kill to protect Praxis, the terrible circumstances of her homeland. Fear for her parents—long since lost to her—the guilt over not reconnecting yet and the gravestone they'd purchased for her, the worry over what would happen to them under Lanali's rule. The secrets that Kaedrich *knew* Praxis was keeping, the layer of ice that had formed between them ever since arriving in Yandosia. What if something had truly happened to Praxis? It's not that Kaedrich *really* suspected it, not if she was being rational with herself, but . . . Perlandra's breath, you just never knew. She remembered, shamefully, the way that she'd attacked Praine, but gods, you just never knew.

Finally, finally, she wiped her eyes with the back of her hand. The last thing she needed was for the Fellows to see she'd been crying. Kaedrich got to her feet, already digging out her handkerchief, when something caught her eye: a flash of white against the blue of the ice, sticking out from beyond the laboratory counter.

She was running forward before her conscious mind had caught up with what she'd seen. By the time the word "hand" entered her thoughts, she could see the rest of Praxis, collapsed onto the floor. A strangled cry escaped Kaedrich, Praxis's name shouted in terror.

Praxis didn't answer, didn't react at all. She was lying on her side, curled tight, like she'd collapsed and then convulsed into the fetal position. Only her hand was extended, as if she'd been clawing to try to reach something just beyond her grasp. She was not wearing her coat. Her pants leg was more than halfway unbuttoned, the cold metal of her brace shining in the light.

All these details flooded Kaedrich at once as she ducked to check on Praxis. She wasn't trying to make sense of any of it, not yet. There was only one question that Kaedrich cared to answer, and so far nothing had settled that. She pressed her fingers against Praxis's neck, and nearly collapsed in relief as a pulse knocked back against her fingertips.

Briefly, Kaedrich squeezed her eyes shut and whispered a fast prayer of gratitude to Perlandra. Her relief was short-lived, however—Praxis's breathing was so slow and shallow that it was difficult to find at all, and no amount of shouting her name or jostling her shoulder was rousing her from this state.

"No, no, no, come on," Kaedrich whispered to herself as she shook Praxis once more. "Praxis. *Praxis!*"

It made no difference. Kaedrich turned Praxis's head and propped her eyelids open, some deep-seated impulse to attempt to *force* Praxis awake—then immediately wished she hadn't. A scream tried to claw its way up Kaedrich's throat, and she only just bit it down.

Praxis's pupils had contracted down to nearly nothing, just a single pinprick of black in a sea of icy blue and white. They stared out, unseeing, ghostly in their emptiness.

Kaedrich vaulted to her feet, already moving toward the door. Her screams for help burst into the corridor before she did. They echoed through the empty tunnel of ice, bouncing with cold indifference against the walls. For a split second, she questioned herself—what would Praxis think, drawing such a fuss, allowing someone else to see her in such a vulnerable state?—but Kaedrich stomped down on that impulse. Praxis needed help, and Kaedrich didn't have the slightest idea what to do to help her. To the darkness with Praxis's privacy right now.

She ran to one end of the empty hall, then the other, shouting the whole time. In the depths of the lapus lumeni division, even guards were sparse. Kaedrich had just turned back, wondering if she had time to run to the main household, when a familiar set of footsteps rang out like chimes against the ice.

"Lord Mannly," Prestina's cold voice said. "*What* is the meaning of—?"

Kaedrich did not question herself, did not care. She lunged forward, grabbing Prestina's hand. "No time!" Kaedrich said as she dragged Prestina back to the lab. "Praxis is hurt, and I don't—I don't know what to—"

"Out of my way," Prestina said. She yanked herself free and moved with remarkable speed for a woman of her station and fashion. Kaedrich only just kept up as the two of them burst back into the lab.

Prestina took in the situation with military precision. She did not even pause before she swept over, crouched down. Pulse, breath, pupils, all noted in an instant. "Oh, Praxis," she whispered. She ran her hand comfortingly along her daughter's arm while she looked around the floor of the lab, as if searching for something that had been lost.

"What are you looking f—?"

"There," Prestina said. She pointed, her arm a sharp line down to her jeweled fingers. Kaedrich followed the arrow they made, her attention landing on an abandoned syringe. It was tucked underneath the edge of a counter, in roughly the direction Praxis had been reaching toward.

Kaedrich scrambled to collect it. She scooped it up, but the flutter of hope in her chest was dashed as she looked down at it. "It's empty!"

"Of course it's *empty*," Prestina snapped. "That isn't how we save Praxis, that's what got her into trouble in the first place."

Fear stole Kaedrich's heart. She clutched the syringe, stained purple, to her chest. "So someone drugged her?"

Prestina snorted. "I think you'll find she took care of that herself. Look." She straightened up, turning so that she could access Praxis's legs. With a sweep of her hand, Prestina moved aside the opened flap of Praxis's trousers.

Kaedrich sucked her breath in through her teeth. At first, just because Prestina had exposed something that Praxis had been trying to keep even more hidden than she usually did—but then, upon seeing Praxis's knee for herself, out of simple shock at how bad things had gotten in such a short time. The muscles around her knee were sunken, the skin drawn. But worse: *above* that, in the solid flesh that plumped out a few inches higher, the skin was littered with tiny red dots.

How had Praxis managed to keep this from her? Kaedrich stood rooted in place, staring at the mess Praxis had made of herself. Hurt and anger and disgust and bitterness twisted themselves around Kaedrich's thoughts, locking up her mind.

She should have seen through it. Praxis had been distant lately, even before the days she'd spent holed up in the lab. Getting ready for bed before Kaedrich, and lingering until after Kaedrich had to leave before dragging herself up again. Shrugging off Kaedrich's advances—feigning tiredness, or irritation with her family, or the start of her monthly cycle—and Kaedrich had *believed* her. But none of it had been true, or at least not the whole truth.

If Prestina could read any of this on Kaedrich's face, she did not show it. She was already drawing herself to her feet, a queen in control of her world. The fanning collar behind her head sparkled like the distant stars, and Kaedrich found herself mesmerized by the display.

"We can't treat her here," Prestina said, and she spoke with such authority that Kaedrich did not even think to question her. "Take Praxis back to your rooms. I'm going to get help—do *not* let anyone in unless I am with them, do you understand?"

Kaedrich nodded.

"Good. Give me two minutes to make the necessary preparations, and then you can start. Take the back passage, up the Amber staircase, to Emerald Level. I should be able to secure the path for you by then, but if *anyone* should see the two of you along the way, I do not want you to answer *any* questions. Is that clear?"

Her instructions were clear, yes, although Kaedrich wasn't entirely sure she understood the need for them. Nevertheless, Kaedrich nodded again.

"Very well." Prestina took one last glance down at her daughter. Her nose wrinkled. "And for sanity's sake, find something to cover her up with, will you? The last thing we need is a scandal right now."

Chapter Thirty-Four

SHE'S GOING TO be fine, she's going to be fine, she's going to be fine.

This was the refrain ringing through Kaedrich's mind as she carried Praxis up the twisting passageways of the Fellows' dwelling. She had to believe it, even if she had very little in the way of facts to support this assertion. There was the steady pulse, at least; and Praxis's breathing, while poor, did not waver. So that was something. And Prestina seemed relatively unconcerned, although that could have just been her frozen exterior lending confidence where none really existed. Kaedrich knew, because she'd seen the same behavior in Praxis more times than she could count.

At this thought, a sharp pang struck Kaedrich. She gripped Praxis even more tightly against herself as she walked. *She's going to be fine, she's going to be fine, she's going to be fine.* Praxis was curled in Kaedrich's arms like a child, her head propped steadily against Kaedrich's shoulder. Her hair brushed Kaedrich's nose as Kaedrich turned to plant a steady kiss on the top of Praxis's head. They were climbing the stairs, one sure step at a time. They were almost to the top.

Once safely in their rooms, however, Kaedrich again found herself with an utter lack of direction. She carried Praxis over to the bed, arranged her so that she would be comfortable, but after that . . . ?

Kaedrich was enormously grateful, then, when a rap sounded on her door a few minutes later. She raced across their rooms, leaping over and around the furniture. Kaedrich cracked the door open, enough to see Prestina's stern face. For once, at the sight of it, relief flooded Kaedrich.

She stepped back, opening the door wide. Prestina bustled in, followed quickly by a small, mousy man who was presumably a doctor. They were talking rapidly in Yandosian as they cut through the sitting rooms, ignoring Kaedrich entirely. Kaedrich hurried to shut and bolt the door behind them, and then raced to catch up. Prestina was standing back, hovering at the foot of the bed, but the doctor had knelt down on the mattress and was already filling a fresh syringe.

"Hang on," Kaedrich said, "what's that?"

Prestina grabbed Kaedrich's wrist, holding her back. "Relax, Lord Mannly. Our doctors have had more than enough practice at treating the effects of overindulging this particular drug in the last few years."

"That's not exactly an answer."

Prestina rolled her eyes, looking so much like Praxis that it was a dagger straight to Kaedrich's heart. "Do I look like a medical expert?" Prestina said. "I can't give you a chemical breakdown of the substance."

"No, but—"

The doctor turned and said something, his soft words lost in the language of Yandosia but his voice lilting up at the end like a question.

Prestina nodded at him. *"Yes,"* she told him, one of the words Kaedrich had learned.

Kaedrich tried to swallow down the knot jumbled up in her throat as the doctor stuck the needle into Praxis's arm. He set it down on the bedside table, and leaned forward to rest his fingers against Praxis's neck. In his other hand he consulted a pocket-sized Yandosian timepiece, sitting still and silent as he measured Praxis's pulse.

Seconds ticked by. Prestina had long since let go of her hold on Kaedrich's wrist, and Kaedrich found herself wishing she could reach over and clutch Prestina's hand instead. Not because of any particular feelings of warmth toward Praxis's mother, but just for something—someone— else to ground herself against. Gods, if this didn't work . . .

No, Kaedrich told herself. *Don't you dare think that.* She reached up, tracing the wavy rays of her pin with nervous fingers.

The first big inhale was so strong that Praxis's mouth gasped open, sucking down air like a drowning woman just hauled up on land. Her body jerked underneath the force of it. Her eyes fluttered, a sea of pure white and icy blue flashing before the lids fell shut once more.

Kaedrich fell to her knees, pressing her forehead against the thick fur blankets at the foot of the bed. She whispered prayers of gratitude and relief as the sounds of Praxis's haggard breaths chimed throughout the room.

"Oh, *honestly*," Prestina muttered from above her. "Have some dignity, sir."

But Kaedrich didn't care about dignity at the moment, or even Prestina's impression of her. She raised her head just enough to watch the rise and fall of Praxis's chest.

The doctor continued to swarm over Praxis. Checking her pulse again, timing her breathing, listening to her heart. He seemed to take forever. Prestina stood sentry at the foot of Praxis's bed, arms crossed over her chest with a poise Kaedrich couldn't fathom. Everything about her was level, even: the cut of her arms and the line of her mouth, the controlled watch of her eyes, the seemingly casual ease of her brow. It was easy to see where Praxis had learned her control. Kaedrich tried to take a measure of comfort in it, tried to make herself even a fraction as collected as Prestina. She sat on the edge of Praxis's bed, holding Praxis's limp hand. Deep breaths, lined up with Praxis's. One and two and twenty.

Finally, the doctor straightened up. Took off his stethoscope and hung it around his neck. He said something to Prestina, and Prestina held her finger up, cutting him off.

"In Durlish, please. He deserves to hear this."

Kaedrich blinked in surprise, though not as much surprise as the doctor showed. He gawped at Kaedrich for a moment, sputtering as if he intended to argue—but one look at Prestina snapped his mouth shut. The doctor nodded, slowly. Began again.

And so Kaedrich listened, although to say that she understood at first would be an exaggeration. Not that the doctor's words were terribly complex, not that she couldn't follow the medical terminology. Kaedrich listened, her breath growing shallow and her chest tightening up, to a diagnosis she could not bring herself to connect with the woman lying next to her. *No* was the only thought in her mind, not even a word so much as an utter rejection of fact. She could not bring herself to understand it, would not bring herself to understand it.

So it was Prestina who asked questions, Prestina who took charge of the logistics of how and when and what. Kaedrich looked away, focusing on the pale hand wrapped up in her own darker fingers. It looked so frail, suddenly, so tiny and vulnerable. What an odd thing, this working of the human body. Muscles and blood and air in the lungs, the delicate interplay of each piece. How slim the lines were, between functioning and not. How closely death hovered at our shoulders.

Not death, though, Kaedrich tried to tell herself, but it made little difference. She knew Praxis would take it as the same thing. Prestina walked the doctor to the door, thanking him, speaking quietly in Yandosian now, and Kaedrich reached out and brushed the hair off Praxis's forehead, gracing her with a kiss.

"I'm going to make this okay," Kaedrich whispered to her, though who could tell at this point if Praxis could hear anything? Her breathing was still shallow, her lips dry. Still, Kaedrich traced the line of her face, the angle of her jaw. "I promise."

If only she could figure out how.

LANALI WAS WAITING for him in the war room.

That's what it was called, anyway, though it was used far more often for petty political disputes, banquets, and budget meetings. It sat on the southern end of the palace, one long wall made of glass that overlooked the whole of Monfort, from the slopes of the elite straight down and across the city's wide embrace of Abbney Bay. The opposite wall held paintings, maps, a crest of the royal family. A long table sat between them, lined with heavy, straight-backed chairs.

Tol entered the room. He was, he felt, exercising great restraint in that he did not kick down the doors and barrel through like a whirlwind from the tropic of Ast.

The first thing he noticed: the crest of the royal family was gone. The middle of the wall stood naked and empty, a faint outline of dust and sun-stains leaving an echo of times gone by.

The second thing he noticed: Lanali had changed her looks again. The slow evolution into luxury had been reversed with whiplash speeds. Her high-necked dress, while blue velvet instead of her older black, was severe with intensity; her hair was pulled taut, pinned in a manner that accentuated the sharp planes of her face. A ring heavy with jewels sat upon her finger. It caught the glow of the electric light as she motioned for him to be seated.

"Welcome back," she said. "We have a lot to catch up on, Tol."

It was a calculated move on her part. Tol saw it instantly, as sure as if a Cloak and Crowns board lay before them. So, too, could Tol see how he could play against her, the strategies he might employ, the countermoves Lanali could make in response. The whole conversation seemed to hang like ghosts in the air around them, just waiting for him to play his part.

Tol did not sit. He was tired of games.

The chair made a satisfying scrape as Tol yanked it from the row.

He knocked it over like an angry wind, one and then another, each one clattering to the floor as toppled game pieces. Lanali watched his approach with infuriating calm, barely seeming to notice the line of chairs scattered behind him.

"You should have discussed this with me," he said as he finally came to a stop in front of her. His chest was heaving now, though how much of it was rage and how much was the weight of twenty solid chairs, he could not say.

"You would have opposed my plan."

"You're damned right I would have! An *invasion*? This isn't what we agreed to!"

Lanali smirked.

What, did she think he wouldn't have figured it out? A map of Rolmstan lay open on the table, pins dotting strategic points along the border. Operations designed to look like attacks by the Rolmish people, the last spark needed to ignite the already fuel-rich paranoia of the neighbors on their southeastern border. The reports—gods, Tol should have seen it coming. Arms production doubled twice in the last two months. Transport seized for use by the Crown. Enlistment numbers in Durland's army expanded by several orders of magnitude. Tol knew the recruitment promises were never meant to last, that eventually they'd be asked to do more than build roads, but *this* . . .

Every piece of Lanali's long game clicked into place at once in Tol's mind. Not just the actions as the Crown—even getting the crown in the first place. The revolution, the anti-magic propaganda, the private security force she'd been slowly amassing piece by piece. It had all been building toward this, and Tol hadn't seen it coming.

How had he not seen this coming?

"I was wondering how long it would take you," Lanali said.

"*Why?*"

Lanali shrugged. "Does it matter?"

"Yes," Tol said. He wasn't even sure it did, until she'd asked, but dammit, *it did* matter. Why? After all these years, all these schemes; after everything they'd been through. It's not that Tol had fooled himself into thinking their relationship hadn't gotten strained in recent years. But for Lanali to plan something like *this*—not just plan it, but work out the details, iron out the kinks, and then to put it into motion, all while hiding it from Tol's notice . . . He needed to know why.

He deserved to understand.

Lanali said nothing, not at first anyway. She studied him, reading his expression. She held her hands in front of her, the points of her fingers pressed together as she considered her answer.

"I want the truth," Tol said. Something he never thought he'd have to say to her, of all people. "You know that I'll know if it's not."

"Yes, I do know that," Lanali said. "But I'm not sure if you really do want the truth. You *think* you do. That's not exactly the same thing."

"Dammit, Frel—"

"Don't call me that!" Lanali said. "That woman is dead!"

"Not to me! It's *who you are*. You may have forgotten, but I haven't. I haven't forgotten any of it."

Not a single day, in fact. Not of *Frel*, the girl Lanali used to be. Before this grand scheme of theirs—no, Tol corrected himself. This was not the time for self-delusion, not anymore. It was never *their* grand scheme to come to Durland. It was only ever hers.

He remembered the night she'd made the decision.

A perfect moon, a perfect sky. The hint of a breeze carried their tiny sailboat across the water, and Frel was laughing at the bow as she tossed the wig she'd been wearing for the past six weeks out to be swallowed by the waves. They'd just pulled off their latest con, swindling an old man out of the money he'd been saving in the hopes that his ungrateful daughter would one day return to beg his forgiveness. He was a surprisingly gentle, surprisingly forgiving soul. He was ready to hand it over. The perfect target for someone like Frel.

Tol navigated the boat. Bags of money bumped into his feet as he avoided the other traffic in the waters between the tightly knit patch of islands known as the Vylla Cluster. The bags were positively stuffed with baks, more of the feathery-thin currency than Tol had ever seen in one place in his life.

"You were brilliant," he called up to her, and Frel turned, a genuine smile shining back at him. Brighter even than the moon. Tol's heart twisted.

"I know," she said, in a voice that sounded singsong to Tol's happy ears. Maybe . . . maybe it was time, he thought, to finally say it. Just *say* it. It didn't have to be complicated. And after all, was he ever going to get a better opportunity than this?

Frel trooped back, dropping cross-legged on the deck and pulling one of the bags of money toward her. She dipped her hands in, the thin baks embracing her fingers like down. Her loose hair blew around her shoulders like mist on a cool morning.

Tol's throat was dry, so he swallowed. And again.

"Frel," he said. His voice was shaky, but that wouldn't matter, surely?

"We can only hope the Durns are as gullible," Frel said as she stretched out, one leg jutting between the bags, her back against the side of the boat. She had a handful of baks in her lap, and she held them up one by one, watching the colors shift in the moonlight.

Tol blinked, thrown by the shift. "The Durns?"

Frel nodded. "I think it's time, Tol. Time for bigger things."

"You . . ." Tol shook his head. "You don't mean you want to *leave Aul*, do you?"

Frel glanced up. "It doesn't have to be forever. Just long enough for people to forget what we've done here lately. We don't want to risk our luck running out, do we?"

"I . . . Well, no. Of course not."

"Good, then it's settled," Frel said, though it was far from settled as far as Tol was concerned. He gripped the boat's tiller, the wood worn smooth from frequent use. Even the sunbaked cracks were softened with time.

But he did not quarrel with her, not then. Oh, he tried to bring it up—in the weeks that followed, as Frel's eyes squinted at the rapidly diminishing money between them, as the plans became set, as they practiced accents, names, as Tol read books of family trees and histories of the nobility of Durland. He tried to bring it up. Tried to suggest something different. Each time, he would open his mouth, and each time, as if sensing what was to come, Frel would offer up another sample of what would be their new life.

"Pon Denli Lanali," Frel said one evening as the sunset stained her copper hair and the sea breeze carried in the smell of salt and fish and home. She stood on the beach, her toes buried in the sand, and held herself straighter and more rigid than any Aul ever bothered with. A glance down at Tol, that was all she offered. Her face was wiped clean of expression, only Durlish composure and manners left to fill the void. "Well? What do you think?"

Tol rolled the name around in his head. *Pon.* "It's not a Durlish title," he said, his only offering at first.

Frel shrugged. "I'll tell them it means 'princess.'"

"*Princess?*" A laugh very nearly escaped Tol then. So fast that it caught in his throat, and he had to cough it out instead. "Do you really think they'll believe that?"

"They'll *believe* whatever I tell them to believe," Frel said, and in that moment her voice was so commanding, so proper, so robust and full of practiced authority that even Tol could almost believe it.

Almost.

Pon was an ancient Aul word for a god of rebirth and creation.

Well, she'd certainly achieved *that*, Tol would have to admit now. Look at her, all of these years later: it was nigh to impossible, even for him, to spot the vestiges of the girl she used to be.

Tol straightened up. He blinked at Lanali, as if seeing her anew. How had he not noticed it before? Had he really been so foolish, so blind, all of these years? He felt as if he'd been looking at her through a special type of spyglass, one designed to superimpose settings and costumes around the figures that you gazed upon, and now someone had taken it away, and this is what was left.

Pon Lanali.

How long had she been playing *him*? Forget Durland and the seizing of the crown—this, by far, was her biggest con. And he'd fallen right for it.

This is what he meant to ask: "Is there really nothing left of her?" But maybe he already knew the answer, finally and for once, because that was not what came out.

"You know that I loved her."

There it was, then. Past tense by now and years too late, but there it was. The truth of them, at last.

Lanali shrugged. "I know. I think that's what made it so easy."

Tol's fists clenched at his sides. He looked to the map, sprawled open across the table, because it was better, easier, than looking at her. The woman that wore Frel's face.

"So what now?" he asked. It was the only question left.

For a moment there was only silence. The lands of Durland and Rolmstan and Marcovalla filled his vision, blurred but manageable chunks, something real to ground himself against.

And then Lanali's palm appeared, upturned as if in offering, between himself and the map. And when Lanali's voice returned, it was so much softer than Tol was used to, so much more like it was when it was *hers*.

"Well, *that*, I think," Lanali said, "is probably up to you."

PRESTINA ANSWERED THE door herself.

The knock came about an hour after the doctor left, soft and timid as a bird tapping against glass. Both Kaedrich and Prestina were sitting near Praxis's bed, a stiff silence resting between them, and both Kaedrich and Prestina looked up, startled, at the sound.

By decree, there were no servants in the room with them. They paused, looking at each other. Kaedrich straightened her shoulders—she would not be bullied, dammit, not here, not now—but Prestina was already rising to her feet, her high collar obscuring her face as she turned away.

Curiosity made Kaedrich lean forward, enough to see around the edge of the doorway that led from the bedroom to the sitting room. Prestina crossed the expanse with the practiced ease of a queen, and when she opened the door, she barely seemed to touch it at all.

"What did I say about being interrupted?"

A maid's voice, soft with remorse: "Forgive me, ma'am, but the Archon is in the lower receiving room. He's demanding an audience with Praxis, ma'am."

"*Now?*"

Kaedrich couldn't see the maid's reaction, but she did see Prestina as she pinched the bridge of her nose.

"Idiot," Prestina muttered under her breath.

"I'll go," Kaedrich said.

Prestina looked back, a sharp puzzle of curiosity drawing her brow together. Kaedrich could see her debating the merits, the costs—though it didn't seem that complicated to Kaedrich. As much as she wanted to stay by Praxis's side, Praxis was going to sleep for a good few hours yet. And if the Archon—Lexthur Delford, the man Praxis had almost married once—was asking for her now, well . . . Kaedrich could admit to being curious. More than curious.

She did not wait for Prestina's approval. It was almost funny, Kaedrich thought as she strode down the long hall, that the one person she felt okay about leaving Praxis with in this state should be her. But even Prestina's hatred for Kaedrich had proven one thing: she cared about her daughter, in her own weird, selfish way.

At the first junction, Kaedrich stopped. She waited for the maid to catch up, and then scurry on ahead. The maid's back was almost as rigid as Prestina, and Kaedrich followed her down a set of stairs, and a long twisting passage.

Finally they reached a door, and the maid stopped. She crossed her arms. "I'll not announce you," she said.

"Fine by me." Kaedrich grabbed the doorknob, and let herself inside.

The room was enormous, like everything else in the Fellows' dwelling. Arched ceilings well above her head were sculpted into what looked like the underside of ocean waves, as if the whole room was underwater. This theme was continued in the carvings of the wall, various sea creatures, both real and mythological, taking subtle shape in the texture. There were even gemstone fish, buried deep in the walls and visible only as glinting shapes.

Kaedrich would have been impressed by it—possibly she even would have adored the room—if it wasn't for her sour mood. Instead, she wrinkled her nose at the obvious display of wealth, the wasted space around them. The entire room held only two small sofas, facing each other in the middle, and a side table laid out with various food and drink.

A solitary man sat waiting, his arm thrown casually along the back of the sofa, one leg propped up loud and proud across his knee. He turned at the sound of the door, his attention resting on Kaedrich for barely a moment before he went back to waiting.

So this was the man Praxis had almost married. Kaedrich's mouth soured—dammit, he was *handsome*. A certain boyish charm hung about him like a good cologne, and his sense of style was understated and impeccable. His shock-white Yandosian hair and beard seemed somehow less severe than the Fellows', and though he wore a little jewelry in the form of two heavy rings, it didn't glare obvious in your face. He felt *genuine*, in a way none of the other Yandosians Kaedrich had met recently did.

Kaedrich made herself approach. She tried not to hate him on sight. He would have made a good match for Praxis, that was the basic problem. His gaze had turned toward the table of food, regarding it with mild interest.

"Lexthur Delford?" Kaedrich asked. She didn't know why she made it a question, except perhaps that a tiny portion of her was hoping there had been a mix-up.

Lexthur glanced up, eyebrow raised. He said nothing.

"I understand you're here to see Praxis Fellows," Kaedrich went on. It occurred to her then that perhaps he didn't speak Durlish—but just as the thought was bubbling up, Lexthur nodded in confirmation.

"That's right," he said. His voice was smooth as ice, his accent barely detectable. "Though someone is getting her now—there's no need to bother me." He was already moving on, leaning over to pick up a particularly delicate-looking dessert, all brushed sugar and fine as crystal.

Kaedrich paused, just for a second, to collect herself. Then she moved to stand tall before him, even though her stomach was doing a thousand somersaults. "Actually, there is. I'm afraid that Praxis isn't available to speak with you at the moment—but you may address your comments to me, if you wish."

A tiny frown marred Lexthur's face as he turned back—but then he blinked, something seeming to connect in his mind. He took in the sight of the fine fur suit that Kaedrich wore, the family ring adorning her finger, and by the time his attention returned to Kaedrich's face, he was smiling. "Oh, of course," he said, his whole manner shifting, as he got to his feet. "You must be Keedrick. Praxis mentioned you." He extended his hand, obviously versed in Durlish customs.

Kaedrich accepted the gesture, though she didn't really want to. "Kaedrich."

"Right, right, Kaedrich. I do apologize—I thought you were one of the grubs." He continued to smile, as if somehow Kaedrich was supposed to feel comforted by this. As if she hadn't just been insulted to her face.

"What did you want to see Praxis about?" Kaedrich asked. It was a much more brusque question than she would normally open with, but she was quickly losing patience with both Lexthur Delford and the rules of polite society. Kaedrich almost smirked, realizing that this must be some of what fueled Praxis's own behavior—until she remembered Praxis sleeping in their rooms, blissfully unaware of the news Kaedrich would have to bear to her later, and that shriveled Kaedrich's amusement right up.

"I'm afraid I was quite interested in speaking with Praxis directly," Lexthur said as he settled back onto the sofa. He gestured for Kaedrich to join him, in the sofa opposing. Lexthur smiled at her. "Are you sure there's no possibility of a meeting at present? It need only take a moment."

Kaedrich shook her head. "I'm sorry, but no. However, I assure you, anything you wish to say to Praxis, you can say to me."

Lexthur quirked one narrow eyebrow. "Is that so?"

"It is. There are no secrets between us."

"Very well," Lexthur said with a shrug. "My business with her is quite simple. I came to inquire as to whether or not Praxis has made up her mind about accepting my proposal."

Kaedrich blinked. "Your . . . your proposal," she said, her voice heavy. She nodded as if she understood. She was trying to arrange her face to make it look as if she knew exactly what Lexthur was talking about, that this didn't come as any kind of shock to her at all. "Of course, I . . ."

"Perhaps there are a *few* secrets between you?"

Kaedrich hated him in that moment. The playful lilt of his voice, the twinkle glinting in his stage-star eyes. Kaedrich fought against the urge to glare at him. "Not at all," she said. "Only, it seems that Praxis thought your discussion was so unimportant that I'm having difficulty remembering the details. Remind me, what was the nature of your proposal again?"

The words, unplanned, shocked Kaedrich as they came out of her mouth. Perlandra help her, being here was turning her *into* Praxis. She barely even recognized herself.

Her rudeness was lost on Lexthur, however. Instead, he burst out laughing. "Well played, sir. Well played. Tell me, have you ever considered a career in politics?"

"No."

Lexthur smiled. "Shame," he said, with a slight shake of his head. "I think you'd be good at it."

"Be that as it may—"

"May we speak like men, Kaedrich?" Lexthur had turned serious, the mirth of his features gone in an instant.

Kaedrich nodded.

"I know this must seem strange to you—my intention to marry the woman you're . . . How do you say it in Durland? 'Courting'?"

Heat flared in Kaedrich's cheeks as she remembered the conversation she'd had with Praxis shortly after arriving. *Are we courting?* She nodded, because the term was what Lexthur was searching for, even if it didn't apply *exactly*.

Though it might.

(It was hard to say.)

"You have to be aware of the difference in our customs by this point," Lexthur continued. "I assure you, any marriage that I make with Praxis would be a financial arrangement. We're not required to be lovers."

This was supposed to be reassuring—it wasn't. Kaedrich's mouth pinched together, and she found herself quite at a loss for words. Or at least, any *polite* words.

"You disapprove." It wasn't really a question, though Lexthur's voice did lilt up just slightly at the end, as if he was surprised, or not quite as sure as he meant to be.

"Let's just say I have a somewhat different definition of marriage than you."

"Do you, though?" Lexthur asked. He held up his hand, halting Kaedrich's reply. "Let me ask you something: you love Praxis, don't you?"

This one was easy. "Yes."

"Then you must want what's best for her."

"Yes."

"Stability?"

"Yes."

"Security?"

"Yes."

"Power and respect?"

"If that's what she wants."

A corner of Lexthur's mouth ticked with the hint of a smile that wasn't quite there. "And you can provide these things?"

"I *will* provide them," Kaedrich said, and she meant it. No matter what it took, no matter how hard she needed to work to make it happen.

Lexthur nodded. "Oh, I have no doubt. But better than she could provide for herself, if she were the head of the company? Because that's what she would become if she accepted." He leaned over, plucking a drink from the edge of the table. "Or didn't she tell you that, either?"

He took a long drink, giving Kaedrich time to absorb this. His attention was on his glass, or on the fish embedded in the walls around them.

It wasn't as much of a surprise as it should have been. Kaedrich was aware enough of bits and pieces of Yandosian law that the news settled itself in her head without the burden of shock. Nor was it surprising that this, too, was something Praxis had kept to herself. For despite all the progress they'd made as a couple, Praxis was still a creature of secrets. She hoarded them, like a fierce dragon, keeping each one tight in her clutches.

Kaedrich's throat went dry. The company. Praxis could have *the company*. The news that the doctor had told her loomed heavy in her mind, and Kaedrich's mouth twisted up as she realized what she was going to have to do next.

"All right," Kaedrich said slowly, "tell me what you had in mind."

THE WHOLE OF Emerald Level had been sealed off, per Prestina's instructions.

Prett found this out the hard way. Stumbling up the stairs at the end of Annelle's disaster of a ball, hoping that Kaedrich had eventually found Praxis—did Prett even really know why he was seeking them out? His thoughts were so muddied by that point it was impossible to tell. When he hadn't had any luck tracking Praxis down in the household, he'd indeed retreated back to the party where he'd left her, only to discover that she'd left when she said she would. Prett had every intention of making the trek home, *again*, but suddenly the prospect had just seemed so exhausting. And really, what was waiting for him there? Kaedrich's worried face, which Prett had inadvertently helped create. Praxis, making her situation worse for herself. Annelle . . .

It was better not to think of Annelle at all. At the party, Prett's guilt had overwhelmed him. He'd collapsed on a couch, accepting the first offering on hand. By the time he'd stumbled back home, hours later, the coming-of-age ball was nearly finished, only the last and most desperate stragglers remaining. Annelle herself, so the word went, had gone to bed ages ago, upset about something she wouldn't discuss. There was nothing he could do to fix that, but he could at least find out what had happened with Praxis. And so, with the bright blue jacket of his suit tied around his neck as a crude cape, he'd dragged himself up the layers of the Fellows household. His thoughts were swirling, his hair was falling in his eyes, and cold snaked down the front of his shirt from when he'd tried to button it back up, somewhere in the haze of the party, and apparently failed. Who knows what had happened to his undershirts.

At Emerald Level, he'd run into the block of his nephew. Micadel's broad shoulders, solid as a boulder, and his strong arm extended in a "that's far enough" posture. His palm against Prett's chest felt as large as the front plate of a suit of armor. This is when the first wave of dread had washed over Prett, and this is when he knew that he *had* to find out what was going on.

"I'm sorry, Uncle," Micadel had said, sounding sincere. "But Grandmother's orders were as clear as diamond."

But Prett was a lawyer by trade, and if there's one thing a Yandosian lawyer is excellent at, it's adhering *just barely* to the letter of the law. Even in his addled state, it took only two minutes of grilling poor Micadel for Prett to establish exactly where the young guard was going to draw the perimeter; and so Prett had walked back over to the staircase and sat down on the top step, like a child waiting for the Star Fairy on Millions Eve. Though what, precisely, he was waiting for now, even Prett could not say. All he knew for certain, right then, is that something terrible had happened, in the time since he'd left Kaedrich and now.

Prett worked the knot of his suit jacket free, drawing it away from his neck and sliding his arms back into the tangled sleeves. On some level, perhaps, he already knew he'd be there a while. His thoughts were every bit as much of a mess as his hair, which he ran his hands through now, trying to sort this out. It seemed unlikely that something as dramatic as a *fight* could have taken place—surely, something that ripe for gossip, the household would be crackling with the news. And the order had apparently come from *Prestina*, not Praxis, so it couldn't have been something Praxis had asked for. So . . . what, was she *sealed in*? Was the guard and the order not so much to prevent other people from getting to Praxis, as it was to prevent Praxis from leaving? But no, Prett shook his head, because the idea of Praxis being contained against her will was incomprehensible. What exactly was Micadel, or any of them really, supposed to do if Praxis wanted to get through?

Unless there was something wrong with her magic. This idea occurred to Prett a few hours later, after his thoughts had paced in endless circles. It struck Prett like a punch to the throat, so hard that he nearly lost his breath. Prett didn't pretend to understand how magic worked—all he knew of it were the legal implications of being born a wizard. He didn't know if it was like a muscle or an organ, something that could be weakened, damaged—killed.

It was around this point he'd bent over, putting his head between his knees and gripping his scalp. He took deep, cold breaths. He dry heaved a little, panicked a little. Got to his feet and paced up and down the first length of stairs, running his hands through his hair so much that it began to stand on end.

And then he thought about the vial, the one Lexthur had given him.

He didn't want to. The instant the thought first appeared in Prett's mind, he had banished it. But it kept slipping back in, like whispers he couldn't block out. The sight of it, how it had seemed to have a sheen not quite normal; and how Prett had pushed *that* thought from his mind, too, as soon as he'd seen it. *Nope,* he'd told himself, not so much a word as a feeling. *Nope,* and he pocketed the vial as if nothing was amiss. *Nope,* and he turned away to dress for the party. *Nope,* and he carried it all the way through Bolt, the vial heavy in his pocket—was it actually any heavier, Prett thought now, or did it just *feel* that way, like he already knew something was wrong, and didn't want to admit it to himself?

He admitted it to himself now, finally, almost an hour after he'd first thought of it and then not-thought of it. The vial had been *wrong*. Lexthur's expression as he'd handed it over had been *wrong*. All of it had been *wrong*, in a way Prett purposefully didn't see. The most wrong of all: that he'd handed it over to his baby sister without a second thought.

She should have checked it, he thought, and then immediately hated himself for thinking it. Guilt broke out like sweat, hot and prickly, and Prett tried to shake it off like an itch. Why would she have? It was supposed to be top grade. Prett had promised so himself.

"Prett?"

Prett whipped his head up. For one glorious, delirious moment, he'd thought he'd been saved, that Praxis was up and fine, that she'd called out to him, that she was here to forgive him. But when his eyes found their focus, it wasn't his sister's face that they settled upon.

It was his mother.

Habit made him scramble to his feet. He smoothed out his hair, tugged his suit back into order. His face was already rapidly contorting itself back into some semblance of control, muscles nearly wrenching themselves in their hurry to appear collected.

"Mother."

Prestina regarded him warily. So she was not going to pretend she hadn't seen. A maid stood sentry beside her, a breakfast tray prepared. Prett started at the sight of it—depths help him, how long had he been sitting there? Prestina motioned for the maid to continue, and Prett watched with annoyance as Micadel moved aside for her.

"What are you doing here?" Prestina asked, after the maid had disappeared. The question was not accusatory, which was a surprise, but not an entirely pleasant one.

"I . . . ," Prett started as he turned back to his mother. Words failed him. Should he admit he was worried? Or would it be better to try to make some excuse, which Prestina would inevitably not believe, but hopefully would pretend that she did?

Prestina's brow crinkled in, as if sensing his thoughts. "Your sister is fine, if that's your concern. She merely needs a little rest."

"Rest."

"Yes. I thought it was best she remained undisturbed."

"I see."

"In the meantime, you should return to your job," Prestina said. She'd folded her hands in front of her, the picture of collected control. "The oversight committee is going to be starting its final deliberations today, and we need you ready to defend us against an unjust ruling."

Prett's face twitched. "Yes, Mother."

She stepped aside.

He eased past her, down the first several steps. A minor indent had been left in the top one, warmed and slightly melted from his having parked himself there for hours. He was sure Prestina had noticed, though he did not explicitly see her attention flick in its direction.

"Oh, Prett," Prestina called after him, just as he'd reached the first landing.

Prett turned, as sure as a marionette. "Yes, Mother?"

"A legal question for you," she said, waving her hand as if it didn't matter. "A minor point of clarification. Tannem has fallen temporarily ill, and there's concern that Prewish may wish to withdraw his name from consideration. He seems to think that, as his father, he's been granted legal claim over Tannem's bid, since he's currently unable to vouch for himself. Is this a concern?"

"Is Tannem okay?"

"Oh, absolutely." Prestina smiled. "It's nothing he won't be over soon enough. But in the meantime, well, I'm sure you can understand the worry. People do all sorts of desperate things, when time is running out."

Prett frowned. "Yes, um . . . hang on, give me a second." He shook his head, trying to sort out his thoughts after all the emotional back-and-forth he'd been subjected to since last night. "Well . . . of course it all depends, I suppose, on how incapacitated he is. Because it's true that even once a child comes of age, his parents are still able to act for him if he's unable to do so himself. I mean . . . Previn . . ."

"Yes," Prestina said, looking solemn.

"But . . . if he's going to be fine that easily, I don't imagine there's much cause for concern. Especially because, if challenged, Tannem can always claim his father had a conflicting interest."

"I see. But it *could* still happen."

"It . . . could, I guess, sure."

Prestina nodded. "Thank you, Prett. That will be all."

"If you'd like, I could talk to Prewish," Prett said. "I mean, I know he's determined to win the bid himself, but even so—"

"That won't be necessary."

"Are you sure? It's no trouble."

"I said it's fine."

Prett's mouth set into a hard line. "You weren't asking because of Tannem," he said. It wasn't a question.

Prestina raised a single eyebrow. "Excuse me?"

"What did you do?" Prett charged up the stairs, stopping just in front of his mother. He was breathing hard, suddenly, rage and worry heaving fast in his chest.

But Prestina did not react to his outburst. In fact, not the slightest trace of surprise was etched into her ice face. She maintained steady eye contact with her son, her voice never once wavering, as she said, "You should know better than most, Prett, to be careful about throwing accusations around when you have no proof."

"I don't care. Mother, I swear it, if I find out that you had one single thing to do with this—"

"You would say nothing," Prestina said.

"Don't be so sure of that."

"Oh, but I am. You see . . . *I'm* not technically the one that did any-thing. Assuming that something was done in the first place."

"What?" Prett asked, but then the truth slammed down in his mind like an iron door clanging shut. He reached out, steadying himself against the wall. "Oh, stars," he muttered.

He remembered the vial again, the sense of wrongness that he'd just *ignored*. He did not know exactly how or why Prestina was in collabora-tion with Lexthur, but one thing was clear: Prett had just been played, as expertly as Prawl dealt a hand in Fiddler's Dash.

"Mother, how . . . how could you? She's your *daughter*."

Prestina smiled. "It's a funny thing, isn't it? Motherhood. You know, there's a species of bat that lives in the south of the Syll peninsula, I believe, where the females cannot reproduce if they've eaten a particular beetle that lives all over that part of the world. It's almost impossible to avoid. So what these bats do, is they select the strongest stock of their daughters to stay in the colony and be the breeders of the next generation. Of course, you can't *make* a bat stay put—which is why the mothers quite literally eat the wings off of their chosen daughters, to keep them where they'd most benefit the colony. Can you imagine? The biggest and strongest offspring, and their mothers have to cripple them to save their lives."

"Praxis isn't a *bat*!"

"Good thing, too," Prestina said. She started off down the stairs, paus-ing beside Prett for only a moment. "Can you imagine how stringy a wing must be?"

Chapter Thirty-Five

$\mathcal{W}$HEN THE ATTACK came—as it must, for make no mistake, the battle lines had already been drawn, the soldiers armed, the generals prepped and ready on both sides—it began as Tol expected: it began with a smile.

It had only been a day, not even, but Tol was ready. When the aide came for him, smiling and disarming, sorry to disturb you sir, beg your forgiveness sir, it's just that the Pon wishes to see you sir, Tol did not even hesitate. He returned the young man's expression in kind. Probably, the aide did not even realize what he'd been sent to do; probably, he was chosen simply for his gentle nature, his friendly mien. It was a quality not many of Lanali's staff possessed, and briefly Tol wondered how long she had searched to find just the right face. He imagined her cataloging them, possibly for weeks, this moment looming larger and larger on the horizon.

The aide shifted his body, arm outstretched to indicate the direction he wished to guide Tol, torso just the slightest bit tilted in deference. Tol brushed past, the wide hall of the palace stretching out before him. He'd been found in a small alcove, at a window that overlooked the garden. The window started low and ended high; the sill somewhere near the waist of an average Durn, the arched top towering well over their heads. Tol had rested his arm comfortably across the sill, affecting a dreamy air of contemplation as the aide had approached him.

Well, he had been wrapped up in thought, but it was not the sort of moony-eyed fancies he'd been portraying. Tol had been going over his plans in his mind, checking the lines of them for any knots or faults. He always found some—no matter how well he'd set things up, no matter how many outcomes he planned for, there were always places where a plan might fall apart—but the weave of this one was strong, at least. He was comfortable leaping into it, confident as much as he could be that it would catch him on the way down.

He would find out soon enough.

They moved at a sedate pace, but steady, like the ticking of a metronome. Every step of this act had been scripted, every breath accounted for. Twice over, in fact. He knew that she knew that he knew. She probably suspected. The only thing left in play was which one of them had outmaneuvered the other, out-anticipated the other. Which of their traps were meant to be traps, and which were meant to be seen and avoided, thus leading to further traps? In his mind—and no doubt hers—there were plans layered upon plans, contingencies for every conceivable outcome. If she struck first, if he attacked from the left; if it happened in the courtyards, or the kitchens, or his bedroom; if he went with magic, if she went with bullets. The only thing neither of them considered was to let the matter lie. Concealed on Tol's person, right at that moment, he had: three knives, two pistols, one rope (coiled around his leg), an old-fashioned water skein filled with lamp oil, a vial of poison, and a dead rat.

At the end of the next hall, they turned right. Tol allowed himself one momentary smile as the walls narrowed in around them, and a cold prickle on the back of his neck indicated they'd reached the outer field of a magic suppressor. A servants' passage, devoid of windows, minimal doors through which to escape.

So she'd be going with brute force, then. Tol had to admit, he was vaguely disappointed.

The click of a door opening did not reach them until they were halfway down the servants' passage, but it was not that sound which truly broke the illusion of peace: the crack of a bullet, bursting through so fast that it was easy to misremember, and think it had been fired before the door was even open.

It hadn't, of course. Tol heard one, and then the other, two distinct and separate sounds that, while linked with the ribbon of Lanali's betrayal like a fine bow on a precious gift, were not in fact the same. By the time the second had begun, Tol had already ducked and so the bullet, blissfully unaware that its target had moved, continued along until it met with the back of the man sent to fetch Tol. A bloom of red erupted from the man's chest, the force of its expulsion knocking him backward, and Tol was already waiting, ready to catch his weight. Tol let him collapse across his own back, the shocked, parted lips of the man's dying breath sliding into view as Tol grunted beneath the brunt of his weight.

No time for sentiment. Even as the man's life slipped from him, Tol dragged himself to his feet. More bullets peppered the air now, a vicious swarm that stung at the corpse across Tol's back. He was already reaching into his jacket pocket, already retrieving the water skein, already popping open the cork. With a deft flick of his arm, the skein was in the air.

He ducked his head, shielding himself, so he did not see what happened as it happened. He knew only the splash of lamp oil on the tiles, the billow of heat as the skein exploded above his head, the lick of flame that raced down the lengths of oil trailing to the floor. One bullet, one spark, was all it took to turn the servants' passage into an inferno.

Tol barely heard the shouts of alarm, over the crackle and spit of the fires around him. Hauling the corpse up, still slung over his back, Tol raced for the end of the passage as well as he was able. He knew that guards would have been positioned at both ends, and so it did not really matter which direction he ran in; he chose based on the fires, based on the weight on his back, based on his whims. Heat chewed down from above, and Tol knew the corpse had been set on fire as well, and so once he drew near enough, he stopped and hurtled the body at the end of the passage.

The guards posted there scattered, like rats exposed in the wall, and Tol slid easily into the chaos.

PRAXIS SLEPT STRAIGHT through that night. Kaedrich stayed in their chambers, watching over her. Not that there was anything to *do*, except to wait. Praxis wasn't sick, Kaedrich kept reminding herself—just asleep. Her breathing was normal by now, her temperature was normal. When Kaedrich nudged her, Praxis half roused, her speech thick and groggy. She would be fine, at least for now, but Kaedrich watched over her just the same. When Prestina offered to stay for a while longer, Kaedrich refused. When someone tried to ask her if she was hungry, Kaedrich ordered a tray in. If anyone was asking questions about where they were, why they utterly refused to leave the room, Kaedrich didn't hear them. A bubble of untouchability had fallen upon them, and though Kaedrich did not have direct confirmation of this, she knew on some level that it had to be Prestina's doing. The only person so much as allowed at their door was a single Yandosian maid, older and quieter, her eyes never once straying inside for a nosy peek at what might be there to see.

So Kaedrich waited. She ate the dinner sent up to her, and when the hour finally drew late she put a chair underneath the knob of their already locked door, changed into her pajamas, and curled up to Praxis's back like this was any other night.

When she woke up, Praxis was still asleep. Kaedrich bathed, dressed, ran her hand across Praxis's forehead. She collected the breakfast tray that had been left outside of her door. Read the note tucked underneath her plate. Kaedrich had on her best suit, one that Prawl had chosen, that he said "fit" her more than the others. It had an unusual cut, for Yandosian style, with a vest and shorter jacket that was reminiscent of Durlish culture. Kaedrich pulled a chair over from the sitting room, and in this manner she waited.

She was still waiting a few hours later, when Praxis finally woke up. The process took several minutes, with Praxis blinking and rubbing the sleep out of her eyes. Once or twice, it looked like she might fall under again, her eyelids fluttering shut, but finally they opened and stayed open. Her gaze fell upon Kaedrich, still and silent in her chair.

"Ella."

Her voice was creaky. Praxis cleared her throat, reached for a glass of water that Kaedrich had left beside the bed. She sat up, the blankets shifting around her. She rubbed at her forehead, as if trying to piece together the circumstances that had led her to this time and place.

When Praxis stilled, this is when Kaedrich knew she'd remembered.

Her hand lowered. Her gaze followed them, as if her nails were suddenly the most interesting thing in the world.

"It's not what you think," Praxis said.

"You really have no idea what I think about it, love," Kaedrich said. She held up the note she'd received with breakfast, pinched between her middle and forefinger. "But believe it or not, that isn't the most pressing issue we have to discuss. Your father's plan has failed. The inheritance is going through whether he likes it or not, and the Minor Conclave has accelerated the timetable. They want to make their decision by the day after tomorrow, so they need *all* bids in today."

A puzzled frown creased Praxis's forehead. "That's . . . unfortunate, but I don't see what it has to do with—"

"When were you going to tell me that Lexthur proposed?"

Silence fell. Praxis closed her mouth, the rest of her sentence apparently forgotten.

"You weren't *going* to tell me," Kaedrich said as she tucked the note away into her breast pocket. "Were you?"

"It didn't seem relevant, considering I would never accept him. And anyway, I . . . I didn't want you to misunderstand."

"In other words, you didn't trust me."

"*No,*" Praxis said. *Now* her attention finally snapped up, locking straight on Kaedrich's face. "No, that's not it. It's just . . . Yandosians—"

"Yeah, I get it. You treat marriage differently than I do. I'm not an idiot, Praxis." Kaedrich smoothed out her already-smooth pants, and drew herself up straight in her chair. She folded her hands across her lap. "So then let's talk like Yandosians. You should do it."

Nothing Kaedrich could have said would have dumbfounded Praxis more than this. Kaedrich could read it in her face: naked shock, the kind of blank-eyed stare that happens when someone is presented with an idea so completely unfathomable that a part of their brain just shuts down, rather than accept the reality in front of them. Praxis's lips parted, a tiny bubble of saliva forming and bursting as they did.

At several different times, Praxis attempted speech. All her early efforts failed, crashing against the shores of her disbelief. When she did finally manage it, all she said was, "You can't be serious."

"I'm dead serious," Kaedrich said. She watched as Praxis flinched at the expression. Kaedrich continued before Praxis could protest. "I had an interesting chat with Lexthur last night, and he laid out the whole thing for me. Even *I* can see the power of the bid you two would make. You'd win. You have to know that."

Praxis pushed herself still farther up the bed. She ran her hands through her hair, already standing up on end. "I can't believe I'm hearing this from you."

"Then maybe you don't yet know me quite as well as you think you do. I'm *realistic*, Praxis."

Praxis laughed under her breath. "No you're not. You're the single most optimistic person I've ever met."

"Not about everything."

"Oh, I see," Praxis said, her voice turning into a cold snap. "So for the safety of Durland, you're willing to whore me out to the highest bidder, is that it?"

Kaedrich paused. "Huh? I don't—What does Durland have to do with any of this?"

"The funding . . . ," Praxis said. She frowned. "Didn't you say you'd spoken to Lexthur?"

"Yeah . . ."

"But . . . if he didn't tell you about my plan, then why—?"

"This has nothing to do with Durland. I'm thinking about *you*."

"Me?"

"Yes, Praxis. Someone has to, since you apparently refuse to do so for yourself. Do you have any idea what an amazing opportunity this is for you? What you'd be able to *do*, with this kind of power? You'd never have to worry about the future again."

"I don't worry about it now."

Kaedrich laughed bitterly under her breath. "Yeah, I know."

"Okay, now what's *that* supposed to mean?"

The answer that Kaedrich gave her wasn't verbal. It didn't need to be. Kaedrich just *looked* at Praxis, and while she did, she remembered the terror that had filled her when Praxis had been lying there. Praxis hadn't been worrying about the future yesterday, when she'd allowed herself to overadminister a drug that she shouldn't have been using in the first place. She hadn't been thinking about the risks. Hadn't been thinking about what it would do to *Kaedrich*, if the worst should happen.

Kaedrich held her look—heavy, angry, accusing—until Praxis broke eye contact. Praxis squirmed in her bed, like a child caught stealing sweets.

"I didn't . . . ," Praxis started, then fell short. She took a breath, trying again. "It was a mistake, all right? I must have measured out more than I intended. But I didn't mean to—"

"Didn't mean to *what*?" Kaedrich snapped. "Didn't mean to lie to me? Again?"

"I didn't *lie*."

"You didn't tell me the truth."

"I didn't tell you *anything*."

"Yeah," Kaedrich said. "I know."

She did not even try to keep the hurt out of her voice.

Praxis shrank down, slumping deeper into the mattress. She didn't look at Kaedrich; instead, she leaned her head back to look at the intricate scrollwork of lapus lumeni threads woven into the ceiling of ice. Her lips were pressed together with the weight of things not said.

"Do you have any idea what I went through, finding you like that?"

Praxis shut her eyes. "Yes," she whispered.

"You scared the hell out of me, Praxis."

"I'm sorry," Praxis said. She turned her head, looking directly at Kaedrich. Just two words, but not ones that Praxis was experienced in saying with any great sincerity. She reached out and Kaedrich, somewhat reluctantly, leaned forward and took Praxis's hand. "Ella . . . I'm sorry."

"I know you are," Kaedrich said. "And I appreciate it. But, love . . . that doesn't magically make everything better."

Praxis cringed. "I know."

Kaedrich sighed. She turned Praxis's hand over in her own, and absently began to trace the lines across Praxis's palm. Just beyond it, the irritation of Praxis's scar stood out, angry red against the shock-white of her wrist. It looked even worse in the icy light of Yandosia. Everything, Kaedrich thought, looked worse in Yandosia. She remembered how she'd tried to argue that they should leave; the desperation in her voice, the longing for home. She still felt it—a tug, just behind her heart, drawing her away from here. She *had* to leave, *had* to return and fight for the restoration of her homeland, she knew that, but . . . things were more complicated now.

Kaedrich tried to steel herself, but there was no good way to do this. She kept her gaze lowered, speaking more to Praxis's palm than anything as she said, "You're going to have to stay in Yandosia."

A cold silence slid into the room. Though Praxis hadn't exactly been *moving*, a more absolute sense of stillness settled across her. Kaedrich knew without even looking up that Praxis's face would have hardened over as she tried to clamp down on her fear and uncertainty.

"What . . . ?" Praxis started. She stopped, took a breath. Started again. "What are you saying?"

"We brought in a doctor while you were . . . unconscious. The poison in your knee has begun to reassert itself."

"That's not possible." Her words were confident, though her tone was not. "Brex—"

"He filtered out the poison at the time," Kaedrich said. "But apparently a drop or two had nestled into your bone, and it's been building ever since. The doctor—the doctor said they could remove the source of the poison, but that enough of it has seeped out already that . . . you'll have to stay here. The cold will keep it from taking hold in your bloodstream."

Kaedrich gave Praxis a minute or two to process this. She knew from experience that it was a lot to take in; Kaedrich had been living with it all night, and she still hadn't accepted it, not really. She kept expecting something to happen, someone to step in and laugh and shake their head, explain that there had been some terrible mistake, *so* sorry to worry you like that, of course everything is *fine* . . .

Everything wasn't fine.

Praxis's hands slid from Kaedrich's grip. Kaedrich stared down at her own empty palms, the pink looking sickly underneath the light of the lapus lumeni, the brown lines dull and chalky—she pulled them back into her own lap, folding them neatly.

"What *exactly* does that mean, they can 'remove the source' of the poison?" Praxis asked.

Kaedrich's voice was small as she said, "They'll try to leave as much of the leg as they can."

A startled cry escaped Praxis before she could stop herself. She clamped her hand over her mouth, but too late.

Kaedrich made herself look up, though Praxis was turned away from her. She was holding herself back, curling into the pillows, as if trying to make herself small enough to disappear. Kaedrich got up, shifting from chair to mattress. She reached out, drawing Praxis away from the pillows, drawing her near until Kaedrich could wrap both of her arms tightly around Praxis's back. Praxis's face buried itself in the warm crook of Kaedrich's neck, her hands clutching in desperation at Kaedrich's shirt.

"Shh," Kaedrich said, though Praxis wasn't even trying to talk. She rubbed Praxis's back, smoothed down Praxis's hair. "I know. I know."

She gave Praxis the moment. Just held her, whispered reassuring nothings—*I love you*s, and *I'm here*s.

Then she pulled back. Then she brushed Praxis's hair off of her forehead. Then she tipped Praxis's chin up, making sure they were on the same level.

"But don't you see, love? That's why you *need* to do this. I can't provide for you here—you know I can't."

"I never asked you to."

"Not in so many words, no," Kaedrich said, a sad smile playing at her lips. "But honestly, Praxis . . . who do you think is going to keep you housed and fed, when your family's money dries up?"

Praxis scowled. "It's not going to—"

"It *is*. One way or another, it is." Kaedrich paused, long enough to draw Praxis's knuckles up for a kiss. "I know you don't want to hear this, but *someone* is going to take over the company soon. Do you really think any of your brothers are going to keep throwing money at your reckless whims? You've been protected all of your life, but the party's ending. Soon you'll be on your own."

"I can work, you know. In Durland—"

"You flounced around with magic, because you needed to be backed by a patron in order to have anyone take your work seriously. It was never about the money. You know it wasn't."

"So?" Praxis said. "The point is that I can do it."

"I know you can. Which is why you need to take over the company. Why settle?" Kaedrich said, talking over Praxis's sharp intake of breath. "Why bother doing *anything* else, when you can shape the *Fellows empire* into whatever you want it to be? Praxis . . . you're not going to be happy doing anything less than grand."

Praxis's face screwed up in discontent. Kaedrich could see the need to argue, dancing somewhere behind the scowl, but for once Praxis was holding it back. Considering what she was going to say, chewing on her thoughts . . . thinking about what Kaedrich had said.

Under any other circumstances, this huge step forward in personal growth would be a cause for pride and celebration. Instead, a heavy sadness draped over Kaedrich—this was exactly the kind of skill that Praxis was going to need to cultivate as head of the company.

"What about you?"

It was the question Kaedrich was hoping Praxis wouldn't ask. Kaedrich forced herself to smile, though it cut her as sharp as a knife.

"I'll be fine."

Fine.

Such an innocent word, for such a deadly concept. Kaedrich could feel the jaws of it closing around her, even now. *Fine.* Trapped in Yandosia for the rest of her life, whittling away her years. Never achieving anything. Unable to help her homeland, even now, in the midst of such crisis.

She couldn't do it. Kaedrich knew this, deep in her heart. But it was what Praxis needed to hear, and if there was one thing Kaedrich had learned from her, it was to lie with a smile. So there it was.

Was this it, then? Their hands were tangled together above the fur blankets, their grip so tight that their knuckles were turning white. Had the decision been made? It seemed impossible, and yet . . . what was the point in denying it? Their fates were sealed, probably had been since the moment they'd set foot on the ice.

All they had to do now was live with it.

LATER—AND EVEN DURING, if there was time to think at all—they would ask the same questions: How had he done it? Where had he slipped by? Why hadn't they seen?

The consensus was magic, for surely it was not error. Lanali had sent only the best, or so she'd said, though the best did sometimes stop to wonder, looking at their ranks, if they hadn't also been lumped in with the second- and sometimes maybe even third-best, if they were being honest, I mean, just look at some of them, and though they would never know it, it turns out they'd been right. But still: decent enough fellows, each of them, and skilled and sharp. And the man—so distinct in appearance, yes, sure he was small, but not small enough to fall through cracks and slip between fingers, not *really*. So where had he gone? How in the world was such a feat possible? Of course it was by magic. It had to be. That terrible, devious, trickster sham. It was no wonder there was talk of banning it outright. Such measures were only reasonable.

In truth, it was a kind of magic, if magic is the means by which our eyes deceive us, by which the world fails to live up to how it Should Be. Which isn't the world's fault, really, when you stop to think about it, or at least that's what Tol believed. The world had been here far longer than him, than anyone. Why should it obey our ideals?

So this is how it was done: all throughout the palace that day, there had been a pair of servants carrying a painting. An ordinary enough painting, a portrait of a long-dead king and his long-dead dog, but quite large; when carried, it hovered inches from the floor, and still cleared the top of their heads. Why were they carrying it? No one bothered to ask. It was assumed, as only made sense to assume, that they had their reasons.

They'd been wandering and listening all day, and so it was easy to determine when and where the attack would take place. As the first shots fired, the first screams rippling out through the corridors, they were carrying the painting down a set of stairs. White stone all around, the wide outer curve of a wall to their backs, they left plenty of room beside them for people to run by. Backup was already on the move, and the two men carrying the painting paused on a landing to let them pass.

It was in this moment, shuffling to the side, that Tol slipped in behind them, pressed between the canvas and the wall. How he made it that far was all his own luck, though stealth had been his friend for years now, and it helped that he wore the same color as so many of the palace walls. Guards were still passing by and, with the ease of further moving out of the way, one of the men handed his half of the painting to Tol's waiting hands. That man then slipped into the crowds—unnoticed, as servants so often are.

The crowd behind them, the painting set off again, down the wide steps. And in a world that works the way it should, someone would have noticed the change immediately. Tol and the servant looked nothing alike, after all, neither in height nor build nor color nor personal style. The fraud was there for anyone to see, but that was the whole point. They were not looking where they could see. Tol had learned this trick, years ago, on the scattered islands of Aul. The painting caught the eye, the imposing look of the king, the humble servitude of his dog. The ostentation of the gilt framing. Few people, if any, stopped to look at the hands that held it, and so Tol kept his head down, his body in shadow of the massive frame towering over him, and he walked right past the soldiers and guards, the ones shouting, *Where had he gone, how could he have escaped, he had to be here somewhere. It must be magic.*

THE PHONOGRAPH HAD run its course.

It sat on Previn's shelf, filling the room with a low hiss, the *thip, thip, thip* of the needle bouncing on nothing. If the wax recordings trapped in music, then what was this, Previn was sometimes forced to wonder. Could this be the true sound of silence?

Unless the explanation was a lie. They did that to him sometimes, as if they thought he wouldn't notice. Told him stories that made no sense, hand-waving away his unspoken questions, ignoring the curiosity in his eyes. Or else they did not bother to explain at all. Why waste their time, they told themselves—sometimes right in front of him, sometimes *right to his face*—when he'd never possibly be able to understand anyway?

The only time they really talked to him was when they were talking about themselves. Sometimes, Previn felt like the mirror that hung in his bathroom: something to be stared at as they sorted themselves out. Previn often stared at himself in that mirror as he waited for his nurse to finish prepping his clothes, or drying his tub, or laying out his bed. He knew he wasn't like the rest of them, that his body couldn't move like theirs, that his voice couldn't work like theirs. He saw them standing, laughing, chatting, but when he tried to do it himself, he faltered. But his mind . . .

His mind was another story.

All his life, Previn had been listening. Listening to the stories they read him, and the conversations they had among themselves as if he wasn't even there. Listening to the music they played, listening to the voices that carried themselves down the halls and into his room. Prenna made a habit of sitting beside him as she read him books, showing him the pictures on the pages, but it wasn't the colorful illustrations that always drew his eye. He listened to her voice, the familiar words as she described the antics of friendly penguins and seals and snow weasels, and he watched as repeating shapes beneath the drawings seemed to follow the rhythm of her story.

He knew right away that there was a pattern to it, even if it took him *years* before he finally broke it, before his eyes could dance ahead and fill in the ending before Prenna said it.

He listened. To their lives, to their troubles. To their games. He listened to Prewish's description of the mines, and Prommel's tales of heroics in the sparring ring, and Praxis's endless complaints. He listened the year Prett became obsessed with an invention called a telegraph machine, to all the seemingly endless list of countries Prett wanted to communicate with now, that he wanted to visit when he grew up. He listened to the news that his sister was gone, that she might be dead, and he listened to the drama of his growing family as they married, had children, as those children married. He listened to the glorious news of Praxis's return, though by the time anyone thought to tell him, she'd already startled him by bursting in and rushing out again.

And he listened now, his blood growing cold, to a tale he almost couldn't bring himself to believe. Only the red-rimmed eyes across from him, normally so controlled, normally so sure, managed to convince Previn of the truth of the words he was hearing. Murder and magic and regret. The need for absolution, the plea on the voice Previn didn't want to hear anymore, couldn't bear to listen to now. He supposed he shouldn't have been surprised, not really, given who it was coming from, and yet he was. He was. When a kiss landed on Previn's head, a goodbye in Previn's ears, Previn knew something terrible was going to happen next. He hadn't been told it, but he knew. He was always listening.

If only someone would ever listen to *him*.

Chapter Thirty-Six

THE NEXT STEP was magic by halves.

In one half of the palace: Tol, uncoiling the rope from around his leg, one eye glancing out the window beside him as he judged distance, visibility, wind conditions. In the other: a visiting group of diplomats from a country across the westward sea, a dead rat hidden in the giant sweep of their plumed hats.

The rat had been slipped in by the same man that Tol had carried the painting down with. They'd parted company on the main floor, in a corner isolated from the chaos. The man had held out his hand, expecting payment perhaps, and Tol had slipped the rat, wrapped in burlap, into his waiting palm instead.

Money came next, of course, money always had to come next. The rat, then, was carried with ease, unnoticed, until the man could deposit it somewhere about their person. "Be very careful," Tol had warned him, voice low and serious. "Do not drop it." And perhaps the man had thought this absurd, but if he did, he at least had the decency to neither show it, nor act upon his disbelief, for he handled the rat with all the care one would normally show a newborn kitten.

Later, when he heard about everything that happened, he would be grateful he had. And would vow to never dismiss anything Tol told him ever again.

What was there to say? Tol needed a distraction, and the visitors had given him one. He had not, as Lanali would probably suspect, arranged for their visit himself—he was not *quite* that forward-thinking. But he'd be damned into the mud if he did not act upon such a ripe opportunity as this. He secured his rope. The doors to the room he was in were sealed by magic and thus, safe for the moment, he waited, and listened. He knew that he would not hear the shriek of alarm as the rat was found on the dignitary. But he would hear the explosion as the rat, yanked from the ensuing hysterics and thrown aside, struck the nearest wall.

The rumble of the palace reached his feet on schedule. Tol smiled to himself. Praxis had called her work a "delayed combustion hex," and Tol had found it, the half-finished notes she'd been working on in the days leading up to her exile from Monfort, what felt like a lifetime ago. Tol had since used it against her once or twice, and quite enjoyed the magic that it took to put it together; how ironic, then, to rely on it now as their enemy became one.

It was not difficult, next, to slip through the window, scale the wall. Chaos reigned in the palace, the guards scattered and divided. They were looking for Tol, they were racing for the source of the explosion, they were struggling to understand how one was not, automatically, the other. By the time enough of them realized the explosion must have been a diversion, Tol's feet were already touching the ground.

THERE WASN'T MUCH time, but Praxis couldn't bring herself to hurry.

Kaedrich was hurrying. She'd gathered up the pieces of Praxis's leg brace and strapped them onto her with mechanical efficiency, her face as cold as the ice around them. Her only words were brisk, professional. "Lift." "Here." "Is that too tight?" "Turn." "Ready?"

Ready?

The idea of being ready was laughable, though Praxis did not laugh. She may never laugh again. Laughter was a thing that belonged with Kaedrich, that existed in the tiny pocket of her life where she'd lived on a ship and there was nothing to do but lie there together, their fingers tracing the lines of each other's faces, sloppy grins dancing between them.

Praxis tore herself away from the memory. She could not even bring herself to look at Kaedrich now, even as Kaedrich helped her up, even as Kaedrich stood there for a moment, making sure Praxis was steady, that she could manage the workings of her own two feet, the complicated mechanism required to make them both work.

This isn't the end, Kaedrich had said, in that damned steady voice of hers. The words had floated around Praxis, untethered by a sense of time or place or purpose. They might have been talking for hours, days, years. They might have been talking for only a few minutes. *Things don't need to change between us.*

It was a nice lie. Probably, Kaedrich even believed it. Praxis would believe it, too—she had to, if she was going to survive the trip into Bolt, if she was going to manage the terrible conversations ahead of her. That didn't make it true. Oh, they would try, of course they would try. Making the best of terrible circumstances was one of Kaedrich's specialties, and Praxis, well . . . Praxis was a survivor.

Surviving is easy, Praxis, she heard her mother say. *Surviving is small.*

"Praxis!"

Prett's voice chased her down the hall, greeting her far sooner than he did. Praxis could see him, restrained by Micadel just at the top of the staircase. A bruise was blooming angry red across Prett's jaw.

"What's going on here?" Praxis demanded as she approached. Gods, look at her: already, she was becoming her mother.

Prett made one more attempt to jerk free of Micadel's grip. "Can't you see that—?"

"Uncle, don't make me hit you again."

"It's all right," Praxis said, though by that point she'd already reached them. She exchanged a curious glance with Micadel, who straightened up underneath her gaze.

"Ma'am," Micadel said, tapping his lips. "Forgive us, but I have orders to—"

Praxis waved off his concern. "It's fine. You can leave us now, though. I'd like to talk to my brother."

Micadel nodded. "Ma'am." He tapped his lips again, as if Praxis was already in charge, and then marched off down the stairs.

Prett watched the whole exchange with a wary gaze. "Praxis . . . ?"

"It's fine," Praxis said. "What did you need?"

Beside her, Kaedrich cleared her throat. "Praxis, we don't have a lot of time."

"Then he can come with me," Praxis said. "And we'll talk on the way."

She didn't look at Kaedrich as she said it. She couldn't. They'd both agreed that if Praxis was going to do this (and she still couldn't believe she was going to do this), then she wasn't bringing Kaedrich with her. Kaedrich hadn't been happy when Praxis first said it—insisted upon it, in fact—but that was, ultimately, the bargain: if Kaedrich really wanted Praxis to do this, then Praxis was going to do it alone.

Despite the rush, there was the slightest hesitation from Kaedrich.

Praxis turned. "Unless you want to call the whole thing off?"

It was an open challenge, and they both knew it. *How committed are you, Kaedrich? There's still time...*

"No," Kaedrich said with a grimace. She gave Praxis a quick, professional kiss, and then started off down the stairs after Micadel. Alone.

"Okay," Prett said, "exactly what the *hells* is going on here?"

Praxis shook her head. "Nothing. Come on."

She clicked her thumb, started to step forward—but Prett's grip wrapped tightly around her wrist, just enough to halt the mechanisms. The tension jerked Praxis's foot up and sideways as a flare of irritation coursed through her.

"Let go of me!"

"Not if you're about to do what I think you are," Prett said.

"What I do is none of your business."

Praxis twisted her arm, up and around the way Prommel had once taught her as a maneuver to free herself. Prett's grip tightened and fell away, though he snatched it right back up again, harder this time. He held it there, near her face, as he took a threatening step forward.

"Praxis, listen to me: you don't know what you're doing."

Praxis rolled her eyes. "Is that brotherly concern?"

"It's the truth."

"I'm fine," Praxis said.

Gods, the last thing she wanted to do right now was stand here and defend a decision she hated, much less to Prett. She jerked her hand again, Prett's fingers so tight with desperation around her wrist that her own were growing numb.

"Prett, I swear, if you don't let me go *right now*—"

"I poisoned you."

He had to have been joking.

This was Praxis's first impulse. Before shock, before outrage, before anything. Prett Fellows: he was a lot of things, a prankster among them, but he was not a dangerous man. Praxis almost laughed, because the very idea was so absurd. Hadn't they always been close, after all? Hadn't they confided in each other as children, played together, rolled their eyes together at the antics of their older siblings? They used to lay sprawled out on Prett's bed sometimes, drawing pictures of what they thought the rest of the world looked like, fat atlases and books of history lending shape to their daydreams. They planned their escape from this frozen world together. They were going to travel together, fend their way together, fight pirates together. Never mind that their dreams had fallen by the wayside as they grew. Never mind that Praxis stormed off without a single word, in the end. That kind of bond didn't just *die*.

So he had to be joking, except that he was just watching her now, and the guilt and anger—so much anger, so long repressed—were plain enough upon his face.

He wasn't joking.

"*Why?*"

"Because I was asked to," Prett said.

Now the shock came. *Now* the world seemed to rip out from underneath Praxis. *Now* the truth of Prett's words knocked the wind out of her. She teetered forward, suddenly unstable, and in her unbalance she found herself grabbing onto him for support, even now. Somewhere in the midst, he had let go of her hand, and now Praxis found herself clutching onto his jacket, an icier blue than he normally wore, cold as his heart. She stared at her gloved hand, her slim fingers tracing the intricate stitching.

"—sorry, I'm sorry, Prax, I swear, I'm so sorry," Prett was saying. How long had he been repeating the tired refrain? His hands held her steady by the shoulders, and Praxis took a step back, out of them, away from them.

She shook her head. Slowly, like she was moving in a daze. "Don't say that," she said. His apologies fell upon her like knives. "Don't say that!"

"All right, all right, sorry—No, sorry, I didn't mean—! Not sorry, just . . . Okay." He took a deep breath. "Okay."

"'Okay'?" Praxis laughed, a single, bitter twist falling between them. "No, Prett, this is not 'okay.' This is about as far from 'okay' as you can get."

"I know. I'm—" He drew himself short, spreading his arms in frustration. "How can I even talk about this if I can't say I'm sorry?"

"I don't know. I don't *care*. Just . . . just stand there for a second, and let me think."

She turned away from him. Ran her hand along her forehead, as if working out a deep headache. A headache would certainly be preferable right about now. Her time was running out, and she did not have any left to waste on the mess Prett had thrown before her, and yet . . .

"Who asked you to?" Praxis said. She spoke at the ice, barely turning her head.

Prett hesitated. "Lexthur. Though I think—I mean, I'm almost certain—that he was working with Mother on this."

Lexthur. Mother.

Praxis shut her eyes. She leaned forward, the cool of the wall pressing against her forehead. When she was a child, it used to calm down sparks of magic behind her eyes, when they sprang up out of anger or frustration. She felt the cold now, let it seep in behind her skin, spread across her face. She tugged off her gloves, dropping them anywhere, and then reached up, pressing her palms flat on the wall beside her. Ten points of contact for her fingers, one more for each palm, one for her forehead, one for the slant of her nose. Praxis soaked in the cold, more and more of it. Her hands shook, her head shook, her body shook, from the effort of stilling the magic inside of her.

It didn't work.

A silent scream of fury tore itself from her throat. Cracks split the ice, splintering out from each point of contact like a spider's web. They raced across the surface of the wall, the whole of the stairwell trembling underneath her power. A chunk of ice, one and then two and then five, rained down and *ping*ed against the floor.

"Praxis!"

Prett wrenched her away from the wall. He spun her around, gave her face a slap hearty enough to rival those of Prestina. Praxis couldn't even see him at first, couldn't even think, her whole head blurred by the magic rebounding back and settling against her like an echo.

She glared at Prett. Kinder looks than that had killed men in the past.

"Get out of my way."

"No," Prett said. "You want someone to hate for this, you hate me. I'm the one who did it."

"Because they put you up to it."

"I wasn't forced to, Praxis. No one put a gun to my head. I think . . ." Prett hesitated. "I think I knew what I was doing. Deep down."

"No," Praxis said. "No, you don't know what you're saying. You wouldn't . . . you couldn't . . ."

"I could." Prett sighed. "Look, I'm not saying it was right, but—you don't know what it was like, Prax. Staying behind. You don't know what it's like, to watch your parents suffer at the loss of one child. What was I supposed to do? I *couldn't* leave, and you're the reason why. And a part of me hated you for it."

"So because you were too spineless to defy our parents, you chose to *poison* me? I could have *died*, Prett! You could have killed me."

"I know!" Prett shouted, desperation lacing his voice. "I know, I'm—"

He bit his tongue. *I'm sorry.* He didn't say it, wouldn't say it, but the shape of his not-saying it filled the space between them as surely as if he'd uttered the words. For a while they just stood there, the silence saying more than either of them could muster. Prett seemed to be chewing on so much more, so many regrets and miseries plain enough upon his face. Even if Praxis cared, there was clearly no time to read them all, their number and depth too much to bear.

But then:

"Listen," Prett said finally, "I understand if you want to hate me right now, but . . . you need to be careful around Mother. This isn't over for her. I don't . . . I don't know what she has planned, but she's not herself right now. She compared you to a *bat*."

Praxis snorted, a messy and dismissive puff. "A bat."

"Yeah, I don't know. Some species from Syll. She was going on about the way these mother bats chew the wings off their babies, to keep them in the colony. I tried to tell her—"

"Wait," Praxis said, raising a hand to cut him off. "They chew the wings off? She actually *said* that?"

Prett grimaced. "Yeah, trust me, I couldn't make something like that up."

"Oh gods," Praxis whispered as the world seemed to pitch wildly beneath her. She caught herself against Prett, the only stable thing within her reach, and his steady arms gave her balance back. Why hadn't she seen it before? *They'll try to leave as much of the leg as they can.* None of the other doctors had said a single word to imply that Praxis's leg was in that bad of shape, not once. Not until *now*, when the decision for control of the company hung in the balance, when Praxis had to take a stand or give it up forever. Kaedrich had told her that Prestina had been the one she'd turned to for help, that Prestina had brought in the doctor, and now the thoughts in Praxis's mind crystallized into a picture as sharp and clear as diamond. There was only one doctor Prestina trusted with her children, only one doctor she knew would handle matters with the discretion Prestina required. He'd been handling Previn's health for *years*, brought onto the payroll full-time when Previn was just a baby. If anyone was embedded deeply enough in Prestina's pocketbook to do a favor like this, it would be him.

Heat flared in Praxis's fingertips, and she shoved herself away from Prett so hard that he stumbled.

"Whoa! Prax, wait, what's going on? Where are you—?"

"To settle something," Praxis said. She felt the weight of time pressing down on her, her window of opportunity with the oversight committee narrowing, but to the depths with that. If Praxis was right, it wouldn't matter if she missed it.

AND WHAT OF Lanali herself? Surely she must have been involved in the whole messy affair of Tol's attempted assassination, more so than simply issuing the orders and waiting to hear if it was done.

Yes, in fact, she was right in the thick of it. In a manner of speaking.

From the solar just off the King's Bedroom, Lanali watched it all. The debacle in the servants' passage. The empty air, where Tol should have been. The mad scramble through the palace, checking hidden corners, secret passages, tower windows. The library, where the visiting dignitaries had been seated for a quiet tea, the smell of seared flesh still hanging in the air from those who had been too close when the explosion—was rumor to be trusted, had it really been a rat?—went off. It was Lanali who had them check all the doors to the palace, sealed just before she'd ordered the attack; Lanali who instructed them in where to look, where to go; Lanali who understood that the explosion, rat or otherwise, had been a mere diversion from the truth of Tol's escape.

Lanali who had spotted him, running between the hedgerows.

This last one, at least, she had done with her own eyes, and thus was granted an extra degree of satisfaction. She'd pulled herself away from her other senses, going to the windows of the solar for a crack of cool air after the effort it took to maintain a link with her inner-circle guards. A newly minted branch of the military, the elite force had been uniformed in crimson and anointed the Steel Guard. They answered only to her. The magic had been stolen from the genius of a man named Deter Vaulsk, on the city of barges—years ago by now, and still it did not work quite right. Anyone else might have given Lanali some credit: she was, after all, working from only observations and impressions, her own hunches, never having seen or experienced his magic for herself. True, she'd stolen his thumb, and even a small bone such as that would house a bit of the spell he'd created. But it had taken Lanali *years* of failed experimentation to get the mental link between her and her knockoff "Silvers" to come even close to the level of control that Vaulsk maintained over his own. Not that Lanali wanted quite the same experience—his Silvers were linked to his own mind so thoroughly that they knew what he knew, and Lanali was not one to give up her secrets.

Still, the fact that she'd come this far would have been something to be commended, if Lanali did not have such a strict rule against failure. This newest breed of Steel Guard, the most steadfast and loyal of her soldiers, had already proven a great success. A heavy blink, a shift in Lanali's mental perception as she focused in on one or another, and when she opened her eyes it was like looking through their own. The world around her was still there, but faded to the background, as if she had wandered into a particularly intense daydream.

In this manner she had watched what was happening, directing the action, and in this manner she retreated now, with the burning memory of Tol's white suit disappearing into thick green. *He's reached the gardens.* She did not know, even now, if they perceived her wishes as a manifestation of her voice inside their head, or if it was more intuitive than that, a deep-pressed *understanding* of what she wanted, but either way she did not care. She watched and felt as her Steel Guardsman absorbed this, as he motioned for the others to follow. As they headed for the greenery.

He was, of course, long since gone from the gardens by the time they got there, but at least they had some sense of where he'd left from. Lanali's men spread out, both those she couldn't directly control, and those few whom she could. She gritted her teeth and jumped repeatedly from the perception of one to the next to the next, a headache building from her efforts.

On the upper slopes of the city, they spotted him again—ducking behind a carriage, hoping to avoid detection. Lanali felt the pounding of her soldier's feet against the sett stones, as fast and steady as her heart, but by the time they caught up with the carriage, a billow of smog had swallowed Tol whole. He led them on a merry chase down the length of Monfort, appearing only briefly, disappearing into crowds, empty buildings, hidden shadows. In the commerce district, a fat band about halfway down the slope, he climbed to the rooftops, his white suit caught against the sun as he leaped from one building to another. Lanali's men climbed stairs just in time for him to shimmy down a drainpipe, and now they clustered together, slamming into each other's backs, as they scrambled to retrace their steps back to street level.

Did he *want* to be seen? This is the puzzle that Lanali futzed with as she kept track of her Steel Guardsmen, wending through the streets. She knew that Tol was better at going to ground than this, but he also knew that Lanali knew most of his tricks for doing so—was is safer, then, to play this game, to taunt her from afar? Hiding in the open, bursting through crowds on purpose, so that her actions would need to be taken in broad daylight. In hiding, in the dark, someone could catch up to him and slit his throat with impunity, dispose of his body before anyone would even know he was dead.

And then, in a plaza by the docks, the game changed again.

For there he was, just standing there, obvious for anyone to see. He'd climbed onto the base of the statue in the middle of the open square, his hand wrapped around the marble reins of a horse reared up in battle. The Steel Guardsman that Lanali was controlling came to a temporary stop, too surprised to understand what to do next.

But it did not matter what he did next, and it did not matter what Lanali told him to do next. Tol decided what came next. Lanali watched, heart in her throat, as Tol waited until he was sure he'd been seen, and then he grinned at the member of the Steel Guard that Lanali spied from, and he placed his fingers to his lips, and he whistled, hard and shrill.

And then, like magic, though there was nothing magical about bribes and preparation: from the depths of the crowds, a mob of street urchins pushed their way through, blooming like an infestation across the square. Each of them was wearing blankets or ragged cloaks, and as Lanali watched, as all of her gathering army watched, they threw this aside to reveal bright white suits, the perfect copy of Tol's. From the depths, a variety of scrappy red wigs appeared, and the urchins donned them with the speed of players changing their costumes backstage, until the entire square was a sea of Tol lookalikes. Not perfect, no, but—close enough, especially in the haze near the bay. Plenty close enough, as Tol leaped from the statue and disappeared beneath the waves of his duplicates.

At this signal, the urchins scattered. Like a splash from his dive, droplets and ripples spreading out through the crowd of the plaza. A chaos of white suits, red heads—too many to check, too many to keep track of. Lanali's men lurched into action, giving chase down the streets and across the square, grabbing them randomly by the shoulder, but Lanali herself did not. *Stop!* she shouted into the mind of her Steel Guardsman, and he stopped. *Turn.*

Under her guidance, he ran to the same statue Tol had used. A quick step up, and he was eye level with the marble horse's saddle, scanning the racing crowd from above, colorful dots in the smog. What was she looking for? Even Lanali could not say, not really. She would know it when she saw it.

There.

Lanali's Steel Guardsman did not need to be told to leap from the statue, nor to race for the docks. Perhaps he had seen what she'd seen, or perhaps their connection was stronger than she gave it credit for, her fury so hot that it had fused her perception across his own. It did not matter: the guard raced to the docks, straight to the end, until he had to skid to a stop and could go no farther. And there, across the widening expanse of water, down a gap in the smog that seemed to exist just for this purpose, there he saw it, and there she saw it. The real Tol, standing on the back of a ship, planted proud like a flag as he waved at her in the breeze. The white of his suit was not surrender, though—it was victory. Lanali's Steel Guardsman stood on the docks, his breath heaving in her chest, his hands tightened into fists, and in the manner of Durns, Tol blew him a kiss, blew *her* a kiss. He shouted something, his voice buffeted by the wind and the waves and the clamor of city life behind them, but Lanali could have sworn that she heard it, and she knew even then that the memory of it would burn in her heart like a splinter, enraging her. *Goodbye, my love. Good game.*

Chapter Thirty-Seven

KAEDRICH DIDN'T REALIZE where she was going until she was already there. In the whirl of her emotions, she'd let her feet guide her, not bothering to stop and ask what they were leading her toward. At first, her destination didn't seem to make sense, but then it did: Kaedrich wanted to get away from the Fellows—the scheming, the backstabbing, the subtle jabs, the layers upon layers of meaning coated on top of the simplest gesture—and while that wasn't strictly possible, there was one person she could talk to, who wouldn't bullshit her, or try to manipulate her the way the rest of his family would.

And yet, as Kaedrich pushed the door to Previn's room open, she did not find the respite she'd been longing for. Quite the opposite, in fact.

She'd walked into the middle of a crisis of some sort. Kaedrich was surprised that she hadn't heard the shouting from the door. Not that she'd be able to understand what the maid or nurse or aide or whoever she was, was saying to Previn—Previn, who was himself wailing, pawing at the neckline of his aide with one hand while the other slammed the end of a pencil repeatedly against the armrest of his wheeled chair.

"What's going on here?" Kaedrich asked. She was surprised at the authoritative tone of her voice, the way it seemed to fill the room without even needing to shout. But nowhere near as surprised as Previn and the aide. In an instant the noise had stopped, both of their heads whipping in her direction, both of their eyes popping wide.

Previn immediately released his hold on the aide's uniform, his hand sprawling out in Kaedrich's direction, but the aide was having none of it. With a snide glare at Kaedrich, she grabbed Previn by the wrist, yanking him down. She told him something stern in Yandosian, but Previn didn't listen to her, wrenching his arm free again.

"I asked what's going on," Kaedrich said, but the aide only had time for another sharp glare.

"This isn't your concern," she said as she wrestled and wrangled in an effort to contain Previn's flailing limb. And always, a constant drumbeat of the pencil against the armrest. Tap-tap. Tap-tap-tap. Tap . . . tap-tap.

"The darkness it isn't." Kaedrich raised her hand, the shifting colors of Prawl's ring easily catching in the light. "I asked you a question. Don't make me repeat it again."

The aide's lips twisted up in a bitter scowl. She made one more attempt at jamming Previn's arm back into his lap, and Previn lunged, teeth flaring. The aide only just managed to jump back before he bit her own arm.

"He's gone mad!" the aide said. Now, at least, she was willing to give him some space. She eyed him warily as she clutched her arm, as if he had actually managed to catch it. "He's never been like *this* before!"

Previn made a grunt. He flailed his arm in the aide's direction, in a way that was almost . . . almost *dismissive* of her, like he was waving her off as folly. He certainly was dismissing her, in his own attentions—his gaze was locked on Kaedrich, eyes wide and wild, yes, but also desperate, hopeful, determined. Pleading.

There was no madness in them.

A chill snuck up on Kaedrich, so fast she almost shivered. "No, that's not it," she said to the aide. Oh, but how Kaedrich wished she could speak Yandosian, that she could simply approach Previn with questions. She *could*, she supposed, ask the aide to translate something for her, but she doubted the aide's integrity, that she would accurately relay not just Kaedrich's words themselves, but the *tone*, the meaning behind them.

Kaedrich approached Previn. The aide squeaked, once, almost as if she wanted to warn Kaedrich to keep her distance, but then she quieted down, as if perhaps she didn't actually care what happened to Kaedrich after all. Just as well. Kaedrich crouched down, resting one hand lightly on the edge of Previn's chair for stability. "I'm sorry," Kaedrich said, her voice billowing with the soft embrace of remorse, "I don't understand what you're telling me. But you *are* trying to tell me something, aren't you?"

Previn slammed his pencil down again, harder and faster, the taps so frenzied that they were starting to lose themselves in the pelting rain of their intensity. Kaedrich looked at the pencil, studying it. That was the key, she was sure of it, but exactly what it was supposed to mean was beyond her.

Behind her, the aide huffed. "I'm going to fetch the doctor. He needs one of his injections."

"No, wait!" Kaedrich said, but even as she turned, the aide was already racing out the door. Kaedrich whirled back to Previn, desperation clear on her face. "I'm sorry, I—I'll be right back, I promise!" She sprang up and held up her finger, wait, hoping that its meaning was clear, even as Previn lurched forward, attempting to grab at Kaedrich.

Kaedrich ran after the aide. *"Wait!"* she called, but the aide was not waiting, and Kaedrich slid as she hurried to keep up. Her heart thundered in her throat, because they did not need to bring in a doctor, Kaedrich was sure that was the last thing they needed. Kaedrich had seen doctors, plenty of times, men in white coats whose eyes glazed over when you spoke, who would be more likely to sedate Previn than try to figure out what was wrong. They did need help, yes—but not this. Never this.

And yet, who else was there? Who would bother to listen, to try to understand? Only Praxis, perhaps, if the stars were aligned and her mood was right, or if Kaedrich could stress the importance. But she would surely be halfway to the Minor Conclave by now, Kaedrich realized, a sick knot tightening in her stomach. Gods, why had she agreed to this? Why had she agreed to any of it? As she chased the aide through the halls of the Fellows household, she felt suddenly choked with regret, and nothing, she knew, would ever be able to make it right again.

But that was her fault, and her problem. In the meantime, there was still this: Previn needed help—real help—and despite her own personal crisis, Kaedrich was not going to stand by and let someone botch it up. So she slid around a corner, barely keeping up, and followed the aide as she barreled straight into the doctor's office.

To Praxis's surprise, the Fellows' current family doctor was not, in fact, the one who lingered in Praxis's childhood memories.

Hers was of a boulder of a man, round to the point of comedy, his face perpetually flushed and dotted with perspiration, his lips forever parted as his stale breath scraped over you. He had a habit of talking over Praxis's head, even when she sprouted and shot up taller than him, even when she had turned from a child into a woman. His bushy, curly hair was thinning out on top, and Praxis used to glare at the sheen of it, grinding her teeth as he gave her mother a litany of things Praxis should and shouldn't be doing—for it seemed to him that her body and her health were never quite right, that her spine wasn't going to be straight enough as she grew, and then once it was, that her hips were going to be too narrow, that her thin bones would somehow end up burdened under the brunt of too much fat if she kept eating sweets, that her eyes were poor, that her teeth were crooked.

She hated him, for being wrong and being arrogant and for the way he watched her, his eyes lingering, as she grew. But the one thing she would grant him was this: he was not one to fold easily under pressure.

It was a surprise, then, and kind of a disappointment if Praxis was being honest, that his replacement was, by contrast, such a spineless leech. She burst into his office, but had barely even begun to threaten him, when he began begging to speak.

At least, that's what Praxis assumed he was begging for, though it may have simply been air. Her gaze had narrowed in, her magic reaching out and tightening around his heart before she'd even had a chance to consider how best to approach him, or indeed whether or not Prestina would even use him the same way she would have his predecessor. Faint little gasps and sputters escaped his lips as he dropped to the floor, and Praxis forcibly shut her eyes, ripping apart the noose of her magic. The doctor sucked in a lungful of air, then lay there gulping silently as a fish for a moment. His eyes were bugged and wild, and he stared up at Praxis from his spot on the floor, and Praxis was forced to wonder if he'd ever have the nerve to rise to his feet again. Probably, he was wondering the same thing.

Praxis flexed her fingers and crouched in front of him. The doctor slithered backward, clawing at the furniture in an effort to drag himself farther from Praxis, but Praxis merely reached out, stabbing a finger down onto the hem of his jacket, and though the act itself did nothing, had no force, the threat of it stilled him as dead as a stone.

He stared at Praxis, terror naked in his eyes. A mouse, pinned senseless beneath the paw of a cat.

"I'm going to make this easy on you," Praxis said. She was surprised, as was he, by the evenness of her voice. "Did my mother tell you what to say, about my leg? Tell me the truth—tell me quickly—and I promise I'll let you go unharmed."

"Yes," the doctor said, so fast that Praxis hadn't even quite finished speaking.

Praxis felt the ripple as it hit her, making her flinch. It was not unexpected, but it still stung. "Okay. Second question, and my last one: was any of it based in truth?"

This time, the answer came more slowly. The doctor's mouth opened, closed. Opened again. He creaked once, before he said, "*Any* of it? Yes. Sort of. That is," he added hurriedly, "the poison that's been embedded does seem to be reasserting itself, a little. At least, that's the general consensus."

"Consensus?"

A tiny spark of fear shone in the doctor's eyes. "You've . . . sought out opinions . . ."

"She had me *followed*?!"

Even as the doctor nodded, head bobbing frantically, Praxis had to admit that this shouldn't have been a surprise. The reach of Prestina Fellows was near-legendary, her spies positioned everywhere within Bolt. Praxis should have known her actions would not go unnoticed, that word would leach back to her mother's waiting ears. Shame and anger, both, heated Praxis's cheeks, and she actually had to look away from the doctor now. It did not help the look she was trying to maintain, the intimidation she hoped to spear through him, but neither could she face the way he might look at her now. Played as easily as he had been—perhaps more so, for after all, wasn't the doctor merely paid off?

Praxis forced herself to look back. "Fine. So if that's the truth, then where was the lie?"

"The cold," the doctor said, and somehow even before he continued, Praxis knew what he was going to say. "The cold isn't going to help you. It seems to be the reason this has happened in the first place, and if you stay . . . if you stay . . ."

"Go on," Praxis said, her eyes narrowed, her voice low and deadly still.

The doctor gulped. "If you *stay*, you'll lose the leg for sure. If you leave, you might be able to salvage it."

That was it. With a snap, something seemed to break inside of Praxis; she screamed, suddenly looming over the doctor. Her arm raised, flames already engulfing her hand. What was she going to do? She did not know. In the moment, the fury at her mother exploding in her mind, she did not care. She could see the fear in the doctor's eyes, and the betrayal, too—*you said you'd let me go unharmed*—but also, deep beneath it all, a sigh of resignation, like yes, of course, it was always going to come to this, with the Fellows.

It was that, more than anything else, which tore into Praxis. That, more than anything else, which made her veer at the last second, hurtling her anger and her flames both. They struck the wall, melting a hole, yes, water and ice bursting out into the room in a glorious spray, but ultimately harmless. Praxis stood there, chest heaving, breath shaking, the hot feeling of magic and dry, unshed tears burning behind her eyes. She could not think in words. All she saw was her mother's face, its superior poise, the haughtiness that Praxis herself had emulated, whether intentionally or not, for so long that it felt almost like her own. Years ago, she'd thought she'd escaped, that she'd won. But where was the victory in turning into your opponent?

Praxis did not know how long she would have stayed here, too broken up to move her tangled pieces. The doctor was surreptitiously attempting to slide his way along the floor, away from her, but it was not him that finally drew Praxis from the depths of her despair.

The door slammed open, a clatter of hurried footsteps running in. First one voice, talking fast in Yandosian, calling for the doctor, and then another, another—

The only other.

"—hang on, I'm telling you, I—Oh! Praxis?" Kaedrich came to a sudden halt, then jerked forward, uncertain. Praxis could feel, through her wizard's sense, as Kaedrich took in the scene before her: the hole in the wall, the boiling rage, the cowering doctor. When Kaedrich spoke next, her voice was hesitant. "What are . . . what are you doing here?"

"Nothing," Praxis said, coming back to herself. Her fury hardened with diamond-clear focus onto what it should have been fixated on from the beginning: her sense was already stretching out, spreading through the tunnels, hunting like a predator for her mother. She shoved past Kaedrich—anything to get moving, to get out from under those damned watchful eyes—but Kaedrich followed, leaving the doctor and the aide behind.

"Praxis—Praxis, wait! Where are you going?"

"Nowhere."

"No, but—*hang on*, blast it, this is important!"

Praxis gritted her teeth. She did not want to, but—she paused. For Kaedrich, she would always pause. She made herself turn, forced her face smooth. She tried to keep her voice from snapping as she asked, "What?"

For a moment, she worried Kaedrich wouldn't tell her. A battle was clearly being waged in Kaedrich's mind, the urgency of what had driven her into the doctor's room chafing against the weight of whatever had enraged Praxis so. She had to have known it was important, whatever it was. She had to have realized it mattered.

Praxis did not know, at first, if she would even listen to whatever Kaedrich had come to say. The need to find her mother was like a physical pull, hooked around her navel. Her limbs *needed* to move, her magic *needed* to seek its revenge. She did not know how long she would be able to contain it, if asked to, even if just for a short while.

But then Kaedrich said it, the only thing that would have ever diverted Praxis, the only thing strong enough to matter, even now. Even now. Always.

"I need your help."

So she listened, following Kaedrich to Previn's room, but then annoyance billowed up fast.

For one, she just didn't have time for this. Kaedrich had said she needed Praxis's help, okay, but for this? Seriously? Praxis's skin still clawed with unspent magic, the fire seeming to burn just beneath the surface. Her wizard's sense hadn't found her mother yet, so maybe Prestina was out, though there were still so many tunnels in the sprawl of the Fellows household and business that it was hard to say just yet. Even as Kaedrich led the way, even as she explained what was going on, a large part of Praxis's mind simply wasn't processing it. It wasn't that Praxis didn't *try*, on some level at least, but . . . oh, hells. What difference did it make what Previn was doing? Certainly, it could not matter—not when stacked against something like *this*, this deep betrayal that had gutted Praxis more thoroughly than anything she'd ever expected. It's not that she'd never considered it before, that her mother would try to manipulate her. Praxis had just never imagined she'd go this far—and she'd never imagined that, once revealed, the betrayal would *hurt* so much.

So it was with limited patience that she had entered Previn's room, and it was with limited patience that she took in the situation: yes, yes, he was agitated; yes, yes, it was unusual for his fits to reach this level of frenzy; yes, yes, he was tapping as if the second devil himself was dancing on his shoulder. It didn't *mean* anything, though, that was what Kaedrich's soft, kind heart couldn't accept.

In the meantime, they were wasting precious minutes. Praxis's attention pulled, her senses stretching ever farther, and she tried to leave, but Kaedrich grabbed her arm.

"Praxis, listen to me. There's something he's trying to tell us."

Praxis shook her head. "Look, I get that you're trying to see more in him than there is, and I *understand* that need, I really do. But I promise you"—she gritted her teeth before continuing; the tapping was reaching a crescendo now, boring into Praxis's skull— "there's nothing there to find, he's just—*oh, for the love of sanity, will you stop that!*"

Had Praxis ever shouted at Previn before? She towered over him, the echo of her outburst still ringing in her ears. It seemed incomprehensible, like kicking a puppy, and yet that damned *sound*, over and over and *over* again, a never-ending series of repeating dits and dots that thrummed like a familiar heartbeat through Praxis's skin. It had driven her just as crazy now as it had when she was a child, the year Prett had—

Praxis froze. Previn hadn't once stopped tapping the arm of his chair, slamming the pencil against it so hard that now tiny cracks were beginning to work their way up the whale-bone frame. He had locked eyes with her, a far more direct look than she was used to, his gaze level and . . . accusatory? It would have been accusatory on anyone else, certainly. But that was impossible, as impossible as the idea that had swept up on Praxis as she stood there and listened, really *listened* to the pattern of the taps. Their repetitive quality, the pauses and variations in length.

"Praxis? Praxis!"

Kaedrich's voice drifted in from a distance, a sound carried by the wind. Praxis held up her hand, indicating both that she was all right, and her need for quiet. *Tap-tap,* went the sound. *Tap-tap-tap. Tap . . . tap-tap.*

"Get me a piece of paper," Praxis whispered. *And a chair,* she wanted to add, because she was almost too weak to stand by now. The chill of realization tickled up her spine, stealing her strength and her breath. All she could do, as Kaedrich scrambled for paper and pen, was to stare at Previn, really *stare* at Previn. It wasn't possible. It wasn't.

"Here," Kaedrich said a moment later, and Praxis was grateful for the excuse to break eye contact. Praxis took the supplies from Kaedrich's hands, then moved to stand beside the shelf with Previn's phonograph. She cleared herself a tiny workspace, smoothing the page out. Her pen shook as it hovered over the paper. Could she even remember the code, after all of this time? Prett had only been obsessed with telegraph machines for a year, a childhood fancy that had burned bright and flared out just as quickly as it had ignited.

For a moment, all thought of her mother receded from Praxis's mind, and even her wizard's sense pulled back. Praxis closed her eyes. Listened, counted. Her pen copied the noises as a series of dots and dashes, and at first it was just a jumble. But then, look: here, she remembered that one. She scribbled the equivalent letter over the marks on the page. Then another. Then she thought she recognized another, though maybe she was wrong. She wrote it down anyway, unwilling to disregard it. Previn's tapping grew faster—excited or frantic, it was hard to tell which. The letters Praxis was writing down seemed to be repeated, so she stopped copying and started trying to transcribe, one and then another—that one repeated, that one was . . . what was it? Yes, she remembered now. She wrote it down.

The process itself was so complicated, dredging up ancient muscle memory, that Praxis forgot at first the circumstances of what she was trying to do. It was only once a completed word—no, a completed *phrase*, two Yandosian words strung together—hung in front of her that the reality of what she'd written caught up with her.

Please listen.

Praxis froze. Her blood rushed in her ears, making it impossible for her to notice, at first, that Previn's incessant tapping had finally stopped. The words swam in front of Praxis, and though the translated phrase only repeated itself one and a half times, she'd copied down the code several more times over, all down the length of the page. *Please listen, please listen, please listen, please listen.*

"Oh gods," Praxis breathed.

"What does it say?" Kaedrich asked. She had come up behind Praxis at some point, craning over Praxis's shoulder to read—but of course, it was all in Yandosian.

Praxis didn't answer. When she turned, she did not look at Kaedrich.

Her brother's eyes were rimmed with red; tears pooled at the corners, naked relief and joy easily read upon his face.

Praxis pressed her hand across her mouth, as if she'd said something embarrassing or vulgar. *"You understand?"* she asked through her fingers.

Previn jerked his head. He started tapping on the armrest of his chair again, a different pattern than before, though still just as insistent.

"Okay, wait, give me a second," Praxis told him in Yandosian. She flipped the paper over, the page blank and expectant. *"Wait, start over. Tell me."*

Previn paused. Longer than a break in the letters. He started over.

Praxis nodded, concentrating on her work. She took down the pattern first, filling the entire page—she had to cramp the last line. She glanced up expectantly when it seemed that Previn was done. He jerked his head again, and Praxis quickly returned her attention to the paper. She was still rusty at translating the code; her memories felt choked with dust. She scratched out one letter and then another, working not in order, but rather in order of her confidence. A letter here, a letter there. She tried to keep her frustration in check, and focus on the job at hand. One word and then another began to morph into understanding, scattered like breadcrumbs across the paper: *Father. In. Effort. The. Forgiveness.*

Death.

Magic.

SHE MIGHT NOT be able to read the words above the dots and dashes, but Kaedrich recognized the pattern of it easily enough. Telegraph code, or something very much like it. It seemed obvious, now that Kaedrich was faced with it, but she had never learned the patterns. She told herself that it was wrong of her to feel smug about being right; she did anyway. Because she *was* right, that much did not need translation. Praxis's utter shock, the way she had looked at her brother—and then, the way Praxis nodded along, really listening. Praxis copied down everything Previn said, and then took several long, agonizing minutes to translate the code into Yandosian.

And then she'd frozen. She stared long and hard at the paper, all the scant color draining from her face until she was as white as the sheet in front of her.

Praxis turned to her brother. Asked him a question that Kaedrich was willing to bet was something like, "You're *sure*?"

Previn nodded. Once, and very directly.

Kaedrich watched the shift in Praxis's throat and the clench of her jaw as she swallowed down hard.

Without another word, Praxis stalked out of the room.

Kaedrich blinked. She hovered, uncertain, for a heartbeat, and then shot Previn an apologetic look and rushed to catch up with Praxis.

She was already halfway down the corridor. Praxis's ragged coat billowed as she swept at her top speed toward the stairwell.

"Praxis!" Kaedrich hurried after her, their footsteps ringing down the empty hallway. "Praxis, what—where are you going? What did he say? What's happening? Talk to me!"

But Praxis didn't talk. Instead, in silence, she ran her fingers lightly over the page she'd taken with her. Kaedrich didn't understand, until Praxis handed the sheet over, and Kaedrich saw as the letters shifted and morphed, bumping into each other, making room, reshuffling.

To Kaedrich's amazement, the Yandosian was gone. Durlish took its place.

Kaedrich read it.

She read it again.

She read it a third time, although by now they'd reached the staircase, and she kept having to look up so that she didn't miss her footing on the slippery steps and topple down to the bottom. "But . . . this means that your *father*—"

"Yes."

"But . . . but how is that *possible*?" Kaedrich asked. She handed the paper back to Praxis, who hastily folded it and stuffed it into a pocket of her coat. Kaedrich rubbed at her forehead, as if a headache was threatening. "I don't understand. Can't you *tell* if someone's a wizard?"

Praxis's jaw set as she hurried down the stairs. She forced a nod of concession. "Usually."

"But—!"

"Kaedrich, please," Praxis said. She came to an abrupt halt, and Kaedrich nearly ran into her back.

The two women just looked at each other for a moment, and Kaedrich could see it now: the hurt and confusion, the *fear* hidden behind Praxis's carefully still face.

"Please," Praxis said, "can we not fixate, right this minute, on *how*? I don't . . . I don't know *how*. You're right, I should have been able to tell. I should have known for my whole life, but I *didn't*, and now people are *dead* because *my father*—"

Praxis's voice broke as she cut herself off. She clamped a hand over her mouth, as if fighting to keep from being sick, as she turned away. She reached out to steady herself against the wall of the stairwell, her fingers pressing firm against the ice.

She looked small, suddenly, in a way she never had before. Compassion thrust its dagger into Kaedrich's heart, her chest seizing up as she watched. Praxis's shoulders had curled forward, her whole body acting like it wanted nothing more than to huddle up into a tiny ball.

Tentatively, Kaedrich reached out. But her hand stopped just before her fingers brushed the back of Praxis's shoulders, something unknown holding her back. She curled her fingers up as she withdrew her arm, retreating.

"Oh, Praxis," Kaedrich said instead.

"Don't," Praxis said. She turned just enough to look back over her shoulder. The plane of her face was as cold as the walls. "Don't say it." Praxis took a deep breath, and in an instant she had folded her emotions down, shoved them into the bottom of her soul to be dealt with later. Her eyes went unfixed, concentrating on her magic.

"Well?" Kaedrich asked a moment later.

Praxis shook her head. "He's not here," she said. They looked at each other, the answer hitting them in an instant. Two sets of eyes widened as a mirror of each other.

They did not need to speak as they set off down the stairs again. Kaedrich ran on ahead, to get a sleigh ready, so that by the time Praxis got there, they could leave immediately for the only other place that Prawl would be.

The Minor Conclave.

Chapter Thirty-Eight

ONCE THERE WAS a boy named Syral Kaston.

He was small for his age, the youngest of eight. No one expected great things from him. No one expected anything from him. He came from a mining family; not the biggest or the best in the business, but proud and steady, having been around for near to a hundred years by the time Syral was born.

There was nothing special about Syral, at least not as far as his family was concerned. He was a quiet kid, quiet and smart, though his family already had plenty of smart, so even that was nothing impressive. His only talent, as far as anyone could figure, was at card games—he was very, very good at card games. All sorts of card games, though his favorite, of course, was Fiddler's Dash.

Still, cards were hardly a solid business skill. And business, more than anything else, was what the Kaston family was founded on. It was what they had spent decades building, stone by stone, tunnel by tunnel, deal by deal. Sound business, solid business. None of the gambles that the other companies tried, none of the trends chased. The Kastons' empire may have been small, but it was made of sweat and tears and hard work. It would endure. While all the others came and went—even the Fellows, one of the mightiest of their field, was rumored to be facing difficulty those days—the Kastons would endure.

It was precisely this strength that drew the attention of a young woman named Prestina.

She took her time. Scouted them out. Prestina, so young, so pretty, wormed her way into parties and dances ... and card games. It was here that they met, and here that Prestina proved herself nearly equal to Syral's own considerable skills. Carefully, she courted the youngest Kaston boy. She managed to keep her identity hidden for several weeks before someone finally found out, but by then she and Syral had come to an understanding.

Their marriage was a quirk of bookkeeping. Use the solid financial backing of the Kaston family to win inheritance of the great and mighty Fellows empire, and then use the might of the Fellows empire to win control of the Kaston fortune. It was a play so bold that none of Syral's other siblings ever saw it coming, and none of them stood a chance. Within months, it was done. Syral's family, bitter at the reckless endangerment of everything they'd fought so hard for over the years, swore off all ties with the young tycoon, but that was fine. He wasn't a Kaston anymore—he wasn't even Syral. From the ashes of his old life, he'd brought forth something new and whole. He changed his name, along with his entire world.

Prawl Fellows was born in his stead.

There was only one problem: it turns out Prawl Fellows wasn't really much better suited to running a company of that scale than Syral had been, and now he had to save it from the brink of ruin.

That's okay, though.

Because Prestina *was*.

It was not, by Prawl's standards, an ideal arrangement. The first year of their marriage soured whatever scrap of genuine affection there might have been between the two of them, but business was business. They needed solutions fast, and Prestina was brimming with them. Within that first year, they stopped the financial bleeding. Within two, they'd managed to turn toward a profit. Within five ...

The golden age of the Fellows empire had begun.

PRESTINA LOOKED OUT at the circle of men who would decide her fate.

Not just *hers*, of course, but—her company. Because it *was* her company, dammit, and she didn't care what anyone, or any law, had to say on the matter. She was the true Fellows. She was the one who had grown up underneath the weight of that enormous legacy. She was the one who had devised a plan to save it, scouting out each of her rival companies until she found exactly what she was looking for. She was the one who had to make it work. It had been her idea, to license the *use* of lapus lumeni rather than outright *selling* them. Price it dirt cheap to install, spread them until Fellows gems lit just about the whole of Yandosia. A modest monthly fee, that they could slowly ratchet up over the course of many years. Recharge fees. Replacement fees. By the time her fourth child was born, the family empire had regained all of its former glory and then some.

But did any of that matter, to the men in this room? Did any of them even know, would any of them even believe her if she told them? Look at them, really stop and look. They were nothing compared to her. Smug, doughy men of limited imagination and middling ambition. Prestina had blackmail material on all of them, had stuffed most of their campaign coffers herself. She should own them. Prawl would own them. The only thing—the *only* thing—that they had going over her was the equipment between their legs. Because some doctor, somewhere, had taken them from their mothers and declared them men, and somehow that meant something.

They sat in silence for now, at least. Heads bowed as they read over "Praxis's" proposal for the company's future. It was a formality, one Prestina had no doubt was skimmed over or outright ignored as each of her bidding sons and grandsons and in-laws had trooped down here over the past few weeks, submitting their own names for consideration. True, the inheritance was decided, in part, by this document—but any submitted proposal needed to have already been independently reviewed and certified by the auditors, so there really wasn't need for any extra scrutiny before the application itself was accepted as valid.

And yet.

Here they were. Glasses on, faces scrunched in concentration. Several ministers had notepads out, scribbling down figures as if double-checking the numbers in front of them. Prestina sat near the end of the table (not at the *head* of the table, as a properly welcomed bidder would be), and tried to keep herself in check. Appearances mattered, after all. She sat with one leg crossed over the other, her hands folded on her knee. She had opted for a shockingly tame dress, by her standards, the better to appear "businesslike" rather than the great hostess they thought of her as. Her collar still rose to the full height that her station commanded, but the jewels were toned down, and the neckline cut rather severely up toward her jaw. Far more fur than normal covered her sleeves and bodice, somewhat mimicking the suit coats that all the men buried themselves under. Prestina did not fidget. She did not sigh, she did not check the time. Every part of this meeting had been planned, every detail of Prestina's appearance scrutinized.

It mattered.

"Well," one of those interchangeable men said finally. He was the first to look up, the first to remove his glasses. With his movement, the spell over the room broke, and the rest of them looked up one by one. He leaned back in his chair, tapping his folded glasses on the pages still spread out in front of him. "This is very impressive, I have to say. Very ambitious."

Prestina gave them the smile they expected to see. As if she'd been given a compliment. "Thank you."

"Perhaps a little *too* ambitious, though?" he asked. He glanced at his colleagues, who gave various nods of approval, before his attention returned to Prestina. "Let's not forget that at the end of the day, we are still talking about a woman here. Forgive me, but I just don't see your daughter being up to this."

Prestina did not forgive him. She was not *surprised*—indeed, she'd have been more shocked if Praxis's bid was accepted without question—but she did not forgive. But she continued to smile at him, this man who had used family money, money he didn't even earn for himself, to secure his position at this table.

"Mr. Thorne," Prestina started (of course she knew his name, she knew all their names), "I appreciate your concern, though I assure you it's quite unfounded. Praxis is fully versed in all areas of operation, and will be aided, as you can see, by only the best hands in the business."

It wasn't a lie if it was going to be true eventually, right?

Mr. Thorne gave a tight smile, bordering on pity. "But will it be enough? I'm sure none of us have anything less than glittering respect for your daughter"—bullshit—"nonetheless, it is an awful lot of responsibility we're talking about here. I'm just not sure she has the disposition necessary to fulfill the role. And what about when she wants to get married? What about when she wants a family?"

Nods were exchanged around the table in earnest now. Prestina gritted her teeth, just long enough to release the smallest bit of her frustrations, not long enough to show her irritation. Depths help her if she ever showed her irritation.

"I can assure you, gentlemen, from personal experience, that pregnancy is not a debilitating condition. The impact on my daughter's workload would be minimal."

The discomfort that radiated from the men around the table was palpable. It was a calculated move, referring to pregnancy so directly, not to cloak it in coy little euphemisms and baby-speak. Had any of these men even said the word "pregnant" in their life? They shifted in their seats, checked their watches.

Mr. Thorne cleared his throat. "Yes, well . . . be that as it may, one can hardly expect her to maintain the same level of interest in business once she's embraced the joys of motherhood. This company is going to need someone *solid* at the head. One whose passion for the job is not going to wane. It would be cruel to ask that of any woman, no matter how outwardly capable she may appear."

Prestina's eyebrow arched. "Is that so?"

"It is," Mr. Thorne said.

"I see. Well, far be it from me to question your assessment of what women are capable of—I mean," she added with a laugh, "what would *I* know about the matter? Nonetheless, I feel the need to point out you do not have the right to outright *deny* Praxis's bid, based on this. The law clearly recognizes her status." Prestina narrowed her eyes. "Or would you like to fight me on that?"

If the men were uncomfortable before, it had nothing on them *now*. A woman discussing childbirth was distasteful to them, to be sure—but a woman discussing business in these halls, as if she belonged? Worse still: a woman discussing business *like a man*? This, compounded by the fact that—woman or no—the threats of Prestina Fellows were not to be taken lightly. She took the table in turn, meeting each of their eyes one by one. Watching them wither. Watching them squirm.

Only Mr. Thorne did not back down. His chin remained oh-so-slightly jutted with superiority, his gaze level.

"No one is challenging your daughter's *right*," he said slowly. "I am only pointing out to you the utter lack of support she is due to receive, should she pursue this foolishness."

"We'll see about that."

"Yes, we will," came a voice from the door, and the entire room jumped. Even Prestina, controlled and prepared, was not prepared for *this*.

Prawl Fellows strolled inside, a glowing orb fixed tight in his hand.

THE HEART OF Bolt was already in chaos when Praxis and Kaedrich arrived.

All up the length of the spiral, people had been rushing and tense, but now here at the top panic truly reigned. Though it was unclear, as they dismounted from the sleigh, exactly what had transpired so far. Clusters of people huddled around a giant pillar, keeping a safe distance but still drawn toward it, the natural shape of disaster. Kaedrich fought against panic, imagining what might be going on inside. The idea that Prawl was a wizard was still so new, so unexpected, that she really couldn't begin to picture what he was capable of. And if he had a Beacon, well . . . okay, at least he couldn't, by nature, seize control of it and become its Lady, but Praxis had paled when Kaedrich mentioned that he was most likely the one who had it. She didn't really want to know what it might mean. They soldiered on instead, in silence, pushing through the crowds with all the authority of a Fellows.

In the pillar, Lexthur Delford was barking orders, struggling to be heard over the commotion swirling around him.

"What's going on?" Kaedrich whispered.

Praxis paused, listening for just a second before translating. "He's telling them not to contact the Major Conclave yet. I guess they think they can handle this on their own." Praxis snorted, listening to something else that Lexthur shouted. "Like that's going to work."

Kaedrich turned back. Lexthur was berating someone, an aide in a turquoise suit. He raised his hand and his voice, both, and for one heart-stopping second, Kaedrich was sure Lexthur was going to strike the aide. But then Praxis cleared her throat, long and loud, and everything in the room dropped. All the noises, all the shouting, all the commotion. Lexthur's hand.

He turned, heaving a weary sigh. Like he wasn't at all surprised.

Praxis planted a hand on her hip, surveying the room. "Having a little trouble, are we?"

Lexthur grimaced. "I was wondering when one of *you* would turn up. I suppose you've heard."

"Actually, the news hasn't spread that far yet. Let's just say I had an inside source."

"Then you are lucky. Trust me, you don't want to know the circumstances."

"Try again," Praxis said.

Lexthur sighed. "Huxley," he said. He waved at Praxis, and Huxley, the aide who'd been the object of Lexthur's tirade, hurried over. His arms were loaded with papers, his jacket rumpled, his cheeks flushed as if he'd been running for days.

"Yes, hello, so," he said. He barely paused for breath as, beyond him, Lexthur turned away and continued to organize his people. "In short, your father has taken over the Minor Conclave. We . . . don't really know the full extent of this yet."

"Do you mean he's holding them *hostage*?" Kaedrich asked. The idea felt preposterous, and yet.

Huxley grimaced. "No one has used that kind of language at this point," he said. "But, well, it's not entirely inappropriate. We've sent for a team of wizards, though it's anyone's guess how quickly they'll arrive, but once they do, we'll send them up to find out exactly—"

"No," Praxis said, loud enough for the whole room to hear. "I'll go."

Immediately, everyone went quiet. Lexthur sighed. He came forward, gripping Praxis's arm and guiding her off to the side of the room, Kaedrich right on their heels. Lexthur glared at her, briefly, but most of his attention lay with Praxis as he lowered his voice.

"Praxis, I didn't want to be the one to tell you this," Lexthur said, "but—"

"My mother is up there, too," Praxis said. "I know."

Kaedrich's heart leaped, hearing this, but of course Praxis would know. Of course her magic would have already told her.

It took Lexthur a moment longer to work this out. He stared at her, confused, and then concerned, and then just deeply, deeply troubled.

"You don't need to be the one to do this," he said finally.

"Yes, I do."

"There are people coming in to handle this, Praxis. They're the best in Yandosia."

Praxis straightened up, jutting her chin forward. "Not anymore."

"*Praxis—*"

"*No.* This is my problem, Lexthur. I'm going to fix it. I need to fix it."

Lexthur sighed. But it was not him Praxis had turned to, not his approval she needed. Kaedrich gave her a tiny nod, the best she could manage, and Praxis returned it with a shaky smile.

"Are you sure?" Lexthur asked, oblivious to all of this.

Praxis turned back to him. She nodded. "I am. I owe him that much."

"All right, then," Lexthur said. He stepped aside, motioning for her to pass. "Good luck, Praxis. Truly. I think you're going to need it."

"Thank you," Praxis said. She looked at Lexthur, the rest of the men. Kaedrich. "Don't follow me. Don't try anything stupid down here. I'm handling this."

If anyone had a problem with this, they didn't speak. In truth, Kaedrich doubted they did. Relief seemed to ripple through the room, emanating perhaps strongest from Lexthur himself, and Kaedrich didn't blame him, not really. She didn't blame any of them.

Still. This didn't mean she *agreed* with them.

Kaedrich gave it a moment, counting up in her head as she envisioned Praxis beginning the long climb up the steps. "Right!" she said, clapping her hands together when it felt like Praxis had gotten a sufficient lead. She turned to Lexthur and all the aides and guards lingering uselessly behind him. "This is what we're going to do."

Lexthur raised a finger. "Um. Forgive me, but didn't Praxis specifically say *not* to get involved?"

"Oh," Kaedrich said. She tipped her head. "Do you not realize how this works yet? You see, Praxis makes her own choices, but then, well . . ." She shrugged. "I make mine."

HIS WIFE.

Of course it would be his wife.

Prawl strolled into the room, removing the orb from his coat pocket as he passed through the door. He tossed it in the air and caught it easily, his reflexes as sprightly as a child.

"Oh, don't let me interrupt," Prawl said as he came to stand at the head of the table. He set the orb down in front of him, the heavy glass reflected on the polished white tabletop. Its gleam ensnared each of the members of the oversight committee in turn, and Prawl could see why. When he'd first gotten it, plucked from the lifeless hands of Trendall, he couldn't stop staring at it either.

Only Prestina was able to ignore it, her attention fixed squarely on Prawl.

Prawl gave her a benevolent smile. "Hello, dear. You didn't tell me you'd be paying a social call today."

"It seems there's a lot we don't tell each other these days," Prestina said. She raised one eyebrow, just enough to show him she'd noticed his new "toy"—not enough to outright pay attention to it, or what it might represent.

Of *course* she'd be so petty.

Of *course* she'd dismiss his achievements.

A sour taste tinged Prawl's mouth, just a little. But fine. He could be the bigger person here, today. He ignored his wife's jab, and reached out and gave the orb a good spin, just for show. His finger rested on top of it to keep it from rolling away, as its odd light danced across the faces of the ministers.

"So," Prawl said, turning his attention to the room at large. "I understand you're here to decide my fate."

Silence split the room. The truth has a funny way of rendering people mute, Prawl mused. This is one trick he didn't need his magic for, when playing Fiddler's Dash. People were so ready to talk, when all they had at their lips were lies.

Finally, one of them—Thorne, if Prawl wasn't mistaken, though he often forgot their names—cleared his throat. "Not *your* fate, no. Your company's."

"It's the *same thing*," Prawl said with a snarl. His fingers curled around the orb. Power surged through him, coursing straight to his veins—oh, such power. Prawl had never known the strength of magic before, not really. His owns skills had remained limited, untrained, untapped. He'd been told, once, that his power was *stunted*, but was it really? Or had the neglect of it in his youth merely allowed it to *wither*?

He would probably never find out.

"No," Prestina said. "It's not the same. It's never been the same."

"Shut up! No one asked you."

"Then maybe someone should! Because it's my company, even more than yours, *Husband*. Or have you forgotten whose ideas put us back on top?"

"As if you would ever *let* me forget."

"Oh, grow up. You've had everything handed to you, and you *still* insist on complaining about your lot in life?"

"Don't act as if you know about my life!" Prawl snapped. "You know nothing. You have *always* diminished me—just like my parents. But I am *not* weak, and I am *not* useless, woman! I have more power in the palm of my hand than you could ever dream of wielding, and I *will not be ignored*. Not anymore."

Prestina sneered. "*Really.* And how, exactly, do you propose to stop this? Face it, Prawl, you're outdated. It's time this company moves forward. It's *going* to move forward, if it's the last thing I do."

Prawl's lips stretched back, each of his glinting teeth revealed in a manic grin. The power in his veins crackled, begging him to *show them, show them, see how they'd cower*, and Prawl nearly laughed from the giddiness of it. Instead, he held himself tall, his shoulders squared as he surveyed the table in front of him, all those faces waiting, waiting. "Is that so?" he asked. He held his hand over the orb, letting the power of it soak up into his palm. When he turned his hand over, it was instinct to let the magic shoot out, unseen, from the tips of his fingers. It struck each of the faces around the table in turn, freezing them in place.

All the faces except for Prestina's. He'd let her escape this round, on purpose, a special move reserved for her. She jerked in alarm, her eyes wide as she took in the thralled state of the ministers. "What did you—?"

"Nothing dangerous, I assure you," Prawl said. He laughed softly. "That honor is reserved for you, my dear."

"You wouldn't." Prestina's voice was sure, her face controlled, but Prawl had been married to her long enough to see the creep of doubt in the corners of her eyes.

Prawl shrugged. "Wouldn't I?"

Would he? Perhaps not, once. The smallest flicker of uncertainty passed through Prawl, the memory of Pranders's face haunting his mind. His stomach turned over, cold shooting through him for just an instant, before the whisper of surety soothed his agitated thoughts. Prawl shut his eyes to gather strength, gather magic out of the orb. Look at everything this power had led him to achieve already. Look at everything he stood to gain.

When he opened his eyes again, the world had changed. Prawl had changed. Whatever doubt or lingering sense of moral queasiness had settled, brushed aside for the clarity of sight before him. The ring of ministers around the table, a weak golden-amber glow nestled inside of them; even that, even now, was frozen in place, locked at Prawl's command. He surveyed the table briefly, satisfied, before he dared to let himself look at Prestina. Prestina, her own glow churning like fire beneath the surface. Never could Prawl have imagined one so furious as this; the control she held over it was masterful, like a god of the raging seas.

And still, when he held his hand toward her, a thread of it slipped even her control. It darted for Prawl, as eager as a puppy, and he gripped the length of it tight in his fist, a surge of satisfaction coursing through him. He raised his hand, ready to pull. He remembered the ease with which he'd stolen Trendall's, how quickly the wizard had fallen. Prestina could not see it, but perhaps she could feel it, because her eyes widened, now, her hand flying to her chest as if her breath had hitched.

When Prawl spoke, he did so as barely a whisper. The kiss of his words graced Prestina's cheek as she turned to glare at him.

"Goodbye, *Wife*."

He did not hear the door when it opened. But he did hear the voice. *"Daddy, stop!"*

Chapter Thirty-Nine

"STAY OUT OF this, Praxis."

"I can't," Praxis said, and never had anything felt more true. She stepped cautiously into the room, one hand held out as if approaching a wild animal and the other held loose by her side, her fingers curling as they guided her steps forward one by one. She had no magic out, nothing aggressive in her appearance or movements.

The room itself was deathly still, and *quiet*. More than two dozen ministers sat around a long table, each one frozen in place as surely as if they'd become part of the ice. Only their eyes remained free of the thrall her father had gripped them in. They swiveled toward Praxis as they stared her down hard, many of them wet and ringed with red, others glaring with enough fury to melt the room.

Fear crept a careful dance up Praxis's spine. It wasn't just the shock of finding out that her father was a wizard. It wasn't just the nerves of finally facing the situation, seeing it for herself. It wasn't even the sight of Prestina sitting trapped before Prawl, glowering up at the man that was poised and ready to kill her at a moment's notice. The magic here was *wrong*. Praxis could feel it, a subtle vibration in the air that set her teeth on edge.

Then she saw it.

Then she knew.

The Beacon was *bleeding*.

Maybe not in the most literal sense. To the naked eye, nothing about it appeared amiss, and certainly the glass was containing it—for now. But Praxis could see its magic leaking through, years of neglect having damaged the balance between it and the mortal world. And there Prawl stood, proudly towering over it, soaking up all the excess magic like some kind of energy vampire. The Beacon itself was screaming on the table, a shrill whine that only Praxis could hear.

It was almost more than Praxis could bear. She fought against a shudder as fear stabbed icicles beneath her skin.

One problem at a time, she told herself, though it was Kaedrich's voice that took shape in her mind.

Praxis took another step forward. "You don't want to do this."

"The hells I don't," Prawl said. "There is nothing I wouldn't do to save my company, Praxis. *Nothing.*"

"I know. Daddy, I know." She took another step, easing around the far end of the table. "Listen to me, though: I've been where you're standing. I know what it feels like, to have that kind of power coursing through you. It *wants* to be used, and you want to use it. But I'm telling you, as your daughter, the certainty you're feeling right now *won't last.* And when it wears off . . . you're not going to like what you find."

Prawl's lip curled up. He still hadn't taken his attention off of Prestina. "I will, if it keeps my company where it belongs."

"No," Praxis said, her throat seizing up on her. "You won't. Choices like this come at a cost—one that stays with you forever."

"If you're trying to scare me—"

"Look at me, Daddy."

A muscle beneath Prawl's beard twitched. His magic was overextended, stretched out to blanket the entire room, but did he know, did he understand, that he did not have to stay looking fixedly at Prestina? For the first time, a twinge of sympathy passed through Praxis; she'd had training, years of study. Who had guided Prawl, when his magic began to manifest itself? Had anyone?

Praxis came to a stop about halfway up the length of the table, behind the chair of a minister who was stuck gripping the table so hard that his already pale knuckles had turned first white, then angry pink.

"It's okay," Praxis said. "Your hold will maintain itself without eye contact."

Prawl snorted. He shook his head, just enough. "You *would* say that."

"I swear on my blood that it's true. I am not trying to trick you. I just want you to look at me."

"Why?"

"Look at me."

Prawl did not—at least, not at first. He licked his lips, considering his options. Prestina continued to glare up at him, their eyes dead set and locked against each other. There seemed to be an entire argument passing wordlessly between them, years of meaning wending together in an instant.

Slowly, slowly, Prawl turned his head.

He saw his daughter.

It was true that Praxis had come into the room unarmed, divested of both traditional weapons and the spark of defensive magic. But while Prawl had been deciding whether or not he believed her, a trace of magic had snapped to life behind Praxis's eyes. She threaded it out slowly, willing it through her blood. Letting truth spread like corruption through her veins. This magic did not manipulate anything, did not change anything. Rather the opposite: as it traveled, it lit up all the dark patches of Praxis's soul, turned her hidden truths inside-out for her father to see. No one else, no one without magic, would be able to tell the difference, and even an ordinary wizard wouldn't necessarily see it. But Praxis knew, without being told, that Prawl's fear had driven him into the cracked and vulnerable corner where the world splits itself open, where a person's life force is revealed. She could see, in the way he held his hand toward her mother, that he was one yank away from stealing Prestina's for good.

So he would see hers.

She didn't like to think about hers. She'd seen it for herself only a few times, those horrible moments when she'd fallen into this view herself. It glowed fiercely like the sun, enhanced to be so much brighter than it was supposed to be by the life forces she'd already stolen from others. Praxis breathed steadily, keeping the magic running through her veins. Truth.

"Do you see, now?" Praxis said. "The damage it does?"

Prawl's eyes widened. The glimmer of the Beacon reflected in them, all the corrupted power he should not have, that was never meant for mortal hands. Praxis cursed herself for not having noticed it before— Prawl had to have been absorbing it for weeks now, but Praxis had been so wrapped up in her own problems that she hadn't taken the time to look for it. Now he was saturated, fit to burst. Praxis looked into his eyes, but it wasn't her father she saw in there, not really.

"It's . . . it's beautiful," he said.

What little hope Praxis had brought into the room with her curdled and died.

"No. No, it's not."

"Yes it is," Prawl said with a wide, sloppy grin. "The *power* of it—like staring into the purest depths of the mines. Can you hear it?" He tipped his head, tapping one finger against his temple. "The way the darkness calls to you?"

"Stop it."

"Oh, no." Prawl laughed. "No, this is perfect! How did you manage it? Tell me, my opal. How do I become like you?"

"You don't," Praxis said. "You don't *want* to. This"—she gestured at herself, at everything she represented—"is what it looks like when you're fundamentally *broken*. Don't you get it? There is something dead inside of me, and I can *never fix it*."

Truth is an ugly thing.

Praxis shut her eyes. A sob tore at her chest, fighting to break free. Had she even realized this about herself, yet? The depths to which the damage ran, the full extent of her broken soul?

"Daddy, please," she said. She looked back at her father, the two of them locked in a standoff. Praxis needed leverage, she needed power, and what she'd thought was her guarantee had faltered. She sighed. "You don't want to be like this. Think about what you've already sacrificed. Think about *Pranders*!"

"Don't say that name!" Prawl shouted as a convulsion seemed to ripple through his body, barely contained. But a portion of his concentration slipped—Praxis saw it, in the slight flinch of the ministers.

"I have to," Praxis said, seizing hold of it before it slipped away from her. "Look at what it's already made you do! Your own *son*. My *brother*."

"He shouldn't have been snooping!"

"So because he made one mistake, he had to die for it?" Praxis shook her head. "This isn't *you*. Please, can't you see that? You have to let it go. It's not worth it."

Prawl shook his head. "No. That's where you're wrong. Don't you *understand*, Praxis? Without the company, I am *nothing*! If this is what it takes, to keep me in control—!"

"It won't."

The voice came from halfway down the table. One of the nameless men in suits, their identical faces impossible to distinguish. They filled the room like a school of fish, each one blending into the next and then the next. Prawl's hold on them must have weakened, just enough. The minister's face was slick with sweat, and his movements were stiff as if fighting to break through. Praxis felt the tension in Prawl's concentration as his magic surged through the room, trying to regain control. But something had loosened, somewhere, and now with a struggle, the minister rose to his feet.

"We will not be terrorized, Prawl," he said. His breath fought for purchase in the unstable footing of the room. "If that is your goal, then you should know now that it will fail. If anything, you've only proven what this Conclave already knew: that your time has long since come."

A twisted smirk curled Prawl's lip. "Is that so?"

"It is. Even you have to see that."

Praxis winced. "Oh, for sanity's sake, shut up!"

"Yes, do!" Prestina added. Her voice was laced with desperation as she looked back and forth between him and Praxis. "Let my daughter handle this."

A tiny wash of gratitude passed through Praxis. It was an odd feeling, to be on the same side as her mother. Especially today.

Unfortunately, it did not help matters. The minister bristled. "Nonsense. I will not be silenced by *women*."

"You will if you value your life!" Praxis said. "So shut up, and—"

"No! I will not be silenced! The Conclave requires a unanimous vote to reverse an inheritance process, and I am here to say Prawl Fellows *will not* be getting that vote! Not unless it is over my dead body!"

Prawl smiled. His whole body seemed to relax, a bit of the fight disappearing from his shoulders. "So be it, then."

He raised his hand. His hold on Prestina's life energy, held slack until now, released as Prawl seized hold of the glow spooling out from the minister.

There was no time—there was only action and reaction. Praxis threw herself forward, until she was right at the table.

"I'll take the company!"

The words were out of Praxis's mouth before she even knew she would say them, but they were enough. Finally, finally, they were enough.

Everyone stopped. The room fell silent.

Prawl was staring at her—startled by her outburst, and obviously not understanding why Praxis had said what she said. But he had paused, his hand frozen in the air, and that was all Praxis needed.

She grasped onto that hesitation, like a life rope thrown to a woman lost at sea.

"I'll take the company," Praxis repeated. She wanted to be slower and calmer, but her voice was still twinged with hysterics, her speech rapid and desperate. "And then you can run it in my name. Do whatever you want with it, I don't care. Or, I don't know, retire if you'd rather, and study magic full-time—whatever you want. Just . . . please, please let me help you. No one has to die today."

It was a long shot, a stab in the dark. Praxis had no idea if it would work, if any of what she was saying would even appeal to her father, much less if it was something that could be put into action once the Minor Conclave was free of his thrall. Still, Praxis had to try.

"But you're leaving," Prawl said.

Actually Prawl. Praxis heard the difference, even if no one else did. For the first time since entering the room, she was speaking to a version of her father that was untouched by the power he'd accessed, that was nothing but Prawl, the man who'd snuck Praxis sweets when she was being punished, the man who'd stood by outside of her bedroom when she'd come home sobbing from her Qol Nar, the man who had warned her not to make choices based on other people's expectations.

The father she'd abandoned. Who had wrapped her in a hug that defied age when she'd returned, who looked across the table at her with tears in his eyes when he thought she wouldn't notice.

Praxis swallowed down a sudden lump in her throat. "I don't have to. I'll stay. If that's what you need me to do, Daddy . . . I'll stay."

"Oh, Praxis."

She could see the way he wanted to agree. Could see the war he was fighting inside, in the downturn of his eyes and the twist of his mouth. Father, businessman, wizard, murderer, husband, Fellows. He had worn so many faces throughout his life, but who was he, in the end? Which voice was going to win?

Prawl's jaw set.

"I can't do that to you."

He pulled.

There was no warning, no time to stop it. The minister was alive one moment, and a corpse the next. He fell to the ground as a *no*-shaped scream ripped itself from Praxis's throat.

And so this was it, the moment where the decision had been made for her. The world around Praxis seemed to slow and crystallize, like water freezing into place in the ice garden when she was a teenager. Her throat still ached with the last of the scream, and the air crackled with unseen magic that hit her tongue like a metallic tang. The minister—she did not even know his name, he was just another face sticking out of just another fur suit—had landed flat on his back, his blank eyes staring up at Praxis with neither accusations nor pleas, neither surprise nor acceptance. He was just *there*, just *dead*, just a pile of meat and bone and blood that was already beginning to cool. And Prawl . . . Prawl stood there, his eyes closed in near-rapture as he absorbed the life that was never meant to belong to him. There was no question left, no hope to cling to. The truth sat between them, as heavy as the glacier they were buried in.

She was going to have to kill her father.

Time ticked forward again as flames sprang to life, unbidden, over Praxis's palms. The sounds of the world crashed back into place: Prawl's triumphant laughter, the faint gasping panic of Prestina, a few strains of what might have been terrified screaming that managed to escape the thrall Prawl had managed to hold on the rest of the ministers.

"This ends *now*," Praxis said.

Prawl's laughter cut off sharply as he narrowed his eyes at his daughter. "Does it?"

In the next moment, a bevy of things happened in rapid succession, too many to distinguish into discrete actions, tumbling into each other like waves breaking on a beach. Praxis flicked her hands forward and open, unleashing wild furls of flame in Prawl's direction; Prawl raised a single finger; the magic oozing from the Beacon flared, combining with Prawl's already enhanced level of untamed power; panic struck at Praxis's heart as her flames parted effortlessly around Prawl, fire transmuting into harmless curls of smoke that framed him from behind. He stretched his hand toward her, palm upturned in a gesture that, in other contexts, might have looked generous and inviting.

It was not generous and inviting.

He curled one finger and then another, beckoning.

Praxis gasped, and staggered forward. Pain flared behind her eyes as her magic crackled to life, harder and faster than any natural summons. It burned like fire as it ravaged across her body. Praxis shut her eyes, tried desperately to clamp down on her magic, but it just kept slipping through her grasp like trying to hold water in her fist. It coursed through her, drawn out, ripped from herself, from her skin, and there was nothing she could do to stop it, she was losing it, she was losing *herself*, she—

"*Please.*"

Praxis just barely managed to eek the word out, squeezed from her lungs as if it was her last breath. She had collapsed toward the table, just barely holding herself on her elbows and knees. She did not entirely know, in that moment, what she was begging for. For it to stop? For the end to come swiftly? For salvation?

It did not matter.

"Shh, don't worry, little opal," Prawl said. His voice filled the room, pounded against her, slithered into her thoughts as if they were her own. "I won't kill you. I'm . . . fixing you."

No, Praxis thought, but couldn't say. She tried to shake her head, tried to choke the word out. All that was left was the pain and the sense of it, *no no no no,* drumming loud in her head, but it wasn't doing any good. It wouldn't stop him. He was shushing her, soothing like a father, and Praxis couldn't hold on much longer, the world was shifting in and out of focus. Fog, dull and gray and cold, seeped into her mind.

A shrill whistle pierced through the veil. Rapid and sharp, like an alarm sounding. Praxis's eyes snapped open, recognizing the pattern, and the hold on her magic snapped off. The release sent it cascading back toward Praxis, so sudden that the force of it knocked her completely backwards, onto her ass.

It roared back to life, safe and angry inside of her.

"Everybody out!" Kaedrich shouted.

Praxis clicked her thumb to reengage her leg brace and hauled herself too fast onto her feet. She wavered, her head spinning.

Kaedrich had charged through an open doorway somewhere behind Prawl, along with half a dozen clerks and administrators, who were currently ushering the ministers out. The whistle she'd used, that she'd learned from Falconridge, had been developed by Syll monks decades ago, the frequency specially aligned to disrupt a wizard's sense of the world around them. Praxis remembered vividly how well it had worked on her the first time, when she hadn't heard of it yet, when she hadn't been prepared, and it seemed to have had a similar impact on Prawl. He stumbled like a drunk, clutching at his head, while the room erupted in chaos around him.

Enough chaos to allow Kaedrich to slip past him. Enough for her to reach out, the Beacon within arm's reach.

Praxis saw what was going to happen—just before it happened, too late to do anything about it.

Prawl turned, grabbing a piece of the Beacon's oozing magic as he swung his fist. The punch connected with Kaedrich's side, a flare of light and a strong gust of wind scooping her straight off her feet. She hit the wall, her shoulder and hip connecting with the ice, her head clonking painfully to the side.

Praxis raged forward. There was no guilt left in her heart, no mercy to cloud her judgment. The world glowed, vibrant and *alive* around Praxis, and Praxis reached through the tangle of energy, seizing her father by the throat. His life force swirled around them both, writhing in confusion until they were steeped in it, as if it didn't quite understand who it belonged to. Praxis saw the moment, disconnected from herself. Prawl's eyes widened in terror. Praxis, Prawl; father, daughter; killer, killer; wizard, wizard. For a moment, was there any difference? Two broken souls. They would never be whole again.

She could do it. She knew that she could do it.

But she did not *want* to do it.

The magic of the Beacon teased itself around them, twisting through Prawl's own like a seductress prowling the room.

Maybe that was the key, then. If the Beacon's magic, bleeding out from its realm, was the temptation and the power that had granted her father both the ability to carry this out, and the madness to want to try, then perhaps cutting it off would cure both problems.

At the very least, it was a better option than patricide.

Before she could talk herself out of it, Praxis released her hold on her father and plunged her arms deep into the magic of the Beacon. She drew it toward her, letting it fill her up, up, up, until it felt as if she would burst of it. Her head spun. Her throat closed up, as if she was going to vomit. The world pitched, and Praxis tumbled forward, landing hard on her hands and knees. But it wasn't ice that met her palms, it wasn't ice that broke her fall.

It was stone.

A voice boomed out across the distance, rolling like a thunderclap.

"Welcome, mortal."

HANDS UNHINDERED BY gloves or controls. Two legs that required no extra gears to maneuver themselves. Praxis pushed herself up, in the threadbare pinstripe trousers she used to wear, the ill-fitted shirt that was once white. Her slate-blue coat settled around her as she stood tall in the realm of the Beacon.

No shadows waited to greet her, no hallways stretched out into endlessness. Instead, she found herself in a sea of freestanding doors, arranged on a series of concentric circles. Tracks carried the doors spinning around the circumference, pausing once in a while, starting up again, layers upon layers of them turning this way and that like some elaborate piece of clockwork. So this was not the domain of the Beacon of Souls, and Praxis was not dead. That, at least, was a small comfort.

A very small comfort. For it did nothing to settle the question of how she had gotten here, or what would be required of her to *leave* once she was done.

The booming voice continued. It echoed out from a central pillar standing tall in the middle of the circles, a Beacon shining bright over the top. Praxis must have been at least a mile from the center, but the voice carried as easily as if the Beacon was standing right beside her.

"Right on time."

Praxis shrugged. "If you say so."

"Such honesty, though," the Beacon said, "to show the truth of yourself to your father. I have to say, I was not expecting that. I suppose this means I'll need to rethink some of your future doorways—but then, you never were a creature of consistency. So much destruction. So much chaos."

"Is this where I'm supposed to be impressed that you know who I am?" Praxis asked.

"Your reverence or lack thereof does not concern me, mortal. I know everyone, but make no mistake: we all know *you*. You're the one that started it all. The *meddler*. The schism child. The Queen of Ice."

"Flattering, I'm sure," Praxis said. "But I'm not a queen."

The Beacon chuckled. Its laughter rippled through the empty land, bouncing from door to door as they spun past her, so that it seemed to be coming from every direction at once.

"Are you so certain?" the Beacon asked.

A bitter chill swept over Praxis, as strong as a surface gust. She gasped and clutched her arms against herself, but it was not fabric that covered her arms anymore, not really. Instead, layers upon layers of frost had been woven together to create something even more exquisite than lace. It fitted over Praxis like a dress, sweeping out behind her into a train of snow. The sleeves hung down and covered most of her hands, leaving only her fingers free, which were wrapped in twisted rings of ice. A high collar of frost and spikes danced on the edge of her peripheral vision, and the weight on her head told her well enough that a frozen crown rested in the sweep of her much longer hair. Disgust wrinkled her nose.

"I don't have time for this," Praxis said. She ripped at the delicate material, shaking off the illusion as easily as brushing snow from her shoulders. She would not be distracted. She stepped forward, her normal look restored. "I need to fix this—I need to fix *you*."

"Indeed?" the Beacon asked, its voice light with amusement. "Then by all means, mortal. *Diagnose* me. If you can."

Praxis took a tentative step forward. Doors trundled past, stuck along their tracks like an endless loop of trains. She needed time, but how much did she have left, here? She didn't even know how she'd arrived, much less how to get out again. Was it the wound itself? In which case, if she did manage to somehow fix the Beacon, stop the bleeding flow of magic . . . would that trap her here? Time, time. *Focus.*

She waited for the ring of doors in front of her to pause, then leapt through the gaps between them before they started up again. One level down, Praxis thought. There were only a few hundred more to go. She looked at the pillar of the Beacon, so far in the distance. It hung beneath a heavy sky, the one patch of light in the whole realm.

"It would help if you told me who you are," Praxis said. "Which part of the world you control."

"Yes," the Beacon said. "I'm sure it would."

"You're not going to, though, are you?"

"I might. Who knows? I can see so much, mortal, yet no creature can see the choices in their own future."

The ring of doors closest to Praxis slowed, then stopped. A single door stood directly before her: heavy with age, simple slats of hardy wood bolted together with iron.

A sudden impulse seized Praxis. She leapt forward, grasping the door latch with both hands. A simple slide-bolt mechanism. It slid open, the door swinging wide in its frame.

There was nothing through the gap. Just an empty frame, the next ring of doors whirling past as if nothing at all had happened. Praxis leaned her head through, wondering if perhaps whatever magic controlled this place required her to pass beneath the arch, but again: nothing happened.

She slammed the door shut, and the Beacon's chuckle echoed throughout the realm. The ring began to turn again, removing that door, replacing it with a blur of others.

"Do not be discouraged, child," the Beacon said. "That choice was not yours to walk through."

"So *someone* could have."

"Of course. People walk through them all the time. Even now. Even as you move among their futures, choices are being made."

Another ring paused in front of Praxis. She took the opportunity to duck quickly between the doorways again, moving farther toward the center. The ring before her was stopped, too, although before Praxis could dart through, something else caught her eye. Several doorways to her left, a small gap had opened up beneath the track, and Praxis watched as a mechanical clamp reached up, seizing the door and sucking it down into the depths. The gap closed up, and the ring slid instantly back into motion, as if the door had never been there in the first place.

"You're saying these doors are people's choices?"

The Beacon said nothing in response, though Praxis felt the wave of an impression drifting off of it, the sensation of a casual shrug.

Praxis tipped her head, studying the doors more closely. So many doors, of all different designs.

Sadly, this knowledge did not seem to help her any. Not yet, anyway, though Praxis tucked it into the back of her mind as she edged past another ring, and then another. The direct approach was never going to work, not here. Praxis chewed her lip for a moment, turning the Beacon's words over in her mind.

"What did you mean, I *started* it all?"

"You awoke her," the Beacon said. "You and the false-faced woman. Did it never occur to you to wonder what would happen to the garden in your wake? Did you never think to visit?"

"The garden?" Praxis asked, though even as she spoke, the answer settled itself in her mind. A layer of reality, running literally underneath the realm of each of the Beacons. Praxis had only been there once, when she'd first been seizing control of the Beacon of Souls away from Pon Lanali. At the time, the garden had been dead and dust, waking up only as the two of them battled their way through. Praxis could have returned, she supposed now, during the time she served as Lady of Souls, but . . .

"Why would I? It's just a garden."

The Beacon's realm shuddered. The doors around Praxis wavered ominously.

"You understand nothing," the Beacon said. Its voice lashed against Praxis like the disciplined strike of a school teacher. "The garden is flourishing, glorious and terrible, and she is tending to her crops."

"She?"

"Sister. Mother. God. She has so many names, all of them wrong." The Beacon sighed. "It does not matter. You will find out soon enough— or not. I have imagined a possibility for that, too, although I fear she fights against it. She is working, though, ohhh, always working. Such vision, even I cannot predict."

Praxis raised an eyebrow. "Right . . . What does any of this have to do with me, again?"

"Nothing," the Beacon said. "Everything. Only fate will tell."

"I don't believe in fate," Praxis said.

"It doesn't believe in you, either. So I suppose one of you will be wrong, Queen of Ice."

"Stop calling me that."

"You cannot avoid the truth forever."

"And I'm not trying to," Praxis said. "It's just not my name."

"Not yet."

"Don't I get a choice in that?"

The Beacon chuckled. "Perhaps."

Praxis shook her head. More nonsense, more riddles. This was, perhaps, one of Praxis's least favorite aspects of the Beacons—for sanity's sake, why couldn't an immortal creature learn to just *say what it meant*? Was that really so much to ask?

Perhaps it didn't matter, though, because finally Praxis had reached the pillar. Far quicker than she should have, far quicker than she would have if this place were real. Praxis couldn't help but feel that the Beacon had allowed her this mercy, though for what purpose, she didn't like to speculate.

At the center of the Beacon's realm was a ring of doors, four of them separated from the others. They stood stationary in their track, so tight around the pillar that at first glance they might have been built directly into the stone. Praxis circled the central pillar, regarding them carefully. Two of them were made of stone themselves, ancient enough that it was a wonder they were still standing. Dust coated them, cobwebs strung like Saint Gildern's Day ribbon across the surface. Another was an elaborate wooden beauty, carvings of trees and foxes and geese etched in such detail that Praxis could easily imagine them springing to life at any moment.

The fourth one was broken.

Something had ripped it from its track. The frame was cracked, the latch on the door itself busted apart as if a thief had been too impatient to pick the lock. It sagged against the pillar, hanging open.

Praxis stepped toward it. There was something familiar about it, though Praxis couldn't place exactly what. It was a fine door, to be sure, sturdy and ornate at the same time, but nothing special. Paneling broke it into upper and lower halves, raised curves adding just a little flair to an otherwise plain design. Chips of white paint littered the ground around it, and the gold doorknob gleamed bright in the pooling light of the Beacon, high above.

And yet, Praxis was sure she'd seen it before. Somewhere, sometime. She felt as if she'd already passed through it, the door itself so inconsequential and easily ignored. She reached toward it and her pulse kicked up, her throat closing over on her. The sound of it slamming shut—again and again, four times in quick succession—rang strongly through her mind. She saw it, suddenly, her memory strong enough to block out the present: this same door had trapped them in a room in the Council's Crescent in Monfort. The same room where Kaedrich had died.

Praxis doubled over, sick with the very thought of it. She tucked her head between her knees, willing herself not to faint. "What's this doing here?" she asked, though it wasn't clear, even to her, if she was asking the Beacon, or merely bemoaning the cruel hand of fate, that it should have cursed her with the distraction here, now, of all places.

"Never mind that," the Beacon said, and Praxis laughed a deranged laugh, that such an ancient creature could imagine such a thing were possible.

Never mind. Praxis could never forget, not for an instant. It hovered forever in the back of her awareness. Everything that might have been. Everything that was unfolding now, as a result.

Never mind.

Praxis forced herself to take a deep breath. *Never mind,* she heard again, though it was Kaedrich's voice this time, not the Beacon's. She straightened up, tucking the memories forcibly into a smaller corner of her mind. She craned her neck back, until she could look straight up to the mighty orb of the Beacon, standing tall over the whole of its realm.

"Very good," the Beacon said. "Now then, it is time to make a choice."

In a tight ring, right behind Praxis, a set of three doors slid up from a gap in the tracks. They spun into place, coming to rest before her. All three were identical: made of ice, polished bright as mirrors. Her own face reflected back at her, slightly distorted. Praxis made herself look away.

"I have indulged you, mortal, because that is what you needed, but now it is time you know the truth: you will not fix me."

"Don't be so sure. If you give me a little more time, I'm sure I could figure out what's—"

"Yes, I'm sure you could. And one day, looking back, you might work it out; it's really not that hard. But no, you misunderstand. You *can* fix me. You *won't*, however. Don't forget, little one, that I imagine all possibilities, and in none of them are you willing to do what is necessary to set things right. That's okay," it added, talking over the beginning of Praxis's protests, "in truth, it does not hurt that badly. And pain is . . . quite the novelty, for a creature such as myself. No, hush. I have spoken. These are your choices."

The doors spun around again, just once, as if trying to draw Praxis's attention back.

"Your father possesses a kind of magic that does not belong to him. Left to its natural course, he will surely die from using it. You could let him," the Beacon said. "That is one choice. His fury will rage hot and fast, leaving destruction in its wake, but in the end there is nothing he can do to hold on to it."

"Pass," Praxis said.

"Very well."

The first door spun away—the whole ring retreated, sight unseen. When it returned, only two doors remained.

A sense of finality struck Praxis, then, seizing her by the throat. First three choices, and now two. What was left for her, hidden behind those doors? She'd been so fast to dismiss the first one, but what if that was the most humane of the options? Praxis stared at the remaining doors, mocking her in their simplicity.

Her fists clenched tight at her sides. "What kind of sick game are you playing?"

"Life," the Beacon said. "Just life, mortal. Nothing more, nothing less. Now then, your next choice: you can carry out the task you had set out to do."

"You expect me to kill my father? After I already decided not to?"

"I *expect* nothing, mortal. It is *your* choice. It still stands before you, and I can see a future in which you would still take it."

"Well, I don't," Praxis said, squaring her shoulders. She looked at the two doors, the only options the Beacon was giving her. Her stomach squirmed, but there was no question. Praxis batted her hand. "Take it away."

The two doors spun away on their ring.

Only one returned.

It drew to a stop, settling in the stone with an ominous grinding sound, cut by the sharpest silence.

The door creaked as it opened—before Praxis could stop it, before she could question it—and from a haze of darkness and emptiness and hopelessness, there fell a gem.

Specifically, a lapus lumeni.

It tumbled out of the open doorway, as if someone was chucking out the trash, and clattered onto the stones by her feet. The door slammed shut in its wake.

Praxis picked it up.

"Behold your future, mortal."

Praxis snorted. "My future is a rock?"

The realm of the Beacon shuddered underfoot, a ripple of discontent emanating from the pillar. "Do not make jest. Few of your kind are ever granted the opportunity to truly see the paths that lay before them."

"And not that I'm not loving this," Praxis said, her wrist flaring with guilt because she wasn't being as sarcastic as she should be, "but seriously, are you ever going to cut the riddles and just tell me what this thing is supposed to be?"

A moment of silence from the Beacon. Nothing but the endless scrape of rings upon rings of doors, whispering like waves against the sand of inevitability. Then:

"That is the lapus lumeni in your father's pocket. Do you truly not recognize it, Queen of Ice?"

"Why would I recognize—?" Praxis started, but then she turned it over. A dusky gray hue marred the crystal's normal sheen. This wasn't lapus lumeni after all; this was something nameless, something dark and twisted, something she'd never intended to craft, not really. Praxis shut her eyes, remembering the drive she'd felt, tinkering with the magic. The pull. As if the ice around her was whispering, teasing her with visions of the glory she'd achieve, the reward she'd be granted from her father. The inspiration that had finally led to its breakthrough. Praxis understood now, in a way she hadn't before: it had never come from her.

A low chuckle thrummed out from the Beacon's pillar, purring in Praxis's bones.

"You mother*fucker*!" Praxis screamed. She turned sharply, glaring up at the twisting mass in the orb above her head. The edges of the crystal cut into Praxis's hand as she clenched her fingers around it. "You did this! This is what you wanted from the beginning! *You* had me craft these, because you *knew* it would come down to this! Didn't you? *Didn't you!*"

She did not wait for an answer. She hurtled the crystal, aiming at the broken glass of the Beacon.

Only at the last second, just before the two pieces struck, did Praxis remember what had happened the last time a Beacon's orb had been shattered from inside its own realm. She lurched, throwing her arm out, and the crystal was struck by her magic and veered off-course, hopping up and over the dome of the glass.

Panic flared through Praxis. Shit, what if she'd been wrong? What if her *reaction*, and not her use of the crystal, had been what the Beacon had been hoping for, all this time? If it could see all of Praxis's future choices, if it could weigh their likelihoods, wouldn't it have known about her temper? How in the seven hells do you fight something that can know what you'll do before you do?

She raced to the other side of the pillar, collecting the crystal before she lost it here forever. The door, her door, came with her, spinning around the tightly wound track. Always in front of her. Waiting.

"Clever little thing," the Beacon said, a touch of amusement in its voice.

This time, Praxis took a second to collect herself. She tried to will her irritation back, tried to ebb the flow of magic crackling through her, begging her to act. To *react*. This time, she held the crystal close against her chest, the whole of her attention on the shape of the door.

"What's my choice?"

"You know what that is used for."

"Storing magic."

"Magic, yes," the Beacon said. "Mortals call it magic. But *you've* seen it for what it really is. You know what it really looks like. You're clever, Queen of Ice. What else can be stored in this?"

Praxis's grip tightened around the crystal. She knew in an instant what the Beacon was talking about—the life force energy that ran through all creatures. Perhaps she'd always known what she was crafting. The whispers from her lab came back to her now, walking on her shoulders and pressing against her face like a contented cat.

Gods, what had she done?

"No," Praxis said. "I already said I wouldn't kill my father. So you must have something else in mind."

"Who said anything about death?" the Beacon asked. "Death is merely a byproduct of severing the tether between the body and its life force. Make no mistake: this was always your path. Your *choice* is merely whether or not you will free him from the prison of his own design."

"I don't underst—" Praxis started, but then the Beacon's words clicked into place in her mind. Praxis's eyes went wide. "Oh. *Oh.*"

"Indeed."

"I can't," Praxis said. The only thing she could say. The only thing she could do. She stared at the crystal in her hand, the inky shade of death that somehow already tainted it. Except what the Beacon said was true: these were merely designed to *house* magical energy. If Praxis siphoned off her father's life force, trapping it in place inside . . . but left the smallest thread, trailing invisibly between them . . .

"He would continue to live," the Beacon said, as if reading Praxis's mind.

"You call that a life?" Praxis asked. She pictured it: unconscious, helpless, the essence of himself encased inside of this, his body left to either be tended to, or to rot. "You can't ask me to do this."

"I ask nothing of you, mortal. I merely offer you what lies in your future. I have seen the affection you harbor for your father. I crafted you this choice."

"Wait . . . Are you trying to tell me you had me create these as a *kindness*?" Praxis asked.

The Beacon's light shifted, almost thoughtfully, in its orb. "If you could not kill him," the Beacon said simply, "then there had to be another way."

A strangled laugh escaped Praxis then, the sound curling toward hysteria. Because, of course, of *course*, a Beacon would see things that way, and of course, of *course*, it was technically right. That was the trouble with them, these beings, these terrible, wonderful, awful, eternal things. They saw things as they were, and yet—they understood nothing.

"How can I do it to him?" Praxis asked, her voice cracking. "He's my *father*."

The Beacon *hmm*ed. "A Beacon would not claim to understand," it said. It spoke slowly, as if, for once, it was choosing its words with precise care. "But I believe it is a thing you mortals call 'love.'"

Chapter Forty

ONCE THERE WAS a young man named Prawl Fellows.

Not so young, anymore. Not that he looked his age: luck and blood-lines had blessed him with a perpetually jovial face that was often mistaken for youth, and of course the soft glow of the lapus lumeni provided an ageless, ethereal air to most Yandosians. But he was starting to feel it, the passage of time, as a slight ache in his bones. He was starting to see it, in the roll of his expanding waistline and the weariness in his eyes that greeted him when he looked in the mirror.

It wasn't unexpected. He was forty-two years old by then, the head of a financial empire that spanned most of the world. Three of his children were adults themselves, and even the youngest, even little Praxis—gods, she was so big now. Eight years old, full of fire and ice. It was all Prawl could do most days not to burst out laughing whenever Praxis would jut her small chin out, sassing one of her brothers, or refusing to listen to her mother's pedantic social instructions.

He watched her now as she entered the party. Late, as usual—Prestina guiding her into the room with an iron grip and a smile of ice.

Prawl made himself turn back to his guests. He'd never hear the end of it, later, if Prestina got wind that he was ignoring his duty, and actually *enjoying* himself at his own *party*. He threw himself into the business of laughing and appearing to drink, schmoozing with all the right people.

The guest list had been curated by Prestina, the better to acquire expansion rights for one of their deepest mines, and it was important they secure the deal tonight.

The evening dragged on, like a knife sliding over Prawl's arm. One time, he looked over to find a guest actually talking to little Praxis, the two of them off in the corner and engaged in such deep conversation that Prawl was forced to wonder what it was they were talking about—but there was no time for that. He glanced at Prestina, who'd also noticed, and she marked her daughter's good behavior with a tiny nod of approval; then she narrowed her eyes at Prawl, and he all but jumped to clap the back of a passing minister. "Hestol," Prawl said, just the right amount of friendly drawing out the name, "it's been too long. How's the wife?"

There was only one enjoyable facet to these little gatherings, and that was the card game. Prawl was still good at them, unnaturally so, and better than that: Prestina didn't play. Hadn't since they'd married.

"Gentlemen, welcome," Prawl said with genuine pleasure as the guests filtered in one by one. He only invited men these days, he'd learned that lesson the hard way. He was standing beside a long table, cards and drinks already laid out, and he motioned to them now. "Help yourself to a chair and a glass; I promise you, there's going to be plenty."

He took his own chair—and was joined, almost immediately, by the man Praxis had been speaking to earlier.

Prawl hid his grimace. He and the man, Moc, had been acquainted for several years now, and while Prawl had nothing in particular against Moc's temperament or family, there was one reason for Prawl to resent him: he's the only man Prawl hadn't been able to beat at Fiddler's Dash in fifteen years.

Well. That was going to change, Prawl thought to himself as the rest of the men settled in place. His fingers were already shuffling the cards, excitement sparking behind his eyes.

Four hours later, determination had soured into resentment as Moc laid down the last of his cards: a full chord.

Prawl did not even try to keep the scowl off of his face as he threw his own cards, facedown, onto the table. "Take it," he snarled.

Moc smiled benignly as he reached forward, drawing the excessive pile of money that lay between them into his own hoard. "An excellent game."

Prawl snorted. "For you."

"You shouldn't be so hard on yourself," Moc said, but Prawl was already starting to ignore him. He stood up, walking over to the sideboard as if he was going to pour himself another drink. Everyone else had long abandoned them by this point, and mostly Prawl just wanted an excuse to put some distance between himself and Moc.

He should have been able to win.

It wasn't ego, or vanity. It was just . . . he was good with cards. *Very* good with cards. So good that at times, it was almost like he *knew* what the other players were holding, like he didn't even need to guess. Except for Moc, damn him. Prawl just couldn't get a read on Moc, no matter how much he tried.

"After all," Moc continued from somewhere behind him, "you're clearly untrained, and going up against a much stronger wizard. Really, it's remarkable you're able to harness your abilities so specifically."

The drink paused in Prawl's hand, lifted halfway to his lips. "What?"

"Your magic," Moc said simply.

Prawl turned around. He was still holding the drink, the one normal thing he had to ground himself against. The ridges of the cut crystal ran so straight that they bordered on sharp, and he ran his thumb along the familiar lines.

"My . . . ?"

"Yes," Moc said. He smiled. "Surely you've realized it, by now?"

Had he? Suddenly Prawl wasn't so sure. His initial reaction was shock and denial, sure, why wouldn't it be, but . . . He thought of his skill at cards, of the headaches that built behind his eyes after a long night spent gambling. Of the way that he just seemed to *know* who was coming to knock on his door, before they entered. Prawl knew next to nothing of magic, so it was easy to dismiss these things, throughout his life, as luck and intuition. He'd never spoken of it to anyone. But standing here now, looking at Moc, the idea began to settle on Prawl in a way that felt . . . *right*.

He licked his lips. *Magic.* Depths help him, he couldn't even imagine the possibilities, but already his mind was churning with potential. The *idea* of it grabbed him—all the things he might do to bolster the company, all the ways he might finally, *finally* be able to outshine Prestina's great contributions, her glorious plans. The look on her face when—

"Of course, it's far too late to help you," Moc said, and all of Prawl's budding enthusiasm soured in an instant. Moc, seeming to sense this (perhaps he did, what did Prawl know?), gave a casual shrug. "And, I'm sorry to say, your base level of power was stunted to begin with. No, no, it's much more advantageous to focus on your daughter."

"My daughter."

"Praxis."

"Yes, I know who my own daughter is," Prawl snapped. It would only occur to him later, much later, that there were technically two that Moc could have been referring to. A rational part of Prawl's brain told him that the reason he'd never even considered Prenna was that Moc had been seen talking to Praxis earlier, but . . . that explanation never felt true to Prawl. He had never considered Prenna, because Prenna could not be a wizard. Prawl knew this in his gut, an instinctive pull that had always made him love Praxis just a little bit more than his other children.

He remembered, suddenly, when Prestina was pregnant with Praxis. By the eighth child, the novelty had worn off, and even what little excitement and shared bond used to exist between Prawl and Prestina surrounding their first and second had long since disappeared. But. There was one evening, Prawl couldn't even remember why. Prestina was resting in her private library, lying on the couch with her feet up. She'd fallen asleep reading, and Prawl was collecting the book before it slid from her fingers. His touch brushed his wife's ample stomach, not even meaning to, but suddenly this *flood* of emotion had seemed to well up out of nowhere: contentment and trust and mercy and joy, delirious joy of recognition. It punched Prawl so hard that he actually staggered backward, and dropped the book with enough force that the sound of it woke Prestina after all. He had never been able to explain it, never understood it. But the minute his second daughter had been born, he knew she was something special.

Now he knew why.

It was too much for him. Prawl rubbed hard along his brow, trying to stomp down on the heat of tears that had suddenly filled his eyes. Too late, Prawl's life made sense. Too late, he knew what had always separated him from his brothers. The world that Prawl might have had opened up inside of his mind: a world of magic, a world of genuine respect, a world of real power at his fingertips. A world of wonder. A world ripe for the taking, adventure waiting around every corner. This was the world he could never have.

This was the world he'd give to his daughter. Her ticket to something greater.

"How do we proceed?" Prawl asked, looking up.

Moc smiled.

PRAXIS OPENED HER eyes and the world hung frozen, just for a moment, around her. Everything exactly the same as the instant she entered the realm of the Beacon, as if no time at all had passed in the interim. Prawl had fallen back, landing in a stagger on his knees. Kaedrich was lurching forward, charging to Praxis's aid. Prestina was being led out of the room by Lexthur, her head ducked as she tried to avoid the fight spilling out behind her. Praxis took in all of it, in a moment before she released her breath. And then she looked back at her father, the man she was about to condemn.

He was looking back at her.

He was looking *right into* her. As if, somehow, he had seen into the realm with her, had witnessed the choices she'd been facing. His eyes were red, rimmed with tears, turned down at the corners with a remorse so deep that it would surely gut him clean out. In the narrow gap of eternity that Praxis had snared for herself, she reached out and brushed her fingers against the whiskers of her father's beard.

"I'm sorry," Praxis whispered, and though he could not answer, could not move or speak, somehow something shifted in those eyes. And there it was, then, the one thing she needed if she was going to step through this door.

Forgiveness.

The world roared back into chaos. Prawl fell, collapsing from his knees to his side, and in that instant his fur coat fell open. Praxis swept in, seizing the modified lapus lumeni from the inner pocket.

She did not have to work for it. The Beacon's magic was still oozing, still pooling around them, unseen to all but Praxis and her father, and so it was only them that truly saw what was happening as Praxis teased the bulk of amber glow from the soul of her father. Madness was reasserting itself with each rapid blink, and so Praxis did not allow herself to question, did not allow herself to dare.

By the time Kaedrich reached her, it was done. The final thread trailed down from the crystal to Prawl as he laid back, his eyes drifting shut. A weary sigh, like falling asleep, slipped from his chest.

A gasping sob escaped Praxis. The crystal slid from her fingers, landing easily on Prawl's open hand, as if it had always been waiting for it. Praxis clamped her hands over her mouth as Kaedrich, taking in the situation with only a glance, came around and wrapped her arms tightly around Praxis's shoulders.

There was nothing more that could be done, no balm to fix this heartache. Praxis did not dare to look upon her father. Instead, she turned until she spotted it, the source of all her troubles, the Beacon which still sat on the table, bleeding, and even now—*even now*—seemed to ripple with a sense of smugness, like a chuckle grating along the nerves. Praxis wrapped her fingers around it, and a surge of magic lapped at her arm, begging like a dog. "Don't you *dare*," she snapped, low under her breath, but it was enough. The Beacon, perhaps abashed, perhaps bored, perhaps so jaded that it simply did not care about the affairs of mortals anymore, even her, pulled away from her perceptions, until it was nothing more than a crystal orb, as dull as the fake one around her neck.

She slid it into her pocket, letting it bleed. She would deal with it, later.

Outside, assembled members of the Minor Conclave were waiting for her, Prestina and Lexthur among them. So many open faces, terrified, anxiously awaiting the news. They looked so small, now, mere dolls, and their problems such trifles. What did any of them know, of fate and magic and heartache? What did any of them know, of real choice? Praxis watched them. She held her face steady, her eyes dry.

She did not need to say it.

Prestina dipped her head. Several of the members of the Minor Conclave followed suit.

Only Lexthur dared to speak, clearing his throat, stepping forward. He held his face down, abashed, already submissive, as he said, "I know this is a small comfort, but it's yours, by the way. If you want it."

Praxis's brow wrinkled. "What?"

"The company," Lexthur said. "We . . . we just discussed it. Honestly, if this doesn't prove your worth . . ."

"Oh, for sanity's sake," Praxis said, as the world suddenly reasserted itself, heavy and unwelcome. All these petty problems, all these petty choices. What did it even matter to her? "You think I honestly *care* about something like that? *Gods.* Sort it out yourselves—or better still, give it to Prommel. He's the only one of us who's ever had half a soul to begin with."

"Was that an *official* request?" Lexthur asked, but Praxis was already shoving past them, bodies shifting as she barreled through. The only answer she gave was the door slamming shut in her wake.

Beside her, Kaedrich reached out, gripping Praxis's hand. Praxis squeezed back.

The door opened again, the sound chasing them like the desperation of the shoes that fought to catch up.

"Praxis Adello Fellows!" Prestina shouted. "Get yourself back here *right now*, or so help me, I'll—"

"You'll *what*, Mother?" Praxis said. She stopped and turned, so suddenly that Prestina nearly crashed into her. "Hmm? Tell me, what could you *possibly* hope to do to me, that hasn't already been done by now?"

"*Don't* talk to me that way," Prestina said. "I understand you're upset—"

"Oh, you do, do you? So you *understand* that I've trapped my father in an essentially endless sleep, until either his life or his magic runs out, and the only hope he might have for ever waking up again is when there's nothing left to trap anymore? You *understand* that? Because I really don't think you do!"

Prestina's face twitched. She waved her hand in front of her, as if swatting away a bug. "That's not the point. You have a duty to uphold— right here, right now. This company—"

"Is not more important than my father!"

"Of course it is!"

The surprise that echoed through the hall then was so sharp it was almost tangible, the taste of blood on Praxis's tongue. She stepped back, staring at her mother. Even Kaedrich had edged aside, as if she didn't dare approach.

Prestina rolled her eyes. "Don't look at me like that. This is bigger than us, Praxis. We *have* to consider the future. Do you honestly think *Prommel*, of all people, is going to have what it takes? To really put the company first, above *everything*? Do you think he would sacrifice, the way we would?"

"You mean the way *you* would."

"Oh, please," Prestina said. "Don't pretend we're any different, Praxis. Deep down, when it really comes to it, there is nothing we wouldn't do to protect what matters to us."

"No, that's true," Praxis said. A cold chill ran down her spine, but for once she could not bring herself to argue with her mother's point. She shut her eyes, just for a second, as all of it came back to her: Kaedrich, dead in her arms; the Beacon, a shining ray of opportunity.

Prestina's voice floated in from all around her. "Then you know what needs to be done."

Praxis's eyes snapped open. Prestina was just looking at her, so sure, so smug. The perfect portrait of what Praxis was—could be—would be— wouldn't be.

She straightened her spine. "No," Praxis said. "I won't."

Praxis saw the slap coming. Of course she saw the slap coming. But this time, she did not accept it; with a single reach, she'd clamped her own grip around her mother's wrist, stilling it in its tracks. Never once did Praxis look away from her mother's face as the two of them glowered across at each other, each so much alike. Too much alike.

"I just want you to know," Praxis said as she threaded a trail of magic down through her arm, out her fingers, "that I am not doing this to you out of revenge, although I *know* what you tried to do to me"—the magic seeped out, wrapping tightly around Prestina like a shackle—"and I think even you would agree that anger would be justified. No, don't speak," Praxis said. "Don't you dare say a word, Mother, not until I've had my say. You put the company ahead of all of us, my entire life, and now I think it's time for your hard work to be rewarded. You want to feel what responsibility feels like? Real responsibility? Here's responsibility: someone is going to need to look after Father now. To feed him, and clean him, and make sure that no harm comes upon his body."

Prestina's eyes were already widening. Could she tell, somehow, even then, what was happening? As Praxis leaned in, lowering her voice to a whisper, Prestina's breath seemed to freeze in her chest, as cold as the heart that beat there.

"So this is what's going to happen, Mother. I've just trapped you in a binding spell. The farther away from him you get, the more pain you're going to experience, until it becomes just too much to bear. I'm sure some of it's probably already seeping in—so you'd better go to him. And get used to staying by his side, because you're going to be there for a long, long time to come."

"How *dare*—" Prestina started, but then a gasp cut her off. She flinched forward, turning up to stare at her daughter's cold, cold face. Genuine fear began to skitter in the corners of her eyes; the first time, perhaps, that Praxis had ever seen it there.

Good, Praxis thought. She grinned.

"You're the one who tried to trap me here," Praxis said. "Now you can see how it feels." She released her grip on her mother's wrist, finally, tossing Prestina aside as she turned her back. She glanced once at Kaedrich, but Kaedrich was only watching, only waiting. Praxis held out her hand, and Kaedrich took it.

"Praxis!" Prestina cried, but Praxis was already moving off, down the winding steps. Prestina's voice trailed after her, racing out across the distance that Prestina no longer could. "Get back here! Take this off of me!"

"Goodbye, Mother!"

"No, Praxis! *Praxis! Praaaaxiiiiis!*"

Chapter Forty-One

THERE WERE NO melodramatic lines playing out in Annelle's head now, though it would have been fair to say that this time she really *was* standing on the threshold of destiny. Her destiny, anyway, taking shape before her as she oversaw the loading of several trunks into the back of a sleigh. She couldn't quite *see* the shape of it, not yet, but that didn't mean it wasn't out there just the same.

In the end, her departure was softer than her aunt Praxis's had been, all those years ago, and yet Annelle felt in some ways this made a more powerful statement. When she'd spoken to her parents about it, she laid out her plans in no uncertain terms, explaining *some* of her reasons for leaving, keeping others to herself. The look in Prenna's eyes made it clear that she knew more than Annelle was probably comfortable with, but in the end it had been her, and not Lorric, who first rose to her feet and wrapped Annelle in a hug. *"I'm so proud of you,"* she'd whispered, and Annelle knew that it was for more than just the success of her coming-of-age ball. This place was a sinkhole, the ground collapsing beneath you so suddenly that you might not have even realized it had been there at all; and then, once at the bottom, the climb out was impossible. A long, angry, tearful, bitter night had shown that to Annelle, and in the end she'd laid there in silence for hours, staring at her ceiling, chewing things over. Really, it only made sense. All this ambition that she harbored inside of herself, all the knowledge she'd gained working for Prett, all the determination she got from her mother and her mother's mother, and she was willing to stay here and use her power to propel someone *else* toward greatness?

In a city-state like Drift, larger and more cosmopolitan, closer to the surface, away from the more conservative politics that the deeper Bolt was known for, she could chase after greatness herself. Her mother had already written a letter for her, which Annelle was to present to the head of Academics at the Symposium. The name Fellows still carried plenty of weight in a place like that. Annelle would find a way to settle in just fine.

"Ready, miss?"

Annelle turned. Her driver, a young man who had often taken her into Bolt or on day trips when her friends invited her to the nearest underground springs, was standing beside the team of bruskers, scratching one of them behind the ear. "Yes," Annelle said absently. She turned back; her parents were there to see her off, her brother Hanshaw wedged between them as if they were trying to pin him forever in his boyhood. Annelle stepped forward, the four of them embracing as one. There were tears, and well-wishes, and promises to write, on all parts.

When she got into the sleigh, the driver helped her up. His hands warmed hers, and Annelle caught her breath as he smiled, broad and sincere. Why, she wondered, had she never noticed before, how nice he always was, how attentive, how kind to the dogs? She felt sure it went beyond duty. There was something *good* about him, something that seemed to hum in the very air between them.

He smiled again as she settled into her seat. "Excited for your trip, miss?"

Annelle nodded. She wasn't sure she *had* been, not really, but now the whole of what she was doing rose up in a giddy bubble around her, and she couldn't help but laugh. There were so many things she was going to do, so much to explore. So much to conquer.

"What's your name, anyway?" Annelle asked. She actually leaned forward, catching the door just as he was going to close it.

The driver tipped his head, almost as if he was surprised that Annelle had thought to ask. "Sebian Delmore," he said. Then the corner of his mouth quirked up. "But since we'll be on this trip together for a while, you can call me Seb."

"Seb." Annelle nodded. She sat back again, folding her hands in her lap like the queen that she was. "Very good, Seb. We can go now."

Seb waved a jaunty salute. "As you wish."

He shut the door for real then, and Annelle let out another private laugh of pure delight as she settled back into her seat. She bit her lip, grinning, and looked out the windows at the familiar walls of the Fellows' tunnels one last time. *Look out, destiny,* she thought to herself. *Annelle Fellows is on the job.*

Oh, the open world. It had no idea what was in store for it.

As ANNELLE'S SLEIGH was beginning to pull out of Bolt, the one carrying Praxis and Kaedrich was heading in deeper still. Although the idea of a swift, dramatic exit held a certain amount of appeal to Kaedrich, Praxis had already gone that route once with her family. Besides, she'd said, there were a few things she needed to tie off this time. Because, although it went unspoken between them, they both knew that this time would be Praxis's final goodbye.

"This still leaves the matter of the Beacon," Kaedrich said. She did not ask about Praxis's father, the exact nature of what Praxis had done to him. She did not dare. Instead, she focused on the orb of the Beacon, glowing bright and otherworldly in Praxis's lap. Praxis had one hand beneath it, cradling it, and the other clamped above, as if she was afraid of what would happen if she dropped it.

Praxis gave a bitter laugh. "Yeah. Any ideas?"

"Do you think you could become its 'Lady'?"

Praxis shrugged. "I don't know. I didn't exactly acquire that title from the Beacon of Souls by normal means, and I still don't know how Lanali managed it."

"It's probably not a great idea, anyway, having control of two of them."

"No . . . ," Praxis said. "I suppose it would be best to get rid of it somehow."

"It would need to be somewhere safe, though. Where no one can ever find it again."

Praxis nodded, unsurprised. "If we detour farther inland before we leave, there's a legendary crevice right at the pole; stories say it leads directly to the heart of the world. I suppose we could drop it in there."

"I don't know," Kaedrich said. "I mean . . . it was dug out of the ice once already."

"True . . . ," Praxis said, tipping her head in thought.

"Could we maybe, I don't know, hang on to it until we're on the boat? Drop it somewhere in the middle of the ocean? Or do you think the depths would crush it?"

Praxis glanced down. "No, that could work," she said, a little too quickly.

"Okay, so . . . that's a plan," Kaedrich said. She forced a laugh. "Of course, we run the risk of water knights getting hold of it."

Praxis raised an eyebrow, looking up curiously. "What?"

"Water knights," Kaedrich said. She sat back, slightly dumbfounded. "Don't tell me you've never heard of the beasts."

"Heard of them, sure," Praxis said slowly. "In passing. But they're a myth."

Kaedrich shook her head. "Nope. Lucan swears his father saw one, when he was in the navy. Showed us a tooth from it."

"And you *believed* that?"

"He wouldn't lie."

Praxis snorted, like she wasn't entirely sure she agreed. "Maybe not. But would his father?"

This, Kaedrich had no answer to. She thought of the tooth, passed between Lucan and Havil and Marlick and her. It was warm from their hands by the time she got to it, but so sharp. *Careful,* they'd all been told. *It can cut your thumb off easy as cheese.*

Kaedrich shook her head. "We'll figure it out," she said finally as she looked across at Praxis. "You and me. Together. We always do."

Praxis looked down. "I'm . . . sorry, that I didn't listen to you. You're right, I should have trusted your judgment. You knew my father was hiding things from us, but I . . . I didn't want to see it. It was *right there,* and I didn't want to see it."

"Hey," Kaedrich said. She'd already started moving, already sliding across the distance between them. She settled next to Praxis, wrapping one arm around her shoulders, tucking Praxis into the crook of her arm. "Listen to me. No one wants to think the worst of their parents. *I* didn't even want to think the worst of him—I certainly never suspected him of this. But in the end, you did what you had to, to save the rest of us." She gave Praxis's shoulder a quick squeeze, planted a solid kiss on the top of Praxis's head. "I'm proud of you," she whispered into the down of Praxis's hair. "You know that, right?"

A brief nod, or maybe it was just the jostle of her head, as Praxis buried her face against Kaedrich. In the end, it didn't matter if Praxis acknowledged this, because the acknowledgment wasn't the point. This was: Praxis Fellows, stoic and remote, the ice queen, bitter and cold, feeling safe enough to cry against the fur of Kaedrich's coat. And this was: Kaedriella Mannly, warm and forgiving, her strong arms both wrapped around Praxis now, letting her have this moment. She kissed the top of Praxis's head again, saying nothing. Saying everything.

In the end, there would always be this.

HISTORY WOULD MARK this as a day of changes in the Fellows empire, but that did not even begin to cover the way the family would remember it. Praxis would make sure of that.

Her first stop was her sister's office, her second was the bank. She had both Prett and Prenna in tow, in their official capacities as bookkeeper and lawyer. The banker had stared at her as she'd laid out her intended course of action, his eyes as wide as if she'd just suggested she wanted to cut her own heart out and have them eat it raw.

"But . . . but . . . *But!*" he kept sputtering, but Praxis would not be moved. Her account, which her father had kept such a tender eye on all of these years, was to be emptied and closed by the end of the day, with all of her funds transferred toward paying off the remaining criminal fees of every single worker in her family's employ. By the workers' standards, the amount was astronomical, though it still left a manageable amount of cash left over. That, then, would be divided up equally among them as the first real and proper wages they'd probably ever received in their lives. She still needed to talk things over with Prommel—ideally, she would get him to agree to let anyone that wanted it to keep their jobs, but this time with proper pay and housing—but that was something she'd have to settle later. For now, he was tied up in paperwork of his own as the company traded hands.

In the meantime, Praxis had other matters to see to.

"So we're settled, then?" Praxis asked, a short while later. She'd returned from the bank with Prett in tow, leaving Prenna to finalize matters. Praxis glanced beside her now. "You're both in agreement?"

Prett shifted, looking uneasy. "I still can't believe this is real. You're sure he understands?"

Praxis crossed her arms. "Don't ask *me*," she said, jerking her head pointedly in her other brother's direction. "Ask *him*."

Prett frowned. "Right, right, sorry." He tucked his hair behind his ear, nervous, as he turned. His attention settled on Previn for a long minute.

As far as arrangements go, it wasn't exactly ideal. But Prett was leaving the country, finally, and Praxis didn't trust anyone *else* in her family to look after Previn's best interest any better than he would. Prett had been brought up to speed on Previn's unconventional method of communicating, and Previn, having gotten the idea from listening to Prett's games as a child, was slightly more warm to him than any of his other siblings.

Except for Praxis. But though Previn wanted to see more of the world, he couldn't follow Praxis where she was going. Not yet.

So Prett it was.

"Previn?" Praxis asked. "Is this acceptable for now?"

Previn jerked his head in a way Praxis was beginning to learn meant "yes."

For now, he tapped out, and both Prett and Praxis wrote down the translation for themselves.

Prett shook his head. "I can't believe I never figured this out for myself."

Didn't listen, Previn tapped.

"No," Prett agreed, a pained twist in his voice. He looked up, from his paper to Previn's face. "I didn't listen. I'm sorry."

Previn's head jerked, *yes.*

"I want *regular* updates," Praxis said. "At least, as regular as I'll have a stable address. Prett, you transcribe letters from Previn, if he wants to write them. It should go without saying that if I find out you've been altering the facts in *any* way—"

"Don't worry, dear sister. I know *exactly* how scary you can be."

The faintest trace of a smile tugged at Praxis's lips. "You'd better. Because I *will* be checking in with you, just as soon as . . ." She glanced at Kaedrich, hovering silently in the doorframe. Praxis swallowed. "Just as soon as we're done."

Prett reached out. He took Praxis's hand, startling her, but he did not let go.

"Praxis. No disrespect to Kaedrich, but you know you don't have to do this, don't you? It isn't your fight."

Praxis shook her head. "You really don't get it, do you? Kaedrich's fights *are* my fights, now. Besides, I helped make Pon Lanali. It's a long story," she added, waving off both of her brothers' obvious curiosity. "I promise I'll tell you both, when I come to get you."

You will come, Previn tapped. It wasn't clear if it was supposed to be a question or a statement. Perhaps it didn't matter, anymore.

Praxis put a gentle hand on Previn's shoulder. "Yes. I will," she said.

Prett crossed his arms. "You're making an awful lot of promises today, Prax. Forgive me, but it's not really your style. Are you sure you're up to all of this?"

It was true—too true, really, an uncomfortable sort of truth that only family can point out. Praxis glanced up again. Kaedrich still hovered in the doorway, waiting, watching. Just the sight of her gave Praxis a nudge, straightened her spine. "I know what I'm doing," Praxis said. She turned back to Prett. "Now, can you give us the room for a minute? There are a few things I'd like to discuss with Previn before I leave."

Prett nodded. "Of course."

"I'm sorry," Praxis said once Prett was gone. "I know this isn't ideal."

Better than now.

"True . . . but you deserve more than that. And I intend to give you more than that, it's just—"

Previn's taps cut her off.

I understand.

And Praxis felt this resonate down to her core, the truth of these words undeniable: Previn *did* understand. He'd always understood. All these years, all this time they'd been ignoring him, belittling him, assuming that because his body didn't work the way theirs did, that his mind was in some way stunted. Even Praxis. The shame of it burned her throat. She had to find a way to make it up to him; they all did.

Previn started tapping again, drawing Praxis out of her guilt spiral. She hurriedly picked her pencil back up, making fast marks across the page.

Your wife is pretty.

Praxis bit down on a smile. She was grateful that the whole conversation—spoken and tapped—was talking place in Yandosian, because for sure she didn't want Kaedrich to overhear this portion. It also didn't surprise her, somehow, that Previn had sussed out the truth of Kaedrich's identity for himself. Praxis stared at the letters, the Yandosian word for "wife" scratched down in her own handwriting. The heat of a flush crept up her cheeks.

"Yes, she is," Praxis said finally, not bothering to correct his word choice. She glanced over her shoulder at Kaedrich, her heart warming, then looked over at her brother, and placed a finger to her lips. "But we must never tell anyone, understand? It's a secret, just between you and me."

Previn grinned. He raised his own finger, landing at a slant just on the side of his mouth.

"Thank you," Praxis said. She leaned over, wrapping her arms around Previn in a careful hug. "Truly, Previn . . . you've saved all of us."

A flush crept up Previn's cheeks, even as his face split into a grin.

"Are you sure you're going to be okay?" Praxis asked. She had stepped back, but made sure to maintain steady eye contact. True, there wasn't much other choice. But she needed to be sure.

Previn studied his sister for a minute, his jaw shifting back and forth as if he was giving this matter serious thought. When he started tapping next, his pace was slower, more deliberate.

Nothing is sure, he tapped, and Praxis's heart twisted hard. But then: *That's the adventure.*

The dry memory of tears heated Praxis's eyes. She made herself nod. "I can't argue with that. And you deserve one more than anyone."

Another grin from Previn. Praxis carefully got to her feet, patting Previn's shoulder one last time.

"Goodbye," she whispered as she kissed the top of his head.

A jerk of Previn's arm, his version of a wave. Praxis walked over toward the door, threading her hand in with Kaedrich's. The two of them looked at each other, a genuine smile passing easily between them, and now Praxis knew they'd be okay. Her chest loosened, filling up like a balloon. One last turn and wave, from both of them, and then they were gone, finally leaving Yandosia for good. Praxis's heart swelled; true, there was still an enormous task ahead of them, and now they were facing it without the support she'd been planning on. But they would manage, somehow. Praxis was not one for optimism, but suddenly she felt the surety of this, straight down to her toes. She squeezed Kaedrich's hand, and Kaedrich squeezed back. Together.

That's the adventure.

THE SPEECH WAS delivered from the balcony of the palace, but it did not stay there. The words sprung forth from the Pon like a flock of released doves sweeping out across the countryside. They were carried in the form of printed reproductions, dutifully copied down and spread to newspapers across the whole of Durland, which in turn were copied and translated, seeping across the borders into Rolmstan and Marcovalla. They were carried in the form of nervous whispers, neighbor and neighbor and neighbor and friend worrying across fences and factory floors and dinner tables. They were carried by official messenger, diplomats in fine suits informing governments of what they'd already heard via other means. And of course, they were carried in the hearts of everyone that had listened to her, the Pon's smoothed-out voice booming forth and washing over the assembled peoples, chilling and enraging them all at once. The dangers of magic, the treachery that Rolmstan had participated in. The need for action, stirring the blood of all true Durns. The words spread.

The words spread through the troops now called into action, lines of men both nervous and determined as they filed through the familiar streets of Monfort and made their goodbyes. They spread through the gleaming new factories, rebuilt by Lanali's reconstruction efforts. Steel sparked, and machines clattered and groaned, spitting forth rifle after rifle, helmet after helmet. Boxes of bullets stacked into the back of heavy-laden carriages, the drivers grim-faced as they clicked their sturdy horses into action.

They spread along the rail lines, which used to be devoted to the daily bustle of ordinary life, now seized by the Crown and put to government work. Packs of cars jammed with soldiers and arms and supplies, barreling straight for the southeastern border.

They spread through the palace. Darting in silent whispers as the whole of Lanali's council went to work. They echoed in the minds of servants as they ducked their heads to avoid the unnatural eyes of Lanali's Steel Guards. They hovered on the edge of the throne room, where Lanali had finally set up residence, commands barked from the seat of power itself. She looked out at the clusters of advisers and officers carrying reports, the first wave ready to move. She did not smile, and yet, a smile was the only thing anyone who looked upon her that day would remember.

They reached the border. The words and the troops and the weapons. The horses. The autocarriages, bulky with extra protective layers, transformed from a plaything of the wealthy into a weapon of war. A sea of set and determined faces, young faces, men enraged by fear and bolstered by promises. The new flag of Durland fluttered high and proud over their heads, dotting the spread that stretched for miles. Thousands of bodies, strapped with guns and swords. An unstoppable tide.

Lanali stared down at the map. Her army was represented by blocks and figures, dozens clustered together along the dividing line between the two countries. A circle of generals surrounded the table, their faces caught by the lamp in determined lines. Miles away, the soldiers paused. The sun was caught behind a veil of cloud; a drizzle dampened their uniforms, but not their spirits. Commanders darted between ranks, inspecting, correcting. Waiting. The order buzzed in the back of their minds, but it had not come in yet, not quite.

The table was warm underneath Lanali's palms. The border—already, it was difficult to see the border, so crowded as it was with troops on both sides. Lanali looked at it, snaking between the figures, between the countries. Such an arbitrary dividing line. Why shouldn't it change? Why shouldn't she reshape the world?

Come and find me. She'd heard those words in a garden, once, and now here they were, always, whispering in the back of her mind.

Lanali took a deep breath as she looked up at the generals, waiting, ready. *I'm on my way,* she thought. But aloud, she said only one thing.

"Begin."

The adventure continues in . . .

THE BEACON CAMPAIGNS • BOOK FIVE

Hope
&
Ashes

Coming Soon

PHOTO BY CORIE KELLEY

About the Author

Jenn Gott spent most of her childhood tromping through her parents' woods, and the rest of it making up fifty imaginary friends at a time. She has never let them go—these days they're just called "characters," and they spend more time on pages than in her head. She is still happiest living in the woods, with her equally nerdy husband and their spoiled snuggle-cat.

🌐 jenngott.com
🐦 @gottwords
📷 @jenngottbooks
✉️ jenn@jenngott.com

Sign up for the latest news and updates at:
jenngott.com/newsletter

www.ingramcontent.com/pod-product-compliance
Lightning Source LLC
Chambersburg PA
CBHW030746030726
47497CB00001B/157